Biggles'
BIG ADVENTURES

CAPTAIN W. E. JOHNS

PRION

This edition first published in 2007 by

Prion
an imprint of the
Carlton Publishing Group,
20 Mortimer Street,
London W1T 3JW

Biggles Flies North First published 1939
Biggles in the Baltic First published 1940
Biggles Sees It Through First published 1941
Biggles in the Jungle First published 1942

Copyright © W.E. Johns (Publications) Ltd.

All rights reserved.

This book is sold subject to the condition that it may not be reproduced,
stored in a retrieval system or transmitted in any form or by any means,
electronic, mechanical, photocopying, recording or otherwise without the
publisher's prior consent.

A catalogue record for this book is available from the British Library

ISBN 978-1-85375-616-0

Illustrations by Alfred Sindall (*Biggles in the Baltic*), Howard Leigh and
Alfred Sindall (*Biggles Sees It Through*), Will Narraway (*Biggles Flies North*)
and Terence Cuneo (*Biggles in the Jungle*).

Typeset by e-type, Liverpool
Printed in India

Contents

Introduction

Biggles – or Squadron Leader James Bigglesworth, to give him his correct name – was the most popular boys' war hero of 20th-century British fiction. He features in almost a hundred books, the first appearing in 1932 and the last in the 1960s.

These books were written by Captain W. E. Johns, who had been a fighting pilot in the First World War when he was a member of the Royal Flying Corps, the forerunner of the RAF – so all the technical details of the warplanes and their flying capabilities are factually accurate. And what about the books' characters, especially Biggles and his comrades-in-arms and friends Algy Lacy and Ginger Hebblethwaite? They epitomise the way British youngsters used to view the fighting men of this country, and were the ones many wanted to copy when it was their turn to join the forces. Decent, brave, tough and fair – and very skilful at their jobs – they are the embodiment of the ability to improvise when things went wrong, which was considered the most British of military virtues.

So what is the appeal of these old-fashioned heroes today?

The main excitement of the books lies in Captain Johns's storytelling skills and his depiction of violent, but never vicious, action. The reader of a Biggles novel is really made to hold his breath, while the familiarity of the favourite characters makes each new book a pleasure to get stuck into.

The four novels chosen for this omnibus embrace two phases of Biggles's career, the years before the Second World War, when he was involved in many adventures helping out old friends and the Second World War itself. Two of the novels in this book – *Biggles Flies North* and *Biggles in the Jungle* – are from the years just preceding this war, while the other two take place at war's very outbreak. All four exhibit their author's brilliant evocation of extreme landscapes – from the steaming jungle to the frozen north – as well as his mastery of thrilling action.

Of course, as with many books from a previous age, these stories do not always match our own views and have sometimes been attacked as outdated. But in many ways Johns's world is better than ours: his heroes neither drink nor swear (although they do smoke a lot), and the action is both realistic and believable.

There is much to admire in these British fighting heroes of days gone by. But the reader of these books will be transported above all by the characters' adventures and the simpler world they sought to defend.

BIGGLES IN
THE BALTIC

CHAPTER I

The Call to Arms

As the momentous words 'England is now, therefore, in a state of war with Germany' came sombrely over the radio, Major James Bigglesworth, D.S.O., better known as Biggles, switched off the instrument and turned to face his friends, Captain the Honourable Algernon Lacey, M.C., and 'Ginger' Hebblethwaite. There was a peculiar smile on his face.

'Well, that's that. It looks as if we are in for another spot of war flying,' he murmured with an affected unconcern which did not deceive the others, who realized full well the gravity of the situation.

'Seems sort of unreal, as if something which you thought had only been a dream had suddenly come true,' remarked Algy quietly. 'What are we going to do about it?'

Biggles shrugged his shoulders. 'For the moment – nothing,' he answered. 'This isn't the time to go worrying the Air Ministry. They know all about us; no doubt they'll send for us as soon as they're ready. As far as we personally are concerned, we have this consolation: we do at least know something about the job – I mean, war flying – and that gives us an advantage over those who don't. We had better stand by in case the Air Ministry tries to get into touch with us. I only hope they'll let us stick together and not send us to different squadrons. I—' He broke off as the telephone bell shrilled. 'Hello, yes,' he went on, answering the call. 'Yes, Bigglesworth speaking – right you are, sir, we'll come right along.' He replaced the receiver. 'I'll give you one guess who that was,' he said drily.

'Colonel Raymond,' suggested Algy softly.

'Quite right. He's already back at his old job on Air Intelligence. He wants us to go along and see him at the Air Ministry right away. Call a taxi, Ginger.'

'Bringing us here doesn't sound as if we're going to an ordinary service squadron,' remarked Algy suspiciously, as they entered the Air Ministry and took the lift.

'We shall soon know,' returned Biggles briefly, as he knocked on the Colonel's door.

Colonel Raymond gave them a smile of welcome as he rose from his desk and came to meet them. 'Glad to see you all looking so well,' he said cheerfully. 'I've got a job which I fancy should suit you down to the ground.'

'Not *too* suicidal I hope, sir,' grinned Biggles.

The Colonel indicated three chairs. 'I wouldn't call it suicidal, although I'm not going to pretend that it's likely to be all plain sailing. If it was I shouldn't waste *you* on it, you may be sure. At a time like this we need our best men for special jobs.'

'Nice of you to put it that way, sir,' acknowledged Biggles.

'I presume that you are willing to come back into the service?' inquired the Colonel.

'What about Gin – I mean Hebblethwaite? He hasn't been in the regular service yet.'

'If you take on the job I'll see that he is gazetted as a pilot officer right away.'

'Good,' nodded Biggles. 'What's the job, sir?'

Colonel Raymond pointed to a map of Europe that nearly covered one wall of his office; its varnished surface was decorated with drawing-pins of different colours, each marking a point of strategical importance. 'I need hardly say that what I am going to tell you must be treated in strictest confidence,' he said earnestly. 'One careless word might undo the work of months. Incidentally, Bigglesworth, I may as well tell you that you were earmarked for this particular job months ago; in fact, it would hardly be an exaggeration to say that the job was specially created for you. What I mean is, had we not known someone capable of handling it we should hardly have dared to formulate such a dangerous plan.'

The Colonel picked up a long ruler and indicated on the map the area of ocean separating northern Germany from Scandinavia. 'Here is the Baltic Sea,' he continued, tracing the coastlines of Germany and East Prussia. 'You will readily perceive that anyone operating in these waters would be within easy striking distance of enemy country.'

A puzzled look came over Biggles's face. 'But the Baltic is Germany's own sea—' he began.

Colonel Raymond held up his hand. 'Not entirely,' he argued. 'Germany does, more or less, control the Baltic, but other countries have an interest in it – Lithuania, Latvia, Finland, Estonia, and the Scandinavian countries. You may say, naturally, that they are all neutral. Quite right, they are, and it would be a serious matter if the neutrality of these countries were violated, either intentionally or accidentally. I am now going to let you into a secret so vital that its importance could hardly be exaggerated. Some time ago, perceiving that war might not be averted, we took the precaution of acquiring from one of the countries I have named an uninhabited island so small as to be negligible. Its name is Bergen Ait. It is in fact no more than a mass of rock, quite useless for any commercial purpose. Nevertheless, it embodies a feature that made it worth the large sum of money we paid for it, although here I should say that no one outside the countries concerned is aware of the transaction – that the island is British property, entitling us to use it as a base. It is remote, and in normal times I don't suppose anyone lands on it year in year out. Naturally, being so small, it could not easily be defended against enemy forces, so its only value to us lies in its secret character. The special feature to which I referred just now is a cave that has been worn into the very heart of the rock by the action of the waves. This cave is large enough to house several aircraft. You will now begin to see what I am driving at.'

'I understand,' replied Biggles quietly. 'The idea is to establish a base right on the enemy's doorstep, so to speak?'

'Precisely. From this base raids will be launched on military objectives, some of which have already been decided on, places which could not very well be reached from England or France. We have been preparing this depot for some time. The aircraft are, in fact, already there, as well as other equipment likely to be required, all ready for "Z" Squadron – as we have decided to call it – to take over. I need not describe the equipment in detail now, but in case you wonder – if you go – what the skis are for, I must tell you that in winter the sea is often icebound, and the squadron will be frozen in. For the rest we shall have to rely on the Commanding Officer to use his initiative in dealing with the difficulties and dangers that will certainly arise – events that are impossible to foresee.'

'How is this officer going to get there, since the Baltic is, anyway, at this moment, controlled by the German fleet?'

'There is only one way – by submarine,' replied the Colonel calmly. 'The submarine will land the party there – and leave them there.'

'I see.'

'You understand that the job is essentially one for volunteers; you needn't take it on if—'

'I don't think we need discuss that, sir,' interrupted Biggles.

'Good. I knew you wouldn't let us down. Make a list of the personnel you think you will be likely to require and I will arrange with the Admiralty for underwater transport. Don't take more men than is absolutely essential. The fewer there are the longer the stores will last.'

'One question, sir. I imagine the base is equipped with radio?'

'It is.'

'That means we shall get orders from time to time?'

'Yes.'

'Are we to confine ourselves to these operations, or am I at liberty to take action on my own account – always assuming that such action is, in my opinion, worth the risk involved?'

Colonel Raymond was silent for a moment or two. 'That's a difficult question to answer,' he said slowly. 'Naturally we are anxious to preserve the secret of the base as long as possible, but if I said "no" to your question it might mean losing a chance to strike a vital blow at the enemy. I shall have to leave it to your judgement. But if you do take on anything on your own account the responsibility will be yours.'

'That's fair enough, sir,' agreed Biggles. 'Are there any special instructions?'

'There are, but I can't give you them now. You'll sail under sealed orders, and receive instructions concerning them by radio when you have established yourself at your base. When is the earliest you can start?'

'Now, sir.'

Colonel Raymond smiled. 'That's a bit too early for me. Today is Sunday; I will arrange for you to embark on Wednesday morning. We'll have another chat before then; there are one or two minor points I shall have to discuss with you. There is one thing ...'

Biggles waited.

'Frankly, I think it is certain that sooner or later the enemy will discover your hiding-place,' continued the Colonel, his eyes on Biggles's face. 'You may last three months – a month – or only a week; it depends upon how things fall out. We must do the best we can with the time at our disposal. As far as we know, the German Intelligence Service has no suspicion of what is afoot, but one can never be quite sure. Bergen Ait is no great distance from Kiel, where an old acquaintance of yours is in charge.'

Biggles raised his eyebrows. 'An old acquaintance? You don't by any chance mean—'

'Von Stalhein. Erich von Stalhein – no less. He was bound to be given an important command.'

Biggles smiled faintly. 'Von Stalhein, eh?' he murmured reflectively. 'You know, I've almost got to like him. He hasn't had the best of luck in his encounters with us—'

'It is to be hoped, for your sakes, that he doesn't have the best of luck this time,' said Colonel Raymond seriously. 'He has old scores to wipe out, remember. He's your worst enemy, and an implacable one. If ever he catches you—'

'We shall have to see to it that he doesn't,' put in Biggles lightly.

'That's the spirit,' agreed the Colonel. 'Well, that's all for the time being. I'll let the Air Chief Marshal know you're going. You ought to be able to do the enemy an immense amount of mischief before he finds you out.' The Colonel held out his hand. 'Good luck.'

'We shall do our best, sir,' promised Biggles.

CHAPTER II

'Z' Squadron Takes Over

Precisely a week later, a little after sunrise, the small party that comprised 'Z' Squadron, R.A.F., stood on a shelf of rock in the sombre heart of Bergen Ait, and watched the submarine that had brought them there creep like a monster of the deep towards the entrance to the vast cavern which the action of the waves had eaten into the islet. From the conning-tower, still open, projected the head and shoulders of the commander, his eyes on those he was leaving behind. He raised his hand in salute. 'Good hunting, boys,' he called. The words echoed eerily round the walls.

Biggles returned the salute. 'Good hunting yourself, sailor,' he replied.

That was all. The naval officer disappeared. The steel cap of the conning-tower sank into its bed; deeper and deeper into the water bored the long grey body of the underwater craft. Presently only the conning-tower could be seen, and as the vessel felt its way into the cove that sheltered the mouth of the cave, this, too, disappeared, leaving the airmen alone in their sinister war station.

Biggles turned and considered the members of his squadron. They were five all told, Algy and Ginger being the only pilots besides himself. Colonel Raymond had pressed him to take more, but Biggles felt that an outsider might upset the unity of a team which, from long and often perilous experience, had proved its efficiency, a team which had been forged in the fire of loyal comradeship. An extra member who was not in entire sympathy with them might easily do more harm than good, he reasoned, perhaps wisely.

In addition to the three pilots there was Flight-Sergeant Smyth, Biggles's old war-time fitter and rigger, whose skill with either wood or metal was almost uncanny, and who could be relied upon to work a twenty-four-hour day without complaint should circumstances demand it. With him was his son Roy, a lad of eighteen who had entered the Royal Air Force as a boy apprentice and had passed out as a wireless operator mechanic. Keen, alert, and intelligent, he promised to follow the footsteps of his father up the ladder of promotion.

The only other member of the squadron was an old naval pensioner appropriately named William Salt, already known to them as 'Briny', a nickname which he had carried for nearly half a century in the Navy. Nobody knew just how old Briny was, but he was apt to boast that he had started life as a boy in the days of sail, when steamers were few and far between. Biggles had applied to Colonel Raymond for a cook, feeling that one was necessary to save the others wasting valuable time in the kitchen. Briny had been, in fact, the cook on Colonel Raymond's private yacht; owing to the war the yacht had, of course, been laid up; Briny had put his name down for service and Colonel Raymond had recommended him confidently, despite his age, saying that he possessed a store of practical knowledge, apart from cooking, that would be useful to them. His only failing was (he warned them) a weakness for 'reminiscencing', but this was balanced by a shrewd cockney wit that might amuse them on their dreary station. So Briny had, to use his own expression, 'pulled up 'is mudhook' and come along.

'Well, here we are,' announced Biggles. 'There's little I can tell you that you don't already know. It may be rather alarming to be stationed in what are practically enemy waters, but no doubt we shall get used to it. We have this satisfaction: instead of being a mere cog in a vast machine, we are, as it were, a detached unit fighting a little war of our own, the success of which will largely depend on ourselves. I'm not going to make a speech, but there is one point I must mention. On a job like this, where everyone is in close contact with everybody else, ordinary service discipline is bound to be relaxed. This calling people by nicknames, for instance – as far as I, as commanding officer, am concerned, this may continue except when a person is actually on duty; or, since we shall all be on duty all the time, perhaps I had better say engaged on specific duty under my direct orders. Cooped up as we are, each is too dependent on the others to bother about ceremony, but I don't think familiarity need interfere with the efficiency of the unit. I know you'll all do your best. In the event of casualties, the next in order of seniority will, of course, take over. That's all. Roy, take over the radio room and stand by for reception of signals. Briny, you'd better get the galley functioning. The rest come with me; we had better make ourselves familiar with the layout of the depot before we do anything else.'

The servicing of the base at Bergen Ait had been carried out by the Admiralty, who, as usual, had done their job thoroughly. The islet itself was, as Colonel Raymond had said, merely a mass of rock rising to several hundred feet above the sea, the nearest land being the enemy coast of East Prussia. Less than a mile in circumference, for the most part the cliffs were precipitous, sterile, the home of innumerable sea-birds. Here and there, however, erosion had caused the cliffs to crumble, so that they lay in terrifying landslides to the water's edge.

One such collapse had flung a mighty spit of rocks some distance into the sea, so that a small cape, perhaps two hundred yards in extent, was formed. This served as a breakwater and at the same time formed what was, in effect, a cove that could be used as a harbour, but only when the sea was reasonably calm. In bad weather, or when the wind was blowing directly into it, the cove (so the Admiralty had informed Biggles) became a seething cauldron, dangerous for any type of craft. Even in fair weather the tides raced into the cove with considerable force, and it was no doubt due to this that the rock had been undermined, forming the cave, which, being at an angle, could not be seen from the open sea. One glance had been sufficient to warn Biggles that should an aircraft be caught out in bad weather it would be utterly impossible for it to get back into the cave. Indeed, as he had surveyed the scene from the submarine, he suspected that the natural risks of operating from such a base were likely to be as dangerous as the enemy. On the other hand, these very hazards had their compensations, in that they were likely to keep enemy shipping at a distance.

Although the entrance of the cave was low – hardly large enough to admit an aircraft at high water – inside it was as lofty as a cathedral, and ran back, diminishing in size, for a considerable distance, although the farther extremity had not yet been explored. It was obvious that, except at one place, the walls of the cave had dropped sheer into the water, but an artificial shelf (promptly named the 'catwalk' by Briny) had been cut to enable those inside to reach the bay. This shelf also served as a quay for mooring the aircraft and a small motorboat.

At one spot, however, a flaw in the rock had left a more or less flat area, about half an acre in extent, and every inch of this space had been utilized for the erection of several low wooden buildings. On inspection these turned out to consist of a small but well-fitted workshop and armoury combined, a mess-room with sleeping quarters and a record office attached, and store-house packed with food, mostly tinned, although there were sacks of potatoes, onions, and other vegetables. The radio room stood a little apart, and from this also was controlled the electrical equipment both for lighting and for running the lathe in the workshop. A small oil engine, dynamo, and storage batteries were housed in a recess cut in the rock. Near by was a rather alarming ammunition dump, long sleek torpedoes lying side by side with bombs of various sizes – high explosive, incendiary, and armour-piercing – as well as cases of small-arms ammunition. Another hut contained spare parts and medical and photographic stores.

'Well, I must say the Navy have made a thorough job of it,' observed Biggles with satisfaction, as the party concluded its tour of inspection. 'Let's go and have a look at the machines. Colonel Raymond told me that they were specially designed for the job. He could only let us have four – one each and one in reserve. Normally they will be used as single seaters, but there is a spare seat for a passenger, or gunner, with a gun mounting, under the fabric just aft of the pilot's seat. The spare seat can be made available by merely pulling a zip fastener. They're amphibians, of course; goodness knows where we shall have to land and take off before the job is finished. The outstanding feature, I understand, is a wide range of speed; what with flaps and slots we ought to be able to land on a sixpence. There are eight machine-guns, operated by a single button on the joystick. Incidentally, you'll notice that they are fitted for torpedo work, as well as with bomb-racks.'

'Well, it's a nice clean-looking kite, anyway,' remarked Algy as they stood on the ledge looking at the aircraft. 'By the way, what do they call them?'

'As far as I know they haven't been named,' returned Biggles. 'The official designation is S.I. Mark I.A. – the S standing for secret.'

'That's too much of a mouthful; we shall have to think of something shorter,' declared Ginger.

'Can you suggest anything?' inquired Biggles.

Ginger thought for a moment. 'What's something that sits in a hole and darts out at its prey?' he asked pensively.

'A rabbit,' suggested Algy.

Ginger snorted. 'I said *darts* out at its prey. Have you ever seen a rabbit dart at a dandelion?'

'What's something that whirls out, strikes, and then whirls back home again?' murmured Biggles.

'Boomerang,' answered Ginger promptly.

'Good,' cried Biggles. 'That sounds more like it. We're the Boomerang Squadron. It wouldn't be a bad idea if we gave each machine a name of its own, too, for identification purposes,' he added.

'In that case mine's *Dingo*,' announced Ginger. 'If we're the Boomerangs we ought to stick to Australian names.'

'An Aussie once told me that the dingo is a nasty, dirty, stinking little beast,' said Biggles, with a sidelong glance at Algy.

'He may be, but he's thundering hard to catch,' declared Ginger. 'I'm sticking to *Dingo*.'

'Then mine's going to be the *Didgeree-du*,' announced Algy.

'What!' cried Ginger incredulously. 'There ain't no such animal.'

'A fat lot you know about it,' grunted Algy. 'The didgeree-du is a bird.'

'As a matter of fact, the didgeree-du happens to be a native Australian musical instrument,' put in Biggles. 'It makes a lot of noise about nothing.'

'I don't care, I'm sticking to it,' insisted Algy doggedly. 'I like the sound of it.'

'Then I'll call mine the *Willie-Willie*,' decided Biggles.

Ginger stared. 'You're not serious? What on earth is a willie-willie?'

'You'll know if you ever run into one,' replied Biggles grimly. 'I flew into one once, some years ago.'

'Flew into one? What are you talking about?'

'A willie-willie, my lad, is a cyclone, typhoon, and hurricane rolled into one. It lurks round the north Australian coast and descends out of the blue in search of its prey, which it smashes, mangles, and finally blows to pieces. That's what I hope to do to the enemy.'

'Then *Willie-Willie* is a good name,' admitted Ginger. 'What about the spare machine? The duck-billed platypus is the only other Australian animal I know.'

'That's good enough,' agreed Biggles. 'But this won't do. We must get on. I'm expecting a signal through at any moment.'

They spent the next hour examining the machines, which, if appearance counted for anything, were capable of all that was claimed of them.

'What was that signal you were expecting?' inquired Ginger as they climbed out of the *Dingo* on to the catwalk and made their way towards the depot.

'That's something I can't tell you, the reason being that we're still under sealed orders. Admittedly they are in my pocket, but I can't open them until I get instructions.'

'I suppose the signal will come through in code?'

'Of course; all messages are in code in war-time,' answered Biggles. 'Well, there's nothing we can do except wait, so we may as well go along and see what Briny has produced for lunch.'

'What about trying out one of the machines?' suggested Ginger.

Biggles shook his head. 'No, for two reasons,' he decided. 'In the first place, it would be folly to show ourselves except when we are compelled to, and secondly, our petrol supply is not unlimited. As far as showing ourselves is concerned, I have an idea that most of our orders will be for night work, so we had better have a good look at the map.'

'It's going to be tricky work finding this lump of rock on a dark night, particularly if, as I presume, we shan't dare to show a light,' murmured Algy.

'It is,' agreed Biggles, 'but we shall have to do the best we can. It certainly wouldn't do to show lights except in dire emergency, because enemy ships might be close in to us without our knowing it, since in war-time ships don't carry lights, either.'

As they entered the mess Roy ran up with a slip of paper in his hand. 'Signal, sir,' he said, saluting briskly.

Biggles took the slip, glanced at it, and taking several envelopes from his pocket, selected one and ripped open the flap. For a minute or two he read in silence. Then, 'Listen to this,' he said. 'It concerns every one. I'll read it aloud.'

' "To Officer Commanding Z Squadron. Standing routine orders.

' "1. These orders must be committed to memory by every officer in your command.

' "2. This document must on no account be taken into the air. It must not be allowed to fall into the hands of the enemy. In case of doubt it should be destroyed.

' "3. As they are at present planned, the duties of Z Squadron will be confined to night operations, details of which will be issued.

' "4. Every precaution will be taken to prevent the enemy from becoming aware of the existence of the squadron, or its base. If an aircraft of the squadron is pursued by hostile aircraft the pilot concerned will not on any account return to his base, but will destroy his aircraft on the open sea.

' "5. Should the base be located by the enemy it must not be allowed to fall into his hands. All war material must be destroyed, no matter what sacrifice is involved.

' "6. Signals. Only in a case of utmost importance should radio equipment be used for transmitting signals. Personal danger does not constitute a sufficient reason to transmit. If information of sufficient importance to warrant transmission is obtained, code will invariably be used.

' "7. Further supplies of food, fuel, and war material will be dispatched as the exigencies of the service permit, but it must be assumed that no such stores will be sent.

' "8. The greatest possible care will be taken not to violate the neutrality of non-belligerent countries." '

Biggles laid the paper on the table. 'That's all,' he said quietly.

'Quite enough to be going on with, too,' murmured Algy.

Briny appeared in the doorway. 'Lunch is ready, gen'l'men,' he said.

CHAPTER III

First Orders

By the following morning all the members of 'Z' Squadron were fairly settled in their new home and were becoming accustomed to the persistent lapping of the sea against the walls of the cave – a mournful, depressing sound that had disturbed Ginger's sleep. However, breakfast of ham and eggs, served by the ever cheerful Briny, soon dispelled the gloomy atmosphere.

'Have you got things sorted out in your department?' Biggles asked him.

'Ay, ay, sir,' answered Briny. 'This is a picnic to some of the places I've served. Why, I remember once in the Red Sea, chasing Arab dhows we was – let's see, it 'ud be about—'

'All right, never mind about that now,' interrupted Biggles.

'Ay, ay, sir!' Briny saluted and departed.

The airmen first went to the signals room, where they found Roy busy fixing up an alarum device that would rouse him should a signal come through while he was sleeping. Leaving him at his task, they made their way to the machines, on which the Flight-Sergeant was already working. Continuing along the catwalk, they reached the mouth of the cave and stood blinking in the daylight, notwithstanding that the sky was overcast.

Ginger climbed on a rock and surveyed his immediate surroundings. It was not a view calculated to induce high spirits. Under leaden clouds, a dark, choppy sea was beating sullenly at the foot of the cliffs, throwing showers of spray over the natural breakwater and nicking hungrily at festoons of black, slimy seaweed that lined the high-water mark. Above him, sea-birds of many sorts gathered on the numerous ledges or soared in the grey atmosphere like scraps of wind-blown paper. A movement a little farther along caught his eye, and he saw a seal drop into the water.

'Strictly speaking, we ought to mount a guard here,' opined Biggles. 'But if we did none of us would do any work or get any sleep.'

'I should go off my rocker, anyway, if I had to stand here and stare at this all day,' muttered Algy.

Biggles considered the heaving water speculatively. 'I should say that a vessel coming from that direction at night' – he pointed to the northeast – 'would see the reflection of our lights. I think it would be a good idea if we got some tarpaulins fixed up over the entrance to the cave.' He glanced up at the sheer face of the cliff. 'I don't think there's any question of exploring the island,' he continued. 'From what I can see of it, only an expert mountain goat could get to the top – not that I imagine there is anything there worth going up for. Well, there seems to be nothing more to see, so we may as well get back.'

On the way he gave the Flight-Sergeant orders about covering the entrance with tarpaulins.

Returning to the depot, they were in time to see Briny walking towards the galley with three fair-sized fish strung on a line.

'Where did you get those?' inquired Biggles.

'Out of the ditch, sir,' was the brisk answer. 'I thought that as 'ow we were living with the fishes, as you might say, sir, they ought to do their bit, so last night I dropped in a line or two to try me luck.'

'Smart work,' complimented Biggles.

'Why, lor luv a duck, sir, that's nothing,' declared Briny; 'I've kept the whole ship's company going on fish before today.'

'*What!*' exclaimed Biggles incredulously.

Briny looked slightly embarrassed. 'Of course, they didn't get much each,' he admitted. 'But talking of fishin', I remember once, off Cape Horn, we got in amongst so many fish that they lifted the ship clean out of the water. I sez to Charlie, a shipmate o' mine, "Charlie," I sez—'

'Yes, all right Briny. Keep the story for a dull evening,' interrupted Biggles.

'Ay, ay, sir.' Briny touched the peak of his weather-soiled cap and went on towards the galley.

'I fancy he must sleep in that cap,' murmured Algy; 'I've never seen him without it.'

Further conversation on the subject was prevented by the arrival of Roy with a signal.

Biggles took the slip of paper. 'This, I fancy, is where we start the ball rolling,' he said, leading the way to the record office, where he unlocked a small safe and took out a red book carrying on the front, in large letters, the word SECRET. He sat down at the table to decode the message, and for several minutes was busy with pencil and paper.

'We do our first show tonight,' he said at last, looking up at the others. 'Zero hour is ten o'clock, weather permitting. Our objective is an ammunition dump on the south side of the Kiel canal, about three miles from the town. The dump can be identified by four long sheds standing close together, end on. The moon rises early, so we ought to have no difficulty in finding them.' Biggles filed the message and put the file in the safe.

'It sounds easy,' ventured Ginger.

'It may *sound* easy, but we may find it otherwise,' replied Biggles. 'In all Germany the worst hotbed of archie is at Kiel. Raymond warned me of that. After all, the Kiel Canal is probably the most important artery the Boche possess, so they've guarded it with their best anti-aircraft equipment. I think this is where we have to play the old soldier on them; if they hear us coming they'll knock us to pieces before we get anywhere near the dump.'

'And what is the "old soldier" in this case?' inquired Ginger.

'We'll climb to twenty thousand, cut our engines fifteen miles away and glide over. With luck they may not spot us until the first bomb bursts. Then the fireworks will start and things will probably get pretty warm. Ginger, you'll be new to this sort of thing, so I'll give you a tip. If you can't get high, keep low – the lower the better as long as you don't barge into anything. The lower you are the more difficult target you make for the gunners, since they can't swing their guns about like rifles.'

'Then we aren't all going over together?' put in Algy.

Biggles shook his head. 'It's too dangerous. We should probably collide in the dark. I think the best plan is to go over at intervals of ten minutes. I'll go first. As soon as I've unloaded my eggs the guns and searchlights will be after me; in the din they won't hear you coming, so you may get a chance to have an unmolested crack at the target. Algy, you'll follow me. Ginger, you'll be last, and if things pan out as I imagine you ought to get a clear shot. Take one bomb – a two-thirty pounder. If you lay it near the dump it

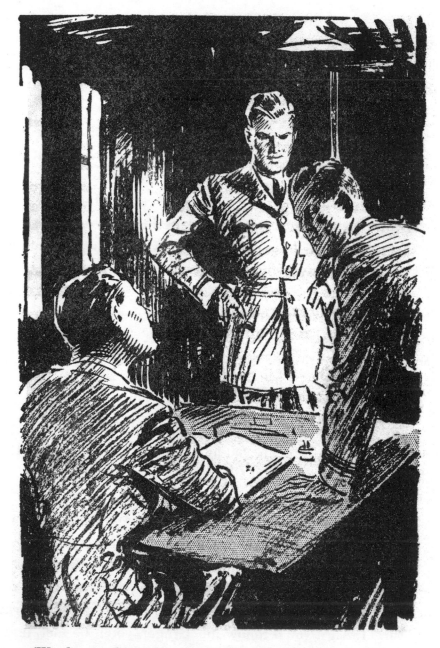

*'We do our first show tonight,' he said at last, looking
up at the others'*

ought to shake things up a bit. The instant you unload, shove your joystick forward and zigzag for the open sea. Then come straight home. To prevent us landing on top of each other in the dark I'll get Smyth to signal three flashes with a green light as an all-clear signal. He can stand by with the motorboat in case any of us makes a dud landing. That's all. We'd better get ready. Let's get the target marked on the map for a start.'

The rest of the day passed quickly, with all available hands preparing the machines for their perilous mission. They floated in line, in order of take-off, Biggles's machine leading, with two 112-pound high explosive bombs under the wings, and a nest of small incendiary bombs between the large twin floats. Algy's machine carried a similar load; Ginger's, the single 230-pounder, as Biggles had ordered.

As twilight fell the machines were towed nearer to the tarpaulins which the Flight-Sergeant and Briny had erected in accordance with Biggles's instructions. Biggles pulled one aside, and stepping into the open, surveyed the deserted sea reflectively; the sun, a ball of glowing crimson, was just sinking into the misty horizon. The wind had dropped and the sea was going down, as it so often does towards evening. He glanced at his watch. The time was eight-thirty. 'Everything seems to be all clear,' he remarked. 'Let's go and have a bite of food. By the time we've finished we shall be all set to give the gentle Hun a taste of his own medicine. I hope he likes it.'

CHAPTER IV

The Raid

At precisely ten o'clock, after a careful survey of the sea for ships, Biggles taxied out into the little cove under a moon that cut a swathe of silver light across the gently stirring ocean. The stars twinkled clear and bright in the autumn sky, into which the black silhouette of the rocky islet reared up like a mighty colossus. Without a glance behind him, he steered the *Willie-Willie* – its name now painted on the nose – into position for a clear run towards the open sea. The engine bellowed suddenly, and the machine surged forward, slashing a line of foam across the face of the water. The line ended abruptly as the aircraft soared like a gull into the air.

Holding the stick back with his knees, for the night air was as placid as a bowl of milk, he took a piece of chewing-gum from a pocket under the instrument-board and chewed it reflectively as he scanned the ever-widening horizon for lights; but neither gleam nor flash broke the sombre pall that war had laid over land and sea. Even the beacons of lighthouses and lightships had been extinguished. Only a weird blue glow illuminated the flickering instruments on the dashboard.

As the needle of the altimeter crept round the dial to the

10,000 mark Biggles turned the nose of his machine due south; still he climbed, but more slowly now as the air became more rarefied. Up and up – 12,000 –14,000 – 16,000 – 18,000 – into a lonely indigo world; and still the machine bored upward. The blue light gleamed coldly on his face as he peered forward through the windscreen, looking for the land which he knew lay ahead. That Kiel would be 'blacked-out' after sunset was only to be expected, yet he thought there was a chance that the lights of moving traffic might reveal a road. But not a spark broke the stygian darkness.

At last the altimeter registered 20,000 feet, and the nose of the machine sank a little until it was on even keel; then, as the muffled roar of the engine died abruptly, the nose sank still lower and the *Willie-Willie* began to glide. The only sound was the soft hum of air passing over the surface of the machine.

Peering forwards and downwards, Biggles soon made out a vague mass which he knew was land, a vast black shadow that spread away until it was lost in the distance. Not a light showed anywhere. Turning to the right, he followed the coastline for a while, and then, after a glance at his compass and the moon, he headed straight towards it, losing height all the time, probing the darkness with his eyes, seeking the unmistakable landmark which he knew was there – the famous canal which connects the Baltic with the North Sea. At last he found it. The enemy might curtain their windows, but they could not curtain the moon, which, climbing higher, reflected itself on the water so that the canal lay like a silver ribbon across the sable land.

Biggles glanced at his altimeter again and saw that he was down to 8,000 feet; he would have wished to have been higher, for he still had some distance to go to reach his objective, but he dared not touch the throttle. One sound, and he knew that the silent atmosphere would be gashed by a score or more of blinding white searchlight beams. On he glided, the altimeter needle falling back as he followed the silver streak still far below.

He was down to 5,000 feet when at last he saw the slight curve in the canal that marked roughly the position of the ammunition dump. He could not see the actual buildings; he did not expect to; but he knew that they were there – assuming that Colonel Raymond's report had been correct, and this he had no reason to doubt.

He eased the joystick back until it was 'sloppy' in his hand, so near was he to stalling; but every mile gained now was of value, and although he hardly dared to hope that he would be allowed to get over the target without being detected, he intended to get as close as possible.

He was about a mile away when a searchlight beam thrust upward into the darkness like a steel dagger; for a moment it remained still, quivering, and then began a methodical quartering of the sky. Another joined it, and another, and he knew that the sound detectors had picked him up, in spite of the fact that his engine was only ticking over. He swerved away from the beams, and then put his nose down steeply towards the objective. In a moment a dozen beams were criss-crossing around him like gigantic scissors, as the operators below strove to get him in their grip. Suddenly one cut a colossal arc across the heavens; for a fleeting instant it flashed on his wings, and he knew that silence would no longer serve him. Almost viciously he thrust the throttle forward, and the engine bellowed its roar of defiance; simultaneously he pushed the nose of the machine down and sped like an arrow towards his target. In an instant the air was split by flashes, some, very close, bright orange; others, farther away, dull crimson, as the anti-aircraft gunners flung up a furious barrage. He did not alter his course, but held straight on in a screaming dive, leaving most of the flashes behind him.

His face, ghostly in the pale blue light of the instruments, was expressionless; his jaw was set, and his mouth a thin straight line. Something struck the machine with a thud that made it quiver. His lips closed a little tighter and his eyes flashed to the tell-tale instruments; but the set look on his face did not alter.

Not until he was down to 500 feet did he pull the machine out of its dive. Then, calmly and deliberately, as he brought it to even keel, he leaned over the side, seeking the sheds. Around him the air was torn and gashed by flame and hurtling metal, but he ignored it, as he knew only too well that to think about it was to court fear. So he concerned himself only with one thing – the sheds.

At last he saw them, stretching in a straight line along the edge of the canal, precisely as they had been described. He kicked out his right foot and dragged the stick in the same direction, side-slipping to bring the machine over them. Satisfied that he had gone far enough, he centralized the controls, keeping his eyes on the leading edge of the starboard plane at the place where it joined the fuselage, waiting for the sheds to appear. There was no question of using bomb-sights.

As the sheds came in line with the edge of the plane his hand closed over the bomb-toggle. An instant longer he waited. Then he jerked it back – one ... two. The machine rocked as its load swung into space. Before it had properly recovered he had kicked out his right foot and was zigzagging at right angles from his original course; at the same time he held the joystick forward for all the speed he could raise, knowing that only speed could save him from the lines of white sparks that were streaming upwards, which he knew were tracer bullets.

He felt the explosion of the bombs rather than saw them, although the whole sky was lit up by a white glare; but the blast of air whirled the machine up like a feather caught in a gale of wind, and he braced his knees against the sides of the cockpit to steady himself. Banking vertically, he snatched a glance over his shoulder in time to see another explosion. The blaze half blinded him, but in the split second before it occurred he had noted that the end shed only was on fire. There was, he knew, a chance that the explosions caused by this fire would set the others off, for contrary to the general impression, an ammunition dump does not necessarily go up in one terrific explosion. It can catch fire and burn for a considerable period, sometimes weeks, with sporadic explosions from time to time.

With the anti-aircraft guns still pursuing him, he zoomed low again at the sheds, releasing his incendiary bombs in a shower; then, banking vertically, he raced towards the open sea. A searchlight picked him up and held him, nearly blinding him with its brilliant glare. For a moment or two he flung the machine about wildly, endeavouring to shake it off, but the beam clung to him like a leech. His nostrils quivered as a wave of anger surged through him. 'All right, if you want it you can have it,' he grated through his set teeth, and shielding his eyes with his left arm, he spun round and raced straight down the beam. His thumb found the button on the joystick and jammed it down savagely, and the machine shuddered like a frightened horse as eight streams of bullets poured down his path of flight. It was an old trick, and it worked. The light went out, either because it had been hit or because the operators had bolted for cover out of the withering hail. Satisfied, he swung the machine round on its original course towards the sea.

Most of the lights and archie flashes were now behind him, and he guessed the reason. The listening posts had heard the other machines. He glimpsed a fast-moving spark, like a firefly, held in a beam above him, and he knew that it must be Algy diving at the target. An instant later two terrific explosions in quick succession lit up the sky like a flash of summer lightning, and again the blast of air lifted the *Willie-Willie* bodily. There were no more explosions, from which Biggles gathered that Algy had missed the sheds, although an ever-spreading crimson glow suggested that he had set some buildings on fire, and since these must have had some connection with the dump the bombs had not been wasted.

The scene was now far behind him, too far for details to be picked out, so he allowed his nerves to relax and devoted his attention to the business of getting home.

Ginger, gliding at 5,000 feet towards the scene of action, had seen all that Biggles had seen. In fact, he had seen more, for so far he was unmolested, and flying on a straight course towards the canal, was able to get a clear view of it. From a distance he had seen Biggles's bombs explode, and, shortly afterwards, the destruction of the end shed. He had watched the archie barrage following him, and then return with renewed violence to the area in which Algy in the *Didgeree-Du* was now taking up the fight. He saw, too, the explosion of Algy's bombs, although by this time he himself was preparing for action.

The wisdom of Biggles's plan was now apparent, for not only was he down to a thousand feet, but he had been able to line his machine up with the sheds, which he could see clearly in the lurid glow of the fires, without his presence being suspected.

This satisfactory state of affairs, however, was not to last. Trembling a little with excitement in spite of his efforts to remain calm, he had commenced a shallow dive towards the objective when a searchlight suddenly swung round and flashed on his wings. It overshot him, and before it could turn back he had steepened his dive so that it sought him in vain. Nevertheless, the damage had been done, and in a twinkling the other lights were probing the air around him.

His mouth turned dry as the first archie shells lacerated the air dangerously close to him. He knew they were close because he could hear the muffled explosions above the roar of his engine, and Biggles had told him that archie was only dangerous when close enough to be heard. He had expected the barrage to be bad, but not quite as terrifying as this. Several times he felt splinters strike the *Dingo*, and although he tried hard not to think about it, his imagination refused to be sidetracked so easily. However, he kept his eyes on the sheds, determined to get a direct hit or die in the attempt. To endure all this danger for nothing was not, he thought, to be borne. Once he caught a glimpse in his reflector of the inferno that raged in the sky behind him, and the muscles of his face went stiff. Still, he reasoned, Biggles had gone through it; so had Algy; therefore, so must he.

An unseen missile crashed through the machine just in front of him with terrifying force. Something struck him on the cheek with the bite of a whiplash, and he grunted with pain. Putting his hand to the place, he stared fascinated by the sight of his own blood. Reaction came swift and strong; and, as so often happens, it took the form, not of fear, but of bitter resentment, and he looked for the target with a personal interest. 'I'll show you,' he muttered furiously, and jammed the stick forward in a kind of fierce exultation.

Down – down – down, he roared, careless now of the storm of fire that raged about him. 'I'm going to get those sheds or bust,' he told himself desperately, and it was no idle boast. A glance at the altimeter gave him a shock, for the needle was nearly on zero; he had not realized that he was so low.

In a sort of daze, feeling that the thing was not really happening and that he would presently wake up, he took aim with calculated deliberation. He was still a little short of the target, and the second or two that he had to wait exasperated his patience. He wanted to see the bomb burst and blow everything sky high.

Slowly, as the wing crept up to the first shed, his hand groped for the bomb-toggle. 'Now,' he muttered, suddenly conscious of a sense of power, and pulled the handle back as far as it would go. The *Dingo* bumped as the steel-clad load of high explosive plunged earthward.

Ginger was torn between a desire to wait and watch what happened and an urge to dive clear; fortunately for him his common sense prevailed, or it is unlikely that he would have lived long enough to know how successful he had been. He had zigzagged away as Biggles had told him, and was about to turn to see the result of his effort when the entire world seemed to blow up, lighting earth and sky in one terrific blaze. He felt the heat of it on his face. The *Dingo*, caught in that fearful blast, soared dizzily, throwing him against the safety-belt with a force that made him gasp. Temporarily blinded and half stunned by shock, he skidded crazily round the sky not knowing which way to go. In a subconscious way he noticed that most of the searchlights had gone out; nor was the archie as bad as it had been. The lattice mast of a wireless tower seemed to leap out of the darkness towards him, and he dragged the stick back into his thigh in a panic. He missed the mast by inches, but the shock did something to restore his senses to normal. 'Gosh! I'm nearly on the ground,' he thought frantically, and made haste to correct the error. He saw the canal, and made for it like a pigeon; for a few seconds he followed it; then, happening to glance at his compass, he saw that he was going the wrong way.

Again it was in something like a panic that he whirled the machine round and sped like a bullet towards the open sea. For some minutes the archie followed him, but in some curious way he had ceased to be alarmed by it. He began to laugh, but pulled himself up abruptly. 'That won't do,' he told himself seriously, and remembering the wound in his face, he felt it carefully. It was still bleeding, but, as far as he could make out, not badly. In any case, he was not conscious of any pain, so he thought no more about it. He did not bother to climb for height, but checking his compass, set about getting home by the shortest possible route. He remembered Biggles and Algy, and wondered vaguely how they had fared, but his thoughts were chaotic and he found it difficult to concentrate. 'I suppose I shall get used to this sort of thing,' he mused philosophically.

He could see the black bulk of Bergen Ait some time before he reached it; indeed, he was surprised that he could see it so plainly. He scanned the sea for ships, but there were none in sight, for which he was thankful, for it permitted him to make straight for the cove.

It was clear when he reached it, but as he glided down he could just make out one of the other machines being towed into the cave. Three flashes of a green light gave him the signal to land, and in a minute or two he was on the water, taxiing towards where he knew the entrance of the cave to be. The *Dingo* seemed strangely sluggish, but he thought nothing of it until the motor-boat dashed out, with Briny in the bows making frantic signals to him to hasten. Obediently he gave the engine more throttle, and roared into the cave, where the motorboat took the machine in tow and dragged it to the catwalk.

He switched off and pushed up his goggles. 'What's the matter?' he asked weakly.

Biggles answered. 'You were sinking. You must have got a float holed. It's all right now; the Flight-Sergeant will attend to it.'

Ginger sprang up in alarm. 'Great Scott!' he cried, 'I didn't know.'

Biggles helped him ashore. 'Good work, laddie,' he said patting him on the back; 'you got it a beauty.'

'How did you know?' inquired Ginger. 'Did you see it?'

'I certainly did – that is, I saw the blaze on the sky. They saw it from here – and heard it.'

Ginger stared. 'Well, do you know, that's a funny thing,' he said shakily; 'I was right on top of it yet I didn't hear a blessed thing.' He staggered suddenly.

Biggles caught him. 'Bear a hand, Algy,' he said sharply, noting the blood on Ginger's face. 'He's been hit. He needs medical attention.'

Ginger laughed foolishly. 'Don't you believe it,' he protested; 'what I want is my supper.'

CHAPTER V

An Unwelcome Visitor

For three days the Boomerang Squadron had no further instructions from London, for which Biggles was grateful, for the respite gave him time to organize things at the base to his entire satisfaction, and gave Ginger's face a chance to heal. The wound turned out to be a very slight one, no more than a cut from a flying splinter. Even so, in his excited condition it was enough to give him a temperature, and much to his disgust Biggles ordered him to remain in bed for a day. The period of inactivity also gave the Flight-Sergeant an opportunity of repairing the machines, all of which had been more or less damaged by gunfire.

Only one signal was received, and this could not have been more brief. It consisted of a single word, 'Congratulations'.

'I suppose that's from Colonel Raymond,' said Ginger. 'How do you suppose he knows how much damage we did – when we don't really know ourselves?'

Biggles laughed shortly. 'He knows all right, you can bet your boots on that,' he asserted. 'We've got agents on the spot, I'll warrant. Somebody told me that we had an agent at Kiel right through the last war. Anyway, since Headquarters has gone to the trouble of congratulating us, we must have made a nasty mess of the dump.'

One other item of news interested them immensely, and this they received on the ordinary radio, a powerful instrument on which they could get all the world's programmes. They rarely had time to listen to music, but the news broadcasts kept them up to date on the progress of the war. The item that pleased them most was the story of the raid by R.A.F. Squadrons on the German battleships at the entrance to the Kiel Canal. It had occurred on the same day as their own raid, and Biggles realized that the two raids must have been part of the same plan to destroy the enemy's equipment in the canal zone.

It was late in the morning of the third day after the raid that the next signal was received. The three pilots were sitting in the tiny mess, listening to Briny, who was describing with a wealth of graphic detail a raid in which he had once taken part against the cannibals of the Solomon Islands.

'Ten thousand of 'em there was, a-dancin' and brandishin' their spears; and only me and my old shipmate Charlie to face 'em,' he declared in a hoarse whisper. ' "Charlie," I sez, "you attack 'em in the flank. I'll tackle 'em in front. Charge!" I yells, and you wouldn't believe it—'

'You're quite right, Briny, I wouldn't,' put in Biggles sadly. 'Personally I could charge a well-done steak right now, so—'

Roy hurried into the room with the signal. He saluted and handed it to Biggles who, after a glance at the coded message, took it to the records room, the others following. He unlocked the safe, took out the code-book, and the envelope to which the signal referred.

'They seem to have got our jobs all ready for us before we came,' remarked Algy.

'The Colonel as good as told us so,' reminded Biggles. 'It was only to be expected. Our people have got spies on the mainland, and probably knew before the war started the most vital objectives which could be reached by a unit stationed here.' He read the orders in silence, the others watching his face anxiously.

'Well?' exclaimed Algy at last, impatiently.

Biggles glanced up. 'Listen to this,' he said quietly. ' "To Officer Commanding Z Squadron, on detached duty. On the first night after receipt of these instructions on which weather conditions are suitable, you will destroy the tunnel on the Berlin-Hamburg railway at Albeck, about sixty miles from the coast, as shown on the enclosed map. Owing to the depth of the tunnel it is not possible to do this by direct bombing. The only way success can definitely be assured is by placing an explosive charge (case W.D. 6. in your stores) in the tunnel. This will involve landing in enemy territory. A suitable field, one and a quarter miles from the tunnel, is marked in red on the map. You are warned that both ends of the tunnel are guarded day and night by double sentries. The guard-houses are situated as follows. At the northern end, a farm building seventy-eight yards north-east. At the southern end, a signal box twenty-five yards south-south-east. Receipt of these instructions will be acknowledged by a double A transmitted on the wave-length allotted to you three times at intervals of three seconds." '

Biggles finished reading, laid the paper on the desk and tapped a cigarette reflectively on the back of his hand.

'Very pretty,' announced Algy cynically. 'Do they think we possess some means of making ourselves invisible?'

'That's all right, old boy, you needn't come,' murmured Biggles casually.

Algy started forward belligerently. 'What do you mean – I needn't come? You can't leave me out of a show like this—'

'I'm sorry,' broke in Biggles blandly, 'but I rather gathered from your remark that you'd prefer to stay at home.'

'Well, think again,' snorted Algy.

'And that's no way to talk to your commanding officer,' returned Biggles. 'All right. We'll tell Roy to send the acknowledgement and then, with the map in front of us, think of ways and means. As a matter of fact, I did a job like this once before,' he added, as they went to the radio room and gave Roy instructions concerning acknowledgement of the orders.

Roy, with earphones clamped on his head, made a note on his pad. 'By the way, sir, I'm picking up a lot of Morse,' he said. 'I think it's being sent out from somewhere not very far away. It's in code, of course.'

'By jingo, if we could read it, it would be useful!' exclaimed Ginger. 'Do you think we could decode it?'

'Not a hope,' answered Biggles promptly. 'What point would there be in using a code that could be deciphered by the enemy? The only way official messages can be deciphered in war-time is with the official key, and that's something we're not likely to get hold of. I imagine the British government would be only too pleased to pay a million pounds for the German secret code at this moment. All the same, Roy, you can keep a record of any Morse you pick up – one never knows. Get that acknowledgement off right away.'

'Very good, sir.'

Biggles led the way back to the office and spread the map on the table. 'All we can do is memorize the spot,' he said, pointing with his forefinger, 'and work out the best way of getting to it. We shan't need three machines; two should be enough, one to do the job and the other to act as a reserve – and possibly a decoy. I'll think about that. If the weather is O.K. we may as well go tonight and get it over. Algy, go and dig out that box marked W.D. 6. I'll go and have a look at the sky. No,' he added as an afterthought, 'there's no need for me to go. You go, Ginger, while I have a look at the map.'

Leaving Biggles pondering over the map, Ginger made his way along the catwalk. He stopped for a few minutes to speak to the Flight-Sergeant, who was still working on the *Dingo*, and then went on towards the mouth of the cave.

Even before he pulled the tarpaulin aside he was aware, from the shrill cries of the gulls, that something unusual was happening outside. Thinking that possibly the cause was a coming change in the weather, for he knew that gulls often get excited at such times, he moved the heavy tarpaulin and looked out. Instinctively his eyes turned upwards to the birds. Normally the majority sat placidly on the ledges on the face of the cliff, but now they all appeared to be on the wing, and he was amazed at the number of them. The air was full of whirling white forms, thousands of them, wheeling and at the same time uttering discordant cries of alarm.

At first Ginger could see nothing on account of the birds, but as he stared he became aware that they seemed to be concentrating at two places, not very far apart. Focusing his eyes on the spot, he caught his breath sharply as he perceived the reason for the uproar. Two men in dark uniforms were creeping along a ledge; in their hands they carried baskets in which they were putting something which they were picking up from the rocks.

It did not take Ginger long to realize that they were collecting the eggs of the gulls, which were protesting at the outrage in the manner already described. For a full minute he stared at the two men as his brain strove to grasp the significance of their presence. Unprepared for anything of the sort, he was for the moment completely taken aback; but as his composure returned he realized that a boat of some sort must have brought them, and he looked along the foot of the cliffs to locate it. It was not hard to find. It was a small collapsible canoe. Sitting beside it, calmly smoking a pipe, was a third man.

Again Ginger's eyes moved, for he knew that such a frail craft could not have made its way to the rock across the open sea, and what he saw turned him stiff with shock. Lying just off the entrance to the cove, not two hundred yards away, was a submarine, its grey conning-tower rising like a monument above the deck. There was no need to question its nationality, for on the side of the tower was painted, in white, the single letter U. Below it was the number 159.

How long the submarine had been there, Ginger, of course, did not know, but it had evidently been there for some time, for several members of the crew were disposed about the deck, sunning themselves in the autumn sunshine, while a line of washing hung between the conning-tower and a circular gun turret.

Ginger was still staring, half stunned by shock, when he heard a noise inside the cave that galvanized him into frantic activity. It was the swish-swish of an engine as its propeller was turned preparatory to starting, and he knew that Smyth was about to test the *Dingo*. Releasing the tarpaulin which he was still holding, he tore back along the catwalk and nearly knocked the Flight-Sergeant into the water with the violence of his approach. He was just in time, for the Flight-Sergeant's hand was already on the starter.

'Stop!' he gasped. 'Don't make a sound.' Leaving the mechanic gazing after him, as if he had lost his reason, he dashed along to the records room, where he found Biggles and Algy still poring over the map.

Their eyes opened wide at the expression on his face. 'What's wrong?' snapped Biggles.

Ginger pointed down the cave. 'There's a U-boat in the cove,' he panted.

There was dead silence for a moment. Then Biggles sprang to his feet. 'The dickens there is,' he said tersely. 'What's it doing?'

Briefly, Ginger described the situation.

'I'd better have a look,' muttered Biggles. 'There seems to be nothing we can do except sit quiet in the hope that it will soon clear off.'

'Suppose these bird-nesters find the cave?' asked Ginger.

'It'll be the last birds'-nesting they do for a long time,' promised Biggles grimly.

'It's the U 159,' Ginger informed him.

Biggles clenched his fists. 'By thunder,' he swore, 'here's a chance. It was the U 159 that sank the liner *Arthurnia* without warning, so it would be just retribution if we handed it a basinful of the same medicine. It must be on its way back to its depot. Come on.'

He dashed off down the catwalk closely followed by the others, but nearing the tarpaulin he slowed down and peered cautiously round the end of it.

The U-boat was still in the same position, but the men who had been ashore, evidently having filled their baskets, were making their way back in the canoe. Reaching the submarine, they climbed leisurely on board.

'They seem to be in no hurry,' observed Biggles anxiously. 'I'm afraid we're going to have them hanging about for some time. Ginger, send the Flight-Sergeant to me.'

Presently the Flight-Sergeant came at the double, and Biggles gave him orders in a low voice. 'Get an armour-piercing bomb on each machine and cast off ready for instant action.' He turned to the others. 'If she finds the cave we shall have to go for her,' he explained. 'There are probably forty or fifty men on board, so if they once got ashore we shouldn't have a chance. They'd radio our position to Germany, anyway, and probably plaster us with that heavy gun on the bows. Our machine-guns wouldn't be much use against that. I'm still hoping they'll go without finding us.'

An hour passed, and still the submarine gave no indication of departure. Another hour went by; the washing was taken in and the deck cleared, but not until mid-afternoon did the sinister craft begin to turn slowly towards the open sea.

Biggles breathed a sigh of relief. 'She's going,' he said. 'That's the best thing that could happen for everybody.'

With her steel deck awash, the submarine ploughed its way slowly towards the south, the airmen watching it with mixed feelings of relief and regret, for such a mark might never again present itself.

Ginger, who had fetched a pair of binoculars, steadied himself against the rock and brought them into focus. 'How far is it away do you think?' he asked Biggles.

'About a couple of miles – why?'

'It's stopped – at least, I think so. Yes, it has,' declared Ginger. 'There seem to be some officers on deck – they're looking at something on the water. By gosh! It's coming back.'

Biggles grabbed the glasses – not that they were really

necessary, for what Ginger had said was obviously correct. The submarine had swung round in a wide circle and was returning over its course.

'What's the idea?' asked Algy. 'What could they have seen to bring them back?'

Biggles snapped his fingers. 'I've got it,' he cried. 'Look!' He pointed at an iridescent stain that drifted from the mouth of the cave and spread in a long wavy line towards the southern horizon. 'They've spotted that oil,' he added sharply. 'They're on their way back to see where it's coming from. It'll bring them straight to the cave. Quick! The machines! We've got to get that sub. or it's all up with us. Pull that tarpaulin out of the way, Smyth.'

There was a rush for the machines. Biggles was away first, as he was bound to be, for the *Willie-Willie* was nearest the entrance and blocked the way of the others. The roar of its engine drowned all other sounds. Leaving a wake of churning water behind it, the machine shot through the entrance to the cave and raced on over the cove. It bumped once or twice as it struck the swell of the open sea, and then, after climbing for a moment or two at a steep angle, made straight for the U-boat.

Biggles knew that there was no time for tactics. In the first place the members of the submarine crew must have heard his engine start, and no doubt they could now see him. That was not all. He knew that he had got to send the U-boat to the bottom before a wireless message could be sent to the shore, or a flotilla of destroyers would be round the islet like a pack of wolves round a wounded deer. It was in an attempt to prevent this happening that Biggles roared straight at the submarine.

From a distance of a quarter of a mile he could see the gun-crew feverishly loading their weapon, and more in the hope of delaying them than hitting anybody, he brought his nose in line and fired a series of short bursts from his machine-guns. Whether it was due to this or an order from the commander he did not know, but the men suddenly abandoned their weapon and bundled into the conning-tower. The top closed and the U-boat began to submerge.

But by this time Biggles was over it. His bomb hurtled down. He zoomed away swiftly, banking steeply on the turn so that he could see what happened. What he saw brought a grim smile to his lips. As quick as he had been, the others were not far behind him. The *Didgeree-du* and the *Dingo*, in line, swept over the patch of swirling water. Two great columns of smoke and spray shot upwards. The stern of the U-boat rose high out of the water, the propellers racing; higher and higher it rose until it was almost vertical; then it plunged downwards and disappeared from sight.

For a little while Biggles continued to circle, the other machines following him, in case there should be any survivors; but there were none, and in his heart he was relieved, for they were in no condition to take care of prisoners. A final glance at the wide patch of oil that marked the last resting-place of the U-boat and he turned back towards the islet. Without waiting for the others to land, he raced straight on into the cave, and, jumping out, ran on to the radio room.

'Did that submarine manage to get out a signal?' he asked Roy sharply.

'Yes, sir. It was very short though – not more than three or four words, I should say, although as they were in code I don't know what they mean. I've got a record of the letters though.'

'I see,' said Biggles slowly, and returned to the catwalk where the others were just coming ashore.

'What you might call short and sweet,' remarked Algy.

'Short, but not very sweet,' answered Biggles. 'Ah, well, that's war. If it hadn't been them it would have been us. That's what they've been handing out to unarmed ships so they could hardly complain. The Admiralty will be glad to know that one raider is out of the way. It seems to be a case where we might risk transmitting a signal. But come on, we'd better get ready for this show tonight.'

CHAPTER VI

A Dangerous Mission

The plan for the blowing up of the Albeck tunnel, as finally decided by Biggles and accepted without demur by the others, was completed, and as the weather remained favourable it was agreed to put it into operation that night. Two machines would go over, the first to be the *Willie-Willie* converted into a two-seater, with Biggles and Ginger in it. This was actually the operative aircraft. It would carry the explosive charge – a time bomb – with which they hoped to destroy the tunnel, and fly at its maximum ceiling, which Biggles thought could not be less than 25,000 feet. This would, of course, involve the use of oxygen apparatus, which had not been overlooked by the Admiralty in fitting out the base. Algy, in the *Didgeree-du*, also converted into a two-seater, was to take off twenty minutes after the others and fly at 10,000 feet with a dual role to play. Primarily, his purpose was to act as a decoy to distract attention from the operative machine by drowning the noise of its engine with its own. Secondly, it could act as a reserve plane to pick up the occupants of the first machine if by any chance it should be damaged in landing. If its services were required Biggles would signal to it by means of a red light; otherwise, it was to return home independently.

Biggles saw clearly that the greatest difficulty to be over-come was to reach the landing-field undetected, for it was too far inland to be reached in a glide after the manner adopted in the attack on the ammunition dump. He knew that if once the machine was picked up by the ever-questing searchlights it would not only be futile to land, but suicidal; so, after giving the matter considerable thought, he had decided on the scheme just outlined as the most likely way of escaping observation. Algy was to fly straight towards the landing-field, drawing both the searchlights and the anti-aircraft gunfire. In this way it was hoped that the other machine, flying 15,000 feet above it, would, by cutting its engine some distance away, be able to reach the field more or less silently. Once the *Willie-Willie* was on the ground matters would have to take their course. Biggles would have to open his engine in order to get off again, but this he did not mind, trusting to his ability to get back in the face of anything the enemy might do to prevent it.

To start with, the watches of both machines would be synchro-nized; both aircraft were to rendezvous over the islet at a prearranged time, at their respective altitudes, and fly on the same compass course at the same speed. This should (as Biggles explained) keep them together, for they would not be able to see each other. He, having to climb to a greater height, would take off first. The scheme was not entirely satisfactory, but he was convinced that it was the best they could do in the circum-stances.

'We'll start as soon as it's dark,' he concluded. 'It may take us some time to get into the tunnel, and it wouldn't do to be caught out in daylight.'

Accordingly, the machines were made ready, and at nine p.m.

the *Willie-Willie*, with Biggles in the pilot's seat and Ginger crouching over a gun behind him, taxied out to the cove. Another minute and they were in the air, spiralling steadily upwards.

For twenty minutes the steel airscrew of the *Willie-Willie* clawed its way into the starlit heavens, by which time the altimeter needle registered 22,000 feet, and the airmen adjusted their oxygen apparatus; then, still climbing slightly, Biggles struck off to the south-west at a steady speed of 280 miles an hour. Half an hour later the German mainland appeared ahead, black, sinister, as mysterious as another world. A finger of gleaming silver stabbed the darkness, and soon the air was cut into sections by the ever-alert searchlights.

Biggles's voice reached Ginger over the telephone. 'Look down,' he said. 'Poor old Algy seems to be copping it.'

Ginger looked over the side. Far below, so far that they appeared to be on the ground, a hundred flickering points of light danced in the darkness, and he knew it was the archie barrage throwing a curtain of fire round Algy's machine. It was hard to believe that the bursting shells were 10,000 feet above the earth. For a time he watched the barrage moving along below them, and from it was able to judge roughly the position of the *Didgeree-du*. Algy was getting the worst of it now, he reflected, but their turn would come later.

Once a probing beam swept perilously close to the *Willie-Willie*, but Biggles side-slipped away, sacrificing a little height in the slip, but keeping on his course.

The minutes passed; one by one the searchlights went out and the barrage thinned, as the coastal batteries were left behind. Below, the earth was wrapped in profound darkness, but the roads showed dimly, like pale threads snaking across the vast panorama.

Woods and forests showed as inky stains on the vague background of the earth. Occasional flashes still followed the course of Algy's machine, and the cunning of Biggles's plan became apparent, for so far not a single shell had come near the *Willie-Willie*, and it seemed fairly certain that its presence had not been suspected by the watchers on the ground. Shortly afterwards the archie trail swung away to the left, and Ginger knew that Algy had begun to circle away in accordance with their plan. That Biggles had noticed it, too, was made apparent when the *Willie-Willie*'s engine died, leaving the machine to glide silently along its lonely course.

Standing up to look immediately below them, Ginger saw what he expected to find – the railway; a long straight line that began in the indistinct distance behind them and vanished into the black horizon ahead. He considered it seriously, knowing that Biggles's skill in pilotage would now be severely tested, for to bring a machine down from such a height on a given landing-ground, at night, without touching the throttle, required more skill than the average pilot possessed.

Once a curious, nebulous ball of fire rolled along the line, and he knew that it must be a train; the lights in the carriages were out, but the fireman could not prevent the glow from reflecting on the smoke as he stoked his furnace.

Ginger thought the glide would never end. It seemed interminable, the more so because, owing to their great height, they did not appear to be moving; nor did they seem to get any lower, although he knew that this was not the case, for the altimeter told a true story and the needle was swinging back all the time.

Staring fixedly ahead, he saw the thin line of the railway end abruptly, as if it were cut off short in open country, and he knew they had at last reached the tunnel. A moment later the machine began a wide, flat spiral, and the details on the ground soon showed up more clearly. The moon had risen, and in its cold blue light he could even see the farm-building at the northern end of the tunnel which he knew must be the guard-house.

Quickly now the greys became less dim, and the outlines of woods and hedges stood out more sharply. A wide river, which he knew must be the Elbe, meandered across a deserted landscape to the north-west, for villages were few and far between.

A current of air on his left cheek interrupted his survey as the machine went into a steep side-slip, and he realized that Biggles must have arrived over the objective with plenty of height to spare; he noted it with satisfaction, for had they undershot they could only have reached the landing-ground by opening the engine. Looking ahead he could see it, a large field roughly triangular in shape, with a group of trees at the apex. He glanced at Biggles, and saw that he was leaning forward as he operated the gear that lowered the undercarriage wheels.

The field was under them now. Almost imperceptibly the nose of the machine came up as Biggles flattened out. The tail sank a little, but still the machine glided on towards the trees, its wheels about two feet above the grass.

Ginger held his breath and waited, praying that there were no unseen obstacles, for on the floor of his cockpit rested a small, square wooden case containing enough high explosive to blow the machine to atoms. He breathed again as the wheels touched, bumped gently once or twice, and trundled on towards the trees. He felt the machine strain slightly as the left wheel brake was applied, causing the aircraft to swing slightly so that it finished its run a dozen yards from the trees, facing the open field ready for an instant take-off should danger threaten. Silence fell.

'Well, here we are,' remarked Biggles quietly.

'Nice work, chief,' acknowledged Ginger.

They both got out of the machine, Ginger taking the explosive charge with him, and stood still, listening, peering with straining eyes into the dim moonlight, for there was just sufficient light for it to be deceptive.

'Everything seems to be quiet; I don't think we were spotted,' said Biggles at last. 'Give me a hand.'

Slowly, and not without effort, they dragged the machine back into the dense gloom under the trees, leaving it with its nose still pointing to the open field. There was no movement of air, so the question of the direction of the wind did not arise.

'Good! She'll do nicely there. We'll get along,' muttered Biggles softly, and picking up the time-bomb, set off down a hedge that led in the direction of the tunnel.

They came to a gap, and crawling through it, came out in a lane, which they followed for some distance; then Biggles cut across country, keeping as close as possible to the hedges, until they came to a slight embankment. 'We're about over the tunnel,' whispered Biggles. 'If we turn right here it should bring us to the entrance.'

In a quarter of an hour, now moving slowly and with infinite caution, they came within sight of the railway line. Lying flat, Biggles surveyed the scene. There was no one in sight. The guard-house, a square black barn, stood about a hundred yards away, but of the sentries there was no sign. He crept forward for a short distance and again lay still, straining his eyes to find the men who he knew must be there.

He was still staring into the tricky half-light when the door of the barn was suddenly thrown open; a shaft of yellow light fell athwart the grass, and a peremptory voice, in German, called, 'Keep your eyes open there; there's been an air-raid warning.'

'*Jawohl*,' was grunted in answer, so close to where he lay that Biggles instinctively stiffened.

The door was closed and the light disappeared. Silence returned. But it did not last long. 'Did you hear that, Fritz?' said the voice that had last spoken.

'*Ja*,' came the reply, heavy with boredom, some distance away. 'Anybody would think that the Englanders were coming here. The corporal's nervous. He ought to go into the trenches for a bit; that'd cure him.'

Biggles smiled grimly and felt for Ginger. 'I shall have to knock this fellow on the skull,' he breathed. 'If he makes one sound we're sunk. Keep close to me.' He drew his revolver, and holding it by the barrel, began to creep forward. He had not far to go. A round forage-cap appeared silhouetted against the sky. Beside it, at an angle, was the black outline of a bayonet.

For several minutes Biggles lay still, trying to work out the best way of approach, for there seemed to be a low growth of brambles between him and the sentry, and to cross these without making a sound was manifestly impossible. He was still lying there when, from far away, came the drone of an aero-engine, its steady purr punctuated by the dull *whoof, whoof, whoof*, of archie. He knew that it was Algy, still cruising about watching for a possible signal.

'Hello, Fritz, here comes the Englander,' called the sentry excitedly. 'Come here, you'll see better.'

The last word died on the man's lips, for knowing that if the two sentries came together his task would be infinitely more difficult, Biggles had risked all on a desperate chance. The sound of the man's voice deadened the slight crunch of briars as Biggles crept swiftly across them, added to which the sentry's interest was entirely absorbed by the approaching aircraft. He was staring up into the sky when Biggles rose like a black shadow behind him and brought the butt of his revolver down on his head. The man dropped without a sound.

Tight lipped with anxiety, Biggles whipped off the man's cap and put it on his own head. Snatching up the rifle, with the bayonet fixed, he rose erect just as the second sentry came over the brow of the slope not half a dozen paces away.

'Ah, there you are,' grunted the German as he came on. 'What are you doing?'

Biggles dropped the point of the bayonet until it was a foot from the man's breast. 'One sound and you die,' he said sharply in German, and there was a vibrant quality in his voice that confirmed his dire threat. 'Drop your rifle,' he added.

After his first gasp of astonishment the man made no sound. The rifle fell to the ground with a thud.

'Now lie down on your face and you will not be hurt,' commanded Biggles.

The man obeyed.

'Ginger, pull his greatcoat over his head and tie it round his neck with the belt,' went on Biggles. 'Now tie his wrists behind his back with your handkerchief – pull it tight.' He opened the flap in the butt of the rifle and took out the cord pull-through used for cleaning the barrel of the weapon. Kneeling, he wound it twice round the sentry's ankles and knotted it.

Now these operations had taken perhaps two minutes, and all the time the aeroplane had been drawing nearer. And that was not all. The door of the barn had been thrown open, and half a

'He was staring up into the sky when Biggles rose like a black shadow behind him'

dozen men poured out, talking excitedly, staring up at the sky. A telephone bell jangled. As if this were not enough, the rumble of a train could be heard approaching the southern end of the tunnel.

Biggles snatched up the time-bomb. 'If either of these fellows moves hit him on the head,' he said grimly. 'If those guards come this way, leave me; make for the machine and save yourself.' Before Ginger could answer he had scrambled down the slope and disappeared into the tunnel.

With his heart beating painfully from suppressed excitement, Ginger squatted beside the sentries, watching the men outside the barn, for in them lay the greatest danger. Once one of them shouted something, presumably to the sentries, but as Ginger could not speak German he did not know what was said, and could only remain silent. Overhead, the aircraft was now turning for home.

Ginger waited. A minute passed; it seemed an eternity of time. Another minute went by. What on earth was Biggles doing, he wondered feverishly? If he wasn't quick he would be knocked down by the train. Then, to add to his panic, one of the men outside the barn detached himself from the group and hurried down the line towards him.

Ginger drew his revolver and curled his finger round the trigger. Why didn't Biggles come?

The man gave a shout and broke into a sprint, and the next instant the reason revealed itself. Biggles came panting up the embankment. 'Run for it,' he gasped.

The man on the line shouted again. It was answered by others. A shot rang out.

'Keep going,' panted Biggles, as they tore through the brambles and made for the hedge that led in the direction of the landing-ground.

Ginger, snatching a glance over his shoulder, saw a line of figures on the top of the embankment, but the next second he was flung flat on his face as the ground rocked to the roar of an explosion that nearly burst his eardrums. Dazed, he staggered to his feet. Biggles caught him by the arm. 'Keep going,' he said again.

If there was a pursuit Ginger saw no more signs of it. His knees were weak under him by the time they reached the field in which the plane had been left. Gasping for breath, for they had crossed a ploughed field and their boots were caked with mud, he staggered on. Biggles, too, was puffed, and had to slow down. The group of trees that concealed the machine was still some distance away, but they plodded on, keeping close to the hedge. Once an aeroplane, its navigation lights ablaze, roared over them.

'They've got fighters up, looking for Algy I suppose,' panted Biggles. 'They'll be after us, too, presently,' he added, as they reached the machine, still standing as they had left it.

'Have *we* got navigation lights on?' asked Ginger suddenly. 'I forgot to look.'

'Yes – why?'

'Then why not switch 'em on and fly low?'

Biggles stared. 'Have you gone crazy?'

'I shouldn't be surprised, but I was thinking that they would take us for one of themselves and leave us alone.'

Biggles laughed aloud as he scrambled into his seat. 'Brilliant idea,' he declared. 'We can always switch the lights off if the dodge doesn't work. Come on – let's go.'

Ginger climbed into his seat; the machine raced across the dew-soaked turf and in a few moments was in the air, heading northward.

As soon as they were at a thousand feet Biggles switched on

the navigation lights, clearly revealing their position to anyone on the ground. He was only just in time, for a searchlight beam was already feeling its way towards them; but as the lights came on it swung away so as not to dazzle (as the operator evidently thought) the pilot of one of his own machines.

Ginger chuckled. The scheme was working. Indeed, it worked far better than they could have hoped, for not once were they challenged either by searchlights or anti-aircraft guns. They had one shock, and that was when an enemy machine, also carrying lights, came close to them, and actually flew for a short distance beside them. But apparently the deception was not suspected by the pilot of the German plane, for presently it turned away and disappeared into the night.

As they crossed the coastline Ginger let out a yell of triumph. Biggles did not answer, and leaning forward to see why, Ginger saw him staring ahead with a tense expression on his face, revealed in the luminous glow of the instruments. 'What's wrong?' he cried.

Biggles's answer was terse. 'I may be wrong, but that looks like fog ahead.'

Hardly had the words left his lips when a wisp of clammy moisture clutched at the machine, and the next instant everything was blotted out.

With his eyes on his instruments, Biggles switched off the navigation lights, which could no longer serve them, and easing the stick back, started to climb. He knew that it was no use trying to get under the fog, for he was already flying so low that to fly lower would be dangerous. There was just a chance, however, that if the fog proved to be no more than ground mist he might be able to get above it and see through it; for it is a curious fact that what at a low altitude may be an opaque blanket, can become transparent from a great height. But when the *Willie-Willie* had climbed to 5,000 feet, and was still fogbound, he knew that height would not help them; still he went on climbing, and shortly afterwards emerged into a cold, tranquil world of utter loneliness, beautiful in a way, but almost terrifying in its desolation. Overhead, the moon and stars gleamed in the dark blue vault of heaven, throwing a silvery sheen on the ocean of cloud that lay below, an expanse as flat as an Arctic snowfield, stretching as far as the eye could see. Just above it roared the *Willie-Willie*, with its shadow, surrounded by a misty halo, keeping it company.

With his eyes on the compass Biggles flew on. Half an hour passed and he knew that they must be somewhere near their base, but no break appeared in the all-concealing blanket that lay below. He dare not go down now for fear of colliding with the rock, so he started to circle, hoping to find a break in the fogbank; but it was in vain.

Two courses now lay open to him. Either he could turn away from the base, and, flying by instruments, endeavour to put the *Willie-Willie* down on the open sea, or he could continue circling in the hope that the fog would disperse before his petrol ran out. This, however, was unlikely, for he had only an hour's petrol left, and he knew from experience that the fog would probably persist until it was banished by the rising sun. If the fog did not disperse, then in an hour he would have to go down anyway, so he decided to go down while there was still petrol in his tanks; otherwise, even if he did get down safely, he would find himself adrift on hostile waters.

The steady roar of the engine died away as he cut the throttle and raised the landing wheels that would not again be needed;

at the same time he pushed the joystick forward. With the air humming a mournful dirge through the slowly rotating propeller, the machine glided down to the silvery plain that seemed to stretch to eternity, as smooth and level as a frozen sea. For a few seconds the floats ploughed into it, tearing it up like cotton wool; then the fog took the machine into its clammy grip.

Biggles sat quite still, his eyes on the altimeter needle. Minutes passed, minutes as long as hours, while the needle crept back round the dial – 4,000 ... 3,000 ... 2,000 ... 1,000. Still the gloom persisted. The acid test was now to begin. The needle continued its backward revolution, quivering slightly, over the hundred-feet mark.

Biggles had this advantage. He was not landing on unknown country where there was a risk of colliding with a hill, a high building, or trees. He had set the altimeter at sea-level, and to sea-level they were returning. He could, therefore, fly to fine limits.

Inexorably the needle sank, ticking off the hundred marks on the dial. Biggles had pushed up his goggles and was leaning over the side of the cockpit, blinking the moisture off his eyelashes as he stared down into the void. Two hundred feet, and there was still no sign of the black water which he knew was there; a hundred....

Ginger held his breath and braced himself for the shock which he felt was inevitable. The altimeter needle came to rest on the pin. Zero! Simultaneously a dark indistinct mass loomed up below.

The machine flattened out as Biggles snatched the stick back and held it level. The dark mass disappeared, returned, and then showed as black as ink. Biggles pulled the stick right back into his stomach. The *Willie-Willie* lurched sickeningly, and then sank bodily. Splash! A cloud of spray rose into the air. For half a minute the machine forged on, drenching itself with water. Then it came to rest. Biggles flicked off the ignition switch; the propeller stopped its rhythmic ticking. Silence fell. Silence utter and complete.

He unfastened his safety belt. 'Well, we are at least on the floor,' he said philosophically.

'So what?' asked Ginger.

'We sit here until the fog lifts,' returned Biggles. 'We can't do anything else. I only hope Algy got home before all this muck came down.'

CHAPTER VII

Combat!

For some time Biggles sat on the back of his cockpit, deep in thought. Actually, he was doing mental arithmetic, going over in his mind the course he had flown, trying to work out roughly how near – or how far – they were from the base. After a while he gave it up, realizing that even if they knew the direction of the islet it would be a most hazardous business trying to get into the cove; the chances were that they would run on the rocks at the foot of the cliff – or be carried on to them by the swell; and even if they managed to secure a handhold, the idea of trying to climb the cliff was not to be considered. It looked impossible in daylight, let alone on a foggy night. The thing that worried him most was that he did not know how fast or in what direction they were drifting. That they were drifting he had no doubt whatever, for there are few places on any ocean entirely free from currents. A four-knot current to the south might, when the fog lifted, leave them in full view of enemy coastguards, with consequences that could hardly fail to be tragic.

His reverie was interrupted by Ginger, who had climbed out and was standing on one of the floats. What the dickens is this thing in the water?' he said.

Biggles had been vaguely aware that the machine had jarred slightly against some floating object, but thinking that it was only a piece of driftwood he had paid no attention to it. He joined Ginger on the float, and, without speaking, stood staring at a round object that was just awash.

'That's the third one of those things we've passed,' said Ginger in a puzzled voice.

'What do you mean – we've passed?' asked Biggles sharply.

'What I say.'

'But the thing, whatever it is, must drift at the same rate as ourselves, so how could we pass it? It must be the same one—'

He broke off, and groping under his leather flying coat, took a box of matches from his jacket pocket. A match flared up, casting a small circle of yellow, misty light. 'Good heavens!' he cried aghast as he peered forward at the object. 'It's a mine. We've either come down in a minefield or we've drifted into one.'

The mystery was now explained. They were drifting, but the mines were stationary because they were anchored.

Ginger dropped on his knees and fended the mine away from the float, actually holding it by one of the horns, contact with which might have caused it to explode. 'For the love of Mike let's get clear of the infernal thing,' he muttered desperately.

Biggles said nothing, but he knelt beside Ginger on the float and helped him to push the machine clear.

'What can we do about it?' questioned Ginger.

'Nothing. This knocks any idea of taxiing on the head. We've only got to bump into one of these things – once. We can't move till daylight, that's certain.' Biggles lit a cigarette and smoked it reflectively.

The night wore on. Several times they saw mines and frequently had to fend the machine clear; but at last came a long interval when they saw none, and Biggles expressed a hope that they were clear of the minefield.

'What's the time?' asked Ginger.

Biggles climbed to the cockpit and looked at the watch on the instrument board. 'Three o'clock.'

'And it won't start to get light until half-past six.'

'About that,' agreed Biggles.

'How far do you reckon we're away from the base?' was Ginger's next question.

'I've no idea,' admitted Biggles. 'We've no indication of how fast we're drifting. I think we must be some way away from the island though, because of these mines. I can't think of any reason why there should be a minefield near the islet. That doesn't mean that the Boche hasn't got a reason, though.'

After that they fell silent again. What seemed to be an eternity of time passed; they could do nothing but sit still and watch for mines, although as a considerable period had passed since they had seen one, it looked as if Biggles's surmise that they were clear was correct.

It was, Ginger judged, about six o'clock when he heard a faint sound in the distance. He noticed that Biggles had evidently heard it too, for he stood up, listening, staring in the direction from which it had come. 'What did that sound like to you?' he asked.

'It sounded like a whistle,' answered Ginger. 'I suppose it isn't possible that we've drifted near the island, and that's—'

'No. Smyth wouldn't whistle if he was looking for us. He'd hail. Hark!'

'I can hear an engine,' asserted Ginger.

'So can I. It's coming towards us, too.'

'Is it the motorboat?'

'No – the beat is too heavy. Great heavens! Look out, it's nearly on us.'

It seemed as if at that moment the fog lifted slightly, for suddenly the muffled beat of powerful engines became clear and strong. Biggles flung himself into the cockpit, and then hesitated. He knew that if they remained where they were they were likely to be run down; on the other hand, if he started the engine the noise would drown all other sounds, and they were likely to collide with the very thing they sought to avoid. A swift glance over his shoulder showed him that Ginger was in his seat. Simultaneously the deep-throated boom of a ship's siren shattered the silence.

Biggles waited for no more. He started the engine, and began taxiing away from the point from which the sound had seemed to come. Hardly had the aircraft got under way when a towering black shape loomed over it. Biggles jerked the throttle wide open and the machine plunged forward. Even so, he thought it was too late, for they were right under the bows of the vessel. He flinched as it bore down on them, and the next instant what appeared to be a monster as large as a cathedral was gliding past them, leaving the plane careering wildly on the displaced water. Above the noise of his engine Biggles heard a bell clanging, and a hail, but he did not stop, for he knew that any ship in those waters was almost certain to be an enemy. A searchlight blazed suddenly, a spectral beam through which the fog swirled like smoke.

By this time the *Willie-Willie* was tearing over the water as fast as Biggles dare take it, for the wake of the huge vessel, which he realized from the searchlight must be a warship, was catching them broadside on, threatening to capsize the comparatively frail aircraft. He could see nothing; even the ship had once more been swallowed up by the fog, and the searchlight with it. For perhaps five minutes he went on; then, satisfied that they were clear, he throttled back, leaving the propeller ticking over. Slowly the machine came to rest and he stood up in his seat. 'Jumping halibut,' he muttered irritably, 'this is getting a bit too much of a good thing.'

'What was it, anyway?' asked Ginger in a strained voice.

'A Boche cruiser I think,' replied Biggles. 'It was going dead slow on account of the fog, or it would have cut us in halves. The lookout saw us, too, but I doubt if they could make out our identification marks, so they would naturally assume that we were one of their own machines, forced down by the fog.'

'In that case they'll probably stop and look for us.'

'They may stop, but I don't think they'll do much looking in this murk. They're more likely to try to give us their position, supposing that we are only too anxious to be picked up. There they go,' he added, as the bellow of a siren boomed across the water.

For half an hour the cruiser remained in the vicinity, sending out frequent blasts; but at the end of that time the eerie sound grew fainter and fainter, and finally ceased altogether – much to Biggles's relief, for the fog was beginning to turn grey with the coming of daylight.

Nevertheless, some time was yet to pass before visibility began to improve. Not for nearly an hour did the luminous white disk of the sun appear, low down on the eastern horizon, to prove that the fog was lifting. Slowly the area of dark-green water round the *Willie-Willie* widened, until it was possible to see a mile in every direction. Knowing that it was now only a matter of minutes before the mist would disperse altogether, Biggles took off and began climbing for height. As he expected, it was possible to see through the fast-thinning vapour, and presently he made out the black mass of Bergen Ait, far to the north-west. He headed towards it and glided down in the cove just as Algy was preparing to take off in search of them.

'I thought you were goners,' he said.

'You'd have thought so if you'd been with us, and that's a fact,' returned Biggles, who was staring at the water in the cove, where a number of seabirds were flapping, as if they found it difficult to get off. Streaks of bright colour showed everywhere. 'Where did all this oil come from?' he asked.

'From the submarine, I imagine,' answered Algy. 'There's oil all over the place.'

'Ah – of course; I forgot.'

'It wasn't only oil that drifted here from the submarine,' went on Algy. 'One of our bombs must have fairly split it in halves, and I fancy the skipper must have been in the act of sending a signal – at least, a whole lot of papers have drifted here. Take a look at this.' He pointed to a book bound in blue oilskin that lay on a rock, with stones between the pages so that the air could dry them.

Biggles took one look at it. 'Sweet spirit of Icarus!' he gasped, slowly turning the pages. 'It's the German secret code. We shall have to let the Admiralty know about this. What a stroke of luck. Hark!'

For a few seconds they all stood motionless in a listening attitude. Then Biggles took a pace forward, staring up at the sky, now a pale eggshell blue. One tiny black speck broke its pristine surface, a speck that grew rapidly in size. Nobody spoke, for they all recognized it. It was a German Dornier flying-boat.

'Get under cover everybody,' ordered Biggles.

He turned and darted along the catwalk towards the signals room, but in a few minutes he was back at the mouth of the cave where the others were still watching the movements of the enemy aircraft through a hole in the tarpaulin. 'It's looking for the submarine we sank yesterday morning,' he said. 'It has sent out several signals; Roy picked them up and I've just decoded them. Incidentally, you were right about the sub; it was signalling when our bombs hit it.'

'The Dornier's coming this way,' observed Algy from the tarpaulin.

Biggles joined him. 'You're right,' he said.

'He's coming lower, too. I'm afraid he's spotted the oil – yes, by gosh, he has. He's coming right down to have a closer look at it. If he follows it to this rock we're sunk.' He stepped back as the Dornier suddenly dived towards the cove. The roar of its engines vibrated through the cave.

'He's going to circle the island,' declared Ginger, with alarm in his voice.

'If the wireless operator starts tapping out a message about the oil there'll be a destroyer here in a brace of shakes,' muttered Biggles. 'Even if he doesn't signal he's bound to report it when he gets back, which will mean the same thing. They are bound to send some sort of boat out to see where the oil is coming from. I'm afraid we've got to stop this chap getting back.' He turned and ran along the catwalk to where the *Willie-Willie* was moored. 'Briny, get that tarpaulin down!' he yelled as he cast off.

The others had followed him along the catwalk. 'I'm coming!' shouted Algy, jumping into his machine.

'Please yourself; the more there are of us the better chance we shall have of getting him. Once we show ourselves we've *got* to get him.'

Biggles's final words were drowned in the roar of his engine, and the *Willie-Willie* surged towards the entrance. To Briny, who was dragging back the tarpaulin, he shouted, 'Where is he?'

'Round the other side of the rock, sir,' bawled Briny.

'Which way did he go?'

'Round to the left.'

Biggles waited for no more; he shoved the throttle open and the *Willie-Willie* tore across the cove in a cloud of spray. Another moment and it was off the water, banking steeply to the left.

Biggles's object was, of course, to come up behind the German 'plane, which he assumed – from the information Briny had given him – was still circling the island in a left-hand direction. He was, therefore, unprepared for what happened next. Actually, Briny's information had been correct, but what he could not be expected to know was that the Dornier had turned about on the far side of the island and was now coming back towards him. The result was that Biggles, rounding the towering black shoulder of the central mass, nearly collided with him. Both pilots saw each other at the same moment; both banked vertically, and in a split second had raced past each other in opposite directions, before there was even time to think of shooting.

With a grunt of annoyance Biggles dragged the *Willie-Willie* round in its own length, and tore along after the Dornier, just in time to see Algy's machine whirl into sight, and nearly meet the Dornier head on, as he had done.

The enemy pilot – wisely, perhaps, seeing that he was outnumbered – put his nose down for speed and streaked away to the south with the two British machines in hot pursuit.

As he roared low over the cove Biggles glanced down, and seeing no sign of Ginger's machine, wondered where it was. An instant later he knew, for it suddenly flashed into sight across the Dornier's bows. There was a streak of tracer bullets, and then the Dornier went on, apparently unaffected.

What had happened was this. In his desperate haste to get off Ginger had not thought of asking Briny which way the Boche had gone, so instead of turning to the left like the others, he had turned to the right, and in so doing had actually done what the others had intended doing. He had found himself behind the Dornier – in fact, behind all three machines; but as they had dived he found himself above them, and was thus able to use his superior height to gain speed and intercept the machine with the black crosses on its wings. He had managed to get in a short burst of fire at it, but his shooting had been hurried, and it was with chagrin that he saw the Dornier proceed on its way, apparently untouched by his bullets. All he could do was join in the pursuit with the others.

Biggles had no doubts about overhauling the Dornier, for their machines were built for speed whereas the flying-boat was designed primarily for coastal reconnaissance. And since it was soon apparent that they were, in fact, catching it, he had little doubt as to the ultimate result. What upset him was the thought that at that very moment the German wireless operator might be tapping out, as fast as he could, the circumstances of the combat – with, of course, the position of the secret base.

The German pilot did all that he could do against three opponents, as did his gunner, who, facing the pursuers, made things very uncomfortable for them. But he could not shoot in three directions at once, for Biggles and Algy were old hands at the game. At a signal from Biggles they separated to press their attack from different directions. Algy, coming within range, opened fire, drawing the gunner's fire upon himself and so giving Biggles a clear field.

The end came suddenly. Biggles swooped like a hawk and poured in a long decisive burst. He held his fire until collision seemed inevitable and then zoomed high, turning on the top of the zoom to see the result of his attack. Not that he had much doubt as to what it would be. With eight guns pouring out bullets at a rate of a thousand rounds a minute, the Boche must have been riddled.

His supposition was correct. The Dornier was roaring straight up like a rocketing pheasant; for perhaps two seconds it hung on the top of its stall, its airscrews whirling; then its nose whipped down in a spin from which it never recovered. Biggles watched it dispassionately, for he had seen the end of too many combats to be disturbed in his mind; and he was too wise to take his eyes off his victim in case the spin was a ruse to deceive him. That the Dornier was not shamming, however, was confirmed when, with its engine still racing, it plunged nose first into the sea. It disappeared from sight instantly and did not reappear; only an ever widening circle of oil marked the spot where it had ended its fatal dive.

Cutting his engine, Biggles glided down, and circled for some minutes in case there should be a survivor, but it was soon clear that the crew had perished in the machine, so he turned towards the island, anxious to find out from Roy if the radio operator in the Dornier had succeeded in getting out a message.

A glance over his shoulder revealed the others taking up formation behind him, so he went on towards the base, now about six miles distant.

Before he was halfway there Algy had rushed up beside him, beckoning furiously and jabbing downwards with his gloved hand.

Looking down, Biggles saw the reason. Ginger was no longer in the formation; he was gliding down towards the sea, which could only mean one thing – that he was having trouble with his engine. They could not leave him, so Biggles throttled back and began circling down, at the same time throwing a worried glance at the sky, the colour of which promised a change in the weather. He watched Ginger put his machine down on the water, and from its jerky movements saw what he already suspected – that the sea was getting rough. However, he landed within hail of the *Dingo*. 'What's wrong?' he called.

Ginger stood up in his cockpit, holding the edge to steady himself, for the machine was rocking dangerously. 'My engine has cut out,' he shouted. 'It began to splutter after they shot at me.'

Biggles taxied closer, while Algy continued to circle low overhead.

'What shall I do?' asked Ginger.

Biggles thought swiftly. To make repairs on the water was obviously out of the question. Had the sea been calm he would have dashed back to the base and sent the motorboat out to tow the *Dingo* in, but low, ominous clouds were scudding across the sky and the sea was rising quickly. In the circumstances he decided to attempt to tow the *Dingo* in himself. 'Catch this line and make it fast!' he yelled, and swung his mooring-rope across the nose of the *Dingo*.

Ginger caught the line and made it fast to his axle strut, and scrambled back into his seat as Biggles started taxiing towards the base.

Before they had gone a quarter of a mile, however, Biggles knew that they would never reach it, for the sea, now capped with vicious-looking white crests, was throwing both machines about in a manner that was definitely dangerous. A nasty cross-wind was dragging at the *Dingo*, and more than once brought it up short with a jerk on the tow-line that threatened to tear both machines to pieces.

He eased the throttle back, for the question of saving the *Dingo* had become of secondary importance; it was now a matter of saving their lives, for he was by no means sure that he would be able to get the *Willie-Willie* off the water. 'Cut the tow-line!' he yelled. 'Get ready to jump. I'm coming round to pick you up.'

Ginger obeyed the orders unquestioningly, although he realized that they implied the loss of his machine. Climbing out of his seat, he clung to a float, waiting for Biggles to bring the *Willie-Willie* alongside.

It was no easy matter, for both machines were now tossing wildly, and should they be thrown together it would mean the end of them. Blipping his engine, Biggles brought the *Willie-Willie* nearer.

'Jump for it as I go past,' he shouted.

Ginger, balanced on the float, jumped for his life. But his weight, as he jumped, was sufficient to cause the *Dingo* to yaw violently, and instead of landing on Biggles's float, as he hoped, he landed short and disappeared under the water. His head broke the surface almost at once, and he clutched at the float. He managed to grasp it, and endeavoured to drag himself on it, but the weight of his thick, water-soaked clothing held him back.

Seeing his plight, Biggles climbed out, and seizing him by the collar, gave him the assistance he needed. He then helped him into the rear seat.

There was still one more thing to be done. He dared not leave the *Dingo* floating derelict on the water, for not only would it certainly lead to inquiries, but it embodied features which German designers would no doubt be pleased to possess. So as soon as he was back in his cockpit he reached for his signalling pistol, and was taking aim at the *Dingo*'s petrol tank when Algy roared low overhead – so low that it was obvious he was trying to attract attention.

Biggles looked up, and saw Algy's gloved hand jabbing frantically towards the south-east. So occupied had he been with his task that he had paid no attention to the horizon; now, looking in the direction indicated, he saw a sight that brought a scowl to his face. Racing towards them through rain that was beginning to fall was a German destroyer.

CHAPTER VIII

Discoveries

It was typical of him that he finished what he had begun. He took quick aim and sent a flare into the *Dingo*'s petrol tank. A tongue of flame spurted out. Satisfied that the destruction of the machine was assured, he pushed his throttle open. Simultaneously a spout of water leapt into the air about fifty yards in front. He had heard the scream of a shell, so he was in no doubt as to what it was. The destroyer, seeing that they were about to escape, had opened fire.

Straight along a trough in the sea roared the *Willie-Willie*, flinging spray high into the air, with spouts of water rising behind it as the German gunners tried in vain to hit the small, fast-moving target. A giant wave loomed up in front, its crest curling ominously, and it was in sheer desperation that Biggles dragged the joystick back, for he knew that the *Willie-Willie* could not meet such a sea head-on, and survive. Its floats left the water, and then sank down again as if loath to leave it; they cut through the foaming wave-crest; the machine shuddered and Biggles thought the end had come. An inch lower, and the *Willie-Willie* must have been dragged down, but as it was the crest thrust the machine upward. For a few seconds it hung perilously near a stall; then the racing propeller lifted the nose and it staggered into the air.

Gasping his relief, Biggles looked for Algy, and saw him about a thousand feet above, firing long-range shots at the destroyer – not, of course, with any hope of causing damage, but to irritate the gunners and perhaps spoil their aim. Seeing that Biggles was safely off the water, he desisted, and roared down alongside the *Willie-Willie*.

Biggles, after a last regretful glance at the destroyer – regretful because he had neither bomb nor torpedo with which to attack it – beckoned to Algy and turned his nose to the west with the idea of leading the captain of the enemy ship to think that they were on their way to England. For one thing was certain: under the eyes that he knew would be watching them he dare not return to the base. In any case, with the sea that was by this time running, he doubted if a landing in the cove was possible. So through a mist of driving rain the two machines roared on into the western sky.

Not until he was satisfied that they were out of earshot of the destroyer did Biggles begin turning in a wide curve, for it was not his intention to get a great distance away from the base; indeed, as he had only about an hour's petrol left in his tanks he dare not go far. He was, in fact, in a quandary, and his problem was this. If the rough sea persisted and they returned to the base, it was likely that the machines would be wrecked trying to effect a landing in the cove. By holding on their present course there was just a chance that they might reach a neutral country, in which case, even if they got down safely, they would spend the rest of the war in an internment camp. But they would at least save their lives.

Biggles did not hesitate for long. He decided to return to the island – if he could find it. He was by no means sure that he could, for the weather was fast getting worse. And it continued to get worse, great masses of cloud rolling across the sky and filling the air with a drenching mizzle that blotted everything underneath. Another thing that worried Biggles was the fact that Ginger was already soaked to the skin, and might well collapse from exposure if he remained much longer in the air. How much petrol Algy still had left in his tanks he did not know, but he assumed that it was no more than he himself had. With one thing and another it was in a very anxious state of mind that he began a wide turn which he hoped would bring them within view of the base.

Twenty minutes passed. The wind was now blowing half a gale, bringing with it occasional sleet, and he had to admit to himself that he had no idea of his position. Only one thing was clear, and that was that their condition was little short of desperate; consequently, when a few minutes later he saw land through a hole in the clouds, he lost no time in diving towards it. He knew that it was not Bergen Ait, for it seemed to consist chiefly of a long sandy beach, with flat, marshy ground beyond it; however, since their lives were now at stake, he glided towards it, thankful for the opportunity of getting down anywhere.

As he drew nearer he was able to make out that the beach fringed a large bay, protected on the windward side by rolling sand-dunes, so that the surface of the water, while not by any means calm, was far less rough than the open sea and offered a fair chance of a landing. Had he been sure that the surface of the marsh was firm he would have risked a landing on it, but he had no means of knowing whether it was hard or soft and he dare not take the chance. The only satisfactory thing about the landscape was that it seemed to be entirely deserted, for he could not see a building of any sort.

After a glance over his shoulder to make sure that Algy was following, he glided down to a rather rocky landing, and at once taxied to the shelter of the lee shore, where, after a searching survey of the landscape, he turned to see how Ginger was faring, and to wait for Algy.

Ginger was standing up. His teeth were chattering. 'Crikey!' he muttered, 'isn't it perishing cold! Where are we?'

Biggles shrugged his shoulders. 'Don't ask me. All I know is that we're in a lovely mess – or we shall be if this muck doesn't clear off. Here comes Algy; let's hear what he has to say about it.'

Algy landed and taxied up to them. He pointed to the sandy beach. 'What country's that?' he demanded.

'Search me,' returned Biggles bitterly. 'As far as I'm concerned it could be pretty well anything except Australia or Canada. We've been going round in circles for the last half hour.'

'You're telling me,' snorted Algy. 'You nearly got me dizzy. What made you land here, anyway? Are you thinking of doing a bit of paddling on the beach, or something?'

'If this sea doesn't go down pretty soon you're likely to have all the paddling you want – and bathing too,' retorted Biggles. 'I don't know about you, but my main tank is pretty well dry. We can't do anything about it until the clouds lift – not that I think they will, until this evening. The dickens of it is, Ginger's wet through.'

'Then why not run up on the sand? There ought to be some drift-wood about; if there is we could light a fire and warm ourselves.'

Biggles rubbed his chin thoughtfully, a harassed frown lining his forehead. 'If it happens to be a neutral country there'll be a fine old stink if anybody sees us.'

'From what I can see of it there's going to be a stink anyway. I'm all for going ashore.'

'All right,' agreed Biggles. 'If the sand is firm we could take off from the beach.'

No more was said. They taxied the two machines to the edge of the surf, where, lowering their wheels, they ran up on the sand. By the time they had looked about them the rain had stopped, although billowing clouds sweeping low over the sea restricted visibility to about a mile.

'If this stuff will lift a little higher we ought to be able to find our way back to the island,' declared Biggles cheerfully, glancing upward before turning to scrutinize the landscape; but all that could be seen was a long strip of drab yellow sand, unbroken by a footmark and backed by bleak dunes that ended in a fringe of coarse grass. A more desolate spot it would be hard to imagine, for there was not a building of any description in sight, or any other mark of human occupation. Which, of course, suited them very well. There was plenty of driftwood along the high-water mark, so in a short time a brisk fire was burning, with the stranded airmen huddled around it. And there they remained all day, going farther and farther to collect fuel as their stock ran low, noting with satisfaction that between occasional storms the weather slowly improved, with a corresponding extension of visibility.

On one such wood-collecting excursion Ginger found himself near the sand-dunes, so more from a spirit of idle curiosity than definite reconnaissance he climbed to the top of the highest and surveyed the view inland. He discovered that, as not infrequently happens, he could see farther across the landscape than he could over the sea, and thus it was that an unsuspected feature was revealed, a feature that at once explained the desolation.

It seemed that they were not on the mainland at all, but on a sandbank about half a mile wide, and of such length that it could almost claim the description of an island. Beyond it lay a narrow strait, with what he took to be the mainland in the background – a foreshore as low and desolate as the sandbank on which he stood. And he saw something else, something that aroused his curiosity more than a little, although the object was commonplace enough. It was merely a notice-board on the edge of the sandbank; but it seemed to be in a well-kept condition, and he wondered, naturally enough, for what purpose a board should be erected in such a place, since it was hard to imagine that anyone would come there unless compelled to do so – as they had been – by bad weather.

The notice-board stood some distance away, facing the strait, and his curiosity was such that he felt compelled to examine it more closely; at any rate, the language used would tell him what country they had invaded, he reflected; it might even give them the name of the locality, which would be a valuable guide to help them to find the base. So, keeping a careful lookout, he set off across the soaking grass.

The board proved to be at a greater distance than he had judged; however, he encountered no obstacles, and the end of ten minutes' sharp walking saw him standing in front of it.

One glance was sufficient to tell him on whose territory they had landed, for apart from the unmistakable German letters, the order concluded with the two familiar words, 'Heil Hitler'. For the rest, unable as he was to read German, he could only recognize the word *verboten*, which he knew meant forbidden.

He made a note of the text for Biggles's benefit, and was about to start on the return journey when, like a colossal apparition, out of the mist at the northern end of the strait came the last type

88

of vessel he expected to see in such a place. It was a liner, and a huge one at that. He wasted no more time, but bending low, raced back towards the camp as fast as his legs would carry him.

As he topped the last rise he saw Biggles coming to meet him, and Algy's attentive position near the machines suggested that they had become alarmed by his absence.

'What is it?' asked Biggles crisply, knowing from Ginger's attitude that something was amiss.

'We're on an island,' puffed Ginger. 'There's a channel on the other side. There's a whacking great liner going through it.'

Biggles's face expressed amazement, but he dashed up the slope, and throwing himself down, peered through the long grass. 'Well, upon my life, if it isn't the *Leipzig*!' he gasped. 'She's the swell German luxury liner. You remember she disappeared after leaving South America about three weeks ago. The Navy's been scouring the seas for her. So she's got away, after all. I should say she's going to Danzig, now the Germans have captured the city. They'll probably use her as a troopship. What a tragedy we haven't a torpedo with us. What a target she makes! But what's the use of talking. Even if we took off now, and found the base right away, it would be dark before we could get back.'

For some minutes they lay still, watching the great ship creeping majestically down the channel.

'Why were you away so long?' asked Biggles presently.

'I went to have a look at that notice-board over there.'

'Notice-board? Where?'

Ginger pointed. 'There it is. I went to see what was written on it. It's in German, so we're evidently in Germany. The only word I knew was *verboten*, but I made a note of the rest.' He recited the words.

'Well, upon my life, if it isn't the Leipzig,' he gasped

'That simply means "landing forbidden – anyone trespassing will get it in the neck" – or words to that effect.'

'Why should people be forbidden to land on a place like this? Who would want to land, anyway?'

'It's no use asking me,' returned Biggles briefly. 'Wait a minute though,' he added. 'There must be something here people are not allowed to see, and if that is so we ought to find out what it is – although goodness knows what it can be.'

They watched the liner disappear into the mist and then returned to the machines.

Algy greeted them impatiently. 'I reckon we could get off now,' he said, jerking his thumb in the direction of the sky. 'It has started to get dark, so if we hang about much longer we shall have to stay all night.'

'Yes, we'll go,' agreed Biggles. 'All the same, there's something queer about this place, so I think we ought to come back later on – probably tomorrow – and give it the once-over. Just a minute.' He climbed into the cockpit of the *Willie-Willie* and took his map from its pocket. Opening it flat on the ground, he studied it closely. 'This must be where we are,' he announced, pointing to the coast of East Prussia. 'This island here must be the island we're on – here's the strait – see? That gives us a line to Bergen Ait. Come on, let's get home.'

In a few minutes both machines were in the air, racing low over the uneasy water on a north-westerly course. The weather was still thick, but the clouds had lifted somewhat and were broken in many places, a condition which suited Biggles well, for although he flew through the open spaces, he kept close to the clouds, prepared to take cover in them should danger threaten.

However, they saw no craft of any sort, either in the air or on the sea, and twenty minutes' flying on full throttle brought them to within sight of their rocky home. The sea, while by no means as tranquil as they would have wished, had gone down considerably, and landing in the cove presented no great difficulty or danger.

Not a little satisfied at their safe return, Biggles taxied into the cave, calling loudly for Briny.

Instead, the Flight-Sergeant answered his hail.

'Where's Briny?' asked Biggles.

'He's gone, sir,' answered Flight-Sergeant Smyth.

'Gone? What do you mean – gone?'

'We thought you were down on the water somewhere. I told him you hadn't enough petrol to remain up all this time, so he took the launch and went to see if he could find you. I stood by here in case you returned.'

Biggles regarded the Flight-Sergeant seriously. 'Then heaven only knows what's happened to him,' he muttered. 'What time did he start?'

'It'd be just before lunchtime, sir.'

Biggles made a despairing gesture. 'Then *he* must have run out of petrol by this time. I expect he found the sea got too rough for him and had to run before the wind. Well, we can't do anything about it now,' he added after a glance at the mouth of the cave. 'It's nearly dark. We'll look for him in the morning – that is, if he doesn't come back during the night. You'd better look over these machines. We've lost the *Dingo*. By the way, before we left I told Roy to send a signal that we had got hold of the German naval code. Do you know if he sent it?'

'Yes, sir. The message was acknowledged.'

'Good.' Biggles turned to Ginger. 'You go and get some dry clothes on,' he ordered, 'then join us in the mess. It's about time we had something to eat.'

CHAPTER IX

What Happened to Algy

When at daybreak the following morning Biggles was informed that Briny had not returned he made immediate arrangements for a search. 'It's a nuisance because there are other things we should be doing,' he told Algy, for Ginger, tired out, had not awakened. 'We ought to explore that sandbank to see what the notice is about,' he continued. 'And there is a chance that we might overtake the *Leipzig* and plunk a mouldy[1] in her ribs. Further, I don't like this flying about in daylight; we are bound to be spotted sooner or later if we go on like this; the original idea was that we should only fly at night. However, while there's still a chance that Briny is drifting about in the boat we can't do other than try to find him. There's no need to wake Ginger. He can do with a rest. Two machines will be enough, anyway; there should always be one in reserve. I'll leave orders that Ginger is to stay where he is until we return.'

'We'd better go in different directions,' suggested Algy.

'More or less,' agreed Biggles. 'The gale came down from the

1 Naval slang for torpedo.

north so the boat should be somewhere south of here. I'll cover the south-west. You take the south-east.' So that there could be no mistake, he marked the two sections lightly on his map with a pencil. 'If we find the boat, and it isn't too far away, we might try to tow it back – providing, of course, that the water is calm. Otherwise we shall just have to pick Briny up and abandon the boat. Come on, let's get off. I'm glad the weather is better, but it's getting late in the year and I wouldn't trust it too far. By the way, I've got Roy on decoding all the Boche messages that he has picked up; they may reveal something that needs our urgent attention so we'd better not be too long away.'

In a few minutes both machines – the *Willie-Willie* and the *Didgeree-du* – were in the air, heading away from the base on their respective courses. The sky was clear except for wind-torn streaks of cirrus cloud at a great altitude, but it was not long before the machines were out of sight of each other.

Algy, as arranged, continued to fly south-east, and, having climbed to 5,000 feet, settled down to study the surface of the ocean, which stretched away to the horizon, unbroken as far as he could see by a vessel of any sort.

For twenty minutes he cruised on, and then began turning in ever-widening circles, but no sign of the missing boat could he see. Far to the southward a dark grey line marked the position of the enemy coast, and for some time he kept away from it, for he was anxious to avoid being seen from the shore. But presently some floating wreckage attracted his attention, and in order to investigate it he had to approach nearer to the coast. He soon ascertained that the wreckage was not that of the motorboat, and he was about to turn back towards the open sea when he perceived – what he had already suspected – that the land to the south was not the mainland, but the desolate sandbank on which they had landed the previous day.

Thinking the matter over, it struck him that it was by no means unlikely that Briny had been driven on to it, for the weather had come from the north, and as he knew from their visit that the sandbank was uninhabited, there seemed to be little or no danger in examining it more closely. With this object in view he began edging cautiously towards it, keeping as far out to sea as would permit a survey of the sandy beach.

He had followed it for perhaps three miles, and could see in the distance the bay in which they had landed, when a dark-coloured speck that could only be a human being detached itself from the dunes and ran down to the water's edge.

Algy could only fly nearer, for, from where he was, recognition was out of the question, but he felt that it was extremely unlikely that an enemy coastguard would expose himself in such a way, or behave in such a manner, for the figure was now gesticulating in a way that could only mean one thing. So he cut his engine and began to glide down; not with the intention of landing immediately, but in order to satisfy himself that the figure was actually that of the missing sailor. He felt pretty certain that it was, for he could not imagine who else it could be, but a doubt still lingered in his mind because there was no sign of the motorboat.

Gliding low over the solitary figure, he saw that it was, in fact, Briny, whose wild manifestations of joy reminded him in some curious way of Man Friday on Robinson Crusoe's island. A quick inspection of the shore satisfied him that it was safe to land, and in a few minutes the *Didgeree-du* had run to a standstill on the beach not far from the stranded sailor.

Briny, grinning broadly, lost no time in reaching the aircraft. 'How did you know I was here, sir?' he inquired, saluting.

'I didn't,' Algy told him frankly. 'How did you get here, anyway? Where's the boat?'

'I don't know where the boat is and that's a fact, sir,' declared Briny. 'I swam here.'

'What do you mean – you *swam* here?'

'Well, sir, it was like this 'ere, sir. The gale caught me a beam, and pretty near swamped me. I couldn't make no 'eadway against it – although I remember once, off Cape Cod—'

'Never mind about Cape Cod. We're here. Where's the boat?'

'Well, as I was saying, sir, I 'ung on as long as I could. Then I ran out of petrol, and there I was, adrift as you might say. Then I see this place and thought I'd better get ashore. I couldn't get the boat in, so I 'ad to leave her and swim for it. I 'ad a job to get through the surf meself.'

'You must have nearly lost your life,' suggested Algy.

'I nearly lost me 'at,' returned Briny seriously.

'It would have been a pity to have done that,' muttered Algy sarcastically. 'What happened to the boat?'

'She drifted away after I got ashore. Then I ran up here as fast as I could.'

'Why run? What was all the hurry about?'

'Well, you see, sir, you wouldn't believe it, but I found meself right up against the German liner *Leipzig*. I knew her in a jiffy. I remember seeing her once, off Cape—'

'Just stick to the story. Where is the *Leipzig* now?'

'She's aground, sir, at the entrance to the channel, about four miles down the coast. I reckon she must have gone ashore in the dark at low water. Maybe they'll float her off when the tide turns.

And there's something else here, too, although you wouldn't spot it if you didn't run slap into it, as I did, in a manner of speaking. There's a big shed round the next bend.'

'What sort of a shed?'

'A building as big as an aeroplane hangar, but not so high. It's painted all over with brown and yellow stripes. It stands on the edge of the water in as neat a little cove as you ever see.'

'What's in this shed?'

'I dunno, sir. It was dark when I was there. I lay down in the dunes near by, reckoning to have a closer look when it got light, in case there was a dinghy in it. I was trying to find a way in when I see you coming, so I ran down on to the beach so as you'd spot me.'

'Did you find anything else on this bit of no-man's-land?'

'No, sir, that's the lot.'

Algy thought quickly. The absence of the motorboat was now explained, but he was more concerned about the shed Briny had described. That it was a secret supply depot seemed certain, and this, no doubt, accounted for the notice-board forbidding people to land. But Briny's description of the shed had been vague, and he felt that while he was there he ought to obtain more detailed information, for the Admiralty would be anxious to have full particulars. 'How far away is this shed?' he asked.

'About a mile, sir, I reckon.'

'And as far as you know there was no guard over it?'

'I didn't see a soul, sir.'

'In that case we'll go along and have a look at it. Get in.'

Briny started, 'Get in what, sir?'

'This aeroplane – what else do you think I mean? You can't see any motorcars about, can you?'

'What, me, sir?'

'Yes, you. Don't argue.'

'You don't mean you're going to *fly* there, sir?'

Algy wasted no more words. He bundled Briny into the back seat, and then, climbing in himself, taxied swiftly along the beach.

'Steady on, sir, me 'at's blowing off,' roared Briny, who was clutching at the sides of the cockpit.

Algy did not take off, for the short distance he had to travel made it unnecessary, and five minutes brought them to within sight of the building. He saw at once that Briny's description of it, as far as it went, was correct. The shed was a large but low structure, covering nearly half an acre of ground, built in a dip in the dunes at the landward extremity of a tiny cove so regular in shape that there was reason to suppose that it was artificial. The building stood at the very edge of the water; indeed, it was obvious that at high tide a boat of shallow draft would be able to moor up against the huge sliding doors; yet so cleverly camouflaged was it, in the same drab colours as the surrounding sand, that it would have been possible to fly over it at a low altitude without suspecting that it was there. It appeared to be absolutely deserted.

Seeing that it was impossible to taxi right up to the shed on the landward side on account of the dunes, Algy took the machine on to the water, and after raising his landing-wheels, made a cautious approach, prepared to take off the instant anyone appeared; but by this time he felt confident that had a guard been on duty he must have heard the approaching aircraft and revealed himself.

Nevertheless, he did not relax his caution as he taxied on, very slowly, until the *Didgeree-du* was alongside a wooden landing-stage that now appeared near the doors.

'Go and have a look round to make sure that nobody's about,' he told Briny. 'I'll stay here in case of accidents. If it's all clear I'll join you.'

Briny was soon back. 'Can't see a thing, sir,' he reported.

'What's in the shed?'

'I can't see, sir. There ain't no winders.'

'That's queer. You'd have thought there'd have been some sort of lighting.' Algy got out and tried the doors, but, as he expected, they were locked.

Meanwhile, Briny had climbed to the top of a dune, high enough to overlook the roof. 'There's skylights on top,' he announced.

'Skylights usually are on top, Briny,' smiled Algy. 'I'd better have a look. Give me a bunk up.'

Algy was soon on the roof which, like the rest of the building, was built of corrugated iron. Crawling to the skylight, he peered down through it. For a few seconds he could see nothing, for owing to the inadequate lighting the interior of the shed was in dim twilight. Presently, however, he was able to make out the broad details, enough to tell him that the shed was, in fact, a naval depot – for submarines, chiefly, he thought, judging by the torpedoes and a formidable stack of oil drums. Having seen enough for his immediate purpose he slid off the roof.

'It seems to be an ideal spot to plant a bomb,' he declared as they went back to the machine. 'And the sooner the better,' he added. 'If we can get rid of this lot, submarines coming here, relying on finding fuel, might find themselves stranded. I should say the sub. we sank was making for this place. Come on, let's get back; the C.O. ought to know about it.'

More than a little satisfied with the result of his survey, Algy turned the nose of the *Didgeree-du* to the mouth of the cove, and opening his throttle, roared away in the direction of the base.

So concerned was he with getting back that beyond keeping a watchful eye on the horizon for shipping he paid little attention to the sea below; so when Briny tapped him on the shoulder and pointed downwards, he followed the outstretched finger with a twinge of anxiety – anxiety that grew rapidly to acute alarm when his eyes found the object that Briny had spotted. Unquestionably, it was the wreckage of an aeroplane.

Cutting his engine, he side-slipped steeply towards it, and at a thousand feet his worst fears were realized, for showing just above the gently lapping waves was the circular red, white, and blue nationality mark of a British aircraft. For a moment he experienced a feeling of relief as he remembered that the *Dingo* had been lost, for he assumed, not unnaturally, that this must be the remains of it; but then he recalled that Ginger's machine had been burnt out, whereas there was no sign of fire on the wreckage.

As quickly as he dared he put the *Didgeree-du* down on the water and taxied up to the wreck. One glance was enough to tell him the worst. The machine was one of their own; and if further proof were needed, the boomerang device on the crumpled fuselage, with the name *Willie-Willie* below, provided it. It was Biggles's machine. And the reason for its present condition was apparent, for through fuselage and wings were the unmistakable gashes of shrapnel.

As white as death, Algy flung off his flying-coat and slid into the water, groping blindly for the cockpit. He found it. It was empty, as was the spare seat. Gasping, he returned to the surface, and climbed up on the nearest float of his own machine, from whence he stared at the wreckage as if he could not believe his eyes. His brain seemed paralysed. Biggles had been shot down. That was obvious. And judging from the number of hits registered on the plane, and the mangled condition of it, the crash must have been a terrible one. He tried not to believe it, but there was no getting away from the grim evidence before him.

It was Briny who discovered that the engine was missing. 'It looks as though it was chopped out with an 'atchet,' he declared in a sombre voice.

'Then that settles it,' returned Algy miserably. 'They shot him down and salvaged the engine for their own use. They would, of course.' He said no more. There was nothing else to say. Minutes passed and still he stood on the float, staring dumbly at the wreck. At last, realizing that no good purpose could be served by remaining, yet hating to leave the spot, he climbed slowly into his cockpit. His eyes wandered over the surrounding sea.

Briny guessed what he was looking for. 'It ain't no use looking for the body,' he said gruffly. 'It 'ud sink. I remember—'

'We'll get back,' broke in Algy harshly, and taking off, he raced on full throttle for the base.

'Where's Mr. Hebblethwaite?' he asked the Flight-Sergeant, who came running along the catwalk to meet them.

'I don't know, sir,' was the unexpected reply. 'We haven't seen him for a couple of hours or more.'

'He didn't by any chance go with the C.O. after all?'

'No, sir. The C.O. hasn't come back yet.'

'I'm afraid he – won't be coming back,' said Algy slowly. He glanced at the *Platypus*, the spare machine, still riding at her mooring. 'Mr. Hebblethwaite must be about somewhere.'

'That's what we thought, sir, but we can't find him.'

Briny and the Flight-Sergeant watched in embarrassed silence as Algy unfastened the strap of his flying-cap and lit a cigarette. 'The war still goes on,' he said evenly. 'It can't stop because the C.O. is – missing. I am now in command here. Get my machine up to the derrick and sling a torpedo on it.'

'But are you going off again right away, sir?' asked the Flight-Sergeant.

'I am,' answered Algy curtly. 'You'd better make a thorough search for Mr. Hebblethwaitehe may have fallen and hurt himself. If he turns up tell him to stand by until I return. Those are my orders.'

The Flight-Sergeant saluted. 'Very good, sir.'

CHAPTER X

Ginger Goes Exploring

Had Ginger been aware of Algy's tragic discovery his state of mind would have been more harassed than it actually was – although he would have found it difficult to believe that possible.

He had been awakened by the roar of the two machines taking off to begin the search for Briny; he had guessed what they were going to do and hastily pulled on his slacks with the intention of confirming it. Outside he was met by the Flight-Sergeant, who gave him Biggles's order that he was to stand fast until the search party returned.

Annoyed with himself for having overslept, Ginger made his way back to his quarters, finished dressing, and had his breakfast. Thereafter he wandered about for the best part of an hour, killing time by examining the stores and visiting Roy in the signals room. Bored, he was on his way to the mess when it struck him that it was a good opportunity to explore the extremity of the cave – not so much for any particular reason as from idle curiosity. So fetching an electric torch from the stores, he started off over the loose rocks which began where the water ended. It struck him that he ought to have told the Flight-Sergeant where he was going, in case the machines returned before he did, but on second thoughts he concluded that this was unlikely, and proceeded on his way.

It is often fascinating, if futile, to speculate what might have happened if certain events had gone otherwise than they did, or to trace the tremendous consequences of incidents which, at the time, seemed of trivial importance. Thus it was with Ginger now. Had he returned and reported his proposed expedition to the Flight-Sergeant, the Flight-Sergeant would have known where he was; he in turn would have informed Algy, who, instead of taking off with a torpedo on board, would have first tried to locate him in order to tell him about his discovery of Biggles's machine. But Ginger did not return, and as he proceeded on over the rocks he would have been incredulous could he have foreseen the result of his failure to do so. It is certain that the history of 'Z' Squadron would have been altogether different from what it actually was.

He discovered, as he rather expected, that beyond the area of flat rock on which the depot was established the cave rapidly diminished in size, closing in on all sides until it was no more than a high, narrow tunnel, the floor of which was strewn with rocks worn round by centuries of erosion. He could not see why this should be, for the sea did not come as far, ending as it did in a rather slimy pool just beyond the depot. However, he assumed that exceptionally high spring tides penetrated farther into the island than they supposed, and made a mental note to warn Biggles of this, for it seemed not unlikely that at such times the floor of the depot would be inundated.

Thereafter the cave narrowed so rapidly that he was quite prepared for it to end abruptly at any moment; so confident was he that this was the case that he almost abandoned his survey, and it was only by the merest chance that he squeezed through a gap and turned the beam of the torch on what lay beyond. To his surprise he found that the cave, while not broadening to any great extent, became very high – so high, in fact, that the light of the torch failed to reach the ceiling.

The picture that now presented itself was in the nature of a gigantic crack, or fissure, the floor of which sloped upwards. Both the floor and walls of the cavity were polished smooth in a manner that suggested that water was responsible, and again this puzzled him not a little, for he could not imagine that the tide would rise so high. Wonderingly he took a few paces forward, and a clue to the mystery was provided when, stepping on something soft and looking to see what it was, the light of the torch revealed the decomposed carcass of a seagull.

On the face of it there was nothing remarkable about finding the body of a gull there, for there were legions of them on the outside of the rock, but his common sense refused to accept the obvious explanation – which was that the gull had made its way right up the cave in pitch darkness. Why should it? He had never seen a gull in the cave, or even one that looked like entering the cave, so why should this particular bird proceed up it so far and then perish miserably?

A few moments' reflection were sufficient to cause Ginger to reject the supposition that the gull had flown up the cave. Yet the gull was undoubtedly there. How had it got there? There could only be one answer to that question. There was another entrance to the cave; it was (he reasoned) through this other entrance that the water had entered, and since water does not run uphill, the other entrance must be higher than the one they habitually used.

This at once presupposed that the gull had been carried to its present position by water flowing down through the rock.

Hunting about, Ginger soon found what he sought – a small pool in a depression in the floor. Dipping his fingers into it, he tasted it, and discovered that it was fresh, without any suggestion of salt. After that, deduction was fairly simple. Somewhere ahead, possibly on the top of the rock, there was a watershed through which rain water made its way down into the cave.

He went on now with renewed interest, for it seemed probable that he had found a way to the top of the rock; and if this was so it would serve a very useful purpose in that they would be able to command a much wider view of the ocean than had been possible from the mouth of the cave. So he pressed on, anxious to ascertain if this was really so.

The floor now began to rise steeply, strengthening his conviction that the fissure went to the top of the rock. It was tiring work, for not only was he travelling uphill, but he was often compelled to put the torch in his pocket to leave both hands free while he climbed a scree of loose shale, or an awkward-shaped boulder. However, he encountered no serious obstacle until he was brought to an abrupt halt by a face of overhanging rock some twelve feet high which completely blocked his path. Examining it closely, he suspected that he must be near the top, for a steady trickle of water flowed over the edge of the rock, which was worn to the smoothness of polished marble. It was covered with green slime, and to make matters more difficult, did not present a single foothold.

Disappointed at the thought of being thwarted just when success seemed assured, he sat down to get his breath and at the same time think out a way of overcoming the obstruction. He soon found one. There were plenty of pieces of loose rock lying about; these he proceeded to collect and pile one upon the other, forming a cairn, from the top of which he was able to reach the top of the obstruction. The rest was comparatively easy. Or so he thought.

How far he was wrong he discovered when, dragging himself up on the rock, his dangling legs struck the top of the hastily constructed cairn and sent it avalanching down the cave with a crash that brought his heart into his mouth, for until he realized what it was he had a horrible thought that the cave was collapsing on him. He perceived at once that this was going to make it very difficult for him to get down again. And it was only the first disaster, for as he was squirming over the edge of the rock, the torch, which he had put in his pocket, fell out, and went crashing down the way of the cairn.

Reviling himself for his carelessness, he dragged himself up and sat panting in utter darkness on the edge of the rock, thoroughly alarmed, wondering whether to go on or to try to get back, realizing that the descent of the rock on which he was perched was not going to be easy. Even if he got down without hurting himself, and then found that the torch was broken – as seemed highly probable – his return was going to be a slow and tedious business. He remembered with relief that he had a box of matches in his pocket, but feeling in it with nervous haste, he discovered to his intense disappointment that there were only three matches in it.

He knew that, as he had already been away from the depot much longer than he originally intended, he ought to start back and leave further exploration for a future occasion, when he could begin more suitably equipped. And he had, in fact, made up his mind to return forthwith when, happening to stare into the darkness ahead, he saw a grey streak not very far away, a patch of reflected daylight which could only mean that he was near the end of his journey.

In the circumstances it was only natural that he should begin walking towards it, feeling his way in order to conserve his precious matches. But he had only taken a few paces when he stepped into a void. Feeling himself falling, he made a terrific effort to preserve his balance; but it was too late, and the next instant, with an abruptly terminated cry of horror, he was splashing frantically in ice-cold water.

To fall into a pool of cold water at any time is bad enough, but to do so in utter darkness, in such a place as Ginger now found himself, was terrifying. Unable to touch bottom he had to swim, and instinctively struck out for the rock from which he had fallen, only to discover to his dismay that it was as smooth as a tombstone and the top was beyond his reach.

Had it not been for the one patch of grey light his plight would have been desperate indeed, and it was probably as much in order to escape the suffocating darkness as any other reason that he struck out towards it. To his unspeakable relief, after swimming a few strokes he found that he could touch bottom, so he staggered on through the water towards the blessed light, which, he felt, was the only thing that saved his sanity.

As he approached the spot it grew definitely lighter, and it was with a prayer of thankfulness that he finally dragged himself towards an aperture through which he could see what he had begun to wonder if he would ever see again – the blue sky. His haste to reach it was nearly his undoing, for he had forgotten all about his steep climb, and he was in the act of stepping forward when a spectacle so unexpected, and so alarming, met his eyes that a gasp of despair left his lips as he recoiled from it. The ground in front of him dropped sheer for a full four hundred feet. Indeed, it was even worse than that, for his precarious perch actually overhung the abyss, and he dropped on his knees in a spasm of vertigo as his eyes surveyed the dizzy height.

For a moment or two he remained still, fighting the weakness, angry that he should have succumbed to it. Then, taking himself in hand, he made a quick inspection of his position. He saw that instead of emerging on top of the rock as he had assumed would be the case, the fissure had ended some twenty feet below the top of the cliff, which he could now see above him. He perceived, too, that although this twenty feet of rock face was sheer, the surface was rough, and offered finger holds by which a skilled mountaineer might have made his way to the top; but he was not a skilled mountaineer, and the mere thought of trying to make the short but terrifying journey to the top made him feel physically sick.

Lying flat, he peeped furtively over the rim of his perch at the rocks far below, but they offered no clue to his whereabouts in relation to the cove. All he could see was a jumble of weed-covered rocks against which the waves – appearing from his height as insignificant as ripples – beat with measured regularity. Above them, minute white specks, which he knew were gulls, soared aimlessly. For the rest, the ocean stretched, an infinite expanse of dark green water, to a hazy horizon.

The next matter that engaged his attention was the source of the water that filled the subterranean lake, for he saw at once that it could not enter the aperture through which he had reached the light of day, so returning a few paces into the cave he examined the roof closely. It was his ears rather than his eyes that provided the solution, for a steady trickle of water told him that tiny invisible streams were percolating through flaws in the rock and finding their way into the natural reservoir, which, at the time of heavy rain, must overflow with the results already noted.

As there was nothing more to see Ginger now gave serious thought to his position. He became aware that he was cold, which was not surprising since he was soaked to the skin – his second wetting within a few hours. He was worried, too, about his long absence from the base, which he knew could not fail to cause alarm, and might upset Biggles's plans. He had dismissed all idea of trying to get to the top of the rock, so it was obvious that the only way he could return to the depot was by the path he had come up, although this now presented difficulties that appalled him.

In the first place it meant a swim across the lake, with no assurance that he would be able to find the fissure on the far side, or to climb up to it if he did find it. Assuming that he was successful so far, he was then faced with the disagreeable ordeal of dropping twelve feet in utter darkness on to a pile of boulders; for his matches, being wet, were now useless. He realized with an unpleasant twinge of fear that if he injured himself in the drop he was likely to die, in circumstances which he preferred not to contemplate. It is not surprising that the more he thought about things the less he liked the look of them, and sought desperately for an alternative.

Turning again towards the sea, it suddenly struck him that the watery sun might have sufficient power in it to dry his matches; if he could only get them dry, he thought, he ought to be able to transport them across the lake by tying them on his head. So with this object in view he took the box from his pocket and laid it, with the three matches beside it, in a sheltered pocket of rock reached by the sun. This done, he stood back prepared to await results. And he was still waiting, cold and uncomfortable, when a sound reached his ears that brought him round facing the sea, tense and expectant. It was the distant hum of an aero-engine; and presently he saw the plane, which he recognized at once for one of their own, heading straight towards the rock. What was more, he perceived that if it held on its present course it would pass fairly close to him. If only he could attract the pilot's attention – for he did not know who was flying the machine, and was unaware of Algy's tragic discovery – it would alter the whole position. Those at the base would then guess what had happened, and presently come to his assistance. Even if they failed to find the fissure, he would, by signalling to them as they flew over, be able to ask for the things he most needed – food, a rope, and a new torch.

Watching the machine, with fading hopes he soon realized that the chances of his being seen were remote. The pilot might glance at the top of the rock in passing, but he would hardly be likely to look closely at the face of the cliff, for there was no reason why he should. But if he, Ginger, could only reach the top, silhouetted against the skyline he could hardly escape being seen. Swiftly, he turned to make a closer inspection of the perilous passage.

Now that he had become accustomed to the dizzy height it did not look so formidable, and almost before he had made up his mind seriously to attempt it he found himself on the bottom ledge, groping with his fingers for a firm hold. Finding one, he shifted his feet, and clawed again for a fresh cleft for his fingers. And so he went on, not once daring to look down, but keeping his eyes on the rim above as it drew imperceptibly nearer.

Gasping with fear and exertion, his clutching fingers at last closed over it, and with a haste made desperate by the now close proximity of the aircraft, he dragged his aching body over the top and rolled clear of the edge.

In a moment he was on his feet, waving frantically. He was just in time to see the machine glide out of sight round a shoulder of the rock.

Sick with disappointment, he sank down, and cupping his chin in his hands, gazed disconsolately at the empty sea.

CHAPTER XI

What Happened to Biggles

When he took off to look for Briny, the only doubt in Biggles's mind, apart from a natural concern about the lost sailor, was that, by force of circumstances, they were doing much more daylight flying than he had ever intended, more than Colonel Raymond had intended, and without question more than was safe if the secret of the base was to be guarded. His natural caution told him that they could not hope to go on flying daily over hostile waters, at all hours, without sooner or later being observed, and the suspicions of the enemy being aroused. Already their activities must have attracted attention, he reflected, as he pursued his allotted course, climbing all the time to obtain a wider field of view.

For the best part of an hour, like Algy, he was unsuccessful, seeing no craft of any sort; and he was contemplating giving up the search when, far to the south, a minute object caught his eye. It was a vessel of some sort, but even at that distance he felt that it was too big to be the motorboat. Nevertheless, he decided to make sure, so he flew on, and presently perceived that the object was not one boat, but two, a fairly large one with a smaller one moored close to it.

A suspicion was already forming in his mind as he throttled back and began a long glide, in this way losing height to get a clearer picture of what was happening; and in a few minutes his suspicion was confirmed. The smaller of the two vessels was undoubtedly the missing motorboat; the larger one, as far as he could make out, appeared to be a trawler or drifter. Considering the situation, he came to the natural conclusion that Briny had been found adrift by the larger boat, which had – as it was bound to – offered assistance, either by taking it in tow or supplying it with fuel.

The question that now automatically arose in Biggles's mind was the nationality of the drifter. If it turned out to be a German ship, then he could do nothing about it, for while he was prepared to take chances, it did not occur to him to attempt such a fantastic undertaking as to try to capture the ship single handed. What concerned him far more was the fact that by this time he was being watched by the crew, who would lose no time in reporting his position.

Instinctively his eyes went to the drifter's stern to see if she was flying her nationality flag; and he saw that she was. What was more important, it was not the flag of the German Mercantile Marine. He was unable to identify it; all he knew was that it was not the German flag. And that was really all he cared about, for if it was not a German vessel it must belong to a neutral country, and since they were on the high seas he had nothing to fear.

Consequently, he continued the glide with the object of landing as close as he could to the two vessels, now lying hove to side by side. It may seem strange – and a few minutes later he was to reflect on this – that not for one single moment did it occur to him that the drifter might be flying false colours. So, with no suspi-

115

cion in his mind, he made a good landing and without hesitation taxied up to the larger craft. It is true that it struck him as odd that Briny was not in sight, but he came to the natural conclusion that he was in the captain's cabin going through unavoidable formalities, in which case there was a chance that he might not have heard the approaching aircraft.

Still without the slightest suspicion of anything wrong, Biggles taxied right up to the drifter; and if he had entertained any doubts the behaviour of the crew would certainly have dispelled them, for they were leaning over the rail, smiling with what he took for amiability. So he made the *Willie-Willie* fast, and stepping out on to a float, climbed aboard.

'Thanks for picking up my—' he began, but he got no farther. Instead he stared in amazement at what he now beheld. The members of the drifter's crew were still smiling, but from all sides he was covered by a whole range of weapons, from automatic pistols to a machine-gun.

Biggles knew that he had made a mistake, but he still did not understand entirely what had happened. His eyes went again to the flag still fluttering at the stern, thinking that he must have been in error in supposing it was that of a neutral country; but what he saw only confirmed his first impression, for the flag was that of a Scandinavian country, although he couldn't remember which. Further, the crew wore no uniforms except the blue jerseys commonly used by merchant sailors.

'What's all this about?' he inquired curtly, slowly looking round the circle of menacing weapons.

'You come this way,' ordered one of the men, who, in peaked cap and double-breasted reefer jacket, appeared to be one of the ship's officers. He beckoned towards the companion-way.

'*From all sides he was covered by a whole range of weapons*'

Unquestioningly Biggles followed. Indeed, he was in no case to argue. Further, he was anxious to get to the bottom of the apparent mystery as soon as possible.

Escorted by two men armed with rifles, he followed the officer down the steps and along a short corridor to a cabin, where he was disarmed and then searched, the contents of his pockets being taken away. There was a brief delay; then the officer returned and ordered Biggles to follow him. They went on a little way down the corridor and halted before a door that stood ajar.

'Come in, Major Bigglesworth,' said a suave voice, which Biggles recognized instantly.

A ghost of a smile flitted over his face as he pushed the door open, walked slowly across the threshold, and turned to face the man who was seated behind a small ship's desk. It was, as he already knew, his old enemy, Erich von Stalhein of the German Secret Service.

A curious expression, half cynical and half triumphant, was on the German's austere face; but his blue eyes were frosty.

Biggles considered him dispassionately. 'Congratulations,' he said.

'On what?'

'On changing your nationality. I can't recognize your new flag so I don't know what you've changed to, but since it couldn't be worse than it was when I last saw you, it must, perforce, be better. In the circumstances I can only congratulate you.'

A flush swept across von Stalhein's prominent cheekbones. 'Still as insolent as ever,' he said harshly.

Biggles helped himself to a cigarette from a box that stood on the desk and tapped it on the back of his hand. 'What have you done with my man – I mean, the fellow who was in the motorboat?'

'Ah! So there was only one.'

'You ought to know.'

'On the contrary, since the boat was empty when we found it we had no clue to the occupants or the number of them. We found the boat adrift – but we recognized its nationality, of course.'

Biggles looked into the German's eyes and thought he was speaking the truth – as indeed he was. 'The poor old fellow must have fallen overboard,' he said sadly.

'What was he doing in the boat?'

'Between ourselves, von Stalhein, he was looking for me. I was delayed on a flight yesterday and he came to the not unnatural conclusion that I had been forced down. When he, in turn, failed to return, I could hardly do other than look for him, could I?'

'Failed to return? Return where?'

'To the place where I expected to find him, of course.'

Von Stalhein leaned forward in his chair. 'Major Bigglesworth,' he said distinctly, 'I would advise you to be frank with me. We know you are operating somewhere near our coast. Where is your base?'

'How do you know I'm operating near your coast?'

'I will ask the questions if you don't mind. I repeat, where is your base?'

'Well, I suppose there's no harm in your asking,' murmured Biggles indifferently, 'but I have a higher regard for your intelligence than to suppose you expect a correct answer.'

Von Stalhein's thin lips parted for a moment in a frigid smile. 'From where did you take off this morning?'

Biggles made a deprecatory gesture. 'Oh, stop wasting time, von Stalhein. What is more to the point, I'm here, which should afford you considerable satisfaction. What are you going to do about it?'

'What do you expect me to do?'

'Hurry back home and tell the world how clever you are. Don't forget to mention that you borrowed a neutral flag, will you, because I shan't.'

'As it happens, I am too busy at the moment to do anything of the sort, but I will take steps to transfer you to a place where you will be safe pending your trial for espionage.'

Biggles raised his eyebrows. 'I suppose to one who doesn't mind sailing under a false flag, false charges are a mere detail.'

'Do you deny that you are a spy?'

'I most emphatically do. How can I be a spy when I am wearing a British officer's uniform? The rules of war demand that I be treated as a prisoner of war.'

'I am not concerned with the rules of war – or any other rules, Major Bigglesworth. You have given me far too much trouble in the past for me to run one single risk of your escaping. I've got you, and I'm going to keep you until I hand you over to those who will know how to deal with you – and if you have any optimistic views as to what that will be I advise you to dispel them. It so happens that my chief is not far away, so perhaps it would be as well to settle the matter immediately. With you disposed of I shall pursue my quest for your base with greater assurance.'

'I'll bet you will,' sneered Biggles.

'For the last time, I will offer you certain considerations in return for information concerning the position of your headquarters.'

'And for the last time, von Stalhein, nothing doing. Save your breath. You'll need it before I'm through with you.'

The German shook his head sadly. 'As you wish,' he said quietly.

He gave a curt order to the escort and Biggles was marched from the room to a fairly comfortable cabin.

He heard a key turn in the door, and other sounds that told him that a guard had been posted.

Having nothing else to do, he sauntered to the porthole, not with any hope of getting through it for it was obviously much too small, but to see what happened to his machine.

Several men were working on it, cutting the engine from its bed. This was soon hoisted inboard, leaving the wrecked airframe floating on the water. The drifter then got under way, leaving the remains of the *Willie-Willie* rocking in its wake.

He was about to turn away when a gun crashed. For a moment he thought that the drifter was being attacked, but then he saw a shell burst near the derelict fuselage of his machine, looking strangely pathetic as it drifted alone on the water, and he guessed that von Stalhein had ordered it to be destroyed. That this supposition was correct was soon confirmed when several shots struck the machine, smashing the floats and causing it to settle slowly in the water.

Biggles turned away from the porthole. As far as he was concerned the *Willie-Willie* was a complete wreck; he gave it no more thought, nor did he look at it again, so he was unaware that the airframe did not entirely disappear, but remained awash, kept afloat by the air in the undamaged portions of the wings and elevators.

He was lying on his bed, smoking, turning his position over in his mind, when he was surprised to hear the drifter's engines slow down, and finally stop, while the clang of bells and shouted orders told him that something was happening. He knew that they could not yet have reached any of the German ports on the Baltic, for it was still twilight – about six o'clock as near as he could judge (his watch had been taken from him when he was searched), so he wondered what was happening. And it was with the object of trying to find out that he crossed again to the porthole. At first he could see nothing but water, but as the drifter slowly swung round he was astonished to see the hull of a big liner come into view. Nor was his surprise in any way diminished when he recognized it for the *Leipzig*.

What business the drifter had with the big ship he could not imagine, but he was soon to know. His door was unlocked. An escort appeared, and he was invited peremptorily to follow it. He had no alternative but to accept.

Across the deck of the drifter, up a gangway, and through a door in the side of the huge ship he was led, and finally halted outside the door of a stateroom. A brief delay, and in response to a sharp order he was marched inside.

He saw at once from the assembled company, and the manner in which it was disposed, that something in the nature of a court, or tribunal, had been convened; and he had no doubt as to the part he was to play. Facing him, seated at a long table, were four officers in German naval uniform. Between them sat an elderly man with iron-grey hair and piercing blue eyes who regarded the prisoner with more than passing interest. It was clear that he was the President of the court. At the end of the table sat von Stalhein, with some papers in front of him, and from one of these he now began to read so fast, in German, that Biggles had difficulty in following what was being said. However, he made no protest, for there was good reason to suppose that the result of the so-called trial was a foregone conclusion.

Von Stalhein finished reading and sat down. 'You understand?'

said the President in English, looking at Biggles with frigid hostility.

'More or less,' returned Biggles; 'but before we go any farther I must protest against this court and the charges Hauptmann von Stalhein has enumerated. I am an officer of His Britannic Majesty's Forces, on active service, and under the rules of war I claim the privileges of a prisoner of war.'

The President smiled grimly, an unpleasant smile which told Biggles at once that his protest was a waste of time. He had expected as much, but still he had felt compelled to make it.

The President looked at the men seated on either side of him. 'I don't think we need waste any more time over this,' he said harshly in German. 'We have heard of this man Bigglesworth before; he is one of the best men in the British Intelligence Service; we have reason to know him, for he has given us a lot of trouble in the past.'

'A man dressed in the military uniform of his own country can hardly be called a spy, I think, if that is what you are trying to make out,' put in Biggles coldly.

'Pah! What is a mere uniform? Can you deny that since the outbreak of war you have been into Reich territory?'

'I don't deny it, but I was in the uniform I am now wearing. If that makes me a spy, then by the same token every German soldier in Poland is a spy, and the French troops in your country on the Western Front are also spies. Are they to stand trial for espionage if they are captured?'

'It is not the same thing,' said the President roughly, although he did not explain where the difference lay. 'You know, of course, the price a spy must pay when he is caught?' he added.

'Yes, of course I know,' replied Biggles bitterly.

The President nodded and made a note on a slip of paper. 'Then the sentence of this court is that you be shot to death in—' He broke off short, in a listening attitude. 'What's that?' he asked sharply.

Von Stalhein had jumped to his feet and hurried to a port-hole. Simultaneously anti-aircraft and machine-guns broke into violent action. Above the din came the high-pitched scream of an aeroplane diving at terrific speed under full throttle.

Von Stalhein turned back swiftly into the room. 'You had better take cover, sir,' he said tersely. Then his eyes turned on Biggles, and his hand dropped to the revolver that he wore in a holster on his hip.

What he intended doing was not revealed, for at that moment the ship heeled over under the impact of an explosion so violent that every one in the room was hurled off his feet. With it came a blinding sheet of flame, followed a split second later by swirling clouds of black, oily, high-explosive smoke.

CHAPTER XII

A Cold Swim

Biggles, coughing convulsively as the acrid fumes bit into his lungs, pushed aside a limp body that lay across him and staggered to his feet. He tried to see what had happened, but the lights had gone out and the room was black with smoke which made his eyes smart unbearably; from the angle of the floor, though, he knew that the ship had taken a heavy list to starboard, a list that was rapidly becoming more pronounced. The air was filled with an appalling medley of sounds – shouts, the hiss of escaping steam, the vicious chatter of a machine-gun, a series of explosions deep down in the ship, and the gurgle of rushing water; somewhere not far away a man was groaning. A sickening smell of scorching mingled with the fumes.

Trying to beat the smoke away from his face with his hands, Biggles groped for the door; he found it, only to discover that it was jammed tight and half buried under collapsed girders. Clearly, there was no escape that way, so in desperation he turned to where he judged the nearest porthole to be. At the same time the smoke began to disperse somewhat, and through a grimy haze several things were revealed. The first thing he noticed was that it was nearly dark outside. Then he saw that a great jagged hole had been torn in the ship's side, and that owing to the list water was already pouring through it in an ever-increasing flood. Instinctively he made towards the hole, and looked out upon a fearful spectacle. He had seen much of war, but never anything on quite such a scale as this, and the deep twilight only served to make it more terrible. The water was full of debris of all sorts, among which at least a hundred men were swimming or splashing. Many were shouting, either from fear, or to make their position known to others. A splintered lifeboat hung vertically by its bows from a single davit, while over all lay a cloud of smoke and steam.

With the water now threatening to sweep him off his feet, Biggles turned back into the room to see what had become of the members of the court, not from mere curiosity, but with the deliberate object of helping any who were unable to help themselves, for it was obvious that it was only a matter of minutes before the stateroom would be submerged. He was only just in time, for in the deepening gloom he saw von Stalhein on his knees, taking aim at him with his revolver. Biggles sprang aside an instant before the weapon blazed, and the bullet ricocheted through the yawning hole in the ship's side.

Biggles snatched up a broken chair and flung it at the German. At the same time he shouted, 'Don't be a fool, man; let's get out of this. We can argue afterwards.'

Von Stalhein ducked and the chair missed its mark; but it served its purpose, for his next shot hit the ceiling.

Biggles waited for no more. It seemed to him that it was neither the time nor place for such a display of venom, so with a curt, 'All right; have it your own way,' he ran to the hole and dived into the sea.

For two or three minutes he put his entire energy into getting away from the ship; then, finding a piece of wreckage capable of supporting his weight, he rested, and took the opportunity of looking back. The sight that met his eyes remained engraved indelibly on his mind. The great liner was so far over on her side that her upper works still projected over his head. On its bulging side men were running about seemingly in an aimless fashion, although a few were jumping into the sea. He could no longer see the hole through which he had escaped – the hole which had wrought the havoc; but standing on a wrecked lifeboat he could see the lithe figure of von Stalhein, revolver in hand, looking out over the frothy water, apparently trying to see him.

'My goodness, how that fellow must hate me,' thought Biggles, for he could not imagine any normal-minded person behaving in such a way at such a time. 'Well, I suppose he can't help it,' he mused, and dismissed the German from his mind, for he had more urgent matters to attend to. He was still much too close to the ship for his liking, for he knew what a tremendous vortex would be created when it went down.

Aware that he would not be able to swim very far in his clothes, he proceeded to divest himself of everything except his vest and pants, and he had just completed this operation when he discovered that he had a companion. He recognized him for the officer who had been in charge of the escort when he had been marched before the tribunal. He saw, too, that he was in a bad way, so he asked him, 'What's the matter?'

'I can't see; the oil has got into my eyes,' was the answer.

Biggles pulled off his silk vest and thrust it into the man's hands. 'See what you can do with that,' he suggested.

Hanging on to the wreckage with his left hand, the man lost no time in following the advice. 'That's better,' he said presently. 'I seem to know your voice. Aren't you the Englishman?'

'That's me,' admitted Biggles cheerfully, as he began paddling the wreckage farther away from the sinking ship.

The man went on wiping his eyes, clearing them of the heavy oil which had clung to the lashes. 'Thanks,' he said, handing the vest back.

Biggles smiled and put it on again.

'Your fellow who did this made a good job of it,' declared the German.

'You're dead right; he certainly did,' agreed Biggles, spitting out a mouthful of sea water. 'What sort of aeroplane was it – did you see?'

'Yes, I saw it,' answered the sailor, and gave Biggles all the description he needed for him to realize that it must have been either Ginger or Algy who had dropped the torpedo.

'What were you doing round here, anyway?' was Biggles's next question.

'We were hove to at the mouth of the channel, waiting for the tide.'

'Channel?' The word made Biggles prick up his ears, for if it was the channel that separated the mainland from the sandbank on which he had landed with Algy and Ginger, then it gave him a rough idea of his bearings.

'How far are we from land?' he inquired, for it was now too dark to see anything.

'About a kilometre – more or less.'

'Which way does it lie?'

The man pointed. 'Over there. That's the German coast, but the sandbank on the other side is nearer, I think. If you're going to swim to it you'd better start.'

'Why – is there any hurry?'

The man was looking past Biggles at something beyond him, and turning to see what it was, Biggles saw the drifter, the existence of which he had completely forgotten. It was moving dead slow through the water picking up survivors; its boats had been lowered and were doing the same thing. He had no desire to be picked up, for he had a shrewd idea of what that would mean in the end – particularly after the sinking of the *Leipzig* by one of his machines. He preferred to take his chance on the sandbank, or even the mainland, where, if he was found, he might pass as a survivor of the ill-fated ship until he could make plans to escape. There was always a chance that he might be able to steal a small boat and get back to Bergen Ait.

'Thanks,' he told the German gratefully, and struck off into the darkness.

'*Lebewohl*! Good luck!' called the German after him.

For some time Biggles did not look back, but devoted himself to getting clear of the danger zone, the position of which he could judge roughly by the frequent hails of men still in the water as they tried to attract the attention of the rescuers. There was no moon, but in the light of the stars he could just make out the dark hull of the drifter. But of the *Leipzig* there was no sign. In a vague sort of way he wondered what had happened to von Stalhein, but he soon dismissed him from his mind, for the water was cold, and although he was a strong swimmer, he knew that if he did not soon reach land he might succumb to exposure. So settling down to a steady breast stroke, which he knew from experience he could keep up for a long time, he struck out in the direction in which, according to the sailor, the sandbank lay. At present he could not see it; not that he expected to, for it was too dark to see far. It was disconcerting, this swimming through the darkness towards an unseen objective, for should he miss it his position would be hopeless; at least, from what he had seen of the Baltic while flying over it, he would not have given much for his chance of being picked up by a ship.

An hour later he was still swimming, but not so strongly, for his body was fast becoming numb from the cold, and he dare not float to rest himself, as he could have done had the water been warmer. Shortly afterwards, however, he found it imperative to change his stroke, and in doing so he heard the sound which he had been hoping to hear – the measured beat of surf on the sandy shore.

With a prayer of thankfulness he struck out with renewed vigour, and a few minutes later found him staggering through shallow water to the beach. Not until he had crawled up on the sand did he realize how far he was spent; but even then what he feared most was that he might collapse from cold, for the night air was chilly. So with the object of restoring his circulation by the only means available, he set off at a jog-trot along the lonely beach, which seemed to stretch to infinity in front of him. He was deadly tired, but still he ran on, deriving some comfort from the warmth that his exercise was producing.

How far he ran he did not know. Nor did he care. He only knew that he seemed to have been running for hours when just ahead he observed some fairly high sand-dunes, and towards these he directed his steps, hoping to find shelter where he could take a breather. Breaking into a sprint to satisfy himself that he still had it in him, he dashed round the foot of the first dune, and collided with stunning force with somebody coming the other way.

Tired as he was he was unable to keep his balance, and after a final stumble, in which he caught a glimpse of a dark human form, he plunged headlong into the loose sand.

Quick as he was getting on his feet, the other was quicker, and he went over backwards again with a gloved hand pressed savagely over his mouth. Gripping his assailant with his hands, and doubling his knees under him, he endeavoured to fling him off, but only succeeded in causing them both to roll over and over down the sloping sand. They arrived at the bottom with Biggles underneath. He saw an arm raised to strike. The butt end of a revolver showed for an instant against the sky, and he clutched at it desperately. His assailant sought to free his arm, but just as furiously Biggles held on to it. Then came the end. But it was not the end Biggles expected, for, the struggle coming on top of his previous exertions, he was on the point of collapse.

It came when his opponent suddenly shouted, 'Hi! Briny! Help!'

'Algy,' gasped Biggles weakly. 'Get off my chest, you maniac!'

CHAPTER XIII

An Alarming Discovery

The pressure on Biggles's chest relaxed with amazing promptitude.

Algy was incapable of speech, and for a while he could only yammer foolishly. 'What are you doing here?' he managed to get out at last.

Biggles lay flat on his back, panting heavily. 'What do you think? Making sandcastles with my little spade and bucket? What are you playing at, anyway?'

'Oh, I'm just collecting pretty pebbles for the kids to play marbles with,' replied Algy. 'As a matter of fact, I'm on my way to blow up the dump.'

'Dump? What dump?'

'Ah! Of course, I forgot, you don't know about that. Briny found a dump.'

'Briny? Where is Briny? What's he been doing? Am I going crazy or are you? You talk as if he'd found a dump kicking about on the beach.'

As if in answer to the questions, Briny himself charged round the dune, swinging a rifle in a most dangerous manner.

'Be careful what you're doing with that thing, you fool,' snapped

Biggles irritably, for what with shock and fatigue he was in no mood to be polite.

Briny stopped with ludicrous suddenness, the rifle poised. Then, slowly, it dropped to the ground. 'Luv a duck, sir, if it ain't the C.O.,' he gasped. 'What have you been doing, sir, if I may make so free as to ask?'

'Riding round the front in a hansom cab with Hitler,' grated Biggles with bitter sarcasm. 'It's time we stopped asking fool questions and got this thing straightened out,' he added with a change of tone. 'I'll start. I found the motorboat, but was captured by von Stalhein in a drifter and arrived on the *Leipzig* just as somebody was thoughtful enough to sling a mouldy in her ribs. I jumped into the sea and swam here. That's all.'

'I slung the mouldy,' admitted Algy.

'Thanks. You'll never sling a better one as long as you live,' declared Biggles. 'I'll tell you why later on.'

'I found Briny stranded on this sandbank,' explained Algy. 'On the way back to the base we found the remains of your machine, so thinking you were a gonner I went mad dog. I had a crack at the *Leipzig* first. Then I went home for a time-bomb. Oh, I forgot to say that when I picked up Briny here we found a dump – a sort of Hun naval store. We were going to blow it up when I ran into you. I brought Briny along to guard the machine while I did the dirty work.'

'I see. That explains things,' said Biggles, rising stiffly to his feet. 'Somebody will have to lend me a jacket. I'm cold. I've been swimming for an hour or more in this perishing ditch.'

Briny took off the flying jacket he was wearing and passed it over. 'I remember once—' he began.

'Then forget it,' cut in Biggles, putting on the coat. 'And now, if somebody would be kind enough to take me home, I should like to warm my tootsies by the stove.'

'What about the dump?' asked Algy. 'I've got the time-bomb here.'

'You can stick it in a crab hole or play hop-scotch with it for all I care. I don't feel like fooling about any dumps, and I've heard all the explosions I want for one day. Let's get back. I'll send Ginger to attend to the dump.'

'You won't,' replied Algy promptly.

'Why not?'

'He's missing.'

'Missing! Since when?'

'Nobody's seen him since we took off early this morning.'

'Is the spare machine still in the cave?'

'Yes.'

'Then he must be on the island somewhere. Suffering Mike! What sort of a squadron have I got? What does the young ass think he's at – a picnic?'

'When you find him you can ask him.'

Biggles thought for a moment. He was not seriously upset about Ginger, for if the *Platypus* was still at its moorings it was obvious that he could not be far away, for the simple reason that he had no means of leaving the base. It struck him, however, that if the dump was to be destroyed, now was the time to do it, for it seemed certain that the Germans would cause a search to be made for him, and the sandbank, being the land nearest to where the *Leipzig* was sunk, would be one of the first places they would look at. He decided, therefore, that if anything was to be done about the dump, now was the best time, for to return later might result in an encounter with a search party sent out to look for him. Indeed, he was only too well aware of how dangerous their whole project had already become. It was, in fact, precarious, now that von Stalhein knew they were operating in the district – assuming that he had survived the *Leipzig* disaster. He knew the German well enough to know that, actuated as he was by personal motives as well as those of patriotism, he would not rest until he had located their base; and it could be only a question of time before he examined Bergen Ait. The fact that the islet was supposed to be the property of a neutral state would weigh little with a man as thorough and relentless as Erich von Stalhein. However, he refrained from depressing the others by communicating to them these disconcerting thoughts.

'All right,' he said at last, 'I'll tell you what we'll do. For the three of us to try to squeeze into the machine is going to be a difficult business, particularly as I'm not dressed for what you might call skylarking. Algy, suppose you take Briny home and then come straight back bringing my spare kit with you. You ought to make the round trip inside an hour. I'll get everything ready here for the big bang the moment you return. That seems to be the easiest way.'

'As you say,' agreed Algy.

'Where is the dump?'

Algy pointed. 'About half a mile along the beach.'

'I see. To save our legs you might as well land a bit nearer to it when you come back. By the way, what exactly does this dump consist of?'

Algy described what he had seen.

Biggles's eyes opened wide. 'It sounds to me as if there ought to be some stuff there that we could use ourselves. I mean, we might find ourselves out of petrol one day, in which case we should be glad to have a reserve supply. Before blowing the place up I certainly think we ought to have a closer look at what it contains.'

Algy nodded. 'I didn't think of that. But you can't get into it. It's locked up.'

'You say it's made of corrugated iron?'

'That's right.'

'Then with a drill and a hacksaw we ought to have no difficulty in cutting a hole through the side. We may as well try it, anyway. You bring the tools back with you. Bring a torch and anything you think might be useful. If we find the job of getting in is too much for us we'll give it up and blow the place sky high as you originally intended. But we mustn't stand here talking any longer. You get off and get back as quickly as you can.'

Algy thought the plan was a sound one, so after settling a few minor details, he returned to the machine, taking Briny with him.

Biggles was left alone on the sandbank. As soon as he heard the machine take off, he picked up the time-bomb, which was still lying where it had fallen when the collision had knocked it out of Algy's hand, and started off towards the dump. The moon was now creeping up over the horizon, so it did not take him long to find the shed and the adjacent moorings, which he examined with considerable interest. He then went round to the rear wall, where he arranged the bomb, for he thought it would be as efficient there as anywhere if it were decided to use it. After that, as there was nothing more he could do, he began making a closer inspection of the building.

He did not learn much, however, for he soon discovered what Algy already knew – that there were no windows. He suspected that there were skylights, but he had no means of getting on the roof – not that he made any serious attempt to do so, realizing that the interior would be in utter darkness.

Having nothing to do now but wait, it was with profound satisfaction that he heard the hum of Algy's engine, really before he expected him. He walked briskly towards the sea, and by the time Algy had landed, and taxied into a sheltered creek about two hundred yards away, he had joined him.

Algy tossed him a vacuum flask. 'Take a swig of that,' he said. 'It's hot coffee – it should warm you up. Here's your kit,' he added, throwing a bundle after the flask.

Biggles began getting into his clothes as quickly as he could, from time to time taking gulps of coffee with grateful relish. 'Is Ginger back yet?' he inquired.

'No.'

Biggles paused for a moment in what he was doing. 'I don't like the sound of that,' he said slowly. 'He wouldn't stay away all this time if he could get back. I'm afraid he's met with an accident.'

'Briny and the Flight-Sergeant have hunted high and low for him – in fact, they're still looking.'

Biggles resumed his dressing. 'This squadron of mine doesn't seem to be living up to its name,' he said bitterly. 'There hasn't been much boomeranging about it lately. Apart from losing two of our machines, we seem to have gone out of our way to scatter ourselves all over the blinking Baltic. We'd better not waste too much time here. Did you bring the tools?'

Algy, who had climbed down from the machine, held them up. 'I've got a length of line in my pocket, too, in case we have to get down through the skylight.'

'Good!' said Biggles, putting on his flying-coat. 'Let's go and rip the hide off this tin toy-shop of Mister Hitler's.'

They were soon at work, choosing the rear wall, with a good deal more noise than Biggles liked, but making such good progress that in half an hour, by levering up the piece they had cut, they were able to crawl through into the interior of the building.

Biggles flashed the torch around as Algy got through behind him. 'Shades of Guy Fawkes!' he ejaculated. 'What a collection. We really ought to save this little lot for firework day.'

He began walking round, turning the light of the torch on bombs, torpedoes, shells, machine-guns, sub-machine-guns, and every conceivable form of ammunition. But what interested him more than these were the fuel tanks, and the carefully labelled collection of spare parts and accessories for all sorts of marine craft. With the painstaking thoroughness of a reconnaissance pilot, he made a mental note of everything he saw as they walked on slowly through the corridors. He pointed to a steel airscrew. 'Aircraft evidently use this place as well as submarines and destroyers,' he said. 'I don't know what to do about it, and that's a fact. It might do us a bit of good one day if we left the stuff here; on the other hand, it might do the enemy a lot more harm if we destroyed it. I've a good mind to radio Colonel Raymond and ask him for instructions. He ought to know about it, anyway. I—'

He broke off suddenly, in a tense attitude. The light went out as he switched it off, leaving them in darkness.

'It sounds as if somebody has found my machine,' said Algy in a low voice, for there was no mistaking the sound that had alarmed them. It was an aero-engine.

'It isn't your machine. There's more than one,' returned Biggles in a hard voice. 'It sounds to me like a formation – flying low, too.'

'They're coming this way,' declared Algy a moment later.

Biggles was still listening intently. 'I don't think it's a forma-tion after all,' he said slowly. 'I should say it's a big multi-engined job.'

As he spoke the roar of the engines died away, but they could still hear the wail of wind through wires.

'It would be a joke if it was coming here, wouldn't it?' murmured Algy.

'It might be your idea of a joke, but not mine,' replied Biggles curtly. 'When I first saw the Baltic I thought it was a pretty deserted place, but lately it seems to be swarming with vehicles of one sort and another. That machine's coming a lot too close for my liking. We'd better get outside.'

'I hope they don't spot my machine.'

'I shouldn't think there's much chance of that in this light. Come on, let's get outside. I daren't use the torch; they'd spot it through the skylight; mind you don't knock your eye out on the blunt end of a crankshaft. Keep close to me. I think I can find my way to the hole.' So saying, Biggles began groping his way towards the spot where they had affected an entrance.

Some time before they reached it, it became obvious that even if the aircraft did not actually intend landing, the pilot was gliding down to survey the spot, for the metal building vibrated with noise. Consequently, it was with more haste than dignity that they scram-bled through the hole and stared up into the starlit heavens.

They were not long finding the aircraft – for, as Biggles had surmised, it was a single machine.

With its navigation and cabin lights ablaze, a four-engined flying-boat was turning with the majestic deliberation of a battle-ship towards the anchorage that adjoined the shed.

'It *would* decide to arrive at this moment, wouldn't it?' said

Biggles savagely, as he forced down the jagged metal flap which they had raised to get inside the building. 'Look out! Get down!'

He flung himself flat, his body pressed close against the corrugated iron, as a parachute flare burst a hundred feet over their heads and flooded the scene with dazzling white light. And thus they were compelled to remain until the keel of the giant flying-boat kissed the water, and surged on towards the wide double doors of the supply depot.

The instant the light exhausted itself Biggles was on his feet. He started to move forward, but pulled up short. 'Where's the time-bomb?' he said tersely. 'I put it down here.'

'I took it inside with me. I thought if we used it, it would make a better job of things there.'

Biggles muttered something under his breath. 'I suppose you acted for the best,' he conceded, 'but we daren't go in there now to fetch it. I doubt if we could find it, anyway, without a light. If they come across it there'll be a fine old hullaballoo. We'd better get back to your machine ready for a snappy take-off.'

By this time the huge aircraft had taxied right up to the building. Its propellers stopped as the pilot switched off the ignition, and it was obvious that the crew were about to come ashore. Its lights reflected on the water, and the sound of voices came clearly through the still night air.

Biggles caught Algy by the arm, and together they ran to the nearest sand-dune, from where they made their way quickly to the place where they had left the *Didgeree-du*. There was no particular need for caution, for they knew that their presence was unsuspected, and it was natural to suppose that the German airmen were too taken up with the task of mooring their machine to worry about anything else.

Biggles doubled round the last dune, and saw the soft gleam of the *Didgeree-du*'s wings. 'Here she is,' he said quickly, and then, as the entire machine came into view, pulled up dead. 'Good heavens! That's done it,' he cried aghast.

Algy joined him. There was no need to ask what had happened: it was too painfully obvious. The incoming tide had flooded the creek to a depth that could be estimated roughly by the fact that gentle waves were lapping against the bottom of the fuselage. The floats were under water, and the machine, for some reason not immediately apparent, had sunk over to one side. Water was still pouring into the creek, turning it into an ever-widening lake.

For perhaps a minute Algy could only stare at the scene as the enormity of the disaster slowly penetrated into his brain. 'I don't understand this,' he muttered. 'Why doesn't she float?'

'Because her wheels have sunk into the sand, that's why,' answered Biggles grimly.

CHAPTER XIV

Von Stalhein Again

For the best part of an hour they strove desperately to drag the *Didgeree-du* from the sand that clung tenaciously to her wheels, but in vain, and Biggles reluctantly gave his opinion that they were wasting their time.

'She's fixed as tight as a limpet on a rock,' he announced disgustedly. 'We shall have to wait for the tide to go down and then dig her out. It must be nearly high water now – I suppose that's why the flying-boat came here just at this time. We can't afford to lose the machine. I should look a pretty fool having to report to Raymond that we were down to a single aircraft.' Biggles sat down on the sloping side of a dune and regarded the *Didgeree-du* with disfavour.

'Waiting for low tide is all right as long as these chaps push off before daylight,' remarked Algy. 'As a matter of fact I doubt if it will be right out before dawn. If the Boche take off in daylight they'll spot the machine for a certainty. D'you suppose they're going to fly calmly round and watch us dig it out? Not likely. They'd shoot us up – or send a radio signal saying that we were here.'

'You're becoming a perishing pessimist.'

'It's no use blinking at facts.'

'All right. Well, there's no sense in sitting here just staring at the blinking thing.'

'What do you suggest we do then – start a sing-song or something?'

'We might creep up to the shed and try to hear what the Boche are talking about. I mean, we might learn how long they propose to stay here. What are they up to, anyway?'

'Refuelling, I expect – unless, of course, they've landed here to make mud-pies,' sneered Algy sarcastically.

'You talk as if you'd had a rush of mud to the brain,' declared Biggles with asperity as he got up and began moving towards the shed, taking care to keep behind the dunes.

Algy followed him, and in a few minutes they were within sight of the building and the big flying-boat.

'They've put the cabin lights out,' observed Biggles. 'If that's anything to go by, they've no intention of moving before daybreak.'

'It looks that way to me,' agreed Algy. 'Judging by the casual way that fellow is coiling up the hosepipe, they're going to stay here for the duration.'

They did not attempt to approach the door, for an occasional figure passed in and out, but from where they were they could see that the big sliding doors had not been opened; instead, a small door let into the larger one – an arrangement frequently used in such buildings – was being used. As there was nothing more to be seen from the position they now occupied they made a cautious advance to the hole in the rear of the building. Biggles had closed it when they had made their precipitate retreat, but it was only the work of a minute to lever it open again. They knew before they did so that some form of illumination had been turned on inside, for a shaft of yellow light poured through the open door, so they were not surprised to find that two large arc lamps, with shades to throw the light downwards, made the interior as bright as day. They could hear people moving about, and – a homely sound – the rattle of crockery; there was also a low buzz of conversation, but they could see no one on account of the high piles of stores that interrupted their view. What they could see, however, was the time-bomb, resting on the floor a few feet away.

'I'm going in to retrieve that bomb; we may need it,' whispered Biggles. 'I'll try to find out what they're up to at the same time. Stay where you are.'

There appeared to be no particular danger in fetching the bomb, for, by bending low, Biggles could keep under cover. Having reached it, he rose furtively and peeped over the top of a stack of shells. The sight that met his eyes brought a smile to his lips, it was so human. Some distance away, perhaps a matter of thirty paces, some boards had been put across two piles of stores, forming a table. Round this were seated seven men, all young, still wearing their flying kit, but with jackets thrown open and helmets on the backs of their heads. They appeared to be in the best of spirits, as they had reason to be, for steaming plates on the table told their own story.

Not until then did Biggles realize how famished he was, and an insane desire to join the party came over him. He dismissed it reluctantly and tried to catch some words of the conversation, but as far as he could make out the men were not talking about their work at all, but – another human touch – were chuckling over a recital of the war rumours then circulating in Berlin.

Biggles remained where he was for some time, but then, as

there was no indication that the conversation would turn to more relevant topics, he went back to Algy.

'I can't hear much, but from their manner I should say they're going to stay here for some time,' he announced. 'At the moment they're having a lovely picnic.'

'Then what about shooting 'em up and having a basinful of soup ourselves?' suggested Algy, ever practical.

'It may sound silly, but that'd be a bit too much like murder for my liking. I've a better idea than that.'

'What is it?'

'I've got a feeling that I'd like to borrow their big boat.'

'And abandon the *Didgeree-du*? Not likely.'

'We could come back and fetch it later on.'

'But they would find it.'

'Not necessarily. Anyway, if we covered it with mud and rushes there's a chance they wouldn't tumble on it. They'll stick around the shed. My feeling is, if we can get hold of that boat we ought not to let the opportunity pass. The *Didgeree-du* may be bogged permanently for all we know, and if that turned out to be the case we should be in a fine old mess.'

'You're right there,' admitted Algy. 'All right then; let's have a dekko at the front of the building and see what's happening there.'

'There's no need for us both to go. You get back to the machine and start camouflaging it while I do the reconnoitring. I'll join you as soon as I can.'

Without protest Algy disappeared into the dunes. Biggles, taking the time-bomb with him, made his way to the front of the hangar, where he found his task even easier than he expected, for the place was deserted, and the great boat rode silently at her moorings, made fast by a single line from the bows. He scrutinized the shadows closely for a sentry, but he could not see one – not that he expected to, for had he been in the position of the chief pilot of the flying-boat he would not have thought it necessary to mount a guard.

Turning his attention to the door, a broad smile spread over his face as he realized how completely chance had played into his hands; for the small door had not only been left open, but there, on the outside, was the key still in the lock. He waited for no more, but hurried back to Algy, whom he found just completing his task, made possible by the fact that the tide was now receding, and the creek was only inundated to a depth of two feet or so. It was now possible to see how hopelessly the *Didgeree-du* was bogged, for her wheels, one lower than the other, were completely under the sand.

Biggles wasted no time in idle contemplation of it. 'Come on,' he said urgently. 'We're all set. The machine's as good as ours.' Briefly he related the circumstances. 'Lend me your pencil, and let me have a page out of your notebook,' he concluded.

'What's the idea?' inquired Algy as he passed them over.

'I'm going to slip a note under the door telling those fellows about the hole in the wall.'

'Why?'

'Otherwise they may never find it.'

'What does it matter?'

'We can't leave the poor blighters to starve to death – anyway, they may be some time getting out, and I'm going to drop an egg on this place at the first opportunity. I should hate to do it thinking they might still be inside. Bombing's all right up to a point, but—'

Algy nodded. 'Yes, to bomb the place after pinching their boat would be adding insult to injury,' he agreed. 'Well, let's get on with it.'

They returned to the store depot, where they found everything just as Biggles had last seen it. You get to the boat and make ready to cast off when you see me coming,' he ordered. 'The engines must still be warm, so they ought to start at the first spark.'

He gave Algy time to reach the boat, and a few minutes' grace after he had gone aboard, and then crept silently to the door. Very gently he closed it. The key turned in the lock without a sound. Then, taking the note he had written from his pocket, he slipped it through the crack. He could still hear the murmur of conversation inside; it had gone on, unbroken, all the time he had been near the door, and he knew that the Germans were in blissful ignorance of what was happening. Picking up the time-bomb, more because they had only one or two at the base and he thought they might need it, than for any immediate purpose, he walked down to the flying-boat and went aboard.

'It's all right, you can relax; there's no hurry,' he told Algy, who had cast off and was now sitting with his hand on the throttle.

'Shall I start up?' asked Algy.

'Go ahead.'

'Are you going to fly her or shall I?'

'You,' returned Biggles briefly. 'I'm going to have a nap. Tell me when we're home.'

With his left hand on the master throttle, Algy started the engines, and the giant boat began to surge towards the open sea.

Biggles opened a side window and looked out, but nothing happened, for reasons which he knew. Still, he smiled at the thought of the consternation that must now be going on within the tin walls of the building.

The flying-boat rocked gently as she struck the swell of the Baltic; then her engines picked her up and she roared into the night sky.

Biggles noticed that Algy was laughing. 'Yes, war's a funny thing,' he remarked, supposing that he knew the cause of Algy's mirth.

'It's funnier than you think,' declared Algy, going off into fresh peals of laughter.

Biggles looked at him curiously. 'Why this sudden flood of hilarity?' he demanded. 'Come on, what's the joke?'

'Did you ever read in the Bible about a camel going through the eye of a needle?'

Biggles stared. 'I don't get it.'

'I'm only wondering what we're going to do with this leviathan when we *do* get her home.'

Biggles frowned suddenly as understanding flashed upon him. 'Stiffen the crows,' he muttered, 'I hadn't thought of that.'

'Neither had I, until we started. She won't go into the cave, or anything like it. Even if we were able to pull her wings off, which I doubt, the fuselage would just about block the entrance.'

Biggles stroked his chin. 'It's just like you to think of something difficult when everything looked easy,' he observed bitterly. 'Work it out yourself. I'm tired. Tell me when we get to the island. I'm going to sleep.'

And sleep he did, until Algy nudged him in the ribs and warned him that they were nearly in.

Biggles woke up and stretched, yawning. 'That's better,' he announced as the flying-boat glided down to a smooth landing, with enough way on her to carry her to the mouth of the cave. Opening a side window he looked out, ready to hail if he saw anyone, for he realized that there was a chance of their being fired on. But the base seemed to be entirely deserted.

'Where the deuce is everybody?' asked Algy.

'I expect they're asleep,' returned Biggles. 'Don't make a noise, there's no need to wake them up,' he went on, as they walked along the huge, tapering wing of the flying-boat and jumped ashore.

'Hm, this is odd,' he continued a few minutes later as they reached the depot, still without any one appearing. 'One would have thought there would have been somebody on duty.'

They went all round the depot, but the only person they could find was Roy, who, with earphones still clamped on his head, lay asprawl his desk, sleeping the sleep of exhaustion. The British and German code-books lay beside him; the pencil with which he had been working was still between his fingers.

'Poor little beggar,' whispered Biggles, 'he's absolutely all in, which isn't surprising considering the length of time he's been at this desk. I suppose he tried to hang on until we got back, but flopped out over his work. You can't keep awake indefinitely. I've been asleep at the joystick before today. I think we may as well let him sleep on. Ginger isn't back, that's certain, but what on earth can have happened to Briny and the Flight-Sergeant.'

'I suppose they've gone to look for Ginger.'

'Yes – of course, that's it. Well, I must say this looks a pretty dead sort of hole. Hullo! What's this?' Biggles picked up a sheet of paper that lay by itself half concealed under Roy's face. Very gently he drew it clear and picked it up. It was marked across the top, in big block letters, URGENT. 'Good heavens, it's a signal,' he said tersely. 'It must have come in while we were away. Roy's decoded it, too – what's this—?'

Biggles read the message aloud. '"Urgent. Enemy naval supply depot suspected on north-east coast of East Prussia, probably among sand-dunes north of the Gutte Channel. It is of vital importance that it be located immediately and destroyed."'

Biggles stared at Algy. 'What do you know about that?' he muttered.

'It must be the place we've just left.'

'Of course it is. There couldn't be two of them so close to each other. What a confounded nuisance we didn't finish the job while we were there. Well, it'll have to wait now. I'm dead on my feet. I couldn't take a machine to that sandbank and back if the Empire depended on it. I can hardly see out of my eyes.'

'You look about played out,' murmured Algy seriously. 'You're certainly not fit to fly until you've had some sleep; you'd only crash and kill yourself if you tried. I tell you what; I'm fresher than you are; you lie down and get some sleep. I'll take the *Platypus* and make a quick trip to the sand-bank. I hope those fellows are not still inside the building.'

Biggles glanced towards the entrance of the cave and saw that it was now grey with the approach of dawn. 'They'll be outside by now,' he said definitely. 'They will have found my note telling them how to get out, so they'll probably be on the beach watching for a ship to take them off. When they see you coming they'll guess what you're going to do and clear off. If they hang around it'll be their own funeral. After all, there's a war on and orders are orders. All right, old lad. I'd be obliged if you would slip back and do the job; one bomb ought to be enough.'

'I'll get along right away,' declared Algy. 'You get some sleep. When I come back we'll hunt round for the others.'

'Good! I'll see you off.'

Without waking Roy, they left the signals room and made their way along the catwalk to the *Platypus*. A single 112-lb. bomb was slung on the central bomb-rack, and Algy was about to get into his seat when Biggles picked up the time-bomb which he had brought back with him. 'You might as well take this,' he suggested. 'If you miss with your bomb, and the Boche are a fair distance away, you might land and do the job with this one. We've got to make sure of the place. It won't take up any room, anyway, so no harm will be done if you have to bring it back.' He placed the square charge of explosive on the rear seat.

'I tell you what would be a good thing to take,' said Algy suddenly.

'What?'

'One of those sub-machine-guns from store. If the Huns are still about, and I expect they will be, they might start shooting at me, and – well, I'd feel happier if I had a mobile weapon in case I had to land, or was forced down.'

'That's true,' agreed Biggles. 'Stand fast. I'll fetch you one.'

He was soon back with a vicious-looking weapon, and some clips of ammunition, which he arranged securely within Algy's reach. 'Don't forget this is our last machine,' he reminded him as Algy climbed into the cockpit.

'I'll try not to bust it,' Algy promised.

Biggles ran to the mouth of the cave and looked up at the sky. 'Don't be too long away,' he called. 'I don't like the look of the weather.'

Algy waved to signify that he had heard and taxied out on to the cove.

Biggles waited for him to take off and then made his way slowly to the mess. He looked into the kitchen as he passed, wishing that he had the energy to get himself some breakfast; but his one over-whelming desire was for sleep, and he lay back on his bed with a sigh of relief, not intending to sleep immediately, but to rest for a few minutes before undressing. But nature, long denied, decided otherwise. His eyes closed, and he sank into a heavy dreamless sleep of utter weariness.

The hour hand of the clock on the mantelpiece ticked its way slowly round the dial, and still he did not awake. Another hour went by and still he slept, unaware that the sun had been blotted out by a dark indigo curtain that rose swiftly from the northern horizon. Presently, too, this curtain was blotted out by whirling flakes of snow that eddied about the entrance to the cave before dropping silently on the sullen water. And still he slept on, unaware of the silence, a sinister silence broken only by the relentless ticking of the clock on the mantelpiece.

He did not hear the tramp of feet that came cautiously along the catwalk. He neither heard nor saw the door open as Erich von Stalhein, an automatic in his hand, entered the room.

The German counter-espionage officer fitted a cigarette into a long holder, lighted it, and blew a smoke ring into the air. On his face was an expression of extreme contempt. For a little while he considered the sleeping figure thoughtfully; then, reaching forward, he tapped him on the shoulder with the pistol.

Biggles's eyes opened. A shadow of amazement swept through them as they came to rest on the German's austere face. Slowly he raised himself on one elbow.

'You know, von Stalhein, you're becoming a positive pest,' he muttered petulantly. 'Why can't you let a fellow sleep?'

Von Stalhein smiled sardonically. 'Don't worry,' he purred. 'Very soon you shall go to sleep for a long, long time.'

Biggles eyed him reflectively. 'Just what do you mean by that?' he inquired.

'I mean that in the past I have too often delayed what – knowing you – should have been done immediately. On this occasion there is going to be no such delay. I trust my meaning is now plain.'

Biggles nodded. 'Well, I expect as you're a German you can't help it,' he murmured. 'But really, von Stalhein, your mother should have taught you that it isn't customary to shoot prisoners of war. It isn't done. I insist on a fair trial.'

'You had one, on the *Leipzig*.'

Biggles realized the futility of protest. 'Purely as a matter of detail, how did you find your way here?' he asked.

The German held up Biggles's map. 'It was most thoughtful of you to make pencil marks that brought me almost directly to Bergen Ait. An officer of your experience should have known better.'

'You're quite right. I deserve to be shot for such criminal folly,' agreed Biggles. 'How did you get here – in the drifter?'

'Of course. It picked me up, so after landing those saved from the *Leipzig* I came straight on here – not alone, of course. I have a score of marines outside. They are just checking your very interesting stores. I suppose you realize that you have committed a flagrant breach of international law in installing yourself here, on neutral territory?'

Biggles did not enlighten the German as to the facts of the case; he would discover them in due course. 'You're a nice one to talk about breaches of international law,' he sneered.

'You know, von Stalhein, you're becoming a perfect pest,'
he muttered petulantly

'Suppose I ask a few questions for a change?' suggested von Stalhein. 'Where are your friends?'

A ray of hope shot through Biggles's mind, for all the time he had been talking, although he had not shown it, one terrible thought was uppermost in his mind. It was Roy, in the signals room, whom he was thinking about, for on his desk lay the most vital document any German agent could hope to secure – the British secret code-book. The German code was there, too, but that didn't matter. At first he had taken it for granted that Roy had been found, and the code-book with him; but now, in view of the German's question, it began to look as if this was not so, otherwise von Stalhein would have commented on it. One of his few weaknesses was vanity, and if he had indeed secured the code-book he could hardly have refrained from gloating over it.

So Biggles merely effected a yawn. 'Why, aren't they here?' he inquired.

Von Stalhein regarded him narrowly. 'No,' he snapped, 'they're not. But doubtless they will return in due course. I'll wait for them – but there is no reason why *you* should. I have a firing party on parade outside. I presume it will not be necessary for me to use force to induce you to report yourself to them. I will make the necessary introduction before the *unteroffizier* takes charge.'

Biggles rose slowly from the bed. 'You won't object to my having a cigarette?' he said politely.

'Of course not,' replied von Stalhein reproachfully. 'Is there anything else I can do for you – any messages – you know the sort of thing? I hate being dramatic, but at such moments as this it is usual—'

Biggles lit a cigarette and flicked the dead match away. 'That's very kind of you, von Stalhein,' he said coldly. 'I hope to do as much for you one day.'

The German smiled confidently. 'Then you will have to be very quick about it. Shall we go?'

Biggles nodded. 'I suppose we may as well.'

Von Stalhein clicked to attention and bowed as Biggles preceded him through the door to the depot.

A squad of marines, under an N.C.O., was in line, waiting.

CHAPTER XV

Happenings on the Rock

Roy was still asleep over his work when the Germans entered the cave, but his door was open, and it must have been some sound made by them that caused him to wake up with a start. For a moment or two, still heavy with sleep, he stared about him uncomprehendingly; then, realizing where he was, he looked at his watch, wondering how long he had been asleep.

To his relief he saw that everything was exactly as he had left it. There was nothing to show that Biggles and Algy had returned and visited the signals room, so he assumed, therefore, that they were still away, and he was still puzzling over their prolonged absence when a sound reached his ears that took him quickly to the side window of his cabin, which commanded a view of the entrance to the cave.

The sight that met his eyes caused him to go cold with horror. He blinked, shook his head, and looked again, hoping that what he saw was merely a dream – a very unpleasant dream – for coming along the catwalk was a file of German marines. At the mouth of the cave he could see the boat from which they had landed, and beyond it, a huge fuselage bearing the swastika of the German Air Force. For two or three seconds he could only stare in wide-eyed consternation, his brain racing and his thoughts chaotic; the one fact that he seemed capable of grasping was that in the absence of everybody the base had been attacked in force by the enemy. Not for one moment did he doubt that he was alone in the depot. There was no reason why he should. He assumed automatically that had anyone else been there some sort of resistance would have been made. He was not to know, of course, that the German flying-boat had actually been flown to the base by Algy.

Trembling from shock, he tried to force himself to think clearly, to decide what he ought to do. At first he toyed with the idea of making a rush to the bomb-store and blowing the whole place to pieces, himself with it. Then his eyes fell on the code-books, still lying on his desk, and he knew that his first duty must be at all costs to prevent the British code from falling into German hands. The German code did not matter so much, although it would be better, he thought, if the enemy were kept in ignorance of the fact that it had been captured. Hastily stuffing into his pockets all the loose messages that lay on the desk, he picked up the two code-books and crept round to the rear of the hut – the only way he could go, for the German marines had now reached the depot.

His one idea was to find a place where he could either destroy or conceal the code-books before he was captured, for he could not see how capture was to be avoided. There was only one direction he could take without being seen, and that was towards the rear of the cave, and up the narrow passage he now made his way.

For some time he stumbled on, bruising himself against unseen obstructions, but relieved to discover that the cave went on farther than he expected. Actually, as we know, it extended a good deal farther, but he was, of course, in complete ignorance of what lay ahead.

Not until he had gone some distance and was sure that he could not be seen from the depot did he start to put into operation the plan uppermost in his mind – the destruction of the code-books. Naturally, his instinctive thought was to burn them, and with this object in view he took a box of matches from his pocket and struck one. Hitherto, not possessing a torch, he had been in darkness, so it was in the light of the match that he first saw his surroundings. Somewhat to his surprise, and to his great satisfaction, he saw that the cave, although it had narrowed considerably, continued, so he decided to follow it to the end in a vague hope that the code-books might be saved after all.

For some time, in his anxiety to get as far as possible from the invaders, he struck matches recklessly, but finding his stock getting low he then began to use them more sparingly; all the same, it was not long before he discovered, by counting them, that he had only four matches left, and these he decided to preserve as long as possible. This was, in the circumstances, a natural and wise precaution, but it was to prove his undoing, for in trying to climb over an enormous boulder without using one he lost his balance on the top of it. He made a frantic effort to save himself from falling, even allowing the books to fall from his hands, but the rock was smooth, and his clutching fingers failed to secure a hold. His head came in violent contact with the hard floor on the far side; something seemed to explode in a sheet of purple flame, a flame that faded quickly to blackness as he lost consciousness.

Had he known that Briny and his father, the Flight-Sergeant, were somewhere in front of him, he might have proceeded up the cave with more confidence. In their search for Ginger they had explored the rocks round the mouth of the cave as far as it was possible to go, but finding no sign of him there, they had turned their attention to the other extremity. They both had torches so they were able to make good progress, feeling that at last they were on the right track.

It was Briny who discovered Ginger's broken torch. He was picking his way through the loose rocks of Ginger's fallen cairn when he noticed it, lying half hidden under a boulder. He recognized the type at once, and knew then without any doubt that Ginger was somewhere in front of them.

'I say, Flight, look at this!' he cried, as he picked up the torch. 'He must 'ave come this way.'

'I don't like the look of that,' said the Flight-Sergeant in a worried voice. 'Something pretty serious must have happened or he wouldn't have left his torch behind. The bulb's broken, anyway,' he concluded, sweeping the floor of the cave with his own torch as if he expected to see Ginger lying there.

'He must 'ave gorn up there,' declared Briny, shining his light on the high mass of rock in front of them. 'How did he get up there without a light I wonder?'

'I should say he dropped it from the top,' reasoned the Flight-Sergeant shrewdly.

'But you'd 'a thought he'd 'a come back for it,' protested Briny.

'You would, but evidently he didn't,' observed the practical Flight-Sergeant. 'Give me a leg up; we'd better have a look up here.'

Briny gave him a shoulder, and the Flight-Sergeant gazed speechlessly on the sheet of placid water which he saw in front of him. 'He didn't go this way,' he announced at last.'

'Why not?' asked Briny from below.

'Come up and have a look.' Bending down, the Flight-Sergeant caught Briny's hands and dragged him to the top of the rock. 'What d'you make of that?' he muttered.

'Strike ole Riley!' breathed Briny in an awe-stricken whisper. 'He must 'a tumbled in and got drownded.'

'That's how it looks to me,' admitted the Flight-Sergeant despondently. 'I don't think it's any use getting ourselves wet trying to get across. Let's give a hail. Hullo, there!' His voice echoed eerily over the still water.

'He ain't 'ere,' said Briny in a low voice as the echoes rolled away.

'We'd better get back and report,' decided the Flight-Sergeant. 'The C.O. ought to know about this. I reckon he's back by now.'

"Ere – 'old 'ard!' ejaculated Briny suddenly, catching him by the arm. 'Ain't that a light I can see over there?'

The Flight-Sergeant switched off his torch and told Briny to do the same so that they could see more clearly. Together they stared at the grey streak that had attracted Ginger's attention.

'That's daylight all right,' declared the Flight-Sergeant. 'It begins to look as if he may have gone across after all – bearing in mind that he'd lost his torch. I'm going over to have a look at that. You'd better stay here; there's no need for us both to go.'

'That suits me,' admitted Briny. 'I've nearly lorst me 'at twice as it is. You know, this reminds me of a place I once struck with my old shipmate, Charlie—'

'I'll sock you on the jaw and give you something else to remember if you don't shut up remembering things,' snarled the Flight-Sergeant, whose nerves were on edge. He started taking off his clothes and piling them on the rock. 'You stay here till I come back,' he ordered Briny.

"Ow long are you goin' to be away?'

'It depends on what I find over there. If I want you I'll shout.'

'Where do you reckon it leads to?'

'The top of the island, I should say. And I guess that's where we shall find Mr. Hebblethwaite – that is, if he hasn't fallen off. Stand fast.' The Flight-Sergeant slid into the water, and holding the torch above his head, swam on his back towards the streak of reflected light.

Ginger was, as we know, on the top of the island. He had been there for some time and was in a bad way.

After seeing Algy's machine disappear round the shoulder of rock he had sat still for some time, thinking that it might reappear and wondering what was the best thing to do. But when the plane did not reappear he set about exploring the place, prompted by the hope that it might be possible to get immediately above the cove and attract attention by shouting.

He soon saw that the top of the island was more or less flat; what slope there was, was towards the place where he stood, which accounted for the seepage of rainwater into the underground lake. Only round the extreme edges was the rock very rough, and here it had been carved into fantastic shapes by the searing wind. There was no herbage of any sort; on all sides the rock lay bare, gaunt, and stark, with the grey edges cutting into the wan autumn sky. The rock, too, was wet from the recent rain, and he found that progress was both slow and difficult. However, after a time he reached the spot he had selected, a place from where he hoped to be able to see the cove, only to discover to his chagrin that it was still out of sight beyond a forbidding *massif* that towered up at the southern extremity of the island.

This mass of rock he eyed with disfavour, for he perceived that to reach the top of it would entail a dangerous climb. Another thing that worried him was the fact that the afternoon was now well advanced, and if darkness caught him still on the *massif* he would find it difficult indeed to get down; and the top of the grim pile was no place to spend the night.

He wondered what the others were doing, and what they were thinking of his long absence. He did not know – and perhaps it is as well that he did not – that Biggles was at that moment on the *Leipzig*, standing before a tribunal, and that Algy was in the cave preparing to take off with a torpedo to sink the liner. When Algy did take off Ginger heard him, but he could not see him, for he had just reached the most difficult part of the *massif*. As the roar of the aero-engine reached his ears he made a hasty descent, hoping to attract the attention of the pilot before the machine was out of sight; but by the time he reached the level part of the island the *Didgeree-du* was a speck in the southern sky – much to his disgust.

Cold and weary, he knew that it would be folly to attempt to rescale the *massif* before darkness fell, so he looked about for the best place to await the machine's return. By the irony of fate, when it did come back it passed within fifty feet of him, but as it was now quite dark it might as well have been a mile away. He wondered who was flying the machine, and what had been its mission, little suspecting that it was Algy returning after torpedoing the *Leipzig*.

Soon afterwards he heard the machine take off again, which was, of course, when Algy set out, with Briny in the back seat, determined to blow up the German store depot. It was, as near as he could guess, two hours later when he again heard the machine returning, and assumed that that would end operations until the following day. To his amazement, within a few minutes he heard the plane go off again, and again he wondered what was going on. This was the occasion when Algy, having flown Briny back to the base, was returning to the sandbank with Biggles's spare kit.

Tired as he was, Ginger did his best to keep awake until the machine returned, for he was not to know that its wheels were stuck fast in the ooze of the sandbank. He was curled up in a fitful sleep between two rocks when the big German flying-boat glided down. Nor did he hear Algy take off again, now in the *Platypus*, on his attempt to bomb the German store depot in accordance with Colonel Raymond's instructions, although the sky was now grey with the dawn of another day. Indeed, he did not awake until the rim of the sun, ominously red, was showing above the eastern horizon.

He was wide awake the instant he opened his eyes, to find that his very bones were stiff with cold. He stamped up and down for some minutes to restore his circulation, and then, with a sort of desperate energy, set about the ascent of the *massif*. Realizing only too well that he might not survive another night on the open rock, he took the most fearful chances to reach the top; but at last he got there, and lying flat on his stomach, peered over the edge of the cliff. He was, as he expected, immediately above the cove, but the hail that was ready on his lips remained unuttered. At first he could only stare unbelievingly, trying to force his unwilling brain to accept the awful truth. But there was no getting away from the fact. There, on the cove, near the entrance to the cave, rode a four-engined German flying-boat.

As far as he was concerned it could mean only one thing – the squadron had been discovered by the enemy. And he must be pardoned for thinking that.

For some minutes he lay still, staring down with dismay. Then, with his face pinched from the cold, and his heart heavy, he rose to his feet and started on the return journey to the flat part of the island. Just what he was going to do he did not know, but at the back of his mind there was a wild idea of getting back to the depot by the only way he knew – the way he had come up.

It took him longer than he had expected to get down from the *massif*; and so taken up was he with his task and his melancholy thoughts that he did not notice the change in the weather until a snowflake settled lightly on his face. He stopped abruptly, glaring up at the leaden sky. 'You would pick on this moment to do the dirty on me, wouldn't you?' he grated impotently.

However, he hurried on, but by the time he had reached his immediate objective, the twenty-foot face of rock above the ledge, the snow was whirling round him so thickly that he could hardly see where he was going. At the edge of the cliff he stopped, half bewildered by the flakes that danced before his eyes. Foolishly, he struck at them with his hands in a futile attempt to see the ledge. 'I'm going down if I fall down,' he told himself grimly, as he dropped on his knees preparatory to starting the terrifying descent.

It is likely that he *would* have fallen down, but even as he groped for the first foothold he heard a sound that caused him first to stiffen, and then draw back hurriedly. It was the muffled roar of an aeroplane which seemed to come from somewhere over his head. His lips parted in sympathy for the pilot, whose feelings he could well imagine, for as if the snow were not bad enough, the engine was missing fire on at least one cylinder, in a manner suggesting that a complete breakdown was imminent.

CHAPTER XVI

Strange Meetings

Straining his eyes into the baffling background of snowflakes, Ginger endeavoured to get a glimpse of the machine, for he could follow its course roughly by the sound. He heard it coming closer, the engine still missing fire, and when it did appear it was so close that he ducked, thinking that it was going to land on top of him. He recognized the machine for one of their own.

It was not difficult to work out what had happened. Either Biggles or Algy had been caught out in a storm, not far from the base, and was now trying to get in. To make the task more hazardous, the engine started to cut out altogether, picking up again in spasmodic bursts, which led Ginger to ascribe the trouble to snow getting into the air intake.

Still watching, he twice saw the vague grey shadow of the machine appear in the semi-opaque pall that hung over the rock, only to disappear again immediately. The second time he actually saw the pilot's head looking down over the side of the cockpit. After that there came a brief lull. The engine was no longer firing, although whether this was due to a complete breakdown, or because the pilot had throttled back, Ginger did not know.

He walked a few paces towards the flat area, and then stood

still again, straining his ears for the noise he fully expected to hear – the crash of the machine striking the sea or the side of the island. He was still staring up when suddenly he heard the whine of wind in wires, dangerously close; then, out of the snow, came the grey shape of the machine, straight towards him, its wheels practically touching the rock. Even as he stared aghast, the wheels bumped, and bumped again, but the machine still ran on.

Thereafter he acted purely by instinct, for there was no time for thought. He knew that the pilot had no means of rising again, and that if it went on, in a few seconds the machine would topple over the edge of the cliff. He was already running to save himself from being knocked over with it as this fact flashed into his mind. He might just have got clear, but now he halted, and as the knife-like leading edge of the port wing reached him, he grabbed it and hung on.

He was, of course, instantly carried off his feet, but he had the satisfaction of feeling the machine swing round, and heard the protesting scream of slewing wheels. Then his fingers lost their grip and he fell headlong. The machine rumbled on, slowly, on a new course, its wheel-brakes hissing.

Ginger picked himself up and limped after it painfully, for he had bruised his knee in the fall. By the time he reached the machine Algy was standing up in his seat, goggles raised, looking back over the tail. His face was pale and drawn with strain, but as his eyes fell on Ginger they opened wide.

'Nice work, big boy,' grunted Ginger. 'Have you any chocolate aboard?'

Algy brushed a hand over his face. 'What is this?' he inquired in a dazed sort of voice. 'Where the dickens are we?'

'On top of the island – where else could we be? Didn't you know where you were landing?'

'Landing my foot,' snorted Algy. 'Didn't you hear my motor packing up? What with a dud engine *and* the snow, I should have been glad to get down anywhere – the right side up. I knew I was near the rock because it loomed up at me once or twice, but I thought I was clear of it, gliding down on the sea. Instead of which I suddenly hit the carpet; I had to run on because I couldn't get off again.'

'You nearly fell off it,' declared Ginger. 'If I hadn't grabbed your wing, in another couple of seconds you would have been over the cliff. This isn't Croydon.'

'You're telling me!' Algy climbed stiffly to the ground, bringing with him a bar of chocolate from the pocket in the cockpit. He gave it to Ginger who ate it ravenously.

'I don't get this,' went on Algy. 'What are you doing up here? Why did you stay up here?'

'Because I can't get down.'

'How long have you been here?'

'Since yesterday morning.'

'Great Scott! How did you get here?'

'Through a hole in the rock. But never mind about that. There's a German flying-boat down in the cove. I saw it when I looked over the top this morning.'

Algy laughed. 'That's all right,' he said. 'It's ours.'

'*What!*'

'Biggles and I pinched it last night. Of course, you didn't know about Biggles being a prisoner on the *Leipzig* – von Stalhein got hold of him.' Briefly, he gave the astonished Ginger a résumé of events of the past few hours. 'So I went off to lay an egg on the

Boche supply depot – which I did; then coming back I ran into this stuff,' he concluded, indicating the snow with a gesture of disgust.

Ginger, in turn, described how he came to be where he was.

'We'd better see about getting down – and the sooner the better,' announced Algy when he had finished. 'We shall have to abandon the machine, for the time being at any rate. Even if we could get the engine right, the weather makes flying out of the question.'

'If you're thinking of trying to fly off the top of this rock, even with the engine right and the weather fine, you'd better forget it. You don't know what it's like. Wait till the snow clears and have a look at it; you may change your mind then.'

'Couldn't it be done?'

Ginger hesitated. 'I suppose it might, at a pinch,' he conceded, 'but it would be a grim business. I should hate to try it, anyway.'

'Then if we can't fly her off we shall have to dismantle her and take her down in pieces,' said Algy optimistically. 'We'd better have a look and see if I damaged her when I bumped.'

They both walked round the wing to the nose of the machine and made a careful examination, but as far as they could see the machine had not been damaged – at least, not enough to prevent her from flying if the engine was put right.

'Smyth will have to come up and attend to the engine,' declared Algy. 'It's our last machine so we can't afford to lose it. Confound this snow! We shall be buried if it goes on. What's the difficulty about getting down?'

'Only a little matter of a twenty-foot drop on to a ledge just about big enough for a seagull to land on. You'd better come and look.' Taking Algy by the arm, Ginger led him to the edge of the cliff. 'That's the ledge we've got to reach,' he said, pointing. 'Do *you* feel like tackling it?'

'Crikey!' ejaculated Algy as he stared down into the void, although the sea was hidden from view by the snow. 'That's not so pretty,' he agreed.

Then, as they both stood staring down, there came a sound from somewhere below them that made them look up and gaze speculatively into each other's eyes. It sounded like a long-drawn-out howl.

'What in the name of goodness was that?' muttered Algy in a puzzled voice.

Ginger moistened his lips. 'There must be some sort of wild beast in the cave,' he whispered. 'Now we *are* sunk. Nothing would induce me to go down there.'

He started violently as a hairy object emerged slowly on to the ledge below. It turned, and a face looked up. It was Flight-Sergeant Smyth. His expression made Algy burst into a yell of laughter.

He recovered himself quickly and addressed the amazed N.C.O. 'What do you think you're doing, fooling about without any clothes on?'

'My togs are just inside the cave, sir,' explained the Flight-Sergeant. 'I had to swim the pond.'

'Pond! What pond?'

Ginger explained about the subterranean lake.

'I see,' went on Algy. Then, to the Flight-Sergeant, 'You've arrived just in time. You'd better go and get your clothes. My machine's up here and I want you to have a look at it.'

'But how is he to get up?' demanded Ginger.

Algy took from the pocket of his flying-jacket the line which he had taken to the sandbank, thinking that he and Biggles might have to enter the shed through the skylight. 'This should help,' he said naïvely.

'By gosh! What a bit of luck! That will do the trick,' said Ginger. 'Look here! I tell you what. We'll get the Flight-Sergeant up here to look at the engine. Then let me down, and I'll let Biggles know what has happened. I want a change of clothes anyway, and something to eat.'

'Yes, I think it's time you went down,' said Algy seriously, giving Ginger's weary face a searching look. 'I think that's a good idea. I'll stay here till you get back. You might as well bring Briny with you.'

The Flight-Sergeant, with his clothes in a bundle, reappeared on the ledge. He dried himself as well as he could with his cardigan and then got dressed. 'Briny's with me, sir,' he announced. 'He's the other side of the pond.'

Ginger looked at Algy. 'I think we'd better tell him to stay there,' he said. 'I don't see that there's much he can do up here, so he might as well come down with me and give me a hand over the difficult places.'

Algy agreed, and they told the Sergeant to shout to Briny to remain where he was, after which they lowered the rope and hauled Smyth to the top.

Ginger, with the N.C.O.'s torch, was then lowered to the ledge. He shouted to Briny to show a light to guide him, and then made the passage across the lake. The sailor helped him up when he reached the far side.

'Lor luv a duck, sir, what a time we're 'aving,' Briny greeted him.

'Yes, aren't we?' agreed Ginger without enthusiasm.

'What 'ave you been doin' up here all this time, sir?'

'Mushrooming,' returned Ginger briefly. 'Come on, let's get down. I've had about enough of this hole.'

Without further conversation they assisted each other down the face of the rock where Ginger had lost his torch, and set off down the tunnel, making all the speed they could.

Ginger, who was leading, didn't see Roy until he fell over him. 'Look out!' he cried as he picked himself up. 'Good heavens, it's Roy,' he went on sharply as the light flashed on the pale, blood-stained face.

'Something must 'ave happened, sir,' said Briny in a hushed voice.

'I can see that,' answered Ginger, staring at the two code-books, still lying where they had fallen. 'Yes, by thunder, something certainly has happened,' he breathed.

'It must be pretty bad to have sent him up here with those books,' whispered Briny. 'What could it 'abin, sir?'

'I can't imagine,' replied Ginger, shaking his head, 'unless, of course, the depot's been attacked. I can't think of any other reason that would send him up here with those two books. He must have been trying to save them when he fell off this rock.'

Briny had taken off his jacket, and after getting Roy into a more comfortable position, pillowed it under his head.

Roy showed no signs of recovering consciousness, and there was nothing more that they could do to help him.

'We'd better carry him down, sir,' suggested Briny.

'I doubt if we can manage it – apart from which, I think it would be dangerous,' muttered Ginger. 'He ought to be moved carefully until we see how badly he's hurt. There's a stretcher down below; I'll go and fetch it.' He spoke slowly, for he was wondering what else there might be below. Algy had told him that when he, Algy, had taken off to bomb the German supply depot, he had left Biggles to sleep off his exhaustion. Why had he not come up the cave with Roy if an attack had been made? Again, there had been no shooting; at least, he had heard none, and he felt certain that if shots had been fired he would have heard them. The more he thought about it, the more inexplicable the affair became.

'I'll tell you what we'll do,' he said at last. 'You stay here and look after Roy. If he comes round before I get back, and is able to walk, try to get him down. If not, wait till I return with a stretcher. I'll go on and see what's happened at the depot.'

'Ay, ay, sir.' Briny touched the peak of his ancient cap. 'I remember once seeing a cave—' he began, and then shook his head sadly as Ginger set off quickly down the fissure.

Ginger hurried on, but as he neared the base he slowed down, for he still had an uneasy feeling that something was amiss. Approaching the final opening, he saw that the lights were still on, so he instinctively switched off his torch and adopted scouting tactics.

He heard the Germans before he saw them, and his heart went cold. Peeping round the final obstruction, he knew at once what had happened, for several German marines were standing on the catwalk. Breathless, he could only stand still and watch, wondering what had become of Biggles.

He was still watching when the door of Biggles's room opened and Biggles himself came out. His manner was nonchalant, but behind him walked von Stalhein, an automatic in his hand. There was a gruff word of command. A file of eight marines, armed with rifles, whom Ginger now saw for the first time, marched forward from the back of the mess that had hidden them.

Von Stalhein halted. With military precision he turned to Biggles, clicked his heels and saluted. Then an N.C.O. in charge of the marines stepped forward. He, too, saluted, and said something in a harsh voice.

Biggles nodded. 'Get on with it and get it over,' he said in English.

The words gave Ginger a clue as to what was happening, and for a moment he was nearly overcome by a sense of his own helplessness. But it did not last long. A look of almost savage determination set his lips in a hard line, and he sidled out of the cave to the rear of the signal room. Pausing only for a moment to make sure that he had not been observed, he then slipped cautiously to the canvas-covered pile of stores behind the mess, where, as it was practically dark, he could only grope for what he sought. With a feeling akin to exultation his hands closed over the barrel of a Bren machine-gun, and he drew it out, holding his breath as it clanked against the rock floor. Blessing his foresight, or the lucky chance – he wasn't sure which it was – that had caused him to examine the stores before exploring the passage, he pulled out a box of ammunition and loaded the gun.

Another surreptitious peep round the end of the mess showed him that he had not a moment to lose, for Biggles, smoking a cigarette, was standing with his back to the wall, with the marines in single file in front of him.

Several other Germans were about, but none of them was looking towards the inner extremity of the cave, which in the circumstances was not remarkable; their eyes were on Biggles, so Ginger was able to creep back to the fissure without being seen or his presence even suspected. There, to his joy, he saw that he had the file of marines in line; only the N.C.O., who was standing a little in front of the others, was clear of his enfilade as he brought the gun to bear and squinted down the sights. Von Stalhein was leaning against the door of the mess, a spiral of smoke rising from the long cigarette holder which he held between his fingers.

At a word of command from the *unteroffizier* eight rifles came to the present.

Ginger was trembling with excitement. Without taking his eyes from the sights, or his finger from the trigger, he shouted at the top of his voice, 'Biggles! Run this way!' Then he squeezed the trigger.

Tac-tac-tac … tac-tac-tac … tac-tac-tac … spat the gun, rolling a hideous tattoo in the confined space and filling the air with the acrid reek of cordite smoke.

To Ginger, the rest was a nightmare in which he seemed to be only a detached spectator. He saw Biggles, twisting and turning as he ran, racing towards him, and he saw that there was a danger of hitting him. So he jumped clear of the cave, and stepping aside, stood in the open, holding the dancing gun while he sprayed everything and everybody in sight.

The marines, those who remained on their feet, bolted for cover. Only von Stalhein stood his ground, shouting orders that were not heeded, punctuating them with snapshots from his automatic in Ginger's direction. A ricocheting bullet tore a long splinter from the mess door not six inches from his face, and he, too, darted back out of sight.

Biggles reached Ginger and snatched the machine-gun from his hands. 'Steady with your ammunition,' he grated, and began to sweep the depot with short bursts of fire. But answering bullets soon began to splash against the rocks around him, and Ginger caught him by the arm. 'Come on,' he cried shrilly. 'Let's get out of this. This way.'

'Where to?' shouted Biggles.

'I'll show you. Keep going. Everybody is up here.' Ginger darted into the fissure and switched on his torch.

Biggles waited only to send a final burst down the catwalk, and then, still carrying the gun, he followed at Ginger's heels.

'This is a useful place,' he observed calmly. 'Knowing that we've got this gun, it'll take a brave man to follow us up this drainpipe. How far does it go?'

'Right to the top of the rock.'

'Is Roy in here by any chance?'

'Yes.'

'Has he got the code-books?'

'Yes.'

'Thank God for that,' said Biggles earnestly; 'that's all I care about. You know the way. Lead on, Macduff.'

CHAPTER XVII

Reunion

For some time they pushed on as fast as they could go, occasionally stopping to listen for sounds of pursuit; but as none came, Biggles called a halt and demanded to know what had happened, and what was still happening, on the top of the rock. So in as few words as possible Ginger described his own adventures, and explained how Algy, Briny, and the Flight-Sergeant came to be where they were. He then told him about Roy.

'He must have seen the Huns coming, and bolted with the code-books,' declared Biggles. 'I wonder why he didn't warn me.'

'Did he know you were there?'

Biggles clicked his fingers. 'No, now I come to think of it he didn't. He was asleep when I got back. I was asleep, too, when von Stalhein walked in on me. I didn't hear a thing. When I opened my eyes and saw von Stalhein there – well, I'll leave you to guess how I felt. But we'd better get on. With one thing and another we seem to be in as pretty a mess as we were ever in.'

'We could hold this cave indefinitely – against an army,' said Ginger emphatically.

'We could – if we could live on air,' agreed Biggles. 'We'll talk about that when we get to the others. Come on. Apparently von Stalhein thinks he's got us bottled up, so he's not in a hurry to chase us.'

'How many men has he got down there?'

'I don't know.'

'Well, we've got to break through them, or we shall be here for the rest of our lives. Two might get away in Algy's machine, but that's all.'

'You seem to have forgotten standing orders,' said Biggles seriously.

'What do you mean?'

'I mean that our first job, now that we've been discovered, is to destroy the depot. That stuff mustn't fall into German hands. After we've attended to that we'll see about getting away – not before. But I shall have to have a word with Algy before we decide anything definitely. Hullo, here's Roy and Briny.'

They found Roy sitting up, looking shaken, but he smiled when he saw Biggles coming. 'Sorry about this, sir,' he said.

'So am I,' returned Biggles. 'How are you feeling?'

'Pretty fair, sir.'

'Able to walk?'

'I'll have a shot at it, sir.'

'Good. Then let's get up to the top.'

Briny looked surprised. 'To the top, sir?'

'That's what I said. It's no use going down because the place is full of Germans.'

Briny took a pace backward, his face a picture of consternation. 'Blimey!' he whispered.

Ginger led the way up the cave until they reached the buttress of rock that dammed the water in the lake. They helped each other up, and from the top Biggles surveyed the water with a curious expression on his face.

'What do you think of it?' inquired Ginger.

'I think it's going to be very useful,' replied Biggles enigmatically. 'You're wet through already so you might as well come across with me. Briny, you stay here with Roy and keep guard. I'll leave this gun with you. If you hear anyone coming up the cave, let drive. We shall hear you shoot and come back to help you.'

Biggles took off his clothes, and holding up the bundle with one hand, followed Ginger across to the ledge, where they discovered that it had stopped snowing, although the sky still looked very threatening. A hail brought Algy to the edge of the cliff above them. He lowered the line, and in a few minutes they were reunited at the top, where Biggles told Algy what had happened at the depot. 'How's your machine?' he concluded.

'We haven't tested it yet, but it should be all right,' answered Algy. 'The Flight-Sergeant found a piece of solder in the petrol lead; he's taken it out, so if anyone feels like taking off he can have a shot at it.'

Biggles contemplated the prospect without speaking, for it was enough to daunt the stoutest pilot. The maximum run over the smooth part of the rock was not more than a hundred yards; and that was not the worst. At the end of it, fluted columns of weather-worn rock rose vertically some ten or twelve feet in the air, which meant that a machine taking off, failing to get that amount of height, would collide with an obstruction that would smash it to pieces.

'It might just be done,' decided Biggles at last.

Algy nodded. 'That's how I figured it. Who's going?'

'You are.'

'Why me? Why should I get away?'

'I'm not thinking about you particularly; I'm thinking about the German code-book. Von Stalhein doesn't know we've got it, and it's worth its weight in gold to the Admiralty. Whatever happens here that code is going home if it is possible to get it there.'

'I doubt if I've enough juice in the tank to get to England,' said Algy dubiously.

'Is there enough to get you, flying solo, as far as the North Sea?'

'Yes, I should think so.'

'Then that's the way it will have to be. If, when you get to the North Sea, you can't spot one of our ships – well, I'm afraid it's going to be just too bad. But there ought to be plenty of shipping about – destroyers, mine-sweepers, submarine chasers, to say nothing of merchant convoys.'

'Why don't you go yourself?'

'Because I've got something else to do here. You've got your orders – don't argue.'

'As you say. What are you going to do?'

'First of all I'm going up to the top of that lump of rock and have a look at the cove.' He pointed to the *massif* up which Ginger had climbed. 'By the way,' he continued, 'you took a machine-gun with you last night. Is it still in your machine? If it is I'll take it. With luck I might get a pop at von Stalhein, if he happens to be standing outside the cave.'

'Yes, it's still in my seat.'

Biggles walked up to the machine, and was lifting the gun out when he gave a cry of triumph. 'By jingo! I'd forgotten that!'

'Forgotten what?'

From the rear seat Biggles lifted the time-bomb, which Algy had not used. 'This squib is the answer to a question I've been asking myself for the last half-hour,' he announced enthusiastically.

Algy stared. 'What's the big idea? I'm not clever at riddles.'

'Does your imagination go far enough to give you a picture of what will happen when I blow this charge against the rock that holds all that water in the cave?'

Algy's jaw dropped. 'You're crazy,' he declared. 'It would blow the cave to pieces. In fact, it might blow half the island to pieces. The tunnel would probably cave in and you'd be stuck up here with no way of ever getting down.'

Biggles laughed shortly. 'That's a detail. What is more to the point, a million gallons of water let loose would sweep every man in the depot into the sea – and everything else.'

'But you don't know which way the explosion would expend itself,' put in Ginger aghast. 'You'd bust the dam all right, but you might blow the top clean off the island – or blow the side out of it, causing the whole place to collapse.'

'My orders are to destroy the depot if we have to abandon it,' answered Biggles grimly. 'Whatever else happened, the explosion would release the water, so von Stalhein and his gang would get their ears wet when they weren't expecting it – not that I care two hoots about them. I'm only concerned with flooding the depot before they can shift the stuff out of it.'

'This ought to be worth watching,' murmured Ginger.

Biggles's manner became brisk. 'Algy, put the code-books in the machine. I'm going up to the top of the rock. If anything unforeseen happens before I get back, take off and head for England. If you have to come down in enemy waters tie something round the British code-book and sink it. Ginger, you come with me.' Putting the machine-gun on his shoulder, Biggles set off up the *massif*.

It was not an easy climb when Ginger had attempted it, but now, with snow about, it was even more difficult. However, by strenuous labour, and by helping each other over the worst places, twenty minutes saw them at the top.

Ginger was the first to reach the edge and look down. He gave an exclamation of dismay.

Biggles joined him. 'That's von Stalhein's drifter down there, in the cove,' he said. 'I knew it was there. That looks like von Stalhein himself standing on the bridge, talking to the captain. I think I'll let him know that we're still alive.' He lay down in the snow, and taking careful aim, poured a stream of bullets down on the drifter.

Von Stalhein made a leap for the companionway and disappeared; some other men who were standing about also darted for cover.

'Rotten shooting,' said Biggles disgustedly. 'I couldn't hold the gun still in this snow; it jumped all over the place as soon as I pressed the trigger.'

A bullet splashed against a rock just below him, and whistled away into the leaden sky.

Biggles drew back. 'There's no sense in making targets of ourselves,' he said. 'They won't show themselves again for a bit. I've seen all I wanted to know, anyway, so we may as well get back.'

Ginger caught his arm and pointed seaward. 'What's this coming?' he cried.

Biggles looked up. 'A couple of German destroyers, I fancy,' he said evenly. 'Von Stalhein must have called them up by wireless. It doesn't make much difference; I don't see how we could have got out, anyway. We couldn't get near that flying-boat without coming under fire of the drifter. Let's hope the destroyers come into the cove.'

'Why?'

'You'll see. I think you'd better stay here while I go down and get the bomb in position. I'll ask Algy to wait until it goes off; then, if he gets back safely, he can tell Raymond what happened. You watch the destroyers. If they come into the cove, let me know by raising your arms above your head. I shall take that as the signal to blow the charge. Is that clear?'

'Clear as daylight.'

'Good. I'll get down now. After the bang you'll be able to watch what happens.' Biggles smiled and hurried down to where Algy was waiting by the machine. His manner was still inconsequential, but his heart was heavy, for he knew that the last hour of the base had come, and he felt that he ought to have made better use of it. He knew, too, that except for something like a miracle, their own time had come. Whether they were blown up by the bomb, or whether they went down through the cave to surrender themselves to von Stalhein, it would come to the same thing in the end. Not that he contemplated going down. His orders were to destroy the base and he was thankful that he had a means at hand to achieve that object. He had always had a feeling that the end might come this way, for it was as obvious to him, as it had been to Colonel Raymond, that such a base, situated as it was practically in enemy country, could not last for any great length of time.

'What's happening in the cove?' asked Algy as Biggles joined him.

'It seems to be getting busy. There's a drifter and a German flying-boat already there, and two German destroyers just coming in,' smiled Biggles. 'Our friend von Stalhein might almost be justified in thinking that he has got us all safely bottled up at last.'

'Have you any reason to suppose that he hasn't?'

'None whatever. Well, that's all. I want you to stand fast and wait for the result of the explosion before you take off. You will then be able – I hope – to tell Raymond that we wrecked the base before the Boche could shift the stuff. You'd better not start your engine yet. Von Stalhein has no idea that we've got a machine up here, and we don't want him to know, or the destroyers might start slinging shells across before you can get off.'

Algy's face was expressionless as he held out his hand. 'Cheerio,' he said. 'I shall fly back here, of course, if I get the code-books home. If I can persuade the Air Ministry to let me have one I'll borrow a flying-boat; so hang on, if you can, on the off-chance.'

Biggles smiled as he squeezed Algy's hand. 'Do your best, old lad,' he said. Then, turning to the Flight-Sergeant: 'Bring the line and help me down to the ledge,' he ordered.

Whistling softly, he picked up the time-bomb and walked towards the cliff.

CHAPTER XVIII

Biggles Strikes Back

Flight-Sergeant Smyth lowered Biggles to the ledge and waited for further instructions.

'Drop the rope,' Biggles told him. 'I shall need it. Thanks. Now listen carefully. You can see Mr. Hebblethwaite from where you are I think?'

'Yes, sir.'

'Very well. There are two German destroyers on their way here. If they come into the cove Mr. Hebblethwaite will signal by raising both hands above his head. You will pass the information on to me via Briny, whom I shall send across to this ledge. I shall send Roy on over here too. I shall be at the far side of the lake.'

'Very good, sir.'

Biggles undressed, coiled the rope about his middle, and picking up the bomb, shouted to Briny to show a light. Arriving at the far side, he was pleased to find Roy looking much better, and sent him across to the ledge. He then ordered Briny to lower him to the bottom of the rock that dammed the water, where he waited until the message had been passed on to him that Ginger had made the signal. He was relieved to get it, for more

185

than once stealthy sounds coming from below suggested that the enemy were scouting up the fissure.

He timed the bomb for a quarter of an hour, and placing it in position, piled around it all the loose rock that he could find. He then ordered Briny to pull him up, and together they crossed over to the ledge, from where, after the rope had been thrown up, they were all hauled to the top.

Biggles ordered every one farther away from the cliff in case the explosion should start a landslide, and then looked about him. Ginger was still on the top of the *massif,* looking down into the cove. Algy was standing by his machine ready to start up at an instant's notice. The others were standing near him.

'How long before the balloon goes up?' shouted Algy.

'I set the bomb for a quarter of an hour, so there are still about ten minutes to go. I'm going up to the top to join Ginger. Don't be in a hurry to take off. If anything unforeseen occurs, get off right away without waiting for me to come down; otherwise hang on, and I'll try to give you some definite information to take to Raymond.'

Algy nodded. 'Good enough. But don't wait too long. I don't like the look of the weather; it may start snowing again.'

Biggles glanced at the sky. 'It doesn't look too good,' he admitted, and then set off up the *massif.*

He was still only halfway up when there was a muffled roar, and the whole island quivered like a jelly. He was nearly thrown off his feet, and for the next minute or two was kept busy dodging rocks that had been shaken loose and were rolling down the steep side of the *massif.*

Ginger, lying at the edge of the cliff, watching the destroyers manoeuvre into position in the cove before dropping anchor, clutched at the rocks on either side of him as his perch shook under the violence of the explosion. Several pieces of rock on the face of the cliff were shaken loose and went hurtling down into the cove; some fell sheer; others struck the cliff again lower down and bounced far out over the water. Shouts of alarm rose from below; men appeared on the deck of the drifter, von Stalhein among them; others appeared at the mouth of the cave. Some were launching a dinghy.

After that there was a brief lull, although pieces of rock continued to detach themselves from the side of the cliff and whirl downwards, sometimes taking minor avalanches of loose shale with them. Then, from the very heart of the rock, it seemed, came a terrifying rumble, like distant thunder. The rock began to tremble anew, and Ginger experienced a feeling of acute alarm not far short of fear, for the sensation was one of lying on a volcano about to burst into eruption. His alarm was in no way lessened when a great mass of cliff broke away, and with a roar like an express train went plunging down into the void.

By this time the destroyers, their propellers threshing the water into foam, were turning towards the open sea. On their decks men were running about in a panic. The drifter followed; being smaller it moved faster, and trying to cut across the bows of one of the destroyers, came into collision with it. There was more shouting.

Ginger turned and saw Biggles coming hand over hand up the *massif*. 'Look out!' he cried shrilly. 'The whole island's falling to pieces!'

The words had hardly left his lips when the cliff in one place started to bulge; it was as if it were made of elastic, and was being forced out under terrific pressure. Then, with a crash like thunder, the bulge burst. A mighty torrent of water shot clear into space. Rocks and water went plunging down together. Simultaneously, from the mouth of the cave there issued a swirling yellow flood.

Ginger felt Biggles throw himself down beside him, but he neither looked at him nor spoke. He was too spellbound by what was happening below. At first the falling rock and water prevented a clear view, but as the first pent-up energy of the water subsided somewhat – although a cataract continued to pour down the cliff – the scene became clearer.

It was a terrifying spectacle that met his eyes, more like an upheaval of nature than an artificial catastrophe. Before the weight of water, the three vessels were being swept about like toy ships. One of the destroyers had rammed the drifter amidships and had stuck fast. Both were grinding against the spit that formed one arm of the cove. The second destroyer, with black smoke belching from its funnels, still had its nose pointing towards the cliff, but in spite of its engines, was being slowly carried backward, and was in danger of colliding with the other two vessels. The flying-boat, being lighter, had already been swept out to sea, and now drifted helplessly.

The flood still pouring from the cave went swirling out to sea, a turgid yellow tide that carried with it all sorts of debris, and made a clear line of demarcation with the deep water. Men were clinging to the wreckage which, Ginger noticed, consisted largely of broken timbers, obviously the remains of the buildings of the depot.

'What a picture,' muttered Biggles in a tense whisper. 'I wish I had my camera. Raymond will never be able to say we didn't go out with a bang. What's happened to the cliff underneath us?' He strained forward trying to see it.

'Mind you don't go over!'

Biggles backed hastily. 'There seems to be a tidy hole there. I hope this piece we're on doesn't collapse; it doesn't look any too safe. Hullo, look at the drifter; she's sinking. The crew are abandoning it judging by the way they're jumping on to the destroyer. There goes von Stalhein. That fellow seems to bear a charmed life.'

'He probably thinks that about you.'

Biggles grinned. 'True enough,' he agreed. 'The other destroyer's going to get away, now that things are a bit quieter.'

'It looks like it. Still, she doesn't look any too happy. I bet her wireless is buzzing, asking for help. They'll have to hang around to pick up the people who are marooned on the rocks.'

Several marines, presumably survivors of the party that had been in the cave, had managed to secure a foothold on the rocks that ringed the cove.

'Well, what happens next?' inquired Ginger, watching the second destroyer back slowly out to sea.

'Ask me something easier. We've done about all we can do. Even if we could get down through the cave, which I doubt, I don't think we could take on a destroyer single-handed.'

'We could stop anybody from getting up here.'

'Yes, I think we could do that, but why need they bother to come up? They know we can't get away. All they have to do is sit where they are and wait for us to fall off from want of food. We've one card up our sleeve though. They don't know we've got a machine up here, so it'll shake them when Algy takes off. I may as well tell him to go; there's no point in him staying here any longer now that the fireworks are over.'

One of the destroyer's guns flashed. A shell whined up and sprayed the rock with shrapnel.

'Who says the fireworks are over?' muttered Ginger drily. 'They can see us evidently. We'd better get down.'

Biggles turned towards where Algy was standing; cupping his hands round his mouth he let out a hail. 'All clear!' he shouted, pointing to the sky. 'Tell Raymond we've flooded the place and bust up a destroyer and a drifter at the same time.'

Algy waved to show that he understood. 'Cheerio!' he yelled; 'I'll be back in a couple of days.'

Biggles caught Ginger's eye and smiled. 'Trust old Algy not to be left out of the finale. All the same, I don't see what he can do if he does come back – but it's no use telling him not to.' He sat down on a rock to watch the machine take off.

Ginger squatted beside him. 'I shall be glad when he's up topsides,' he said anxiously. 'I am by no means sure that he's got enough room to get off. If he touches those spikes of rock with his wheels—'

'Don't think about such things,' protested Biggles.

Algy was now in his seat. The propeller came to life.

'I hope there isn't another piece of solder in that petrol pipe,' murmured Ginger.

'He's testing her now,' put in Biggles, as the noise of the engine rose to a crescendo, and then died away again as it was throttled back.

'It doesn't sound too good to me,' declared Ginger, with his head on one side.

'She's giving her revs, anyway, or he wouldn't be so crazy as to try to take off,' returned Biggles. 'There he goes.'

The *Platypus* was racing across the flat part of the rock, apparently to certain destruction. Fifty yards from the jagged teeth that barred its path the wheels had not lifted.

'He's deliberately holding her down,' said Biggles, whose face was deathly white.

Twenty yards from the edge of the cliff the *Platypus* jerked into the air, its wheels missing the rocks with a foot to spare.

Ginger wiped imaginary perspiration from his brow. 'Phew,' he gasped, 'I can't stand much of that. I—' He broke off suddenly and started to his feet.

Biggles, too, sprang up, his lips in a straight line. Comment was unnecessary. The engine was spluttering. There came the explosion of a backfire. The engine picked up again, but only for a moment. Another splutter, and it cut out dead.

As soon as the engine had started missing, the nose of the machine had tilted down. Now it went into a glide, and began a flat turn back towards the rock, about a hundred yards behind it.

'He'll never do it,' said Biggles in a dull voice. 'He can't get back. It's impossible. He'll go nose first into the cliff if he tries.'

What he had said was obviously so true that Ginger did not answer. He was incapable of speech. With his muscles as taut as if he were flying the machine himself, he could only watch. He saw the machine turn away from the island as Algy, too, realized that he was attempting the impossible. A moment later the *Platypus* disappeared from sight below the level of the cliff.

'He's going down on the sea – it's all he can do,' snapped Biggles, and started off down towards the place where the machine had disappeared, jumping from rock to rock in a manner that was little short of suicidal. The Flight-Sergeant, Briny, and Roy were also racing towards the place. With his heart in his mouth, Ginger followed Biggles.

Breathless, they arrived at the edge of the cliff just as the snow began to fall again, although it was not yet too thick to prevent them from seeing the machine land heavily on the water. But the captain of the destroyer had also realized what was happening, and now the long grey hull, flinging a bow wave high into the air, came racing towards the helpless aircraft.

'I'm afraid it's all over bar the shouting,' said Biggles heavily. 'He hasn't a chance.'

'He seems to be mighty busy doing something,' observed Ginger, staring at Algy, who was now standing up in his cockpit. 'What's he doing?'

'I know what he's doing,' said Biggles bitterly. 'He's tearing the British code-book to pieces so that he can set fire to them.'

'What! In the machine! He'll have the whole thing in flames in a couple of minutes. If his tank catches fire he'll blow himself up.'

'He'll risk that as long as he destroys the book,' declared Biggles. 'Confound the snow,' he added viciously, as the blizzard suddenly thickened and blotted out the sea. They could not even see the water.

For a minute the watchers on the cliff stood still, listening, vainly straining their eyes.

'I thought I heard a shout,' muttered Ginger.

The words had hardly left his lips when a violent explosion again shook the rock, although the noise was muffled somewhat by the snow. A moment later came the sound of debris falling into the water.

'That's his tank gone up.' Ginger's voice was little more than a whisper.

Biggles said nothing. With his chin cupped in the palm of his hand he sat staring, white-faced, into the driving snow.

CHAPTER XIX

Marooned on the Rock

For some time nobody spoke. The only sound was the chugging of an invisible motorboat somewhere on the sea below.

At last Ginger tapped Biggles on the shoulder. 'Come on,' he said. 'There's no sense in sitting here getting smothered with snow. If we don't soon get back to the cave we may not be able to find it.'

Biggles got up. 'I was trying to work out a way of getting that code-book back, but it's got me stumped,' he said despondently. 'However, as you remark, it's no use sitting up here in the snow, unable to see a blessed thing; we may as well have a look at the cave – if it's still there. If it isn't – well, it'll be interesting to see how they propose to get us off this rock. They won't just sail off and leave us here, that's certain.'

'The only thing they could do would be to shoot us up from the air with machine-guns.'

Biggles reached for their own gun. 'Two can play at that game,' he said grimly. 'Poor old Algy; if only he could have got away with those books I shouldn't have minded so much what happened here. Ah well! I suppose it was bound to come to this sooner or later. Let's get back to the cave.'

They all made their way through the drifting snow to the edge of the cliff.

'The ledge is still there, anyway,' observed Biggles, looking over the top as he tied the rope round his waist. 'Let me down first.'

With the gun in his hands he was lowered to the ledge. The others followed, Ginger, who came last, scrambling down at the end of a running line, with the rope looped round a projecting piece of rock at the top of the cliff.

Entering the cave, they saw at once that the lake was no longer there. Where the water had been yawned a wide black crater, but the passage across it offered no great difficulty. At the far side they found that the rock that had dammed the water had been shattered by the explosion; beyond it, the fissure was almost choked with debris, and Biggles looked at it dubiously before he advanced.

'Take it quietly everybody, or we may have the whole place down on our heads,' he warned the others.

Moving with extreme caution, taking care not to disturb loose rocks, they went on, noting the results of the escaping flood.

It was Ginger who saw the new exit first. Biggles had just pulled up with a cry of warning – or it may have been dismay – for they had reached a place where the fissure was almost completely blocked with pieces of loose rock, jammed together by the colossal weight of the water. All their torches were on, and it was no doubt due to this that the grey light which entered the cave from the left at first passed unnoticed. Ginger, happening to look that way, let out a shout. 'Here, what's this?' he cried. 'It looks like a hole. It must be the place where the water burst through the side of the cliff.'

As quickly as they dared they made their way to the spot, and soon saw that what Ginger had surmised was indeed the case.

A large portion of the side of the cliff had been forced out by the sudden weight of the released water, leaving an enormous cavity into which the snow now drifted.

Biggles made his way cautiously to the edge and looked down. 'I can just see the cove,' he announced. 'I should say it's about eighty feet below us.'

'Is there anybody about?' inquired Ginger.

'I can't see anybody.'

'Then they must be back in the cave, trying to get up to us.'

'I don't think they'll get past that mass of rock – the place where we were held up.'

'If they can't get up, it also means that we can't get down.'

'I'm by no means anxious to get down just yet, anyway,' said Biggles slowly. 'I think the snow is getting thinner. Let's sit here for a bit until it clears. We'd better see what's happening below before we do anything else.'

Resting the gun against a boulder, Biggles sat down to wait. Ginger squatted beside him, and the others leaned against the rock. As Biggles had remarked, the snowstorm was passing, and presently it was possible to see most of the cove.

'Where the dickens has everybody gone?' muttered Ginger, scanning the scene below in search of the Germans whom he fully expected to see there.

'Don't ask me,' replied Biggles. 'I can only think that the second destroyer must have picked them up.'

'But it was making for Algy's machine. Surely it wouldn't have tried to get back into the cove through all that snow. Visibility must have been zero.'

'There's the destroyer, and the drifter, at any rate,' observed Biggles, as visibility improved and it became possible to see the two vessels, still locked together against the spit. The destroyer had sunk by the stern, with her bows still in the drifter's hull. Both appeared to be deserted.

'This has got me whacked,' went on Biggles, with a puzzled expression on his face. 'Where the dickens have the crews gone?'

'The lifeboats aren't there,' the Flight-Sergeant pointed out. 'They must have taken to the boats when the destroyer started to founder.'

'But where could they go? Why can't we see them? You'd have thought they'd have come ashore.'

Briny stepped forward. 'Excuse me, sir, I didn't like to mention it before, but when you was a'sittin' on the top there, just after Mr. Lacey flopped down in the ditch, I thought I 'eard a motor-boat. I've got a pretty good ear for engines, and I said to myself, I said, if that ain't the blooming motorboat wot let me down, then I never 'eard it.'

Biggles stared, trying to grasp the significance of what Briny had said.

'Just a minute,' put in Ginger sharply, turning to Biggles. 'Didn't you say that the drifter had picked up the motorboat? If so, it might have brought it here.'

'That's right,' conceded Biggles.

'Then they might have cleared off in the motorboat – or taken the lifeboats in tow.'

'Even so, that doesn't explain why they should suddenly rush off, knowing that we were on the island.'

'They may have gone to the other destroyer.'

'Yes, but where *is* the other destroyer?' cried Biggles, indicating the open sea, for the snow had now practically stopped, and it was possible to see for two or three miles.

'Great Scott! Look! There's Algy's machine,' shouted Ginger suddenly.

Biggles stared as if he could not believe his eyes; but there was no possibility of mistake. The *Platypus* had drifted into sight, close to the rocks below them. It seemed to be in an undamaged condition, but of Algy there was no sign.

'He must be in the water – unless he managed to get ashore,' ventured Roy.

'Hark!' said Biggles suddenly.

Over the water came a hail. 'Ahoy there!'

'What the dickens! That wasn't Algy's voice,' swore Biggles.

'It certainly wasn't,' agreed Ginger emphatically.

Then to their ears came the muffled beat of an engine, and they all stared at the shoulder of rock from beyond which the sound seemed to come. And as they stared, moving very slowly, a long, sleek body came into sight, just above the surface of the water.

'Look out! It's a U-boat,' snapped Biggles, grabbing the gun. Then he stopped, staring incredulously as the rest of the steel deck came into sight. On the deck was a gun, and behind it stood a crew of British bluejackets. Nobody spoke as the conning-tower came into view, and then Ginger let out a yell, for standing talking to two British officers was Algy. The submarine forged on, its white ensign fluttering.

'Ahoy there!' yelled Ginger, nearly going over the cliff in his excitement.

They saw Algy look up and point, and in a moment a dozen faces were staring at the hole in the rock.

'Talk about fairy godmothers, they aren't in it,' declared Biggles, a flush on his pale face. 'Where have you sprung from?' he shouted.

'We've come for that code-book!' shouted the submarine commander.

Biggles remembered his signal to Colonel Raymond and understood what had happened. The Admiralty had sent for the valuable document. 'Watch out!' he roared. 'There's a Boche destroyer about somewhere.'

'It won't worry us,' answered the naval officer. 'It's—' He jabbed his thumb downwards.

'That must have been the bang we heard,' said Ginger. 'It wasn't Algy's tank; it was a mouldy hitting the destroyer.'

'Come down – I've got to get back. I daren't hang about here!' shouted the submarine commander. 'Where are the people off that other destroyer?'

'They must have seen you and pushed off in their lifeboats. They had a motorboat with them.'

'I see. Come on down.'

'Stand fast. We're not sure that we can get down.'

Biggles made his way quickly to the cave, but it did not take him long to ascertain that any idea of getting down that way was out of the question. How far the blockage extended it was impossible to say. At some risk he dragged a few small pieces of rock aside, only to reveal more rock, apart from which he nearly brought the roof down on his head. 'It would take weeks to clear a way through here,' he told Ginger, who had followed him.

'But that means that we can't get down at all.'

'It begins to look like that,' admitted Biggles. 'Maddening, isn't it, with the submarine so close.'

'Perhaps they can get a line up to us?' suggested Ginger.

'We'll ask them.'

They hurried back to the opening and informed the naval officer of the position. 'Can you get a line up to us?' concluded Biggles.

The submarine commander conferred with his officers. 'No!' he shouted up. 'We haven't a line long enough. Even if we had we couldn't get it up to you.'

'That means we're stuck here,' declared Biggles, looking round the horizon which, now that the snow had cleared, could be seen. His eyes fell on a line of lifeboats heading southward, and the mystery of the abandoned ships was explained. He realized that von Stalhein must have seen the destroyer torpedoed, and had promptly fled in the motorboat. Biggles's roving eyes picked out something else, a smudge of smoke far beyond the boats. 'What's this coming!' he shouted, pointing towards it.

The submarine commander studied the distant hull with his binoculars. 'It's a German cruiser,' he announced. 'If you're coming with me you'll have to buck up. I daren't risk my ship by staying here.'

Biggles thought desperately, but he could find no way out of their quandary. 'All right skipper,' he shouted at last, 'you get off and take the code-books. We shall have to take our luck.'

'Sorry – but you can see how it is.'

Biggles waved good-bye.

Suddenly Algy cried, 'Can you get back to the top?'

'Yes,' Biggles told him, whereupon Algy spoke rapidly to the naval officer, at the same time pointing towards the German flying-boat, which was still drifting about half a mile away. Then he looked up.

'Get back to the top of the rock,' he bellowed. 'You'll have to buck up.'

'I don't know what he's thinking of doing, but we'd better do as he says,' declared Biggles. 'It's no use staying here, anyway.'

A parting wave and they were on their way back to the summit of the island. Panting with exertion, they made their way across the empty reservoir to the ledge, and then, by means of the rope, to the top.

'I've got it,' said Ginger, as they ran across to a position from which they could look down on the submarine. 'He's going to fetch the flying-boat.'

'But he can't land a boat up here,' protested Biggles, as they reached their immediate objective and scanned the sea for the submarine. But it had gone. The German cruiser was still coming at full speed, and was now not more than five or six miles away. The *Platypus* was a smouldering wreck, burnt to water-level. The big flying-boat was racing over the sea towards the island.

'He must have set fire to the *Platypus* to prevent it from falling into the enemy's hands, so he must be pretty confident of getting away,' declared Biggles.

A moment later the aircraft left the water and roared up towards the top of the rock. Five pairs of eyes watched it anxiously as it climbed rather higher than the island, and then swept round with the obvious intention of flying straight over them. As it passed over the level area a bulky object fell from it and plunged downward. Another followed, and another. There was no time for more, for by this time the machine had overshot the island; but it banked steeply and retraced its course. Two more objects detached themselves to bounce on the rock.

'I've got it!' yelled Biggles. 'They're brollies.'

Ginger stared aghast. 'Does he think we're going to jump off the top of this place?' he gasped.

'That's it. There's no other way.' Biggles ran forward to retrieve the parachutes, the others following him.

By the time they had each picked one up the flying-boat had cut its engines and was gliding down. It landed, and taxied nearly – but not quite – under the overhanging ledge, which, fortunately, happened to be on the side farthest from the cruiser.

Algy's voice floated up. 'Come on!' he shouted. 'I'll pick you up. Get a move on. It's that or nothing.'

'Where's the submarine?' called Biggles.

'Gone.'

'Has it got the code-books?'

'Yes.'

Biggles gave a sigh of relief and started getting into his harness. Ginger and the Flight-Sergeant were doing the same thing. Afterwards they helped Briny and Roy, neither of whom had ever made a parachute jump.

Biggles looked down, and judged the distance to be a little over four hundred feet. 'We shall have to pull the ring as we jump,' he announced. 'Jump out as far as possible to get clear of the rocks.'

Briny's face was ashen. 'You don't mean to say, sir, that I've got to go over there?' he whispered plaintively.

'That's just what I do mean,' answered Biggles firmly.

'I daren't do it, sir, s'welp me, I daren't.'

'Be a man, Briny. Think what a tale you'll have to tell when you get home. Think of how you'll be able to start your stories: "I remember the day I jumped off the top of Bergen Ait—"'

Briny's eyes opened wide. 'Why, yes, that's right, sir,' he gulped.

'And I'll tell you something else,' declared Biggles. 'When we get back I'll let you tell a yarn right through without interrupting you.'

'Don't forget to pull the ring!' he screamed as Briny
tottered into space

'You will, sir?'

'Honest. Only buck up about it. If you hang about much longer you'll find yourself landing down the funnel of that perishing cruiser.'

Briny advanced to the edge of the cliff. He looked down and shuddered. 'It's no use, sir,' he moaned. 'I daren't—'

'Over you go or I'll throw you over,' snarled Biggles, pretending to fly into a fury. 'Don't forget to pull the ring!' he screamed as Briny tottered into space.

Ginger put his hands over his eyes. He couldn't bear to watch. He held his breath, waiting for the splash.

'Phew! He's all right,' said Biggles, drawing a deep breath. 'The brolley's open, so he can't take any harm now. Algy will attend to him. Your turn next, Roy. Don't forget to slip your release gear as soon as you touch the water.'

'Very good, sir.' Roy stepped forward, and waited until Algy had dragged the dripping Briny into the flying-boat. Then he jumped clear.

His father gasped his relief as the parachute mushroomed out.

'You go next, Flight-Sergeant,' ordered Biggles.

The N.C.O. jumped without a word.

'You'd better wait a minute before you go, to give Algy time to pick them up,' Biggles told Ginger.

Ginger grimaced. He had made many jumps, but never one like this. However, he clutched the rip-ring with his right hand and launched himself into the void, head first, in the professional manner.

A shell screamed over the island; it burst in the air, spraying the rock with shrapnel.

Biggles ignored it. He jumped out as far as he could, and slipped the quick-release gear the instant his legs dragged in the water. Slipping off the harness, he swam to the door of the flying-boat just as Algy was dragging Ginger in.

'Get a move on,' he told Algy. 'That cruiser's coming up fast. Keep low for a bit when you take off, then she won't be able to see us on account of the island being in the way.' He pulled himself on board and sank into the spare pilot's seat, wiping the water from his face. 'Lucky thing those chaps carried brollies,' he told Algy seriously.

'Lucky thing I remembered seeing them, too,' snorted Algy. 'You might give me credit for something once in a while.'

'Good work, old lad,' agreed Biggles, 'but we'll talk about that when we get home. Just see about getting us there.' He turned to Briny, and noticed that there was something different about him, although he could not make out what it was. His expression was disconsolate. 'What are you looking so miserable about?' he inquired.

'I've lorst me 'at at last,' answered Briny in a broken voice. 'It fell orf as I was comin' down. You don't know what that 'at's been through, sir. I remember once—'

He stopped as if from force of habit.

Biggles nodded encouragement. 'Go on,' he prompted. 'What did you and your old shipmate Charlie do?'

'Well, would you believe that,' muttered Briny, scratching his head in confusion.

'Believe what?'

'I've forgotten what I was going to say.'

His confession was greeted with a yell of laughter.

'Tough luck, Briny,' said Biggles sympathetically. Then he

turned back to Algy. 'You'll have to watch your step when we get over the North Sea,' he warned him. 'Don't forget that we're carrying swastikas and black crosses, and there must be a whole crowd of our fellows fairly pining to get their sights on one.'

"That's all right,' replied Algy. 'When I left the submarine Sparks was tapping out a signal warning all ships and aircraft not to shoot at a four-engined Dornier flying-boat flying at a thousand feet. If Roy will get to the wireless cabin and get into touch with the Air Ministry, no doubt they'll tell us where to land.'

'That was well thought out,' declared Biggles. 'Good enough! Let's get home.'

The four engines of the flying-boat burst into song, and she streaked away from the secret base that was a secret no longer.

CHAPTER XX

Home

Forty-eight hours later, after landing at an R.A.F. Marine Base on the East Coast, Biggles, Algy, and Ginger reported to Colonel Raymond at the Air Ministry. They found him waiting for them.

Biggles, who was in rather low spirits at what he regarded as his failure to keep the secret base going, was more than a little surprised at the reception they received. It was certainly not what he had expected. Instead of criticism he found only satisfaction amounting to jubilation.

Colonel Raymond waved aside Biggles's apologies for losing the base and his machines. 'My dear fellow, that code-book was worth a hundred machines to us, apart from which you certainly made things hum for a little while. The work you have done more than repays us for what we spent on the base – in fact, you managed to do a lot more than we expected.' He smiled. 'Did any of you get any sleep at all?'

'Not much,' admitted Biggles. 'But I don't see that we did an awful lot—'

'Rubbish. What did you expect to do – destroy the entire German Navy and Air Force? If any one unit achieves greater success than yours I shall be very much surprised. Directly or indirectly, you were responsible for the destruction of an ammunition dump and a marine store depot; you interrupted lines of communication which has held up the movement of German forces from Poland to the Western Front; you have sunk a submarine, a drifter, and a liner that was to have been used for troop transport in the Baltic. Two destroyers have been sunk, and you have captured one of the enemy's latest marine aircraft. On top of that you get hold of the latest naval code – all without a single casualty and for the loss of only four aeroplanes which can easily be replaced. You certainly didn't waste any time.'

'But we've lost the secret base.'

Colonel Raymond smiled knowingly. 'A secret base – yes; but not the only one we possess. We've been busy in the Baltic for some time past. Bergen Ait isn't the only island that threatens Germany. But that's for your private ear – perhaps I shouldn't have told you. We sent you to Bergen Ait – I'll be quite frank with you – because it was nearest to the German coast, and consequently the most dangerous – for the enemy as well as you. D'you know how long the Higher Command estimated the base would last after you took it over, before it was located by the enemy?'

'Six months?'

'Twenty-four hours at most.'

'You didn't tell me that,' murmured Biggles reproachfully.

'Naturally – we didn't want to discourage you,' Colonel Raymond informed him coolly. 'But work it out yourself. You were in enemy waters, with hostile craft all round you, both on the sea and in the air.... No, Bigglesworth, it couldn't last more than a few days at the very outside. When you went out of this door I never expected to see you again.'

'We're difficult people to kill,' murmured Biggles, winking at Ginger.

'Evidently. Well, that's all. Believe me, we're grateful for what you've done, and no doubt your work will be mentioned in dispatches when it becomes safe to do so. At the moment we prefer to keep quiet about it. Now take yourselves off and let me have a full report in writing on what happened at Bergen Ait; after that you can take a few days' leave – but don't go too far away.'

'Why not?'

'Because – well, you see, we may need you again.'

Biggles nodded. 'I had an idea you might,' he said slowly as he walked towards the door. 'Good-bye, sir.'

The Colonel smiled. 'Perhaps it would be better to say *au revoir*,' he suggested softly.

BIGGLES SEES IT THROUGH

CHAPTER I

An Eventful Reconnaissance

From twenty thousand feet Squadron-Leader James Bigglesworth, D.S.O., better known to his friends as 'Biggles', looked down upon a world that revealed no more signs of occupation than the moon. From time to time his eyes, whimsical and faintly humorous, switched to the atmosphere around him, and then settled for a moment on the bewildering array of dials that smothered his instrument board. His eyes ran over them swiftly, for years of experience enabled him to read them as easily as a schoolmaster reads a book. Once in a while he glanced at his companion sitting in the second pilot's seat, Flight-Lieutenant the Hon. Algernon Lacey, D.F.C., and, still more rarely, behind him at the slim, watchful figure of Flying-Officer 'Ginger' Hebblethwaite, manning the centre gun-turret of the Bristol Blenheim. The fourth occupant of the aircraft, Flight-Sergeant Smyth, master mechanic, he could not see, for he was squatting humped up over a gun in the tail.

For nearly four hours these positions had been maintained with practically no variation, each airman concentrating on his particular task to the exclusion of all else, knowing full well the penalty of relaxation in the most deadly form of warfare devised by human ingenuity – war flying, wherein mercy is never expected and rarely encountered. During the whole of the four hours nothing had happened; the engines roared, the propellers slashed their way through air that was frozen into immobility, the instrument needles quivered. Far to the north the rim of the sun, a slip of glowing crimson, just showed above a jagged horizon that was the Arctic Circle, and shed an eerie twilight on a world of ice-bound desolation.

So this, thought Ginger, surveying the frozen panorama from his glass-protected turret, was Finland. He had been eager enough to go with the others when the Air Ministry had allowed Biggles to accompany a party of volunteers to help the Finns in their struggle against Soviet aggression, but now that he was there he saw no reason to congratulate himself. They had been in Finland only a week, but as far as he was concerned it was enough. Practically forbidden to fly over Russian territory, their work had been confined to long-distance reconnaissance raids along the frontiers, and since they encountered little opposition, and there was nothing to see on the ground except snow, it was becoming monotonous. Presently they would return to their base at Oskar, where they would have to spend an hour swathing the machine in rugs to prevent the oil from freezing. Tomorrow there would be another uneventful reconnaissance. Yes, it was becoming monotonous. He yawned.

At the same moment Biggles's voice came from the internal communication transmitter at his elbow.

'Enemy aircraft on the starboard quarter. Stand by to attack.'

Simultaneously with the words the Blenheim banked and dived steeply for speed.

Faintly above the roar of the racing engines came Biggles's voice, singing: 'Roll out the barrel....'

As he swung his turret to face the field of attack, Ginger's lips pursed up to echo the catchy tune. He saw the enemy aircraft at once, a Polycarpov bomber, one of the type being used by the Russians for the bombing of Finnish towns. It was also diving – for home, proving that the pilot had seen them.

Biggles's lips parted in a smile, for he knew that he had the 'legs' of the Russian.

Steeper and steeper became the Russian's dive as he sought escape in sheer speed, but steeper, too, became the dive of the Blenheim.

Ginger aligned his gun, bracing himself against the terrific drag of centrifugal force, and waited. The Russian seemed to swim towards them, sideways. But still he waited. The distance between the two machines closed; the Russian was no longer misty grey, but clear and dark. Jabs of orange flame showed where the Russian gunners were already firing.

Straight under the enemy machine Biggles dived, and then rocketed upwards, and the Blenheim vibrated slightly as its guns began to stutter.

The front gun having fired its burst, the Blenheim turned slowly, giving Ginger and Smyth in the rear seat their chance. Both took it: their guns roared as one.

The dive of the Soviet bomber steepened for a moment, then its nose jerked upwards. Ginger gave it another burst – he was very close now. Smyth's gun took up the staccato chatter, and a stream of bullets played a vicious tattoo on the Russian's cockpit. It dropped a wing and fell sideways into a spin. The fight was over.

Biggles brought the Blenheim to an even keel and watched

the Russian go down, ready to renew the attack should the spin turn out to be only a trick; but it was no sham. Black, oily smoke began to pour from its side; the cantilever wing broke across the middle, and the fuselage plunged earthward like a huge torpedo. It seemed to go on falling for a long time, long after it looked as if it must have reached the ground. But the end came at last. Clouds of snow mingled with the black smoke as it struck the frozen earth and spread itself in a thousand splinters over an acre of ground.

Biggles glanced at Algy, and for a moment their eyes met. Both faces were expressionless, for they had seen the same thing happen too many times to be upset by the dreadful spectacle. It was an unpleasant but inevitable part of air fighting.

Humming quietly, Biggles turned away and began to climb for height, but his eyes were on the ground, making a hasty reconnaissance while they were so close to it. Suddenly his tune broke off short and his body stiffened, his eyes focused on a speck that moved slowly across a flat sheet of ice which he knew to be the frozen surface of one of the hundreds of lakes that form a major part of the Finnish landscape. On one side of it a ridge of black rock projected through the snow like a crocodile's back; near it was a small dark object that seemed to stagger, fall, and then stagger on again, only to fall once more.

Biggles spoke tersely. 'What d'you make of it?'

'It's a man,' returned Algy briefly, his eyes on the object.

'That's what I thought.'

The Blenheim's engines faded into a moan that was like the death-cry of a dying giant, and the machine sank earthward. The wind sighed over wings and fuselage.

At a height of a hundred feet Biggles circled the man on the ground, now lying where he had last fallen.

'He's all in, whoever he is,' remarked Algy.

Biggles made a swift survey of the lake's icy surface.

Algy guessed what was in his mind. 'Are you thinking of going down?'

'I don't like it, but I think we must. We can't leave the poor blighter to die.'

'It seems silly to risk four lives to save one – particularly when ten thousand men are dying every day along the Mannerheim Line.'

'I agree, but this isn't quite the same thing. If I don't try to save him, the thought of that poor wretch lying out here in the snow will spoil my sleep tonight. It'll spoil yours, too, so don't kid yourself.'

'All right – go ahead.'

'Stand by to land,' called Biggles into the microphone to warn the gunners of his intention.

He brought the machine down very carefully, his hand on the throttle ready to zoom again the moment an obstacle showed itself. But there was none; the surface of the frozen lake was like powdered glass, and the Blenheim ran to a smooth standstill some thirty yards from where the motionless form was lying.

Biggles studied the sky carefully in all directions before he would allow anyone to get out; then he slipped his emergency brandy flask into his pocket, climbed down, and with Algy and Ginger following, walked quickly towards the body. Over everything hung the silence of death. Nothing moved.

Biggles was first to reach the unknown man, who, it was now seen, was old and grey. He dropped on his knees, and lifting up the limp head, stared down into a face that was pinched with cold and thin from suffering. The eyes were open. Unscrewing the top of his spirit flask with his teeth, he coaxed a little of the brandy between the blue lips. The man coughed instantly as the fiery liquid stung his throat; its effect was instantaneous and he struggled into a sitting position, muttering something in a language that none of them understood.

Biggles had picked up a few words of Finnish since he had been in the country, and he tried them, but they appeared to convey nothing. He tried French, but the man only shook his head. Finally, in desperation, he tried English. 'Who are you?' he said.

To his amazement the man answered in the same language.

'Are you – English?' he said.

Biggles replied, 'Yes, we're English. Who are you, and what are you doing here? But perhaps you'd better not try to talk yet; we'll carry you to our 'plane and get you somewhere safe.'

The old man shook his head. 'No,' he breathed with difficulty. 'It's – too late.'

'Too late? Surely not.'

'You don't understand. I am wounded – by – a bullet. What I have to say I must say now, or it will be – too late – and it is – important.'

'We'll get you into the machine, anyway,' declared Biggles.

'No – I implore you. When I die you must leave me here.'

Biggles stared.

'If you take me somewhere – I may be – recognized – by a spy, and then it would be known – that I had – escaped. It would be better if it were thought that I had died – without speaking.'

Biggles looked nonplussed, but he nodded. 'Very well,' he said. 'I gather there is something you want to tell me. Here, have some more brandy; it may help you.'

The old man drank the spirit gratefully, and it brought a

faint flush into his sunken cheeks. 'Yes; listen carefully,' he said. 'I am a Pole. I was a scientist working for the government in Warsaw. When the Germans marched into Poland I was on the point of concluding important experiments with metal alloys for aircraft – experiments that might well revolutionize the whole business of metal aircraft construction. Rather than destroy the fruits of seven years of labour, I put all my papers in a portfolio, and sought to escape so that I could give them to the Allies. But then it was hard to get out of my unhappy Poland. To make matters more difficult, the Germans knew all about me and my work, and when they found that I had gone they pursued me; they hunted for me everywhere. All frontiers were closed. There was only one way I could get out – by air. Our pilots were flying to neutral countries to save their machines. I found one willing to help me, and we fled to Russia, only to find that the Russians, too, had marched against us. We had only a little petrol left, so we tried to get to Finland. But the German Secret Service learned of my escape by aeroplane and traced it to Russia; they knew the number of the machine, and we had no means of painting it over. German pursuit 'planes flew over Russia to catch us, and they were close enough to shoot at us when we flew into a blizzard near Lake Ladoga. I had been hit by a bullet, and, although I did not know it, so had my pilot; but he flew on until the petrol gave out. Where we came down I don't know, for we had been lost in the blizzard, but we crashed into the side of a frozen lake, which must be one of the smaller lakes near Lake Ladoga.'

'In Finland or in Russia?' put in Biggles quickly.

'I'm not sure – Finland, I hope. But let me finish. My brave pilot died there. I knew that the German and Russian 'planes would still be looking for us, so rather than risk the papers falling into their hands, I hid the portfolio under some rocks near the wrecked 'plane. Then I started walking westward, hoping to meet some friendly Finns. But I saw no one. I had no food. It began to snow. I have been walking for three days, I think – I don't know how long. Give me – brandy.'

Biggles saw that the old man was near the end, for the shadow of death had already settled on his pale face. There was nothing more he could do except try to prolong the old man's life for a little while with the brandy.

'What is your name, sir? We ought to know,' he asked.

'Petolski. England knows of me. You must get the papers, but you must be quick or the Russians or the Germans will find them.'

'Can you give me any clearer directions for finding them?'

'They are about fifty paces east of the broken 'plane, under a large rock.'

'And how far is the lake from here?'

'Twenty – thirty – perhaps forty miles. I don't know. I may have – wandered. Tell – tell—' The old man's head had begun to droop. A shadow had crossed his eyes, which were staring unseeingly into the sky.

Biggles moved the flask nearer to the lips, but stopped suddenly as the body went limp in his arms. 'He's gone – poor old fellow,' he said quietly, and allowed the body to sink slowly to the snow-covered ice.

'What are we going to do with him?' inquired Algy. 'I know he said we were to abandon him, but I hate the idea of just leaving the poor old chap lying here—' He broke off short as a yell came from Smyth.

The three airmen sprang to their feet. Simultaneously they heard the roar of an aero engine suddenly switched on. One glance was enough. Flying low, racing towards the spot, was an aeroplane, a German Messerschmitt.

'Quick!' snapped Biggles. 'Get aboard!' He dashed to the Blenheim.

Had the Messerschmitt pilot been a little less impetuous, or had he been a better shot, the affair might well have ended there and then, for he got in his first burst while the Blenheim was still on the ground. True, Biggles, realizing his danger, jerked the throttle wide open, and the instant the machine began to move he jammed on one wheel brake, producing a skid so violent that Smyth, sitting in the tail, was nearly sick. Before the Messerschmitt could turn and fire again Biggles had his machine in the air, following the German and keeping underneath him, thus rendering his deadly front guns ineffective, although from this position Ginger had a clear view of the sleek fuselage. It may be that some of his shots took effect, for the Messerschmitt swerved away. Biggles seized the opportunity to bank steeply in the opposite direction, so that in a few seconds the two machines were a mile apart. He knew his business too well to fool about with a machine of higher manoeuvrability so far from home.

Keeping the stick forward, he tore westward with his wheels only a few feet from the ground, a position calculated to hamper the German pilot should he resume the attack, in that his speed would be chopped for fear of overshooting his mark and hitting the ground. The Messerschmitt did, in fact, chase the Blenheim for a little while, but it did not press the pursuit home, and when the German pilot suddenly turned back on his course Biggles guessed the reason: he had spotted the lonely figure on the ground.

'They heard the roar of an aero engine suddenly
switched on'

Biggles actually turned the Blenheim, hoping to catch the Messerschmitt at rest on the lake as he himself had nearly been caught, but his ever watchful eyes picked out several other specks in the sky coming from the Russian frontier and he decided to let well alone. He pulled his nose round again to the west and headed for Oskar, which he reached some time later without further incident.

Leaving the others to attend to the machine, he borrowed a car and went straight down to Helsinki, no great distance away, where he reported to the British Consulate, feeling that the information he now possessed was too valuable to be lost.

It was nearly dark when he got back to Oskar, where he found the others congregated round the stove in the general mess, for the aerodrome was used by several units of the Finnish Air Force beside the International Squadron. However, he took them on one side and gave them the result of his mission.

'The Consul rang up London,' he said quietly. 'Ten minutes later Intelligence came through and I spoke to Colonel Raymond. It seems that our people know all about Petolski and his researches, so I wasn't surprised when Raymond asked me to try to get hold of the portfolio. He seemed mighty anxious about it, too. We've got to spare no effort to get those papers. If we can't get them ourselves we must at all costs prevent Germany getting hold of them.'

'How?' inquired Algy naïvely.

'How the deuce do I know!' returned Biggles. 'If we get them ourselves the Boche *can't* get 'em.'

'The Boche know about these papers?'

'Yes, Petolski told us so himself.'

'Then we look like having a lovely time playing hide and seek in the snow with a bunch of Huns.'

'I shouldn't be surprised at that,' admitted Biggles. 'Pity that confounded Messerschmitt came along. We can reckon that they found Petolski's body.'

'Which means that since they knew he escaped by air, they'll be looking for his crashed 'plane, hoping the papers will still be in it.'

Biggles nodded. 'We've got to get to it first.'

'When do we start?'

'At dawn. It's no use sitting here thinking about it; that won't get us anywhere. We may not come back.'

'You're telling me!' sneered Algy.

'What I meant was, not immediately. We'll take enough grub to last for two or three days, and some spare cans of petrol. I'll make a list of other things that might come in handy – things like skates.'

Algy started. 'Skates! Say, what *is* this – winter-sports?'

Biggles smiled. 'You've said it, laddie. Incidentally, it wouldn't be a bad idea if we took some white sheets to wrap ourselves in, for camouflage, as the Finns do.'

'Ha! Corpses on skates,' gibed Algy. 'I don't know what war's coming to.'

'You'll find out,' Biggles grinned.

'Why not paint the tops of our 'planes white, so that if any Huns come along they won't be so likely to spot us?' suggested Ginger.

'That's an idea,' agreed Biggles. 'I'll get the fellows on to it right away.'

'How about some snow-shoes, some skis, and a sledge or two?' suggested Algy sarcastically.

'Don't be a fool. This is no laughing matter – as you may discover if we run out of petrol and have to start walking.'

'I always did hate walking – you don't seem to get any place,' muttered Algy disgustedly.

'I'm not so keen on hiking myself,' admitted Biggles.

'You get your feet wet.'

'Absolutely. Ah, well, it may not come to that. Let's turn in; we may as well start fresh,' advised Biggles.

CHAPTER II

Ginger Makes a Discovery

The stars were paling in the sky the following morning when the Blenheim took off from the bleak aerodrome on its dangerous quest. Algy still persisted in adopting a facetious attitude about the whole thing, but he knew well enough the hazardous nature of the enterprise. Biggles had, of course, taken the Station Commander into his confidence to account for their temporary absence, for the supposed site of the crashed Polish machine was nearly three hundred miles from their base at Oskar, and since snow had fallen recently he suspected that it was going to be hard to spot the wreck from the air. But what concerned him most was the probability of running into hostile aircraft on the same mission as themselves, for while he had no fear that they would not be able to hold their own if it came to combat, too frequent encounters would not only diminish their petrol supply, but would seriously interfere with their search.

He flew in a straight line towards a point some distance north of Lake Ladoga, his objective being the area due east of where they had found the dying professor. This was actually about twenty miles inside the Finnish border, but the old man had been so hazy as to his whereabouts that it seemed just as likely that the crash would be in Russia as in Finland.

Reaching the spot, he started to circle, exploring with his eyes the many lakes over which the Blenheim passed; but it was obvious from the start that the search was not going to be easy. Owing to the snow it was difficult to see what was frozen water and what was snow-covered land. In the case of large lakes, the flat surface was, of course, a pretty good guide, but even so it was not easy to see where the water ended and the land began. Many times Biggles brought the machine nearly to the ground in order to make a closer examination of rocks that occasionally formed the shores of the lakes.

'I don't think it's any good going on like this,' he told Algy at last. 'We might go on doing this sort of thing for weeks without spotting the crash. Apart from the spare juice in the cans we're carrying, we've only just enough left to get home. We're over Russia now, anyway.'

'What are you going to do about it?'

'Land. We shall have to start working these lakes systematically – at any rate, the big ones. We'll land as near the bank as we dare and then explore on foot. If we draw blank we'll hop on to the next lake.'

Algy shook his head sadly. 'Seems a crazy business to me.'

'Can you think of anything better?'

'No.'

'Then don't be so infernally pessimistic. There is this about going down: the machine won't be so likely to be seen if we run into a bunch of Russians or Boche. Look at that.' The sun had just broken through the mist, and he pointed at the shadow of the Blenheim, huge and distorted, as black as pitch against the white background of snow, as it raced along below them. 'That shadow can be seen for miles,' he added.

Algy touched him on the arm. 'Take a look,' he said, pointing ahead.

Peering through the windscreen, Biggles saw five black specks against the sky high overhead; they were in arrow formation, and were obviously Messerschmitts. Instantly he cut the throttle and glided down, and the shadow on the ground seemed to come to meet the machine. As the wheels touched the surface of the frozen lake, machine and shadow came together and ran on to a stop.

'We'll sit here for a bit and hope they don't spot us,' said Biggles. 'I can't look for a crash and fight five Messers at the same time. I'm not a perishing magician.' He switched off and the propellers hissed viciously to a standstill. In the silence that followed the drone of the machines overhead sounded like the buzzing of angry hornets.

They watched them for some time without speaking. Then, 'They're going over,' said Algy. 'What do we do next?'

'I think we'll taxi over to those rocks,' returned Biggles, nodding towards a mass of black basalt that erupted out of the snow on the edge of the lake. 'Then we'll have a look at the map and start checking off the lakes one by one.'

'Okay,' agreed Algy.

Biggles took the machine to the spot he had indicated and then called the other two members of the crew forward. 'Well, here we are,' he said. 'We shall have to do a bit of exploring on foot. Smyth, you'll stay with the machine – keep your eyes skinned. Algy, you and Ginger go one way; I'll go the other; we'll meet at the far side, and if we don't find anything we'll come straight back and hop on to the next lake. Put a white sheet over your shoulders in case those Messers come back.'

They found nothing on the edge of that lake; nor did they find anything at the next, or the next, or the one after that. By mid-afternoon they were weary, and all they had done was to put a number of strokes on the map, indicating the lakes that had been searched.

'If we're going back we'd better start,' opined Algy.

'We're not going back,' returned Biggles, glancing at the sky. 'The weather looks settled so we may as well stay where we are.'

'And sleep in the machine?'

'Unless you prefer the snow,' smiled Biggles.

'To the deuce with that. I'm no Eskimo.'

'I suggest that we have a bite to eat, a few hours' rest, and then go on with the job,' put in Ginger. 'The sky is clear so it won't get dark.'

'That's true,' agreed Biggles. So far north, at that season of the year, it would not get really dark, as it would do farther south.

They made a satisfying but not particularly appetizing meal from the stores they had brought with them, after which they lay down in the roomy fuselage to rest.

Ginger, however, could not sleep. Try as he would he could not get comfortable, with the result that he was soon in that unhappy state when he knew that, so far from sleeping, he was getting wider awake. The cold was intense, too, and the silence trying to the nerves. He knew that there was only one thing to do to break the spell, and that was to get up and have a walk round. Very quietly, therefore, he opened the door and stepped down into a twilit world so utterly devoid of life that he shivered. Buffing his arms, he walked up and down for a little while regarding the lonely landscape, wondering, naturally, about the quest on which they were engaged and if they would be successful.

Near at hand, where the ice-surfaced lake met the land, the ground rose steeply to a ridge. He did not know what lay beyond it, and the thought occurred to him to find out. Possibly there was another lake, in which case there was just a chance that it might turn out to be the one they were looking for; and it was really in the hope of finding a speedy solution to their problem that he made his way to the top of the ridge.

Before him stretched a panorama so awe-inspiring in its utter desolation that for a minute or two he stared at it aghast. Seen thus it looked much worse than it had done from the air. Snow covered everything, even the drooping firs that here and there clung to the stark hillsides.

He was about to turn away when a movement caught his eye, and looking round again quickly he saw that it was a flicker of light. At first he supposed it to be the aurora borealis, but soon dismissed this thought, for he perceived that it was much too low down, and of a warm yellow tint. It appeared to come from behind the next ridge, about a mile away, and as he stood staring he thought he heard a faint sound. Seized by curiosity, he at once determined to investigate. He glanced at the machine, but apparently the others were still sleeping, so without further delay he set off across the snow in the direction of the light.

Before he reached the ridge he had a pretty shrewd idea of what he would see on the other side, for the flicker of yellow light was now much brighter, and it could only mean one thing. Beyond the ridge a fire was burning, and a fire indicated the presence of human beings. Even so he was hardly prepared for the sight that met his startled gaze when, on hands and knees, he topped the rise and looked over.

He found himself staring down into a wide, flat depression, which he knew from experience, was another of the numerous lakes with which the district abounded. On the near side of it was a camp of six tents, arranged in a circle round a brightly burning fire, near which also a number of men were congregated. They were only about a hundred yards from where he lay. Faint snatches of conversation reached his ears, and although he could not speak Russian, he recognized the sounds of that language. Ginger noted a line of sledges, six in all, close by the tents. Six tents suggested that there were not less than thirty or forty men in the party, and it shocked him to think that they had been so close to danger without being aware of it. Clearly, Biggles would have to know about this at once.

He was about to turn away when a sound reached his ears that for a moment threw his brain into a whirl. It was the soft hum of wind over the fabric of a gliding aeroplane. The Russians evidently heard it too, for there was a sharp cry and more fuel was thrown on the fire, causing the flames to leap high; all of which suggested at once that the men were desirous of attracting the attention of the 'plane. In fact, it implied that the 'plane was expected.

Ginger lay still, resolved now to learn as much as he could before returning to the others. He had not long to wait. The 'plane passed low overhead and made a smooth landing on the lake, finishing its run not far from the camp. Men ran from the fire and dragged the machine still nearer. Two men got out and walked into the camp, where another man, evidently the leader of the ground party, was standing a little apart from the others.

The first words spoken by the newcomers struck Ginger like an electric shock, for they were in German, in which language the leader of the ground party replied. Stiff with amazement and dismay, Ginger heard one of the newcomers speak again, and at the sound of the voice the muscles in his throat seemed to restrict. The voice was unmistakable. It could belong to only one man. He had heard it too often to have any doubt about it. It was the one man whom they had most cause to fear – their old enemy, Hauptmann Erich von Stalhein, head of the Special Branch of the German Secret Service.

What on earth could have brought von Stalhein to a place like this was the thought that flashed into Ginger's head. The answer to the question was almost automatic. Obviously he had come to recover the missing portfolio.

For a few minutes longer Ginger watched; then the leaders went into the tent, and as soon as he realized that he was unlikely to gather any further information, he slid back off the rise and raced to the machine.

The others were still asleep, but he awakened them with scant ceremony.

'Biggles!' he cried tersely, shaking Biggles's shoulder. 'Hi! Wake up. Things are happening – get a move on.'

The others scrambled hastily to their feet, for there was a vibrant ring in Ginger's voice that bespoke real urgency.

'What is it?' asked Biggles sharply.

'There's a party of Russians on the other side of the hill. What's more, von Stalhein is with them.'

'*What?*'

'It's a fact.' Ginger described swiftly and briefly what he had seen.

For a moment even Biggles was speechless in the face of this astounding – not to say alarming – piece of information. 'My sainted aunt!' he muttered, 'this is developing into a more desperate business than I bargained for. How far away are they?'

'Only about a mile. If they happen to march this way they'd be right on us before we could do a thing.'

'All right – all right. Don't get excited. We shall have to do something about this. Let me think.'

For a few minutes there was silence while Biggles stared intently at the floor, deep in thought. At last he looked up. 'Von Stalhein is on the same job as we are, that's certain,' he said. 'If we take off he'll hear us. Further, he'd hear us every time we tried to get down anywhere near here. In short, once we're in the air we're stumped.'

'If we stay here and they happen to find us, we shall be knocked for six,' put in Algy grimly.

'You needn't tell me that,' returned Biggles crisply. 'As I see it, our only chance is to get this party on the run before they know we're about. If we could do that it ought to give us a little while to carry on the search unmolested.'

'Yes, but how are you going to do that?'

'There's only one way. We've got to attack them.'

'Attack them!' cried Algy. 'Four against forty? You're crazy.'

'Not so crazy as you might think. We've got two machine-guns and a couple of rifles. The enemy won't know that there are only four of us. Suppose you were in that camp, unaware of a hostile force in the district; then, suddenly, from close range, a brisk fire was opened up on you by machine-guns and rifles. What would you do?'

'Run,' answered Algy promptly.

'Exactly. Those Ruskys will run, too. They'll suppose that they're being attacked by one of those flying columns of Finns that have been doing so much damage lately. In their anxiety to get away they'll abandon their stores. We'll destroy them, which means that since they can't stay here without food or shelter they'll have to return to where they can get fresh supplies. While they're doing that we shall take the opportunity of finding the papers.'

'It sounds easy,' agreed Algy dubiously.

'Isn't it a bit thick to open fire on a sleeping camp?' put in Ginger.

Biggles laughed sarcastically. 'What d'you think this is – a Sunday-school party? Forget it. This is war, and a surprise attack is what every general dreams about. D'you suppose that if they'd tumbled on us they'd have invited us to pick up our guns and fire the first volley? Not on your life. After the trouble we've caused him in the past, if von Stalhein got hold of us he'd shoot us with no more qualms than if we were rabbits – you know that as well as I do. This is a chance we may not get again, and I'm in favour of taking advantage of it. One thing is certain – we've got to drive them out before they drive us out; otherwise we might as well pack up and go home.'

'I think we ought to give them a chance,' protested Ginger. 'After all, as long as we can get rid of them, that's really all we're concerned with.'

Biggles thought for a moment. 'Maybe you're right,' he said slowly. 'If we wounded any of them, we should find ourselves cluttered up with prisoners – unless we just left them to die, which isn't a nice thought. I'll tell you what. We'll try shooting high first.

If they bolt, so well and good, but if they return our fire we shall have to let 'em have it, and no argument. After all, it's our lives against theirs.'

'What about von Stalhein's 'plane ?' inquired Algy.

'We'll attend to that at the same time,' declared Biggles. 'A can of petrol should do the trick. Come on, let's get the guns out.'

In ten minutes they were ready, armed with the two mobile machine-guns they had brought with them, rifles and revolvers, in addition to which Biggles carried a two-gallon can of petrol with the cap already loosened.

From the spot where Ginger had lain they surveyed the enemy camp and saw that it was now sleeping; at least, only one man could be seen, a sentry, who, with a fine indifference to his task, was standing near the fire warming his hands. A yellow light showed through the canvas of the tent von Stalhein had entered.

Biggles gave his orders in a whisper. 'You stay here,' he told the others. 'I'm going to make a detour to get to the 'plane from the far side. As soon as you see the flames, let drive at the tops of the tents – and keep on firing. Yell at the same time. Try to make as much noise as a squadron of cavalry. I shall probably be about a quarter of an hour.' He glided away below the brow of the hill and was soon lost to sight.

Algy took one machine-gun and Smyth the other. They aligned them on the tents. Ginger had to be content with a rifle. After that there was nothing they could do except wait. The minutes passed slowly. Not a sound broke the silence.

'The fireworks are about due to begin I think,' murmured Algy at last.

Hardly had the words left his lips when a blue flicker of flame lit up the air over the machine; it grew swiftly in volume; then came a *whoosh*, and a great sheet of flame leapt skyward.

'Okay,' snapped Algy, 'let 'em rip.'

Instantly the still air was shattered with the demoniac rattle of machine-guns. After the silence the din was terrifying. Above the clatter rose the yells of the attackers. The blaze of the now burning aircraft, and the crackle of the bullets in its guns, added to the turmoil.

The effect on the camp was only what was to be expected in the circumstances. Utter confusion reigned. Blind panic followed, and in less than a minute the Russians were in flight, streaming across the snow with bullets whistling about their ears. Never was victory more swiftly or more easily achieved. Complete success had crowned the enterprise.

Biggles dashed up. 'Cease fire,' he ordered. 'They've gone and we'd better go steady with the ammunition.'

They waited for a little while to give the Russians a chance to get clear, and then went down to the camp.

'See what's on those sledges,' ordered Biggles. 'If there's nothing of any use to us pitch them on the fire. Do the same with the tents.' He himself went to the tent in which von Stalhein had been in consultation with the Russian leader. He came out stuffing some papers in his pocket, and then helped the others to drag the tent to the fire. In a few minutes all that remained of the enemy camp was a blazing pyre in the centre of an area of trampled snow. Most of the enemy had abandoned their rifles in their haste, and these, too, were flung into the blaze. The 'plane was a glowing heap of metal.

'I fancy that's cramped their style for a bit, anyway,' remarked Biggles with satisfaction as he surveyed the scene. 'We may as well get back to the machine.'

'What are you going to do next?' asked Algy as they approached the Blenheim.

'As it must be pretty nearly morning, we may as well go on with the search,' returned Biggles. 'I'll just have a look at these papers first.'

Reaching the machine, the others gathered round while Biggles examined the documents he had found in the enemy camp. All except one were in Russian, so as he could not read them he buried them in the snow. The exception was in German, and this he perused with interest, for there was good reason to suppose that it had been brought by von Stalhein.

Actually, it told them little they did not already know. It described the dead professor, referred to the papers containing the results of his experiments, and gave vague directions for finding them. It included a sketch-map showing the position where the professor's body had been found, proving that – as Biggles had surmised – the body had been located the day before by the Messerschmitt pilot. But there was, of course, no guide to the actual locality of the missing papers, for this was something the professor did not know himself, and Biggles derived a crumb of comfort from the fact that the enemy was in as big a quandary as he was regarding their whereabouts.

Having read the letter aloud, Biggles folded it and put it in his pocket. 'That doesn't help us much,' he remarked. 'The only thing we can do is to proceed as we did yesterday; but we'd better keep our eyes skinned for any stray Russians who may be about. Von Stalhein of course will come back. He's that sort of fellow.'

'By gosh! Won't he be in a tearing rage, too,' remarked Ginger.

'As he's three parts a rattlesnake at any time, I don't see that he can be much worse,' returned Biggles. 'We'd better keep clear of him if we can.'

'How far will those Russians have to go for fresh stores, d'you think?' queried Ginger.

'I don't know,' answered Biggles. 'I don't think it can be less than a couple of days' march. Come on, let's get busy while we've got the chance.'

CHAPTER III

Success – and Disaster

For the whole of that day they pursued their quest with energy and speed, knowing that it was only a question of time before von Stalhein would return with reinforcements – to say nothing of sending aircraft to locate them; and it was for this very reason that Biggles concentrated his efforts in an easterly direction – that is to say, over Russia, feeling that it was the most difficult as well as the most likely locality. They could, he reasoned, fall back inside the Finnish frontier and carry on the search there when they were seriously interfered with by von Stalhein.

It was about four o'clock, and they were circling in the Blenheim looking for a suitable place to pass the night, when Biggles's ever watchful eyes noticed an unusual scar that ran in a straight line across the untrodden snow, and coming lower, he soon saw that it was a track made by a body of men. The line it took gave him a clue to the identity of those who had made it, for the line came from the scene of the camp which they had attacked. Coming still lower – so low, indeed, that his wheels were only a few feet from the ground – he perceived that the track had been made by the Russians subsequent to the attack, and not on their outward journey, a fact that he deduced from the absence of sledge-marks. He pointed this out to Algy.

'We do at least know which way they've gone,' he remarked.

'How about following the track to see how far they've got?' suggested Algy.

'Good idea. It may give us a line on where they are making for, and consequently let us know roughly how long we may expect to be free from interference.'

Biggles was climbing steeply, following the track, when suddenly he gave a cry. He said nothing, but Algy was not long spotting what had called forth the exclamation. Some distance ahead the track started to traverse a long, narrow lake. But it did not proceed very far. It turned at right angles and made straight for the bank, where the snow was all trampled down as if a halt had been made.

An unpleasant sensation crept over Biggles as he circled low over the spot. Already in his heart he knew the reason for the sudden turn in the line of march, and why the halt had been made, but he hoped that he was wrong.

'What can you see down there?' he asked Algy in a curious voice.

Algy threw him a sidelong glance. 'It's no use kidding ourselves,' he said evenly. 'That's a crashed aeroplane under that pile of snow; you can see that from the shape of it.'

'Then it looks as if von Stalhein has tumbled on what we were looking for – by accident.'

'It looks that way, but there's still a chance that it isn't the Polish machine – or if it is, that von Stalhein didn't find the papers,' said Algy, trying to be optimistic.

Biggles said no more. He cut the throttle, landed on the ice, and taxied up the track made by the Russians to the wreck. Without a moment's hesitation, such was his anxiety, he jumped down, and closely followed by Algy, ran to the scene of the trampled snow. In the centre of it, still half buried, although a good deal of the snow had been dragged away, was the remains of a crashed aeroplane. Biggles tore more of the snow from one of the crumpled wings and exposed Polish military markings.

'That settles any argument about that,' he asserted harshly, and remembering the Professor's instructions for finding the papers, he ran straight to the spot. His heart was sick with anxiety, for footmarks were everywhere, and it was obvious that the search had been thorough. He knew only too well that von Stalhein was nothing if not efficient. Within a minute he knew the grim truth, for exactly where the professor had described it was a large rock. Around it the snow had been trampled. Under the rock was a cavity, but it was empty. The portfolio had gone. Presently they found it, half buried in the snow a little distance away. The flap was open. It was empty.

Biggles took out a cigarette and tapped it on the back of his hand. 'What d'you know about that?' he said bitterly. 'Von Stalhein never had a bigger stroke of luck in his life. He must have been going across the lake when he spotted the crash. The irritating part of it is, if we had left him to go on searching where he was when we attacked him, the chances are that he wouldn't have found it. That was ten miles from here. The poor old professor no doubt meant well, but actually he couldn't have chosen a worse hiding-place. It was so obvious. The rock was so conspicuous.'

Algy, too, lit a cigarette. 'All the same, I don't see where else he could have hidden it,' he said slowly. 'He couldn't very well just tuck it into the snow, where it would have been exposed as soon as the stuff melted. Well, it certainly is von Stalhein's lucky day. As far as we're concerned – well, it's a tough break. Von Stalhein wins the game after all.'

'What d'you mean – wins the game?' snapped Biggles. 'This is only the first round. He can't have got back to his base yet, and while he's walking about Russia with those papers on him he can't claim to have won – not while we're still on our feet, anyway.'

Ginger and Smyth had come up. They did not need telling what had happened. The picture told its own story.

'It looks as if this is where we go home,' observed Ginger.

'On the contrary, this is where we go after von Stalhein,' returned Biggles curtly.

Algy smiled wanly. 'Biggles old top, there are moments when I wonder seriously if you didn't crack your skull in one of your crashes.'

'Meaning what?'

'You're daft to think of tackling—'

'You said that last night,' cut in Biggles.

'I know, but it's one thing to attack a sleeping camp, and quite another for us to take on that bunch of stiffs in cold blood. There can't be less than forty of them.'

'You haven't forgotten that when they bolted quite a number of them left their rifles behind?'

'No, I haven't forgotten that either.'

Biggles's face was grim. 'I'm going to get those papers, or—'

'Or what?'

'Oh, stop arguing. Let's get going.'

They hastened back to the Blenheim and got aboard. Just what Biggles was going to do he didn't say. Possibly he wasn't sure himself.

His first action was to locate the Russians, and, since they were on foot, this did not take long. The party appeared as a small black column moving slowly across the waste of snow. As soon as he saw it Biggles turned away.

'They'll have heard us,' remarked Algy.

'Possibly, but we're too far off for them to recognize the machine,' answered Biggles. 'Bear in mind that ours isn't the only 'plane hereabouts. For all they know it may be one of their own.' As he spoke Biggles turned away from the track at right angles.

He flew on for about five minutes, during which time the Blenheim had covered ten miles. Then he turned sharp left, flew for another five or six minutes, and then left again, a manoeuvre which, if the Russians had held on their course, put him well in front of them. From a thousand feet he started to examine the ground carefully, and apparently he found what he was looking for, for he turned away and landed on a convenient lake, running the machine on until it was close against the sagging pines that came down on all sides to the edge of the ice.

'Get the guns out,' he ordered crisply, and the weapons that had been used for the attack on the camp were again produced.

'Start cutting some sticks – straight ones if possible,' was Biggles's next command.

'What's the idea?' inquired Algy, taking out his pocket-knife.

'You'll see,' returned Biggles briefly.

It took them about a quarter of an hour to find a dozen good sticks and strip them of their twigs. Biggles then gathered them under his arm, picked up a rifle, and telling the others to follow with the rest of the weapons, set off on a course that, as Algy soon realized, would intercept that of the Russians. A halt was called while Biggles climbed to the top of a hill to reconnoitre. He soon came running back.

'It's all right,' he said, 'they're coming. This way.'

A short walk brought them to a narrow depression between two banks, rather after the manner of a railway cutting. To enhance this effect, through it ran a number of lines in the snow, obviously the tracks of sledges.

'This must be the track the Russians made on their outward journey,' Biggles explained. 'I spotted it from the air, and unless my judgement is at fault, the Russians are now cutting across to strike it, obviously with the intention of returning along it. The party should therefore pass through this cutting – in fact, they're already within a mile of us. I'm going to ambush them here. Algy, you'll take one of the machine-guns and stay where you are. Ginger, you take a rifle and get behind those rocks on the other side. Smyth, you take the other machine-gun and find a place near Ginger. Don't let yourselves be seen. For the love of Mike keep your heads down until I give the signal.'

Biggles waited for the others to take up their allotted positions, and then, picking up the sticks, he worked them horizontally into the snow along each side of the cutting, pointing slightly downwards until they gave a fair representation of rifles covering the track. He then went down to judge the effect, and came back announcing that it was even better than he had hoped. He then took up his own position, one from which he could watch the approach of the Russians without being seen. 'No shooting unless I give the word,' he told the others. 'Show yourselves when I go down to have a word with von Stalhein.'

'Watch out he doesn't plug you,' warned Ginger anxiously.

'He'd be a fool to do that, with nearly twenty rifles covering him,' grinned Biggles. 'If I know von Stalhein, he's got more sense than to commit suicide.'

They hadn't long to wait. Ten minutes later the Russians came into view, marching in column of fours, about forty men in all. Von Stalhein, with the Russian leader, a man conspicuous by his height, and another officer in German uniform, presumably the pilot of von Stalhein's 'plane, stalked along just ahead of the main body.

Biggles smiled faintly as they strode unsuspecting into the trap, for it was a situation after his own heart. He waited until they were within a score of paces, and then stood up.

'Halt!' he called crisply in German. 'Von Stalhein, tell those men to drop their weapons. One shot, and I'll tell my men to mow you down where you stand. You're covered by machine-guns.'

Von Stalhein's hand flashed to his pocket, but he did not draw the weapon he obviously had in it. His blue eyes moved slowly round the half circle of supposed weapons that menaced him.

Algy got on his knees and dragged his machine-gun into view. Smyth did the same. Ginger, too, could be seen. There was no reason why von Stalhein should for one moment doubt the truth of Biggles's assertion. The Russians stood still, like a flock of sheep, staring at the ridge.

Biggles walked down the slope into the gully. Von Stalhein watched him, his eyes on Biggles's face. His own face was expressionless.

'We've met in some queer places, but I little thought that we should bump into each other in this out-of-the-world spot,' began Biggles pleasantly, as he strolled up to the German. 'But there,' he added, 'I suppose it's only natural that we should so often find ourselves on the same job. I shouldn't have troubled you, though, if you hadn't been lucky enough to strike by accident what we were both looking for.'

'Major Bigglesworth,' said von Stalhein coldly, 'there are times when I seriously wonder if you were created by the devil just to annoy me. I confess that nobody was farther from my thoughts at this moment.'

'And nobody was farther from my thoughts than you, until you dropped into the game a few hours ago,' replied Biggles. 'It was like old times to hear your voice again.'

'Then it was you who attacked our camp last night?'

'Yes; but I don't think attacked is the right word.'

'What do you mean?'

'Well, we took care not to hurt you. You don't suppose that it was by accident that all our shots went over your heads, do you? I know that isn't your way of doing things, but as I told you once before, I should be genuinely sorry if anything happened to you – you're always the life and soul of the party. But we're wasting time. You must be anxious to get back, and so am I. D'you mind handing over the papers?'

'What papers?'

Biggles looked pained. 'Really, von Stalhein, it isn't like you to start that childish sort of talk. Don't make me resort to violence – you know how I hate it. It's my turn to call the tune. Pass them over and look pleasant.'

Von Stalhein's eyes never left Biggles's face. He allowed a frosty smile to part his lips. 'Yes,' he agreed bitingly, 'it's your turn to call the tune, but the game isn't over yet.' He put his hand in his breast pocket and produced a bulky envelope with the flap loose.

Biggles took the papers and glanced through them to make

sure that they were what he was looking for. Satisfied that they were, he put them in his own pocket. 'Thanks,' he said; 'I won't detain you any longer. Go right ahead.' Biggles looked up at the ridge. 'All right,' he called, 'let them pass, but at the first sign of treachery open fire.' He stood aside.

Von Stalhein bowed, smiling sardonically. 'We shall meet again before very long I think,' he predicted.

'The pleasure will be yours,' smiled Biggles. '*Auf Wiedersehen.*'

Von Stalhein said something Biggles did not understand, presumably in Russian, to the leader of the party, who, while this conversation had been going on, had not said a word. His face expressed a mixture of consternation and amazement. However, he gave an order and the party moved forward. Von Stalhein did not glance back. They went on through the gully, and soon the party was again a black column tramping across the snow.

Biggles beckoned to the others and they hastened to join him.

'Nice work, laddie,' grinned Algy.

'Not so bad,' smiled Biggles. 'Let's get back to the machine. The sooner we're out of this the better I shall be pleased. There's a look in von Stalhein's eye that I don't like.'

'But what could he do now?'

'I don't know, but I've a feeling that he's got something up his sleeve.'

'D'you suppose that he's sent somebody on ahead for reinforcements – I mean, before we stopped him?'

'Don't ask me, but it struck me that he wasn't so upset as he ought to have been. Let's go. Once we get in the machine he can do what he likes. Ten minutes should see us on our way.'

That a lot can happen in ten minutes Biggles was well aware, but he was certainly not prepared for what was to happen in the next short interval of time. In fact, the success of the mission seemed assured.

Twilight was closing in as they started back, a cold, eerie half-light that spread like a stain from the west over the dreary scene. Even the trees, drooping under their weight of snow, seemed to bow under the dismal depression that hung over everything like a blanket.

The airmen reached the Blenheim without misadventure, and Biggles was just opening the door when from the east came the low, ominous rumble of heavy bombers. At first the sound was no more than a deep vibrant purr that rose and fell in the still air, but it increased rapidly in volume, and it was obvious that the bombers were heading directly towards the spot where the airmen stood staring up into the sky.

'There they are,' said Biggles, pointing.

'Five of 'em,' muttered Algy, following the direction of Biggles's outstretched finger. 'We'd better push off.'

'You're right,' agreed Biggles tersely. 'Von Stalhein must have sent a messenger on ahead, or somehow got in touch with an aerodrome. From the way they're flying, these big boys are looking for us. Let's go!'

Later on Biggles felt that he made a mistake in taking off as he did, for had the machine remained stationary there was a good chance that it would not have been seen. But it is easy to be wise after an event. The truth of the matter was – and Biggles in his heart knew it – that with the menace drawing swiftly nearer, he took off in too great a hurry. He did not fail to survey the line of his take-off before opening the throttle, for this was automatic, but instead of his usual intense scrutiny, he gave the surface of the lake no more than a cursory glance. It may have been that as, during the last twenty-four hours, he had made a dozen landings and take-offs from frozen lakes without seeing anything in the nature of an obstacle, he subconsciously took it for granted that this one would be no different from the rest. Be that as it may, Algy was no sooner in his seat than he opened the throttle, for by this time the bombers were nearly overhead.

It was not until the Blenheim was racing tail up across the ice at fifty miles an hour that he saw the little pile of snow directly in his path. For an instant he stared at it, trying to make out what it was, hoping that it was only soft snow; then, in a flash, he knew the truth, and it was the shape of the snow that revealed it. A floating branch or log had been frozen in the ice, and against it the snow had drifted.

Now to change the course of an aircraft travelling at high speed over the ground is a highly dangerous thing to do at any time; the strain on the undercarriage becomes enormous, and is transmitted to the whole machine. The designer cannot make allowances for such strains, and stresses the machine on the assumption that it will take off in a straight line.

As far as Biggles was concerned, it was one of those occasions when a pilot has no time to think. His reaction is instinctive, and whether or not he gets away with it depends a good deal on luck as well as skill. Thus was it with Biggles. To stop was impossible. To try to lift the machine over the obstacle before he had got up flying speed would be to invite disaster. Yet, at the same time, to touch either of his brakes would be equally fatal; so he pressed the rudder-bar lightly with his left foot, hoping that it would give him just enough turning movement to clear the obstacle. Had the machine been on a normal aerodrome he might have succeeded, but on ice it was a different matter. Instantly the Blenheim started to skid, and once started there was no stopping it. It did what would have been impossible on turf. Propelled by the sheer weight it carried, the machine kept on its course, but in a sideways position.

Knowing that a crash was inevitable, and with the fear of fire ever in the background of his mind, Biggles flicked off the ignition switch, and a split second later one of the wheels struck the log. The result was what might have been foreseen. The undercarriage was torn clean away, while the machine, buckled under the force of the collision, was hurled aside. There was a splintering, tearing series of crashes; the metal propellers bit into the ice and hurled it into the air like the jet from a fountain; the fuselage, flat on the ice, with one wing trailing, spun sickeningly for a hundred yards before coming to a stop.

No one moves faster than a pilot after a crash – that is, of course, assuming he is able to move. He is only too well aware that a fractured petrol-lead and one spark kicked out of a dying magneto can result in a sheet of flame from which nothing can save him.

Biggles flung Algy off his lap, where he had been hurled by the collision, and yelling to the others, fell out on to the ice. Algy followed. Ginger, wiping blood from his nose with his sleeve, tumbled out of the centre turret. Biggles dashed to the tail seat. Smyth was in a heap on the floor. They dragged him out, moaning and gasping for breath.

'He's only winded, I think,' said Biggles tersely, kneeling by the mechanic and running his hands over him.

Smyth, still gasping, tried to sit up. 'I'm all right,' he panted.

In the panic of the moment they had all forgotten the bombers, even though their roaring now seemed to shake the earth.

Ginger was the first to turn his face upwards. 'Look!' he screamed.

From each of the bombers men were falling, one after the other, turning over and over in the air. Then their parachutes started to open, and a swarm of fabric mushrooms floated earthward. The sky seemed to be full of them. Biggles calculated that there were at least fifty.

For a moment nobody spoke. There seemed to be nothing to say. The awful truth was all too plain to see, for already the parachutists were dropping on to the ice and, freeing themselves of their harness, were converging on the crash.

CHAPTER IV

A Grim Ultimatum

Biggles's first thought was of the papers in his pocket. He remembered Colonel Raymond's words, 'At all costs they must not be allowed to fall into the hands of the enemy.' Yet even then he hesitated to destroy them, for once burnt they were gone for ever, and with the professor dead, the vital information they contained could never be recovered. He realized, too, that the papers would directly affect their own fate. Once they fell into von Stalhein's hands his first precaution would be to silence those who might, if they escaped, say what had become of them. On the other hand, without the papers von Stalhein would hesitate to destroy the only people who knew where they were.

Yet where could they be hidden? All round the ice lay flat and bare, and to attempt to hide them in the wreck of the machine would be as futile as if he had retained them on his person. There seemed to be only one way, and Biggles seized upon it. In the crash one of the wings had collapsed, with the result that an engine had broken loose from its bearers; the manifold exhaust had snapped off, and had slid some thirty or forty yards from the machine, where, being hot, it had already half buried itself in the thick ice which, of course, had partly melted. It was obvious that in a few seconds the manifold would disappear from sight altogether; but as it grew cold the water would quickly freeze again and entomb it.

In a moment Biggles tore a piece of loose fabric from the damaged wing, wrapped the papers in it, and hastening to the pool of water that marked the spot where the manifold was swiftly disappearing, he threw the manifold aside and into the water-filled cavity it had created he dropped the packet, forcing it to sink under the weight of his automatic, which would in any case, he knew, soon be taken from him. This done, he marked the spot by taking a line on landmarks on either bank, and then rejoined the others, who were still standing by the crash waiting for him to give them a lead.

Resistance was clearly out of the question. It would have been suicidal, for they were completely encircled by the Russians who had dropped from the sky and were now closing in on them. It is true that they could have put up a fight, for they were well armed, but the end of such a one-sided affair would have been a foregone conclusion. Even if the Russians were driven off they would only have to line the banks of the lake to starve them into submission.

Biggles was anxious to avoid being killed, if it were possible, for more reasons than one; and one reason was the papers. He alone knew where they were hidden, and if he failed to return, that would be the end of any chance of their ultimately reaching home. While he was still alive, whatever the Russians might do, there was still a hope – a slender one admittedly, but even that was better than no hope at all – that he might one day return and recover the papers. A bullet whizzing over the ice decided him, and he put his hands up.

'It's no use,' he told the others. 'We can't fight this mob. We shall have to surrender.'

Algy looked surprised, for the decision was not like Biggles; however, he did not question the order, but slowly raised his hands. The others did the same, including Smyth, who was now nearly normal. The Russians closed in, and Biggles, looking round the circle, saw that von Stalhein was not with them.

'What have you done with the papers?' asked Algy.

'I've hidden them,' returned Biggles.

'Where?'

'Never mind. If you don't know, the information can't be got out of you,' replied Biggles evenly. 'I may tell you later on.'

The Russians now came up and crowded round the prisoners, who were quickly disarmed. Their pockets, too, were emptied, everything being put into the leader's haversack. Whether this man was an officer or an N.C.O. Biggles could not make out, for as they had no common language conversation was not possible. However, he didn't seem badly disposed towards them; in fact, after looking at the crash, he shrugged his shoulders and smiled sympathetically at the British airmen. Several of the Russians gathered round the log that had caused the disaster, for they, as parachutists, knew a good deal about flying, and understood exactly what had happened.

While this had been going on the five bombers had circled, slowly descending, and now they landed one after the other on the ice, afterwards taxiing into position for a take-off near the crashed Blenheim. There was a fairly long delay while the Blenheim was searched from end to end, the maps going into the Russian leader's haversack. There then appeared to be a discussion between him and the pilots of the bombers as to the disposal of the stores, armament, and equipment; from their gestures Biggles was able to follow the debate fairly well, and he formed the opinion that the pilots were unwilling to carry so much extra weight – a supposition that was confirmed when they all moved off, leaving the crash exactly as it lay.

Night had now fallen, and while it was not really dark, Biggles hoped that camp would be made and the take-off postponed until the next morning, for this would give them a chance to escape – not a very good chance perhaps, but a better chance than they would have once they had been handed over to von Stalhein, who would, he felt sure, claim them when he heard of their capture.

In this hope, however, Biggles was to be disappointed, for the whole party moved over to the big machines, where the British airmen were separated, presumably to distribute the weight. The bombers then took off and roared away in an easterly direction.

The flight, as near as Biggles could judge, lasted only about twenty minutes, in which time he estimated that they had covered about fifty miles. They then glided down and landed. Looking through a window, Biggles could see landing lights put out to guide them, from which he supposed that they were not at a regular aerodrome. This, he presently saw, was only half correct. The place was evidently used as an aircraft base, but canvas hangars suggested that it was only a temporary and not a permanent aerodrome. For the rest, in the short time he had to survey the scene after he had got out of the 'plane he saw that the landing-ground was, in fact, yet another lake, but one so large that the extremities were lost in the distance. He thought it might be Lake Onega, which, next to Lake Ladoga, was the largest lake in the district.

At the point where they had landed the bank rose steeply for a hundred feet or more, and it was at the base of a rocky hill that the hangars had been erected. A short distance to the right the lights of a village, or a small town, glowed dimly, and above, silhouetted against the sky, he could see an imposing fort or citadel. He could not make out the details, but at any rate it was a massive building of considerable size, and this, he suspected – correctly, as he soon discovered – was their destination.

He was relieved when he was joined by the others, for he was afraid they might be separated, and under an armed guard the party moved forward between the hangars to a road that wound a serpentine course upwards towards the fort. A march of some twenty minutes brought them to it, when it became possible to see that it was a medieval-looking structure rising sheer out of rock which had obviously been used in its construction. At a gloomy portal they were challenged by a sentry, but after a brief halt they moved forward again. Heavy gates clanged behind them.

'I know now what it must feel like to be taken into Dartmoor,' murmured Algy.

'Judging from the outside of this place, Dartmoor is a luxury hotel compared with it,' growled Ginger. 'If we can crack our way out of this joint we need never fear being locked up anywhere.'

The Russian leader made it clear by gestures that they must not talk, a command that was obeyed, for the man had not treated them badly.

Their way now lay through a series of stone corridors, cold and depressing, lighted by an occasional lantern. Another sentry met them and conducted them on, their echoing footsteps adding to the atmosphere of gloom. The sentry halted before a heavy, iron-studded door; he knocked on it and, in answer to a command from within, opened it. A shaft of bright yellow light fell athwart the corridor. The leader of the party that had captured them beckoned to the prisoners and entered the room, carrying in his hand the haversack containing their personal belongings. This he placed on a great, antique table; he then saluted and withdrew, closing the door behind him.

There were three men in the room – two, judging from their uniforms, being Russian officers. The third was von Stalhein. He eyed Biggles with a whimsical smile, in which, however, there was more triumph than humour.

'I told you the game was only beginning,' he said with a sneer, in his perfect English.

Biggles nodded. 'Go ahead,' he invited. 'It's your lead – but don't get the idea that this is the end of the game.'

'Nearly – very nearly,' said the German softly. 'This is the last hand. It was unfortunate for you that I had the foresight to send a man on ahead of my party to fetch the bombers.'

Von Stalhein pulled the haversack towards him and emptied the contents on the table. He went through them quickly, but without finding what he sought. Again he raised his cold blue eyes to Biggles's face. 'Where are the papers?' he demanded curtly.

'What papers?' returned Biggles blandly, using the same words that von Stalhein had used earlier in the day.

The German smiled grimly. 'I get your meaning,' he said. 'But don't forget I was polite enough to hand the papers over.'

'So would I – if I had them,' answered Biggles evenly.

The Russian who had captured them was brought back into the room and closely questioned for some time. As soon as he had gone von Stalhein turned again to Biggles.

'Where did you put them?' he demanded in a manner that

was now frankly hostile. 'They weren't on your person and they weren't in the machine. What did you do with them?'

'That's a fair question so I'll give you a fair answer,' countered Biggles. 'I hid them. They now repose in a place where – unless I am flattering myself – you will never find them.'

The German's eyes switched to Algy, and then to Ginger.

'It's no use looking at them,' remarked Biggles quietly. 'They don't know where they are. Such a vital piece of information I kept to myself.'

Von Stalhein toyed with his monocle for a moment. He fitted a cigarette into a long holder, lit it, and sent a cloud of grey smoke curling towards the ceiling. 'You know, Bigglesworth, in the past you've had a lot of luck,' he said reflectively.

'Now don't try to do me out of what little credit my efforts have brought me,' protested Biggles.

'But luck,' continued von Stalhein imperturbably, 'can't last for ever, and I think you've about come to the end of it. You've given me more trouble than the rest of the British Intelligence Service put together, and I find you irritating. Still, there are qualities about you that I, who try to be efficient, admire, and for that reason I'm going to give you a chance. Tell me where the papers are and I will see that you are handed over to the authorities as ordinary prisoners of war. Refuse, and I'll see to it that you're shot for carrying arms against a nation with whom you are not at war.'

'We seem to have had this argument before,' replied Biggles. 'We are British subjects – yes; as such we are volunteers in Finland, a fact that is born out by the Finnish uniforms we are wearing. Among those papers on the table you will find our commissions in the Finnish Air Force; by International Law they make us belligerents, and in the event of capture we claim the privileges of prisoners of war.'

Von Stalhein picked up the documents in question. He rolled them into a ball and deliberately dropped it into the fire. 'They are easily disposed of,' he said quietly. 'Let us now assume that you are not fighting for Finland, but are acting as spies for the British Government.'

'Have it your own way,' murmured Biggles. 'But I still hold the trump card. Shoot us, and you've lost the papers for ever.'

Von Stalhein stroked his chin. 'I wonder,' he said softly. 'It rather looks as if I shall have to employ more persuasive methods. I am going to give you until eight o'clock tomorrow morning to remember where you put those papers; if by that time you have not recovered your memory, then your companions will be taken into the courtyard and shot. Since they don't know where the papers are there is really no point in my keeping them here. I will see that you get a room overlooking the courtyard, so that you will be able to watch the proceedings. I think you know me well enough to appreciate that when I say a thing I mean it. In effect, you will sign your friends' death warrants. Think it over. That's all – until eight o'clock.'

'You might see that we get a respectable dinner,' requested Biggles. 'We've had a busy day and we're hungry.'

'I'll attend to it,' promised von Stalhein. 'By the way, where are the rest of your men?'

'What men?'

'The crowd you had with you when you took the papers from me.'

'Oh, those! There weren't any men – just the four of us. The rest of the rifles were sticks.'

Von Stalhein started. A pink flush stained his pale cheeks and his lips pressed themselves together in a straight line. It was clear that, being entirely German and lacking in sense of humour, he hated the manner in which he had been tricked. 'Very clever,' he sneered. 'But not clever enough. We'll see who laughs last.'

'Yes, we shall see,' agreed Biggles.

The Russian guard was called and the prisoners were led away.

After traversing several corridors, slowly mounting, they were shown into a large, sparsely furnished apartment with a number of trestle beds arranged round the walls, with blankets folded at their heads. It seemed that the place had been used before as a prison cell, but there were no other prisoners. A deal table stood in the middle of the room, and on it an iron bowl and a can of water. There was only one window; it was heavily barred, and it overlooked a paved courtyard enclosed within high walls. In fact, the fort was built round the courtyard, but a flight of steps gave access to ramparts with which the whole was surrounded. So much the prisoners saw at a glance.

Biggles sat on one of the beds. 'It looks as if we're in a jam,' he announced.

'You're telling us!' muttered Algy.

'What's the matter? It isn't the first jam we've been in, is it?'

'No, but from what I can see you'll be a bright lad to get out of this one. It would have put the tin hat on Jack Sheppard's career as a prison-buster. What are we going to do?'

'Obviously, I'm going to show von Stalhein where the papers are hidden.'

'What?' There was a chorus of dissent.

'But don't be silly,' argued Biggles. 'You heard what von Stalhein said about bumping you off at eight o'clock? He'll do it too, as sure as fate, unless I tell him what he wants to know.'

'Well, let him,' declared Algy desperately.

'And you think I'm going to stand here and watch you lined up against a wall? Not if I can prevent it,' declared Biggles. 'I'm going to tell that rattlesnake that I shall have to *show* him where the papers are hidden, for I can't describe the place to him. I shall have to go myself – get the idea? That will give me a little longer to do something – perhaps a chance to get away.'

'For sheer cold-blooded optimism you certainly take the cake,' remarked Algy.

'Well, try to think of something better,' invited Biggles. 'Meanwhile we may as well get some sleep while we can.'

Reluctantly the others agreed.

CHAPTER V

Biggles Takes a Trip

They were up and washed, sitting on their beds the following morning when the door opened and von Stalhein, followed by two Russian guards, entered. Von Stalhein, as usual, was immaculate, and his monocle gleamed coldly. He addressed Biggles.

'Well?' was all he said.

Biggles nodded. 'All right, I agree,' he answered. 'You've got me in a tight spot and I can't refuse – you know that.'

The German smiled frostily. 'Where are the papers?'

'I can't tell you,' answered Biggles. 'Just a minute,' he went on quickly, as von Stalhein's face darkened with anger. 'Let me explain. I know where the papers are because I hid them, but I couldn't possibly describe the place to you because there was no feature, no landmark, to mark the spot. In the circumstances I can only suggest that you take me to the place, and then I'll show you where the papers are.'

'How far away is this place?'

'About fifty miles – quite close to where we were picked up. The best thing would be for you to fly me back to the lake where we crashed yesterday. From there it's a short walk through the snow. We ought to be able to get the papers and return here in a few hours.'

For a moment von Stalhein regarded Biggles suspiciously. 'Very well,' he agreed slowly, 'I will order an aeroplane immediately. But if you try any tricks—' His eyes narrowed.

'I'm not a madman,' protested Biggles. 'By the way, have I your word that if I hand you the papers you will treat us as prisoners of war?'

'That is what I said,' announced von Stalhein curtly.

In half an hour Biggles was getting into the machine – one of the big Russian bombers. In spite of his protests that it was unnecessary – for the German had provided an escort of six Russian soldiers – he had been handcuffed. But von Stalhein was taking no chances, and he refused to take them off. A small hand-sled, lightly loaded with what Biggles supposed to be food, was lifted aboard, and the machine took off. Twenty minutes later, under a leaden sky, it landed on the lake where the Blenheim still lay, a twisted wreck.

Biggles's brain had not been idle during the journey. He had no intention of taking von Stalhein straight to the spot where the papers now lay frozen in the ice, which was, as we know, only a short distance from the crash; but what had upset his plan was the handcuffs. With steel bracelets on his wrists he was absolutely helpless, so the first problem that exercised his mind was how to get rid of them.

'Well, where are they?' demanded von Stalhein as they got out. The Russians followed them, leaving the pilot sitting in his seat.

Biggles had, from the air, made a swift survey of the landscape. To his right, from the edge of the lake, the ground rose in a steep, snow-covered slope perhaps a hundred feet high. Beyond the ridge the ground dropped away into a valley nearly a mile wide, with an even steeper range of hills beyond, a formidable barrier that rose for several hundred feet, the whole being covered with smooth, untrodden snow.

Von Stalhein was waiting.

Biggles nodded towards the nearest ridge. 'That's the way we shall have to go,' he said.

'Good,' answered von Stalhein, and the party moved off, Biggles and the German walking in front, followed by two Russians dragging the sled, and then the remaining four guards with rifles over their arms.

Handicapped as he was by the handcuffs, Biggles had a job to get up the first slope; actually he made it appear much more difficult for him than it really was, floundering in the deep snow and sometimes falling, so that he had to be helped to his feet by the Russians, who seemed to sympathize with his plight, for even they found the going by no means easy. The consequence was, by the time they got to the ridge Biggles was puffing and blowing, and generally affecting all the symptoms of exhaustion.

Von Stalhein, now that they were so near their objective, got more and more impatient at every delay, particularly when Biggles insisted on resting before going on. 'Can't you see that I'm nearly all in?' he said plaintively. However, after a short spell he got on his feet, and after descending the far slope, set off across the valley.

'Where are we going?' demanded von Stalhein.

Biggles nodded towards the towering hills ahead. 'Just over the other side,' he answered.

Von Stalhein said no more, but stalked on, curbing his impatience as well as he could – which was not very well.

They crossed the valley, in the bottom of which the snow had drifted in places to a depth of three or four feet, and while the crust was frozen hard enough in most places to support their weight, sometimes it broke through, when Biggles had to be extricated. As a matter of fact, his frequent stumbles were deliberate in the hope that repeated delays would cause von Stalhein to release his hands. He took care not to suggest this himself, however, for fear the suspicions of the German were aroused. But still von Stalhein refused to take the bait.

The valley traversed, the ascent of the big hill commenced, and here Biggles was seriously handicapped. However, he puffed along, apparently making a genuine attempt to keep up with the party, which, naturally, had to lag back for him. Nearing the top the snow became harder, so hard, indeed, that it was little better than a sheet of ice, and the climbers had to dig their heels into it to get a foothold. Progress became little more than a snail's pace, and von Stalhein began to lose his temper. Twice Biggles slipped, and glissaded wildly for thirty or forty yards; on such occasions he lay gasping until the Russians came back, helped him to his feet, and literally dragged him up the slope to where von Stalhein was waiting.

Biggles knew that something had got to be done pretty soon, for all this time they were getting farther and farther away from the papers, and he could not keep up the deception much longer without von Stalhein becoming suspicious. They were now nearly at the top of the hill, and as he had no idea of what was going to happen when he got there, he determined on one last attempt to get his hands free. He slipped, and after staggering for a moment like a drunken man, he fell heavily and began to slide backwards. This time he really could not stop, so he covered his face with his arms and allowed himself to slide, thankful that there were no obstacles against which he might collide. He went halfway down the hill before he was brought to a stop by a patch of soft snow, and there he lay, exhausted – but not so exhausted as he pretended to be. He made no attempt to get up, so the party halted while two of the Russians came back and tried to get him on his feet. But Biggles flopped like a sack of flour, and since it was only with the greatest difficulty that the Russians could get him along at all, they shouted something to von Stalhein. What they said he did not know, but his heart gave a lurch when one of the guards smiled and hurried up to von Stalhein. Presently he returned, bringing with him the key of the handcuffs, which were removed. On the face of it, there was no real point in keeping them on, for he was one unarmed man among seven, six of whom carried rifles and the other an automatic.

Still playing for time, Biggles dragged himself wearily up the steep slope, and after a considerable delay reached the others who, with the exception of the German, were squatting on the snow, having turned the sled sideways on so that it could not run down. The men had leaned their rifles against it.

Reaching von Stalhein, Biggles collapsed in a heap, gasping for breath; but his eyes were taking in every detail of the situation, for the moment for which he had been waiting had arrived. Slowly, as if it were a tremendous effort, he began to get up. Then, suddenly, he moved like lightning. He jerked to his feet, slammed his right first against the German's jaw, knocking him over backwards, and dived at the sled. It took him only a split second to drag the nose round so that it was pointing down the hill. The rifles, except one which he grabbed, he kicked aside. Then, flinging himself on the sled in a flying leap, he tore away down the hill.

'*He slammed his right fist against the German's jaw*'

In an instant he was travelling at a speed that alarmed him; but apprehensive of the shots that he knew would follow, he eased his weight a little to one side so that the sled swerved slightly. He was only just in time, for bullets zipped into the snow unpleasantly close to his side; but a small mark travelling at nearly sixty miles an hour is not easy to hit, and he made it more difficult by altering his weight so that his course was anything but straight. He did not attempt to look behind; he was much too concerned with where he was going, for a spill at such speed might have serious consequences. He took a small mound like a ski jumper, and grunted as he came down flat on his stomach; but the sled still tore on at dizzy speed, which ultimately carried him three parts of the way across the valley. His great regret was that the others couldn't see him, for it was the most exciting ride he had ever had in his life, and he made a mental note that he would take up tobogganing when he got too old for flying.

At last, as it met the gentle slope on the far side of the valley, the sled began to lose speed. He remained on it while it made any progress at all, but as soon as it had stopped he picked up the rifle, and smiling with the thrill of the mad ride and at the satisfactory outcome of his trip, he looked back across the valley. Von Stalhein and the Russians, looking like black ants, were slipping and sliding down his track more than a mile away. He abandoned the sled that had done him such good service and hurried on.

His one fear now was that the Russian pilot who had remained in the 'plane would have heard the shots, and reach the ridge in front of him first, to see what the shooting was about. Actually they arrived at the ridge together, but the Russian was unarmed – or at least, no weapon was visible. Almost colliding with

Biggles, he merely stared in astonishment, evidently wondering, not without reason, how the miracle had been accomplished.

Biggles tapped the rifle meaningly, and then pointed to the opposite hill.

The pilot took the tip; he was in no position to argue. In any case, he did not seem particularly concerned about the affair, feeling, perhaps, that it was not his business to worry about a prisoner. He nodded pleasantly and walked on to meet his comrades. Biggles watched him for a little while to make sure that there was no hanky-panky, but seeing that he did not even look back, he turned towards the lake and, reaching the ice, made for the spot where he had hidden the papers. There was no difficulty in finding it, for the ice was a slightly different colour where it had been melted.

Getting the papers out, however, was not such a simple matter, and in the end he achieved it by shattering the ice piecemeal with the butt of the rifle. He recovered his automatic at the same time, so having no further use for the rifle, he sent it spinning into the wreck of the Blenheim. Both the canvas-covered bundle of papers and the automatic had pieces of ice adhering to them, so he went over to the Russian bomber and laid them on one of the still warm engines to melt. He then went into the machine and examined the cockpit; he did this unhurriedly, knowing that von Stalhein and the Russians could not possibly get back to the ridge overlooking the lake in less than half an hour. What pleased him still more was the realization that without an aircraft it would take von Stalhein and the Russians at least two days to cover the fifty miles that lay between the lake and the fort.

Satisfied that the flying of the machine presented no difficulty, he fetched the papers and the pistol from the engine on which he had laid them, and was glad to see that they were now free from ice. He looked hard at the sky, which, from a dull leaden colour, had deepened to almost inky black. Subconsciously he had been aware of the fading light for some time, but now, with a flight before him, he regarded it with a different interest, and some apprehension. 'There's snow coming, if I know anything about weather,' he told himself. For a moment, but only for a moment, he was tempted to fly the papers straight back to Helsinki, but the idea of abandoning the others to the tender mercy of von Stalhein, who would, in view of what had happened, be more than usually vindictive, was so repugnant to him that he dismissed the thought instantly. He knew that none or all must be saved, or the rest of his life would be spent in remorse.

His plan, briefly, was to fly back to within a few miles of the fort, land the machine where there was little chance of its being found, and then, in some manner not yet decided, attempt to rescue the others, after which they would make for the 'plane and fly home together. Yet now even the elements seemed to be conspiring against him, for should snow begin to fall he was likely to lose himself. The machine was not equipped for blind flying, and in any case the country was absolutely unknown to him.

He was about to get into the pilot's seat when he saw, lying under a wing, the parachute that had evidently been dropped by the rightful pilot of the machine. Having no definite purpose in mind, but neglecting no precaution, he put it on, and then got into his seat. The watch on the instrument board told him that it was now nearly three o'clock.

It began to snow just as he took off, not the small driving flakes of a blizzard, but big, heavy flakes that dropped like white feathers straight down from the darkening sky. He might well have cursed it, but knowing that this could serve no useful purpose, he merely regarded it with thoughtful brooding eyes.

In a minute he was in the air, roaring eastward, keeping low so that he could watch the ground, for once he lost it he might have a job to find it again – without colliding violently with it. Thicker fell the snow as the minutes passed, and by the time he was halfway back to the fort the ground was no more than a dark grey blur. Still he roared on, hoping for the best. There was nothing else he could do. But the snow fell even more thickly, until it seemed that the heavens were emptying themselves over the desolate land.

He was down to a hundred feet when he got back over the aerodrome; he could just see the giant hangars and the hill that rose behind them. He cleared the fort by only a few feet.

The position now seemed hopeless, for he knew that once he lost touch with the aerodrome he would be utterly lost, and landing would be a matter of extreme danger. He had one stroke of luck. It seemed that the ground staff at the aerodrome had been alert, and assuming that the machine would want to land, they had turned the beam of a searchlight into the sky, and to this Biggles clung as a drowning man clings to a plank. Yet to land on the aerodrome was out of the question, for the second he was down the mechanics would be certain to run out to him, when he would instantly be discovered. Desperately he racked his brain for a solution to the problem. He could think of only one, and that was not one that would have appealed to him in the ordinary way. However, his plight was so desperate that he was in no position to choose.

Turning the bomber, he headed back towards the beam, at the same time climbing up to a thousand feet. The earth of course had disappeared; all he could see was the beam, and that only faintly. With professional skill he adjusted the elevators so that the machine would fly 'hands off' on even keel; and opening the emergency tool kit under the seat, he took from it a file and a pair of pliers, which he thrust into his jacket pocket. Then he opened the door, and when he judged that he was over the fort, he launched himself into space. Instinctively he counted the regulation 'one – two – three' and then pulled the ripcord.

He had made many parachute jumps, but none like this. He could see nothing; he could feel nothing except the harness taut round his limbs, telling him that the brolly had opened; all he could hear was the drone of the bomber as it ploughed on untended through the murk. One thing only he had in his favour – there was no wind. A dark mass loomed below him. Bending his knees and folding his arms over his face, he waited for the shock.

When it came he fell headlong, clutching wildly at anything he could catch, while the billowing folds of the fabric settled over him. Apart from being slightly winded by the impact he was unhurt, for which he was truly thankful, for a broken bone, or even a sprain, would have been fatal to his project. Throwing the fabric impatiently to one side, he slipped out of the harness and looked about him. To his intense satisfaction he saw that his judgement had been correct – or nearly so. He had hoped to drop into the courtyard, but instead, he had landed on the ramparts, which suited him even better, for these ramparts were, in fact, actually the flat roof over the occupied part of the fort.

In order that his position should be understood precisely, a brief description of the fort, as seen from above, becomes necessary. Like many military buildings of the late medieval period, it took the form of a hollow square. That is to say, the buildings, instead of being constructed in a solid block, were built round a central courtyard of about an acre of ground, which served the garrison as a parade ground. In other words, the buildings were really a fortified wall in the form of a square with a parapet on the outside. It was on the top of this wall that he had landed, so that a sheer drop occurred on both sides. On one hand was the outside of the fort; on the inside, the parade ground.

On this wall the snow had, of course, settled, and he examined it quickly, for footmarks would suggest that it was patrolled by a sentry; however, he found none. Then, suddenly, the snow turned to sleet, and then to rain, big heavy drops that hissed softly into the white mantle that lay over everything.

'Snow – sleet – rain – there isn't much else it can do,' he told himself philosophically, crouching low as he surveyed the scene in order to locate the room in which the others were confined – unless they had been moved. This was no easy matter, for by now it was practically dark; still, the darkness served one useful purpose in that it would hide him from the eyes of anyone who happened to cross the courtyard.

The room in which they had been locked was on the inside of the rampart wall; that he knew, for the window overlooked the courtyard; from it that morning he had remarked a well, and this now gave him a line on the position of the window he was anxious to find. Rolling the parachute into a ball, he put it under his arm and made his way cautiously towards his objective. Presently he was able to see that only one window was barred, and that told him all he wanted to know. But a new difficulty now presented itself. The window was a good six feet below the coping, and except for a narrow sill, there was nothing, no projection of any sort, by which he might descend to it. The solution of this problem was at hand, however; twisting the parachute's shrouds into a skein, he wound the fabric round one of the projecting battlements, made it secure, and then lowered the shrouds so that they hung in front of the window. In another moment his feet were on the sill. Bending, he looked in through the window.

CHAPTER VI

Biggles Comes Back

After Biggles had gone the feelings of the others can be better imagined than described. Their confidence in their leader was tremendous, but they could not deceive themselves, and without discussing it they knew in their hearts that the task with which he was now faced, the recovery of the papers and their escape from the fort, was, on the face of it, so tremendous that it seemed fantastic even to contemplate it. So they passed a miserable day; they saw it start snowing, and were glad when darkness began to envelop the gloomy scene outside. What had become of Biggles they did not so much as conjecture, knowing it to be futile.

'He'll turn up,' remarked Ginger confidently. 'I don't know how he manages it, but he always does.' He started violently, peering forward in the direction of the window. 'Great Scott!' he went on. 'Can you see what I see, or am I going crazy?' His voice was so high pitched that it bordered on the hysterical.

The others both stared at the window. Neither of them spoke. Algy got up from the bed on which he had been sitting, and walked, a step at a time, towards the window. 'It's Biggles,' he said in a funny voice. 'If it isn't, then it's his ghost.' He seemed bewildered, which is hardly a matter for wonder, for even if Biggles had escaped and returned to the fort, which seemed unlikely enough in all conscience, Algy could not imagine how, without wings, he had got to the window, for below there was a sheer drop of thirty feet. He reached the window just as Biggles tapped on it sharply with the file, which he had taken from his pocket.

Algy opened the window, which was only fastened by a simple latch, the frames opening inwards because of the bars. 'So here you are,' he said in a dazed voice. It seemed a silly thing to say, but he could think of nothing else.

'As you remark, here I am,' answered Biggles cheerfully. 'Now listen. Here's a file. One of you stay near the door so that you aren't caught in the act, while the others get to work on these bars. You'll have to cut one of them clean out. It's half-inch iron, but it should be fairly soft and shouldn't take you more than an hour. I daren't stay here in case anyone comes into the courtyard and looks up, so I'm going back on the ramparts. I shall stay handy, so as soon as you're through give a low whistle. There's no time for explanations now.'

'Okay,' agreed Algy eagerly, and took the file, while Biggles's dangling legs disappeared upward as he dragged himself back to the ramparts.

The others had all heard what Biggles had said, so there was no need to waste time in bartering words. Ginger went to the door, while Smyth, who was the handiest man with a file, set to work on the centre bar. He went at it with a will, and the steel fairly bit into the rusty iron.

Biggles squatted on the ramparts in no small discomfort, for it was bitterly cold and he had no protection from the rain. However, there was nothing he could do except blow on his hands to prevent them from becoming numb, as he listened to the file rasping into the iron. In this way nearly an hour passed. Nothing happened to interrupt the work. Occasional sounds below suggested that guards were being changed, but no sentry came to the ramparts.

Biggles lay down and peered over the edge of the wall. 'How are you getting on?' he whispered hoarsely.

'Fine! We're through the bottom and nearly through the top. Ten minutes should do it,' answered Algy.

Biggles lay still, waiting. The filing ceased. A moment later there was a soft snap as the iron parted.

'We're through,' came Algy's voice. 'How do we get up?'

'I'll lower a rope,' answered Biggles. 'It's a bunch of parachute shrouds. Grab the lot and I'll pull you up. It's no use going down into the courtyard because we may not be able to get out. We've got to get down the *outside* of the wall. As far as I can see it's about thirty feet, and ends on some rocks.'

In a few minutes they were all on the ramparts; Algy was last up, having closed the window behind him. 'I'd like to see von Stalhein's face when he calls and finds the room empty,' he chuckled.

'Let's save the laughter until we're the other side of the frontier,' suggested Biggles. 'I've got those confounded papers on me and they give me the heebie-jeebies. I'm scared stiff at the thought of being caught with them.'

'Where did you get this brolly?'

'Borrowed it,' returned Biggles tersely, as he pulled up the shrouds and lowered them again on the outer side of the ramparts. He peered down, but although the rain had nearly stopped, it was too dark to see anything distinctly. 'You'd better go first Algy,' he said. 'Let us know if it's all clear.'

Algy took the shrouds in a bundle in his hands, and forcing his feet against the wall in the manner of a rock climber, went down backwards. His voice, low and vibrant, floated up: 'All right – come on.'

The others descended in turn, and found themselves on a narrow ledge about a hundred feet above the village. The ledge appeared to follow the walls of the fort, but there were several places where a descent was possible.

'What about the brolly?' asked Ginger. It was still hanging on the wall.

'Leave it where it is,' decided Biggles. 'It's too bulky to carry about and I don't think we shall need it again. It won't be seen until it gets light, and by that time we ought to be clear away.'

After scrambling down the rock to the level ground below, Biggles instinctively headed for the hangars, hoping to find an aircraft outside, but, no doubt on account of the weather, they had all been taken in. What was even more disturbing, there seemed to be a good deal of activity; lights glowed dimly through the canvas walls of the hangars, and men, singly and in parties, moved about them. Biggles backed away into the shadows.

'It's going to be a dangerous business trying to get one of these kites,' he muttered anxiously. 'They're all big machines – too big for just the four of us to handle on the ground. The ground staff here use tractors to haul them about – I've heard them. It's difficult—'

'Gosh! It's a long walk home if that's what you're thinking,' whispered Ginger.

'It must be getting on for fifty miles to the lake where I crashed the Blenheim, and then a fair distance to the frontier.' Biggles seemed to be speaking his thoughts aloud.

'We should never make it without grub,' declared Algy.

'There's food in the Blenheim.'

'But that's nearly fifty miles away!'

'Still, it would help us on our way if we could get to it. We've got to try. As far as I can see we've no choice.'

They crouched back from the narrow track that passed behind the hangars as a sound could be heard approaching. Presently a sledge drawn by a pony went past.

'By Jove! If we could get hold of that —' whispered Algy.

'We'll follow it,' decided Biggles instantly. 'It's ten to one that it will stop in the village, and the fellow may leave it to make a call.'

Keeping at a safe distance, they followed the sledge to the outskirts of the village, where, as Biggles had predicted, the driver stopped outside a house; boisterous conversation and the clinking of glasses suggested that it was a tavern. Leaving the vehicle, the driver went in. Yellow light flashed on the road as he opened the door, and was cut off again as it closed behind him.

'Stay here!' Biggles's voice was crisp. He glanced quickly up and down the road; there was nobody about. Walking quietly up to the pony, he took the bridle in his hand and led the animal back to where the others were standing. 'The next thing is to get on the lake,' he announced. 'If we can do that we can make a bee-line due west.'

It took them some minutes before they found a lane descending to the lakeside. On the way they had to pass several houses, or rather hovels, and they had a bad moment when the door of one of them opened and a man came out. However, he appeared to see nothing unusual in the sledge, for he said nothing, and disappeared into the gloom in the direction of the tavern.

As soon as they were on the ice Biggles climbed into the driver's seat. 'Get aboard,' he ordered, and the others scrambled up on what turned out to be a load of hay. Biggles took a bearing from the stars, which here and there flickered mistily through breaks in the clouds, and shook the reins. The pony walked a few paces and then broke into a trot.

What none of them expected, having had no experience of this mode of travel, was the noise made by the sledge-runners on the ice. They hummed like circular saws as they cut through the layer of rain-softened snow into the hard ice underneath, and Biggles looked apprehensively in the direction of the hangars, which were only about a hundred yards away. However, having started there was no going back, and he drew a deep breath of relief as the lights gradually faded into the darkness behind them. He realized that the snow was both a blessing and a curse, for while it gave grip to the pony's hooves, it marked a track that could not be missed. All around lay a flat, seemingly endless expanse of greyish snow, with coal-black patches of sheer ice where, for some reason not apparent, the snow had melted. Such patches were as slippery as glass, as Biggles soon discovered when the pony ran on the first one and nearly fell, so thereafter he avoided them. He called Algy up beside him, and as he did so a searchlight stabbed the sky behind them. For a moment it flung its beam towards the stars; then it swooped swiftly down and began playing on the ice, sweeping the surface like a white sword.

'What does that mean?' asked Algy sharply.

'I imagine it means that our escape has been discovered,' replied Biggles quietly. 'The owner of the sledge may have missed it, or the Commandant of the fort has discovered the room empty. The hunt is on.'

'They'll spot our tracks, even if they don't see us.'

'I'm afraid you're right.'

'Shouldn't we abandon the sledge?'

'Not yet – this is a lot better than walking.'

As he spoke, Biggles flicked the pony with the whip; it broke into a gallop, and they went flying over the ice with the runners fairly singing. Twice the searchlight nearly caught them in its dazzling beam, but, as if it sensed the danger, the pony tore on, and soon they were beyond the reach of the blinding radiance, a tiny black speck in a world of utter desolation.

'How wide is this lake?' asked Algy.

'I don't know exactly, but from what I saw of it from the 'plane this morning it must be pretty wide – not less than forty miles I reckon. We've got to be off it before dawn, though, or those bombers will be on us like a ton of bricks. They'd be bound to see us, when they could please themselves whether they landed and picked us up, or just bombed the ice so that we fell in.'

'Gosh,' muttered Algy, 'what a cheerful bloke you are!'

'The clouds are our salvation so far,' resumed Biggles. 'They make it just too dark for safe flying. The moment they go it will start to get lighter. What we really want is a spot of snow to keep the bombers out of the air.'

'What I want,' returned Algy bitingly, 'is a hot drink and a fur coat. Jumping rattlesnakes! Isn't it cold?'

'We've got to stick it for a bit,' Biggles told him. 'When we get to the other side and start running we shall be warm enough. We shall have to watch out that we don't bump into von Stalhein. I left him out here this morning with a bunch of Russians, but I fancy he's a bit to the north of us.' Biggles gave the others a brief account of his adventures earlier in the day, and after that they fell silent. The pony, tiring, steadied its pace. The only sound was the hollow thud of its hooves and the whine of the runners on the ice. Ginger and Smyth, deep down in the hay, dozed uneasily. Biggles, his face expressionless, stared into the gloom ahead.

CHAPTER VII

The Avalanche

awn saw the rim of a hazy red sun peeping over the horizon behind them, throwing a strange pinky glow over the flat surface of the lake. After the darkness it was a relief to have the light, for it enabled the weary travellers to see where they were, although Biggles several times looked anxiously to the rear.

They could now see the edge of the lake in two directions, to the north and to the west, in which direction they were moving – moving slowly, for the pony was near the end of its endurance. To the north the land showed as low, snow-covered hills. Ahead, at a distance of perhaps four miles, a barrier of steeper hills rose sharply and formed a jagged skyline, with dark patches of rock showing where the rain had washed away the snow. Sweeping forests of spruce and fir, which had also shed much of their white mantle, could be seen.

Biggles urged the pony on, not without a qualm of conscience, for it had proved a willing little beast and had served them well; but out on the ice as they were, he knew that they were as conspicuous as a fly on a white ceiling. Once they reached the trees they would find cover, both from above and from the surrounding country, so that was the first consideration. Gradually the forest for which

Biggles was heading drew nearer, but the pace had dropped to a walk, for the pony could obviously do no more. Twice aircraft could be heard behind them, and Biggles wondered why the pilots did not strike the trail and follow it – until Ginger called attention to what none of them had noticed; a sharp thaw had set in, causing the snow to start melting, and thus obliterate the trail except for a short distance behind them. Indeed, the snow was now soft and slushy, and as soon as he realized it Biggles got down, made the others do the same, and ran beside the sledge. Relieved of their weight, the pony put on a spurt, and reached the edge of the lake just as a bomber appeared in the distance.

Biggles led the stout little animal in amongst the trees where he thought they would be safe, unharnessed it, and flung the hay out on the snow. 'There you are, laddie,' he said, patting its neck. 'That ought to keep you going till the snow melts.'

He insisted on remaining under cover until the bomber, whose circling progress left them in no doubt as to its mission, passed on; then he turned to the ridge of hills which, running from north to south, lay across their path. 'This is where we start walking,' he announced.

'D'you know where we are?' inquired Ginger.

'No, but as long as we keep heading westwards we ought to be all right. From the ridge in front of us we should be able to see the lake where we crashed the Blenheim. I made a note of it yesterday from the air. I'm aiming to strike the Blenheim in order to pick up some food.'

The climb up the steep, snow-covered slope was a severe one, particularly as the thaw was now perceptible; indeed, after the intense cold the air seemed muggy, and they were soon perspiring freely. A steamy mist began to form.

'Phew, take it easy,' muttered Algy, taking off his jacket and sitting down on a rock to rest. 'There's no need for us to break our necks.'

Biggles agreed, so they all took off their jackets and sat on them while they got their breath preparatory to tackling the last climb, which, as is usually the case, was the hardest part. Refreshed, with their jackets over their arms, they went on, and after a sharp tussle reached the top.

Biggles was first on the ridge; he gave a cry and pointed triumphantly, for the ground fell away again to another lake, and there, no great distance away, lay the twisted remains of the Blenheim. Sliding and slipping, and sometimes jumping over difficult places, they hurried on down the steep bank towards the ice, anxious to secure the food which they hoped was still in the Blenheim.

Suddenly Biggles remembered something; in fact, it was a patch of loose snow that slid away under his feet that recalled to his mind what he had often heard, but of which he had so far had no personal experience – that a sharp thaw is liable to cause an avalanche. 'Steady!' he cried urgently. 'Steady, everybody.' When first he spoke he only sensed the danger, but now he saw it, for in several places the snow was beginning to slide. Unfortunately Algy was poised on an awkward-shaped piece of rock; he slipped, and to save himself he jumped clear.

'Stop!' yelled Biggles – but it was too late.

Slowly at first, but with ever increasing momentum, the whole slope on which they were standing started to slide, and once started there was no stopping it. Biggles did not waste time trying to stop it. 'Run!' he shouted, and began running sideways along the slope to get clear of the danger area.

The others looked up, and went deathly white as, too late, they realized what was happening. With a mighty roar a thousand tons of snow and rock broke loose. Tearing up trees as if they had been so much brushwood, the mass thundered down the slope towards the ice.

Now it happened that Biggles was some distance to the right of the others and, naturally, he took what appeared to be the shortest cut to safety. The others went in the opposite direction – anywhere to escape the awful thing that was happening. In their wild rush they took the most desperate chances, jumping over obstacles which in the ordinary way would have made them pause. Algy practically got clear. So did Smyth, although he was bowled over. For a moment it seemed that Ginger, too, might escape the terrifying wave of death that was roaring down the slope; but he was outflanked; he had been nearest to Biggles and consequently had farther to go. Caught in the fringe of the tumbling mass, in a flash he was whirled away. For a moment Algy and Smyth could see him rolling over and over amongst the snow; then he disappeared from sight.

Algy stared like a man stunned, gazing blankly at the confused jumble of snow, ice, rock, and timber as the avalanche swept past them, swirling and tossing like water in a ravine flooded by a cloudburst. Dimly he was conscious of a great noise without actually hearing it. He reeled under the suddenness of the calamity. The scene was engraved on his mind like a photograph.

Slowly the avalanche exhausted itself, the lip far out on the ice. Silence fell. Snow which had been flung high into the air began to fall silently on the bare bedrock.

Algy turned a stricken face to the side of the slope where he had last seen Biggles. There was no sign of him. Nor could he see Ginger. He turned to Smyth. 'We'd better look for them,' he said in a hopeless sort of voice. 'You try to find Ginger – I'll look for the Skipper.'

Before he had reached the place where Biggles had disappeared Smyth was yelling to him to come back. Shaking like a leaf from shock, he hurried to the spot, to find Smyth clawing frantically at a great pile of loose snow from which projected a leg. It took them only a few minutes to drag Ginger clear. He was unconscious and bleeding from the nose, but a quick examination revealed no broken bones.

'We shall have to leave him where he is for the moment,' muttered Algy. 'Let's see if we can find the Skipper.'

They made their way over the lacerated ground to where Biggles had last been seen.

For some minutes they hunted in vain, and then Smyth saw him. Either he had just escaped the avalanche and then fallen, or had been overwhelmed by it and flung clear, for he lay motionless, face downwards, among the debris of rocks and uprooted trees which had surged far out on the ice of the lake. Half sick with dread, Algy turned him over and got him into as comfortable a position as could be arranged. He was unconscious.

Algy caught his breath when he saw a livid bruise, seeping blood, on the ashen forehead. 'My God! That looks like concussion,' he whispered through lips that were as white as Biggles's. 'This is awful. What are we going to do? We've got to get him off the ice, both of them, or they'll die of sheer cold.'

Algy spoke in a dazed voice. He was, in fact, half stunned by the shock of the catastrophe. Their position had been difficult enough before, but now, with two casualties on their hands, it seemed hopeless, and he was in a fever of dismay. The ghastly part of it was that there was so little they could do.

As they stood staring down at Biggles's unconscious form a weak hail made them look up, to see Ginger reeling down the hill.

'Stand still, you fool!' yelled Algy. 'You'll fall and break your neck.' He raced up the hill, for the warning went unheeded. He caught Ginger and dragged him back from the edge of a steep rock on which he was staggering, and forced him to sit down.

'Did Biggles – get clear?' asked Ginger weakly.

'Yes, but he's knocked out. How do you feel?'

Ginger shut his eyes and shook his head. 'I don't know,' he muttered. 'My legs are a bit groggy – but I don't think I've done myself – any real – damage. Great Scott! What a dreadful mess.'

Smyth came up. 'We'd better get them under cover, sir, until we see how badly the Skipper's hurt,' he said seriously.

'Under cover?'

Smyth pointed to the fuselage of the Blenheim lying flat on the ice. 'Let's get them inside,' he suggested. 'That will be better than lying out here. Otherwise they're liable to freeze, particularly as the Skipper hasn't got a jacket. He was carrying it, wasn't he? I wonder what happened to it.'

Algy looked around. 'I don't see it,' he said dully. 'I suppose it's buried under all this snow. Well, we haven't time to look for it now – we'll get them into the Blenheim. Now I come to think of it, there's a first-aid outfit there – or there should be.'

They helped Ginger out on to the smooth ice, where they found that he was able to walk unaided, although, in spite of his assurances to the contrary, it was obvious that he had been badly shaken, if nothing worse. Biggles was still unconscious, and as he was a difficult load on the slippery ice, they made a rough bed of fir branches and, taking the thick ends in their hands, began to drag him towards the Blenheim.

They were just about halfway, in the most open part of the lake, when, faintly at first, but developing swiftly, came the roar of an aircraft; and the beat of the engines told them what it was even before it came into view – a Russian heavy bomber. Algy, realizing how conspicuous they were, threw up his hands in dismay. 'We're sunk,' he cried bitterly.

'Algy!'

Algy started as if he had been stung, for the word came from the improvised stretcher. He saw that Biggles's eyes were open.

'Listen,' went on Biggles. 'Do exactly as I tell you. There's a gun in my hip pocket – get it out. You've no time to get under cover, so lie down, all of you, as if you were dead. Don't move a muscle. There's just a chance that if the pilot spots you he'll land to see what's happened. If he does, stick him up and grab the machine. It's our only chance.' Biggles tried to get up, but his face twisted with pain and he fell back again. His eyes closed.

It took Algy only a moment to secure the pistol. 'You heard what he said,' he told the others tersely. 'Lie down and don't move.'

They all collapsed on the ice just as the bomber swept over the trees. The pilot saw them at once, as he was bound to, and Algy, whose eyes remained open, watched the movements of the machine with breathless suspense.

Three times the bomber circled, coming lower each time; the third time his wheels nearly brushed them. A white face, fur-rimmed, evidently that of the second pilot, projected from the cockpit and stared down from a height of not more than twenty feet. The bomber went on, reached the end of the lake, turned, and then, cutting its engines, glided back, obviously with the intention of landing.

'Don't move, anybody,' hissed Algy. 'Wait till I give the word.'

'Very quietly Algy stood up, pistol at the ready'

The bomber's wheels rumbled as they kissed the ice, and the massive undercarriage groaned as they trundled on, the machine finishing its run about fifty yards from the fugitives. There was a brief delay; then a door in the cockpit opened; two men descended and began walking quickly over the ice towards the bodies. Algy's nerves tingled as their footsteps drew nearer. He half closed his eyes.

The Russians were talking in low tones, evidently discussing the situation. Then one of them must have noticed the avalanche, for he pointed to it. They both stopped, held a brief discussion, and then came on again. In short, their reaction to the situation was perfectly natural. There was no reason for them to suppose that they were walking into a trap.

To his joy Algy saw that neither of them carried a weapon; their hands were empty – except that one carelessly swung his gauntlets. They went first to Biggles. The leading pilot knelt to examine him while his companion looked on, a position in which their backs were turned to the others.

Very quietly Algy stood up, pistol at the ready. 'Don't move,' he said curtly.

It is unlikely that the Russians understood English, but they knew the meaning of the squat black weapon that menaced them, for the message it conveys is universal. Their eyes opened wide in amazement. Slowly they raised their hands.

As Ginger and Smyth joined the party Algy stepped nearer to the two Russians and tapped their pockets; then, satisfied that they were unarmed, he indicated that they were to start walking towards the bank. A pilot himself, he felt a certain sympathy for them, and realizing that they had a long walk in front of them before they could get home, he pointed first to the crash and then to his mouth in the hope that they would grasp what he was trying to convey – that there was food to be found there.

The Russians looked at each other, and then back at Algy. One nodded; the other waved his hand in a manner that suggested that he understood.

All the same, Algy watched them as they walked on, while Ginger and Smyth got Biggles to the bomber and lifted him inside. They called out that they were ready.

Algy hastened to join them. The engines were still ticking over. He climbed into the pilot's seat and slammed the door. His hand closed over the throttle. 'We're away!' he cried jubilantly.

The propellers swirled as he opened the throttle and turned the machine to face the longest run that the lake provided. His eyes explored the surface of the ice, for he didn't want a repetition of the Blenheim disaster; but there were no obstructions. The engines bellowed. The bomber surged forward; its tail lifted, and in a minute it was in the air heading westwards.

Grinning all over his face, Ginger joined Algy in the cockpit. 'This,' he declared cheerfully, 'is something like it. We ought to be home in a couple of hours.'

Algy nodded, but without enthusiasm, for he was still a trifle worried. He was wondering what would happen when they came to the Finnish anti-aircraft batteries.

CHAPTER VIII

A Bitter Blow

Algy breathed a sigh of relief when they roared across the frontier, for now, he thought, if the worst came to the worst, they could at least land with reasonable promise of security. In his heart he was aware that he was taking a risk in remaining in the air, and that in order to be quite safe he ought to land, perhaps near an outlying homestead where they could lie snug until a relief party came for them. Yet every minute they remained in the air took them three miles nearer home, and the temptation to fly on and get as near to their base as possible was irresistible. He flew with one hand on the throttle, every nerve alert; not for a moment did he abandon his attentive scrutiny of the sky or the white landscape that flashed underneath.

Ahead lay a wide bank of indigo cloud, and he eyed it suspiciously, only too well aware of the perils that might lurk in it, for in war, unless he is driven into them by force of circumstances, a wise airman gives clouds a wide berth; they provide cover for prowling scouts. He was now within a hundred miles of home and his common sense warned him to take no chances, so he decided to run under the cloud and then land at the first reasonable landing-ground that he could find, preferably one near a house or village.

He left it just a minute too long. Where the Gladiator came from he did not see; but a wild yell broke from Ginger, and simultaneously a slim grey shape carrying Finnish markings seemed to materialize out of nothing. In a flash the Gladiator was on him, its guns rattling like demoniac castanets.

Algy flicked back the throttle and made for the ground; he would have done so in any case, but he spotted the number 13 painted on the Gladiator's nose, and he knew the man to whom it belonged – Eddie Hardwell, an American volunteer from their own aerodrome, and perhaps one of the most deadly fighter pilots on the front. He had already shot down five Russian bombers.

Ginger, too, saw the number, and threw up his hands in impotence, for although he had a gun he could not, of course, use it.

The Gladiator's first burst made a colander of the bomber's tail; it swept up and past in a beautiful climbing turn, and then came back, a spitting fury.

Ginger's presence of mind saved the situation. He knew that this time the Gladiator would rake them from prop-boss to tailskid, in which case only a miracle could preserve them. Breathless from suspense, he climbed out on a wing, scrambled on to the back of the great fuselage, and raised his hands in the air in an attitude of surrender.

The fighter pilot swerved, suspecting a trick, but as no gun was brought to bear on him he flew closer and, leaning out of his cockpit, jabbed his hand downwards in an unmistakable signal that the bomber was to land.

Algy did not need telling to go down; he was already going down as fast as safety permitted. He had half a dozen lakes to choose from, for from the centre to the southern end of Finland there is as much water as land. He chose the largest, and as soon as he saw that he was in a satisfactory position for landing he switched off his engines to prove to Hardwell that he was in earnest. A minute later the bomber was trundling over the ice.

The Gladiator circled it once or twice while the occupants, with the exception of Biggles, got out and stood with their hands up. After that the Gladiator made a pretty landing. Revolver in hand, the pilot climbed down and walked over to the party. Suddenly he stopped dead. He blinked, passed his hand over his eyes and looked again.

'Suff'rin' coyotes!' he cried. 'What's the big idea?'

'Easy with the gun, Eddie,' returned Algy. 'We're all here.'

The American put the revolver in his pocket and came on. 'You guys are sure aimin' ter spill yerselves over the landscape, barnstorming in that Rusky pantechnicon. What's the racket?'

'No racket, Eddie. We crashed our Blenheim the wrong side of the frontier, and borrowed this kite to get home in.'

'Okay – I get it.'

'What are you doing around here, anyway? It isn't your usual beat,' inquired Algy.

'I was looking for you,' replied Eddie surprisingly.

'Looking for us?' Algy was incredulous.

'Yeah. There's a guy arrived from England asking for you. We told him you hadn't come back, which seemed to upset him, but he asked one or two of us to have a look round to see if we could spot you. The guy he was most anxious to find seemed to be Bigglesworth. Where is he?'

'He's inside. He got knocked about a bit. What was the name of this fellow from England, did he say?'

'Sure – said his name was Raymond.'

Algy gasped. 'Great Scott! Look, Eddie, this is serious,' he said confidentially. 'We've been on a special mission – to get something for Raymond. He's one of the heads of British Intelligence. Well, we've got what we went for, and he ought to know about it right away. Will you do us a favour?'

'Sure.'

'Then fly back to Oskar, get hold of Raymond and tell him that we're here. At the same time you might ask somebody to fly out in a Blenheim and fetch us home.'

'Okay, buddy; I'll get right along.'

Eddie returned to his machine. It raced across the ice, swept into the air and nosed its way into the western sky. In a minute it was out of sight.

The others returned to the bomber. Ginger was now practically normal, but Biggles was still in a bad way, and seemed only semi-conscious. The others did what they could to make him comfortable. Some peasants, seeing the Finnish uniforms, went off and came back with a doctor. A woman brought a can of hot soup.

The doctor examined Biggles thoroughly, and finally announced that apart from the blow on the head he was suffering only from shock. At least, no bones were broken. The blow on the head had been a severe one, and had it not been for the fact that Biggles's skull was exceptionally hard, it would certainly have been fractured. He dressed the wound, bandaged it, and gave the patient a pick-me-up. The effect of this, followed by a bowl of soup, was instantly apparent, and Biggles's condition improved visibly. In two hours he was able to sit up and announce that, except for a splitting headache, he was all right.

It was at this moment that the roar of aircraft overhead announced the arrival of the relief party – Eddie's Gladiator followed by a Blenheim. Eddie, it transpired, had come back to show the Blenheim just where the Russian bomber had landed. In a few minutes Colonel Raymond could be seen walking over the ice. He nodded a greeting to Algy, but was too perturbed for conventional pleasantries. He went straight to Biggles.

'Are you all right?' he asked quickly.

Biggles smiled wanly. 'Not so bad,' he answered. 'Silly, wasn't it, giving myself a crack on the nut just as the show was practically over. It was a sticky business, too, largely as a result of running into our old friend von Stalhein.'

Colonel Raymond started. 'What! Is *he* here?'

'Too true he is.'

'Then those papers must be even more important than we at first supposed. Did you get them?'

'Of course – otherwise we shouldn't have come back.'

'Where are they?'

Biggles held out his hand to Algy. 'Give me my jacket, laddie, will you.'

Algy looked puzzled. A strange look came into his eyes. 'Your jacket – yes – of course. I – er – well, that is – Ginger, where did you put Biggles's jacket?'

Ginger looked round the cabin, then back at Algy. 'Jacket?' he echoed foolishly. 'Now you mention it, I don't remember seeing it.'

An awful look came over Biggles's face. He staggered to his feet, glaring at Algy. 'Did you come back here without my jacket?' He spoke slowly, in a curiously calm voice.

Algy had turned pale. 'I – I suppose we must have done,' he faltered.

Biggles sank back like a man whose legs will no longer support him.

'I remember now,' resumed Algy. 'You see, after the avalanche we were too concerned about getting you to the Blenheim to bother about your jacket. I remember looking for it, but it didn't seem to be about, so – well, we didn't bother any more about it.' In a few words he described what had happened. 'After all, I didn't know the papers were in your jacket pocket, although I suppose I might have guessed it,' he concluded.

'It was muggy, and we were carrying our jackets over our arms when the avalanche hit us,' Biggles told Colonel Raymond bitterly. 'I shouldn't have taken my jacket off, of course, but how the dickens was I to know that we were going to get smothered under a perishing landslide?'

The Colonel's face expressed disappointment, but he was too much of a soldier to waste time in useless recriminations. He spoke to Algy. 'You say you couldn't see the coat after the avalanche?'

'No, sir. Had it been there I could hardly have failed to see it.'

'Then it comes to this. The jacket must be still there, buried under the snow.'

'I don't think there's any doubt about that,' answered Biggles gloomily. Then, suddenly, he laughed. 'Forgive me,' he implored the Colonel, 'I can't help it. It's the daftest thing I ever did or ever heard of. If you only knew what we went through to get those confounded documents – and now we rush back home and leave them lying in the snow like a lot of waste paper. You must admit it has its funny side.'

Colonel Raymond looked doubtful.

'It's all right, Colonel – don't worry; I'll slip back and fetch them,' promised Biggles.

'Oh, no, you won't. I'll go,' declared Algy.

'Better let me go,' put in Ginger. 'I know exactly where Biggles was lying, and the jacket can't be far away.'

Biggles raised his hand. 'When you've all finished arguing maybe you'll remember who's in charge of this flight,' he said curtly. 'We've got to get the papers – there's no question about that. The thing, then, is to find the most expeditious way of getting them, and I've already decided that. For reasons which I needn't go into it would be unwise to go back in this machine. In any case, it would be foolish for all of us to go back in *any* machine. We four are the only people who know where the papers are, and if we were shot down or captured, the information would disappear with us. I'm going – alone. I'm going to borrow Eddie's Gladiator. With luck I ought to be back in a couple of hours, although that depends, of course, on how long it takes me to find the jacket. The rest of you will go home, get some food inside you and have a good night's rest. If I'm not back at Oskar by this time tomorrow you can reckon that something's gone wrong. Then one of you can have a go – but don't go together. Toss up for it – that's the fairest way. If number two fails to return, then number three goes. If he fails, then number four gets his chance. One of us ought to succeed. If we all go west, then we must be a pretty poor lot. That's the sane way of tackling it – don't you agree, Colonel?'

Colonel Raymond smiled lugubriously. 'Yes,' he said, 'I think it is; it's certainly wiser than putting all our eggs in one basket. One stands just as much chance as four going together, so by going one at a time we quadruple our chances. The only thing that worries me, Bigglesworth, is this: are you fit to fly with your head in that state?'

'While I'm conscious I can fly,' declared Biggles grimly.

'All right; if you say so then it's not for me to say no. When are you going?'

'Right away,' returned Biggles promptly. He turned to Eddie, who had been listening to the conversation. 'D'you mind flying back in the Blenheim with the others, so that I can have your machine?'

'Go right ahead,' agreed the American. 'But as I figger it, you guys have done enough for one day. What about letting me have a go at—'

'Hey, wait a minute, Eddie,' broke in Biggles. 'That's very kind of you and we all appreciate it, but this is our pigeon. Anyway, you don't know where the avalanche occurred, and it would take us a long time to describe the place even if we could, which I doubt.'

'Okay, buddy – but don't lose my kite if you can help it. You'd better have my leather coat, too.'

'I'll try to get the machine home in one piece,' promised Biggles.

'What are you going to take with you?' asked Algy.

'My gun and a couple of biscuits should be enough,' answered Biggles. 'I could do with a spade, in case I have to dig.'

'I should think one of these peasants would lend you a spade,' cut in the Colonel, indicating the men and women who had been slowly congregating on the ice to have a close look at the enemy bomber.

Inquiry soon produced the required implement, which Biggles stowed away in the Gladiator's fuselage. The others stood round while he got into his seat and fastened the safety belt. He waved his hand. 'See you later,' he called cheerfully.

The Gladiator roared across the ice like a blunt-nosed bullet, swept into the air and disappeared into the haze that hung in the eastern sky.

The others watched Biggles go with mixed feelings. They could not fail to see the wisdom of his plan, but none of them liked the idea of splitting up the party.

Colonel Raymond turned towards the Blenheim. 'I expect the Finns will take care of this Russian machine,' he said. 'Let's get back to Oskar. You all need a rest. Tonight you can tell me how you got hold of the papers.'

CHAPTER IX

'Grounded'

Biggles flew straight back to the lake on full throttle, for it was now mid-afternoon and he was anxious if possible to get back before dark. Naturally he kept a sharp lookout for hostile aircraft, but he had no fear of them, for alone in a highly manoeuvrable single-seater he felt well able to take care of himself whatever he might encounter in the air – with the possible exception of a formation of Messerschmitts, which, apart from being faster, were equipped with cannon. His head still ached and he felt tired, but the very urgency of his mission did much to allay his minor discomforts. As he flew he instinctively considered such contingencies as might possibly occur, in order that he might be prepared for them if they did. He saw one Russian bomber, far away to the south, near the north-eastern end of Lake Ladoga where fighting on the ground was in progress, but as he had a more pressing matter to attend to he ignored it, and soon afterwards it disappeared in an easterly direction.

There were many signs to indicate that the thaw had now properly set in; faces of rock were exposed where the snow had vanished, the trees showed darkly green, and the lakes, on which the thin coating of snow had disappeared, were as black as tar.

This, he thought, would be to his advantage, for it meant that the snow that formed the avalanche would be diminishing, with the result that it would be easier for him to find the missing jacket. With luck it might even now be exposed, and so save him the labour of digging.

Reaching the lake, he made a swift reconnaissance, flying low over the wrecked Blenheim and circling the banks at a height that could not fail to reveal enemy troops if they were there. The lake, like the rest, was black, its sullen surface broken only by the remains of the crashed aircraft. There was not a movement anywhere. Satisfied that all was well, and reckoning now that the recovery of the jacket was only a matter of minutes, he lost no time in landing.

He had a shock when his wheels touched, for he was unprepared for the cloud of spray that shot into the air. Indeed, his alarm was such that he nearly took off again; but as the machine settled down he felt the hard ice under his tyres, so he allowed the Gladiator to run on. From the splash of the water and the speed with which it pulled him up, he judged that there could not be less than four inches of water on the ice, and this astounded him, for he could not understand how the ice had melted so quickly. Then, as the Gladiator stopped, seeming in some miraculous way to stand poised on water, he thought the thing out, and presently realized that it was not so much the melting ice that had produced the water, as water running down the banks and flooding it. Naturally, as the snow thawed it would run downhill and so flood the lake.

This was a contingency for which he had certainly not been prepared, and it rather worried him, for there seemed to be a risk of the ice melting and becoming too thin to support the weight of the machine before he could recover the jacket and get off it. Seriously concerned, he taxied up to the lip of the avalanche, where he jumped out and splashed through the icy water to the bank.

The scene that met his eyes appalled him. He had expected something pretty bad, but not as bad as he actually found, for now that much of the snow had disappeared the debris that remained, earth, rock, and trees, looked far worse than it had done originally. The snow that remained was dirty slush, through which trickled rivulets of water. He began to wonder if the papers would be any use even if he found them, and he could only hope that the varnished fabric in which they were wrapped would preserve them.

There was no sign of the jacket, but this did not surprise him, although he had hoped that it would now be exposed; moreover, he perceived that his chance of finding it by digging was not very bright, to say the best of it, for he had no idea whether the jacket had caught in some obstruction at the top of the hill, or whether it lay buried under the mass of rubbish at the bottom. There was this about it, however: the slush was fast melting, and the faster it went the easier his task would be – or so he thought.

He fetched the spade from the Gladiator and set to work exploring the chaos, not concentrating on any one spot, but making a general survey, and digging only round trees in the branches of which the jacket might have been caught. Darkness closed in, the gloomy twilight of northern latitudes, and finally compelled him to desist – at least, it made the search so difficult that it seemed hardly worth while going on with it, for not only would the jacket be hard to see, but there was a chance that he might slip in the mush and do himself an injury. Several times, as the snow that supported him gave way, rocks went plunging down the slope.

He lit a cigarette and for a minute or two gazed at the wild scene ruefully. He looked at the Gladiator; it was well in near the bank and there seemed little chance of its being seen from above; still, he did not feel inclined to pass the night cramped up in the tiny cockpit. The big fuselage of the Blenheim looked more inviting, so he made his way to it, not without trepidation, for he found that walking over the invisible ice was disconcerting. However, he reached the machine and went inside, to find, as he expected, that the bottom of the fuselage was just high enough to be clear of the water. Nothing appeared to have been touched, so he made himself as comfortable as possible and prepared to wait for morning.

A more depressing spot would have been hard to find. Inside the cabin it was practically dark, and he dare not risk a light for fear it might be seen by a wandering enemy scout. All round lay the water, still, silent, black, and forbidding, with the sombre firs clustered like a frozen army on the sloping banks. His head ached. His feet were wet through, and consequently icy cold, and he had no means of drying them. There was this to be thankful for, though: everything inside the machine appeared to be exactly as it had been at the time of the crash, except that the food store had been depleted, presumably by the two Russian pilots. Still, there was more left than he was likely to require.

He was not in the mood for sleep. Indeed, he felt that it would be futile to try to sleep, so he sat in the seat under the centre gun-turret, occasionally smoking a cigarette, waiting for the dawn – a tedious way of passing a night at any time and in any place. Ultimately he must have dozed, for he was suddenly aware that the sky was turning grey. With a sigh of relief he stretched his cramped limbs, but then stiffened suddenly, staring aghast at the floor – or rather, the water that now covered it. Trial soon revealed the alarming fact that there was a good six inches of water in the cabin, and he realized instantly what this implied. The water over the whole lake had risen, and could not now be less than a foot deep.

For a moment he was staggered by the calamity, and wondered why he had not foreseen it. Cursing his stupidity, he prepared forthwith to evacuate his refuge and return to the Gladiator, which he could see standing just as he had left it, although it seemed to be lower in the water.

Cautiously he lowered himself on to the ice, and as he did so the full enormity of the disaster struck him for the first time, for the water came up to his knees. He did not mind that. What did upset him – to put it mildly – was the realization that he would not be able to get the Gladiator into the air, for with such a depth of water dragging at its wheels it would not be able to achieve flying speed. The water, he knew, must be getting deeper every minute.

He made his way to the bank, which was a lot nearer than the Gladiator, for the prospect of wading knee-deep across the middle of the lake was not inviting. As it was, he walked with his heart in his mouth, for his weight was sufficient to cause the fast-melting ice to rock, and send tiny ripples surging towards the shore. He fully expected it to collapse at any moment and let him through. However, he reached the bank without mishap and set off at a run, following the edge of the lake towards the scene of the avalanche.

It took him nearly half an hour to reach it, or what was left of it, for the snow had nearly all disappeared. And then the first thing he saw was his jacket, tangled up in a small branch about fifty yards from the shore. The branch was sinking under the sodden weight of the garment, and he realized with a further shock that had he not arrived at that moment the papers would have been irretrievably lost. Quickly he waded out, dragged the jacket off the branch, and carried it back to the shore. The packet was still in his breast pocket, intact. 'Phew, that was a close thing,' he muttered, as he pushed the precious documents into the pocket of the flying jacket that he had borrowed from Eddie – the pocket in which he had found the cigarettes and matches.

There was nothing now to detain him, so he splashed out to the Gladiator, dragged himself, dripping, into the cockpit, and started the engine. In his heart he knew that he would never get the machine off the water, for its wheels were submerged, but he felt that he must try. He tried in vain. Up and down the lake he roared, cutting the water into a white, swirling wake, and in his anxiety taking the most desperate chances of turning a somer-sault. He saw that if he persisted in his efforts this was what would happen, with disastrous results. He made one last attempt, opening the throttle until the tail cocked high in the air, and the airscrew flipped up great clouds of spray; but the drag against the wheels was too much, and the machine was no more able to get up flying speed than if it had been in deep snow or soft sand – both equally fatal to an aeroplane. Reluctantly he taxied back to the bank, running the machine high and dry, and there he was compelled to abandon it, for it could be of no further service to him. As far as he knew there was not a level stretch of ground for miles, and even if there had been he had no means of getting the machine to it.

He prepared to walk home. There was nothing else for it. And he had, in fact, covered a hundred yards when a thought occurred to him, a thought so disturbing that he shook his head in dismay. For he saw that he dare not leave the lake. He would have to remain there, for this reason. When, in a few hours, he failed to turn up at Oskar one of the others would set out to look for him, and on arriving at the lake, probably not realizing that it was now water instead of ice, would attempt to land on it, with a fatal result. From the air the motionless water would doubtless look like ice; he himself might well have made this same mistake had he not known what had happened. In the circumstances the only thing he could do was to remain where he was in order to warn Algy or Ginger, whichever of them came, that there could be no more landing on the lake. By the irony of fate, the very circumstance that had exposed his jacket now made it impossible for him to leave the place. There was this about it, he mused, as he hurried back to the Gladiator; whoever came would understand his plight and in some way attempt a rescue, although how this was to be achieved he could not imagine, for he knew of nowhere where an aircraft could land. A flying-boat or seaplane, or even an amphibian, would be able to get down on the water, but he had seen no such aircraft the whole time he had been in Finland, and did not even know if the Finns possessed such machines. There was certainly not one anywhere near Oskar.

Reaching the Gladiator, he took the signalling pistol from its pocket and, loading it with a red cartridge, prepared to wait. As a secondary precaution he gathered the driest twigs he could find. As soon as he heard the aircraft approaching he would light a fire; the pilot would see the smoke, and fly low over it to investigate before doing anything else. That would be the moment to fire the pistol. At the same time he could throw lumps of rock into the water, and the splash and the ripples would reveal it for what it was.

Having nothing more to do he climbed to the ridge above him, no great distance, from where he would be able to watch the western sky for the aircraft that should arrive some time during the afternoon.

He was relieved to see that the landscape was deserted, so there did not appear to be any immediate peril, for now that he again had the papers on his person he was filled with doubts and anxiety. Everywhere the snow was melting and water was gushing down to the lake; it was an ironical thought that, although the thaw was directly responsible for his present plight, had it not occurred he might never have found the papers. That, he ruminated, was always the way of things – the good luck balancing the bad.

Slowly the day wore on, and he looked forward to the time when he could discharge his obligation to whoever was on his way to the lake, so that he could start making his way home, for inactivity at any time is trying, but with wet feet it becomes irritating.

Then, suddenly, from a distance a sound reached his ears that brought him round with a start of alarm. It sounded like a shout or a laugh. At first he could see nobody; then, surprisingly, dangerously close, he saw a column of men marching over the brow of a hill that had previously hidden them from view. They were Russian soldiers, and they were making straight towards the lake.

CHAPTER X

Awkward Predicaments

Biggles sank down so that he could not be seen and stared at the Russians in something like dismay, for their presence put an entirely new complexion on the whole situation. It was obvious that they were making for the lake, and a number of sledges suggested that they were likely to stay for some time. He suspected – correctly, as it presently transpired – that it was a salvage party coming to collect the contents of the Blenheim, or such component parts as were worth saving.

Biggles tried to sort out the hundred and one thoughts that rushed into his mind, and the first was, what was he himself going to do? The Russians were unaware of his presence; there was no reason for them even to suspect that he might be there; and in the ordinary way he would have had no difficulty in keeping them in ignorance. But what about Algy, or whoever came to the lake? If he were not warned it was almost certain that he would try to land, in which case he would be drowned. Yet if he, Biggles, tried to warn him, he would instantly betray himself to the Russians. It was a difficult problem. Really, it came to this: by leaving Algy or Ginger to his fate, he could probably save the papers; conversely, he could save Algy and probably lose the papers. If only he could think of some way of getting the papers into the machine without the machine landing, that would get over the difficulty, but it was not easy to see how this was to be achieved. There appeared to be only one possible way, and not a very hopeful way at that; still, there was no alternative, so he decided to try it. Success would largely depend on the initiative of the pilot. If he perceived what was required of him, then the matter presented no great difficulty – but would he?

Biggles's plan was the employment of the device long used in the Royal Air Force by army cooperation machines for picking up messages from the ground, a system that for years was demonstrated to the public at the R.A.F. display at Hendon. It is comparatively simple. Two thin poles are fixed upright in the ground some twenty feet apart in the manner of goal-posts. Between them a cord is stretched, and to the cord is attached the message. The message in this case would, of course, be the papers. The machine swoops, picks up the line and the message, with a hook which it lowers for the purpose. Here, however, the machine would not be fitted with such a hook, but a clever pilot should have no difficulty in picking up a taut line on his undercarriage wheels. Biggles had no cord, but here again the difficulty was not insuperable. Under his sweater he had a shirt which, torn into strips and joined together, would serve the same purpose, and might even be better than a line since it would be easier to see.

Having reached his decision, Biggles went to work swiftly. First, he found two branches which, stripped of their twigs, would form the posts. There was some difficulty in fixing them in the ground, but he got over this by piling pieces of rock round them. He then took off his shirt and tore it into strips. It was still a bit short, so he made it up to the required length with the lining of his jacket. Having fastened the packet of papers to the centre, he stretched the line across the posts, not tying the ends, but holding them in place with light pieces of wood. Had he fixed the ends, the poles would, of course, be dragged up with the line, and perhaps damage the machine.

All this took some time, and he had barely finished when he heard the machine coming; and presently he made it out, a grey speck in the west, which quickly resolved itself into another Gladiator. The Russians were marching along the far side of the lake and had nearly reached the point nearest to the Blenheim; they had quickened their pace, having realized, apparently that owing to the water their task was going to be harder than they supposed.

With his signalling pistol in his hand, Biggles dashed down the hill to the bonfire, not caring much now whether the Russians saw him or not, for in any case they would see him when he fired the red light. Strangely enough, they were so intent on their task that they did not once glance in his direction, but went on with what they were doing. Two men, carrying a rope, waded out to the Blenheim, while the rest lined the other end of the rope as if with the intention of dragging the fuselage bodily to the shore. There were cries of alarm, however, when the Gladiator, carrying Finnish markings, suddenly swooped low over the trees and raced across the black water.

Biggles had already lighted his fire, and as there was no wind a column of smoke rose like a pillar into the air, making a signal so conspicuous that the pilot could hardly miss it. He now ran to the edge of the water, clear of the trees, and sent the blazing red flare across the nose of the Gladiator, which swerved to avoid it, and then turned sharply so that the pilot could see whence it came.

Biggles saw Ginger's face staring down at him; he just had time to heave a rock into the water and beckon frantically before the machine was compelled to zoom in order to avoid the trees.

Biggles knew that the warning signal had been seen, so he tore back up the hill. He fully expected that he would be shot at, but either the Russians were slow to comprehend what was happening or were too surprised to do anything, and he reached the trees without a shot being fired. When he broke clear of them again on the ridge the Gladiator was circling as if looking for him, and he knew that there was no longer any risk of the machine trying to land. Quite apart from his own signal, the Russians who had waded out to the wreck were now splashing back, and they, too, would have been seen.

From the ridge Biggles first looked down to see what the Russians were doing; as he expected, they were running along the bank in order to reach his side of the lake. Overhead the Gladiator was in a tight turn, whirling round and round, with Ginger staring down from a height of about a hundred feet.

Biggles jabbed his hand frantically at the goal-post arrangement, but Ginger continued to circle, clearly at a loss to know what to do – which in the circumstances was hardly to be wondered at. Biggles groaned as the machine turned away and tore up and down, apparently looking for some place to land – which again was natural enough. Presently it returned, with Ginger waving his arm in a manner that said clearly, 'I can't do anything.'

Biggles snatched up the jacket and waved it. He then ran to the line that supported the papers and shook it; the shirt being pale blue, he thought it ought to show up fairly well. Conversation was, of course, impossible, so the antics, which to a spectator would have appeared ludicrous, continued. In sheer desperation

Biggles spread the jacket wide open on the ground, pointed to it, and then, running to the line, made 'zooming' motions with his hands.

At last Ginger understood. He turned away, banked steeply, and then, cutting his engine, glided at little more than stalling speed towards the line. He missed it, but as he had come to within a few feet of the ground he saw clearly what was required of him and climbed up for another attempt.

Pale with anxiety, Biggles looked at the Russians and saw that they had reached the scene of the avalanche, up which they were scrambling. In ten minutes they would reach him. Shots began to smack against the rocks.

The Gladiator was now coming down again, gliding straight along the ridge, its wings wobbling slightly as they encountered the air currents so near the ground. Again Ginger missed. Worse, one of his wheels struck a post and knocked it over. Biggles, forcing himself to keep calm, put it up again, by which time the Gladiator had circled and was in position for the third attempt. Biggles saw that it must be the last, for the nearest Russians were not more than two hundred yards away. If Ginger failed this time, then he determined to grab the papers, dash down the hill, and throw them on the fire which was still burning. At all events this would prevent them from falling into the hands of the enemy.

This time Ginger did not miss. His wheels went under the line fairly in the middle, and as he zoomed up the line went with him, the ends flapping behind the axle.

Biggles gasped his relief, and then fell into a fever as Ginger began to turn, either to make sure that he had picked up the line or to see what Biggles was doing. Biggles pointed to the west in

a peremptory gesture. Ginger waved to show that he understood, and turning again, disappeared over the trees.

Now Biggles had no intention of being taken prisoner if he could avoid it; he took one look at the Russians, now within shouting distance, snatched up his jacket and fled. Yells rose into the air, but he did not stop, nor did he look back. A few shots whistled past him, and then he was under cover of the far side of the ridge, going down it like a mountain goat. He knew that in speed alone lay his only chance of getting away, and he thought he had a fair chance, for he was only lightly clad whereas his pursuers were encumbered with full marching kit – greatcoats, haversacks, rifles, bayonets, and bandoliers. Instinctively he headed for the west, keeping to the trees that hid him from those behind.

It was not easy going, for the ground was rough, scored deeply in places by storm water; there were also fallen trees and outcrops of rock to cope with. Sparing no effort, he raced on, deriving some comfort from the fact that the shouting was growing fainter, from which he judged that he was increasing his lead; but after a while, as his endurance began to give out, he steadied his pace to a jog-trot, and finally to a fast walk. Once he stopped for a moment to listen, but he could hear nothing.

He now began to give some thought to his position. He was a good thirty miles inside the Russian frontier, travelling over much the same route as the unfortunate professor had taken on his dying effort to get the papers to a safe place. Beyond the frontier the country was still wild, so he reckoned that he had not less than fifty miles to go before he could hope to find succour. The only food he had was two biscuits; whether these would be sufficient to keep him going he did not know; he thought they would, for he was in an optimistic mood following the relief of getting rid of the papers. 'It all depends on the weather,' he mused. 'If it holds fine it won't get dark enough to hinder me, so I ought to be able to cover twenty miles before daylight.' Glancing up at the darkening sky, he saw that it was clear of cloud; in fact, if anything, it was a little too clear, for the evening star was gleaming brightly, in a manner that hinted at a return of frosty conditions. There was already a nip in the air. However, he was warm enough while he kept going, and he had no intention of stopping while he was able to go on.

Another comforting thought was this. Assuming that Ginger would get back safely to Oskar, he would lose no time in telling the others what had happened, in which case they might do something about it, although what they would do was not easy to predict, for the ground was much too broken to permit the safe landing of an aircraft. Still, it was reassuring to know that they were aware of his plight. From a high escarpment which he was compelled to climb since it lay across his route, he looked back, but he could see nothing of the Russians, so he strode on, happy in the thought that every minute was taking him nearer home.

An hour passed, and another, but still he kept going, although by now he was beginning to feel the strain. His limbs ached, as did his wounded head, which, in the excitement, he had temporarily forgotten. His rests became more frequent, and he knew that he would soon have to find a haven where he could enjoy a really sustained halt; otherwise he would certainly exhaust himself.

He was now walking through a forest that covered the slope of a fairly steep range of hills. For the most part the soft carpet of pine needles made walking easy, but occasionally a great outcrop of rock would retard his progress, for there was not much light under the trees and he was compelled to pick his way carefully, knowing that a fall must have serious consequences. The country through which he was passing was as savage as the wildest part of Canada, and as uninhabited, and should he break a limb he would certainly die of starvation. He decided that he would explore the next rocks he came to for a cave, or some form of shelter, when he would make a bed of pine needles and have a good rest. There was something disconcerting about the idea of just lying down in the open.

He was not long coming to another mass of rock, and forthwith started to explore the base of it. A dark fissure invited, and he took a pace towards it, only to recoil hurriedly when he was greeted by a low growl. It gave him a nasty turn, for the very last thing in his mind was any thought of wild animals. He had even forgotten that they still existed in Russia.

He was reminded in no uncertain manner. Following the growl, a black mass slowly detached itself from the shadow of the rock and advanced menacingly towards him. It was a bear. It was a large bear, too, and in the dim light it looked even larger than it really was. All the same, it was a formidable beast, and Biggles backed hurriedly. The bear followed. Biggles went faster, whereupon the animal rose on its hind legs and, uttering the most ferocious growls, began to amble after him at a shuffling run.

Biggles bolted. True, he had a pistol in his pocket, but apart from a disinclination to fire a shot which in the still air would be heard for a great distance, and might betray his whereabouts to the Russians, he had more sense than to take on a beast notorious for its vitality with such a weapon at such close range. Finding his way barred by a wall of rock, he went up it with an alacrity that surprised him, to find that the top was more or less level. He looked down. The bear, still growling, made a half-hearted attempt to follow, and then squatted on its haunches, gazing up at him, its forepaws together in an attitude of supplication. Presently it was joined by another, with two cubs. They all sat down, growling softly in their throats, blinking up at the intruder.

'Sorry if I've disturbed the family,' muttered Biggles in a voice heavy with chagrin, for he was angry at being thus held up. He guessed that the thaw had awakened the bears from their winter sleep.

He was answered by more growls.

Biggles shook his head sadly. 'What does one do in a case like this?' he mused. He appeared to be in no immediate danger, but it was obvious that any attempt to leave his perch would be resented by the party underneath; and quite apart from other considerations, the futility of trying to kill outright two full-grown bears with a pistol was only too obvious. He lit a cigarette to think the matter over, hoping that the bears would return to their den and leave him free to go his own way. But evidently the creatures did not like the idea of a stranger being so near their home, for they made no move to depart. The cubs eyed him with frank curiosity, the older ones with hostility.

Biggles considered them moodily. 'Oh, go home,' he told them impatiently.

The bears growled.

Biggles puffed at his cigarette thoughtfully, wondering what madness had induced him to undertake such a crazy quest, a quest that now promised to go on for the duration of the war. A little breeze got up and stirred the pines to uneasy movement. From one of them something that had evidently been lodged on top drifted sluggishly to the ground. It was a strip of pale blue material, frayed at the ends.

Biggles stared at it wide-eyed with consternation. There was no mistaking it. It was a piece of his shirt. Clearly it had broken off his improvised line, but on consideration he felt that this did not necessarily imply that the whole line had come adrift from Ginger's machine. It was quite possible that the end of it had been torn off by the slipstream. After all, he reasoned, Ginger would have flown due west. He himself had run in the same direction, so if a piece of the shirt had come adrift – as it obviously had – it was not remarkable that he should find it. Still, it was an uncomfortable thought that the papers *might* be lying somewhere in the forest. There was nothing he could do about the piece of material, for the bears prevented him from fetching it – not that he was particularly anxious to have it, for there was nothing more it could tell him even if he held it in his hands. So he stayed where he was, stayed while the night wore on interminably to dawn, grey and depressing. The cubs, their interest in the stranger beginning to wane, grew restless, and presently their mother led them off to their lair.

The male parent seemed unable to make up his mind whether to go or to stay. Once or twice he shuffled towards the den, and then, as if loath to lose sight of the intruder, came back, rubbing his paws, and from time to time muttering threats deep in his throat. Finally, however, he made off, and sat just inside the entrance to the cave; Biggles could just see him sitting there, his little piggy eyes sparkling suspiciously. The cave was about forty yards from the rock on which Biggles was perched, and he felt that, provided he did not go near the den, he ought to be able to creep away without upsetting the Bruin family. In any case he would have to try, he decided, otherwise he might sit on the rock indefinitely, which he could not afford to do. So, moving very gently, he slithered to the rear of the rock and dropped quietly to the ground. For a minute he listened, but as he could hear nothing he began to move away. But, quiet as he had been, the bear had heard him, for happening to glance behind, he saw the animal pursuing him at a rolling gait that covered the ground at a surprising speed.

Biggles took to his heels and ran for his life, looking about desperately for a refuge. Trees there were in plenty, but knowing that any tree he could climb the bear would also be able to climb, he left them alone and sped on. For a hundred yards the chase continued, and then ended abruptly. Biggles's foot caught in one of the many roots that projected through the mat of fir needles. He made a desperate effort to save himself, but he was travelling too fast. He stumbled and fell headlong. Even as he fell he whipped the pistol out of his pocket, but in a flash the bear was on him, and with one sweep of a hairy paw knocked the weapon flying. He felt the animal's hot breath beat on his face. Helpless in its ferocious grip, he gave himself up for lost.

CHAPTER XI

Ginger Loses His Temper

Had Biggles, when he had sat upon the rock outside the bear's den, known what had happened to Ginger he would have been more upset than he was. He supposed him to be safe back home, and not for a moment did any other thought occur to him. This was far from the truth.

As a matter of detail, when he arrived over the lake Ginger saw the Russians before he saw Biggles's smoke-signal, for his eyes had gone instinctively to that part of the lake where the wrecked Blenheim lay, and this unexpected factor alone would have prevented him from landing even if it had been possible – unless, of course, he had seen Biggles waiting to be picked up. But this, as we know, was not the case. He saw Biggles's rock splash in the water, and this gave him a pretty shrewd idea of what had happened.

With the events of the next few minutes we are already acquainted, and it may be said that Ginger's relief when he saw the shirt-line on his undercarriage was no less than Biggles's. But his anxiety for Biggles was painful. He felt that he ought to do something, but what could he do? To land was manifestly impossible. It occurred to him to shoot up the Russians with his guns – not that this was likely to help Biggles very much; anyway, Biggles's peremptory signal to him to return home put all other schemes out of his head, and he set about complying with the order. At the back of his mind there was a wild idea of getting a Blenheim and bringing the others over to drop by parachute to Biggles's assistance.

By leaning out of his cockpit he could just see the end strip of shirt; it was flapping wildly in the violent slipstream, and it did not look very safe, for which reason he kept a watchful eye on it as he climbed for height. He had, of course, no means of getting the packet of papers into the cockpit.

He had covered about ten miles of his return journey, and was cruising along at six thousand feet, when to his horror he saw that the end of the line was now so far extended that it reached halfway along the fuselage, trailing back from his right-hand wheel – still far out of reach. This could only mean that the 'drag' on that side of the line was greater than on the other side, in which case it was only a question of time before the whole thing blew off altogether. Here again there was absolutely nothing he could do about it except fly on and hope for the best – that by some miracle the line and its precious burden would hang on at least until he was well inside Finland. But this was not to be. He was actually watching the length of shirt fluttering in the tearing wind when the whole line slipped off and went whirling away behind him.

Immediately a sort of madness came upon him. He felt that the papers were bewitched, possessed of some fantastic influence which made their recovery impossible. He began to hate the sight of them. He had already turned, and staring ahead, he saw the length of rag, sagging under the weight in the middle, sinking slowly earthward. Thrusting the joystick forward savagely, he went at it like a bull at a gate, knowing that he would have no difficulty in overtaking it before it reached the ground; but just what was going to happen when he did reach it he could not think. He had never attempted anything of the sort before; not in his wildest imaginings had he visualized a chase so utterly ridiculous.

The frayed strip of rag seemed to float towards him. At first he aimed his nose straight towards the middle of it, but then, terrified lest the flashing airscrew should hit the papers and cut them to shreds, he gave the joystick an extra push, and at the same time thrust an arm into the air, hoping the strip would catch on it; but this was expecting too much. He ducked instinctively as the crazy line, strung out across the sky, flashed over his head. It missed his hand by about a foot. Looking back to see what had happened to it, to his unspeakable joy he saw that it had caught across the fin, and was now streaming back on either side of his tail. Gulping with emotion, he steadied his pace and began to climb steadily back to his original altitude, all the time watching the streamer. He felt that the whole thing was becoming preposterous – ludicrous. 'I'm going crazy,' he told himself.

Indeed, the recovery of the elusive papers had assumed a similarity to one of those frightful nightmares when one goes on and on trying to do something, but all the time getting farther and farther away from success. It is hardly a matter for wonder that he began to ask himself if the absurd situation was really taking place or whether he was dreaming. If, at this juncture, he had encountered an enemy fighter, things would certainly have gone badly with him, for he did not even glance at the sky. Every nerve, every fibre of his body was concentrated on the papers.

He covered about five miles and then, for no apparent reason, the rags slipped off again, and went spinning away to the rear. He nearly screamed with rage, and as he tore after them he grated his teeth with fury. Never had he hated anything so wholeheartedly as he hated those papers, for which reason his antics, to a watcher, must have raised serious doubts as to his sanity.

In his first charge Ginger missed the papers altogether. In the second he caught the line with a wing-tip, causing the other end to whip round so that the packet actually hit him on the head before bouncing clear again into space. A sound that was something between a groan and a howl of mortification broke from his lips. 'I'm balmy!' he told himself pathetically. 'Balmy! The thing's got me down.'

His final effort was the most hair-raising, for by this time he was perilously near the ground and it was now or never; furthermore, his nose was tilted down at an alarming angle. The rag caught on one of the blades of his propeller, spun round for a moment like a crazy windmill, and then flew to pieces. The packet, detached, described a graceful arc, and then, bursting like a star-shell, shed the papers over the landscape; they floated slowly earthwards, like seagulls landing on smooth water.

Ginger dragged the joystick back just in time. His wheels brushed the tree-tops as he levelled out and then shot upward in a terrified zoom. Perspiration broke out on his forehead, and his expression was that of a man whom – as the Romans used to say – the gods had deprived of his wits. At that moment his rage was such that had he had the papers in his hand he would have torn them to shreds with his teeth. He loathed them and everything to do with them.

Swallowing hard, he cut his engine and began to glide back

towards the place where the papers had fallen, forcing himself to some semblance of normality. He knew that somehow he had got to recover the documents – but how? He could see them clearly, little white spots on the ground near a group of pines that stood alone at the end of a valley.

He began to fly round looking for a place to land. Actually, there was nowhere where a pilot in his right mind would have attempted to land, but in his present mood Ginger was not particular. Desperate, he was ready to take almost any chance – which, in fact, is what he did. Farther down the valley there was a brook. Beside it a strip of comparatively level ground offered possibilities. It was so narrow that a landing could be attempted in only one direction, but as there was no wind this really did not matter. He doubted if the strip were long enough for him to get down and run to a stand-still without colliding with something, for there were more trees at the far end; but he could at any rate try. Cutting his engine again, he began to go down, side-slipping first one way and then the other in order to lose height without an excess of forward speed.

'If I get down without busting something I shall be the world's greatest pilot,' he told himself grimly.

Judging by results he was not the world's greatest pilot, although his effort was a creditable one. The wheels touched, and the winter-browned grass, which turned out to be longer than he had thought, at once began to pull him up. For a moment a genuine hope surged through him that he had achieved the apparently impossible; but alas for his hopes! Hidden in the sere, tussocky grass were small outcrops of rock, and he saw them too late. He missed several by inches, and again he hoped that luck might favour him and all would be well. Slower and slower ran the Gladiator; and then, just at the last moment, his wheel struck a rock. There was a terrific bang as the tyre burst; the machine swerved wildly and then stopped.

With the slow deliberation of a martyr going to execution, Ginger got down, walked round the wing and looked at the wheel. The tyre had been torn clean off and the rim was buckled. That was the only damage the machine had suffered, but it was enough. He might as well have smashed the whole machine to pieces for all the chance he had of getting it off the ground again.

'Well, that's that,' he told himself in a curiously calm voice, for now that the worst had happened there was no need to worry about it.

In a mechanical sort of way he collected a rifle from the bottom of his cockpit, a weapon which he had brought against emergency; then, leaving the machine where it stood, he walked up the valley to recover the papers. He had no difficulty in finding them, for they lay close together, so he collected all he could see and folded them in a bundle, which he wrapped in the original piece of canvas. He was putting it in his pocket when a horrid thought struck him – the same thought that had occurred to Biggles the previous day. Up to this moment he had assumed that all he had to do now was walk home, but he realized suddenly that this would take some time; in the meanwhile, when he did not return, Algy would take off and fly to the lake, in which case, if he did not drown himself trying to land on the water, he would probably fall into the hands of the Russians.

Ginger sat down abruptly, sick with apprehension. He had not forgotten Biggles, but he could not see how he could help him, although if (as he hoped) he had escaped from the Russians, he should now be on his way home; indeed, he might be only a few miles away.

This put an entirely new idea into Ginger's head. If, in fact, Biggles was travelling westward, and he, Ginger, set off eastward, or even waited where he was, they ought soon to make contact, when they could go home together. Then yet another thought occurred to him. Somewhere near the lake must be Biggles's Gladiator. Assuming that it was intact, it ought to be possible to get one of the wheels and put it on his own machine, which would then be in a condition to fly home.

With all these conjectures racing through his mind, he found it hard to make a decision. The point he had to decide was this: should he push on alone and try to reach Finland, or would it be wiser to walk back over his track in the hope of meeting Biggles? In the end he decided on a compromise. He would walk back a few miles, find a high spot that commanded a view of the country, and there wait for Biggles. If when morning came Biggles was not in sight, he would make for the frontier. He did not overlook the possibility of colliding with a party of Russians, which made him disinclined to keep the papers on his person, so his first action was to find a hiding-place for them. If he failed to locate Biggles he would pick them up again on his way back. The group of trees at the end of the valley offered possibilities, and after hunting round for a little while he found a hole under the root of one of the trees; in it he placed the packet, and sealed the mouth of the hole with a large stone. This done, he set off towards the east, making his way up the side of a hill, from the top of which he hoped to get a good view of the country beyond.

Darkness, or comparative darkness, fell before he reached the top, so that he found his view somewhat restricted, but as far as he could make out he was surrounded by rugged, untamed country. A feeling of loneliness assailed him; it was, moreover, cold on the desolate hill-top; so, still heading eastward, he made his way thoughtfully down to the forest that clothed its flank. It was warmer under the trees, but darker, dark enough to make travel both tedious and dangerous, so he found a fairly snug corner under an overhanging rock and settled down to pass the night as well as he could.

For a long time he lay awake, not trying to sleep, but after a while nature triumphed and he passed from restless dozing to real sleep. And during his sleep he had an extraordinary dream – extraordinary both on account of its nature and vividness. He dreamed that Biggles called to him from some way off, telling him to go home. He remembered the words distinctly, for so real, so ringing had been the voice that it was hard to believe that it had occurred only in a dream. Biggles had cried out, 'Oh, go home.'

Not a little disturbed by this strange, not to say startling, occurrence, Ginger sat up and saw that the grey light of dawn was penetrating the tree-tops, flooding the forest with a wan, weird light. He felt refreshed after his rest and better able to tackle the situation, so he picked up the rifle and was about to move off when he heard a sound he little expected to hear in such a lonely place. It sounded like a man running – not only running, but running for his life. The swift patter of feet flying over the fir needles came swiftly towards him, and he crouched back against the rock trusting that he would not be seen, holding the rifle at the ready should it be required.

Suddenly the runner burst into sight round a buttress of rock, so close that he could have touched him. It was Biggles. Looking neither to left nor right, he tore on.

Ginger was so astounded, so shaken, that he could only stare, his jaw sagging foolishly. He barely had time to wonder what

Biggles was running away from when it appeared – a fur-clad fury in the form of a bear. Hardly knowing what he was doing, he raced after the brute, hesitating to shout in case he called the bear's attention to himself. And so for a moment or two the curious procession tore on through the trees, the bear chasing Biggles and Ginger chasing the bear, with perhaps a score of paces between them. Then, to Ginger's horror, Biggles stumbled and sprawled headlong. In a flash the bear was on him.

It is doubtful if Ginger could have stopped even had he wanted to. The impetus of his spurt carried him right up to the animal. Without hesitation he clapped the muzzle of the rifle to its ear and pulled the trigger. The report shattered the silence. The bear, with a grunt, collapsed, and then, toppling over sideways, went rolling down the hill, down and down, until it was finally brought to a stop by the trunk of a tree.

Ginger never forgot the expression on Biggles's face as he sat up. He was as white as a sheet. Utter incredulity struggled with profound relief.

'What in the name of all that's crazy are *you* doing here?' he gasped.

CHAPTER XII

Another Blow

Before Ginger could reply there came growls, fast approaching, from the direction of the rocks.

'Here, come on, let's get out of this,' muttered Biggles, and dashed off through the trees followed by Ginger.

Not until they had put some distance between them and the bear-infested rocks did Biggles pull up. He found a log and sat on it. His first question, asked in ones of biting sarcasm, was, 'Where are those thrice bedevilled papers?'

'They fell off. I tried to land to pick them up, and bust a wheel,' answered Ginger mournfully.

Biggles buried his face in his hands and groaned.

Ginger described in detail what had happened while Biggles listened in mute resignation.

'You know, kid,' murmured Biggles in a strained voice when Ginger had finished, 'this business is getting me dizzy. It's uncanny; it's crazy; it's one of those stories that goes on and on always coming back to the same place. Writers have made a big song about Jason and the Golden Fleece. Pah! Jason did nothing. He ought to have had a crack at this job. I don't often give way to despair, but by the anti-clockwise propeller of my sainted aunt,

330

I'm getting to the state when I could throw myself down and burst into tears – like a little girl who's lost her bag of sweets. Well, I suppose it's no use sitting here. Let's go and look for the papers – we shall probably find they've been eaten by a rabbit.'

'What do we do in that case – catch the rabbit?' grinned Ginger.

'Let's wait till we get there, then I'll tell you. Only one thing I ask you if you have any respect for my sanity. Don't, when we get there, tell me that you've forgotten which tree they're under. It only needs one more little thing to give me shrieking hysterics.'

'Oh, I reckon I can find the place all right,' returned Ginger moodily.

'By the way, why were you coming this way?' asked Biggles. 'Why didn't you make for home?'

'I aimed to find your Gladiator, get a wheel off it, put it on my own kite and fly back.'

Biggles started. 'Say, that's an idea! We might do that. In fact, I think we shall have to go to the lake anyway, because Algy will be over this afternoon, and we ought to let him know that we're all right.'

'The Russians may still be there.'

'We shall have to risk that. You know Algy; if we're not there to send him home he's likely to go on to Moscow. Well, we'd better make a start. I reckon it's a good twelve miles to the lake. If we keep going we ought to get there before Algy; then all we have to do is take a wheel off the Gladiator, come back and pick up the papers, put the wheel on your machine, and fly home – I hope.'

They set off, Ginger carrying the rifle, and after making a detour round the bear-den, bore due east. Both were beginning to feel the need for food, but they said nothing about it, knowing that none was available. They plodded on steadily, stopping only to reconnoitre the country from the tops of the hills that lay in their path. However, they saw no movement of any sort, and shortly after midday they reached the western edge of the lake.

They now proceeded with greater caution, moving quietly from tree to tree, often stopping to listen and scouting the ground thoroughly as they advanced. However, everything was silent, from which they judged that the Russians had departed; otherwise so large a number of men would, they felt, have given some sign of their presence. At last they reached a point from where they could see the fuselage of the Blenheim, now hauled up on the bank, apparently as the Russians had left it.

'Let's go across and have a forage round,' suggested Ginger.

'I doubt if we shall find any food; I expect the Russians will have stripped the machine of everything portable,' answered Biggles. 'However, we may as well go round that way.'

Still keeping sharp watch, they advanced, not a little relieved to find the lake deserted, for it simplified what, had the Russians been there, would have been a difficult task. At last they reached the Blenheim, only to find, as Biggles had predicted, that it had been stripped of everything of value. Even the instruments had been taken.

'Well, it was only to be expected,' observed Biggles. 'After all, the salvage was too valuable to be left lying here.'

There were some odd scraps of food, chiefly pieces of broken biscuit, lying on an empty case in the cabin, where the Russians had obviously made at least one meal out of the provisions the Blenheim had carried. These odd scraps the airmen ate with satisfaction.

'There seems nothing more to stay here for,' remarked Biggles when the last scrap had been consumed. 'Let's go across to the Gladiator. We'll get a wheel off, and then gather some twigs to light a fire as soon as Algy shows up.' They set off again, following the bank.

Now up to this point Biggles had not been concerned at not seeing the Gladiator, although he had several times looked in its direction, because he had forced it as far as possible under the trees. But as they drew nearer and he still could not see it, although he knew exactly where he had left it, a puzzled expression dawned on his face.

'That's a funny thing. We ought to be able to see it from here,' he said once as they hurried on.

'Just where did you leave it?'

'Under the trees – near the foot of the avalanche.'

'Perhaps it's behind that tangle of rubbish.'

'If it is then I didn't put it there,' declared Biggles.

'Maybe the Russians found it.'

'I don't think there's any doubt about that; they'd see it when they were chasing round after me – at the time when you were trying to pick up my shirt. But it didn't occur to me that, since they were unable to fly it off, they would do anything with it.'

'It was a valuable machine, and intact,' Ginger pointed out.

'Yes, I agree, but even so—'

When they reached the spot the matter was settled beyond all doubt or question. The Gladiator had gone; apparently it had been removed in sections, for round the place where it had stood the ground was trampled into mud by those who had done the work.

Ginger looked at Biggles. Biggles looked at Ginger. He smiled. 'We certainly ought to have looked at our horoscopes before we started on this jaunt,' he observed. 'Did you ever know things go so awkwardly? I must say the Russians were pretty smart shifting all this stuff; they can't have been gone very long.'

'Let's have a look.'

They scrambled up the ridge above the avalanche – the same ridge from where, so short a while before, they had looked down on the frozen lake at the end of their sledge-ride.

'There they go,' said Biggles, pointing, but taking care to keep below the skyline.

In the distance a large body of men, with several vehicles, was moving eastwards across an open plain. The vehicles were piled high, and even the men were heavily loaded.

'Yes, there they go – and there goes the Gladiator,' said Ginger bitterly.

'There is this about it,' resumed Biggles. 'They have at least left us in possession of the lake. I only hope von Stalhein has given up the search for the papers and gone back to Germany. I should feel easier with him out of the way.'

'H-m. I wonder what happened to him? It isn't like him to give up so easily.'

'He isn't here, anyway, and that's all that matters at the moment,' asserted Biggles. 'We'll stick around until Algy comes; we'll give him the O.K. and then make for home. Let's get a bit of a fire together and then sit down and rest while we have the chance. We've got a long walk in front of us.'

So they sat down and discussed the situation until they heard the sound for which they were waiting – the roar of an aeroplane coming from the west.

Biggles stared for a moment at the approaching aircraft. 'It's Algy,' he confirmed. 'At least, it's a Gladiator, and I don't know who else it could be. Let's light the fire.' Suiting the action to the words, he put a match to the little heap of twigs, which soon sent a coil of smoke curling upwards. This done, they stood on the ridge in as conspicuous a position as they could find.

Algy, in the Gladiator, was not long spotting them; the machine, after roaring low over the smoke, glided back with the pilot waving.

Biggles raised his arms with his 'thumbs up' (a signal that is universally understood to mean that all is well), and then pointed to the west. To emphasize this last point, that they were starting for home, he began to walk quickly in that direction.

But Algy did not go. He merely circled round, in much the same state of mind that Ginger had been in on the previous day. After a while he climbed higher, flew straight for a minute or two, and then glided back, very low. As he passed over the two white faces staring up at him his arm appeared over the side of the cockpit and a small object dropped like a stone.

Biggles ran and picked it up. It was Algy's cigarette case. Inside was a message written on a page torn from a pilot's notebook. He read it aloud.

'Understand you have both crashed. Am returning home to fetch food; light fire when I come back so I can see you. I will drop grub. If you reach possible landing field, wait, and make signal. I'll come down. If this is O.K. raise both arms in the air.'

Biggles looked up. The machine was still circling. He held up his arms. Instantly the machine dipped its wings to show that the signal was understood and then bore away to the west.

Biggles and Ginger watched it go. 'Well, that's something achieved anyway,' declared Biggles. 'He does at least know how we're fixed; and knowing the line we shall take, he ought to be able to keep in touch with us. If he can keep us going with food we shall take no harm – in fact, getting home ought to be a fairly easy matter. Say, what's that?' He spun round in alarm as the noise of the Gladiator's engine seemed suddenly to become intensified. Then his face grew pale. 'Look!' he gasped, pointing.

Ginger was already looking, and had seen what Biggles had seen. Three Messerschmitts were dropping out of the sky like bullets on to the tail of the cruising Gladiator.

'Good heavens! He hasn't even seen them,' said Biggles in a strangled voice.

Ginger said nothing. He could only stare.

But if Algy hadn't seen the Messerschmitts when Biggles had spoken, he very soon did so, as the behaviour of his machine proved. He was too old a war pilot to be caught napping. As the German machines came within range, the Gladiator swept up in a tight half roll, turned as it came out, and sent a stream of bullets at its nearest aggressor.

The three Messerschmitts broke formation instantly and the leader went into a glide as if his engine had been hit. Nor did he return to the combat. But the two that remained attacked the Gladiator with skill and ferocity, keeping one on each side, but as the lone machine gave neither of them a sitting shot the battle remained indecisive. In his heart Biggles knew that such an unequal combat could not continue long, for neither in performance nor armament is the Gladiator, which is now an old type, a match for the Messerschmitt. Further, Algy had to press on towards home, or try to, for his petrol supply was limited; but every time he tried to break away the Messerschmitts, being faster, were on him, and he had to resort to aerobatics to keep out of their fire, which he returned as often as occasion offered. Then, suddenly, the Gladiator seemed to draw away.

'They've had enough!' cried Ginger jubilantly. 'Good old Algy!'

Biggles shook his head. 'Forget it,' he said bitterly. 'They're keeping away from his fire, that's all. They'll keep out of range and get him by using their cannon. Algy won't be able to get close enough to do them any harm.'

The truth of this assumption was soon all too apparent. The Messerschmitts, keeping out of range of the Gladiator's machine-guns, opened fire with their cannon. As soon as Algy realized this he took the only possible course open to him – he put his machine in a turn and held it there, to prevent the Messerschmitts from getting their sights on him. Yet whenever opportunity offered he darted in and attacked. This was all right up to a point, but Algy's trouble was his limited fuel supply, which made it imperative that he should cross the frontier before it gave out. Twice he made a dash for home, but each time he was compelled to turn and face his opponents as they closed in on him.

The end of such a fight was inevitable. Several times shells appeared to burst right against the Gladiator, causing those on the ground to hold their breath in anguished suspense. All three machines had now drawn away to the west for a distance of two or three miles, so that it was not easy to follow the battle, Several times the machines appeared to pass very close to each other, and after one such encounter the Gladiator was seen to falter; then its nose went down and it dived in a straight line for the treetops. More than that Biggles and Ginger could not see, for rising ground and intervening trees obstructed the view. The two Messerschmitts circled for a minute or two over the place where the Gladiator had disappeared, and then made off to the south-east.

'He's down,' said Ginger in a dull voice.

'It was bound to end that way,' muttered Biggles harshly. He was as white as a sheet. 'Come on, let's find him,' he added, and broke into a run.

Panting, scrambling over obstacles that lay in their path, often stumbling and sometimes falling, they ran on, still hoping against hope that by some miracle Algy had escaped death, but in any case anxious to know the worst. Twilight closed in as they ran on.

'The crash must be somewhere about here,' declared Biggles at last, slowing down. 'It was over these trees that he went down.'

'Thank God the machine didn't take fire, anyway,' whispered Ginger fervently through dry lips. 'If it had we should have seen the glow. I—' He broke off and turned a startled face to Biggles as a shrill whistle pierced the trees. 'Why, that must be him!' he cried joyfully.

Biggles's face lighted up. 'He's got away with it after all,' he shouted excitedly. 'Hi! Algy! Where are you?'

'This way.'

They dashed in the direction of the voice, and presently they saw Algy coming towards them. He seemed a bit unsteady on his feet, and he was mopping blood from his chin, but he was grinning broadly.

'What have *you* got to laugh about?' demanded Biggles. 'You gave us the fright of our lives.'

'The bloke who can walk away from a crash has always got plenty to laugh about,' declared Algy.

'Are you hurt?'

'Nothing to speak of.'

'Well, you obviously haven't any bones broken, and that's the main thing,' said Biggles thankfully. 'What happened?'

'They got my engine, so I pancaked on the treetops, which, as you will notice, are pretty thick hereabouts. I've made harder landings on open ground.'

'Where's the crash?'

'Just over here.' Algy led the way to the spot where the Gladiator, its fabric badly torn, still hung balanced precariously on the pliable tops of the fir trees. Drops of oil, or petrol, or both, dripped steadily from the machine and splashed on the carpet of fir needles.

'I think I did myself most damage getting down the tree,' remarked Algy. 'That's how I damaged my chin – stubbed it on a dead branch.'

Biggles regarded the aircraft sympathetically. 'Well, she'll never fly again,' he announced.

'No, but she might help another machine to fly,' cried Ginger hopefully.

Biggles started. 'By jingo! You're right there,' he agreed enthusiastically. 'That's an idea. We'll shake her down and borrow one of her wheels.'

Algy stared in amazement. 'What's all this?' he demanded. 'What the dickens do you want a wheel for? Are you thinking of playing hoops on the way home?'

Biggles laughed, and briefly explained the situation.

'But surely you've got the papers?' burst out Algy.

'No. We had them and lost them again,' confessed Biggles. 'That is to say, I had them and passed them on to Ginger, and he's hidden them. He's tucked them into a hole under a tree somewhere.'

Algy screwed up his face in an expression of agony and leaned weakly against a tree. 'Suffering alligators!' he lamented. 'And after all this you *still* haven't got those blithering documents. I thought you'd got them in your pocket. I shall go off my rocker if this goes on much longer, and spend the rest of my days crawling about looking for scraps of paper.'

'I reckon we all shall,' agreed Biggles. 'However, Ginger knows where they are, and as far as we know there's nothing to stop us getting them, so that's something to be thankful for. Let's get this machine to the ground for a start, and pull one of her wheels off.'

Getting the machine to the ground, however, was by no means easy, and in the end Ginger had to climb up a tree and shake. 'Hush-a-bye baby on the tree top,' he crooned, as he swayed to and fro, allowing the machine to sink slowly through the branches.

'Don't play the fool,' cried Biggles. 'We don't want to have to carry you home – we've plenty on our hands without that. Look out, she's coming.'

With a rending of branches and a tearing of fabric, the machine crashed to the ground. After that it did not take long to knock out the pin and remove a wheel.

'That's grand,' declared Ginger. 'It was most thoughtful of you to drop in like this, Algy, old pal; otherwise we should have had to pad the hoof all the way home.'

Biggles picked up the wheel. 'You know where the papers are, so lead on,' he told Ginger. 'I shall feel happier when they're in my pocket.'

'How long have we been on this job?' inquired Algy as they set off through the trees.

'Oh, about four days,' returned Biggles.

'That's what I made it, but it seems more like four months.'

'Don't worry, we're on the road home now,' said Biggles reassuringly.

'I suppose you haven't overlooked the possibility of the two Messerschmitt pilots going home and reporting a crash hereabouts, in which case somebody might come over to look for it?'

'No, I haven't lost sight of that possibility,' answered Biggles, 'but I don't think we need worry about that. Even if somebody did come, by the time he reached here we should be miles away. He's welcome to what's left of the Gladiator.'

'We ought to have set fire to it,' said Ginger.

'I did think of it, but it seemed crazy to light a beacon which would have been seen for miles, and bring anybody who happened to be about straight to the spot.'

'You're dead right,' agreed Algy. 'The thing is to get home.'

As they topped the last rise that overlooked the valley wherein Ginger's Gladiator stood, and at the near end of which was the clump of trees where he had concealed the papers, Ginger started back with a cry of consternation. He looked at the others with an expression of agitation. 'Keep back,' he said tersely.

'What is it?' asked Biggles quickly, sensing that something was wrong.

'Take a look, but be careful not to show yourself,' replied Ginger in a voice that was tremulous in spite of his efforts to keep it calm.

The others knelt and peered over the ridge into the valley below. Dotted with tents and fires, around which numbers of men were moving or resting, the valley was now a camp. What the Russians were doing there, or why they had come there, none of them could at first imagine, but they were there, and that was all that really mattered.

Biggles sat down on a rock and threw the wheel aside. 'To think that I've carried this blessed thing all this way for nothing!' he exclaimed disgustedly.

'Yes, that certainly has torn it,' muttered Algy.

Biggles looked at Ginger. 'Couldn't you think of any other place to hide those papers than in the middle of a Russian camp?' he said with bitter sarcasm.

'And couldn't the Russians, with the whole blessed country to choose from, find a place to camp without choosing the spot where I hid the papers?' answered Ginger bitingly.

'Where did you leave the machine?'

'Up the far end of the valley.'

'That means that the Russians will have found it, so what they'll leave behind when they go – if they go – won't be worth picking up. There even seems to be a tent among the trees where you say you hid the papers. Somebody will only have to find them and take them away to finish a really good job of work. I suppose there was no possibility of anybody finding the papers, was there?'

Ginger looked dubious. 'Well, I couldn't do more than I did. I shoved them in a hole and put a stone on it. Anyway, I thought no one ever came here. I wasn't to know that a blinking army was going to take up residence on the spot. What are we going to do about it?'

'I suggest that we all go and jump into the nearest lake and put ourselves out of our misery,' suggested Algy gloomily. 'If anyone ever mentions papers to me again I'll—'

'Yes, I know,' interrupted Biggles. 'We all feel that way. Let's rest for a minute or two and get hold of ourselves. Maybe I can think of something.'

Biggles cupped his chin in his hands and gazed unseeingly across the dreary landscape that they had just traversed.

CHAPTER XIII

Von Stalhein Again

For some little while Biggles sat still, deep in thought, while the night slowly grew darker; but at last he drew a deep breath.

'Well,' he said evenly, 'we may as well face the facts. Let's get them in order. To start with, we can wash out all idea of flying home in Ginger's Gladiator. The camp extends right down the valley, so it would be foolish to suppose that it hasn't been discovered. Even if it were just as Ginger left it, we couldn't hope to get a wheel off it without being discovered, and even if we did we couldn't get it off the ground because the tents are in the way. That means we've got to walk home. Point number two is, we must try to get the papers. It's dark enough to prevent our uniforms being recognized, so it shouldn't be impossible to get to the tree, recover the papers, and get away without being spotted. It depends largely on what's happening in the trees. There's a tent pitched there, and as it stands apart from the others we may presume that it belongs to the commanding officer. If that is so, we shall have to keep an eye open for messengers and orderlies. Another point which should not be overlooked is this. I may be wrong, but I don't think these troops are concerned with us. It looks more like a concentration getting ready to attack the Finns in a new theatre of war. The Finns ought to know about it, and it's up to us to get the information to them. After all, until we started this scatterbrain business of chasing a bunch of papers our job was reconnaissance, to spot just such troop movements as this.' Biggles paused for a moment.

'This is my scheme,' he continued. 'I'm going down to get the papers, and since delay won't make the job any easier I'm going right now. Ginger will have to come with me to show me where they are, otherwise I might be groping round on my hands and knees for an hour or more. Algy, you'll stay here. If by any chance we fail to come back, abandon us and the papers; make your way back home as fast as you can, tell the Finns about these troops, and explain to Raymond what's happened. If after that you feel like snooping back here in the hope of finding out what has become of us, do so, but if you take my tip you'll keep the right side of the frontier. That's all. Are you ready Ginger?'

'Ay, ay, sir.'

Biggles took out his pistol, which he had recovered after the bear incident, and examined the mechanism to make sure that it was working properly. 'Leave your rifle here with Algy,' he told Ginger. 'It'll be in the way. In any case, he's more likely to need it than you are. Let's go.'

There was no great danger in approaching the camp, for although it was not absolutely dark, visibility was reduced to a short distance, and it was unlikely that they would be seen. Even if they were, it appeared probable that they would be mistaken for Russians, for a number of troops were wandering about outside the camp, apparently fetching wood for the fires.

With the coppice between them and the main camp, they went

slowly down the hill, keeping sharp watch for sentries. However, they saw none, and presently stood within a score of paces of the group of pines wherein Ginger had hidden the papers. It was now possible to see more clearly what was happening inside the coppice. A tent had been erected, and yellow light penetrating through the fabric proved fairly conclusively that it was occupied. Close to the tent a fire smouldered between two pieces of stone on which stood a soup-kettle.

'Now, which is the tree?' said Biggles quietly.

Ginger grimaced. 'Well, it's a bit difficult to explain,' he whispered. 'There are so many trees so much alike that whatever I said might refer to any one of them. Once in the trees I could go straight to the spot. You'd better let me go – or let me come with you.'

The wisdom of this was so apparent that Biggles did not dispute it. He looked round cautiously to make sure that nobody was near. 'Come on,' he said softly.

Like Indians, taking advantage of every scrap of cover, they made their way into the trees. Nobody saw them – or if they did they took no notice. Yet within hailing distance were several hundred enemy troops; the babble of their voices drowned all other sound. Biggles smiled grimly at this example of slack discipline, but he was not surprised, for he had heard something of Russian military methods from the Finns. On the face of it, the recovery of the papers appeared now to be only a matter of seconds.

Ginger went straight to the tree under which he had hidden them, then stopped abruptly with a quick intake of breath.

'What's wrong?' asked Biggles tersely.

'The stone I put over the hole has been moved.'

'Are you sure?'

'Certain. It was a big one. I should see it if it were here.'

'But who would move it, and for what? Are you positive this is the tree?'

Ginger pointed to the stones that flanked the cooking fire. 'It was one of those,' he said.

'Never mind, get the papers.'

Ginger dropped on his knees and thrust a hand into the hole. He turned a distraught face upwards. 'They've gone!'

'Impossible!'

'But I tell you they have.'

'You must be mistaken in the tree.'

'No. This was the one. The hole is here to prove it.'

'How far inside the hole did you put the papers?'

'Only just inside. I was afraid to push them too far in in case they slipped farther – too far for me to get my hand in.'

Biggles clicked his tongue. 'The fellow who moved the stone must have seen them and taken them out. He probably lit the fire with them, not realizing their importance. Few of these Russians can read.'

Ginger stood up and brushed the dirt off his hands. 'Well, that settles that,' he said. 'Unless you're going to walk into the camp looking for the cook, we might as well go home.'

Biggles stood still, staring down at the empty hole. And as he stood there a laugh burst from the tent. It seemed so close and so unexpected that he spun round, gun raised. Then he turned a startled face to Ginger. 'You heard that?'

'Yes.'

'Did it – remind you – of anyone?' Biggles's voice was hard.

'Yes.'

'Who?'

'Von Stalhein.'

'You're right. He's in that tent. But he doesn't often laugh. What's he got to laugh at?'

'I should say he's got the papers.'

Biggles nodded. 'That's about it. He's here with the Russian Commander. The cook found the papers and had the wit to take them to the tent. Von Stalhein would recognize them at once. No wonder he's laughing. That's twice he's tumbled on them by accident. He certainly has had all the luck this time. Have you got a knife on you?'

'Yes.' Ginger took it out – a small pen-knife – opened it and passed it to Biggles.

Biggles crept up to the back of the tent.

Ginger crouched back against a tree just behind him. 'Look out!' he hissed.

Biggles dropped flat. He was just in time. A Russian soldier appeared out of the gloom carrying a long butcher's knife in his hand; he went straight to the fire, thrust something into the pot and then sat down, presumably to wait for the stuff, whatever it was, to cook.

Biggles rose to his feet like a shadow and crept up behind the Russian. He was in no state to wait there for perhaps an hour until the dish was ready. At the last moment he trod on a twig. It snapped. The Russian turned sharply, saw Biggles, and with a startled exclamation half rose to his feet. But Biggles moved like a flash. His arm swung down. There was a thud as the butt of his pistol struck the Russian's head. With a grunt the man fell across his own fire. Biggles dragged him clear and returned to Ginger.

'I hate doing that sort of thing, it's so primitive,' he said disgustedly, 'but there was nothing else for it. We couldn't squat here for an hour or more while he was making a stew – or whatever he was doing. Stand fast.'

With the pen-knife now in his right hand Biggles went again to the tent. Very slowly he forced the point through the fabric, and then withdrew it. He put his eye to the slit. For a moment he stood motionless, then he returned again to Ginger.

'Von Stalhein is there with a Russian – he looks like a general. They've got a table between them and the papers are on it. Stay here.'

'What are you going to do?'

'Get the papers – what else? You look after things outside.'

Before Ginger could express the alarm he felt at this drastic step, Biggles had gone, and there was no longer anything furtive about his manner. He went straight to the flap that covered the entrance, threw it aside, and went in, his pistol held just in front of his right hip.

The two men looked up sharply at the intrusion. They half moved forward, but the tone of Biggles's voice halted them – or perhaps it was the expression on his face.

It was one of the few occasions when Biggles saw the German look really surprised. 'Keep still,' he rasped. To von Stalhein in particular he added, 'Tell your pal that one squeak from either of you will be the signal for me to start shooting – and keep your hands in sight. I'm in no mood for monkey business and you'd be wise to believe that.'

Grim-faced, his eyes as hard as ice, his lips pressed in a straight line, Biggles stepped forward, collected the papers with his left hand into a heap, and rolled them into a wad. 'I'll take care of these,' he said. Then he called Ginger.

Ginger appeared in the tent doorway looking somewhat shaken.

'*The two men looked up sharply at the intrusion*'

Biggles thrust the papers at him. 'Take these,' he said. 'Get going.'

Without a word Ginger put the papers in his pocket, turned about and disappeared.

'Now listen, von Stalhein,' said Biggles quietly, 'and listen carefully. A little while ago you accused me of outplaying my luck. You've had more than your share of luck in this party, but don't overdo it. I'm going outside now. You'll stay here. Try leaving this tent and you're apt to meet a slug coming the other way.' Biggles backed out.

The moment he was outside he went quickly round the tent loosening all the guy ropes except two; he then went to the fallen Russian, snatched up his knife, and slashed at the remaining cords. There was a startled cry from within, but before the occupants could get out the tent collapsed. Two jerking humps showed where von Stalhein and his companion were struggling to free themselves from the heavy canvas.

Biggles waited for no more. Turning, he dashed through the trees and raced up the hill to where he had left Algy. He found Ginger waiting; they were both in a state of agitation and uttered exclamations of relief when he appeared.

'Come on,' snapped Biggles, 'jump to it. We've got to get all the start we can before von Stalhein gets his mob on our heels, and that won't take very long. I'm going to make a dash for the frontier.' With that he set off at a steady run towards the west. There was no road, no path, not even a track, so all he could do was to set a course in a westerly direction.

'Here, you'd better have these papers,' said Ginger.

Biggles took them and put them in his pocket.

It was not long before a clamour in the camp told them that von

Stalhein was mustering all his forces for the pursuit, but this was only to be expected and it left Biggles unperturbed. Endurance would now decide who reached the frontier first, and in this respect he felt that, in spite of all their handicaps, they ought to be able to hold their own with the Russians. None of them wasted breath in conversation; with their elbows against their sides they ran on, up hill and down dale, through woods, splashing through swamps formed by the melting snow, round unclimbable masses of rock, and sometimes making detours to avoid lakes. Later they struck a lake that lay right across their path, forcing them to turn to the north seeking a way round it. That there was a way Biggles knew, for he had marked the lake from the air.

They were still running, following the bank, when, unexpectedly, they came to a lonely farmhouse, or the house of a charcoal burner – they didn't stop to inquire which. A dog rushed out at them, barking furiously. Biggles snatched up a clod and hurled it at the animal, whereupon it retired, growling furiously.

'This way!' he cried, for he had spotted something that pleased him more than a little. It was a boat, a rough, homemade dugout moored to a tree-stump. A man was shouting, but he took no notice. 'In you get,' he told the others, and they tumbled into the primitive craft. Biggles untied the painter and picked up the oars – such as they were. The boat surged out on the placid water, leaving its owner raging on the bank.

'This is better,' declared Algy. 'I always did prefer to do my travelling sitting down.'

'You can have a turn at the oars in a minute,' grunted Biggles. 'You won't find that so funny. They're as heavy as a couple of barge sweeps, and the boat feels as if it had a ton of bricks hanging on the bottom.'

'How far is it across the lake, d'you know?' asked Algy.

'You must have seen it from the air.'

'I've seen hundreds of lakes from the air – which one is this?'

'I think I know. I reckon it's about two to three miles across, which should help us a lot, assuming that there isn't another boat in which the Russians can follow us. They'll have to make a detour of seven or eight miles to get round to the far side.'

'By the time we get home we shall have employed pretty nearly all the methods of locomotion known to mankind,' grinned Ginger. 'If we could finish up on roller skates we ought to be able to claim the record. When should we get to the frontier?'

'If we can average three miles an hour, in about six hours,' replied Biggles. 'It can't be more than twenty miles – I fancy it's rather less.'

The boat surged on across the water making a wide ripple on its tranquil surface. The only sound was the soft splash of the oars and the gurgle of the wake.

Presently Algy looked down. 'Great Caesar!' he ejaculated. 'I thought my feet felt cold. Water's coming in somewhere.'

'I'm not surprised at that,' answered Biggles. 'The thing is only tacked together with bits of wire. Look for a bailer – there ought to be one.'

'I can't find one,' muttered Algy, a tinge of alarm creeping into his voice.

'Then use your hat.'

Algy was, in fact, still wearing his flying cap with the earflaps rolled up. 'My hat! That's a bit thick,' he grumbled. However, he took it off and started bailing out the water.

The boat forged on. In front and behind the land showed only as a dark grey shadow.

CHAPTER XIV

Slow Progress

In spite of Algy's efforts more and more water seeped into the boat. Ginger joined in the work of bailing, and although the ingress of water was very slight it still gained on them.

'Can't you pull a bit harder, Biggles?' pleaded Algy, staring at the still distant shore. 'The idea of swimming in this perishing water gives me the horrors.'

'You wouldn't swim very far in it,' returned Biggles. 'You'd be frozen. Here, take a turn at the oars.'

They changed places, and while Biggles bailed, Algy threw all his energy into the rowing. For a while the boat made better progress, but Algy soon used up all his strength, after which the pace became slower than ever. Biggles returned to the oars.

'Either we're going slower than I imagined or else the lake is wider than I thought,' he remarked. 'We don't seem to be getting anywhere.'

'It's probably a bit of both,' put in Ginger.

'We've got to get to the other side before daybreak, that's certain, or we shall be seen by everyone from one end of the lake to the other,' declared Biggles.

In spite of all they could do, and they worked feverishly, the water in the boat rose still higher, and it soon became clear that, far from reaching the bank before dawn, they would be lucky to reach it at all. Biggles's efforts at the oars became desperate, for as the boat filled it became more and more sluggish. At last grey light began to steal up from the eastern horizon, and it revealed something that they had not suspected. For some time past Biggles had noticed a piece of land which, from its more definite outline, appeared to be closer than the rest, and taking it to be a promontory, he had pulled towards it. But in the growing light he now saw that it was not a promontory but an island. It was quite small, embracing perhaps two acres of ground, covered for the most part with bulrushes, but with a clump of trees at one end. This suited them nearly as well, if only because it would enable them to rest and empty the water out of the boat, and so make a fresh start; and for this reason Biggles put his last ounce of strength into the task of reaching it before the boat sank under them.

It was touch and go. Ginger and Algy bailed for all they were worth and Biggles pulled as hard as he dared, but he had to be careful, for the gunwales were only a few inches above water. As the keel touched the shelving bottom Biggles called to the others to follow him, and stepping out, he hauled the boat up as far as he could. As soon as its safety was assured they tilted it on its side and so got rid of the water, after which it was an easy matter to pull it up high and dry.

'Phew!' gasped Biggles as he made the boat fast. 'That was a close thing. We'd better get under cover or we may be seen from the shore.'

Three wet, cold, and hungry airmen made their way to the stunted pines that crowded together at the far end of the islet.

'D'you know,' murmured Algy sadly, 'I remember the time when

I used to do this sort of thing for fun. We called it a picnic.'

'Don't grumble – we were lucky to get here,' Biggles pointed out. 'How far do you think we are from the shore?'

'Half a mile.'

'At least,' put in Ginger. 'Hadn't we better push on?'

'We might, but it would be dangerous,' answered Biggles. 'We don't know who's about, and it's light enough for anyone on the bank to see us. There's always a risk of an aircraft coming over, too, and then we should be in a mess. Our safest course would be to lie low here until it gets dark before we go on.'

'It's going to be a miserable business sitting here all day with nothing to eat.'

'It would be a still more miserable business sitting in a Russian prison waiting for a firing party to arrive,' said Biggles quietly. 'We've nothing to grumble about.'

From the shelter of the trees they surveyed the mainland, but they could see no movement of any sort apart from a few water-fowl. As the day wore on the sun broke through the clouds; there was little warmth in it, but it made the place look more cheerful, and their spirits rose accordingly. They smiled as they looked at each other. Dirty, unshaven, dishevelled, they were, as Biggles said, a pretty lot of scarecrows. Just before noon an aircraft could be heard, and shortly afterwards a Russian bomber went over, flying very low and steering an erratic course.

'What does he think he's doing?' asked Algy curiously.

'Looking for us, I should say,' replied Biggles laconically.

Presently another bomber appeared farther to the north, and yet another, a mere speck in the southern sky.

'If they are looking for us, how do they know about us so soon?' queried Algy.

'Ask me something easier. Perhaps the crowd von Stalhein was with had a portable wireless transmitter. Most modern armies carry radio equipment.'

'What could they do if they spotted us?'

'They might bomb us.'

'Or machine-gun us,' put in Ginger.

'And don't forget that the Russians specialize in parachute units,' reminded Biggles. 'We've already seen an example of that. There might be a score or more of men in each of those machines ready to jump on us the moment they saw us.'

'That's cheerful, I must say,' murmured Algy.

'Well, you asked for it.'

The bombers disappeared towards the west, and for a little while there was silence; then a hail floated over the water. It brought the castaways round with a rush, facing the direction from which it had come.

'Take a look at that,' whispered Algy hoarsely, pointing to the northern end of the distant shore.

The others looked, and saw a large body of Russian troops moving along the bank. Some followed the water's edge, others kept to the higher ground.

'Looks like the crowd von Stalhein was with,' remarked Biggles calmly. 'It's a pity they've got between us and home, but it couldn't be prevented.'

For a long time they lay and watched the soldiers, who, after marching for some distance down the bank, disappeared into the forest in a westerly direction.

'They're going to patrol the frontier, I guess,' said Algy.

'That's about it,' replied Biggles. 'No matter,' he added smiling, 'it will add zest to our homeward trek.'

'Zest, eh?' snorted Algy. 'Hullo, what's this coming? It must be one of the bombers coming back – but it doesn't look like one of those that went over.'

The aircraft was as yet a speck in the sky, flying fast and very low, but as it drew nearer Biggles sprang to his feet. 'By glory!' he cried, 'it's one of ours!'

'You mean a Finn?' Algy asked the question. 'No, British. Look, you can see the markings. It's a Short flying-boat.'

'But what on earth—'

'It's looking for us. Smyth must be flying it.'

'But where the dickens did he get it?'

'I should say there's only one answer to that question. Colonel Raymond, as soon as he realized that the ice had melted, must have radioed for one as the only means of getting us home. He would guess how we'd be stuck when the thaw came.'

The flying-boat roared over the lake about a mile to the south of the island, too far away for there to be any chance of the pilot seeing them. Algy wanted to light a fire, but Biggles forbade it.

'To start with,' he asserted, 'it's by no means sure that the pilot would see the smoke – he's already gone too far over. Secondly, if he did, there is no reason why he should suppose it was us. And thirdly, we've no guarantee that there are no Russians within sight of the lake. They'd spot the smoke, and they'd soon be over to investigate. We should look fools then, shouldn't we?'

The flying-boat roared straight on and soon disappeared in the eastern sky.

'But if it's looking for us why didn't the pilot circle round?' argued Algy.

'Obviously, because it didn't occur to him that we might be so near the frontier. After all, why should it? He's going on to the lake where we crashed the Blenheim. Naturally, that's where he'd expect to find us.'

'That's a bit thick,' muttered Ginger. 'Had we stayed where we were we should have been all right.'

'I agree it is maddening, but "ifs" don't count in this game,' was Biggles's last observation on the matter.

A little while later two Messerschmitts passed over the lake, some distance to the north, and shortly afterwards the Russian bombers came back.

'Great Scott! The sky is absolutely stiff with machines,' declared Algy.

'Yes, we've certainly stirred things up,' agreed Biggles smiling. He glanced at the sun, now far down in the west. Twilight was beginning to settle over the inhospitable land. 'We haven't much longer to wait,' he added. 'As soon as the sun goes down we'll be on our way.'

Nothing more was said. The aircraft disappeared like birds going home to roost. Silence returned. There was no sign of the Russians on the distant shore, and Biggles was justified in hoping that they had left the vicinity. The others were now impatient to be off, but Biggles was too wise to take unnecessary risks by making a premature start. He insisted on waiting until the sun sank behind the hills and darkness fell. As far as they could see there was no sign of human occupation, in all the surrounding landscape.

They launched the boat quietly and took their places. Biggles picked up the oars. He was beginning to feel weak from want of food, but he said nothing about it, and the boat, now free of water, made good progress. Nearing the land he began to proceed with more caution. 'Keep your eyes skinned,' he warned the others. 'If you see anything suspicious let me know; otherwise keep quiet.'

It was a tense moment as the boat crept up to the silent shore; they had no proof that they had not been seen, and for all they knew a score of Russian rifles might be waiting to receive them. Water was gurgling softly in the bottom of the boat, but none of them noticed it; they were too intent on what they were doing. At a distance of twenty yards Biggles turned the boat about and backed in, very slowly, ready to pull out again the instant danger threatened; but nothing happened, so he shipped the oars and allowed the little craft to glide on. It came to rest under the bank. For a minute they all sat still, nerves strained to catch the slightest sound. Then Biggles got out. 'I think it's all right,' he said softly.

Hardly had the words left his lips when voices could be heard approaching. Biggles crouched flat against the muddy bank; the others remained in the boat which Algy, by pulling on a root, drew right in flush with the bank.

How many men there were in the party that came along the lakeside they did not know; nor could they see who they were. They spoke – indeed they seemed to be talking excitedly; but what they said was unintelligible; presumably they were talking in Russian. They crashed along, making a good deal of noise. Once they stopped and were silent. It was a nasty moment for the fugitives. But then the conversation was resumed; brushwood crashed and the footsteps receded. Presently the sounds died away in the distance.

Biggles wiped his forehead. 'This is making an old man of me,' he breathed. 'For the love of Mike don't make a noise – it looks as if the whole blessed country is swarming with Russians. That must have been a patrol just gone past. All right, come on. Leave the boat under the bushes where it won't be seen in the morning.'

Presently the others joined him. For a little while they stood motionless, listening.

'Single file, but keep close together. Stop if I stop,' whispered Biggles.

In front of them the ground rose steeply. What lay beyond the ridge none of them knew, but their way lay in that direction so they took it unhesitatingly. Biggles led. Like Indians on the warpath they crept up the slope, stopping every few minutes to listen. At length, moving like shadows, they breasted the ridge and looked over. Beyond, the ground fell away into vague mysterious shadows, which they could only assume was rugged country similar to that which they had crossed on the far side of the lake. Straight in front, on the line they would have to take, a dim light could be observed. It did not move, and appeared to be shining from the window of a dwelling-house. Biggles glanced at the heavens, picked out a star to guide him on a straight course, and resumed the march.

For an hour they went on steadily, not relaxing their caution, and still halting frequently to listen. Once, in the distance, they heard a sound like someone chopping wood with an axe; on another occasion a wolf howled. That was all. Progress in these circumstances was, of course, slow, and Biggles reckoned that they had covered about a mile, which was not unsatisfactory, for they still had several hours of darkness before them, and he felt that if they could keep up the same pace dawn ought to see them very close to the frontier.

During one of the frequent halts Ginger whispered to Biggles, 'We didn't see the flying-boat come back.'

'It may be staying the night on the lake, or, what is more likely, it went home by a different route,' answered Biggles softly, and then went on again.

In front of them the light, which they now saw came from a window of a substantial house, glowed ever more strongly, and it became clear that if they held on their present course they would pass within a short distance of it. Biggles, however, had no intention of doing this, so he began to edge away to the right in order to miss it by a fairly wide margin. He knew that at such a lonely residence there would certainly be a dog, perhaps several, and not lap-dogs either, but the big husky wolfhound type of animal common in northern Europe – a house-dog in the true sense of the word. Apart from the risk of being attacked and perhaps badly bitten, if they passed too near the house the dog's keen ears would detect them, with the result that there would be a commotion. So he decided to steer clear.

Then, suddenly, the light went out.

'What does that mean?' whispered Algy.

'I should say it means that the people have gone to bed,' answered Biggles without stopping.

As they drew level with it, at a distance of some two hundred yards, it was possible to see the building silhouetted against the sky, for it stood on high ground, and it turned out to be a much larger establishment than they had at first supposed.

It put an idea into Ginger's head. He was hungry, very hungry; indeed, he was weak from hunger. In fact, they were all feeling the strain, although none would be the first to admit it. Biggles's wounded head was beginning to throb again; he was exhausted, and only forced himself to continue the march by sheer will-power.

'I wonder if we could get any food from that place?' whispered Ginger.

Biggles halted and then sat down. 'Let's rest for a minute,' he suggested.

Algy glanced at Ginger and made a grimace. It was unlike Biggles to suggest a rest, and he guessed the reason – that he was very near the end of his strength. He himself was feeling anything but bright, for he had been more badly bruised and shaken by his crash than he admitted. He sat down near Biggles.

Ginger looked at both of them. 'There was a time years ago, before you found me wandering about without visible means of subsistence, when I was pretty good at foraging for food,' he said quietly. 'We need food badly.'

'We can do without it,' said Biggles in a hard voice. 'We're too near the frontier to take risks.'

'That may be so, but we've got twenty miles to go after we cross before we can hope to find food, don't forget. Remember what happened to the professor – he was wandering about for days without finding help.'

'The weather conditions were worse then,' argued Biggles obstinately.

'Food, even a few raw potatoes, would put new life in us,' persisted Ginger.

'Listen, laddie,' said Biggles tersely. 'I know something about this escape business. In nine cases out of ten, when fellows are caught they slip up in the same way. They get desperate for food, and give themselves away trying to get it.'

'Well, I can understand that,' agreed Ginger.

'You're suggesting that we make the same blunder.'

'You think we can last three or four more days without food? It can hardly be less, and it might even be longer.'

Biggles hesitated. The truth of Ginger's argument was not to be denied, and he realized that none of them could go on much longer without food and not crack up. 'What d'you suggest?' he asked.

'I suggest that you two stay here while I have a scout round the house. I won't take any risks. A place that size ought to have outbuildings, and there should be food stored in them, if only field crops. Cut off as they are from anywhere, the people here would be certain to have enough food to last them through the winter.'

Biggles looked at Algy. 'What d'you think?'

'Well, I think it's a risk, but there's no doubt that we need food badly; in fact, if we don't soon get some there seems to be a serious risk of our passing out from sheer starvation. In any case, unless we get some food we shall be too weak to put up any sort of resistance if we happen to run into a bunch of Russians. We should be more in the mood to give ourselves up – if only for the sake of getting something to eat.'

'The danger is dogs.'

Algy shrugged his shoulders. 'Of course – but there it is. It's up to you to decide if the risk is worth while.'

Biggles turned to Ginger. 'All right,' he said slowly. 'Have a shot at it, laddie, but for the love of Mike be careful. If a dog starts barking come straight back here and we'll push on.'

Ginger smiled. 'I'll be careful,' he said, and disappeared into the gloom.

CHAPTER XV

A Staggering Discovery

Never had Ginger approached a project with such excessive caution as he now employed; the need for it could hardly be exaggerated, for it seemed highly probable that on his success or failure the lives of all of them depended. When he had promised to take no risks he had meant it, but he knew that the whole enterprise was a risk, a ghastly risk. Still, it was a risk that had to be taken if they were to avoid the greater risk of dying of starvation, or sinking into such a low condition that they would be unequal to the task before them. No Indian on a scalp-hunting expedition, no felon engaged in a nefarious operation, ever approached an object with greater stealth than he observed in his advance upon the lonely dwelling that loomed like a great black shadow in front of him. Without giving the matter any serious thought, he had assumed it to be the residence of the local landowner, a prosperous farmer, or, as we might say, the lord of the manor, and it was not until he drew close that he realized that it was something even larger. It could nearly lay claim to the title of castle. In the days before the revolution it must have been the country seat of some noble family.

The building stood in the centre of what had once doubtless

been extensive gardens, the whole surrounded by trees, many of them ornamental evergreens that had obviously been imported; but the gardens were now a jungle, and a tangle of briars and bushes, brown and sere from the icy grip of winter, had advanced almost to the walls. This undergrowth offered a certain amount of cover, an advantage that was largely offset, however, by its liability to snap when trodden on.

The building itself was in a bad state of repair, and presented a woebegone appearance. All this Ginger noted as he stood on the inner edge of the encircling belt of trees. Motionless as a statue, he surveyed the structure section by section, window by window, making a picture in his mind of the most salient features, and noting particularly such windows on the ground floor as might lend themselves to his purpose. And as he stood there a chain rattled, a harsh metallic jangle, somewhere at the rear of the house. His eyes flashed to the spot and he perceived a group of outbuildings. The sound furnished him with a useful piece of information; it told him that a dog was there; it also told him that the dog was chained up. He could judge pretty well where it was, so he made a mental note to avoid the spot. It was for this reason that he first turned his attention to the front of the house.

Slowly, exploring the ground with his feet for twigs before putting his weight down, he went on, and presently stood close against the wall. All was silent, as, indeed, was only to be expected, for the hour was late, and it was reasonable to suppose that the occupants of the house were in bed. Had it not been for the lighted window, which proved conclusively that somebody was inside, he would have thought that the house was deserted. Unhurriedly, eyes and ears alert, keeping close against the wall, he moved across the front of the house, trying the front door – a massive portal – on the way. It was locked. He went on to the far corner, and then stopped suddenly, his heart beating faster. Faintly to his ears came the sound of voices, and peering round the corner he made a discovery for which he was not prepared. The light that they had seen as they approached the house must, he now realized, have been in one of the front windows, for the house faced in that direction; and when this light had been extinguished he had supposed, not unnaturally, that the household had retired. But from the corner where he now stood he was able to look along the side of the house farthest from their line of approach – that is to say, farthest from the place where the others were now waiting for him; and to his surprise he perceived that someone was still about, and, moreover, on the ground floor. A shaft of pale orange light issued from a window and fell across the tangle of shrubs outside. Advancing a few more paces, he saw that the window was curtained; the curtains had been drawn, but as they did not meet in the middle a narrow space was left uncovered, and it was from this that the light proceeded.

This at once altered Ginger's plan. He had intended to explore the ground floor for the kitchen, and with everyone upstairs he had imagined that this would be no difficult matter; but if people were still downstairs it would be extremely risky. The kitchen of course would be at the back of the house, but he had avoided making an entry from the rear on account of the dog. Now he hardly knew what to do for the best, but after giving the matter some thought he decided first of all to take a peep through the window in order to see who it was with whom he had to deal, and with this object in view he moved on down the wall towards it.

As he drew nearer to it the sound of voices increased in volume.

Then words reached his ears that stunned him into immobility, for they were spoken in English. This, he told himself, was past belief. He expected the conversation would be in Russian. He would not have been surprised had it been in German, or Finnish, or any Scandinavian tongue; but English! Who in the name of heaven could be talking English in such a place? Surely he had been mistaken – his ears had deceived him; but then he distinctly heard a man say, 'Very good.' And at the sound of that voice his lips turned dry. He crept on and looked through the window.

In his life Ginger had had many shocks, but never one such as he now received. His nerves all seemed to tighten like elastic, causing the sensation known as pins and needles to prickle his skin. For this is what he saw.

There were five people in the room, seated round a large table on which still rested the remains of a substantial meal. Three of the men were Russian officers; another was von Stalhein, although Ginger was not particularly surprised at that, for the German had doubtless been with the Russians who had circumnavigated the lake while they had been rowing across it, and had later gone on towards the frontier. This house had apparently been his objective. It was the presence of the fifth man that numbed Ginger with shock. He knew him only slightly, but he had seen him many times; in fact the man had more than once endeavoured to engage him in conversation, but he was a type that repelled rather than attracted him, and the acquaintanceship had never ripened. He was, in fact, a member of the International Squadron fighting for Finland, a Swede named Olsen who had lived most of his life in Canada – at least, that was what he had said; and this was to some extent borne out by the fact that the only language he spoke was English, and that with a Western accent. Presumably it was for this reason that English was the language employed in the present conversation with von Stalhein – with whom, incidentally, he seemed quite at home.

Ginger listened horrified as he heard the alleged Swede describing in detail the Finnish plans for defence, leaving no doubt whatever that his real business in the Finnish Air Force was that of a spy, acting on behalf of either Germany or Russia. He spoke volubly, while von Stalhein, nodding occasionally, made notes on a sheet of paper. The Russians seemed content to listen. Ginger could hear everything that passed.

When Olsen had finished von Stalhein took several envelopes from his pocket. 'Take these with you when you go back,' he said. 'Deliver them in the usual way. I should like them delivered tomorrow.'

The spy smiled as he took the letters. 'No difficulty about that,' he said.

'You came over in the usual way I suppose?' queried von Stalhein.

'Sure. I'd rather fly than walk. I always leave my crate at the same place – the valley just east of the frontier – and then walk across. By the way, what's going on? The frontier is stiff with troops. If I hadn't known the password I should have been in a mess.'

Von Stalhein sipped his wine, fitted a cigarette into a long holder, and lit it before he replied. 'I've had some trouble,' he said curtly, 'with a fellow named Bigglesworth – you may know him. He's in the International Squadron.'

Olsen started. 'Sure I know the skunk. Because he shot down a few of your crack fliers in the last war he acts like he's running the show.'

Von Stalhein smiled faintly. 'He's a British agent.'

'*What!*' Olsen half rose to his feet. 'Him and them three pals of his always fly as a team. Now you mention it, I ain't seen them for the last day or two. What have they been up to?'

'I wish I had a team like it,' confessed von Stalhein frankly. 'They've been over here and they've got away with some important documents. I have good reason to believe that they're still in Russia, trying to work their way home on foot, having crashed their machines. Hence the troops on the frontier. I'm hoping to catch them when they try to cross.'

Olsen emptied his wineglass. 'Say, what d'you know about that!' he exclaimed. 'Why didn't you grab him before?'

Again a suspicion of a smile crossed the German's austere face. 'Have you ever tried to grab a live eel with your bare hands?'

'Aw shucks! He can't be that clever.'

Von Stalhein leaned forward in his chair. 'Would you like to have a shot at catching him?'

Olsen winked. 'Why not? What's it worth if I do it?'

The German's manner became crisp. 'I'll tell you what I'll do,' he said. 'As I told you, I'm trying to catch Bigglesworth and his friends myself, and it's probable that I shall; but should he slip through my fingers – and he's got a trick of doing that – he'll make straight for Oskar to hand the papers over to his employers. Bring those papers back to me and I'll pay you a thousand pounds. I'll pay you another thousand for Bigglesworth, dead or alive, and five hundred for each of the others.'

The spy grinned delightedly. 'That sure sounds like easy money to me,' he declared. 'Next time I come over they'll be with me – dead or alive. Come to think of it, though, they'd make rather a heavy load for a single-seater. Would the heads be enough?'

Von Stalhein frowned. He looked disgusted. 'Olsen, I fancy you are living about four centuries too late.'

'War's war, ain't it? I ain't squeamish.'

'So I observe,' returned von Stalhein drily. 'Very well, we'll dispense with the bodies. I'll pay for the heads. But be careful you aren't suspected.'

'Me? Suspected? Why, the Finns reckon I'm as good a Swede as ever came out of Sweden.'

Von Stalhein made some notes and handed the paper to one of the Russian officers, with whom he conversed for some minutes in his own language. Then they all finished their wine, got up, pushed their chairs back, and filed out of the room. One of the Russians was the last to leave. He closed the door behind him.

Ginger had had time to recover from his first shock, but as a result of the conversation he had just heard he still felt a trifle dazed. Dazed is perhaps not quite the right word. His brain was racing so fast that he wanted to do several things at once. He wanted to rush into the house and shoot the treacherous spy before he could do further damage; he wanted to rush back to Biggles and acquaint him with the horrid facts; he wanted to tear back to Finland and warn the people there that their plans were known to the enemy; and he wanted to fulfil the original object of his expedition, which was to get some food, plenty of which remained on the table within a few feet of him. The temptation to get some of it was too great to be resisted; he felt that it would make such a difference to them if he could get even a little food, and he made up his mind to try.

With this object in view he attempted to open the window. It was fastened. For a moment he was dismayed, but only for a moment. The panes were small and lead-framed, and the lead being of great age, it had weathered to the thinness of paper. He found a loose pane near the inside catch and prized away the lead until he could remove the glass intact. Having disposed of this, he put a hand through the aperture thus made and slipped the catch. In a minute the window was open and he was inside. Leaving the window open and the curtains drawn ready for a quick evacuation should it become necessary, he went straight to the table, for nothing else interested him. Half a roast chicken looked tempting, as did the carcass of a goose. He gathered together several large pieces of bread, and was making ready to depart when he saw a dish in which still remained a number of baked potatoes. The question was, how to carry them? A napkin answered it. He opened it out flat, and was about to empty the dish into it when a sound from the direction of the window brought him round with a jerk. A hairy face above a Russian uniform grinned at him. A bandolier crossed the man's chest, and a rifle hung by its sling from his shoulder. Obviously he was a sentry. To Ginger's consternation, he crawled clumsily over the windowsill and stood just inside, still grinning amiably and pointing at the table.

At first Ginger could not get the hang of such peculiar behaviour. Then, suddenly, he understood. The fellow took him for one of the servants, and supposed that he was clearing the table. The question was how to get rid of him. On the table stood several long-necked wine bottles. Ginger tried two or three in quick succession, but they were all empty; then he found one that was still half full. He held it up to the man, at the same time raising his eyebrows questioningly above a rather nervous smile.

The man said something – what it was Ginger had no idea – and held out his hand for the bottle. Ginger crossed the room swiftly and gave it to him, and then tapped him on the shoulder with a gesture which he hoped would convey the impression that

*'He stood just inside, still grinning amiably and
pointing at the table'*

his instant departure would be appreciated. The man understood. He stuffed the bottle inside the breast of his greatcoat, said something, and went off – still grinning.

Ginger's relief was such that he nearly collapsed, but he had no intention of leaving the food. He crept back to the table and gathered it up. The bread he stuffed into his pockets. Nor did he leave the potatoes. He emptied the lot into the napkin, caught up the corners, and with the skeleton of the goose under his arm, the chicken in one hand and the napkin in the other, he returned swiftly to the window. He was only just in time, for footsteps could be heard approaching.

He was outside and in the act of closing the window when the door opened and a servant came into the room. However, the man appeared to see nothing unusual, for he started collecting the dishes. Ginger paid no further attention to the window. Picking up his loot, he took one quick look round for the sentry, and not seeing him, stepped stealthily into the cover of the trees, like a fox departing from a plundered farmyard.

Now that he had reached comparative safety his reaction following the last few hectic minutes was so intense that his legs nearly gave way under him, and he had to rest for a moment to recover his composure; then, happy in the knowledge of the success of his mission, and the tremendous information he had to impart, he sped on. He fairly staggered to the place where the others were waiting.

'Sweet spirit of Icarus! What's he got?' gasped Algy.

Ginger thrust the goose carcass into his hands. 'Hold that,' he panted. He held out the chicken to Biggles. 'Lay hold,' he implored him. 'Let's get away from here. I've got news for you that will make you jump.'

'You've got some grub, and that's enough to make me break any jumping record, without anything else,' declared Algy emphatically.

'Don't you believe it,' said Ginger in a voice vibrant with emotion.

'What is it – is von Stalhein in there?' guessed Biggles shrewdly.

'You bet your life he is, and that's not half of it,' panted Ginger. 'Here we are, this will do.' He led the way into a small gully between some rocks. 'Now get an earful of this,' he continued tersely, and forthwith in as few words as possible related what had transpired at the house.

'Good work, laddie,' said Biggles when he had finished. 'It seems that von Stalhein is a bigger skunk than I thought, to put a price on our heads; but as for that foul traitor, Olsen, hanging would be too good for him. There are moments when I regret that torture has gone out of fashion, and this is one of them. Once or twice we've had to sail near the wind in this spy business ourselves, but we don't stoop to murder. Nor do we line our pockets with dirty money. We'd better not stop to eat here. We've got to get Olsen. He knows the password, and if for no other reason we've got to intercept him. If we know what it is—'

'You don't suppose he'll tell you, do you ?' broke in Algy.

'Won't he!' The others had never heard Biggles's voice so hard. 'By the time I've finished with that skunk he'll be ready to tell anything, I'll warrant,' he continued. 'There must be a path running westwards from the house, leading to the frontier – unless Olsen walked across country, which doesn't seem feasible. There's bound to be a drive of some sort leading to a house of this size, and since it isn't on this side it must be on the other. If we strike straight across the rear of the building we should come to it. Let's go.'

Biggles set off, still carrying the chicken; the others followed close behind. Over rocks, through bushes, between trees where it was nearly pitch dark, and even across a watercourse, they pushed on until at length, as Biggles had surmised, they struck a track which clearly led to the house. They came upon it at a distance of rather less than a quarter of a mile from the building itself, and Biggles reconnoitred in both directions before he stepped on to it. 'All clear,' he said. 'This must be it. The track should run straight from the house to the frontier, and unless I'm mistaken Olsen will walk down it on his way back. We'll wait for him here; we shan't find anything better suited to our purpose.'

At this point the track, which had a terrible surface but was wide enough for a wheeled vehicle, ran through a shallow gully, with tall trees on either side.

'We can wait, listen, and eat at the same time,' said Biggles, mustering the food.

Algy clicked his tongue when he saw the bread and potatoes. 'This exceeds my wildest hopes,' he announced in a voice heavy with satisfaction.

'I should think it jolly well does,' returned Biggles. 'I thought we should do well if we got a few raw potatoes, but roast chicken, roast goose, potatoes, and bread – Ginger, you're a wizard.' With scant ceremony Biggles divided the food, tearing the remains of the two birds apart with his hands. Real hunger makes short work of conventional politeness. 'No more talking,' warned Biggles. 'We've got to listen. Eat fast in case he comes.'

'You're telling me,' grunted Algy, tearing at a goose leg with his teeth.

For ten minutes nothing could be heard but the steady munch of jaws, and by the end of that time every scrap of Ginger's haul, with the exception of a few bones, had disappeared.

Algy wiped his fingers on his trousers. 'By James! That's better,' he breathed.

The others smiled but said nothing. They found comfortable positions just inside the trees. Biggles took out his gun, and Algy, with the rifle across his knees, sat down to wait.

CHAPTER XVI

A Desperate Flight

For the remainder of the night the comrades kept their lonely vigil, and it was not until the eastern sky was turning grey that they heard someone coming from the direction of the house. A stone rattled; footsteps crunched on the rough gravel, and presently Olsen could be seen, a leather flying jacket over his arm and cap and goggles swinging in his left hand, coming down the track.

'Good, he's alone,' whispered Biggles. 'Don't move until I give the word.'

Not until the spy drew level did Biggles stir. Then he got up, and with his hands in his pockets strolled out on to the track.

'Hullo, Olsen,' he said casually; 'what are you doing here?'

Olsen sprang back as if he had been struck. For a moment he looked confused, but then, with what must have been a tremendous effort, he recovered himself. But his face had turned pale, and his eyes flashed round as if seeking to ascertain whether Biggles was alone.

'Why – I – er – I had a forced landing,' he stammered.

'In that case, aren't you taking a bit of a risk, strolling about like this in a hostile country as if the place belonged to you?'

'What are you doing here, if it comes to that?' asked Olsen belligerently.

'Oh, I had a bit of business to transact.'

'Is that so?'

'Yes, that is so – but not your sort of business.'

Olsen's right hand was creeping towards his pocket.

'I shouldn't try that if I were you,' resumed Biggles quietly. 'Right now there's a rifle pointing straight at you, and I don't think it would require much excuse to make Algy Lacey pull the trigger.' Biggles's voice hardened. 'It's no use, Olsen. We know your business.'

Olsen blustered. 'What are you talking about?'

'You know what we're talking about. You were a trifle premature selling our heads to von Stalhein. I'm thinking of sending yours to him instead. Hand over those letters.'

'Letters – what letters?'

Biggles drew his pistol, and without turning addressed the others. 'You can come out,' he ordered. 'Algy, take that gun out of Olsen's pocket – and the letters. Put your hands up, Olsen – and keep them up. I'm giving you better treatment than you deserve, so don't try any funny stuff. It wouldn't take much to make me change my mind.'

Olsen, as white as death, his nostrils distended and the corners of his mouth dragged down with rage and fear, slowly raised his hands. Algy took a revolver from his side pocket, and the letters. The revolver he passed to Ginger.

'Olsen,' continued Biggles, 'there are moments when I am tempted to commit murder, and this is one of them, but against my inclination I'm going to take you back to Finland for a fair trial. We've got to get through the Russian lines. You know the password. What is it?'

Olsen shrugged his shoulders. 'How should I know?'

Biggles showed his teeth in a mirthless smile. 'There's a good reason why you should know, and you know that, so we needn't discuss it. It happens that your conversation last night was overheard. I've no time to waste talking. What's the password? Say you don't know again and I shall no longer have any reason for keeping you alive, so make up your mind.'

The spy looked at the three faces that confronted him. They were grim and hostile. There was no mercy in the accusing eyes. Nobody knew better than he the extent of his guilt, and he knew what he would have done had the position been reversed. Possibly it was this knowledge that made him weaken.

'Okay,' he said slowly, 'I guess you've got the works on me. If I tell you, will you let me go?'

'No, by thunder, I won't,' flashed back Biggles harshly. 'You're coming with us. If we run into any Russians, and you make one false move, I shall fire the first shot, and it will be at you. So make up your mind to it, Olsen; whatever happens you're not going to get away to go on with this dirty work. You can tell us the password and come with us, or keep your mouth shut and take what's coming to you.' Biggles raised his pistol.

Olsen shrank back. 'No – don't do that,' he faltered, white-lipped. 'The password's "Petrovith".'

'For your own sake I hope you're not lying,' said Biggles evenly. 'All right – let's go.'

He inspected the track in the direction of the house, and then pointed down it towards the frontier with his pistol.

The party moved off, Olsen walking in front with Biggles's pistol pointing at his back, and in this manner they proceeded for some distance. Then, without warning, a shout rang through the air.

Biggles sprang round. The others did the same. It was now light enough for them to see for some distance, light enough to reveal a startling picture. Just emerging out of the thin veil of mist that clung to the top of the hill on which the house was situated was a party of Russian soldiers. That they had seen the fugitives was at once obvious from their attitudes.

Of the four who stood on the track Olsen was the first to move, and he moved like lightning. He gave Biggles a violent shove, and then, ducking low, and twisting as he ran, he dashed towards the Russians.

Biggles steadied himself. War was war, and he had no intention of allowing the spy to escape; he owed it to the Finns whom Olsen had betrayed, quite apart from the man's promise to von Stalhein that he would bring him their heads. He shouted to Olsen to stop, or he would shoot. Olsen's answer was to whip out a small automatic from under his arm and let drive. Biggles jumped aside the instant he saw the weapon and the bullet whistled past his head. He threw up his own weapon, took deliberate aim and fired. Olsen staggered; his knees crumpled under him and he sprawled face downwards across the track.

By this time the Russians were within two hundred yards and running towards the spot. Biggles thrust the weapon in his pocket, and shouting 'This way!' dashed off through the trees. The others followed.

Now although the Russians were so close, the comrades had this advantage: once within the trees they could not be seen, so it would not be known what direction they had taken. At first Biggles chose the easiest way, for his paramount thought was to put as much ground as possible between him and the Russians, for he realized that, now it was known definitely that they were still

'He threw up his own weapon, took deliberate aim and fired'

inside the frontier, it would only be a question of time before all the troops in the vicinity would join in the hunt, and by that time the password would be useless. After his first spurt, therefore, he turned in a westerly direction, hoping to reach the frontier before the news of their escape was known; if they could do that there was still a chance that they could bluff their way through on the strength of the password. So, still heading west, he pressed on at top speed until the edge of the wood revealed itself ahead. The trees did not end abruptly, but first began to stand farther apart; they then straggled out over country more in the nature of open heath; between the trees lay dense growths of bracken, gorse, and heather, brown from the winter frosts.

Reaching this open country, Biggles pulled up for a moment and made a swift reconnaissance, which he was well able to do by virtue of the fact that the ground fell away in a slope, some-times gentle and sometimes steep, for a considerable distance. Here and there grey rocks, rising to some height, broke through the undergrowth, and towards the nearest of these Biggles made his way.

'Keep your eyes open,' he told the others, and then scrambled up the rock. For a few moments he lay flat, his eyes exploring the scene ahead; then he slid back to the ground.

'There are troops all over the place,' he said quietly. 'We must be very close to the frontier even if we're not already on it, although I can't see any sign of the actual boundary. All we can do is to go on; we'll avoid the troops if we can, but if we're accosted we'll give the password and hope for the best. I can see the track Olsen was following – at least, I can see a track, and it's hardly likely that there are two. It disappears into a forest about a mile ahead. We'll make for the forest and march parallel with the track in the hope of finding Olsen's machine – he would be bound to land as near the track as possible.'

'Lead on,' said Algy briefly.

Progress was now slower, for while crossing the open country it was necessary to scout every inch of the way. Several times they passed close to small detachments of Russian soldiers, and once they had to lie flat while a patrol went past within fifty yards of them. However, they moved steadily nearer to their objective, and they had in fact almost reached it when suddenly and unexpectedly they came upon two soldiers sitting smoking near an outcrop of rock. The Russians saw them at once and jumped to their feet.

Biggles, looking as unconcerned as possible, went straight to them and announced the password. He was anxious to avoid hostilities if it were possible. It was a nasty moment, for up to that time they had no means of knowing if Olsen had told the truth; but it was soon obvious that the password was the correct one. Nevertheless, the Russians seemed somewhat mystified and held a low conversation, whereupon Biggles took the letters from his pocket – the letters which he had taken from Olsen – and after pointing to the addresses, he nodded towards the west in the hope that the two simple fellows would grasp what he was trying to convey – that the letters had to be delivered. This seemed to satisfy the Russians, who made a joke of the travellers' unkempt appearance, apparently under the impression that this was a disguise, and indicated that they might proceed. They needed no second invitation.

Their relief at this simple evasion was short-lived, however, for they had not gone very far when Biggles, happening to look behind, saw the same two Russians coming after them at a run; following them were several more.

Biggles instantly grasped what had happened. The newcomers had brought news of their escape, with a result that the complacent soldiers were now hastening to rectify their mistake. The position was desperate, but Biggles did not lose his head; he maintained the same pace and the same unconcerned attitude until he reached the trees, knowing that if he started to run the Russians would shoot. As he went on he told the others what had happened. But as soon as they were under cover inside the trees he broke into a sprint, striking diagonally through the forest in order to reach the track, the position of which he still carried in his mind.

'Are we over the frontier yet?' panted Algy, as they dashed between the sombre pines.

'I don't know,' answered Biggles. 'It's hard to say. Not that the actual frontier counts for much now there's a war on. The only real advantage of being in Finland is that we might strike a patrol of Finnish troops.'

As Biggles anticipated, they soon reached the track, but he was not so foolish as to expose himself on it; instead he sped on keeping parallel with it, and just within sight of it. There was little undergrowth beneath the trees, so they were able to travel as fast as if they were actually on the track.

By this time the hue and cry could be heard. Shouts came from several points; whistles blew and shots were fired, although what the Russians were shooting at Biggles could not imagine, for he was positive that they could not be seen. He could only conclude that the troops were firing blindly into the trees in the hope that a lucky shot would halt them.

It was Ginger who spotted the aircraft – a Gladiator carrying Finnish markings. The trees ended abruptly and gave way to a flat, low-lying valley large enough to enable a machine to land. The Gladiator stood close in under the trees, presumably so that it could not be seen from above, and might easily have been passed unnoticed had not they known definitely that an aircraft was in the vicinity.

Now the Gladiator is a single-seater, so it was at once obvious that it offered escape for one only. It did not take Biggles long to decide who it should be.

'You'll fly it, Ginger,' he said as they raced towards it. 'Take the papers and the letters straight to Colonel Raymond at Oskar and tell him what has happened. If he can send help, well and good; otherwise we shall have to go on trying to get home on foot.'

Ginger knew Biggles too well to attempt to argue with him at a time like this. 'Right!' he said, taking the elusive papers, and the letters, and thrusting them into his pocket. He swung up into the cockpit. 'Good luck,' he cried in a strangled voice. The engine started at the second attempt; the propeller flashed, a whirling arc of light; then the Gladiator surged forward and, after bumping once or twice on the uneven ground, roared into the sky.

A babble of voices and the crashing of bushes told Biggles and Algy that their pursuers were closing in on them, so they wasted no time watching the machine. Some distance to the right was one of the many lakes with which the country abounded, and towards this Biggles now led the way. Why he chose the lake he really did not know, unless it was because he felt that the steep, reed-lined banks offered more promise of a hiding-place than the open country. In any case it would have been fatal to attempt to cross the open ground in front of the Russian rifles. He ran straight into the rushes until he was ankle-deep in water, and then started to follow the bank, still heading in a westerly direction. Algy kept close behind him. And they were only just in time taking cover, for hardly had they entered the reeds than a number of Russians appeared on the edge of the forest a hundred yards or so away, where they halted, apparently uncertain which way to take. Curiously enough, the very number of them made matters easier for the airmen, for the Russians had evidently outstripped their officers, and as no one seemed able to keep order, they argued among themselves, each man advocating the direction that made most appeal to him. In this way Biggles and Algy got a fair start, and for a little while it looked as if they might actually get clear away.

But then a new factor appeared on the scene, one that made a lot of difference; it was von Stalhein with two Russian officers, all on horseback, and the German lost no time in organizing the pursuit on efficient lines. The troops were formed into detach-ments, and these were set into motion to sweep the landscape so that no part of it remained unsearched.

It was the bomber that finally located them. Where it suddenly appeared from neither Biggles nor Algy knew, but there was a roar overhead, and then the machine, flying low, swept into sight, quartering the ground like a well-trained hound. It was obvious that in some way von Stalhein had managed to get into touch with the pilot, who had brought his machine to the spot.

Biggles and Algy were now compelled to adopt a slower method of procedure. When the aircraft approached near to them they lay still in the reeds, and only when it was some distance away did they dare to continue their flight.

'We shall have to go faster than this; we've wasted too much time lying still,' said Biggles after a quick reconnaissance through the reeds in the direction of the Russian troops, who he saw were drawing perilously near them. Some were actually beginning to search among the reeds at the point where they had entered them.

Algy glanced up at the bomber; it seemed to be a safe distance away. 'Then let's make a dash for it and try to reach those trees at the far end of the lake,' he suggested.

They were now within sight of the far end of the lake, which was not much more than a quarter of a mile away, and there the ground rose steeply to form one of the many rocky ridges that divided several lakes. Trees clothed the flanks of the ridge, and it seemed reasonable to suppose that if they could reach them the task of their pursuers, including the pilot of the aircraft, would be made much more difficult. Biggles saw the wisdom of Algy's advice, and ducking low, he at once broke into a run. Unfortunately they soon came to a place where for some reason the reeds were very short, too short to afford any real cover. However, they made a dash for it, but hardly were they in the open when the aircraft turned. From the manner in which it suddenly came towards them Biggles knew that the pilot, or a member of the crew, had seen them. Straight over them the bomber roared; a small object detached itself from the bottom of the fuselage; it dropped like a stone and burst with a muffled roar about fifty yards away. A mighty cloud of smoke rose high into the air.

'Smoke-bomb,' snapped Biggles. 'That's to tell the crowd where we are. I only hope that von Stalhein is the first to show up – I've got a little present for him.' Biggles took out his pistol. He still continued to run, but it was now obvious from the clamour that the smoke-bomb had done its work.

'It looks as if this is where we fight it out,' observed Algy calmly, clicking a bullet into the breech of the rifle he still carried. He glanced up, wondering why the bomber had not returned to circle over them, and what he saw brought a wild yell to his lips. 'Look!' he shouted.

The bomber was still there, but it was no longer alone in the air. Dropping on it like a torpedo was a Gladiator, and that was not all. Some distance behind the single-seater, looking strangely out of place, and diving as steeply as it dared, was a flying-boat.

'Ginger must be flying that Gladiator – it couldn't be anyone else,' gasped Biggles. 'He must have spotted the flying-boat and brought it here.'

'We must let them know where we are!' cried Algy in a voice which excitement pitched in a treble key.

'Get up on the bank and try to hold off the Russians with the rifle,' ordered Biggles crisply. 'Concentrate on the horsemen first – they're the biggest danger.'

Algy scrambled up the bank, and throwing himself flat, opened fire. There was no further point in trying to hide.

Biggles tore up a quantity of reeds which, like most of the vegetation, were brown and dry from the recent killing frosts, and throwing them into a pile, put a match to them. A thin column of smoke at once rose into the air. Working with frantic speed, he tore up more and more reeds and flung them on the blaze, torn between attending to his task and watching what was happening in the air, for that something lively was happening was certain. Machine-guns chattered shrilly; bullets punctured the placid surface of the lake, and some even plopped into the mud unpleasantly close to where he stood.

Thrilled, as every airman must be when he watches a combat, he looked up at the machines overhead and took in the situation at a glance. The Gladiator was on the bomber's tail now, its guns stuttering in short, vicious bursts. The bomber was diving steeply, banking first one way and then the other in a desperate but futile effort to escape its more agile adversary. Straight on past the bomber the Gladiator roared, and then after a sharp turn swept up underneath it. Biggles could see the tracer bullets like little white sparks of light raking the bottom of the big black fuselage. A feather of smoke, growing swiftly in size, spurted from the bomber's side, and trailed away behind to mark its erratic course. By this time it was obvious that the pilot of the big machine was concerned only with reaching the ground, and he did in fact succeed in doing so. There was a rush of flame and a splintering crash as the wheels touched the rough turf, and Biggles smiled sympathetically as the pilot and crew jumped out and flung themselves clear. The Gladiator turned away at once, but instead of climbing to a safe height, it began sweeping low over the ground with its guns still going.

'What does the young fool think he's doing?' yelled Biggles.

Algy, from the top of the bank, replied, 'He's driving back the mob on the ground.'

Biggles, running up to the ridge, saw that this was true. He had his pistol ready, but a glance told him that it would not be needed – not yet, at any rate – for those men who were not lying flat on the ground to escape the leaden hail were racing for the cover of the trees. Some distance away a horseman was trying to steady a badly frightened horse.

'That's von Stalhein,' muttered Biggles. 'He must be fairly swallowing his tonsils with rage.' Without waiting for Algy to give his opinion, he ran back to the edge of the water and stood clear in the open, waving his arms to attract the attention of the flying-boat pilot. But a moment later he saw that this was unnecessary, for the aircraft was coming in to land on a course that should end near to where he stood. Its keel cut a line of creamy foam on the smooth water; its engines roared with short, spasmodic bursts of sound. Over it now circled the Gladiator. The flying-boat, no longer airborne, surged on towards the place where Biggles stood, reducing its speed as it neared the land.

'Come on! Let's go out to him!' Biggles flung the words over his shoulder to Algy.

Abandoning their position, they splashed out into the icy water and waded knee-deep towards the aircraft. A side window of the cockpit opened, and Smyth's face appeared. 'Come on, sir!' he shouted.

'Good old Smyth; trust him to be in at the death,' declared Algy. 'That man's a treasure. He doesn't talk much, but he's on the spot when he's wanted.'

With the Gladiator still on guard overhead, Biggles and Algy reached the machine; it rocked as they clambered aboard and sank down, panting with exertion and excitement.

'Okay, Smyth – let her go!' shouted Biggles.

Algy looked at Biggles with affected amazement. 'Don't tell me that we're going to get those perishing papers home at *last*,' he muttered. 'I can't believe it.'

'I imagine Ginger still has the papers in his pocket,' returned

Biggles anxiously. 'I wish he'd push on home. If his engine chose this moment to pack up—'

'He'd make a pretty landing and we'd have to start all over again,' jeered Algy. 'Forget it. I'm going home.'

Further conversation was drowned in the roar of the flying-boat's engines as Smyth opened the throttle. The water boiled as the machine swung round to face the longest run the lake provided. Then, majestically, it forged forward, faster and faster, cutting a clean white line across the surface of the lake as it lifted itself slowly from the water. The wake ended abruptly as the keel, after a parting pat, rose clear. The machine turned slowly towards the west.

The Gladiator closed in and took up a position near the wing-tip. Ginger's face could just be seen, grinning. Seeing the others looking at him, he gave the thumbs-up signal, and held the papers for them to see.

Algy turned away. He couldn't bear to watch, for he had a horrible fear that Ginger might drop them overboard, and the bare thought made him shudder. He looked down at the ground and saw that the Russian troops were all converging on one spot. Some of them seemed to be waving to the aircraft; others danced as if in a transport of joy; one or two threw their hats into the air. He turned an amazed face to Biggles.

'I say, what's going on down there?' he asked in a curious tone of voice. 'From the way those fellows are behaving one would think that they are glad to see us go.'

Biggles, too, looked down. He shook his head. 'I don't understand it either,' he observed. 'They look as if they'd all gone crazy. Maybe they have. There have been times in this affair when I thought I'd go crazy myself.'

Algy nodded. 'It's a funny war,' he remarked philosophically.

Biggles stretched himself out on the floor. 'As far as I'm concerned, it can be any sort of war it likes,' he yawned. 'I'm going to sleep. Wake me when we get home.'

CHAPTER XVII

The End of the Cruise

Two hours later the flying-boat landed on a lake near Oskar. The lake was just beyond the aerodrome, so Ginger in the Gladiator was down first, with the result that when Biggles and Algy stepped ashore, Colonel Raymond, with Ginger, was there to welcome him. He had raced over in a car. As he shook hands with them he smiled, presumably at their appearance, which, after what they had been through, can be better imagined than described.

'You look as though you've had a tough time,' he observed.

'Tough!' Algy laughed sarcastically. 'Oh, no. We got ourselves in this mess just to make it look that way.'

'The main thing is, you've got the papers, sir,' put in Biggles.

'Yes, thanks. Good show.' Then the Colonel looked serious. 'I'm sorry you've had so much trouble,' he said. 'I'd no idea it would turn out to be such a difficult and dangerous business. No matter – all's well that ends well.'

'There were times,' answered Biggles reflectively, 'when it looked like ending badly – for us. We only got away by the skin of our teeth.'

Colonel Raymond patted him affectionately on the shoulder.

'Never mind, you're building up a wonderful reputation in Whitehall,' he said comfortingly. 'You may be sure that you'll get the credit for what you've done when I submit my report. Now go and have a bath and a clean-up. Dinner is on me tonight.'

'Where did you produce that flying-boat from so miraculously?' inquired Biggles.

'Produce it? Why, that's the machine that flew me out from England – how did you think I got here? Your man Smyth knew it was here; when you failed to return he came to me in an awful state and asked me to let him have it – he said he thought he knew where he could find you. He's been in the air ever since – I think he must have flown over half Russia.'

'I spotted him in the distance soon after I took off,' explained Ginger. 'He might have found you without me, but in the circumstances I led him to the spot where I took off. That smoke-bomb so kindly dropped by the gent in the Russian bomber showed us where you were.'

'So that was it,' murmured Biggles. 'I thought something of the sort must have happened.'

'If you like you can all fly home with me tomorrow,' offered Colonel Raymond.

Biggles looked puzzled. 'Home with you? Why home?'

'Well, there isn't much point in staying here any longer, is there?'

'But – what about the war?'

'What war?'

'This war.'

A light of understanding suddenly leapt into the Colonel's eyes. He laughed aloud. 'D'you mean to say you haven't heard?'

'Heard what?' cried Biggles. 'What's the joke?'

'The war's over – at least this one is. Peace was declared between Finland and Russia three hours ago.'

Biggles looked thunderstruck. 'Why, less than three hours ago we were still going hammer and tongs.'

'I know. You must have fired the last shots in the war.'

'So *that's* why the Russians stopped shooting and started cheering instead!' cried Biggles, suddenly understanding.

The Colonel smiled. 'Of course. Most sensible people would rather cheer than shoot each other. Are you coming home with me?'

Biggles glanced at the others. 'Well, there seems to be nothing more to stay here for so we may as well,' he said. 'There's only one thing.'

'What is it?'

'Don't, if you value my sanity, send us on any more of these wild paper-chases.'

'That won't be necessary, now the papers are in the bag,' laughed Colonel Raymond. 'Come on, let's be going. As a matter of fact, the day I left England I heard a certain member of the Air Council asking for you.'

Biggles looked up. 'Asking for me? What did he want me for?'

Colonel Raymond coughed apologetically. 'Well – er – I seem to remember him saying something about a job in France.'

Biggles shook his head sadly. 'Now I understand the hurry to get us home,' he murmured with a sigh of resignation. 'I might have guessed there was a trick in it.'

BIGGLES FLIES NORTH

CHAPTER I

Biggles Gets a Letter

Biggles was whistling softly as he walked into the break-fast-room of his flat in Mount Street, but he broke off as he reached for the letters lying beside his plate. With the exception of one they all bore halfpenny stamps, suggesting that they contained nothing more interesting than circulars, but the exception was a bulky package with Canadian stamps, while across the top was printed in block letters, 'CONFIDENTIAL. IF AWAY, PLEASE FORWARD.'

'What's Wilks doing in Canada, I wonder?' murmured Algy, from the other side of the table.

Biggles glanced up. 'Been doing a bit of Sherlock Holmes stuff with my correspondence, eh?'

'As I happen to know Wilks's fist, and am able to recognize a Canadian stamp when I see one, I put two and two together,' replied Algy casually.

'Smart work,' Biggles congratulated him, with cheerful sarcasm, as he tore open the flap of the envelope.

'Wilks? Who's Wilks?' Ginger asked Algy. He had finished his breakfast and was sitting by the fire.

'Wilks – or rather, Captain Wilkinson – was a flight commander in 187 Squadron, in France,' answered Algy. 'He was in South America, an officer in the Bolivian Air Force to be precise, when we last saw him,' he added. 'I wonder what sent him up north?' He said no more but winked at Ginger significantly as a frown settled on Biggles's face, a frown that grew deeper as he turned over the pages of the letter.

There was silence for several minutes. 'Your coffee will be stone cold,' observed Algy at last.

Biggles read the letter to the end before laying it on the table beside him and reaching for the toast. 'Poor old Wilks is in a jam,' he said quietly.

'I suspected it from your expression,' returned Algy. 'What's the trouble?'

Biggles drank some coffee and picked up his letter again. 'I'll read it to you, then you'll know as much as I do,' he said. 'Listen to this. He writes on paper headed "Arctic Airways, Fort Beaver, Mackenzie, North-West Territories, Canada."'

' "My dear Biggles,

' "I am writing this on the off-chance of it reaching you, but knowing all about your nomadic habits I shall be surprised if it does. As you probably remember, letter-writing is not in my line, so you no doubt guessed before you opened this (if ever you do) that things must be pretty sticky. Believe me, they are all that, and more. To come to the point right away, having heard odd rumours of your adventures from time to time in one part of the world or another, it has just struck me that you might not be averse to starting on a fresh one. I do not know whether it is for fun or for profit that you go roaring round the globe; possibly both; but if you hunt adventure for the sake of it, well, old boy, right here I can supply you with the genuine article in unlimited quantities. But make no mistake. This isn't a kid-glove game for the parlour; it's knuckle-dusters in the wide open spaces; and I don't mind telling you that out here the wide open spaces are so wide that you have to fly for a long, long time to get to the other side of them.

' "Before I start on the real story I may as well say that the odds seem to be against my being alive by the time you get this. If I just disappear, or get wiped out in what looks like a genuine crash, find a fellow named McBain – 'Brindle' Jake he is called around these parts – and hand him a bunch of slugs from me, as a last service for an old pal." '

'By gosh! Things must be pretty grim for old Wilks to write in that strain,' broke in Algy.

'Grim is the right word for it,' broke in Biggles shortly. 'But don't interrupt just listen to this.'

' "You remember I was in Bolivia a few years ago. Well, there was a change of government, and as I didn't like the new one – or maybe the new one didn't like me – I packed my valise and headed north, thinking that the most likely point of the compass where I should find a concern in need of a pilot who had learned to fly by the seat of his pants, and not by these new-fangled instruments. I knocked about the States for a bit without getting fixed up with anything permanent, and ultimately drifted over the border into Canada, which is, I may say, a great country, although I have little to thank it for as yet.

' "One day I struck lucky – at least, it looked that way to me at the time, although I am not so sure about it now. I got a charter job flying a mining engineer up to some new gold-fields which were then being surveyed. The concern has since been put over in a big way under the title of Moose Creek Gold-fields Corporation – Moose Creek being the name of the locality. You may have heard tell of the 'last place on earth'. Well, I can tell you just where it is. Moose Creek. It is well inside the Arctic circle. Why they call it Moose Creek I do not know, for no moose in its right mind – or any other animal, for that matter – would go within a hundred miles of the perishing place. But that's by the way.

' "Having got the low-down about these gold-fields, I had one of my rare inspirations. Moose Creek is eight hundred miles north of the nearest railhead, and the journey, made by canoe in summer and dog-sled during the freeze-up, takes about six weeks' heavy going. I had saved a bit of money while I was in Bolivia, and it struck me that since there was certain to be a fair amount of traffic to and from the gold-fields, an air line might be worked up into a paying proposition. I counted on flying up staff, stores, mails, machinery, and so on, and bringing back the gold and the people who would rather ride home than walk eight hundred miles. In an aircraft the journey could be done in a day instead of six weeks. To make a long story as short as possible, I put all my savings into the venture, opening up my own landing-field and shed at Fort Beaver, which is the railhead. I called it Arctic Airways.

' "For a year or so it was touch and go. I was just about broke and preparing to pack up when real gold was struck at the Creek. That sent the balloon up. Traffic jumped.

Things began to hum, and it looked at last as if all I had ever hoped for had come to pass. I got into the money, and with my profits I bought a second machine. Then, out of the blue – literally, as it happened – came the smack in the eye; one which, I must admit, I wasn't expecting. Another fellow jumped my claim – the same Brindle Jake that I have already mentioned. It seemed a bit thick after all I had been through, blazing the trail and all that, for some one else to step in and start reaping my harvest. However, it couldn't be helped, and I decided to make the best of a bad show. I figured it out that there ought to be enough money in the game for two of us, anyway; as it happened, Brindle had his own ideas about that. He decided that two in the game was one too many – and he wasn't going to be the one to go. From that moment I learned that the gloves were off.

' "I must explain the position in regard to Fort Beaver Aerodrome. (The one at the other end of my run, Moose Creek, belongs to the gold company, so I have nothing to do with that.) There is only one possible landing-ground within fifty miles of Fort Beaver, and that's mine. I bought the land off a fellow named Angus Stirling, who had decided that he preferred prospecting for gold to farming. I paid him cash, whereupon he headed north with his traps and hasn't been seen since. I cleared the ground, put up a shed, and the land became Fort Beaver landing-field. There was never any question about the title of the land until recently; every one in Fort Beaver regarded it as mine until one day a bunch of toughs rolled up, and, in spite of my protests, without paying a cent, or so much as a by-your-leave, built a larger shed than mine on the edge of my field. A couple of days later two Weinkel Twelve transport planes landed, and out stepped Brindle Jake and his two pilots, Joe Sarton, a tall chap, good-looking in a rugged sort of way, and 'Tex' Ferroni, a slim, dark little fellow who looks – as, indeed, his name suggests – as if he came from one of the Latin states. McBain himself is a big, broad-shouldered bloke, with odd patches of grey in his hair and beard. That's how he gets his nickname, I am told. A half-breed French-Canadian named Jean Chicot trails about after him like a dog, and I've got my own idea as to *his* real job. I reckon he's McBain's bodyguard. Naturally, I asked Brindle what was the big idea, and you can guess my surprise when he calmly told me to clear off the land. I can't go into details now, but for the first time I learned that there was some doubt as to the title of the land I had bought off Stirling. For some extraordinary reason which I don't understand there seems to be no record of his having paid the Government for it. Anyway, the record has not yet been found, although, being so far away from the Record Office, correspondence is a slow business. He – that is, Stirling – told me that he got the land for a nominal figure under a settler's grant, but it looks to me as if he forgot to register it – or forget to collect the transfer. The fact remains he didn't give it to me, which was, I suppose, my own fault, for it went clean out of my head. I'm afraid I'm a bit careless in these matters. I took his word for it that it was O.K. There is this about it, though. If I don't own the land, neither does Brindle, although he tries to bluff me that he does.

' "He started operating to Moose Creek right away. I flew up and saw the traffic manager of the gold-fields company, a decent little fellow named Canwell, and lodged a complaint, but it did not get me very far. Canwell's point is – and I suppose he is right – he is only concerned with getting his stuff to the railhead, and he doesn't care two hoots who takes it as long as it goes, or as long as he gets efficient service. He was born and bred in the north, and he as good as told me that in this country it is up to a fellow to work out his own salvation. If he hasn't the gumption to do that – well, it's his own funeral. That was that.

' "I got my first ideas of Brindle's methods when, a day or two later, one of my machines shed its wing just after it had taken off; yet I'd stake my life that that machine was airworthy the night before because I went over it myself. Brindle or his men tampered with it, I'm certain, but of course I can't prove anything. The pilot, a nice chap named Walter Graves, was killed. I bought another machine and hired another pilot. Two days after taking delivery the machine went up in flames during the night. My new pilot was 'got at' by the other side, and had the wind put up him so much that he packed up. I've no money to buy another machine. The one I have left is a Rockheed freighter which I fly myself. I sleep in it – with a gun in my hand – but I can't stand the strain much longer. One by one my boys have left me, scared by Brindle's threats, so that I have to do my own repairs. That's how things stand at present. Brindle is operating two machines and is gradually wearing me down. I've been nearly killed two or three times by 'accident'. Brindle wants the aerodrome and my shed. I've told him he'll only get 'em over my dead body – and that isn't bluff.

' "The fact is, old lad, it goes against the grain to be run out of the territory by a low-down grafter. I'm fighting a lone hand, for the 'Mounties'[1] have other things to do besides interfering in what, to them, is a business squabble. With one man whom I could rely on absolutely, to take turn and turn about with me, I believe I could still beat Brindle and his toughs. The trouble is, I daren't leave the place; if I did, I'd never get back; Brindle would see to that. Meanwhile, I'm hanging on. I'm in this up to the neck and I'm going to see it through to the last turn of the prop. It isn't just the money that matters now; I won't be jumped out by a crooked skunk. That's all. If you want a spot of real flying, flying with the lid off, step right across and give me a hand to keep the old flag flying. We did a job or two together in the old days. Let's do one more. All the best to Algy (remember that first E.A. he shot down? The laugh was certainly on you that time).

Yours ever,
WILKS." '

Biggles's face was set in hard lines as he tossed the letter on the table and picked up the envelope, to examine the postmark.

'How long ago was it posted?' asked Algy.

'Nine days.'

'Anything could have happened in that time.'

'I was just thinking the same thing.'

'What are you going to do?' put in Ginger, looking from one to the other.

'That remains to be seen,' replied Biggles curtly. 'For the moment we are just going to Fort Beaver as fast as we can get there. Algy, ring up and find out when the next boat sails. Ginger,

[1] North-West Mounted Police

pass me that directory. I'll send a few cables. We shall want a machine waiting for us when we land – with the props ticking over. If I can get the machine I want we'll show that blighter McBain how to shift freight. Get your bags packed, everybody, and put in plenty of woollen kit. I've never been to Canada, but I seem to have heard that the winters there are inclined to be chilly.'

'Then let's go and see if we can warm things up,' murmured Algy.

CHAPTER II

Fort Beaver

A little before two o'clock, sixteen days after Wilks's SOS had been received in London, a Bluewing 'Jupiter' airliner circled low over the cluster of log huts which comprised Fort Beaver, preparatory to landing.

Biggles sat at the controls, Algy beside him, with Ginger braced in the narrow corridor that connected the pilot's control cabin – it could hardly be called a cockpit – with what normally would have been the main passenger saloon. Behind, amongst the luggage in the rear compartment, sat Flight-Sergeant Smyth, Biggles's old fitter and sharer of many of their adventures.

The 'Jupe' – as Ginger had already nicknamed the machine – was Biggles's first choice, and he accounted himself fortunate in being able to get a commercial transport machine with such a fine reputation. American built, the Jupiter, latest model of the Bluewing Company, was a twin-engined cantilever high-wing monoplane fitted with two 850 h.p. 'Cyclone' engines, one power unit being built into the leading edge of the wing on either side of the fuselage. The undercarriage was retractable. In the standard model there were four mail compartments forward of the main cabin, which normally provided accommodation for eighteen passengers, but Biggles, realizing that eighteen seats would rarely, if ever, be required, had had this number reduced to six, the space thus made available being cleared for freight. As he pointed out to the others, extra passengers, if any, could always travel in the freight compartments. The manufacturer's figures gave the maximum speed of the machine as 230 miles an hour, with normal cruising speed 205 miles an hour.

Negotiations for the aircraft had been carried on by wireless while they were on board ship. Not for a moment did Biggles contemplate taking a machine out with him, although, from choice, he would have preferred a British aeroplane, but that would have meant crating it for an ocean voyage, which is a very expensive business. The result of the negotiations was that when the party had landed at Quebec they had found the machine awaiting them, it having been flown up from the United States by a delivery pilot.

Three long hops had seen the Jupe at Fort McMurray, the base aerodrome of northern fliers, and another long journey northward over the 'bad lands' had brought the airmen to Fort Beaver, which lies midway between the north-east arm of Great Slave Lake and the Mackenzie River, some fifty miles south-east of Bear Lake. They all wore heavy flying kit, with the fur outside, for although it was not yet winter it was already cold, and the annual freeze-up could be expected in the near future.

Behind the pilot's cabin, in the mail compartment, was piled their luggage – valises and suitcases. Stacked in the freight cabin were bales and bundles of spare parts, chiefly engine components; but perhaps the most striking item was an enormous pair of skis, so long that the ends projected into the doorway of the lavatory, which was situated in the tail. It had been left open for that purpose. These would, of course, be needed when the snow came.[1] Until that time the ordinary retractable-wheel undercarriage would be used.

Biggles regarded the landing-ground dispassionately as he throttled back and prepared to glide in. Since it was the only level piece of ground within view it was unmistakable, although two blocks of wooden buildings on the edge of the field provided confirmation, were it needed.

'What do you think of it?' asked Algy.

'Not much,' returned Biggles briefly.

'I never saw a more desolate-looking spot in all my life.'

'What did you expect to find – concrete runways?' inquired Biggles sarcastically. 'This isn't a European terminus.'

'No, I can see that,' declared Algy warmly. 'Wilks was certainly right about the wide open spaces – although he needn't have used the plural. From what I've seen of this country from topsides, it's just one big, wide open space, and nothing else.'

'I fancy we shall find something else when we get on the carpet,' observed Biggles, smiling faintly. 'Is that old Wilks I can see, mending his hut?'

Algy peered through the side window. 'That fellow is too tall for Wilks,' he declared. 'And he seems to be tearing the place down, not mending it, anyway.'

Biggles glanced across quickly. 'The dickens he does. That doesn't look too good. However, we shall soon learn what we came to learn.'

Nothing more was said, and a minute later the wheels of the

---

1 'Wheel undercarriages give way to skis during winter in all northern countries, where every lake, when frozen, becomes a potential landing-ground.

big machine were trundling over the rough surface of the landing-ground, scored in a hundred places with tyre tracks.

Biggles allowed the machine to run to a standstill, and then, using his brakes, turned towards the smaller of the two sets of buildings. Moving slowly and majestically, the Jupiter roared up to where a little group of men stood staring at them from in front of a rough but stoutly built hangar, roofed with corrugated iron.

'Funny, I don't see Wilks,' murmured Algy.

'Which means, obviously, that he isn't here,' returned Biggles.

'Maybe he's in the air.'

'Maybe. We'll soon know. This is his shed, for there is the board with the name of his company on it leaning against the wall. It looks as if it had just been taken down. That being so, what is McBain doing here – for that's who the nasty-looking piece of work in the fur cap is, I'll bet my boots. I don't like the look of things; we'd better leave the engines running in case we want to go up again in a hurry. Tell Smyth to come here and take over, and keep an eye on us. Let's get out.'

As the three airmen stepped down from the saloon door, leaving Smyth in the control cabin with the engines idling, four men walked to meet them. A fifth, obviously an Indian, remained standing near the hangar. One of the four, a little ahead of the others and clearly the leader, was a tall, burly man, whose bristling, square-cut beard was curiously streaked with grey. There was something unnaturally cold about his pale blue eyes, which were set rather far apart, and, as is often the case with pale eyes, looked larger than they really were. Nevertheless, he was a powerful and arresting figure. On his head he wore a fur cap, with flaps hanging loosely over his ears, a check-patterned lumber shirt of blanket-like material, and dark corduroy trousers tucked into half-Wellington boots. A broad belt, with cartridge-pouches thrust through loops, was buckled tightly round his waist.

The man who walked close behind him was an entirely different type, although he was dressed in much the same fashion. Slight in build, undoubtedly good-looking in a rather effeminate way, his delicate features might have passed for those of a woman but for a wisp of black moustache that decorated his upper lip. His eyes, set under finely drawn eyebrows, were dark, but held a quality of restlessness that made it difficult to ascertain what object most occupied his attention – the aerodrome, the aircraft, or the airmen, for he seemed to be watching all three at the same time. The fur jacket he wore was thrown open, revealing a beautifully worked Indian belt, through which he had hooked his thumbs in such a way that the bowie knife which hung on one side could just be seen.

At a distance of two or three paces behind strolled two other men, their hands thrust carelessly into their trousers pockets. One was a fresh-complexioned man of perhaps thirty-five years of age, with a fair moustache; his companion was younger, and as swarthy as the other was fair. Despite the fact that his jaws were working steadily, suggesting the gum-chewing habit acquired by residents in the United States, 'southern Europe' was written clearly on his dark skin.

Before a word was spoken, Biggles, remembering the descriptions in Wilks's letter, could have named them all. The big man was obviously Brindle McBain; the man who walked close behind him, keeping at his heels like a dog, was Jean Chicot. The other two were the pilots, Joe Sarton, the fair man, and Tex Ferroni, the 'slim, dark little fellow'. Wilks's description had been brief, but singularly apt, thought Biggles, as he walked slowly to meet them, at the same time drawing off his gauntlets. His eyes wandered along the front of the hangar and the adjacent offices, now not more than twenty yards away, hoping to see Wilks, but there was no sign of him or of any member of his staff, despite the fact that the buildings were without question those of Arctic Airways. An atmosphere of desertion, almost of desolation, hung over them.

McBain was the first to speak. Seeing Biggles and his companions walking towards him, he stopped and waited for them to come up. The man with him did the same.

'Ten bucks, stranger,' he demanded curtly.

Biggles raised his eyebrows in genuine surprise. 'Meaning?' he queried.

'Just ten dollars,' returned McBain harshly.

'Yes, I had gathered that much,' nodded Biggles. 'What I meant was, what for?'

'Landing fee.'

'Oh.' Biggles reached the four men, who had formed a little group, and stopped. 'Are you the authorized collector for Arctic Airways?' he asked.

McBain's big eyes rested broodingly on Biggles's slight figure. 'No,' he said shortly, 'I'm collecting for myself.'

'I see. And who might you be?'

'McBain's the name.'

'Mine's Bigglesworth,' returned Biggles evenly.

'Englishman?'

'Guess again and you'll be wrong.'

'Smart guy, eh?'

'No, just as ordinary as they make them,' said Biggles, smiling faintly. 'But aren't you making a mistake, Mr. McBain?'

'What gave you that idea?'

'This field belongs to Arctic Airways.'

'Yeah? Well, you're making the mistake. It belongs to me,' grated McBain.

'What gave *you* that idea?' inquired Biggles easily.

McBain hesitated. He took out a pipe and began to fill it. 'What are you doing here, anyway?' he asked in a curious voice.

'Oh, I just dropped in to take a look at my property,' replied Biggles casually.

The other started. 'Your property?'

'Well, I've just put a lot of money into Arctic Airways, so I seem to have some right to take a look at things at close quarters,' observed Biggles.

There was a moment's silence in which McBain's swarthy companion took out a little bag of tobacco and rolled a cigarette with deft fingers.

'Did you say you'd put money into this concern?' McBain jerked his thumb towards Arctic Airways' hangar.

'That's what I said, Mr. McBain.'

'And you've come here to see where your money's gone?'

'No, I've come here to help spend it.'

'You mean – you've come here – to *work*?'

'That's how I figured it out.'

'Then your figgerin' ain't good, Swigglesworth.'

'Bigglesworth, if you don't mind. Awkward name, I know, but it's the best my father could do for me, and as we're likely to see quite a bit of each other, we might as well get things right at the start. It saves misunderstandings later on – if you get my meaning?'

The other nodded thoughtfully. 'Yeah,' he said, 'I get your

meaning. Do you know the guy what ran this Arctic Airways outfit?'

Biggles noted the use of the past tense but he did not reveal his anxiety. 'Ran?' he questioned. 'Isn't he still running it?'

'Don't look like it, does it?'

'I haven't had a chance to look round yet, so I can't say. Still, you seem to know. What's happened to him?'

'Say, what do you think I am – a nurse?'

'I hadn't thought about it,' murmured Biggles. 'If Captain Wilkinson has disappeared it looks as if it's time somebody tried to find him, doesn't it?'

'It may look that way to you.'

'Any reason why it shouldn't look that way to you?'

'Plenty.'

'Pity about that; maybe you'll tell me why, sometime.'

'I sure will, and there ain't no need to wait. Get this, stranger. This airfield is bad medicine for visitors, and if you're half as smart as you think you are, wise guy, you'll pull your freight right now.'

Biggles's grey eyes found McBain's and held them. 'That goes for you too, McBain – if you want it that way,' he said in a voice that was as hard and brittle as ice. 'But before you decide how soon you're going, turn this over in your mind. I'm not greedy. There should be plenty of work here for two operators, and if they work together things could go easier for both. I'm willing to go ahead on that arrangement if you are. Naturally, as the field belongs to Arctic Airways you'll have to pay landing fees for the privilege of using it. If, on the other hand, you'd rather have things the way you've been trying to run them—'

'Yeah?' broke in the other, the muscles of his face twitching. 'I guess that's how I'll have 'em; and I'll start by collecting them ten bucks.'

Biggles shook his head. 'Not a cent, McBain,' he said quietly. 'You can't get away with that bluff – not with me. My lawyers in Montreal are straightening out the title deeds of this property, and when we hear to whom it does belong I'll let you know how much you owe Arctic Airways. That's all – except that I'd rather you kept a bit farther away from my sheds.'

Biggles nodded curtly and moved towards what was obviously Arctic Airways' reception office. For a moment it looked as though McBain would intercept him, for he took a pace forward, clenching and unclenching his hands; but then his companion said something to him that the others could not catch, and he stopped, scowling.

Algy and Ginger followed Biggles into the office. There was nobody there, although by this time they did not expect to find any one. Everything was in confusion. Files had been pulled out and papers were strewn everywhere.

Algy's face was grim as he looked around. 'I don't like the look of this,' he said quietly. 'I'm afraid we've come too late.'

Before Biggles could answer there was a whip-like crack, followed instantly by a splintering thud. Several splinters flew across the room, one striking Biggles on the cheek and drawing blood.

'That was a shot!' snapped Algy, and then darted after Biggles, who had already flung open the door and was striding towards McBain and his companions, who had not moved. The effeminate-looking man, whom Biggles knew from Wilks's description must be Jean Chicot, was sitting on a chock, smiling, a small automatic held in his two hands. McBain and the two pilots were all grinning, but the humour went out of their eyes at the expression on Biggles's face.

Biggles went straight up to Chicot. 'Did you fire that shot?' he snapped.

The half-breed looked up, the affected smile still playing about his thin lips. He shrugged his shoulders and sent a puff of cigarette smoke up into Biggles's face before he replied, at the same time rising slowly to his feet. 'Eet vas an accident,' he smirked. 'I clean my gun – so; he go off. These accidents come sometime – yes?'

Biggles did not answer. His fist flew out in a vicious uppercut. Every scrap of the pent-up anger that was in him went behind the blow. There was a snap like a breaking twig as his fist caught Chicot on the point of the jaw.

The half-breed did not stagger. The blow lifted him clean off his feet. He went straight over backwards and crashed across the concrete apron, his cap going one way and the pistol another. He twisted for a moment and then lay still.

Biggles's face was white, and his lips were set in a straight line as he looked down at him.

'Keep your hands away from your belt, McBain.' It was Algy who spoke. Seeing what was coming, he had whipped out his automatic the instant Biggles struck the blow.

Biggles looked round and saw McBain hesitating; his hands, with the fingers clawed, were a few inches above his belt. 'Plug him if he moves, Algy,' he said grimly. 'If this gang of crooks want it hot, by thunder, they can have it!' Then, to McBain, 'I've killed a lot better men than you in my time, McBain,' he said harshly, 'so I shouldn't lose any sleep on your account.'

'Say, what's going on?'

Biggles spun round and saw that a newcomer had arrived on the scene. There was no need to ask who it was, for his uniform told him that. It was a constable of the North-West Mounted Police.

'What's going on here?' said the constable again, looking suspiciously from one to the other.

'Nothing to speak of,' replied Biggles. 'My friends and I have just arrived by air. For some reason best known to himself – although I've a pretty good idea what it is – McBain objected to our landing and tried to scare us off by getting his half-breed playmate to pull a gun on us, so I had to hit him. That's all.'

The constable regarded Biggles speculatively. 'What are you doing in this out-of-the-way place, anyway?' he inquired.

'Any reason why I shouldn't come here?'

'I don't know – yet.'

'Then you'd better get in touch with your headquarters and find out. If they don't know either, tell them to get into touch with the Department of Aviation – they know. I'm putting money into Arctic Airways, which belongs to a friend of mine, Wilkinson. You probably know him. I want to know where he is.'

'I don't know where he is.'

'Then ask McBain – I reckon he does.'

The constable turned to McBain. 'Where's Wilkinson?'

'Search me, Delaney.'

'When did you last see him?'

'Four days back.'

'Where?'

'Here.'

'What was he doing?'

'Taking off – heading north, I guess.'

'For Moose Creek?'

'Why should he tell me where he was going?'

'And he hasn't come back?'

'I ain't looked for him.'

'You had a good look at the inside of his office, at any rate,' put in Biggles coldly.

'Who said it was me?'

'I do. I saw you come out as we landed.'

'I figger—'

'Wait a minute – I haven't finished figuring myself yet. You knew Wilkinson wasn't coming back, McBain – or you had good reason to suppose he wasn't – or you wouldn't have broken into his office and turned his papers upside-down. Nor would you have started to dismantle his shed.'

'Who said I was dismantling his shed?'

Biggles pointed. 'There's the board – Arctic Airways. I have witnesses who saw you taking it down.'

McBain looked at Biggles evilly. Then he turned to the constable. 'Well, what are you going to do about it?' he inquired. 'I've got something else to do besides stand here gassin'.'

'So have I,' returned the constable. 'You ought to have reported Wilkinson missing, McBain. I shall have to ask fellows going north to look out for him.'

'Don't worry, constable; I'll do that,' said Biggles quickly.

'You mean you're going to look for him?'

'I am.'

'When?'

'Right now. If I don't find him before dark I shall come back here and make another search tomorrow. Meanwhile you might ask McBain to stay in his own sheds; and, while we're away, you might keep an eye on these.'

The constable looked at McBain. 'You stay on your own property,' he said. Then to Biggles, as he moved away, 'Let me know if you find Wilkinson.'

Biggles nodded. 'I will,' he said, and turned towards the Jupiter. 'Come on, you fellows,' he went on quietly to the others, taking no further notice of McBain. 'Wilks must be down somewhere between here and Moose Creek; we've got nearly four hours of daylight left, so the sooner we start looking for him, the better.'

CHAPTER III

A Satisfactory Trip

'So that's Mister McBain,' observed Ginger, as they got back into the machine.

'Yes, and now we know just how we stand,' answered Biggles. 'We shall have to watch our steps with that gentleman. A man with eyes like that was born to be a crook. I must confess that I'm a bit worried about old Wilks.'

'Was McBain telling the truth, do you think, when he said Wilks had flown north?' asked Algy.

'I believe he was. Neither he nor his machine are here, so he must have gone off somewhere, and I imagine Moose Creek would be the most likely place for him to go.'

'He might have gone to Moose Creek and decided to stay there.'

Biggles shook his head. 'I can't agree with that. Knowing the state of things here, if he had to go north my own feeling is that he would get back as quickly as he could. It is quite possible that his machine was got at; anyway, McBain had jolly good reason to suppose that Wilks wasn't coming back, otherwise he wouldn't have dared to take possession of his hangar – for that is what it amounts to, and he would have done it had we not arrived on the scene. If McBain wanted Wilks out of the way – and we know he did – the most certain way to bring it about was to tamper with his machine. Wilks was quite aware of that danger; he told us as much in his letter. It's a hundred to one that he is on the ground somewhere between here and Moose Creek. I only hope the trouble was nothing vital, like structural failure; if it was, then I'm afraid we can say goodbye to Wilks. On the other hand, there is just a possibility that he had to make a perfectly natural forced landing, in which case he would get the machine down somehow. With all his experience the chances are that he would be able to do that without hurting himself, even if he damaged the machine. The only thing we can do now is to try to find out. Fortunately, we've plenty of petrol left in the tanks, so come on; let's get away. All right, Smyth; get back aft, will you.'

As he finished speaking, Biggles took out his map and studied it intently. Both Fort Beaver and Moose Creek were shown, so it did not take him long to work out a compass course, and in five minutes the Jupiter was in the air again, heading northwards, with Algy watching the ground on the starboard side and Ginger on the other.

It soon became evident that the task of picking out an aircraft on the ground, particularly a crashed one, was likely to be a good deal more difficult than they had supposed, for the country was rougher than any they had yet seen in Canada.

For a long time they flew over almost continuous forests of fir, with great outcrops of grey rock thrusting upwards like spurs, while here and there a river wound a tortuous course through gorge and valley. Then the country started to rise, and although the altimeter registered a thousand feet, the Jupiter was soon skimming over the treetops. Biggles eased the stick back and climbed slowly to a safer height.

At the end of an hour the forest had become broken into small, isolated groups of wind-twisted trees, and shortly afterwards even these failed to appear, giving way to a dismal panorama of gaunt rock. Ahead, and on either side, mountains towered upwards majestically, their peaks white with the first snow.

'I don't know about a forced landing, but if Wilks had to go down and land on that stuff I should say he hadn't a hope,' observed Biggles moodily, as he stared down at the weather-worn rock. 'From the time we started I haven't seen half a dozen places where there was the slightest chance of getting a machine down without a crack-up. Goodness me! What a country!'

'It looks as if it levels out a bit farther ahead,' remarked Algy, who had turned to look forward through the windscreen.

'Yes, I agree, it does,' returned Biggles. 'But what sort of surface is it? I shouldn't care to have to put a machine down on that stuff. It wouldn't be so bad if you had engine power to fall back on in an emergency – but with a dead stick[1] it would be an anxious business. Hello, what's that ahead? That looks like something on the ground there … is it? Yes, by heaven, it is! It's a machine. There's somebody beside it – look, he's moving. He's seen us. He's waving.'

The roar of the Jupiter's engines died away abruptly as Biggles cut the throttle and began gliding down to what, by this time, was obviously an aeroplane.

'It's on even keel, anyway,' remarked Algy, who had opened a side window in order to see more clearly.

'It's got its tail cocked up, which looks to me like a broken undercart,' cried Ginger.

---

[1] Dead stick. A flying expression meaning that the propeller is not revolving.

'It must be Wilks,' declared Biggles. 'Nobody else would be flying up here. As long as he's all right I don't care much if he has smashed the machine. Give him a wave.'

With Algy hanging out of the window with an arm outstretched – for to wave literally in the open air when one is travelling more than a hundred miles an hour is practically impossible – the Jupiter dropped lower and lower until at last it was circling in a steep bank at not more than fifty feet above the other machine.

'What's the ground Iike, Algy?' asked Biggles anxiously. 'Can you see a decent place to get down? It all looks pretty rotten to me.'

'Wilks is pointing. I think he means that there is a place over there where we can get down. He's moving off in that direction – but he's limping. He must be hurt.'

The man on the ground was, in fact, hobbling away from the stationary machine, from time to time stopping to pick up a piece of stone and throw it aside.

'He's clearing a runway for us,' declared Algy.

'So I see,' answered Biggles, with a worried frown. 'I don't relish the thought of getting down on it, all the same.' Nevertheless, he started lowering his undercarriage, which had, of course, been drawn up during the flight. He looked at the ground on which he would have to land, and shook his head.

'We can't leave Wilks down there,' murmured Algy.

'Of course we can't,' agreed Biggles irritably, 'but I don't want to bust a perfectly good aeroplane costing me the best part of forty thousand dollars. Nor do I want to walk home.'

'I don't think it's too bad,' muttered Algy, who was still staring down at the ground. 'Wilks is beckoning, so it can't be as bad as it looks.'

Biggles turned the big machine slowly until it was in line with the runway; then he allowed it to sink slowly towards it. Flattening out a few inches above the ground, he held the stick firmly, holding the machine off as long as he dared.

The Jupiter vibrated from nose to tail-skid as her wheels rumbled over the uneven ground, but they stood up to the strain, and the machine finally came to rest about two hundred yards from the lone figure which at once began hurrying towards them. There was no longer any doubt about who it was.

'Biggles, by all that's wonderful!' cried Wilks enthusiastically.

'Well might you say "by all that's wonderful",' grinned Biggles, as he shook hands with his old war comrade. 'What sort of a country do you call this?'

'It's a grand country when you get to know it,' declared Wilks firmly.

'Maybe you're right,' agreed Biggles doubtfully. 'What happened to you?'

'How the dickens did you know where I was?'

'Just a minute, old boy; let's take one thing at a time,' suggested Biggles. 'I'll tell my story first, if you like. We've been to Fort Beaver – landed there about lunchtime today. We found McBain, and I might tell you that he and I had a few sharp words. He didn't seem overjoyed to see us; in fact, we parted on anything but the best of terms. Constable Delaney blew in while the argument was in progress, and under interrogation McBain admitted that you'd flown off and hadn't come back. In the circumstances we decided that you must have started for Moose Creek but failed to reach it, so we came along to pick up the pieces. What happened to you?'

Wilks's smile faded as he told his story. 'You were right about me starting for Moose Creek,' he said bitterly. 'Somebody was kind enough to put a handful of loose cotton-waste in my second tank and it choked the petrol leads. The engines packed up and I had to come down. As it happened I had enough juice in my gravity tank to enable me to reach this place, which I knew all about, having flown over it several times. Naturally, as it is one of the few places between Fort Beaver and Moose Creek where it is just possible to get a machine down, I had made a note of it. All the same, I was lucky to make it.'

'The cotton-waste was McBain's work, I reckon?'

'Of course.'

While they had been speaking they had been moving slowly towards Wilks's machine.

'Did you knock your leg when you came down?' asked Biggles, noting that Wilks was still limping.

'I hit my knee a crack against the dashboard when we tipped up,' returned Wilks briefly.

'Machine damaged?'

'Busted tyre and a bent prop; luckily, being metal it didn't break. But of course there was no question of getting off again. With a groggy knee I was in no shape to start walking three hundred miles back to Fort Beaver, so I just sat here and waited, hoping that I should be missed and that some one would pass the word to the Canadian Airways fellows. They're a grand lot of chaps, and would have come looking for me when they heard I was down.'

'You would have waited a long time, I'm afraid,' replied Biggles. 'Only McBain and his gang knew that you were missing, and they told no one. Indeed, they were so certain that you were gone for good that they were making free with your office when we landed.'

'The dickens they were!'

'I told Delaney about it and he warned them to keep off, so I don't think they'll touch anything – not for a little while at any rate.'

'I don't wonder they didn't expect me back,' observed Wilks. 'This is no country for a forced landing.'

'So I've noticed,' returned Biggles dryly, as he examined the damaged machine with professional ability. Smyth was already at work on it. 'I see you've got a load on board,' continued Biggles, as he looked into the cabin.

'Yes. I was running some spare machine-parts up to Moose Creek; they were wanted urgently, so I am afraid the people up there will be fed up with this delay. They'll probably refuse to give me any future work as I have let them down once or twice already, through no fault of my own you may be sure.'

Biggles bit his lip thoughtfully. 'It's too late to get the stuff up to them today,' he said slowly, 'but we might be able to manage it tomorrow. I think this is our best plan. We've brought all our tools and spare parts with us; luckily we hadn't time to unload them at Fort Beaver. We'll put all your stuff into my machine and fly it back to Fort Beaver. Tomorrow I'll take it up to Moose Creek. Ginger can come with me. Smyth and Algy had better stay here and get to work on your machine. There's nothing you can't fix up, is there, Smyth?'

'I don't think so, sir.'

'Good. All right, let's get to work. Algy, you'd better stay here with Smyth, and as soon as the machine is ready fly her back to Fort Beaver. We'll leave you some grub and you can sleep in the cabin. I shall take Wilks back with me. He needs a rest. How long will it take you to fix things up, Smyth?'

'I think I can get her finished by this time tomorrow, sir,' was the confident answer.

'Then we'll expect you back tomorrow evening, but don't take off unless you can get back to Fort Beaver before dark; it would be better to stay here another night than risk that. Is that all right with you, Algy?'

'As right as rain.'

'Fine! Then let's see about shifting this cargo into the Jupiter. I'd stay here with you but I don't like leaving Fort Beaver for too long with McBain on the warpath. I'll fly low over you tomorrow on my way up to Moose Creek, but I shan't land unless you signal to me to do so. Come on, let's get to work; we've no time to waste.'

It took them, all working hard, about half an hour to transfer the freight from the damaged machine to the Jupiter, and once this was done Biggles lost no time in getting off, for the sun was already low over the western hills. In a few minutes the Jupiter was roaring back over her tracks.

In spite of the fact that Biggles flew on full throttle nearly all the way, it was practically dark when the scattered lights of Fort Beaver came into sight.

Suddenly Biggles started and stared ahead through the wind-screen. 'Don't tell me that McBain has thought better of it,' he jerked out. 'Are those landing flares on the aerodrome, or am I dreaming?'

'They're flares,' declared Wilks, who was as surprised as Biggles. 'I've never known him do that before, and I've had to land after dark more than once.'

Biggles said nothing, but a curious expression came over his face as he stared intently into the gloom. A moment or two later he cut the engines and glided down towards the lights, only to open up again an instant later and roar up into the darkening sky. 'He must take me for a fool,' he snarled savagely.

Wilks stared. 'Who?'

'McBain.'

'Why?'

'To fall into such an elementary trap as the one he has set. Those lights are in the wrong place. Had I landed up the line I should have bashed straight into our hangar. Ginger, drop a signal flare and let's have a look at things. I'd rather trust to my own eyes than McBain's flares – the cunning hound. What sort of fellows can his pilots be to try deliberately to crash another machine?'

The signal light burst below the Jupiter, flooding the earth with its brilliant glare, and the trap was exposed to view. As Biggles had said, a machine trusting to the flares must have crashed to destruction in the Arctic Airways hangar. However, Biggles made no further remarks, but concentrated his attention on bringing the Jupiter down safely, and this he succeeded in doing. Taxiing swiftly up to the shed, he opened the cabin door and jumped down, looking sharply to left and right. Not a soul was in sight. And the flares had disappeared.

Without speaking they got the machine safely into the hangar, but they did not leave it.

'Where do you usually sleep, Wilks?' asked Biggles, as he took off his cap.

'I used to sleep in my hut, in a room next to the office; but lately, as I told you in my letter, I have been sleeping in the hangar. It isn't safe to leave the machine.'

'I can well believe that,' answered Biggles, nodding thoughtfully.

'Very well, we'll fix up quarters in the hangar, then the machine will always be in sight. Where's the pantry? I'm hungry.'

'Not so hungry as I am,' replied Wilks. 'I've had precious little to eat for the last three days. By gosh! – that reminds me – I'm almost out of stores. Is there any food left in your machine?'

'Very little except hard tack – emergency stuff – and I don't fancy that. In any case, I don't feel like touching it except in real emergency. You know what happens when you do that. When the emergency arises you go to the locker and find it empty. Where do you usually get your food supplies?'

'At the stores down in the village.'

'Whereabouts?'

'In the main street. There's only one place where you can get grub – the Three Star Saloon.'

'Then I'll go down and lay in a stock. We can't keep running up and down every day. Will you be all right here alone?'

'Why not? I've had to handle things by myself for a long time.'

'Good enough. Then I'll take Ginger with me to help carry the parcels. You get your cooking-things out and fix up sleeping-quarters while we're away. We shan't be long. After we've had a bite we'll have a talk about the position.'

CHAPTER IV

At the Three Star Saloon

I t was a walk of about two miles to the village of Fort Beaver, most of the way being across rough uncultivated country, from which in many places rugged masses of limestone rose up, worn by the storms of ages into fantastic shapes. Still, there was no risk of losing the way, for a vague footpath wound through the boulders towards the occasional yellow lights that glowed feebly from the log or frame huts which for the most part formed the houses.

Nor was there any mistaking the Three Star Saloon, a long building of rough-hewn timber, for three lanterns hung at regular intervals above the broad platform which ran along in front of it, enabling the sign to be read.

Without any misgivings Biggles pushed open the door and went inside. He had not given a thought to the possibility of McBain being there – not that he would have stayed away on that account. Nor did he imagine that the bar would be so well attended as it was. The loud buzz of conversation that greeted the ears of the two airmen as they walked in came, therefore, as a mild surprise.

The room was lit by several paraffin lamps, mostly of the hanging sort, around which eddied a mist of rank tobacco smoke that set Ginger coughing. Along the entire length of one side ran a counter, or bar, one half of which was devoted to the serving of drinks, and the other half to dry goods – mostly foodstuffs.

Biggles's eyes wandered over the occupants without particular interest. He did not expect to know any one, nor was he anxious to make new acquaintanceships, for he had no intention of staying. As far as he was concerned the shop happened to be a bar, and his one idea was to get what he came for and depart in the shortest possible time.

With this object in view he started walking down the saloon towards the far end, which, as it so happened, was the section devoted to the sale of food; and he was nearly halfway down before he saw McBain, with the other members of his gang, sitting at a table near one of the two circular stoves which heated the room. He noticed that McBain saw him at the same time, and his conversation ended abruptly. However, Biggles took no notice, but went on until he came to that part of the bar where the counter merged with the food department.

'Give it a name, stranger,' said the barman, who, judging by his clothes, was also the proprietor.

Biggles hesitated for a moment. 'As a matter of fact, boss, I didn't come in for a drink,' he answered in a friendly tone. 'I came in to get a supply of grub, but since you mention it I feel that a drop of something hot would not come amiss while I have a look round to see what you can supply in the food line. Have you got any beef extract or malted milk?'

'Both, though we don't get much call for it,' grinned the proprietor.

'Then we'll help to clear your stock. I'll have a Bovril; you can give me a packet of biscuits to munch with it. What about you, Ginger?'

'I'll have some malted milk,' decided Ginger.

The barman nodded and set about preparing the drinks, while Biggles took an old envelope from his pocket and started jotting down selected items from the things he saw exposed for sale – bread, biscuits, cheese, corned beef, tinned salmon, sardines, dried beans, and the like. By the time the barman returned with the drinks he had made a fairly lengthy list, and this he handed over for the things to be put together while he had his drink.

Ginger picked up his cup of malted milk, and realizing that there would be some minutes to wait, took it across to a vacant seat near the second stove; that is to say, the one other than that at which McBain and his company were sitting. The two stoves were some eight or ten yards apart. Actually, he did not see McBain until he was on the way to the stove, or it is possible that he would not have left Biggles; but having started he saw no reason for turning back, so he went on to the seat.

Several, men, trappers or prospectors judging from their clothes, were sitting near the stove engaged in conversation, but he paid no attention to them, beyond glancing at them curiously, until a name reached his ears. The name was Wilkinson – pronounced Wilkson by the man who had uttered it.

He was an old man, certainly not less than sixty years of age, and he was dressed in the traditional garb of a prospector – thick boots, woollen trousers, and fur jacket. On the back of his head was balanced precariously an ancient and battered hat of the Stetson type. Around his neck was wound a white-spotted red scarf, held together in front – incongruously, Ginger thought – with an opal-headed tie-pin.

'Ay, trust Angus to think o' somethin' for me to do,' continued the old man in a wheezy voice, as Ginger regarded him with sudden interest. 'I'm pullin' out agin termorrer, and I near forgot. "If yer see that feller Wilkson," ses Angus, "tell 'im I forgot to give 'im the transfer, but I've still got it." Maybe 'e'll need it and maybe 'e won't, so I guess I've got to trail across to that pesky airydrome.'

'Leave word 'ere, Mose,' went on one of the others. 'There ain't no call for you to go across to Wilkson yourself. One of us is bound to see 'im sometime, and we'll pass word on about the transfer.'

Ginger butted in. 'Excuse me,' he said, 'but are you referring to Captain Wilkinson of the aerodrome?'

'Sure I am, boy,' answered the old man, stuffing tobacco into a short clay pipe with a grimy thumb.

Ginger realized at once the significance of the old man's message, knowing that the Angus of whom he had spoken could be no other than Angus Stirling from whom Wilks had bought the land; and the transfer to which he referred must be the Government title-deed transferring the property to him – that is, to Angus Stirling. 'That's all right,' went on Ginger, not a little excited by this stroke of good fortune. 'I'm a friend of Captain Wilkinson's. My boss – over there at the bar – is his partner. I'll give him the message. As it happens, we need the transfer. Where is Angus now? We shall probably go and see him.'

The old man uttered a cackling laugh, in which the other men joined. 'Sure, go ahead,' he grinned. 'You'll find him on Muskeg Bend.'

'Where's that?' asked Ginger doubtfully, perceiving that his inquiry had provoked mirth, and suspecting the reason.

'On the south corner o' Eskimo Island,' chuckled the old man. 'Me and Angus are working on a claim there.'

Ginger shook his head ruefully, feeling a bit self-conscious at his ignorance. 'I'm afraid I've never heard of Eskimo Island,' he said, smiling apologetically.

'Don't cher worry about that, son; nor ain't a lot of others,' nodded the old man. 'It's farther north than a lot 'ud care to go; nor me, neither, if I hadn't got Angus with me – for which reason I've got to start back termorrer.'

It may have been a movement, or it may have been instinct, that made Ginger glance over his shoulder, and he experienced a sudden pang of apprehension when he saw a man standing so close behind him that he must have overheard every word that had been said. It was the Indian who had been on the aerodrome with McBain's party when they landed.

For a fleeting instant Ginger's eyes met those of the Indian, who then turned suddenly and glided away towards McBain.

Ginger turned quickly to the old man. 'Just a minute,' he said. 'I'd like to bring my boss over here.' So saying, he got up and walked quickly to where Biggles was still standing, checking the parcels as they were piled up on the counter. 'Biggles,' he said quietly but crisply, 'I've had a bit of luck. You remember what Wilks said in his letter about Angus Stirling, the man from whom he bought the land, and not getting the proper transfer?'

Biggles stiffened. 'What about it?'

'Stirling's partner is in here. I've just been talking to him. Apparently they're working a claim together up north, and Stirling asked his partner – that's him, the old man in the slouch hat – to tell Wilks that he still has the transfer. It struck me that we might fly him up and collect it. You'd better come and have a word with him.'

There was no need for Ginger to repeat his suggestion; almost before he had finished Biggles was on his way to the stove.

'Careful,' whispered Ginger, as he followed close behind. 'McBain and Co. are watching us.'

Biggles nodded to show that he had heard, but he did not so much as glance in McBain's direction.

'You're Angus Stirling's partner?' he began without preamble, addressing the old man.

'Sure,' was the brief reply.

'Is it correct that Angus asked you to tell Wilkinson that he still has the transfer of the land he sold him?'

'Ay, that's right enow. That's what he said.'

'I'm glad to hear it,' Biggles went on quickly. 'As it happens we need that paper badly. How far away is this claim of yours?'

''Bout fifteen hundred miles.'

Biggles's eyes opened wide. 'Gosh, that's a bit farther than I bargained for,' he admitted frankly. 'Still, that doesn't matter. Is it anywhere in Moose Creek direction?'

'Pretty near due north of it – 'bout twice as far, I guess.'

'And you're going back there?'

'Sure.'

'When?'

'Termorrer. I aim to catch the freeze-up. She'll be froze by the time I get to the water.'

In a vague sort of way Biggles realized that the old man meant that ice would have to form over a certain stretch of water so that he could get to the claim where Angus was working. 'How are you going to travel?' he asked.

The old man smiled and turned a bright eye on Biggles. 'There ain't no trains where I'm goin', mister,' he grinned. 'It's canoe to Moose River, where I aim to pick up my dogs.'

'Is Moose Creek somewhere on Moose River?'

'Sure.'

'I asked because I'm flying up to Moose Creek tomorrow,' went on Biggles. 'I reckon to make it in a day. If you care to come along with me that should save you quite a bit of time. Maybe we could go right on to the claim. How does that idea strike you?'

A childish grin spread slowly over the old man's face, and he scratched his ear thoughtfully. 'You mean – you aim to take me up in an airyplane?'

'That's it.'

'Well, I ain't never thought about travellin' that road, but I'll try anything onst. Termorrer, did you say?'

'Yes.'

'All the way to Moose Creek?'

'We'll go right on to the claim if there is any place where I could land. Is there a flat patch anywhere near the claim?'

'Sure.'

'How big is it, roughly?'

'About ten thousand square miles.'

'*What!*'

"Tain't nothin' else but flat patch as far as yer can see – when it's froze.'

'You mean this flat patch is ice?'

'That's it.'

'Ah! I understand.'

'Will there be room for the grub?' inquired the old man. 'I've got a fair load to get along – 'nough to last me and Angus till the break-up.'

'You can take anything up to a ton,' returned Biggles.

'I ain't got that much.'

'That's all the better. Be on the aerodrome at the crack of dawn and we'll make Moose Creek in one jump. Is that a deal?'

'You betcha.'

'See you in the morning, then.' Biggles turned, and saw McBain's Indian backing stealthily away. 'Was that fellow listening?' he asked Ginger quietly.

'I'm afraid so. I didn't notice him, though, or I'd have warned you.'

'Well, I don't see that McBain can do anything to stop us,' murmured Biggles as they returned to the bar. 'I've got to go to Moose Creek in the morning, anyway, and it won't be much extra trouble to go on to this claim, wherever it is. I'll get the old chap – what did they call him, Mose? – to mark the place on my map when he comes up in the morning. But we'd better finish our drinks and be getting back; Wilks will wonder what has happened to us.'

Biggles paid the score and, subconsciously aware that a curious silence had fallen on the room, reached for the cup that contained the remainder of his Bovril. Simultaneously there was a deafening roar and the cup flew to smithereens, splashing the liquid in all directions.

For a moment Biggles stared with startled eyes at the spot where the cup had been. Then, recovering himself quickly, he looked round. McBain was standing farther along the bar, a smoking revolver in one hand and a bottle of whisky – which presumably he intended taking away with him – in the other. From the offensive leer on his face, and his heavy-lidded eyes, it was clear that he had been drinking.

No one spoke. The only sound in the room was the soft shuffle of feet as the other men in the bar began to back away out of the line of fire.

'Give me another drink, boss,' requested Biggles quietly.

Silence reigned while the barman prepared another cup and set it on the counter in front of Biggles, whose hand had barely started moving towards it when McBain's gun roared again and the cup flew to pieces as the first one had done.

Unhurriedly, Biggles turned a reflective eye on McBain, who was now holding a glass in one hand while with the other he felt in his pocket, presumably for money to pay the score. The revolver, an almost imperceptible coil of smoke creeping from the muzzle, and the bottle of whisky rested on the bar in front of him.

'Give me another drink, boss, will you?' repeated Biggles, and put his hand in his pocket as if to take out the money to pay for it.

The barman set the cup in front of Biggles and then stepped back quickly.

McBain stood his glass on the bar. His hand moved towards the revolver, but on this occasion things did not go in accordance with his plan. Biggles's hand jerked out of his pocket. There was a double report, the two shots coming so close together that they almost sounded like one. There was a crash of shattering glass and a metallic *ping* as McBain's bottle of whisky splintered into a hundred pieces and his revolver spun along the polished bar before falling behind it.

Dead silence followed the shots. For a full ten seconds McBain stared unbelievingly at the puddle where the bottle had been, his right hand groping for the revolver that was no longer there. The face which he then turned to Biggles was white, mottled with dull crimson blotches. His eyes glared and a stream of profanity burst from his lips.

'What's the matter, McBain?' asked Biggles evenly. 'Any fool can play a game single-handed; you don't mind me joining in, surely?'

The other did not answer. With his big eyes on Biggles's face, very slowly he began creeping along beside the bar, his right hand, with the fingers clawed, sliding along the shiny surface.

'That's far enough, McBain,' Biggles warned him curtly. He knew that it would be fatal to come to grips with the man, who was nearly twice his weight and clearly had the physical strength of a bull. Once in McBain's grip and he would stand no chance whatever. Knowing this, he had no intention of allowing McBain to get his hands on him.

Biggles addressed the barkeeper. 'What is the usual procedure in a case like this, in this part of the world?' he inquired presently. 'Do I shoot him?'

"Ere, wait a minute,' snapped the bartender. 'I don't want no shooting 'ere.'

'I didn't start it,' Biggles pointed out.

'I know you didn't.' The bartender whirled round and snatched a heavy Colt revolver from a shelf behind him. He turned to McBain, scowling. 'That's enough, Brindle,' he said harshly. 'I ain't taking sides, but you asked for what you got. Now get this. You're always a causin' trouble in my bar. If yer can't carry yer liquor, go some place and learn, but yer ain't bustin' up my bar while I'm here.'

McBain ceased his bear-like advance towards Biggles, and turning slowly to the barkeeper, called him by an obscene name.

'I'd better plug him and rid the world of a dirty beast,' suggested Biggles, wondering at the back of his mind why McBain's friends did not take a hand. Snatching a glance in their direction, he understood. Ginger's automatic was covering them.

'Very slowly he began creeping along beside the bar'

How the matter would have ended it is impossible to say, but at that moment the outside door was flung open, and Delaney, the police constable, stood on the threshold, a carbine in his hands. 'What's the shooting?' he inquired bluntly.

'Only me and McBain seeing who can spill most liquor,' replied Biggles.

'You two at it again?' The constable's eyes went from one to the other. 'See here, stranger,' he went on, observing that Biggles was still holding his automatic in his hand, 'gun-play's finished in these parts – savvy? It went out with Buffalo Bill. This is a law-abiding township.'

Biggles nodded. 'Yes, I've noticed it,' he answered, smiling faintly.

'And I don't want any lip. Who pulled first?'

Biggles shook his head. 'Not me. I can't afford to waste ammunition.'

'McBain shot his drink,' shouted old Mose shrilly. 'I seen 'im.'

'Any more shooting between you two and I'll take away your firearms certificates,' declared the constable, eyeing Biggles and McBain in turn. 'And that goes for every one else in this room.'

'Quite right,' murmured Biggles, putting his automatic back into his pocket and then drinking his Bovril. 'Come on, Ginger; grab some of this stuff. Let's be going.'

As they went out he nodded to Mose. 'See you tomorrow – start at daylight,' he called.

Then the door closed behind them and they hurried back to the aerodrome.

CHAPTER V

Ginger Goes Scouting

They said little on the way back beyond congratulating themselves on the discovery of Angus Stirling's whereabouts, and adding a few words about McBain's behaviour.

'One of these days somebody will plug the drunken swine – and the sooner the better,' growled Biggles, as they strode into the hangar and deposited their parcels on a bench.

'I was just beginning to get worried about you,' Wilks told them. 'You were a long time.'

'McBain was there, and he tried to be funny,' replied Biggles, and reported the shooting incident at the saloon. 'But forget about that,' he continued quickly. 'What is far more important, we've got on the track of Angus Stirling. He is working a claim somewhere up north with an old fellow named Mose, who is now in Fort Beaver collecting stores for the winter. Angus actually sent a message to you by Mose – which he gave to us – to the effect that he has got the transfer of the land you bought off him, and you can have it when you want it.'

Wilks sprang to his feet. 'Want it! Why, that document is the key to the whole situation,' he cried. 'With that in our possession we can give Mr. Nosey-Parker McBain his marching orders, and call in the police to eject him if he doesn't clear off.'

Biggles nodded. 'That's the way I see it,' he agreed. 'That being so, I've arranged to collect the transfer just as quickly as possible.'

'How?'

'Mose is starting back for the claim tomorrow, so I've offered to fly him up. We'll land at Moose Creek, where I'll dump the freight for the gold people, and Mose can pick up his dog-team. Then I'm going to fly him on to the claim. He says there is plenty of room to get down.'

'That's marvellous,' declared Wilks enthusiastically. 'What a stroke of luck! I reckon I'm about due for a break; your arrival seems to have turned the tide. Is Mose coming up here in the morning?'

'At dawn.'

'Fine!' A shadow of anxiety crossed his face. 'You said McBain was there,' he muttered. 'Did he hear all this? If he did he may try to stop Mose—'

'I think he heard, but I don't see what he can do,' answered Biggles thoughtfully. 'From the way he chipped in over the shooting affair I don't think he has any great love for McBain. We'd better turn in early; we've got a long day in front of us tomorrow. Have you managed to get things fixed up here?'

'Yes, they're a bit rough, but I think we can manage.'

Some of the tinned food was soon opened, and the three airmen, sitting round a candle-lighted table near the big machine, said little more while they enjoyed their overdue meal. At last Biggles set down the tin mug from which he had been drinking quantities of steaming coffee made over Wilks's Primus stove.

'All we want tomorrow is a fine day,' he declared. 'With any luck Algy and Smyth will be back with the other machine. The next day – or the day after – we ought to be back with the transfer. Then, having mustered our forces, we'll see what McBain has to say. He'll find things a bit more difficult now that there are four of us instead of you by yourself. I wonder what the weather's doing?'

'The prophets forecast an early freeze-up,' Wilks pointed out.

'It was clear enough when we came in,' returned Biggles.

'I'll go and have a look at the sky,' offered Ginger, and leaving the table, he walked slowly to the hangar door and looked out.

He shivered a little as he stepped on to the tarmac, for there was a real nip in the air that suggested that frost or snow was not far away. However, the sky was clear, and although there was no moon, the stars glittered hard and bright in the heavens. For a moment or two he stood with his face turned upwards, glad that he would be able to tell Biggles that there was every promise of a fine day on the morrow, and he was about to return to the others when a dull yellow gleam appeared in the darkness not very far away. Instinctively he looked at it, and an instant later realized that it came from McBain's hangar or the workshops or office adjoining it.

'It would be interesting to hear just what's going on there,' he mused. 'Plotting some dirty business, I'll warrant.' The idea flashed into his mind that if his assumption was correct it would indeed be worth taking a little trouble to find out. There appeared to be no risk. 'Shan't be a minute,' he called over his shoulder quickly to the others, and then began walking cautiously towards the light – not in a straight line, but in a curve that would bring him to his objective from the rear.

He slowed down and moved with more caution as he neared the square of yellow light, which he now saw came from the window of one of the smaller buildings attached to the hangar. Step by step he advanced, every nerve keyed up, for he was quite prepared to find a sentry on guard. He decided that if he were challenged he would bolt for it.

But what he had feared did not happen, and a moment later he was crouching against the rough log wall of the hut, from the inside of which came a low, confused murmur of voices. Inch by inch he edged along the wall until he came to the window. He held his breath as he peeped into the room, for there was no blind or other obstruction to interfere with his view.

A glance showed him that four men were in the room, all sitting in various attitudes round a packing-case on which stood various glasses and a black bottle. They were the two pilots, Sarton and Ferroni, Chicot, McBain's bodyguard, and the Indian. McBain himself was not there.

At first Ginger could not hear what was being said, but he found that by pressing his ear close to a chink in the log wall he could follow the conversation fairly well.

Sarton was speaking. 'He's a long time,' he muttered, picking up his glass. 'I reckon you'd better go and look fer 'im, Jean.'

'No. He say "go on",' protested the half-breed. 'I stay here.'

The words had barely left his lips when Ginger heard the sound of heavy footsteps approaching. His heart gave a nervous leap, but his fears were allayed when he heard the footsteps halt on the far side of the hut. There came the sound of a door being opened and closed.

To his satisfaction he found that by placing his eyes level with the chink in the logs he could see into the room, which was far less risky than peeping round the edge of the window, where he might be seen if any one in the room looked in that direction.

Through his peep-hole he saw that, as he suspected, the newcomer was McBain. Clad in a long and rather dilapidated skunk-skin coat – Ginger recognized the fur by the characteristic white blaze – he was standing just inside the door, glaring at the four who were already there. It struck Ginger that he seemed agitated about something, for his face was pale and his movements abrupt. There was definitely an atmosphere of tension in the room, and, if proof of this were needed, McBain's first words confirmed it.

'Waal,' he growled, 'ain't yer never seen me before? What's biting yer?'

'Why – er – nothin', boss,' replied Sarton nervously.

'Waal, go on gassin' and don't stare at me,' growled McBain, dragging off his coat and hanging it on a peg on the inside of a cupboard door which he opened for the purpose.

'We was just figgerin' that you'd been a long time,' continued Sarton, in an explanatory sort of voice.

McBain jerked round with an abruptness that made the other start. 'That's a lie,' he fired out. 'I ain't been five minutes. Get that?'

'O.K. if you say so, boss,' agreed Sarton in a conciliatory way.

'Fact is, I came up here when you did,' went on McBain more quickly. 'I've just bin outside watchin' the weather, that's all. Remember that; if any one arsts you if I came back 'ere with you, you'll have to say yes or you'll be tellin' a lie. Savvy?'

'Sure,' agreed the others, in a sort of chorus.

'All right,' continued McBain, pouring himself out half a glass of what Ginger took to be neat spirit and throwing it down his throat. 'We're getting' busy tomorrow,' he added.

'Dey send de gold, ha?' asked the breed quickly.

'In a day or two,' answered McBain. 'About time, too.'

The word 'gold' made Ginger prick up his ears, and a moment later, for the first time, he saw McBain's activities in a new light.

'I reckon we'd have had it by now if this fool Wilkinson hadn't clung on so long,' went on McBain. 'It was just a fluke he collected and brought down the last two loads that was worth while. These buddies of his may make things harder. I don't like the look of that thin guy – Bigglesworth. He's a wise guy – and smart. But he won't be smart enough for me. I'll tear him in 'arves before I've done with him.'

'Do you think he'd come into the game if we gave him the low-down?' suggested Sarton.

'Not 'im. He ain't that sort,' growled McBain. 'Anyway, four's enough to split, without takin' in four more. I wouldn't 'a' minded one, when Wilkinson was alone, but I didn't trust 'im. No, we'll play as we are. Everything's all set. All we've got to do now is weigh in next time there's a heap o' dust ready to be brought down.'

'I donta like thees new guy, Bigglesworth,' muttered Chicot. 'I think, mebbe, it better if we fineesh heem soon.'

'Wait till Delaney's out on patrol,' said McBain. 'Then we'll see. Are they over there now?' He jerked his head in the direction of Arctic Airways' hangar.

'They all went in; we watched them go,' declared Sarton.

'O.K. Then I'll think about the best way of handling 'em between now and tomorrow. Got the ship ready to start?'

'All set.'

'Everything on board you'll be likely to want?'

'Everything.'

'Then I'll tell yer what to do in the mornin'. I'm goin' to turn in. I'm tired. Don't stay gassin' here half the night.' McBain picked up the bottle, and putting the mouth of it to his lips, emptied it.

The others stood up.

Ginger waited for no more. He had learned more than he had hoped for, so, after backing quietly away until he was what he considered a safe distance from the hut, he hurried back to the hangar, where he found the others just starting out to look for him.

'Where the dickens have you been?' asked Biggles sharply.

Ginger's manner was terse as he waved them back to the table. 'I've been indulging in what is generally reckoned to be a very questionable pastime. Some people might call it eavesdropping, but in time of war, like this, the best people call it scouting. I've been listening to McBain's little party over the way.' He turned and regarded Wilks with a curious smile. 'If you think those guys are here simply to run you off your aerodrome, Wilks, you've been thinking wrong. That isn't what they're after.'

There was a moment's silence.

'What *are* they after?' Biggles almost hissed the words.

Ginger drained his cup of half-cold coffee before he replied. 'Gold,' he said quickly. 'The little bags of yellow metal which the people at Moose Creek are digging out of the ground.'

Wilks nodded slowly. 'Kick me, somebody,' he said weakly. 'I never even thought of it.'

CHAPTER VI

A Staggering Blow

The stars were still twinkling in the sky, although those in the east were paling, when, the following morning, Biggles, Wilks, and Ginger pulled the Jupiter out of the shed and forced her head to wind ready to take off as soon as Mose arrived. A hearty breakfast, and Biggles and Ginger got into their flying kit, for it had been decided that it would be advisable for some one to remain on guard, and as Wilks was still feeling a bit shaken from his recent crash, he was to be the one to stay behind while the others took the delayed freight to Moose Creek.

While they were waiting they discussed the situation in the new aspect revealed by Ginger's opportune scouting expedition the previous night.

'It would be no use telling Delaney,' remarked Biggles quietly. 'Knowing that there is no love lost between us he'd think that we were just shooting a cock-and-bull story to put McBain and Co. under suspicion – and you couldn't blame him for that. At this stage it would be better to say nothing. Having got our own clock set right – so to speak – our game is to keep a closer watch on McBain's movements until we've got proof of his intentions.'

'How about warning the people at Moose Creek?' suggested Wilks.

'No use at all,' declared Biggles. 'They'd be less likely to believe us than Delaney. They would think, naturally, that it was simply a scheme to keep McBain out of the airline business. They might even tell McBain that we had reported them for a gang of crooks, in which case he would guard his movements more closely and make our task of exposing him more difficult. No, at this juncture we say nothing to anybody.' Biggles glanced at his wristwatch as he finished speaking. 'Old Mose is late,' he observed. 'I thought he would be here before this.'

'Who's this coming?' asked Ginger, who was staring in the direction of the village.

'Some one on a horse,' put in Wilks.

'Looks like Delaney – yes, it is him,' declared Biggles. 'He seems to be in a hurry, too.'

It soon became obvious that the Irish-Canadian 'mountie' was making for the Arctic Airways buildings, and a minute later he pulled his horse up and dismounted beside the waiting airmen. His blue eyes flashed to the Jupiter and then came to rest on Biggles's face.

'You pulling out?' he questioned crisply.

'Not exactly,' answered Biggles.

'What do you mean by that?'

'What I say. I'm going away, but not for good. As a matter of detail, I'm going to slip up to Moose Creek with some stuff they're waiting for.'

'Where did you go after you left the Three Star last night?'

Biggles raised his eyebrows at this change of subject. 'I came straight back here,' he said wonderingly.

'Could you prove that?' Delaney fired the question like a pistol-shot.

Biggles smiled faintly, and shrugged his shoulders. 'Well, naturally I don't clock my movements about, but if you are prepared to take Wilkinson's word, no doubt he's got a rough idea of what time I got back here. You saw how I was loaded up when I left the Three Star; it is hardly likely that I should go for a stroll at that time of night and with that load, is it?'

Delaney switched his eyes to Ginger. 'How about him?' he asked tersely.

'He came with me, of course,' declared Biggles. 'He had as many parcels as I had. What's all this about, anyway?'

'What were you three standing here for when I came along? You looked like you were expecting somebody.'

'We were,' agreed Biggles.

'Who?'

'Mose – I don't know his other name.'

'What did you plan to do with Mose?'

'Fly him up to Moose Creek, and then on to the claim he shares with Angus Stirling. Between ourselves, Delaney, Angus has still got the transfer of this property. If we can get it, it should enable us to give McBain the run-along.'

'I see,' said the constable slowly. 'Well, Mose won't be coming.'

'Why not?'

'He's dead.'

Biggles paled. 'Dead!' he cried incredulously. 'Why, he was as right as rain last night.'

'No doubt he would have been this morning, too, if some one hadn't clubbed his brains out.'

'You mean – he was *murdered*?'

'People don't beat their own brains out.'

'Great heavens!' Biggles's brain raced as he tried to focus the situation in its new aspect. 'You don't think we did it, by any chance, do you?'

'I'm going to find out who *did* do it.'

'Well, we had everything to lose and nothing to gain by his death,' Biggles pointed out. 'We want that transfer badly, and now he's gone we don't even know where the claim is.'

'Yes, I know,' broke in Ginger. 'He told me before you spoke to him. It was – dash it, what was the name of the place? – Eskimo Bend – no, Eskimo Island, wherever that may be.'

'By gosh, if we can't find the place, things will look bad for Angus. Mose was taking up the winter grub,' muttered Biggles.

'If he's on Eskimo Island he will be snowed in for six months when the freeze-up comes; so, as he won't have much grub left by this time, he's as good as a dead man,' declared Delaney.

'I'll take the grub up,' stated Biggles. 'I'll find his shack.'

'Then you've no time to waste,' said Delaney harshly. 'The snow's on the way. Don't all go. One of you had better stay here in case I want you. I'll go and have a word with McBain.'

'You've no objection to me going to the claim?' asked Biggles.

Delaney thought for a moment. 'No,' he said at last. 'Get back as soon as you can, though.'

With a curt nod, leading his horse, the constable strode away in the direction of McBain's shed, where McBain himself and his assistants were now pulling an aeroplane from the hangar.

As soon as Delaney was out of earshot Ginger swung round to Biggles. 'McBain killed him,' he whispered tensely. 'That's why he was so agitated when he came in to the others. I thought his manner was odd – I mentioned that when I was telling you what took place in the room.'

Ginger had, of course, described in detail to the others what had transpired in McBain's hut while he had been watching.

'I wonder,' murmured Biggles. 'Well, if he did, he certainly had a motive. No doubt he was told by that Indian of the arrangement I made with Mose, so by killing the old man he might have reckoned on stopping us making contact with Angus. So certain was I that Mose was coming with us that I didn't bother to ask him the name of the place. It's lucky he told you, Ginger. What's the name of it?'

'Muskeg Bend, on Eskimo Island, he called it.'

'That ought to be sufficient to enable us to find it,' muttered Biggles. 'The question is, does McBain know that we know where Angus is? It's no use guessing, anyway. We'll fly up there and let McBain do what he likes. You look after things here, Wilks. I'll take Ginger with me. With luck we ought to be back in two or three days – four at most. The first thing we've got to do is to get poor old Mose's grubstake up here, although it wouldn't surprise me if Angus packs up and pulls out when he learns what has happened. I imagine that Muskeg Bend isn't the sort of place where Angus would want to spend the winter alone. Let's see about fetching this grub.'

The business of fetching the food occupied some time, for it necessitated a journey to the village; more than one scowl was thrown at Biggles and Ginger as they walked through Fort Beaver, suggesting plainly that they were suspected of the crime that had cost Mose his life, but they took no notice. By the time they got back to the aerodrome Delaney had gone. So had the machine – one of McBain's Weinkel Twelve Transports – which had been outside the other hangar when they had left for the village.

'Where's that machine?' Biggles asked Wilks as they loaded the food in the Jupiter.

'It took off about twenty minutes ago, and headed north.'

'McBain go with it?'

'No. Sarton was flying. I think he only had Chicot with him.'

Biggles nodded, but made no comment on this piece of information as he climbed into the control cabin of the big machine. He was chiefly concerned with getting to Moose Creek as quickly as possible. He spent a minute studying his map, then folded it up and put it away. 'Eskimo Island isn't marked,' he told Ginger, who had got into the seat beside him. 'We shall have to ask where it is when we get to Moose Creek. I expect they'll know up there.'

He started the engines, ran them up, and tested his controls carefully. Satisfied that all was well, he waved to Wilks, who was watching them from the hangar, and then with his left hand moved the throttle slowly forward.

With its engines nearly under full power the Jupiter raced across the aerodrome, rose steadily into the air and sped away to the north.

CHAPTER VII

The Jupiter Heads Northward

Biggles only spoke twice during the next two hours; once, to tell Ginger to keep his eyes open for the Weinkel, and, some time later, to comment on its possible destination.

'I fancy we shall find it at Moose Creek,' he concluded, and in this he was correct.

They roared low over Wilks' Rockheed, which was still standing as they had left it the day before, but receiving the O.K. signal from Algy, they did not land. Biggles tilted the Jupiter's nose upwards as he climbed to his original height.

The country over which they now passed both fascinated and appalled Ginger, who had never seen anything like it before. He realized that he was looking at one of the forbidding sections of the world's surface, a vast area that was absolutely untouched by the hand of man. For the most part it was gaunt grey rock, twisted into a thousand fantastic shapes by vast upheavals when the earth was young, and later cut and scored by glaciers into rifts and gorges both great and small. Occasionally a clump of sparse, wind-twisted bushes mottled the rock; that was all. Once or twice he saw moving objects, which showed that there was a certain amount of wild life even in this wilderness, but the plane was too high for him to identify the animals. Only a small herd of elk did he recognize by their antlers. 'No wonder they call this the "bad lands",' he thought dismally. Instinctively – as most air-men do when flying over such country – he kept a lookout for possible landing places, but he saw none that he would have been willing to try except in the most extreme emergency.

The sun was hanging low over the western mountains like an enormous ball when Biggles picked up the river, which, judging from his map, would lead him to their destination. Soon afterwards the country became a little more open, but they were beyond the world of trees, and the stark barrenness persisted. They passed one or two isolated huts, and then, looking ahead, Biggles saw what he knew must be the gold-field. The river bayed out into a wide lagoon, on the banks of which were clustered a number of huts with corrugated iron roofs. Near them the ground was flat, rather like a marsh, and as they glided down they were able to discern wheel tracks which told them where machines usually landed – for the place could hardly be called an aerodrome.

In ten minutes they had landed and taxied up to the buildings – log huts of the most primitive description – where a man in a fur jacket was waiting for them.

'You Canwell?' called Biggles, guessing that it was the traffic manager.

'You've said it,' was the curt reply. 'You seen anything of Wilkinson?'

'Yes. I'm his new partner. I've brought your stuff along.'

'About time, too. If you fellows can't do better than this, I'll have to find another way of handling my output.'

'We shall do better in future,' Biggles promised him. 'We've had a little trouble, but we're all set now for a regular service.'

Canwell blew a whistle, at which some men appeared and began unloading the equipment. 'I've had one of McBain's machines here,' he told Biggles.

'When was it here?'

'Just now. It's just gone off.'

It struck Biggles as odd that they had not seen the Weinkel on its homeward journey, but he did not comment on it. 'What did the pilot want?' he inquired.

'He has offered to carry all my stuff – all of it, you understand – at fifteen cents a pound.'

Biggles was a bit taken aback by this 'cut' rate, but he did not show it. A smile broke over his face. 'Why, the fellow's a profiteer,' he said lightly. 'I'll do it – all of it – at twelve cents.'

Canwell registered surprise. 'You *will?*'

'Sure I will. We shan't get very fat out of it, but on the off-chance of you developing into a big concern we'll take a gamble on it – if you'll give us a contract and a monopoly.'

'Sounds fair to me,' agreed Canwell. 'I'll think that over and give you an answer tomorrow. You'll stay here the night, I reckon?'

Biggles looked at the sun. 'How much daylight have I got left?' he asked.

'What do you mean – how much daylight?'

'Well, what time will it get dark?'

'In about a week or ten days it will get properly dark, not before.'

Enlightenment burst upon Biggles. He realized that they were so far north that the disc of the sun did not drop below the horizon for the whole twenty-four hours, until it went for good for the long winter months. This meant that he could continue on his way without being overtaken by darkness.

'How far is it to Eskimo Island?' he asked.

'Best part of five hundred miles – as *you* travel.'

Biggles was relieved. He had supposed that it was even further.

'What direction?' he asked.

'Due north as near as makes no difference – why, what's the idea? There's only two white men north of us here – Angus Stirling and Mose Jacobs. There aren't two, now I come to think. Mose has gone out for grub.'

Biggles nodded. 'I know. Mose won't be coming back, either.'

'How so?'

'He was murdered last night.'

'The deuce he was!'

'Angus is expecting him back before freeze-up. Well, he won't be coming, which means that if Angus gets snowed in without grub, he's a goner.'

'By thunder! You're right there,' declared Canwell. 'Poor old Angus. He's a bit daft, but I'd be sorry to see him go. Who's paying you to take the grub up?'

'Paying me? Nobody. You don't suppose I'd let a man die unless some one paid me to save him, do you?'

'Nice work, feller. Can I help?'

'You've got petrol here?'

'Sure.'

'Then that's all I want. I'll give Angus his grub, or bring him back if he decides not to stop on.'

'He won't come, I reckon. If I was you I'd drop the stuff overboard near his shack; that'd save you landing.'

'I shall land if I can.'

'Why?'

'He's got a paper I want.'

Canwell's eyes clouded with suspicion. 'What sort of paper?'

'Wilkinson bought his landing-ground off Angus but Angus forgot to hand over the transfer. We've got a fellow trying to jump our claim—'

'Meanin' McBain?'

'Quite right. If we get the transfer we can ask him to find his own field.'

Canwell nodded understandingly. 'I get you,' he said. 'I heard something from Wilkinson about this dirty deal he's trying to put over. Well, you can handle my stuff in future – always provided that you are here on time to take it. Gold doesn't earn nothin' till it's in the bank, you understand, so the sooner it's in, the better. We can't afford to leave it lying about here. I aim to have a big shipment boxed ready to travel tomorrow, so if you're here you can take it down. I guess you'll be tired, though, if you're going up to Angus's shack.'

'Not too tired,' smiled Biggles.

'Fine. I shall expect you back here tomorrow, then. But whatever happens the metal's got to go to the bank, you understand that?'

'You mean – if I'm not here and McBain is, he'll take the stuff?'

'That's what I mean. My job is to make this concern show a profit, so personal tastes don't come into it.'

'Naturally.' For a moment Biggles was tempted to warn Canwell to be careful of McBain, but he thought better of it, realizing that the traffic manager was the sort of man who would take offence at any attempt to undermine a rival's character.

Biggles therefore turned away and attended to the refuelling of the machine. By the time this was completed Canwell had gone back to his work, so Biggles and Ginger climbed into their seats ready to renew their flight northwards.

'The thing that beats me,' muttered Biggles as he started the engines, 'is how Sarton got back past us without us seeing him.'

'He might have gone on to where we are going,' suggested Ginger.

Biggles started. 'Gosh! I never thought of that,' he admitted. 'Still, I don't think that's likely.'

'If he got to Angus first and induced him to part with the paper we should find it difficult to get it back.'

'That's true,' agreed Biggles. 'Well, we shall see.' He turned and looked Ginger straight in the face. 'You know, kid, I really ought to leave you here.'

Ginger opened his eyes wide. 'Why?'

'Because I imagine that the country we shall have to fly over is pretty grim; the sort that if we *do* hit trouble and have to come down, there'll be no getting off again. I doubt if we should be able to get back on our feet. Some of these tough lads, like Angus and Mose, might, but we're not used to it. We—'

'Just give her the gun and let's get off,' broke in Ginger impatiently. 'We're wasting time.'

A ghost of a smile played about Biggles's lips for a moment. Then he lifted a shoulder in an expressive gesture. His left hand felt for the throttle, and in a moment or two the big machine was nosing up into the sky, which had taken on a dull, leaden hue.

'Canwell was right when he said we had no time to lose,' he said.

'Why?'

Biggles nodded towards the sky. 'Take a look at that. It's going to snow before very long – and when it starts it's going to snow for a long, long time.'

CHAPTER VIII

A Grim Encounter

For more than two hours Biggles held the Jupiter on its northerly course, flying by compass since there were no landmarks – or rather, no landmarks which could be identified. For the most part the land below appeared to be a sterile wilderness, broken up frequently by mountain groups and ranges, depressing in their utter desolation, their flanks scarred by forbidding glaciers. Several times he made rapid calculations on his writing block, checking compass variation, as was necessary so near the Pole.

At length the ground became concealed under wide stretches of snow, or ice – they could not tell which. These stretches became wider and wider in extent until at last they merged into a continuous landscape of dull white. The sun appeared to be resting, motionless, on the horizon, flooding the scene with a wan light. Stars appeared in the heavens, glittering like chips of blue ice, but it did not get darker.

Ginger shivered suddenly, conscious of a terrifying solitude. He thought of Angus, and marvelled that any man should choose to live in such a place of death, even with the possibility of finding a fortune in gold.

He was about to remark on this to Biggles when a sound

reached his ears that caused every muscle in his body to stiffen. He had heard the sound before and knew what it was. It was the unmistakable rattle of a machine-gun. Before he could move, almost before he had thought of moving, the sound came again, this time much more distinctly, and almost simultaneously the Jupiter quivered as if it had been struck by a cat-o'-nine-tails.

Ginger's throat turned dry, and the next instant he was clinging desperately to his seat as the Jupiter soared upwards in a wild climbing turn. Bracing himself against the side of the cabin, he looked out of the window, and was just in time to see a Weinkel Transport go tearing past. The window nearest to him was open, and from it projected what appeared to be a short black stick, from the end of which danced a tiny streak of flame. Behind it was the face of the half-breed Chicot, his lips curled back from his teeth in something between a grin and a snarl.

'Use the signal pistol – it's all we've got.' Biggles's voice was like cracking ice.

Ginger glanced at him and saw that his face was white; his eyes glittered curiously.

'Get a move on,' continued Biggles. 'I'll try to put you into position for a shot. If you can hit 'em it may set 'em alight. You might hit a prop.'

A signal pistol against a machine-gun! Even Ginger was experienced enough to know that the odds were nearly hopeless. 'Need we stop and fight?' he asked tersely.

'They've got the legs of us by ten miles an hour,' was the curt reply. 'Use your pistol. Careful you don't fall out – I may have to throw the machine about.'

Ginger snatched the short large-bored signal pistol from its pocket, and taking one of the thick cartridges from its loop, thrust it into the breech. Forcing the hammer back with his thumb so that the weapon was at full cock, he put his arm through the window and waited. All he could see was sky, but the pressure inside his stomach – a force that seemed to glue him to his seat – told him that the machine was in a tight climbing turn.

Suddenly the Weinkel flashed into view, travelling like a meteor in the opposite direction, streaks of orange flame dancing from the muzzle of Chicot's gun.

Ginger took swift aim and fired, and knew at once that he had missed. A ball of green fire flashed across the nose of the other machine.

Sarton, the pilot, must have seen it coming, for he swerved sharply, which probably spoilt Chicot's aim. As he reloaded Ginger heard the burst of bullets strike the Jupiter somewhere near the tail.

In an instant the Weinkel had disappeared from his field of view, and he could only wait for it to reappear. It needed all his strength to brace himself against the window, for the Jupiter was never still for a moment. Subconsciously he wondered how long the heavy transport machine could stand such handling without falling to pieces.

Again the Weinkel whirled into view, this time coming at him almost head-on. The half-breed was no longer at the window. Apparently he had decided that from the cabin his field of fire was too restricted, so he had climbed up so that the top half of his body projected through the upper part of the fuselage between the wings, a position from which he would be able to fire in any direction.

Ginger realized at once the advantages of this all-round gun-platform, and determined to copy it if his shot missed. He took careful aim at the on-coming machine; unluckily for him, just as his finger was tightening on the trigger, a bullet struck the window frame near his face, and a tiny splinter stung his cheek, causing him to flinch, with the result that his shot went wide. In a flash, following his shot, for which Biggles had waited, the Jupiter whirled upwards and the Weinkel was hidden from view.

Ginger scrambled back into the cabin and grabbed the remaining cartridges – there were only four – and thrust them into his pocket.

'What are you going to do?' snapped Biggles.

'I'm going outside,' returned Ginger crisply.

'Hang on tight.'

'I'll watch it.'

Another moment and Ginger had flung back the emergency trap in the roof and was climbing out. With one hand gripping the edge of the trap, and the pistol ready in the other, he looked round for the attacking machine, and saw it on the opposite side of the narrow circle round which both aircraft were racing. The icy blast of the slipstream smote his face and tore at his body as if he had been naked, and he knew that he would not be able to endure the exposure for long without becoming frozen. Furthermore, it was as much as he could do to hang on, for the Jupiter did not maintain a straight course for a moment, for which reason, no doubt, Chicot had failed to score a vital hit.

Twice Biggles took the big machine into position for a shot, but each time the tearing slipstream spoilt his aim. However, it had this effect; the erratic movements of the Weinkel showed that Sarton was nervous of being hit by a missile which would probably send him down in flames, and his jumpiness, combined with Biggles's manoeuvring, made Chicot's task no easy one.

Ginger had now only two cartridges left, and he determined to make the most of them. He had his automatic, of course, and he knew that Biggles also had one, but he also knew that in air combat such weapons are practically useless. His first chance came when Biggles whirled like lightning and tore straight under the Weinkel, passing under it so close that Ginger instinctively ducked, thinking that he was likely to be knocked out of the Jupiter by the Weinkel's undercarriage. He fired straight up, but the shot, failing to strike a rigid member, went slap through the fabric and out the other side, without doing any more damage than making a neat hole which did not affect the Weinkel's performance.

With the tears that the icy blast forced from his eyes freezing on his cheeks, he thrust his last cartridge into the breech. He had to put the pistol in his pocket in order to hang on with both hands while Biggles did an Immelmann turn, but he grabbed the weapon again as the Jupiter came out in the position this manoeuvre is designed to effect – on the tail of the opposing machine.

Sarton must have known that Biggles was screaming down on his tail, and in his panic dived to such an extent that, although Chicot continued to fire short bursts at the Jupiter, now not more than twenty yards from his tail, he could not properly control the jumping gun.

Ginger clenched his teeth, and taking deliberate aim, fired down between the whirling circles of the Jupiter's propellers. To his dismay the cartridge misfired. As quickly as his numbed fingers would permit he opened the breech, moved the cartridge slightly so that the firing-pin would strike another place, and fired again. Once more the expected report failed to occur.

By this time the Jupiter was almost immediately above the

Weinkel and fast overhauling it; so much so that Chicot was compelled to turn completely round in order to bring his gun – a squat submachine-gun – to bear. Ginger realized with a horrible choking sensation of fear that if Sarton, unaware of their close proximity, pulled his stick back, both machines would collide with such force that they would be reduced to matchwood. He did the only thing that was left for him to do. He flung the now useless pistol.

It was only by a matter of a few inches that he did not succeed in what he hoped to achieve; but a miss, they say, is as good as a mile, and so it was in this case. The pistol struck the port engine cowling just behind the propeller, bounced harmlessly, and then dropped off into space. At the same moment Biggles dragged the Jupiter away from its dangerous position, and Ginger, half dead with cold, slid back into the cabin.

Biggles looked at him inquiringly.

'Missed!' shouted Ginger. 'No more cartridges. Can you put us in that position again?'

Biggles merely nodded. He did not seem in the least perturbed, and something of his calm confidence transmitted itself to Ginger, who smiled as far as his frozen cheeks would permit and then staggered into the main cabin, from where he returned an instant later carrying a foot-square box branded with large black letters:

20 LB. CORNED BEEF

STOW AWAY FROM ENGINES

Not without difficulty Ginger dragged this unwieldy weapon up into his recently held position above the fuselage. Biggles had already begun the Immelmann which starts with a steep climbing turn, so that it seemed to Ginger that the world had suddenly broken adrift from its orbit and was spinning with dizzy speed.

Steadying the box with his left hand, he stared about him through streaming eyes for the Weinkel, and saw it some distance below, circling as if the pilot had temporarily lost them. Then, as if up-borne by a current of air, it seemed to float upwards towards him. He knew, of course, that this was simply the effect of Biggles's dive, which had now begun.

Wondering if he would be able to force his fast-numbing muscles to act when the crucial moment came, Ginger waited for his opportunity. He had a feeling that he was mad, hoping to knock down an armed adversary with a weapon so prosaic as a box of corned beef. Still, by taking a big risk he did not see why it should not be done, and as far as risk was concerned it was a case of neck or nothing now.

With a calmness that surprised him he saw Chicot feverishly reloading his gun; saw him train the weapon on him; saw the tiny spurts of flame start leaping from the black muzzle. Twice he heard the vicious crack of a bullet boring through the machine, and found time to pray that Biggles had not been hit. For a ghastly moment, as the Jupiter suddenly steepened its dive, he feared that he had, and it may have been the horror of this suspicion that caused him to stake everything on one desperate chance. Raising himself on one knee, he waited while the two machines closed up as though drawn by an invisible magnet; then, as the Jupiter swooped low over the Weinkel, he stood upright and with all his force flung the heavy box outwards and downwards. For one terrible second he thought that he was going too, for he almost lost his balance. Dropping on to his knees, he clawed frantically at the smooth fabric; his questing fingers found

*'He stood upright and with all his force flung the
heavy box outwards and downwards'*

a rib under the canvas, and although as a handhold this was poor enough, it stayed his progress long enough for him to grasp the edge of the trap and drag himself back to comparative safety.

Now during the brief instant of time in which this had occurred his eyes had never left the box; they had followed its course with a sort of morbid fascination. It was clear from the start that it would not hit the fuselage of the other machine; in fact, he thought that it would not hit it at all. Nor would it have done so but for the fact that at the last moment Sarton must have moved his joystick. The movement was so slight that it could hardly be regarded as such; but it was enough. The Weinkel's wing-tip seemed to move towards the box, which was turning so slowly as it fell that subconsciously Ginger re-read the words on it as they came into view – 20 LB. CORNED BEEF ...

The box struck the Weinkel's wing about four feet from the tip. The impact occurred just behind the leading edge, and from what immediately happened it was clear that the weight, falling on the main spar where the strain was greatest, caused it to break instantly. The whole wing-tip seemed to crumple up like a piece of tissue paper, twisting back on itself like a worm under a clumsy gardener's heel.

Fortunately, the effect of this was at once exercised on the whole machine. The fractured wing, losing a great percentage of its lift, sagged, causing the machine to fall in that direction. Ginger could imagine the wretched Sarton fighting to right his machine, but in such a case an aircraft is as helpless as a bird with a broken wing. For a second or two the plane zoomed this way and that as the pilot tried to hold his crippled machine on even keel; then the nose followed the dropping wing, and an instant later the Weinkel was spinning earthward.

In fascinated horror Ginger watched it go; he saw the damaged wing 'balloon' as the air rushed into it; saw it rip off at the roots and follow the rest sluggishly, like a piece of torn paper; saw the fuselage spin faster and faster; saw the half-breed flung off and go plunging down beside it, clutching vainly at the air ...

He turned away and fell back weakly into the cabin, limp from reaction now that the danger had passed. He felt no sympathy for the two doomed men in the Weinkel, for the fate that was theirs was what they had intended for those in the Jupiter. The poetic justice of it could not be denied. Dragging himself into his seat he turned a white face to Biggles and saw that he was looking down out of the side window, and the roar of the engine died away. From the angle of the floor he knew that the Jupiter was going down. Following Biggles's eyes he was just in time to see the Weinkel hit the snow and crumple to a thousand fragments. A great pillar of fire leapt heavenwards.

Biggles turned an expressionless face to Ginger. 'They got what they asked for,' he said grimly. 'It's no use our risking a landing.'

His hand went to the throttle; his engines burst into their full-throated bellow again and the nose of the Jupiter crept up until it was level with the horizon. With the machine levelled out Biggles turned again to Ginger. 'Good work, laddie,' he said. 'You'll find some hot coffee in the thermos; you look as if you need it.'

CHAPTER IX

Down in a Frozen World

For some minutes neither of them spoke. Ginger literally gulped the hot coffee, for he was so cold that his lips were stiff and numb. Then he began a vigorous massage of his face and hands to restore the circulation.

He did not expect any great praise from Biggles for what he had done; nor did he get any – which did not mean that Biggles did not appreciate it. Biggles himself did whatever circumstances demanded; Algy did the same, and this example Ginger had learned to follow.

At last Biggles spoke. 'Even now I can hardly believe that McBain would put over a show like that,' he observed bitterly. 'I knew he was pretty bad, but I thought there were limits to how far he would go. Well, it's taught me a lesson. I'll never move without a machine-gun in future. That devil Sarton deliberately waylaid us. But we had better start looking out for Eskimo Island; we can't be far off it, but how on earth we are going to tell where it is or which it is I'm dashed if I know. In some silly way I had imagined that we were going to see an island with water round it, but everything seems to be frozen up. Some snow must have fallen, too, so we can't tell which is land and which is water.

Judging by its extent, and the flatness of it, I should say that that's ice under us now. Those humps ahead should be land, but they may be icebergs frozen into the pack-ice. I don't know. This is going to be a lot more difficult than I thought. I'm half sorry I started. Keep a sharp lookout; I'm not going to hang about long and risk running out of juice. This sort of landscape gives me the heeby-jeebies.'

Ginger, somewhat restored, caught his breath as he looked down at the scene of appalling desolation and loneliness underneath them. He was about to remark on it, to say that they must be off their course since it was inconceivable that a man should leave civilization with all its comforts for such a dreadful place, when one of the engines spluttered, picked up, and then spluttered again.

Biggles was already turning. 'A pretty spot for an engine to pack up,' he muttered viciously. 'I—'

Whatever he had been going to say was left unsaid, for at that moment the port engine cut out dead. But it was not that alone that caused Ginger's lips to part in dismay. The other engine was also spluttering.

A horrid suspicion flashed into his mind. Throwing open the narrow door that led into the freight compartment, he darted in, but was back in an instant, face ashen. 'It's petrol,' he cried, in a high-pitched voice. 'There is petrol everywhere; it's slopping over everything. One of Chicot's bullets must have holed the main tank.'

Even as he spoke the second engine, after a sullen backfire, died out. Both propellers stopped, and a weird silence fell, an unnerving silence broken only by the faint whine of the wind over the wings.

Biggles pumped frantically at the hand-pump that filled the gravity tank; but it drew its supply from the main tank, and the main tank was empty. Nothing happened, so he abandoned the useless task and concentrated his attention on bringing the machine down; it was, of course, already gliding towards the frozen wilderness below.

Ginger looked down to see where they were going. In a subconscious way, without actually thinking about it, he was quite certain that they were as good as dead. He did not give up hope easily, particularly since they had found a way out of so many tight corners, but try as he would, he could think of no possible way out of their present dilemma. Suppose Biggles did manage to put the machine down without breaking anything; what then? The only thing that could get them into the air again was petrol, and that was something they would certainly not find where they were going. To walk all the way back to Moose Creek, a matter of four hundred miles, across such country as they had flown over, was so utterly out of the question that he did not even think of it.

The Jupiter continued to sink with that curious floating feeling customary in such cases, accompanied by the usual soft whine of wind blowing past the wings. As they sank lower it grew perceptibly darker, until, near the ground, the plane was moving through a peculiar twilight, dim, yet light enough to see clearly and for a considerable distance.

The need to choose a landing-place did not arise. The ground was all the same, a never-ending expanse of snow in all directions as far as the eye could see; only to the north a jagged ridge – ice or rock, they knew not which – showed clear and hard against a sky of dark, steely blue.

Ginger braced himself as Biggles flattened out to land. He could see no obstruction, but he had a feeling that the dead-flat surface looked almost too good to be true. Again, there was no way of telling if the snow was hard or soft; if it was very soft, then the wheels of the now lowered undercarriage would certainly sink into it and cause the machine to pull up so suddenly that it would inevitably tip up on its nose.

Nothing of the sort happened. The wheels bumped softly, running through the snow with a gentle hissing sound; then, very slowly in the still air, the tail dragged and the machine came to rest.

For a little while neither of them spoke. Biggles yawned and rubbed his eyes. 'Lord!' he muttered, 'I'm tired. I could go to sleep easily.'

'From what I can see of it we shall shortly be going to sleep for a long, long time,' answered Ginger bitterly. 'Strewth! What a place! If I'd just woke up I should have thought I was on the moon.'

Biggles grinned. 'It isn't exactly what you'd call a hive of activity, is it?' he said evenly, feeling for his cigarette case. Then, the reek of petrol warning him of the danger of lighting a match where he was, he opened the door and jumped down.

Ginger followed him, noticing that their feet rested on black ice under an inch or two of snow. Looking about him, he was appalled by the stark desolation of the scene. They might have been the only people on earth. The only familiar object he could see was a narrow rim of the sun, blood-red, just showing above the horizon. But it was the silence that affected him most; it seemed to worry the eardrums, and the noise of Biggles's match, as he struck it to light a cigarette, sounded like a crash.

Biggles nudged his arm. 'Look!' he said.

Half a mile away two whitish-grey shapes, one large and the other small, were moving in a tireless lope towards the south. Ginger started back in alarm as he recognized them for polar bears, a mother and a cub, but he recovered his composure when he perceived that they took not the slightest notice of them. They might have been accustomed to seeing aeroplanes standing on the ice all their lives. At a perfectly even speed they continued on their way, leaving a faint wake of smoky breath hanging in the air to mark their passage. Presently they seemed to fade into the surrounding gloom, and were seen no more. To Ginger they seemed like the living spirit of the frozen north, and he shivered as he turned back to Biggles, for the cold was intense.

'Well,' he said, 'what do we do next?'

'To tell the truth, laddie, I was just wondering,' replied Biggles. 'There doesn't seem to be an awful lot we can do, does there? But we needn't give up hope. The position may not be so bad as it appears at first sight.'

'Well, that's comforting, anyway,' muttered Ginger. 'How did you work it out?'

Biggles blew a puff of smoke into the still air before he replied. 'First of all, we've got enough grub inside to last us a long time. I'm afraid it's going to be a bit tough on Angus if we eat it, but since he is never likely to find us here, and we are unable to find him, we should be fools to starve ourselves to death on that account. We have also got the cabin to sleep in. It isn't much protection against this perishing cold, but it's better than nothing.'

'And when the grub's all gone?' prompted Ginger.

'Don't be so confoundedly pessimistic,' Biggles chided him. 'I haven't finished yet. As I see it, we've got two fairly sound chances. The first is, obviously, that Algy and Wilks will come to look for us in Wilks's Rockheed. We should hear their machine a great way off in this atmosphere, and if we lit a fire – which we could, easily – they could hardly fail to spot it. The place doesn't exactly bristle with illuminations, as you can see. The second chance is that we shall see or hear something of Angus. We must be somewhere near Eskimo Island, and we must be pretty close to the track he would follow if he started off to meet Mose. Not knowing the facts, he might think that he'd had a mishap, and come looking for him.'

'That's true enough,' acknowledged Ginger. 'Gosh! It's cold! I'm going—' He broke off, staring at the sky. He raised a quivering forefinger. 'Why – look! There's a searchlight,' he cried. 'It must be Algy. There's another – three – four – why, there's a dozen. What the dickens is going on?'

Biggles looked round sharply, then laughed. 'I've never seen it before in my life, but having read about it I should say it's the aurora borealis.'

Ginger nodded. 'Of course,' he said. 'I didn't think of that. My goodness! Look how the colours change. I could watch it for a long time.'

Biggles grinned. 'Well, you'll have plenty of opportunity,' he observed cheerfully.

'But *that* isn't the aurora borealis, I'll swear,' cried Ginger emphatically, pointing in the direction of the distant ridge. 'That's a fire, or I never saw one in my life.'

Biggles turned quickly. 'Where do you mean?' he asked tersely.

'Well, that's funny. It's gone now,' said Ginger in a puzzled voice. 'You see those two extra sharp peaks a little to the right? It seemed to be at the foot of those.'

'Are you sure you're not imagining things?' asked Biggles doubtfully.

'I'm absolutely certain I saw a light,' declared Ginger. 'It just flared up, remained steady for a moment, and then went out again. It was as if somebody had opened the door of a lighted room and then shut it again.'

'I hope you are right,' said Biggles. 'If you are, it can only mean one thing – Angus. It is unlikely that there are two men up here. Those peaks must be Eskimo Island! What a stroke of luck.'

'What shall we do?'

'It's no use staying here,' answered Biggles. 'I wonder if Angus is keeping watch for Mose to return. Let's light a fire. We shall soon get an answer if he spots it, in which case we'll load up some food and make for the shack. He'll probably help us to fetch the rest. Come on, let's get a fire going.'

With some pieces of petrol-soaked rag and packing-paper they soon had a bright fire burning at a safe distance from the machine, all the time watching the steely-blue haze that seemed to hang at the foot of the peaks, obscuring the physical features of the island – if, indeed, it was the island.

Nothing happened. There was no answering flame.

'He must have gone inside,' muttered Ginger in a disappointed voice.

'I should feel happier if I had seen the light myself,' said Biggles.

'You can take it from me that there was one,' returned Ginger.

'It wasn't a reflection of the aurora on a piece of ice, or anything like that?'

'Definitely not. What I saw was yellow lamplight.'

'All right. I'll take your word for it. If Angus won't come to us we had better go to him. It's not much use staying here.' Biggles turned towards the machine.

Nothing more was said. They both loaded themselves up with as many of the food boxes as they could conveniently carry, and then set off towards the distant peaks. How far away they were was difficult to judge. Ginger said two miles. Biggles guessed five. As it turned out, he was the nearer of the two, but he was a good deal out in his reckoning.

CHAPTER X

A Desperate Meeting

'Well, I don't know, but those hills seem no nearer to me now than when we started.'

It was Biggles who spoke, and they had been walking for a good hour when he made the observation.

Ginger stopped and set his load down on the thin blanket of snow that covered the ice under their feet. 'I didn't like to mention it, but I also had noticed that,' he said, massaging his lips, on which his breath had caused a film of hoar-frost to form. He turned and looked at the Jupiter, standing alone and forlorn at a distance which he would have judged to be not more than half a mile, although he knew from the length of time they had been walking, and the pace, that it could not be less than three miles.

There was just a hint of anxiety in Biggles's voice when he spoke again. 'Judging by the distance we must be from the machine, those hills ahead must be ten miles away. Still, it's no use sitting down; that won't get us there. Let's keep going.'

Ginger picked up his luggage again.

Biggles was watching him. 'What's the matter – tired?'

'Just a bit,' admitted Ginger.

They said no more, but trudged on towards the still distant hills.

Another hour passed.

'Angus doesn't seem to be about,' observed Ginger. 'I wish he'd show that light again. It would – sort of – cheer one up.'

'By the clock it's somewhere about the middle of the night,' Biggles told him. 'He's probably fast asleep in bed.' He glanced up at the sky.

'What do you keep looking up at the sky for?' asked Ginger. 'That's the twentieth time you've done it.'

'I was just looking at the stars,' answered Biggles. 'It may be my imagination, but it struck me that they weren't quite so bright as they were.'

Ginger glanced up. 'They're not,' he said shortly. 'What's that a sign of?'

'I don't know,' confessed Biggles. 'I know nothing about the meteorological conditions in this part of the world, but if I was nearer home I should say that there's snow on the way.'

'Then we'd better move a bit faster,' rejoined Ginger. 'Things won't look too rosy if we get caught out here in the snow.'

Biggles did not answer, but, picking up his luggage, set off at an increased pace.

At the end of another hour it was apparent that the peaks towards which they were marching were definitely nearer. They could no longer see the Jupiter; it had merged into the vague background.

'Not much farther,' said Biggles brightly, taking a surreptitious glance at Ginger, for he had noticed for some time that he was lagging. This did not surprise him, for he, too, was conscious of an increasing weariness.

They toiled on again, both of them dragging their feet through the snow, whereas at first their trail had been clear cut. Biggles took one of the largest parcels from Ginger's pile and added it to his own. Ginger started to protest, but Biggles silenced him with a word. 'When in a jam, all pull on the same rope,' he added. 'I'm as fresh as when I started.' This was not strictly true, but Ginger was too tired to argue. His hands and feet had begun to pain him.

Another half-hour brought them to their objective, and as Ginger looked at it his heart sank. It was darker than when they had started; the world was bathed in a sort of cold blue twilight, dim, yet sufficient to reveal the silent crags that rose straight up from the frozen sea, and formed the coastline of the solitary island. The silence was unnerving; so profound was it that it seemed to Ginger that it should be possible to hear the stars twinkling. Nothing else moved. All around was a land of death, as devoid of life as the earth must have once been.

Biggles eyed the cliffs with disfavour. 'I've seen more cheerful spots in my time,' he remarked lightly. 'We can't climb that stuff; we'd better walk along the base until we come to a break.'

They set off again, now following the foot of the cliff, and soon afterwards came to a gigantic gorge, like a vast split in the rock's face. It was not very wide, but the sheer walls were nearly a thousand feet in height, so that the airmen, as they stood at the entrance, looked like two microscopic insects in comparison.

Biggles regarded the chasm doubtfully. Nothing moved. Not a bush or a blade of grass grew; only, here and there, on the rock, a sort of grey lichen or moss. Not a sound broke the eerie silence but their laboured breathing. 'It doesn't seem possible that a human being would willingly exist in such a dreadful place as this,' he said quietly. 'But in the absence of any other way into the island, this must be – what did Mose call it? – Muskeg Bend. If it is, is the shack on the top or at the bottom? Well, I suppose we might as well go in a little way; we can always come back if we find we are wrong.'

They had proceeded a little way into the gloomy ravine when Ginger let out a sudden cry. 'Tracks!' he shouted excitedly. 'This must be the place!'

They hurried towards a long straight mark in the snow, but when they reached it Biggles stopped suddenly. There were two tracks, one wider than the other. 'They weren't made by human beings,' he said firmly. 'I've got it. Those two bears we saw must have come this way.'

Ginger's face fell. 'Confound it,' he muttered, 'I thought we'd struck lucky at last. Hello! What's that?' He looked ahead at a tiny moving object that was floating slowly downward in the still air in front of him. It was not unlike a small grey feather.

'Snow,' said Biggles, grimly. 'That's the first flake. We've got to find Angus pretty soon – or else—'

'How about shouting?' suggested Ginger. 'I should think sound would carry a long way in a place like this.'

'We can try it,' agreed Biggles. 'I think this will be better than shouting, though.' He put his hand in his pocket and took out his automatic. Pointing the muzzle in the air, he pulled the trigger three times at equal intervals.

Ginger flinched as the shots crashed out, reverberating again and again between the towering rock walls. The noise was more like a salvo of artillery fire than mere pistol reports. 'Gosh!' he murmured in an awestruck voice, as the echoes finally rolled away to silence. 'What a din! If Angus is within fifty miles I should think he'll hear that.'

Biggles smiled. 'A little hectic, wasn't it?' he agreed. 'The question is, do we go on or do we wait here?'

'We'd better go on a bit,' suggested Ginger. 'If he comes here he'll see our tracks and follow us. The trouble is, even if he showed a light it is doubtful if we should see it down here in the bottom of this gully.'

They moved on again, pausing from time to time to listen.

They had covered perhaps a hundred yards in this way, with big flakes of snow falling regularly, when Ginger suddenly pulled up short. 'There's something moving ahead,' he said quietly.

'I can see it,' came the swift answer. 'Stand fast. It's a bear. He's coming this way – following the tracks of the others. Don't shoot whatever you do. Gosh, what a monster! He must be the father of that cub we saw. Here, let's get over to one side; he may go past. If he comes for us then we shall have to use our pistols – not that they'll be much use against that brute.'

Dropping their loads, they both ran as fast as they could towards the side of the ravine, giving free passage to the bear, which was following the tracks down the middle, snuffling and grunting to itself as it ambled along without any great haste. When the airmen could get no farther on account of the cliff, they turned to watch.

The bear, an enormous shaggy brute that looked grey in the half-light, snuffled along until it came to the place where the two airmen had stood. For a moment there seemed to be a chance that it would go right on, but the human taint seemed to upset it, for it sat up on its haunches and looked around. After a moment or two spent like this, during which time it did not appear to see the airmen crouching against the cliff, it dropped on to all fours again and began following their tracks towards where they waited breathlessly. It moved hesitatingly, grunting and snuffling in the footmarks, occasionally stopping to sit up and look around in a manner which, in a small animal, might have been funny. But a full-grown polar bear is a very large animal, and neither Biggles nor Ginger saw any humour in the situation as the huge beast slowly drew near to them.

Then, suddenly, during one of its sitting-up periods, it saw them. Instantly it raised itself on its hind legs and let out a deep snarling grunt.

'Look out, he's coming!' jerked out Biggles. 'It's no use running. Wait until he gets close and then make every shot tell.'

With his heart hammering against his ribs, Ginger whipped out his automatic and waited. The pistol seemed a futile weapon against such a great beast, but it was all he had.

When the bear was about twenty yards away Biggles let out a yell, which caused it to pull up dead, emitting a rumbling growl deep in its throat. Then, with its head held low and muzzle thrust forward, it came on again.

Biggles took a pace to the right. 'Keep to the other side of it,' he jerked out.

As the words left his lips the beast rose up on its hind legs and ran forward in a stumbling charge. Biggles fired, and a choking grunt told them that the bullet had found its mark. But it did nothing to stop the beast's progress. At a distance of five or six yards Biggles fired again, at which the animal let out a roar and turned to bite at the place where the shot had struck. But its halt was only momentary, for with a roar of fury it darted forward again.

Biggles side-stepped and blazed point-blank at the pointed head, but without stopping its berserk progress. Then, in his haste to step aside, he slipped and measured his length in the snow. In a flash the bear was over him.

'In a flash the bear was over him'

To Ginger the moment was one of stark panic. His one conscious thought was that he must save Biggles. Hardly knowing what he was doing, he rushed up to the bear and, thrusting the muzzle of the pistol into the thick fur behind the animal's ear, pulled the trigger. The next instant he was swept off his feet as the bear turned on its new aggressor; a hairy paw caught him a sweeping blow on the shoulder and he went over backwards, the pistol flying out of his hand as he fell. A sickening stench of bear filled his nostrils. A roaring report almost deafened him. Then a great weight seemed to settle on his body, crushing the life out of him. He felt himself being pressed farther and farther into the snow, but he still fought with the panic of despair. Something seized him by the arm and he let out a scream, thinking that it was the bear's jaws. Then the scene seemed to change and he scrambled to his feet, panting and muttering incoherently.

'Ach, now! Take it easy,' said a strange voice in a strong Scots accent.

Ginger stared at a short, broad-shouldered figure, with a rifle in the crook of its arm, that suddenly appeared in front of him. Out of the corner of his eye he saw Biggles picking himself up out of the snow. Then he understood.

'Are you Angus Stirling?' he blurted out.

'Ay, mon, that's me name,' was the casual reply. 'And what might *ye* be doin' in these parts, if I may ask?'

Ginger rubbed his shoulder ruefully. 'We were looking for you,' he said, thinking how silly the answer sounded. 'Did you shoot this brute?' he went on, pointing to the body of the bear.

'I did so,' replied Angus. ''Twas about time, too, I reckon.' Beyond that the bear did not appear to interest him. 'And what might your name be?' he inquired.

'Let's go to your shack and I'll tell you all about it,' put in Biggles.

'Ay, mebbe that'd be best,' agreed Angus, and, turning, led the way up the ravine.

CHAPTER XI

An Unpleasant Shock

It was not far to the old Scotsman's cabin, which was situated on the side of a hill which faced south, for which reason it had been seen by the airmen out on the icefield when he had opened the door to bring in some peat for the fire. He told them that he was just going to sleep when he heard the three shots fired by Biggles, and three shots at equal intervals being a universal summons for help, he had at once set off expecting to find Mose, even though it was early for him to return.

After they had shaken the snow from their clothes, Biggles asked the question that was uppermost in his mind. 'What about the weather?' he said. 'Is the snow going to keep on?'

Angus threw some lumps of peat – the only fuel available – into his stove before he replied. 'It might only be an early flurry, and stop again presently, or it may be the real fall,' he said.

'What's your opinion?' asked Biggles.

'I ain't got none; and it would be a wise man as 'ad any in these parts,' was the non-committal reply.

'If it's the real fall – what then?' inquired Biggles.

'We shall all be dead afore the break-up,' returned Angus with disconcerting frankness.

'We've got some food out yonder,' Biggles told him.

'Eh, mon, if this is the big snow it'll be buried afore morning. 'Twouldn't be no use thinkin' o' fetchin' it.'

'And there wouldn't be enough here without it to last us till spring?'

'Not half enough,' said the old man calmly. 'Where's Mose? Did he tell you I was here? What did you come up here for, anyway?'

'I'm coming. to that,' replied Biggles, realizing that in his anxiety to try to discover what the weather was likely to do, he had told Angus nothing about his mission. For another moment or two he hesitated, wondering how to begin.

'I've got some bad news for you, Angus,' he said at last.

The Scotsman threw him a sidelong glance. 'Hm?'

'Mose won't be coming back.'

'That means he's dead.'

Biggles nodded. 'Quite right. Mose is dead.'

'How did it happen?'

'He was murdered.'

Angus started. 'Got drunk, I reckon, and talked about – talked too much.'

Biggles noted how the old man checked himself and wondered why. 'No,' he said. 'At least, I only saw him once, and he was sober enough then.' And thereafter he told the whole story; how Ginger overheard him inquiring for Wilks and the events that followed. This involved, naturally, an explanation of the state of affairs at the aerodrome.

'You reckon Brindle done the killin'?' put in the old man shrewdly, when Biggles had finished.

'I'm pretty sure of it,' replied Biggles. 'But that doesn't mean that I could prove it,' he added.

'So you aimed to bring up the grub and get the transfer at the same time?'

'That's it.'

'What happened? How come you to be walking?'

Biggles had to disclose the incident of the air attack by Sarton – not that he had any desire to conceal the fact that he and Ginger had been responsible for the death of Sarton and Chicot.

When he had finished the old man stared at the stove for a long time in silence. 'I reckon you're tellin' the truth,' he said at last. 'I know Brindle. He's bad medicine. Poor old Mose. I never reckoned he'd go out that way. Well, it was mighty kind of yer to come up, stranger, but I guess you was just a day or two too late. You're here, and here you'll stop, I reckon. When the snow stops we'll go and dig out the bear meat; that'll last us for a bit. There's just a chance that we might dig the grub out of the aeroplane; mebbe we could make do with that. And since you're liable to be stoppin', I'll tell yer something else. Mose was a rich man.'

Biggles looked surprised. 'He didn't look like that to me.'

'No? Mebbe he wouldn't. To make my meanin' plain, me and Mose struck it rich.'

Biggles understood then. 'You mean you've found gold here?'

'Ay, mon, dust aplenty. A power o' good it's like to do us, though, now. Mose had a tidy poke here; he wouldn't take it with him 'cause he was afeared he might get rubbed out for it. Yet he gets rubbed out anyway. Well, it all depends on the weather now; let's see what it's doin'.'

Angus crossed over to the door and flung it open. Outside the world lay still and white under the fresh fall, but it was no longer snowing. Once more the stars were twinkling brightly in the cold blue dome overhead.

Biggles went past him out into the snow, and found that it was only six or eight inches deep. 'This looks like our chance to get the grub up from the machine,' he said. 'We shall have to have an hour or two's sleep first, though. We're about all in.'

'Ay, I can see that,' replied Angus. 'You take a snooze then, while I go out and fetch the bear meat. Then, if you're willin', we'll go to the airyplane.'

Biggles would have preferred to have gone straight back to the machine for fear the snow started again, but there are limits to human endurance, and he was at the end of his.

Angus took some furs from a heap in the corner and threw them on the floor near the stove. 'Make a shakedown out of these,' he said.

Ginger followed Biggles's example in arranging a rough bed on the floor. He threw himself down on it and was asleep in a moment, so soundly that he did not even hear Angus go out and shut the door.

When he awoke he had no idea of how long he had been asleep. It did not seem long, but he knew it must be several hours because a great pile of raw meat was stacked on the far side of the room, the remains of the polar bear. There was more than a man could carry in one load, so he realized that if Angus had made two journeys it must be the next day. Neither Biggles nor Angus were in the room, but it did not occur to him that they were far away, so he got up leisurely and went outside to look for them. Instinctively his eyes went out across the open plain that lay between the shack and the Jupiter, and he was not a little surprised to see two figures moving across it. Presently he made them out to be Biggles and Angus, and what surprised him even more was the fact that they were returning.

'Gosh! What a time I must have been asleep,' he muttered, realizing that the others must have made a trip to the machine. He did not waste any more time in idle conjecture, however, but built up the fire, put the kettle on, and, finding a frying pan, started to fry three large bear steaks, which were just cooked to a turn when the others came in with their loads.

After a hearty meal Angus announced his intention of making another journey to the machine. 'It's a bit of luck, the snow holding off like this,' he explained, 'and we ought to make the most of it. If it starts again it might go on for a week or more.'

The others agreed with this project, for they realized that their lives depended on their getting sufficient food in to last them through the long Arctic winter. Coats and gloves were, therefore, donned, and they set off towards the distant machine.

As they trudged in single file through the snow, with Angus leading, Ginger discovered that he had lost all count of time. With so little difference between day and night he found that he had completely lost track of how many hours or days had passed since they had left Fort Beaver. Not that it mattered. Their actions in future would be ruled by the weather, not by the clock.

Vaguely he wondered what Algy and Wilks were doing, and what they thought of their non-return. As Biggles had said, it was certain that, weather permitting, they would set off in Wilks's machine to look for them, but there were long odds against them succeeding in locating them, with such a vast territory to cover. In any case, once the snow started again it would put an end to any idea of rescue, in which event Wilks and Algy would have to fight McBain as best they could.

The newly fallen snow appeared to have raised the temperature considerably, but it started to freeze again just as they reached the machine, a detail which would, Angus said, make their return trip easier, since it would harden the snow so that they would be able to walk on it, instead of ploughing through it as they had on the outward journey.

To Ginger's surprise the Jupiter was not half buried under the snow as he had expected to find it, but Biggles explained the mystery. On his previous visit, while the snow was still soft, he had brushed it off the exposed surfaces of the machine, so that, on the remote chance of Algy or Wilks finding it, it would be in a condition to fly – provided, of course, that it had petrol in the tanks and the bullet hole was mended.

The chances of the machine ever taking the air again seemed so slight that Ginger, although he did not say so, felt that Biggles had wasted his time. He himself thought no more about it, but set to work with the others unloading the remaining stores. This done, he was about to suggest to Biggles that they drained the crank cases of oil, which would be useful in many ways, when he heard the distant hum of an aeroplane. The sound was unmistakable, and his heart leapt when he heard it.

'Good old Algy!' he shouted gleefully.

Even Biggles had flushed with excitement. 'A fire!' he yelled. 'Let's get a fire going!'

They rushed into the cabin and threw out any odd scraps of packing they could find. An old map, a spare pair of gloves, and even the patching fabric went on the pile as Angus put a match to it. A tongue of orange fire leapt upwards, and in a moment the odds and ends were blazing like a beacon.

'It should be possible to see that for fifty miles,' declared Biggles, peering into the sky in the direction from which the sound had come. 'There he is! There he is!' He pointed with a quivering forefinger at a black speck that had materialized out of the dull haze concealing the southern horizon. 'He's seen us!' went on Biggles gleefully. 'I saw him turn. He's coming – coming—' His voice died away in a curious manner.

Ginger, staring at the fast approaching machine, knew why. It was not Wilks's Rockheed. It was McBain's second Weinkel that was roaring low towards them.

CHAPTER XII

A One-sided Duel

To say that Ginger was flabbergasted would be to express his feelings only mildly. He was thunderstruck. For some reason the possibility of this development had not occurred to him, although he realized now that there was just as much reason for McBain to come searching for Sarton and Chicot, as for Wilks and Algy to come looking for them.

He turned to Biggles who was still staring at the oncoming machine with an expression of mingled chagrin and disgust. 'He was looking for Sarton, I expect,' he muttered.

Biggles nodded thoughtfully, 'And we were kind enough to light a fire and show him where we were,' he murmured.

'He may still think we're Sarton and Chicot.'

'If he does, he'll realize his mistake when he gets a bit closer,' returned Biggles bitterly. 'Hello – see that turn? He's spotted who we are. It will be interesting to see what he does,' he added. 'He'll hardly risk landing.'

Ginger did not reply. He was watching the movements of the Weinkel with a good deal of trepidation, for he felt that whatever McBain did – assuming that he was on board – it would be unpleasant.

That he was right in this assumption was soon made apparent. The Weinkel banked sharply, and putting its nose down, dived at the stranded Jupiter.

For an instant longer Biggles watched it. Then he let out a warning yell. 'Lie flat.'

Ginger flung himself down just in time. Above the bellow of the Weinkel's engines there came the vicious chatter of a machine-gun, and the line of the bullets could easily be followed by the splinters of ice and flecks of snow that leapt into the air in line with the machine.

As it swept past Ginger clearly saw McBain himself behind the gun, which he had thrust out of the side window of the control cabin.

A stream of belligerent imprecations from Angus made Biggles turn. 'You hit?' he asked anxiously.

'Och, mon, not I,' shouted Angus. 'If I ever get ma' hands on that—'

'You keep down,' shouted Biggles, seeing that the Weinkel was coming back.

Angus's rifle cracked as the Weinkel roared past again, cutting a trail in the snow with its gun. Some of the shots went very near the prone airmen.

'You'll never hit him with that,' Biggles told Angus. 'He'll hit one of us in a minute if we aren't careful. We'd better scatter.'

The third time the Weinkel hurtled past the gun was silent. Instead, a small square object crashed down near the Jupiter; it bounced over and over and came to rest very close to the machine. Biggles started forward with the idea of finding out what it was, but before he could reach it, the Weinkel, which had swung round almost on its wing tip, was coming back. A signal light cut a flaming line through the air; it struck the snow very near the square object, and a sheet of flame leapt upwards.

'It's petrol!' yelled Biggles. 'He threw a can of petrol with the cap off. Now he's fired it with the pistol. He's trying to burn the Jupiter.'

Two gallons of petrol make a considerable flame. The scene was bathed in a lurid glow, but it was soon clear that in this case, at any rate, the Jupiter would not be damaged. Owing to the snow the petrol did not spread far, and the flame was ten yards from the machine.

Seething with impotence, Biggles told the others to get farther away in order to reduce the chances of any one being hit. It was as well that he did so, for thrice more the Weinkel dived at them, the gun spitting. Another can of petrol was thrown down, and Ferroni, who was actually flying the machine, almost stalled as he turned slowly above the Jupiter in order to allow McBain to take careful aim.

Biggles sprang to his feet and blazed away with his automatic. It is probable that he hit the machine, for it dived away and climbed up out of pistol range. A signal flare came screaming down, but Biggles had not wasted the brief delay; running forward, he had snatched up the can, still nearly full, and carried it clear. The flare burnt itself out harmlessly in the snow.

For the next few seconds the movements of the Weinkel puzzled the watchers on the ground. The plane turned away sharply and began climbing steeply.

'I think he's going,' said Biggles, rising to his feet. 'He's thought better of it. Maybe he was afraid of running out of petrol himself.'

'No, that isn't it,' cried Ginger. 'Look!'

Biggles followed the direction indicated. What he saw made him catch his breath sharply. 'It's Algy!' he muttered hoarsely.

Heading straight towards the scene was a Rockheed Freighter, attracted, no doubt, by the signal flares.

In normal circumstances this would have given Biggles and Ginger cause for jubilation, but now they both went cold with horror, for the Weinkel was racing towards the other machine, and they both knew that whatever Algy might have in the way of weapons, he would certainly have nothing capable of competing with a machine-gun.

'Judging by the way he flies, I don't think Algy has seen the Weinkel,' muttered Ginger, in a hopeless voice.

'He's probably got his eyes fixed on us,' returned Biggles tersely.

Helpless, they could only stand and watch.

The affair – it could hardly be called a combat – was over even more quickly than they had imagined it would be.

The Weinkel, confident, no doubt, of its superior armament, climbed straight up under the tail of the Rockheed, which had now cut its engines and was gliding down slowly, obviously looking for a place to land. An arm appeared out of the window, waving, making it obvious that those inside the machine had not the slightest suspicion of danger.

Ginger groaned aloud in his misery.

Biggles ground his teeth. 'What would I give for a single-seater and just one drum of ammunition – just one,' he forced out through his set teeth.

The two machines were within a quarter of a mile of the stranded Jupiter when the end came; the horrified watchers on the ground saw the whole thing clearly. They saw the Weinkel's side window open and the gun appear; saw McBain take slow and careful aim; saw the jabbing tongues of flame dance from the muzzle of the gun; saw the Rockheed shiver as the burst of fire struck her.

Ginger could hardly bear to watch, but he could not tear his eyes away. A kind of fascinated horror kept them glued to the machine. He was not quite certain what had happened, but it seemed that either whoever was flying it had been hit, or else the controls had been damaged.

The Rockheed fluttered like a wounded bird, careering from side to side with a sickening skidding movement. Its nose swung upward and sagged in turn.

Biggles said nothing. He did not move. With a face nearly as white as the surrounding snow he stared at the swaying machine with brooding eyes. Never in all his experience had he felt so utterly powerless; never before had he found himself in a position where he could do absolutely nothing. Instinctively, aware of the futility of it, he swayed with the machine as if by sheer will power he could correct the faults, leaning back when the nose dropped and pushing an imaginary joystick forward when the machine looked as though it must stall.

It was now so close that they could see the two men in her; could see Wilks fighting at the controls.

'He isn't hit, anyway,' muttered Ginger through dry lips.

Biggles did not answer. He knew the end was not far away.

The Rockheed stalled, came out, and stalled again, this time missing the ground by inches. It was obviously out of control. The port wing sagged as it stalled again at the top of its zoom, perhaps a hundred feet above the snowfield. Instantly it began to fall again, the sagging wing heading towards the ground – the first movement of a spin.

Then, as if by a miracle, the machine righted itself. Neither Biggles nor Ginger could understand why. There seemed no reason for it. The machine turned sluggishly towards them, and the reason for the apparent miracle became revealed. Algy was out on the starboard wing, lying flat, clinging to the leading edge with his hands as, with his body, he counterbalanced the port wing.

The Rockheed swept down like a tired bird, nearly on even keel, but not quite. The port wing-tip touched the ground first, flinging the snow up like the bow-wave of a ship. After that the result was a foregone conclusion. The whole machine cart-wheeled, flinging Algy over and over across the snow. The nose buried itself. The fuselage tipped up, hanging poised for a moment, and then fell back. Movement ceased.

The Weinkel, its engines roaring triumphantly, swept up into the sky. It levelled out, its nose pointing to the south.

Neither Biggles nor Ginger paid any attention to it; they were both racing at full speed towards the crashed machine, which lay about a hundred yards away from the Jupiter.

'Get to Algy; I'll look after Wilks,' yelled Biggles. His great fear was that the machine would go up in flames before he could reach it, for that is what happens all too often in such cases. He tore open the cabin door and disappeared inside.

Ginger went on to Algy, who, he was overjoyed to see, was moving, although ineffectually. Reaching him, he dropped on his knees beside him. 'Algy,' he cried, in a voice high-pitched with anxiety. 'Algy, old man, are you badly hurt? It's me – Ginger.'

Algy managed to get up on his hands and knees, his head thrust forward. His face was twisted in agony. A long-drawn groan burst from his lips.

Ginger's blood ran cold. The groan convinced him that Algy was mortally hurt. In desperation he looked round for Biggles, but Algy, who apparently divined his intention, shook his head, at the same time groaning again. 'I'm – I'm – I'm—' he stammered, 'on – on – only – winded.'

Ginger gasped his relief and waited for him to recover. There was little he could do. Fortunately, although the symptoms of 'winding' can be terrifying while they last, they do not last long, and once Algy managed to get an intake of breath, he recovered quickly.

'Gosh!' he groaned, smiling wanly. 'Sorry to make such a fuss. How's Wilks? Is he hurt?'

'I don't know,' replied Ginger. 'Take your time. I'll slip across and find out.'

He found that Biggles had managed to get Wilks out of the wreckage. He was sitting in the snow near by, very pale, while Biggles mopped blood from a cut in his forehead. Angus was binding a bandage tightly round his left wrist which, it subsequently transpired, he had sprained slightly.

'How's Algy?' Biggles asked Ginger as he ran up.

'Not bad, apart from being winded. I don't think there is much wrong with him.'

'Snow probably broke his fall,' returned Biggles shortly.

'I expect so,' agreed Ginger.

Algy, his back slightly bent so that one hand rested on a knee, came limping over to them. 'I've had nearly enough of this "farthest north" stuff,' he declared. 'One thing and another, we seem to be in a pretty bad way.'

'Not so bad as it looks,' grinned Biggles cheerfully. Actually, he was so relieved that neither Algy nor Wilks had suffered serious injury that he did not worry about anything else. 'By the way,' he went on, 'this is Angus. Angus, this is my partner, Mr. Lacey. You and Wilkinson are already acquainted.' He stood up and looked round.

'Did you see that skunk McBain shoot us down?' grated Algy.

'Saw the whole thing,' replied Biggles. 'He was having a go at us when you arrived on the scene.'

'Did he shoot you down, too?'

'No. Sarton was responsible for that. He's down, too – dead – and Chicot with him.' Briefly Biggles described the incident.

'Well, what are we going to do?' asked Wilks.

'We'd best be makin' tracks for the shack,' chipped in Angus. 'If it starts to snow we may have a job to make it, and the snow's due to arrive at any minute.'

'Do you mean that we're here for the winter?' cried Algy aghast.

'Looks that way to me, mister.'

'I'm not so sure about that,' put in Biggles. 'We may have a chance yet. Had you got plenty of juice in your tanks?'

'Fifty gallons, I reckon.'

'Then if we can find the hole in our tank, and mend it, and swop the petrol over, we can still get back in the Jupiter.'

Algy looked from Biggles to the Jupiter's wheels, more than half buried in the snow. 'You'll never get her off out of this stuff,' he muttered. 'Those wheels must be frozen in by this time.'

'I agree,' answered Biggles, 'but we've got a pair of skis inside, don't forget. If we can jack up the undercart while we get the wheels off, and put the skis on, we might still do it – if the snow will hold off for a little while longer.'

Algy sprang to his feet, his stiffness forgotten. 'Then let's get at it,' he cried. 'It's our only chance.'

'See if you can find that bullet hole, Ginger,' ordered Biggles. 'It's a race against time now.'

CHAPTER XIII

Southward Again

For three hours the airmen worked feverishly. Ginger repaired the punctured tank, bemoaning the fact that Smyth, who was an expert sheet-metal-worker, was not there to help him. Algy explained that he had decided to leave him at Fort Beaver – where they had arrived as arranged in the Rockheed which now lay smashed in the snow – for two reasons: first, to leave a guard at the aerodrome, and, secondly, to reduce the load of the aircraft, and consequently the petrol consumption.

The others laboured at the undercarriage, the transformation of the Jupiter into a ski-plane being impeded to no small extent by the cold. However, at last it was done. Ginger had already repaired the tank, so the labourers' task of transferring the petrol from the Rockheed to the Jupiter began.

'Is there anything at the cabin you'll be wanting?' Biggles asked Angus, who was helping as far as he was able.

'Meanin' what?' answered the old Scotsman.

'Well, I take it you'll be coming with us.'

'Na, mon. I'm staying here.'

Biggles stopped work long enough to stare unbelievingly. 'Do you mean that?'

'Ay.'

'You'd rather stay for months in this forsaken place than come back to civilization?'

'Ay, I'll stay.'

Biggles shrugged his shoulders. 'Well, I suppose you know best what you want to do. All right; we'll taxi you back to the shack as soon as we are ready; that will save you dragging the stores through the snow. You can then give us the transfer and we'll get away before it starts to snow.'

Angus cocked an eye heavenward. 'Then ye've no time to waste,' he observed dispassionately. 'Here she comes.'

Following his eyes, Biggles saw one or two big flakes floating downwards languidly. He made no comment. There was no need. The others had seen the dreaded flakes, and were working with desperate speed.

It took them some time to start the Jupiter's engines, for they were stone cold, but a little petrol inserted into each of the cylinders finally did the trick. They all got aboard. A few moments to take the chill off the engines and the Jupiter began gliding across the snow in the direction of the island.

By the time Angus's stores were thrown out for him to collect in his own time, and the old man had returned from the shack with the precious transfer, it was snowing steadily.

The last few seconds on the ground were hectic. Angus heaved into the cabin an object that looked like a small sack.

'What's that?' yelled Biggles, who was itching to be off.

'Old Mose's poke,' shouted Angus.

'Mose's *what?*'

'Poke.'

'He means that it is Mose's gold,' called Wilks.

'What do you want me to do with it?' Biggles asked Angus, not very pleased about the responsibility.

'Mose didn't want the gold for himself. He's got a darter down in Vancouver. I reckon he'd like her to have it. Find her and give it to her.'

'All right,' shouted Biggles, without enthusiasm. He was not in the least concerned about the gold; all he cared about at that moment was getting away.

'Stand clear!' he yelled.

The cabin door slammed.

A parting wave to the old Scotsman, who did not seem in the least concerned about his lonely fate, and the Jupiter swung round. There was no horizon, but Biggles did not hesitate. The engines bellowed, and the big machine raced across the snow. A moment later it rose slowly into the air. The ground disappeared from sight immediately, and Biggles fixed his eyes on the instruments.

'We ought to run out of this in ten minutes,' he told Wilks, who was sitting beside him.

Wilks agreed, knowing precisely what Biggles meant; which was that the snow was coming from the north, and, as it had only just started, and the Jupiter was heading south for Moose Creek, it would quickly pass beyond the snow area. The thought led to another. They had managed to get off safely, but how about getting down – if there was no snow at Moose Creek? He asked Biggles this question.

'I hadn't overlooked that,' replied Biggles. 'We'll work that out when we get there. The skids may stand up to a turf landing, but whether they do or not, I'd sooner take the risk – even if we bust the machine – than stay in Angus's shack for six months.'

Wilks nodded. He felt the same about it.

Already the snow through which they were flying was thinning, and a minute later they caught their first glimpse of the ground. Shortly afterwards they ran into clear weather, although the landscape was still snow-covered, the result of the earlier fall. Flying, however, was now a comparatively simple matter, and Biggles, relaxing, began to think of other things. With the major problem answered, that of their escape from being snowed-in, minor worries presented themselves, as usually happens.

'Pity we've lost the Rockheed,' he remarked. 'That leaves us only one machine to operate with.'

'Never mind; we've got the transfer,' Wilks reminded him. 'If we can use that to get McBain off the aerodrome we shall manage all right. By the way, what are we going to do about McBain?'

'What do you mean – do about him?'

'Well, this attack on us. He tried to murder us; are we going to let him get away with it?'

'It's a bit hard to know what to do,' replied Biggles thoughtfully. 'It's our word against his. He thinks we are out of the way, certainly for the winter, possibly for good. He'll get a shock when we turn up. He'll probably accuse us of murdering Sarton, but since the remains of the machine will probably be buried under snow for the next six months, he will have nothing to support his story. We've got a witness in Angus, but he won't be available for six months, either. I think our wisest course would be to submit a report of the whole affair to police headquarters and let them do what they like about it. Delaney, single-handed, can't do much. There is this; our reputation will at least stand investigation, which is more than can be said for McBain, I imagine.'

They said no more, for it was obvious that the future was so problematical that it was impossible to make plans with any assurance.

The snow on the ground was now very patchy, and while they were still some distance from Moose Creek it died away altogether. Within a few days the snow coming down from the north would bury everything under a deep blanket, but for the present the ground was clear.

'There's just a chance that the Creek will be frozen over,' said Wilks, referring to the almost land-locked stretch of water from which Moose Creek took its name. 'It has been freezing pretty hard.'

'How shall we know?' asked Biggles.

'I always use the lake in winter,' replied Wilks. 'If the ice is safe they shift the windstocking across to it, because the ice has a much better surface than the aerodrome. Being boggy, during the summer it gets churned up by the wheels, and when these ruts get frozen hard in the winter they are awful. However, we shall soon see which it is to be. There's the creek, in the distance. It wouldn't surprise me if we found McBain there.'

'It would surprise him, I'll bet,' grinned Biggles.

'He's been there, anyway,' declared Wilks, who was staring down through the window. 'There are his wheelmarks on the ice – at least, those are aeroplane tracks, and it's unlikely that any one else has been up here. And there's the windstocking by the side of the creek; that means it is all right to land on the ice.'

'Well, that's better, anyway. I wasn't feeling too happy at trying to put this big bus down in a frozen field on a pair of skis. Can you see McBain's machine anywhere?'

'No.'

'Then he must have gone off again.'

'Looks like it.'

'We'll find him at Fort Beaver, no doubt.'

Nothing more was said while Biggles concentrated on putting the Jupiter down on the lake on her new type of undercarriage.

To those in the machine the difference was barely perceptible, apart from the fact that the machine ran a long way before coming to a standstill.

'What are we going to do?' asked Wilks.

'Refuel, put our wheels back on again, and head south for Fort Beaver,' replied Biggles shortly. 'There is no telling what lies McBain will spread about us if we leave him too long alone – particularly if he thinks we aren't coming back to refute them.'

Leaving the others to attend to the refuelling and the replacement of the undercarriage wheels, Biggles walked across to the traffic manager's office.

'Here we are again, Mr. Canwell,' he observed cheerfully.

The traffic manager looked up from a book in which he was just making some entries. 'Sorry,' he said, 'but you are just too late.'

'Too late – what for?'

'To take the gold down.'

Biggles nodded slowly. 'Ah – of course. I remember. So it's gone, eh?'

'Yep. Biggest shipment we've ever made in one go. I waited as long as I could for you. McBain blew in, so I let him take it. I'm sorry—'

'You will be, I fancy,' put in Biggles dryly.

Canwell started. 'What do you mean by that?'

'Oh, nothing,' murmured Biggles. 'I fancy you would have found us a bit more reliable in the long run – that's all. How long ago did McBain leave?'

'About ten minutes.'

Biggles nodded. 'Right-ho, then. We might as well be getting along, too. See you later, maybe.'

Biggles walked slowly to the door, but once outside he strode swiftly to where the others were waiting for him. 'It looks as if McBain's got away with the boodle,' he said crisply. 'He's got ten minutes start. Not expecting to be followed, he'll cruise; if we run on full throttle we may overhaul him. Get aboard – step on it.'

CHAPTER XIV

An Unexpected Landing

Not until the Jupiter was in the air, roaring southwards on the trail of the Weinkel, did Biggles settle down to contemplate the situation. The gold was temporarily in McBain's charge; if he intended stealing it, this, clearly, was his opportunity. In the circumstances it seemed unlikely that he would return to Fort Beaver, where transport from the railhead would be waiting to take the gold on to the bank at Edmonton. Where, then, would he go? The more Biggles thought about it the more he became convinced that unless he overtook the Weinkel he would never see McBain again. He, with the machine and the gold in it, would disappear. In one way this would be to Wilks's advantage, for the feud for possession of the aerodrome would cease; nevertheless, it was not unlikely that the Moose Creek Company would be so sore at losing the gold dust that they would never again trust gold to an aeroplane, in which case Arctic Airways would die for lack of business. If they could overtake the Weinkel and see where it went they might succeed in bringing the gold thieves to justice, which could hardly fail to cement their friendship with the Moose Creek Company. This opinion Biggles passed on to Algy, who was sitting beside him in the control cabin.

The Jupiter was now once more in the region of day and night, with the 'bad lands' gliding past underneath them. Biggles was staring ahead, striving to pick up their quarry, when Ginger, his eyes alight with excitement, pushed his way into the cabin.

'Starboard!' he yelled. 'The Weinkel's bearing west.'

Biggles did not answer. His eyes switched to the right, far away from the line he had been following. For a moment or two they studied the sky, section by section, before they settled on a tiny moving speck travelling on a south-westerly course at a slightly lower altitude than themselves. It was the Weinkel.

'I was right,' he said crisply to Algy. 'McBain isn't going to Fort Beaver; the course he is on will leave Fort Beaver miles to the east.'

As he spoke he touched the right-hand side of the rudder-bar with his foot, bringing the Jupiter round on a new course to follow the other machine.

For an hour the respective positions of the two machines did not change. Although in the circumstances it was hardly likely that the Jupiter would be seen by the men in the leading machine, Biggles kept at a safe distance, quite satisfied to watch. The only fear he had was that McBain should be carrying more petrol than they were, in which case they might ultimately be compelled to give up the chase for lack of fuel. He was, therefore, more than a little relieved when he saw the Weinkel going down. Grabbing his map, he studied closely the area they were over, then he turned a bewildered face to Algy.

'There's nothing there,' he said.

'Not even a village?'

'Absolutely nothing.'

Algy stood up and surveyed the ground right to the horizon; it was all the same: open prairie broken by wide areas of fir forest, with a small lake here and there. 'No,' he agreed, at the end of his scrutiny, 'there's nothing in the shape of a town or village. What are you going to do?'

That was a question Biggles could not answer at once, for the problem facing him was a difficult one to solve. While the Weinkel was in the air it was extremely unlikely that McBain would see the Jupiter, but once it was on the ground, with its engines stopped, the noise of the Jupiter's engines would certainly give them away. The Weinkel was still in the air, but it was now losing height rapidly, and it seemed only a matter of minutes before it would land.

His brain raced as he sought a solution to the puzzle. Studying the ground intently, he saw that to the right the ground was fairly open, and that it fell away quickly to the left, the locality in which the. Weinkel looked as if it would land. It struck him that if he could put the Jupiter down on the high land behind one of the patches of timber, it might be possible for them to watch the Weinkel without being seen. Anyway, it seemed worth trying, so he at once proceeded to put the plan into execution. He cut the engines, and not until the Jupiter's wheels trundled over the turf did the others realize what he had in mind.

The machine had barely come to a standstill before Biggles was out, running for all he was worth towards a line of spruce and fir that hid the whole of the country to the south. They were a mile or more from the Weinkel, so there was little risk of them being seen or heard. Ducking low under the drooping fir branches, they pushed their way to the far edge of the timber from where the country to the south lay open to their view.

'There they are!' Biggles's voice was tense as, keeping under cover, he pointed out the Weinkel, which was now standing on the ground by a small log cabin near the edge of a lake. It so happened, however, that from their coign of vantage the Weinkel was between them and the cabin, so although they could see figures moving, they could not see exactly what was going on.

'I should say they are unloading the gold,' declared Ginger.

'I don't think there is any doubt about that,' returned Biggles.

Several minutes passed during which no more was said; then, not a little to their surprise, the Weinkel's engines suddenly opened up again, and almost before the watchers realized what was happening, the machine had taken off and was racing low over a south-easterly course. The cabin was deserted; or, at least, it appeared to be.

'Gosh! We shall lose them if we are not careful. Come on.' Suiting the action to the words, Biggles led the rush back to the machine.

In three minutes they were in the air again. But the Weinkel had had five minutes' clear start, and an aeroplane can travel a long way in that time. There was no sign of it.

'They were heading south-east. That's the direction of Fort Beaver,' Algy pointed out.

'I know, but I don't get the hang of this at all,' muttered Biggles, with a worried frown. 'If they've hidden the gold, they've got a bit of a nerve to go back to Fort Beaver.'

'Maybe they'll just land to pick up the things that belong to them, and, perhaps, refuel. Then they'll come back, put the gold on board, and go straight on south to the United States,' suggested Algy.

'Possibly,' agreed Biggles. 'Yet, somehow, I don't think that's the answer. It's got me beaten, and that's a fact. One thing is certain;

we've got to get back to Fort Beaver ourselves or we shall run out of petrol. Another forced landing would just about put the tin hat on things.'

'Suits me,' agreed Algy. 'A night's rest wouldn't do any of us any harm.'

That closed the conversation for the time being. It was half an hour later before any one spoke again, by which time Fort Beaver aerodrome was in sight.

'There's the Weinkel,' said Biggles. 'And unless my eyes deceive me, that's McBain and Ferroni standing beside it, talking to – it looks like Delaney.'

'Yes, it's Delaney,' put in Ginger. 'If he is asking them what has happened to the gold we'll be able to enlighten him,' he added.

'It will be interesting to see just what is happening,' observed Biggles smoothly, as he cut the Jupiter's engines and glided down.

Their run in carried them very close to the Weinkel. McBain and Ferroni stared at them as they taxied past.

'Yes, you might well stare,' said Biggles quietly to himself, eyeing McBain and his pilot grimly. 'You didn't expect to see us back so soon – if at all – I'll warrant.' His eyes went past the two crooks and came to rest on something that lay on the ground beyond them. A strange expression crept over his face, but he made no further observation until he had switched off in front of their hangar. 'Well,' he said, in an odd tone of voice, 'what do you make of that?'

'Make of what?' asked the others together.

'Those are the Moose Creek gold boxes that they're unloading,' went on Biggles. 'They haven't stolen the gold after all. They'll never get a better chance.' He passed his hand wearily over his

face and then shook his head. 'That seems to knock all our calculations sideways, doesn't it?'

'I – I don't understand it,' blurted Wilks.

'You'd be a clever fellow if you did, I think,' muttered Biggles
dryly. 'According to Ginger, those chaps are crooks, waiting for a
chance to get their hands on a pile of gold. They've actually had
the gold in their possession, with nothing as far as I can see to
prevent them from getting clear away with it. Yet they bring it
back here and quietly hand it over to the bank messenger – that
looks like him coming now – like law-abiding citizens. There's a
weak link somewhere in that chain of events. We had better go
inside and put our thinking caps on and see if we can find it.'

CHAPTER XV

Under Arrest

For the remainder of the day and far into the night they discussed the problem that seemed to admit of no solution. At daybreak the following morning they resumed the debate. They could talk of nothing else. Biggles broke off long enough to send Smyth to the village, shopping, then he continued the discussion.

'You can't get away from it,' he declared, staring out across the now deserted aerodrome. 'If McBain stays here for ten years he won't get a better chance to lift a load of gold than he had yesterday. If he is a crook, why did he deliver the gold instead of pushing off with it? That's what I want to know. Had he wanted to, he could have been two thousand miles away by now. I give it up.'

'The only answer seems to be that McBain isn't a crook after all,' suggested Wilks.

'I tell you I heard them discussing ways and means of getting the gold,' declared Ginger emphatically. 'You're not suggesting that I dreamed—'

'Of course we're not,' broke in Biggles.

'Maybe the haul wasn't big enough, and they are waiting for another lot,' suggested Algy.

Biggles shook his head. 'That won't do,' he said. 'Why, they might have to wait months. You remember that Canwell himself told us that it was an unusually big cargo of metal; and consider the other circumstances. The freeze-up has set in up north, and it's only a question of days – perhaps hours – before it reaches us here. McBain must know by this time that something has happened to his other machine. He must know that we suspect him of the murder of old Mose. He probably guesses that we have got the transfer from Angus. Any one of those factors should be sufficient to send him scuttling out of this locality as fast as he can go. Why is he waiting? What is he waiting for? If he had hidden yesterday's cargo of gold we might suppose that he is hanging about in order to pick up a second lot before clearing out, but with our own eyes we saw him hand the boxes over. There is something fishy about the whole thing. Talking of gold reminds me that we've still got Mose's "poke" in the machine – the dust Angus handed over to us. We'd better put it somewhere safe pending such time as we can hand it over to the authorities. No doubt they'll find Mose's daughter. I don't feel inclined to tear around at this moment looking for her. We'll tell Delaney about it next time he comes up here.'

'I've got a place where we can hide it,' said Wilks. 'There's a secret cavity under my office floor; I had it specially made for valuables.'

'With McBain and Co. about I think it would be a good thing if we put it in right away,' declared Biggles.

The small bag of gold was accordingly fetched from the machine and put into Wilks's hiding place. The task done, they returned to the tarmac.

'To get down to brass tacks, what is the next move?' inquired Algy.

'The most important thing is that we now have the transfer,' answered Biggles. 'As far as I can see, there is nothing to stop us from showing it to Delaney, and asking him to order McBain off our property.'

'Yes, I think that is the right procedure,' agreed Wilks.

'Then we'll hang about for a bit to see if Delaney comes along; if he doesn't, then we'll go and find him,' declared Biggles. 'Go and brew a dish of coffee, Ginger. Bring it in the office when it is ready.'

Ginger nodded, got up, and made his way, deep in thought, to the back of the hangar, where the cooking stove had been installed.

The others sat outside the office door, smoking and discussing the situation. They were still waiting for the coffee when, to Biggles's astonishment, Constable Delaney appeared at the entrance to McBain's hangar.

'What do you make of that?' jerked out Algy.

'I wonder how long he has been there,' said Biggles.

'It must have been a long time or we should have seen him go in,' Wilks pointed out.

'I thought everything was very quiet over there,' muttered Biggles suspiciously. 'He's coming over to us now, by the look of it.'

Delaney was, in fact, walking towards the Arctic Airways hangar, followed by McBain and Ferroni.

'What the dickens do *they* want?' growled Algy.

'We shall soon know,' murmured Biggles, rising to his feet to greet the constable. 'Morning, Delaney; looking for something?' he called cheerfully.

Delaney nodded curtly. 'Yes,' he said shortly.

Biggles experienced a twinge of uneasiness. There was something about the constable's manner he did not like. However, he did not show it. 'Make yourself at home,' he said. 'What can I do for you?'

The constable, carbine across his arm, came to a halt a couple of paces away and regarded the three airmen with an expression of shrewd suspicion. His eyes came to rest on Biggles.

'Were you at Moose Creek yesterday?'

'I was,' replied Biggles frankly. 'Any reason why I shouldn't be?'

'I'll do all the questioning.'

'Go ahead,' invited Biggles cheerfully.

The constable turned to Wilks. 'Any objection to my searching your outfit?' he inquired. 'I'm searching it, anyway,' he added.

Wilks waved a conscience-free hand. 'Help yourself,' he said. 'Maybe if I was told what you were looking for I could help you.'

'I shan't need any help,' rejoined the constable.

'You've had a look round McBain's outfit for whatever it is you've lost, I presume?' put in Biggles.

Delaney threw him a sidelong glance. 'I have,' he admitted.

'And you didn't find it?'

'No.'

'You won't find it here.'

'You talk like you know what I'm looking for.'

'If I had one guess, and if I hadn't seen the boxes being unloaded on the aerodrome yesterday, I should say it was the Moose Creek parcel of bullion.'

McBain took a quick pace forward. 'What are you suggesting?' he growled.

'Work it out for yourself,' replied Biggles evenly. He turned to Delaney. 'You won't find the Moose Creek gold here,' he said. 'Funny thing,' he went on easily, 'I should have thought that if those boxes had been empty you'd have noticed it.'

'They weren't opened till they got to Edmonton,' returned the constable curtly.

'I see. And what was in them?'

'Lead.'

'Oh!'

'The dust was taken out of those boxes between Moose Creek and Edmonton.'

In a flash Biggles understood the meaning of McBain's detour. The gold had been taken out of the boxes at the cabin, and lead substituted. There was one thing he did not understand, though, and this for the time being remained a mystery.

'I thought the boxes were always *sealed* at Moose Creek?'

'Quite right,' returned the constable. 'When these boxes were taken out of McBain's machine the seals were intact, or I should have noticed it.'

'If the seals were unbroken, then lead, not gold, must have been put into the boxes in the first instance.'

'Any reason why the Moose Creek outfit should send out a parcel of lead?'

'None that I can think of.'

'Nor me.'

'I don't see how or where *we* could have got near it,' protested Biggles.

'You're the only other outfit besides McBain's that was at Moose Creek yesterday – and here. That being so you're under suspicion till the dust's found,' said Delaney firmly.

While he had been speaking he had walked into the office,

'Whipping out his revolver, he covered the three
airmen menacingly'

his keen eyes scrutinizing the walls, floor, and furniture. He came striding towards a cupboard when he stopped dead in his tracks, in the middle of a small rug. He stamped. The boards rang hollow. In a flash he had bent down and whipped the rug aside, disclosing the trap-door of Wilks's secret locker.

'Hello, what's this?' he exclaimed.

Biggles remembered Mose's gold, which had temporarily escaped his memory. He saw their danger instantly, and hastened to try to rectify the oversight, but his very haste was in itself suspicious.

'Oh, yes – I forgot – there is some gold in there,' he said quickly.

Delaney started. His eyes hardened and he reached for his revolver. 'Oh yeah? Just remembered it, eh?'

'Believe it or not, but that's the truth.'

'A pile o' gold's the sort of thing you easily forget – huh?'

'I was waiting for you to come along to tell you about it,' said Biggles, realizing with dismay how thin the story sounded.

The constable knelt down, lifted the trap aside, put his hand into the aperture and lifted out a heavy doeskin bag. As he stared at it, turning it round and round, his whole manner became tense. Suddenly he tossed the bag on to the table and, whipping out his revolver, covered the three airmen menacingly. 'So that's it, eh?' he snarled. 'You dirty skunks! Stand still.'

'Why, that's the sort of poke old Mose allus used,' cried McBain. 'He allus used doeskin.'

'Yes, and his initials are on it,' grated Delaney. 'Now we know who killed Mose – and why. This isn't the dust I was looking for – but it'll suit me better than the other.'

'Just a minute, Delaney, you've got this all wrong,' protested

Biggles desperately. 'Don't jump to conclusions. I know how this must look to you – naturally; but you're making a mistake. I can explain it.'

'You wouldn't have the nerve to suggest that this isn't Mose's poke, I reckon?'

'Of course not. We were going to give it to you to hand over to his next-of-kin – he has a daughter—'

McBain burst into a roar of laughter. 'By thunder, that's a good one! It's your turn to tell one, Delaney.'

The constable's lips were dragged down at the corners. 'So you killed an old man for his poke, did you?' he sneered.

'Angus Stirling gave us that gold yesterday when we told him that Mose was dead,' said Biggles quietly.

'What's this? You trying to tell me that you saw Angus yesterday?'

'I *am* telling you.'

'Oh – shut up. He's on Eskimo Island, and he's froze in.'

'He may be now, but he wasn't yesterday.'

As he spoke Biggles realized with increasing horror just what the fact of Angus being frozen in was likely to mean to them. Not for six months would it be possible to make contact with him. As a witness he might as well not exist. The only scrap of evidence they had in support of their story was the transfer, and even so there was nothing to prove that Angus had given it to them with his own hands.

Delaney jerked his head towards the door. 'Get going,' he said.

'Where to?' asked Biggles.

'You'll see,' was the harsh reply. 'We've got a place for your sort.'

'But—'

'Cut it out. Anything you've got to say you'd better save for the court.'

'Wait a minute. There's another one of 'em,' cried McBain suddenly. 'Where's the kid?'

As if in answer, the Jupiter's engines burst into life.

Delaney cursed and dashed outside, but the big machine was already on the move. 'Stop!' he yelled. Seeing that his words had no effect, he blazed away with his revolver, McBain and Ferroni joining in with theirs.

'You kill that kid and it will be the worst day's work you've ever done!' shouted Biggles furiously. In the swift sequence of events he had forgotten about Ginger and his coffee-making. To his heartfelt relief he saw the Jupiter run across the aerodrome untouched. A faint smile played about the corners of his mouth as he watched it climb into the air. 'You'll have a job to catch him now,' he told Delaney, with savage satisfaction.

The constable whirled round furiously. 'You won't crow so loud presently,' he snapped.

'Nor, I fancy, will you,' replied Biggles, with a good deal more confidence than he felt.

'That's enough. March,' ordered Delaney. 'Any one of you who tries to make a break won't know what hits him.'

CHAPTER XVI

Ginger Acts

When Ginger had gone through to the rear of the hangar to make the coffee he had little reason to suspect the desperate events that were soon to follow. As it was, he whistled softly under his breath as he waited for the pot to boil.

There is an old oft-used proverb to the effect that a watched pot never boils and, while this may not be literally true, there is no doubt that whoever first coined the expression had good reason for it. So it was with Ginger. Impatient to return to the others, he was about to pump more pressure into the Primus stove when the sound of voices reached his ears. From the loud and concise tones he realized that visitors had arrived, and unfriendly ones at that. With pardonable curiosity he decided to find out who it was; meanwhile the pot could take its own time to come to the boil.

He did not go round to the front of the office. Had he done so, this story would certainly have ended differently. A few paces from where he stood a small square window allowed light to enter the back of the office, and towards this he made his way.

A description of the scene which met his astonished eyes is unnecessary. He was just in time to hear Delaney accuse Biggles of the murder of the old prospector. And, looking from the tense faces of his friends to the grim countenance of the constable, he realized the desperate nature of the trap into which they had unwittingly fallen. He forgot all about the coffee. The trend of the conversation, which he could hear distinctly, banished everything from his mind except the dire necessity for immediate action. While he had his freedom he might be able to do something. Just what he hoped to achieve he did not know; he had no time to think about it; he only knew that if all four of them were put behind prison bars anything could happen, and for this reason he decided to avoid arrest if this were possible. But how?

On the spur of the moment he could think only of the machine. If he could get it into the air he would be safe – anyway, safer than in any hiding-place on the ground. He lingered only long enough to assure himself that Biggles and the others were, in fact, under arrest; then, dropping everything, he retraced his steps to the rear of the hangar and so reached the machine, which, in accordance with their usual custom, during the hours of daylight, had been left on the tarmac.

Working quietly and methodically, he made his preparations for a swift take-off. He realized that there would be no time to run up the engines; once they were started the noise would bring Delaney out with a rush – as we know was the case.

The whir of the self-starter was the first sound that broke the comparative silence, to be followed almost at once by the choking backfire of the engines as the propeller jerked into life. With the left wheel braked hard, Ginger slowly opened the throttle. The nose of the big machine swung round until it was facing the open turf. With both wheels free he risked a glance at the office, determined to remain where he was as long as possible in order to reduce the risks of taking off with cold engines; but the sight of Delaney racing towards him settled the matter. Picking a mark on the far side of the aerodrome in order to hold the machine straight, he pushed the throttle wide open. He heard the whang of a bullet somewhere behind him, but he paid no heed to it; indeed, there was nothing he could do now but hold straight on.

His heart missed a beat as the port engine signified its disapproval of this treatment by coughing twice in quick succession; but then it picked up and the Jupiter bored up into the still air.

At a thousand feet he turned, wondering which way to go. Looking down, he could see the little group outside the office staring up at him; watching, he saw Biggles wave, and he derived some comfort from the gesture, for he was by no means sure that he had done the right thing.

Still circling, and climbing steadily for height, he switched his thoughts to the immediate future. Where ought he to go? What ought he to do for the best? It occurred to him to go to Edmonton, or some other big town, and there lay the whole story before some important official – if he could find one; but he soon dismissed this plan as too risky. He thought of Angus. If only he could get hold of Angus, and fly him back, the Scotsman's story would confirm their own; then he remembered the snow. He might be able to reach the shack; he might even be able to land without hurting himself or seriously damaging the machine; but once the wheels had sunk into the deep snow no power on earth could get the Jupiter off again. He could see no point in going to Moose Creek, even if the snow had not yet reached there. Canwell would be unable to do anything even if he was willing to come back to Fort Beaver, which did not seem likely. Where else could he go with any hope of finding evidence to bear out the story which he imagined Biggles would tell – the true story?

He remembered the log cabin where the Weinkel had landed on its way down from Moose Creek. Thinking about it, he realized that in some way it was connected with the gang – possibly a hideaway in an emergency should their plans miscarry. It had appeared deserted when last he had seen it. It had this advantage; it was not far away. Provided he could locate it, for he was by no means confident that he could, forty minutes should be ample time for him to reach it. There was just a chance that he might find something there: a clue, perhaps, that would lead to something more important. Anyway, he decided, there was no harm in trying. It was better than submitting quietly to arrest at Fort Beaver.

Satisfied that he was at least doing his best, he swung the Jupiter round until its nose pointed to the north-west, the direction of the cabin.

Looking down, he observed the sterile desolation of the country below and was conscious suddenly of the loneliness. Not without alarm he passed over several patches of fresh snow; however, the sky was fairly clear except to the far north, where a heavy indigo belt of cloud promised more snow in the near future.

He picked up a landmark which he recognized, a diamond-shaped wood, and flew on with more assurance, watching for others. Soon afterwards a silver gleam, almost on the horizon, caught his eye, and presently he made it out to be the lake on a bank of which the log cabin was situated.

Ginger flew on, feeling that it was no use doing anything else; for, if any one was below, the roar of the Jupiter's engines would make any attempt at concealment futile. He picked out the cabin; it looked pathetically forlorn, he thought, in its lonely surroundings; still, he was relieved to see that there was no sign of movement near it.

Cutting the engines, he began gliding down, passing, on his way, the higher ground where they had landed while they were trailing the Weinkel. A sleek animal was running low along the edge of the wood. As he got lower he realized it was a wolf. Presently it turned into the timber and was lost to sight. For a moment or two he wondered if it were better to land where they had landed on the previous day, or to go on to where the Weinkel had come on the same occasion. However, there seemed to be no point in giving himself an unnecessary walk, apart from which he did not like the idea of walking about in wolf country. True, he had an automatic in his pocket, but he preferred to avoid using it as long as possible. For these reasons he went on to the cabin, which he was now seeing at close quarters for the first time.

If the cabin was McBain's, and presumably it was, since he had called there, the reason for the selection of the site – apart from its isolation – was at once apparent. On the southern side stretched a wide expanse of open prairie land, large enough for any type of aeroplane to land on in any sort of weather. He noted this subconsciously as he lowered his wheels and glided towards it; actually, he was more than a little concerned with putting the machine down safely, for a broken undercarriage at this stage was the very last thing he wanted.

With his nerves braced with anxiety he flattened out for the landing; but he need not have worried: the wheels rumbled for a moment, the tail dropped, and the machine came to rest about a hundred yards from the cabin, which he now saw was an almost new, well-constructed building.

He did not bother to taxi up to it. There was no real need to do so. Switching off the engines, he glanced round to make sure that everything was in order, then he opened the door and jumped out. For a moment or two he stood watching the building keenly, feeling certain that if any one had been there he would by this time have shown himself. However, as there was no sign of life, he started walking briskly towards it.

He was still about twenty yards away when a sudden noise pulled him up short. He stood quite still, his eyes running over the building, seeking the cause of the sound, which was very slight, and like the creaking of a tight door or a window being opened. Seeing nothing, he concluded that the sound – if, indeed, he had actually heard anything – was a natural one, such as a piece of loose board giving way, or two branches rubbing together in the belt of fir which began just beyond the hut and skirted the northern edge of the lake.

He was about to move forward again when a shadow flitted across the one window that faced in his direction. This time he knew that there was no mistake; some one was in the cabin. And an instant later all doubt was removed when the light flashed on the window as it was opened. He had no time to think. Regretting his rashness, he looked swiftly around for cover, for the furtive manner in which the window had been opened was at once suggestive of danger; but there was nothing, not even a bush behind which he might hide.

He opened his mouth to call a greeting – but the sound did not reach his lips. Still staring at the window, he saw something emerging; a split second later he realized what it was – a rifle barrel. He braced his muscles to jump aside, but such movement as he made was still little more than an impulse when the rifle cracked. For a brief instant he swayed on his feet. Then he crashed forward on his face and lay still.

The cabin door was thrown open and an Indian, a smoking rifle in his hands and a leer of triumph on his face, strode towards the motionless figure with cat-like tread. A few paces away he halted and looked carefully around, presumably to make sure that there had been no witness of what had transpired; then, as if satisfied that all was well, he leaned his rifle against a tree stump, and, drawing a short curved knife from his belt, advanced confidently towards his victim, who was still lying as he had fallen. With his lips parted in a savage smile, the Indian bent over Ginger.

CHAPTER XVII

A New Peril

While these events were in progress, Biggles and his two companions had been marched by Delaney towards Fort Beaver. It was a grim journey. Algy raged. Wilks strode along, glowering his annoyance. Biggles was irritated, but endeavoured to preserve a calm front. The fact of the matter was, not one of them realized the real seriousness of their position. They were angry at being taken to the jail like common felons, but this, at the worst, would only be temporary. It had not yet occurred to them that they might not be able to prove their innocence of the crime for which they had been arrested. Nor did they imagine it possible that they would be tried by any but an official court of law.

Approaching Fort Beaver, McBain hurried on ahead. Biggles attached no special significance to this at the time, but before very long he realized what the man's purpose had been. Except for this, things might have turned out differently.

The first indication of McBain's errand – although this was not made apparent until some minutes later – occurred while the prisoners were still some distance from the town. Several men appeared, hurrying towards them in a manner that was definitely hostile, if not openly threatening. Muttering and casting malevolent glances at the prisoners, they joined the party. Others appeared, with a sprinkling of slatternly-looking women amongst them. At first vague murmurings were heard; then insults and imprecations were thrown at the three airmen.

Accustomed to civilized administration of justice, Biggles was amazed. He had not supposed that they would be condemned without a fair trial. He noticed that Delaney looked worried, and remarked on it.

'You keep close to me; I don't like the look of things,' said the constable. 'I'd turn back if it wasn't too late. If this crowd decides to take things into their own hands you won't stand a dog's chance. I don't know what's set 'em off like this.'

'McBain, probably,' replied Biggles, suddenly understanding, for he could see the man deliberately egging the crowd on to take the law into their own hands.

Yells, and not a few curses, reached the prisoners' ears. Presently a stone was thrown.

Algy looked at Biggles with startled eyes. 'I don't like the look of this,' he said anxiously. 'Delaney shouldn't have brought us here knowing that the crowd might behave like this.'

'He didn't know. McBain is responsible.'

'The sooner we are under lock and key, the better I shall be pleased,' declared Algy. 'Things look ugly.'

More and more men were hurrying out from the village to meet them and the noise swelled in volume. Above the medley of sound, odd phrases would be heard.

'String 'em up, the dirty murderers!' yelled an old man with a ferocious expression. 'String 'em up like we did in the old days.'

'Murdered Mose for his poke. Hand 'em over, Delaney,' roared another.

'A rope. Fetch a rope, somebody.'

'Hoist 'em up.'

'Old Mose once did me a good turn; now I'll do him one.'

'Hang 'em, hang 'em! Hang 'em!'

These were typical of the threats hurled at the three airmen by the crowd as it surged round them and their escort.

'That's it, hang 'em!' roared McBain.

Delaney halted and held up his hand for silence, but the gesture produced little or no effect. 'Get back to your work, all of you!' he bellowed. 'If this is a hanging job the right people will look after it.'

Those who heard the words only redoubled their demands for the prisoners to be handed over to them.

Delaney was past the stage of being worried. His face was pale and his manner distraught; it became increasingly clear that the situation was beyond his authority or ability to control. 'I can't do nothing with 'em,' he told Biggles hoarsely.

'You've got a rifle, man; why don't you use it? The law's on your side,' Biggles pointed out harshly. Inwardly he was disgusted at the revolting exhibition of hysteria which the cunning McBain had been able to foster.

'They'd tear me to bits if I so much as fired a shot into the air,' yelled Delaney above the uproar.

'I suppose it doesn't matter what they do to us?' sneered Biggles.

A stone was thrown. As it happened it was Delaney that it struck. It caught him on the temple, making an ugly wound. At the sight of the blood the noise died down for a moment, and the constable seized the opportunity provided by the lull to voice another protest. 'What's gone wrong with you?' he shouted furiously. 'What's the idea? Would you hang a man without a fair trial?'

'Yes!' bellowed a red-headed miner. 'Give 'em a trial and the lawyers will help 'em to dodge the noose. We've seen it happen before. Old Mose made his home in Fort Beaver; then it's up to us in Fort Beaver to see justice done.'

'Hear, hear! Hurrah!' shouted the crowd. 'They killed Mose.'

'Who said they killed Mose?' roared Delaney. The stone seemed to have stung him into action.

'Brindle McBain says so,' screeched a woman.

'He seems mighty anxious to get 'em hanged,' answered Delaney. 'It strikes me that he's a sight *too* anxious. Maybe he's got a reason.'

All eyes turned to McBain who, for a moment, looked uncomfortable. 'If they didn't do it, why did you arrest 'em?' he demanded shrewdly.

This was a poser the unfortunate constable found it difficult to answer, a matter which the crowd was not slow in observing.

'Come on, boys. String 'em up!' yelled McBain. 'They'll get off else.'

'You've got one chance; it's a poor one, but I'll try to bring it off,' Delaney told the airmen through set teeth. 'We've got to humour them. Anything so long as we can cause a. delay. Maybe later on they'll come to their senses.' He faced the crowd, hands aloft. 'All right,' he shouted. 'If they killed Mose then they'll hang, but I ain't standing for murder. Let's take 'em down to the Three Star and hear what they have to say.'

McBain objected, declaring that this suggestion was only a trick to get the airmen away. A discussion followed and in the end McBain was overruled. Possibly the blood on the constable's face had sobered the crowd somewhat. If Delaney had been struck, it was not likely that the whole affair would be allowed to pass without some one being called to account when the chief constable of the area arrived – as he certainly would, sooner or later. Possibly Delaney's aggressive attitude had something to do with it. Be that as it may, the crowd, still grimly demanding the prisoners' lives, quietened down somewhat, and the procession moved off in some sort of order towards the Three Star Saloon.

Another delay occurred at the entrance, where the proprietor, fearful, no doubt, of damage to his property, endeavoured to keep the crowd out. But once a number of people get out of hand they seem to lend each other a sort of false courage to do what in normal circumstances they would not dare do. The door of the saloon was forced open and the crowd surged inside like a wave rushing through a breach in a sea wall. The proprietor took up his position behind the bar, revolver in hand, to prevent looting. He threatened to shoot the first man who attempted to touch a bottle without first paying for it, and from his manner he meant it. Delaney got up on the bar itself, made the prisoners line up under him, facing outwards, and from this commanding position, supported by his carbine, he called the crowd to order. Satisfied, perhaps, that it was now getting its own way, the uproar subsided, and presently a comparative silence fell. McBain and Ferroni, smugly complacent, pushed their way to the front near the prisoners. McBain bit the end off a cigar, spat the end away, and lighted it.

'Make it short and sweet,' he demanded.

'One more word from you, McBain, and I'll put you under arrest, too,' snapped the constable.

'Yeah?' drawled McBain. 'For what?'

'For inciting a crowd to riot.'

McBain laughed as if this was a huge joke, and such was the power of his personality that the crowd laughed with him. He blew a cloud of smoke in the direction of the prisoners. 'How are you going to try 'em – all together or one at a time?' he questioned. 'Not that it makes much difference,' he added casually.

'You can leave that to me,' replied Delaney crisply. 'I'll say my piece first – but I want you all to know that this isn't a legal—'

'Cut out the legal stuff,' shouted a young farmer. 'We want the man – or the men – who killed poor old Mose, and we're going to have him. And when we're satisfied that we've got him we're going to *hang* him. Am I right, folks?'

A roar of approval greeted these words.

Delaney held up his right hand. 'All right,' he said. 'I'll start. First of all, most of you know by now that a packet of gold has been stolen in transit between Moose Creek and Edmonton. Brindle McBain and his pilot flew the gold down, and I saw him hand the boxes over with my own eyes. What was inside those boxes I'm not prepared to swear because my eyes can't see through half-inch timber. But I'll swear this: the seals what was put on each box at Moose Creek hadn't been broken.'

'What's all this got to do with Mose?' drawled McBain in a bored voice.

'Yes, let's stick to the business,' muttered several others.

'I'm coming to that,' announced Delaney. 'I was asked to locate the metal, so I started by inquiring at the aerodrome. First I searched McBain's outfit, where I found nothing. I then went on to Arctic Airways outfit where I found more than I bargained for. I found, hid under the floor, six bags of gold-dust, done up as a single poke, them bags being the same as we all know Mose made for to carry his dust in. His initials was burnt on to the hide to prove that they was his. Mose must have struck it rich. I didn't know he had such a poke; he didn't say nothing about it when he was here a week or so ago; but it seems as if somebody else must have known. We all know Mose was murdered, and how he was murdered – now we know *why* he was murdered.'

'That's where you're wrong, Delaney,' put in Biggles quietly.

'I can't think of no better reason for killing a man than a heavy poke,' snapped the constable.

From the chorus of jeers that broke out it was evident that the crowd thought the same.

'On the strength of that poke I arrested every one in the outfit where it was found,' continued Delaney. 'And unless the prisoners can explain how they came to be hiding a murdered man's poke, particularly as at least one of 'em was with Mose on the night he was killed, then I reckon any court would find 'em guilty. This ain't a properly constituted court and nobody here has any right to take the law into his own hands. These prisoners will have a proper trial, but, as I say, unless they can prove that Mose *gave* 'em his poke – which I doubt – then they'll hang.'

On a point of law Delaney was, of course, incorrect, but none of the airmen thought it worth while to argue. They knew as well as any one how damning the evidence was, and Biggles, for one, could not find it in his heart to blame the crowd for its line of thought.

'It is one of the privileges of British justice,' he said loudly, 'that no man is condemned without being allowed to make a statement in his own defence.'

'I reckons we've heard enough,' sneered McBain.

'You shut your face, McBain,' cried Delaney angrily. Then to

Biggles: 'Speak up,' he cried. 'You'd better get up here where every one can see you.'

Biggles climbed up on the bar and faced the sea of scowling faces in front of him. Perhaps it was his quiet manner, or the steadiness of his eyes, that had some effect on the crowd. A hush fell.

'First of all,' he began, 'let me say that I don't blame any one of you for feeling as you do, or for thinking as you do. Were I amongst you, and another man was standing where I am now, faced with such evidence as has been given by Constable Delaney, I should say "that man killed old Mose for his poke". But I should be wrong.'

The expressions on the faces of some of his hearers changed, suggesting that the words had had the desired effect. Biggles noticed it. Delaney noticed it, and breathed a sigh of relief, realizing that if once the hot indignation of the crowd could be calmed they would be more likely to listen to reason and allow the law to take its course in the usual way.

But another man had noticed it too – McBain. And he perceived, apparently, that if Biggles were allowed to continue, his plans for the swift and easy disposal of his enemies might even yet fail.

'Don't take any notice of him,' he sneered. 'He reckons we're a lot of suckers. Let him talk and he'll put one over. Come on, boys, we're wasting time. We know he killed Mose, and he ain't goin' to get away with it.'

'Cut the gas!' snapped Delaney, but his words were drowned in a fresh uproar started by the more headstrong elements of the crowd. The cry went up, 'Lynch 'em!' and it was echoed on all sides. The mob surged forward towards the prisoners.

'Stand back!' The barkeeper was on the counter, the muzzle of his heavy revolver threatening the upturned faces below. 'You'd better get 'em down to the jail, Delaney,' he said in a swift aside. 'I'll hold this rabble. Go the back way.'

Biggles and the others did not know it, but the proprietor of the Three Star was a retired sergeant of the 'mounties', which no doubt accounted for his partisanship on the side of the law. The habits of twenty years are not easily cast aside.

Delaney looked at the now clamouring crowd, and what he saw convinced him of the futility of further argument. He turned to Biggles. 'If we don't make the jail they'll hang you, and I shan't be able to stop them. Follow me. If you try to get away I'll plug you.'

Algy and Wilks, now pressed by the crowd, climbed up on to the counter. Instantly there was a yell of 'Stop 'em', and a shot was fired from somewhere in the rear of the mob. The barkeeper's left arm fell limply to his side. Without a word he blazed back at the man who had shot him. The red-headed miner collapsed in a heap on the floor. Pandemonium followed. A revolver barked again and the barkeeper pitched head first into the crowd. Delaney, white with fury, shot the man who had fired. He waited for no more. 'Come on,' he yelled, and dashed to the rear of the bar, followed closely by the prisoners.

There was a brief respite as they dashed pell-mell out of the back door of the saloon, for most of the crowd was inside, and those who had run out of the front door had not yet had time to get round to the rear.

'The jail is our only chance,' snapped Delaney. 'If we can get inside we may be able to hold it. This way.'

They dashed down the rear of some frame buildings and cut back into the main street of the village, just as the crowd surged into sight round the end of the saloon. Several shots were fired,

'They dashed down the rear of some frame buildings'

but they went wide, flecking up the earth or ripping splinters from the wooden buildings.

The constable and his prisoners did not stop. With Delaney leading, they raced towards a heavily built log cabin which stood in the middle of the track facing the direction from which they had come. A single iron-barred window plainly announced its purpose.

Delaney was feeling in his pocket for the key even before they reached it. He was fumbling with the lock as the crowd, led by McBain, poured into sight. McBain fired, and a bullet thudded into the logs. Biggles fired four quick shots over the heads of the crowd, and while it did not stop their progress, it delayed the leaders long enough for the constable to get the door open.

They all rushed inside, Delaney slamming the massive door behind them and locking it.

'Where did you get that gun?' he asked angrily.

'It was the barkeeper's,' answered Biggles simply.

The constable did not pursue the subject. He closed two shutters on the window and bolted them, but a dim light still came through the numerous cracks in them.

'Well, we've made it,' he said moodily, 'but I don't know what good it's going to do us. We can't hold it for ever. McBain's got that crowd into a good enough state for anything.'

'Well, at least it gives us breathing space,' replied Biggles, looking round the single large room which comprised the jail. 'I reckon we've got one chance left.'

'What's that?'

'Ginger.'

'You mean that kid who got away in the 'plane?'

'That's right.'

Algy looked up. 'Gosh! I'd forgotten all about him,' he confessed. 'What can he do, do you suppose?'

Biggles shrugged his shoulders. 'Goodness knows. But he'll do something, you can bet your life on that. By the way, I wonder what became of Smyth? He must have seen Delaney marching us towards the village, and guessing what had happened, found some place to hide. He'll take care of himself. I'm more worried about Ginger. I should like to know what he's doing at this moment.'

CHAPTER XVIII

Trapped!

'Well, whatever it is he's doing, he'll have to be quick about it,' remarked Delaney coldly.

'You think the crowd will attack us here – in a Government building?' asked Biggles.

A bullet thudded against the side of the cabin; a splinter of wood jerked out into the room.

'There's your answer,' said Delaney.

From a safe place Biggles looked through the barred window at the sky, now pink-flushed with the approach of sunset. He could not imagine what Ginger was doing or where he had gone, but as Delaney had said, if he was coming back he would have to be quick, if for no other reason than that it would soon be dark.

Biggles looked back at the constable. 'Curious situation, isn't it?' he observed. 'Are we allowed to defend ourselves? I mean, if we kill any one in defending our lives, are we liable to be charged with murder?'

'Not while I'm here, I reckon,' replied Delaney dubiously, as though he was not quite sure himself. 'It's McBain who is causing the trouble; but for him I think the others would clear off.'

'Why don't you go out and arrest him?' suggested Biggles.

The constable started. 'That's an idea,' he confessed.

'They're not likely to shoot *you*,' urged Biggles.

'Maybe not, but they're likely to shoot you if I open this door,' returned Delaney grimly.

He ducked as a stone whirled through the window. It struck the opposite wall with a crash, and fell to the floor. They all looked at the missile and observed at once that there was something unusual about it. Biggles picked it up. 'Hello,' he said, 'this looks like a message.'

A piece of paper had, in fact, been tied to the stone with a piece of string.

Delaney, asserting his authority, took it out of Biggles's hands, unfolded it, and, in the fast waning light, read something that had been written on it.

'What is it?' asked Algy, unable to restrain his curiosity.

'It's from that fellow of yours – Smyth,' said Delaney. 'He says he's found and saddled my mare and is going to Blackfoot Point for help.... There's an officer and four troopers there,' he added, by way of explanation. 'Somebody in the crowd must have given him the tip.'

'How far away is this place?' asked Biggles.

'Twenty miles – a bit over.'

'Well, that's a hope, anyway; but twenty miles – it means that if Smyth gets there we couldn't expect help much before dawn.'

'And I reckon that'll be about six hours too late,' returned Delaney. 'What are they up to outside?'

There was little need to ask. While the foregoing conversation had been taking place the crowd had surged round the jail, and the demands for the prisoners had reached an alarming pitch of frenzy. 'We want the men who killed Mose,' was the gist of the cries.

'Bring 'em out, Delaney, or we'll tear the jail down,' yelled a strident voice.

'This is Government property and I'll plug the first man who lays hands on it,' roared the constable. 'Go home, the lot of you.'

'Not till we've hung the murderers,' was the reply.

'You won't come in here while I'm on my feet,' declared Delaney wrathfully.

The crash of another bullet against the door was the answer.

'Look here, Delaney, you'd better go,' suggested Biggles. 'There's no sense in your getting killed from a mistaken idea of duty. Leave us to it. We'll hold 'em off as long as we can.'

'The Force has never lost a prisoner yet and I ain't going to be the first,' was the curt rejoinder.

'Get a log, somebody,' came from outside. 'Bring a log, and we'll soon have the door down.'

The words were taken up on all sides. 'A log – a log.' McBain's voice could also be heard demanding torches.

By this time it was quite dark, so the need for some means of illumination was easily understood.

'Well, I'm afraid it means bloodshed,' said Delaney regretfully. He took up a position beside the window and waited.

'Here they come with a tree,' he answered presently, and levelling his revolver, fired two shots.

There came a yell from outside. The two shots were answered by a dozen, and Delaney staggered back, clutching at his shoulder.

'Have they hit you?' cried Biggles anxiously. 'Got me through the shoulder,' snarled the constable, leaning back against the wall.

Biggles went to the window, shouted out that the constable had been hit, and demanded a truce while bandages were fetched.

A howl of execration was the reply, and he ducked back just in time to escape a fusillade.

'Their blood's up,' groaned Delaney. 'Nothing will stop 'em now. I know. I've seen this sort of thing before.'

'Maybe we'd better surrender,' suggested Biggles. 'I don't like this idea of you losing your life to save us.'

'I've never lost a prisoner yet, and I ain't starting now,' returned Delaney obstinately.

Biggles shrugged his shoulders.

A moment later the building shook as a heavy weight struck the door with a crash.

Delaney cursed, and snatching up his revolver with his left hand, emptied it into the middle of the rough-hewn pine logs from which the door was made.

The shots were followed by a sudden silence.

'They've killed Fred,' said a voice charged with passion. Instantly such a yell arose as made the others weak by comparison. Again the building shook as the attack on the door was resumed.

Biggles's jaw set. Revolver in hand, he crept to the window and peeped out, hoping to see the man who had been responsible for the riot. But if McBain was there he was too wise to show himself. Four men were just lifting the heavy log which was being used as a battering-ram. The eyes of the spectators were on them. Biggles took careful aim at the nearest man's arm and pulled the trigger. The man staggered, and released his hold on the log, which fell on the feet of the next man to him. Again Biggles fired, shooting at the legs of the other three. Another man fell, and there was a general dash for cover. Biggles jumped aside as the answering shots came, and coughed as the acrid smell of cordite drifted back into the room.

Several times as the night wore on the attack was resumed, but on each occasion it was beaten off by the defenders.

'With luck we shall just last one more attack,' announced Delaney during a pause.

'How so?' asked Biggles.

'I've only one cartridge left.'

'And I've none. My gun's empty,' said Biggles quietly, tossing the now useless weapon on the floor.

'What do you reckon the time is?' asked Wilks, who had spent most of the night leaning against the wall smoking, since there was nothing he could do.

'Can't be far short of dawn,' said Delaney. 'I wonder what they're up to out there. They seem to be sort of quiet.'

'We shall soon know, I fancy,' replied Biggles, as the sound of stealthy footsteps, accompanied by furtive muttering and whispering, came from outside.

There came a sudden rush, and then again silence.

An orange light flickered on the window frame, faint at first, but growing rapidly brighter. A crisp crackling told the defenders the worst.

'They've set the place on fire,' gasped Biggles.

'That's the end of it, then,' announced Algy calmly. 'Either we go out or we stay here and fry.'

'Of the two I prefer to go out,' said Biggles.

'And me,' nodded Wilks.

Delaney swore soundly, but it did no good. Smoke oozed under the door and eddied in through the window. Presently they were all coughing.

Delaney went over to the door. 'I'm sorry,' he said, 'but I can't do any more. If you can save yourselves, do it, but if you should get clear give yourselves up at the nearest police post. I shall be after you again, else.'

Biggles nodded. 'We're ready to stand our trial when the time comes,' he said. 'But I'm afraid the crowd thinks otherwise. Come on. Let's get it over.'

Smoke and flames poured into the room as Delaney threw open the door against which faggots had been piled. A yell went up.

'I'll go first,' said the constable, and took a running jump over the blazing faggots.

Biggles followed. Almost before his feet touched the ground on the far side of the fire many hands had seized him and borne him to the ground, where, helpless, his wrists were tied behind his back. He was then dragged to his feet and marched off.

The same fate befell the others, and presently the three of them were assembled in the middle of a jubilant throng. Only the constable had not had his wrists tied together. He remained with his prisoners, protesting in the strongest possible terms at the crowd's behaviour, but he might as well have saved his breath for all the effect the words had. The crowd had nothing against him, so beyond a certain amount of horseplay he was left alone.

A shout went up for ropes, which were soon produced, whereupon a move was made up the main street, the crowd surging along with the prisoners in its centre.

'Where are we going?' Biggles asked Delaney, who was walking beside him.

'There ain't no sense in telling you lies,' answered the constable. 'There's a tree up on the top there, on the way to the aerodrome, with a convenient branch.'

'Thanks,' replied Biggles, not without bitterness.

The eastern sky had already been grey with the approach of dawn when they had evacuated the jail; by the time they reached the tree – which was, in fact, near the edge of the aerodrome – it was comparatively light.

The prisoners were led under a branch, which projected at right-angles from the trunk. Three ropes, with nooses already made, were thrown over it.

'It's hard to believe that this is really happening, isn't it?' said Algy, looking at the tree and then at the eager crowd in a dazed sort of way.

'It is,' agreed Biggles.

'Silly sort of way to die,' complained Algy.

'And all my fault for bringing you out here,' muttered Wilks, in a voice heavy with remorse.

'Rot!' said Biggles. 'You've nothing to blame yourself for. It's just a bit of luck that nobody could have foreseen. My greatest regret is that that hound McBain looks like getting away with it.'

'No use trying to get the crowd to listen to us, I suppose?' suggested Algy without enthusiasm.

'Not the slightest,' returned Biggles. 'I should have tried it had there been any hope of them listening, you may be sure. Look at 'em. They won't even listen to Delaney, who most of 'em must have known for years. No, I don't usually give up easily, but I must confess that there seems to be no way out of this pickle.'

A noose was slipped round his neck. Turning, he watched the

others being treated in the same way, regardless of Delaney's frantic expostulations.

'Keep your eyes on McBain, Delaney,' called Biggles loudly. 'He's the man who murdered Mose.' Then, quick to the others, 'Poor old Ginger. Looks as if he's not coming back after all.'

CHAPTER XIX

A Life Or Death Struggle

When Ginger had fallen outside the remote cabin he had not been killed. He had not even been hit by the shot which had been fired at him. He felt the whistle of the bullet as it passed his cheek, and the shock had caused him to stumble. And even as he stumbled he realized with a lightning flash of inspiration that the moment he recovered himself he would be a mark for a second shot. So he dived headlong to the ground.

This was, primarily, an act of pure self-preservation, for in this position he offered a smaller target than in any other, and he was well aware of it. In moments of extreme peril the brain often works faster than at any other time, and hard upon Ginger's first thought came another, the recollection of a trick that is as old as the hills. Men have practised it from the beginning of time. Animals still practise it – some regularly. Indeed, after one of them has the ruse been named – playing 'possum. In short, Ginger feigned death hoping that the man who had fired at him would be deceived and might give the pretended corpse a chance to turn the tables.

Lying absolutely still on the turf, Ginger heard the cabin door open, heard some one emerge and walk towards him. It was a nasty moment, and it required all his fortitude to remain as he was, because, for all he knew, the man was even then sighting his rifle to make sure of his work. It was not to be wondered at that Ginger's scalp tingled – almost as if it was conscious of what was about to happen to it.

The grass rustled as the unseen man approached. There was a momentary pause, then a hand closed over the back of Ginger's head, and he knew it was time to move.

With a grunt he sprang to his feet, looking wildly for his attacker, and saw a man whom he recognized at once – the Indian member of McBain's gang.

With the scalping knife in his hand, the Indian had instinctively started back at Ginger's unexpected return to life; but the withdrawal was only momentary; with his smile of victory replaced by a snarl of disappointment and anger, he leapt forward again to the attack.

But the brief respite had given Ginger a chance to get his balance. His right hand flew to his pocket and came up grasping his automatic, but before he could pull the trigger the Indian, with a lightning sweep of his left arm, had knocked the weapon aside so that the bullet crashed into the end of the cabin. What was more, the blow knocked the automatic clean out of Ginger's hand; it described a short flight through the air and came to rest on the turf some ten yards or more away.

Ginger did not attempt to run, for he knew that the fleet-footed Redskin would quickly overtake him. In desperation, he leapt forward to seize the arm that held the knife; he did this before the Indian had time to recover fully from the blow he had struck at the automatic, with the result that they both went down with a crash, Ginger falling across the arm which he had seized so that the knife was not six inches from his face. To prise the weapon from the Indian's hand would be, he knew, beyond his strength, so he resorted to a method which he once saw employed during a fight between two drunken miners. He used his teeth. Taking the bones in the back of the brown hand between his jaws, he bit with all his strength. Under the excruciating agony the Indian let out a scream, and the hand jerked open convulsively. But before Ginger could possess himself of the knife, the Indian, with a tremendous effort, flung himself sideways, with the result that they both rolled over away from the weapon.

Both were now disarmed, but of the two the Indian was the heavier and Ginger knew that in the end this must tell against him. The automatic was his only chance. Somehow he must reach it, although, having by this time rolled over several times, he was by no means sure of its exact whereabouts. Meanwhile, all his strength was needed to keep the Indian's hands from his throat.

For perhaps a minute the struggle continued without marked advantage on either side. Sometimes the Indian was on top, and sometimes Ginger, who, knowing what his fate would be if he weakened, was now fighting with the fury of despair. He managed to get on top again, but before he could break free and make a dash for the automatic the Indian had flung him off again, this time with such force that he rolled some distance away. He was brought up by a stone against which he struck his head with a force that made him gasp. Yet even in his sorry plight he had the wit to realize that it was a stone, and that a stone can be a useful weapon in emergency.

By the time his wildly groping hand had found and closed over the stone, the Indian was more than half-way towards him, so slightly raising himself, he flung the missile with every ounce of his fast-waning strength, and then twisted sideways.

The stone caught the Redskin full in the mouth, producing an animal snarl of rage and pulling him up short, spitting blood. For a brief moment his sombre eyes blazed into Ginger's; then they went beyond him, and he darted forward.

Ginger was on his feet in an instant, and it took him not more than a split second to see what his adversary was after. It was the rifle which had been left against the tree stump, and which Ginger now saw for the first time. To reach the weapon first was obviously impossible. Frantically his eyes scanned the short turf, seeking the automatic. He saw it, made a rush for it, and reached it at the precise moment that the Indian grabbed the rifle. Both weapons came up together and two reports rang out, one following the other so closely that the sounds blended. But Ginger's shot had been fired first, by an interval of time so short as to be immeasurable. But it was enough.

Where the rifle bullet went Ginger did not know. It had not hit him, and that was all that concerned him. He was staring at the Indian, whose behaviour was unlike anything he had ever seen before. At Ginger's shot he had appeared to throw the weapon up into the air before taking several running steps backward, then he fell and finished up flat on his back.

Ginger, gasping for breath, concluded, not unnaturally, that he had killed the man. Reeling with exhaustion, he took a pace towards him, whereupon to his amazement and dismay the Indian sprang to his feet and dashed away.

Ginger was in no mood to let the man get away; he represented too big a danger. Jerking up his weapon, he let drive at the running form, and missed. At least, the Indian continued running;

furthermore, as he ran he twisted and turned in a manner that made shooting almost a waste of powder. Three times Ginger fired without any of the shots taking the slightest effect, and by that time the Redskin was out of effective pistol range. Still running, he disappeared from sight in the belt of timber that skirted the water's edge.

With a grunt of mortification Ginger dropped the muzzle of the automatic and walked across to where the rifle was lying; on picking it up he perceived the cause of the Indian's strange behaviour. His – that is, Ginger's – first shot had not hit the man; it had hit the rifle. By a strange chance the bullet had struck the trigger-guard, and the force of the impact had, of course, knocked the weapon from the man's hands. Also, it must have spoilt his shot. Considering the matter, Ginger could not make up his mind who was the luckier – he or the Indian.

Looking at the sky he saw that the day was fast drawing to a close, so he made his way towards the open door of the cabin in order to pursue the quest that had brought him to the spot.

He did not intend to stay long. The surprise of his encounter with the Indian had left him not a little shaken; moreover, he was rather worried for fear the Indian would find some means of turning the tables on him; he saw that it was going to be difficult to search the cabin thoroughly and at the same time keep a close watch on the trees in which the Redskin had disappeared. To make matters worse, the light was failing. It would soon be dark, and the possibility of his being benighted in the cabin had not previously entered into his calculations. He still hoped to avoid it, particularly as the Indian was at large. Standing the rifle against the door, ready for action should it be needed, he looked around.

The first thing he saw was a fur coat hanging from a peg on

the opposite wall. Its presence gave him something of a turn, for he recognized it at once from its unmistakable white blaze. It was McBain's. He had worn it, he recalled, on the night of the murder of old Mose. What it was doing there he did not know, but it seemed evident that McBain had either left it behind by accident or else he had lent it to the Indian – probably the latter. Anyway, he reflected, its presence proved, if proof were needed, that McBain was closely concerned with the cabin even if he did not actually own it.

A preliminary examination of such objects as were in view revealed nothing more of particular interest. There were a few pieces of furniture, mostly homemade, and of the roughest possible character. A packing case, on which were strewn some odds and ends of food, served for a table. Two chairs, a bench, an iron stove of the covered-in variety, a heap of firewood, a lamp of the hurricane type, a small pyramid of stores – that was all.

In the ordinary way Ginger would have looked no further, for there was nothing suspicious about such articles; indeed, they were normal camp equipment, and it would have been more surprising had they not been there; but two circumstances combined to make him feel sure that there was more in the cabin than met the eye. In the first place, why had McBain's machine landed there when there was every reason to suppose that it had the gold on board? Secondly, why had the Indian been left there? McBain was not the sort of man who would do anything without a good reason, certainly not when he was in the middle of a carefully prepared scheme. The presence of the Indian indicated that there was something in the cabin that needed guarding, and, in the circumstances, what could be more likely than that it was the gold?

Satisfied that his reasoning was correct, Ginger broke off in his ruminating and looked steadily in the direction of the trees, but there was no sign of the Indian, so without further loss of time he proceeded with the search. If the gold was there, then he would not rest until he had found it, he decided.

There was no question of there being a concealed cavity in the walls, for they were of solid tree-trunks set one above the other in single thickness. The roof was of split pine, through which daylight showed in many places, and clearly offered no hiding-place. There remained only the floor, and this, as far as it was visible, was solid enough.

Ginger regarded the heap of firewood reflectively. 'If the gold is here it is under this pile,' he told himself confidently as he began dragging the branches aside. It took him some time to get down to floor level, for he was still rather worried about the Indian, and he broke off from his task several times to study the landscape. However, at last he pushed the remaining few branches aside and dropped on his hands and knees, feeling for the trap door which he felt certain was there. He could hardly believe it when he discovered that nothing of the sort was there. Again and again he examined the floor inch by inch, but in the end he was compelled to admit to himself that he had been mistaken. The floor at that point was as solid as the rest.

Half sick with disappointment, he stood up and stared down at the spot as though he still found the obvious truth difficult to believe. If the gold was not there, he thought with fast sinking hopes, then it must be buried somewhere outside, in which case he would be very lucky indeed if he found it. It might be anywhere within a hundred yards, which meant that he might dig for a week, or even a month, without striking the spot. The more he thought about it the more depressed he became. It was infuriating to be so near and yet so far, for he was still convinced that the gold was there. He began to hate the sound of the word.

Remembering the Indian, he crossed again to the window and looked out over the darkening landscape. Somewhere out there was the Indian, he mused, unless he had started off on foot for Fort Beaver to warn the others of what had happened, which did not seem likely.

He started as a thought flashed into his mind. The Indian! He would know where the gold was hidden. What a pity he had got away; otherwise he would have made him divulge the hiding-place. Perhaps he was not so far away – perhaps – Ginger caught his breath as the idea took root. 'It's my only chance,' he muttered. 'I've got to find that blighter. I've got his rifle, so it shouldn't be very difficult.'

Three swift strides took him to the door, where he had left the rifle. He put his hand out for it, confidently, only to draw back with a little gasp of amazement. He stopped, staring at the place where it had been – where he was certain he had put it. But it was no longer there.

CHAPTER XX

Lost

Ginger's first sensation on discovering his loss was one of utter amazement. He was incredulous. It was followed by one of doubt. In his mind he was absolutely certain that he had leaned the rifle against the doorpost. True, he had performed the action subconsciously, for at the time his thoughts were concentrated on the interior of the cabin; but, nevertheless, casting his mind back – as one often can in such circumstances – he had a clear recollection of standing the weapon against the doorpost as he surveyed the interior of the room. Was it possible that he had been mistaken? Had he, without thinking what he was doing, moved it again afterwards? He could not remember doing so, but it was just possible. With a frown of perplexity lining his forehead, he looked at all the likely places in turn – the walls, the table, and even the stove. But there was no sign of the rifle.

As he stared, almost bewildered, vaguely into his mind came stories he had read of the stealth with which an Indian could move; skill in the art of self-effacement, born of a thousand years of inter-tribal warfare, had been the theme of many of the stories he had read in his not-very-distant schooldays. Without giving the matter serious thought, he had always regarded this alleged cunning with a certain amount of scepticism. It made good reading, but that did not necessarily mean that it was true. It now began to look as if it were. Somehow the Indian must have crept up to the cabin and recovered the rifle. There was no other explanation.

For nearly a minute Ginger stood still, deep in thought, conscious that the loss of the weapon completely altered the circumstances. It meant that he would have to abandon his recently formed plan, for to go out into country which he did not know, armed only with a pistol, to look for a man who probably knew every inch of the ground, and was, moreover, in possession of a rifle, would be sheer lunacy. Still pondering, he became aware that it meant a good deal more than that. If the Indian was still in the vicinity, which seemed most likely, the chances were that he would remain as near to the cabin as possible, covering the door, waiting for him – Ginger – to step outside. With a fresh twinge of alarm, he perceived that he would not be able to get back to the machine without running the gauntlet of the Indian's fire.

Reproaching himself bitterly for his carelessness, he looked up, and saw that he was standing in line with the small window, not much more than a loophole, that looked out from the rear of the cabin. Instinctively he stepped aside. He was only just in time. A bullet ripped a splinter of wood from the side of the window and buried itself with a crisp *zut* in the opposite wall.

Although thoroughly startled by the narrow margin of his escape, Ginger realized that the shot settled any remaining doubt as to the whereabouts of the weapon. The Indian had got it, and the direction from which the shot had come gave him a rough idea of his position; and since the ground on that side of the cabin

was level as far as the trees, he realized that the Indian had probably taken up a position on the edge of the wood.

Ginger, keeping well away from the window, examined the situation in this new light. He no longer entertained the idea of going
out to look for his enemy. He was more concerned with preserving
his life, and the machine; and he experienced a fresh pang of
apprehension when the thought flashed into his head that the
Indian might, under cover of darkness, set fire to the Jupiter, or
put it out of action in some other way. At all costs he must prevent
that, he thought desperately.

Still racking his brain for a solution to the difficult problem
with which he was now faced, he fell back on his old resort. What
would Biggles do in such a case? A careful reconnaissance near
the door confirmed his belief that it was possible, by making a
rush, to reach the machine; but the idea of becoming the fugitive,
leaving the Indian in command of the situation, was repugnant to
him, quite apart from which it meant, definitely, that his mission
had failed. In any case, it was nearly dark, and his common sense
told him that it would be an act of the greatest folly to try to find
his way back to Fort Beaver in the dark. Even if he found the
aerodrome, which was not very likely, the business of landing
the big machine without lights of any sort was a responsibility
he preferred not to shoulder. If he started and lost his way, the
machine would probably be wrecked in the inevitable forced
landing when his petrol was exhausted. Having seen the country,
he knew that it would be hopeless to try to get down anywhere in
the inhospitable region between the place where he was and Fort
Beaver. If he crashed it might be months before he was found. He
might never be found.

To make matters worse, it had turned bitterly cold, and there was a feeling of snow in the air. Torn by indecision, he tried to make up his mind what to do for the best. Suppose by a miracle he did get back? What then? He would be in the same predicament as the others. Fortunately, he did not know that their plight was as desperate as it actually was, or his anxiety would have turned to something worse.

Now as he stood near the cabin door busy with these worrying thoughts, he perceived something which hitherto he had not noticed, possibly because up to the present moment it had held no significance. Not far from the door there was a depression, a slight fold in the ground. As a feature of the landscape it was negligible, but he knew that by lying flat in extended order a regiment could have taken cover in it. He recalled that once, years before, he had watched a troop of boy scouts practising taking cover in just such a trifling depression. At the time he had not known that the depression was there. From the edge of the field where he stood it could not be seen. When the scouts stood up they appeared as one would expect to see them, a definite and unmistakable party of human beings; yet when they lay down they disappeared from sight as if the ground had opened and swallowed them up. After they had gone, his curiosity was such that he had examined the place, and was amazed to find that the depression was so shallow that he was by no means sure when he had reached it.

Standing on tiptoe, Ginger now tried to see how far the depression extended, but was unable to do so with any degree of certainty; but he saw that it swept round in such a way that if it persisted in its course it would pass near the northern extremity of the wood in which, if his deductions were correct, the Indian had taken cover.

He made another critical survey of the weather, for he knew

that he could not afford to leave it out of his calculations. Should it begin to snow in earnest, then that would be the end of the undertaking. It might be the end of everything, for the machine would certainly be snowed in, in which case he would be marooned as effectively as if he were on a desert island. The sky was about three parts covered, with occasional stars beginning to twinkle through the broken masses of cumulus. Still, visibility was fairly good. It had settled down to a deceptive twilight, and he knew from experience that, as far north as he was, it would get no darker; it might even get lighter, for the northern sky was faintly suffused with the mysterious ever-moving glow of the aurora borealis; he knew that should the sky clear the rays would become stronger, and reflect more light over the landscape.

Filled by doubts and misgivings, for he was by no means certain that he was doing the right thing, he darted swiftly to the depression, where he threw himself flat on the ground and endeavoured to make out what course the shallow place of concealment took. But it merged into an indistinct background, and his scrutiny told him nothing. Behind him, the cabin showed up against the sky as a square black silhouette. The machine, looking forlorn and deserted, stood about a hundred yards to his right.

Now that the moment had come to leave these recognizable objects he hesitated, but comforted himself with the thought that if anything went wrong he could return to them. Anyway, he decided, he would keep them in sight as long as possible. Stealthily, sometimes crawling, and where the depression was particularly shallow pulling himself along flat on his stomach, he began to make his way along the fold, pausing from time to time to listen or take a surreptitious peep at the cabin. For he had not overlooked the possibility of the Indian playing the same game as himself. He knew that it was not at all unlikely that his enemy was even then endeavouring to creep unseen to the cabin; but what the Indian would not expect, he told himself, was that he had left it. In fact, if that were so, then of the two positions he preferred his own, for it seemed to hold a certain advantage.

He had made his way for what he judged to be about two hundred yards when a gust of wind brought a flurry of snow-flakes with it. He stopped at once, almost overcome with dismay. It was no use going on. Not that there was much point in going back, he reflected bitterly. If there was going to be a heavy fall it would mean the end of everything. 'Still, I suppose I shall be better off inside than out here,' he thought morosely, as he stood up in the whirling flakes, knowing that there was no longer any need for him to remain prone. The snow effectually blotted out everything outside a radius of a few yards. Turning up his collar, he walked swiftly towards the cabin – or, since he could not see, where he imagined it to be.

It surprised him to find how far he had gone. Surely he should have reached the cabin by now? He began counting his paces. When he reached fifty he stopped, knowing that he must have passed his objective. Irritated, but without any alarm, he began to retrace his steps. Presently he broke into a run, only to pull up abruptly as he realized that he was lost. Even then he was not unduly perturbed, for he knew that the cabin could not be more than a hundred yards from where he stood. There was no need for him to lose his head, he told himself. Obviously, the thing to do was to retrace his steps in the thin mantle of snow which now covered the ground. But he soon discovered that this plan, while satisfactory in theory, was, in fact, impracticable, for his trail was obliterated almost as fast as he made it.

He did not attempt to deceive himself any longer. He knew that he had not the remotest idea of where he stood in relation to the cabin. He did the only thing left; he started quartering up and down, this way and that, counting his steps so that he did not go too far in any one direction.

A sharp blow in the face pulled him up with a jerk. Indeed, he staggered back, hand to his face, for the blow had hurt. What had he walked into? It was certainly not the cabin. It was not the machine, for there was no projection on it so sharp as whatever it was that had struck his face. Holding his hands in front of him, he moved slowly forward, feeling his way. They encountered the object, and he knew at once what it was. The blunt end of a twig. His hands groped their way along it until they were met by a tangle of branches, and finally the trunk of a tree. He realized that he had wandered to the wood, but what part of it he had no means of knowing.

And while he stood there, thrown into confusion by his discovery, the snow stopped as suddenly as it had started. The moon broke through the clouds and shone whitely on the snow that lay like a spotless sheet over everything. He saw the cabin and the machine. With a sigh of relief he took a pace forward, for the thought of getting back to the cabin was still uppermost in his mind; but then he backed hurriedly, realizing that the hazard was more dangerous than the one he had first embarked upon. There was no sign of the Indian. Not that he expected it. But that did not mean that his enemy had gone away. On the contrary, in view of the uncertainty of the weather, he would be even more anxious to recover the shelter of the cabin.

Still turning the matter over in his mind, his body stiffened suddenly as a dreadful cry was borne to his ears. It was the howl of a wolf, and at the long-drawn-out cry his blood ran cold. Of course there were wolves there! He had seen them when he had first landed there with Biggles, when they had been following McBain. All the gruesome stories he had heard about wolves pursuing and tearing lonely travellers to pieces rushed through his mind. One wolf, two wolves, or a pack, he hated the whole tribe. He was terrified of them, and he knew it.

Again came the ghastly howl, nearer this time, and before it had come to a quavering end it was taken up by another.

Ginger forgot the Indian. He forgot everything. His one idea now was to get inside the sheltering walls of the cabin and shut the door. The next instant he was flying for his life across the snow in the direction of the haven of refuge. A score of paces, and a chorus of howls broke out behind him. A frantic glance over his shoulder told him the worst; a line of black shapes had broken cover some distance higher up the wood and were streaking after him, running diagonally in such a way that they would, he knew, cut him off before he reached the hut. Hardly knowing what he was doing, acting from an instinct of self-preservation rather than thought, he swerved away from his original objective and raced towards the machine. He ran as he had never run before, for he could hear the soft patter of footsteps and the panting breath of his pursuers.

And as he ran Ginger knew that his life depended upon a circumstance so trivial that he could not have imagined it. The wolves were so close behind that he knew that if the cabin door of the Jupiter was shut he would not have time to open it and get inside before they pulled him down. He could not remember whether he had closed it or left it open. Nor could he see until he was within a dozen paces whether it was open or shut. It was open. With a last convulsive effort he took a flying leap at the aperture and slammed the door behind him just as the leading wolf launched itself through the air. It struck the door with a crash that made the machine rock. Ginger, on his back, still half crazed with panic, snatched out his automatic and blazed at the door from the inside. There was a shrill yelp, followed instantly by a dreadful snarling and scuffling. He knew all about wolves killing and eating one of their number that was wounded or incapacitated, and that is what he imagined was going on outside. He hoped it was true. Nothing would have given him greater pleasure than to see the wolves tearing each other to pieces.

Panting, he made his way through into the cockpit, where he sank down in the control seat to consider the situation in its latest form. He was tired. He was cold. He felt weak and hungry. In fact, he was sick of the whole business. Things seemed to be going from bad to worse, and it is not surprising that he found himself wishing that he had never undertaken a mission which was fast proving to be beyond his ability to fulfil. He could hear the wolves outside. Looking through the side window he could see them, some sitting on their haunches staring up at the cockpit, others sniffing round the undercarriage. One, bolder than the rest, made a leap at the window, only to fall back again as Ginger's pistol cracked. Again came the ghastly business of the wolves devouring their wounded companion.

Ginger felt that he was safe where he was. He would, he decided, stay there until the morning; as soon as it was light enough for safe flying he would abandon his project, and return to Fort Beaver, no matter what the result might be. Searching about, he found a few pieces of broken biscuit in the pocket on the inside of the door, and it was while he was munching these ravenously that he noticed a

'Conspicuous against the snow on the roof was a dark object'

change in the behaviour of the wolves. One of them, sniffing about some distance from the rest, suddenly threw up his head and let out its hateful howl, after which it loped off towards the log cabin where, as Ginger now noticed for the first time, several wolves were already prowling. One by one the others broke away from the machine and joined the party now circling the hut.

Ginger watched them with a new interest, wondering what it was that had attracted their attention. At first he thought that they had simply found his trail, the scent he had left behind when he had started off on his last ill-fated enterprise; but then, seeing that they were all looking upwards, he, too, raised his eyes. Then he understood. Conspicuous against the snow on the roof was a dark object. Even as Ginger watched he saw it move, and he was no longer in any doubt as to what it was – or rather, who it was. It was a man, and there was only one man likely to be in such a place at such a time. The Indian!

CHAPTER XXI

The Prisoner Speaks

How long the Indian had been there, or how he had got there, Ginger, of course, did not know. He did not particularly care. One thing was certain, and that was what concerned him most. The man was 'treed' by the wolves as effectively – in fact, more effectively – than he was himself. His plight was a good deal more precarious.

Twice, as he watched, Ginger saw the Indian slip, and climb back to the ridge by what seemed to be an effort. He wondered why the man had not fired at him, or why he did not fire at the wolves. Watching the man's hands as he clung to the ridge, he suspected the reason; and presently he became fairly certain that his assumption was correct. The Indian had not got the rifle with him. Either he had dropped it in his haste to climb on the roof out of reach of the wolves, or he had accidentally let it slip after he was up. Either way, as far as Ginger was concerned, the effect was the same. If the man was unarmed it put a very different complexion on the whole situation, and he began to take a fresh interest in the proceedings; particularly when, a minute or two later, he heard what he took to be a cry for help.

Opening the side window quietly, he looked out. 'Hi!' he yelled.

'Have you got the rifle?' The words seemed strangely loud in the icy silence. The wolves stopped their prowling and stared at the machine.

'No ... on ground,' came the reply, rather faintly.

'Can you hold on until the morning?' was Ginger's next question.

'No.'

'Why not?'

'Too cold. Die with cold here,' came the tragic announcement.

It did not occur to Ginger to doubt the word of a man whose position was obviously far too precarious for him to hope to gain anything by lying. 'Hold on!' he shouted.

The last thing he wanted now was that the Indian should die, and carry the secret of the gold with him to the grave – or, as seemed more likely, into the stomachs of the brutes prowling below, who appeared to sense that, of the two men, this was the one more likely to satisfy their appetites.

It did not take Ginger long to make up his mind what to do. There was, in fact, only one thing he could do; for, whether the Indian died or not, he had no intention of taking on the pack single-handed, on the ground, armed only with a pistol. And he lost no time in putting his plan into execution. The self-starter whirred. It did not surprise him when the engines refused to start, for he knew that they must be stone cold. However, it was only a matter of time.

Actually, it took him nearly ten minutes to get the first kick out of one of the propellers. A minute later one engine started with its customary roar. A streak of blue flame shot out of the exhaust. He did not bother about the other engine. One, he hoped, would be sufficient for his purpose. And he was right.

If he had any doubts as to how the wolves would behave in the face of a roaring aero-engine they were soon dismissed. Even before the machine moved, most of them were skulking towards the wood, and by the time it was halfway to the cabin, with Ginger making the night hideous with occasional bursts of throttle, they were in full flight. Slowly, on the alert for any sign of treachery, he taxied the machine right up to the cabin wall and then switched off. 'Stay where you are until I tell you to move,' he called to the Indian; and then, jumping down, he picked up the rifle, which he could now see lying near the cabin wall half buried in snow.

'All right, come down,' he said curtly. 'Be careful what you are doing or you'll get shot.'

He stepped back as the Indian slid off the roof, bringing a small avalanche of snow with him, and fell heavily to the ground. Ginger did not take his eyes off him for a moment, but he saw that, unless the man was a clever actor, he was at his last gasp. He was so stiff with cold that he had difficulty in getting him to his feet.

Ginger, stooping down, took the Indian's knife from his belt and tossed it, with the rifle, into the machine. He kept him covered with his pistol, and with some difficulty managed to get him into the hut, where he allowed him to sink down again near the stove. Still keeping one eye on him, he lit the lamp, by the light of which he saw that the man was really in a bad way. There was blood on his left arm, from which he assumed that his bullet must, after all, have wounded him. The stove, he discovered, was out, but he did not bother about lighting it. The lamp would give a certain amount of heat.

'Now,' he said, turning to his prisoner, 'I am going to ask you some questions. If you are wise you will answer them truthfully. You can understand English, I think?'

'Sure,' returned the Indian weakly, with a soft American accent.

'Where is the gold?'

The Indian did not reply.

'Where is the gold?' asked Ginger again.

'Gold? No gold.'

'Don't lie to me!' snapped Ginger. 'You know the gold is here. I know it's here. You'd better remember where it is – unless you want to go back outside to the wolves. You needn't be afraid to speak. McBain won't worry you.'

The Indian started, and Ginger knew that his shot had gone home.

'By the time this business is over McBain will be hanging by the neck,' he announced confidently. 'He is probably under arrest by now.'

The Indian looked up. 'What for, huh?' he asked.

'For murdering Mose Jacobs. You were in that too.'

'No! No – no! Not me!' flashed back the Indian quickly.

'We'll talk about that presently,' declared Ginger. 'What I want to know first of all is where McBain has hidden the gold. Speak up. You'd better tell me what you know. It's your only chance of escaping the rope.'

The Indian looked worried, but he did not answer.

'They'll make you speak when they try you for murdering Mose,' went on Ginger remorselessly. 'You killed him, didn't you?'

'No.'

'Was it McBain?'

'Yes, McBain,' agreed the Indian sullenly.

'How do you know?' fired back Ginger.

'I know.'

'How do you know? Did McBain tell you?'

'No. I guessed. Then I found the—'

'The what? Come on, out with it.'

'He hit Mose with – the butt end of his gun.'

'How do you know?'

'I saw him cleaning blood and hair off his gun afterwards.'

'What did he clean it with?'

'A towel.'

'Where did he put it?'

The Indian hesitated.

'Come on,' prompted Ginger.

'He put towel under some sacks in the corner of office.'

Ginger was more than pleased about this piece of additional evidence – always assuming that the Indian spoke the truth, and he could think of no sound reason why he should lie. 'Of course, there is a way you can save your own neck if you like,' he went on insinuatingly.

'How?'

'By turning King's Evidence. You tell the truth to the police and maybe they'll let you off. If you don't tell all you know it makes you as bad as the actual murderer. Remember that when we get back tomorrow.'

The Indian started. His dark eyes sought Ginger's. 'Back – tomorrow?'

'Yes. You're coming back with me. What else did you think you were going to do?'

Again the Indian did not answer.

Ginger was not particularly concerned about the Indian's fate. What he wanted was all the evidence he could muster against McBain, particularly the gold that would prove his guilt, so he spent some time in planting in the Indian's mind the idea that if he confessed all he knew there was a chance that the law would take a lenient view of his association with McBain. He assured him that McBain would certainly be hanged, and in this belief he was sincere. 'If you won't tell me where the gold is, you'll jolly soon tell Constable Delaney when he gets his hands on you,' he concluded. 'For the last time, where is the gold?'

The Indian turned his face slowly towards the stove. 'Under there,' he said simply.

Ginger could have kicked himself for not thinking of it; or rather, for overlooking such an obvious place. Looking at the stove now, he saw that it stood on a small piece of thin iron sheeting, which had probably been supplied with the stove. Seizing the upper part, he dragged it aside. He swept the iron sheeting away with his foot and a cavity was revealed. Reaching down, his hand came into contact with a small bag, or sack, of harsh material. He dragged it up into the room, and knew from its weight that it contained gold.

There were eight sacks, each tied and sealed. On the side of each one was printed in black letters MOOSE CREEK GOLDFIELDS INC. There was only one other thing in the cache, a small iron object, and for a moment he wondered what it could be; but when, on the base, he saw the brand of the Moose Creek company, he understood. 'A spare seal, eh?' he murmured. 'So that's how McBain was able to do the trick. And he came here to do it. Well, when we get back to Fort Beaver with this little lot several people are going to get a shock.'

The Indian said nothing. Ginger, having obtained what he wanted, had nothing more to say. The only thing that remained was for him to wait until daylight and then get back to Fort Beaver as quickly as possible.

The lamp had taken the chill off the room, but it was by no means warm, and although the Indian had recovered somewhat he looked far from happy. Ginger examined the wound in his arm; it was only a flesh wound, but sufficient to cause the Indian to lose a good deal of blood, which, with the exposure he had experienced on the roof, accounted for his weakness.

Ginger remembered McBain's fur coat. He did not need it himself, but it struck him that his prisoner would be more comfortable in it, so he lifted it from its peg intending to hand it to him. As he took it down, something sharp pierced his forearm, bringing an exclamation of pain and surprise to his lips. The object, whatever it was, seemed to be in the sleeve, so thinking that it was possibly a thorn, he examined the sleeve carefully in order to remove it. He was some time finding the object, but at length he located it in the turned-up fold of the sleeve. Taking it out, he regarded it for some moments in silence, an extraordinary expression on his face. He glanced quickly at the Indian, but the man's back was turned towards him and it was clear that he had not noticed the incident. Slipping the object quickly back into the turn-up of the sleeve, he spread the coat over the shoulders of his prisoner.

The night passed as slowly as any he could remember, but at long last the grey dawn for which he had waited shed its feeble light through the window. There had, of course, been no question of going to sleep with a dangerous character like the Indian in the room.

He went over to the window and looked out. Nothing moved. There was no sign of the wolves.

'Well, it's daylight and I don't see any wolves,' he told the Indian.

'The wolves go back into the wood at dawn,' was the cold reply. 'They not come out again now.'

'Well, come on; on your feet. We'll get along,' ordered Ginger.

The Indian pleaded to be left behind, to be given his freedom, swearing that he would never work for McBain again. But this was something Ginger was not prepared to grant. He compelled his prisoner to help him to carry the gold across to the machine.

When the last of it was safely on board, he closed the hut and made the Indian sit beside him in the Jupiter, reckoning that once in the air the Indian would be powerless to do any harm – unless he deliberately did something calculated to crash the machine and kill them both, which hardly seemed likely.

It took Ginger some time to start the engines, for they were very cold, but in the end he got them going, and just as the first rays of the rising sun flashed up over the horizon the Jupiter roared into the air on its return journey to Fort Beaver.

Had Ginger known what was happening there his cheerful confidence would have received a rude shock. As it was, he was so pleased with the success of his mission that he hummed softly to himself as the landmarks he recognized slipped away behind.

'They must have wondered what has happened to me,' he thought seriously.

CHAPTER XXII

At The Eleventh Hour

As we know, the others had more than once wondered what had happened to him. But now, as they stood under the fatal tree with the end so near, he slipped from their minds.

It was Biggles who knew first that the machine was coming; his keen ears picked up the drone of the motors before he saw it.

'Here comes Ginger,' he said, by which time others in the crowd had heard it too.

There was a quick babble of excited conversation. The immediate preparations for the hanging were temporarily abandoned, and several people pointed to the fast approaching Jupiter.

'Never mind about that,' shouted McBain. It was almost as if he sensed that the oncoming aeroplane was a danger to the success of his plans. Ferroni, who was with him, raised his voice in a demand that the hanging should be proceeded with, but the attention of the crowd was distracted by the behaviour of the machine.

At first it seemed that the pilot was going to glide straight to the aerodrome and land, but at the last moment the machine turned suddenly, as if the pilot had observed the crowd and wished to see it at close quarters. Straight over the tree at a height of not more than fifty feet the Jupiter soared, and then went into a tight circle. The watchers on the ground could see the pale face of the pilot looking down at them.

'Come on; ain't yer never seen an airyplane before? Let's get on with the hangin',' roared McBain. But the noise of the Jupiter's engines so drowned the words that only those in his immediate vicinity heard them.

'What does he think he's up to?' Delaney asked Biggles, who was watching the side window of the control cabin.

'I don't know,' he answered, 'but I rather fancy that he is going to throw something out. Yes, he is,' he went on quickly, raising his voice, as a bulky object blocked the cabin window. 'Watch your heads, everybody.'

The next moment a dark object was hurtling downwards, turning slowly as it fell. There was a yell of alarm from the crowd, each member of which took steps to make sure that it did not hit him; only the prisoners and Delaney remained still, eyes on the falling object, which finally crashed to earth in the middle of the scattered spectators, but, fortunately, without hitting any one.

The actual moment of impact produced a curious effect: so curious, in fact, that it is doubtful if any one of the watchers had the slightest idea of what had happened. There seemed to be a sort of brilliant yellow flash, almost like a tongue of flame, which licked along the short turf for a brief moment before it disappeared. The phenomenon had occurred about ten or twelve yards from the tree.

'What the dickens was that?' ejaculated Algy.

'Goodness knows,' replied Biggles, who was still staring at the spot; he could see a small, buff-coloured object, and beside it a yellow streak. Then the crowd converged on it and it was hidden from his view. There was an excited whisper, almost a hiss, and then a shout went up.

Delaney had run forward with the others. 'Stand away there!' he ordered crisply.

Curiously enough, the crowd gave way to him, as though it once more respected his authority. Mass hysteria is a strange thing; it can die down as quickly as it can arise; and thus it was in this case. It was as if the crowd had been shocked by what it saw on the ground.

Delaney perceived his opportunity, and was not slow in taking advantage of it. 'Stand clear!' he snapped. 'Don't touch it, anybody. And that goes for you, too, McBain,' he went on curtly.

One of the first to reach the fallen object had been McBain, and he stared at it as if he could not believe his eyes. Delaney stooped and picked up something from the ground; it looked like a piece of torn sacking. 'Moose Creek Goldfields!' he cried in an amazed voice. Then, a tone higher, he added, 'Boys, it's the Moose Creek gold!'

The words were received with a loud buzz of excitement, and every one pressed forward to see the pile of yellow dust that had burst from the bag when it had hit the ground.

Delaney placed two men on guard over the gold. They obeyed without question. Then he strode to where the prisoners were still standing, the ropes around their necks. The crowd, its anger melting in the face of this new mystery, surged after him.

'What do you know about this?' Delaney asked Biggles sternly.

'Not much more than you do,' replied Biggles. 'I suggest that you let the boy tell his story in his own way. Here he comes, now.'

Ginger, who by this time had landed, was, in fact, marching towards the crowd; and he did not come alone. In front of him, covered by his automatic, walked the Indian, draped in a long skunk-skin coat.

The crowd fell silent as it watched the approach of this curious procession. On all faces was astonishment not far from incredulity.

Straight through the crowd to where Delaney was standing Ginger marched his prisoner, the spectators forming a lane to allow them to pass. His eyes opened wide when he saw the dangling ropes and for whom they were intended.

'What's the idea?' asked Delaney, the words sounding strangely loud in the hush that had fallen.

'I've brought back evidence to prove that my friends, who have been arrested for the murder of Mose Jacobs, or the theft of the Moose Creek gold, or both, are innocent,' cried Ginger. 'I have brought back the gold,' he went on. 'Some of it you have seen.' He pointed in the direction of that which lay on the ground. 'The rest is in the aeroplane.'

'Where did you find it?' asked Delaney.

'I found it under the floor of a cabin up on the edge of the bad lands – where the thief had hidden it until such time as it suited him to collect it. This Indian was left on guard over it, and he will tell you to whom the cabin belongs. It belongs to Brindle McBain.'

McBain, white with passion, pushed his way to the front. 'What are you saying?' he snarled.

'I'm saying that you stole the gold,' answered Ginger in a hard voice. 'Instead of flying it straight down here you landed at your cabin, broke the seals of the boxes, took out the gold, substituted lead which you had already prepared, and then resealed the boxes. Here is the seal with which you did the job.' Ginger handed Delaney the duplicate seal.

'That's a lie!' roared McBain.

'We shall see,' retorted Ginger imperturbably. He raised his voice. 'Does any one here recognize the coat the Indian is wearing?' he asked.

A dozen voices answered: 'It's McBain's.'

'Do you deny that the coat is yours, McBain?' asked Ginger.

McBain hesitated. It was quite certain that he could not deny it without proving himself to be a liar, for the peculiar white blaze on the coat would have identified it in ten thousand.

'This coat was in McBain's hidden cabin,' declared Ginger, taking the garment from the Indian and tossing it carelessly to its rightful owner, who caught it and flung it over his shoulder.

'Now,' continued Ginger, 'I want to recall something to the minds of those who were in the Three Star the night Mose was killed. Are the two men here who were sitting by the fire talking to Mose when I joined in the conversation?'

The two men pushed their way to the front.

'You would remember what Mose was wearing that night?' Ginger challenged them.

'I reckon so,' they agreed.

'Very well. You will remember that after the row between my friend, Major Bigglesworth, who stands over there, and McBain, we went home. Mose and McBain were still there.'

'That's right. I was there myself, so I can vouch for that,' declared Delaney.

'After that, who went out first – Mose or McBain?'

'McBain.'

Ginger turned to McBain. 'Did you ever, from the moment you left the Three Star, see Mose again?'

'No.' McBain's denial was emphatic.

Ginger nodded. 'I see,' he said. 'On the night Mose was murdered I believe I am right in saying that you were wearing the coat you now have on your arm.'

Again McBain hesitated. It was as if he suspected a trap, but could think of no way of avoiding it. He could not deny that he had worn the coat, for nearly every man present had been in the saloon that night, and must have seen him in it.

'Well, what if I *was* wearing it?' he snarled belligerently.

'Has any one else but you ever worn that coat – except the Indian who was wearing it when I arrived here?'

Again a moment's hesitation. The atmosphere was electric.

'Had any one but you worn the coat it is likely that it would have been noticed, isn't it?' prompted Ginger.

'It's my coat, and nobody else has had it – if that's what you're getting at,' grated McBain.

Ginger pointed to the turn-up at the bottom of the fur sleeve. 'Just feel in there and take out what you find,' he said quietly. 'And then, since you did not see Mose again after you left the saloon, perhaps you will tell us how it got there.'

Like a man in a dream, almost against his will it seemed, McBain's finger went down into the turn-up. The silence was such that every member of the crowd might have been holding his breath. A look of relief passed over McBain's face as he found what was evidently an insignificant object; with a short laugh he took it out and looked at it. As he did so his face blanched. Yet the object was simple enough. It was merely an opal-headed tie-pin.

'Does any one recognize that pin?' called Ginger loudly.

Had he said, 'Does any one *not* recognize that pin?' there would have been fewer to answer. Nearly every one present recognized it, and knew to whom it belonged – the murdered prospector.

Delaney raised his hand for silence. Then he took a revolver from the hand of a man standing near him. The man did not protest.

'McBain,' said Delaney, 'I reckon I know why you were so anxious to lynch three innocent men.'

The crowd surged forward, muttering ominously. Nor did it heed Delaney's orders to stand still. Possibly the fact that most of the men felt that they had been duped by McBain had something to do with it. Be that as it may, McBain evidently suspected what his fate might be and it rather seemed as if he lost his nerve. Accompanied by Ferroni, with a wild rush he swept those who stood around him from his path, and drove a lane through the outskirts of the spectators, heading for safety.

'Stop!' roared Delaney above the uproar, but the fugitives took no notice.

'Look out, they're making for the machine,' shouted Biggles. 'And the gold's in it. If you don't stop them they'll get away and take the gold with them.'

McBain and Ferroni were, in fact, running like hares towards the Jupiter, which was still standing out in the middle of the aerodrome where Ginger had left it. And it seemed likely that they would have succeeded in their object but for an unexpected development.

From the far side of the aerodrome, riding at a gallop, came five uniformed figures.

Delaney yelled a warning. He had now reached the outskirts of the crowd, a position from which he dare use his revolver without the risk of hitting the wrong man, and although he emptied it at the fast retreating figures, the range was too long and the shots did not touch their mark. But they served another purpose, just as useful. They gave the oncoming horsemen at least an inkling of what was happening, as was revealed by the manner in which they swerved to cut them off.

McBain and his pilot swerved too, but they could not hope to compete with horses. Seeing that they were trapped they both drew their revolvers and tried to shoot their way to the machine. They did succeed in emptying one saddle, but then a fusillade of shots rang out and McBain pitched face downward on the turf. Ferroni, evidently seeing that his case was hopeless, threw down his weapon and raised his hands above his head.

The crowd started running towards the new scene of action.

'Here, Delaney, haven't we been trussed up like this long enough?' asked Biggles reproachfully.

The constable took out his jack-knife and cut the prisoners free. 'That kid of yours was just about in time,' he said gravely.

'He usually is,' grinned Biggles. 'Who are these newcomers?'

'Captain Lanton and the troopers from Blackfoot Point,' answered Delaney. 'That mechanic of yours must have got through to 'em. Phew! What a report I shall have to make. You'd better not go away; the Captain will want to see you too.'

CHAPTER XXIII

Conclusion

'I suppose you are no longer in any doubt as to who killed old Mose?' Biggles asked Delaney as they walked across the aerodrome towards the Jupiter, near which the crowd had reassembled.

'None whatever,' replied Delaney.

'Then in that case I assume we are no longer under arrest?'

'No, you're free as far as I'm concerned.'

'Then if it's all the same to you we'll get our machine inside its hangar, and tidy things up a bit. I suppose I ought to fly up to Moose Creek and tell them there that the gold is safe.'

'Better not go away until you've had a word with the Captain,' advised Delaney.

'They stood still as a little procession passed them, carrying a body. They learned that it was McBain, and that he was dead. A bullet had gone through his heart, killing him instantly. Ferroni, with handcuffs on his wrists, was standing near the troopers, towards whom Delaney now continued his way.

'You'll find us in Arctic Airways shed if you want us,' Biggles told him, as their paths separated, the airmen making for the Jupiter with the object of putting it in the shed. This they did, after which, over a hastily prepared meal, Ginger gave an account of his adventures at the cabin. When he had finished, the others, for his benefit, described what had happened in Fort Beaver.

They were concluding the meal with coffee when Delaney and his superior officer entered. At the officer's request Biggles narrated the entire story of their adventures from the time they had received Wilks's letter in London. The tale took a long time to tell, but both the officer and the constable listened breathlessly, particularly when Biggles related the events that had occurred near Angus Stirling's cabin.

'And what are you fellows going to do now?' the officer asked, when at last the story was told.

'As far as I can see our work is finished,' answered Biggles. 'The transfer which we got from Angus Stirling settles any doubt as to who owns the aerodrome, and now that there is only one line operating between Fort Beaver and Moose Creek, the gold-fields people will be glad enough to use it. Anyway, they should be grateful for the recovery of that last consignment of metal, because, but for Arctic Airways, they would have lost it. I reckon that Canwell, when he hears what has happened, ought to give Arctic Airways a contract for handling all their freight.'

'I think so, too,' agreed the officer. 'I know the chairman of the company; I'll have a word with him about it at the first opportunity.'

Which, in fact, he did a day or two later, with the result that the contract was soon forthcoming, as well as an offer of extra finance for spare equipment should it be required.

And that is really the end of the story. Wilks implored the others to remain on at Fort Beaver and share the profits of his enterprise which had been so nearly wrecked, but Biggles was adamant in his refusal to tie himself to any one spot. However, they stayed on until Arctic Airways was reorganized on proper lines, which did not take very long, for Wilks found no difficulty in getting staff once McBain and his gang had been removed.

Wilks flew the party back to Quebec in one of the two Jupiters the firm now possessed, and it was there that goodbyes were said.

'Let me know how things go on,' shouted Biggles from the deck of the ship that was to take them back to England.

'I will,' promised Wilks. 'Thanks for coming over.'

'Don't mention it,' grinned Biggles. 'It's been a pleasure.'

BIGGLES IN
THE JUNGLE

CHAPTER I

Biggles Meets An Old Friend

With its altimeter registering six thousand feet, a travel-stained amphibian aircraft nosed steadily southward under a Central American sky of azure blue. To port lay the deep green of the Atlantic Ocean, rolling away and away to the infinite distance. To starboard, the primeval forest sprawled like a great stain, filling the landscape until at last it merged into the purple haze of the far horizon. Immediately below the aircraft a white, irregular line of surf marked the juncture of land and sea.

There were three passengers in the machine. At the controls was Squadron-Leader Bigglesworth, D.S.O., better known as 'Biggles'. In the spare seat beside him, regarding the vast panorama with dispassionate familiarity, was his protégé, 'Ginger' Hebblethwaite. Behind, plotting a compass course, sat their mutual friend and comrade, Captain the Honourable 'Algy' Lacey. He completed his calculation and came forward.

'I make us out to be off the coast of British Honduras,' he announced.

Biggles smiled faintly. 'You're a bit late in the day, old boy. Unless I'm mistaken, that's Belize, the capital of the colony, just ahead of us.'

'Are you going down?' asked Algy.

'We shall have to,' answered Biggles. 'That confounded headwind which we ran into this morning was outside my calculations; it lost us so much time that we shall have to fill up with fuel and oil before we go on. This is no place for a forced landing.'

'You mean – you'll go down at Belize?'

'Yes. There's a Pan-American Airways maintenance station there. They're a decent crowd. They'll let us have some juice.'

'Do you know anybody there?'

'I don't know the Pan-American staff, but I know a fellow in the Government House – that is, if he's still there; a chap named Carruthers. I did him a good turn some years ago, when he was British Vice-Consul at La Paz, in Bolivia, on the other side of the continent. We might look him up. If he's still here no doubt he will be glad to repay an old debt by offering us hospitality. He'll probably be glad to see us in any case; I don't suppose he gets many visitors at an off-the-map place like Belize.'

As he spoke Biggles retarded the throttle and allowed the aircraft to lose height in a steady glide that carried it on towards a little town that nestled on the edge of the sea, backed by the sombre forest. He was in no hurry, for – for once – the party was on a pleasure cruise, with no particular object in view beyond seeing something of the world, in fair weather, as an alternative to remaining in London through a dull winter.

Ginger had been largely responsible for the trip. Bored by a spell of inactivity, he had threatened to go off alone, taking the aircraft, an amphibian named *Wanderer*, if the others refused to bestir themselves. Biggles, always tolerant, had proposed a trip to Central America to examine the possibilities of an air service between British possessions on the mainland and the West Indies. This project, he declared, need not necessarily be definitely pursued. It provided an object for the flight, as opposed to aimless wandering.

So far the trip had been uneventful. The adventures which in his heart Ginger had hoped they might encounter had failed to materialize. He was getting slightly bored, and made no secret of it. As a form of relaxation on the ground he had decided to collect butterflies, the beauty of which at some of their ports of call had entranced him, with the result that he was taking a new interest in entomology.

Biggles glanced at him. 'Do you know anything about Honduras?' he asked.

Ginger shook his head. 'No. I once saw the name on a postage stamp, otherwise I shouldn't have known that the place existed. Is there anything remarkable about it?'

'No, I can't say there is,' replied Biggles reflectively. 'It's much the same as the rest of Central America. Outside the capital I imagine it's a pretty wild spot. I'm told there's some fine timber there – some of the best mahogany comes from Honduras. The most interesting thing about it from our point of view, having done a bit of aerial exploring, is the Unknown River.'

'Unknown River? But that doesn't make sense,' protested Ginger. 'Either there is a river or there isn't. If there is, well, it must be known. If there isn't, why worry about it?'

'Nobody's worrying about it as far as I know,' returned Biggles. 'The mouth of the river is known, but from what I can make out the upper reaches have never been explored. It's supposed to rise somewhere in Guatemala, which backs on to Honduras.'

'Why hasn't it been explored?'

'Presumably because nobody has had the energy, or the money, or any reason to do so.'

'Then why are people concerned about it?'

'Because the river crops up from time to time in the newspapers in connection with the lost Carmichael treasure. There was a talk on the radio about it not long ago.'

Ginger started and sat up. 'Treasure! Why didn't you say that at first? That sounds more my mark. Tell me about it.'

Biggles smiled sadly. 'I was afraid you'd get excited if I mentioned the treasure. Don't get any wild ideas – I'm not going off on a treasure-hunt.'

'Of course not,' agreed Ginger airily. 'Still, there's no harm in my knowing about it, is there?'

'I suppose not,' assented Biggles. 'It's an old tale, not much more than a legend. This country is stiff with legends about treasures. Speaking from memory, this particular yarn started away back in 1860, or thereabouts, when a fellow named Carmichael, travelling up-country, saved the lives of two Indians. In return they promised to show him the spot where Montezuma hid his treasure from the Spaniards. They went, and found a ruined city. Carmichael cut a cross – or made a mark – on a temple, or the ruins of a temple, under which the Indians said the gold was buried; then he came back for help. When he returned he couldn't find the temple – or the city, for that matter. Nobody ever has found it, although they've discovered quite a number of other old cities. The fact is, there are so many of these old cities now swallowed up by the jungle that they can't work out which is the right one. Anyway, most people in Central America have heard of the Carmichael treasure. Several attempts have been made to locate it, but all people find are the traces of a vast and very ancient civilisation – that's all.'

A thoughtful look came into Ginger's eyes. 'While we're on the spot we might collect what facts there are available,' he suggested hopefully.

'To what purpose?' inquired Biggles coldly.

'Well – I mean – of course, I'm not suggesting a definite trip, or anything like that; but if we happened to be near the place—'

'If I have my way we shan't be near it,' declared Biggles. 'All you'd be likely to find in that jungle would be mosquitoes, leeches, ticks, snakes, and a few other horrors. If you didn't find them they'd find you. Tropical forests may sound great fun, but they can be very, very uncomfortable. Believe me, I know.'

'Does no one ever go into this forest?'

'Oh yes. Rubber collectors and chicle-hunters – mostly natives.'

'Chicle? What's that?'

'The stuff they make chewing-gum out of – at least, chicle is the base. Like rubber, it's the sap of a tree. Chicle is the colony's most important export.'

Ginger shook his head. 'Sounds a sticky business to me.'

And there the conversation ended, for Biggles had to concentrate his attention on putting the aircraft on the water. This he did on an open stretch marked by buoys and a wind-stocking pole, which, as he expected, turned out to be an emergency landing-ground for the big Pan-American Clippers that operated up and down the coast from the United States to Argentina. The local superintendent was helpful, giving them a mooring and promising to fill the tanks. Well satisfied with this arrangement, the airmen went into the town to have a meal, seek accommodation for the night, and, if he was still in the colony, call on Carruthers.

As it happened, they met him just leaving his office, and after greetings had been exchanged, and introductions effected, he insisted on their making their home in his roomy bungalow while they were there.

Ginger, although he did not comment on it, was rather disappointed in the size of the town, considering that it was the capital of a British colony. He realized that there was nothing remarkable in meeting Carruthers as they did, for the administration of the colony was carried on by a small staff. Normally, it turned out, Carruthers was senior Resident Magistrate, but at the moment, the Governor being away on leave, he was acting for him. He was a fair, good-looking young man in the late twenties, with keen blue eyes and a closely clipped moustache. His manner was debonair, but behind it was an alert, authoritative bearing.

'You know, Carruthers,' observed Biggles, as they sat over their after-dinner coffee, 'you've aged a good deal since I last saw you.'

'Do you wonder?' Carruthers' tone was rather bitter.

'You mean – it's the climate?'

'Not entirely, although it's certainly enervating. To turn your hair grey, you should try keeping order in thousands of miles of jungle with a handful of men. That's what I'm up against all the time. I know it sounds easy, and you may think I haven't much to do, but believe me, my hands are full.'

'How does the jungle make so much work for you?' put in Algy.

'It isn't the jungle; it's the people in it.'

'Hostile Indians?'

'There are plenty of those, of course, but left alone they wouldn't give us much trouble; but lately they've been playing Old Harry with the upriver stations, and with chicle-collectors and other travellers from the coast. Something seems to have happened. It's almost as if the Indians are organized. In fact, the coastal natives say that is the case, but it's hard to find out just what is going on. There is wild talk – rumour, of course – about a fellow who calls himself King of the Forest, or some equally fantastic title; but what his game is, if he really exists, I haven't yet been able to discover. It's practically impossible to separate rumour from fact. All the same, if half the rumours I hear are true, then there are brains behind the scheme. I'm responsible for the country, so it gets me worried. If anything goes wrong, I have to take the blame.'

'But as long as this so-called King of the Forest doesn't interfere with you, what does it matter?' queried Biggles.

'But he is beginning to interfere with me – or somebody is, although I'm still in the dark. For instance, as you probably know, chicle is an important commodity here. It's collected by natives. They are jibbing at going up the river, consequently the stuff isn't coming in as it should. Yet the amazing thing is, there are indications that Honduras chicle is still reaching the U.S.A. in quantities as large as usual. Where is it coming from? Who's collecting it? On top of all this I get an inquiry from the Home Office about three white men who are supposed to have disappeared into the interior. I haven't all the facts yet, but apparently they were on a crazy treasure-hunt.'

'Then there is a treasure?' put in Ginger quickly.

Carruthers shrugged his shoulders. 'I suppose there must be some foundation for the rumour. It was alleged to have been seen years ago by a fellow named Carmichael. Beyond that I know no more than you do about it. How these three men got into the interior without official permission, or why they should go without first reporting to me, so that in the event of trouble I should know roughly where they were, I don't understand. They were last heard of on the Unknown River. With two of them I'm not particularly concerned, but the other, a young fellow, happens to have a wealthy and anxious father in the United States, and he's kicking up a nice row because I can't find his son.

'If this fellow who calls himself King of the Forest really exists, and if these Americans have fallen foul of him, they may have had their throats cut. So you see, with one thing and another, I'm having a pretty worrying job. It takes my small staff all its time to handle the ordinary business of the country, without wandering about the jungle looking for lost Americans, chicle-collectors, and self-appointed kings. There is talk of the American archaeological survey people coming back here to resume their work. If they do they may be murdered. Yet if I refuse to grant permission there'll be a scream from the Foreign Office.'

'What do these people want to do?' inquired Biggles curiously.

'Go on with their survey work – delving into the old ruins that exist in the jungle. As a matter of fact, they've made some very interesting discoveries on the sites of two ancient cities called Tickal and Uaxactun. They now want to locate some more sites which they feel sure exist. It shouldn't be hard, because most of these old cities are marked by pyramids like those of Egypt. They're enormous, and although they are buried in the jungle, the tops are often higher than the highest trees.'

'Obviously, what you'll have to do is ascertain if this King of the Forest fellow really exists,' declared Biggles. 'If he does you'll have to arrest him. You won't have any peace until you do.'

Carruthers laughed bitterly. 'Arrest him? How? Who is going to find him, for a start?'

'There's no indication of where he hangs out?'

'None. The natives tell a ridiculous story about a secret town in the forest, which doesn't strike me as being likely.'

'Still, if that were true, it shouldn't be hard to find.'

'You might look for years without finding it.'

'In a search from ground level, I agree. I was thinking of reconnaissance from the air.'

'That would be an entirely different matter,' asserted Carruthers. 'Unfortunately, I don't happen to have an Air Force. I can't get a new launch, much less a plane.'

Biggles smiled. 'I have one,' he reminded. 'You can borrow it with pleasure.'

'Thanks, but who's going to fly it? I'm not a pilot – nor do I know of one in this part of the world.'

Biggles took a cigarette and tapped it thoughtfully on the back of his hand. 'We're not in a hurry,' he said pointedly. 'We might find time to have a look round for you – if the idea makes any appeal. There seems to be plenty to look for – pyramids, ruined cities, lost Americans, the king's secret town – treasure – we ought to be able to find *something*. If we did spot anything we could pinpoint the place on the map and let you know. That would be a help.'

'A help! I should jolly well think it would,' declared Carruthers. 'Do you seriously mean you'd do this?'

'Why not? We're doing nothing in particular. We might as well do something useful. In any case, although I hadn't mentioned it to the others, I was contemplating a survey flight up the Unknown River, just as a matter of curiosity.'

'That would be an important piece of work even if you found nothing else,' remarked Carruthers. 'I'd really be most grateful if you'd do this.'

'Then you can consider it settled,' affirmed Biggles.

'Fine. You have official sanction for the undertaking. When do you propose to start?'

Biggles shrugged his shoulders. 'It doesn't really matter. As far as I'm concerned I could start tomorrow. If the others aren't too tired—'

'I'm not tired,' put in Ginger quickly. 'This promises to be interesting. I always did like looking for things.'

'Very well. If it's all right with you, Algy, we'll start in the morning,' concluded Biggles.

An hour later, to the serenade of bull-frogs croaking in a nearby swamp, Ginger went to bed, to sleep and to dream of kings and lost Americans fighting for a treasure on the summit of a pyramid.

CHAPTER II

An Unexpected Encounter

As the first rays of the tropic sun splashed the eastern sky with gleaming gold and turquoise, the thin miasma of mist which hung over the silent lake began to rise, revealing a number of things that floated on its placid surface – a giant water-lily with thick, circular leaves, each as large as a table; over the snow-white blossom a humming-bird, a living ruby with an emerald breast, hung motionless on whirring wings, its three-inch bill probing the nectary for honey; a log, with two protuberances at one end – or what appeared to be a log, although it had a curious trick of submerging and reappearing in another place. There was also an aircraft, an amphibian, which bore on its nose the single word *Wanderer*.

The aircraft rocked gently, so that ripples lapped its sides, as Ginger's head appeared above the central hatchway, to be followed a moment later by the barrel of a rifle. For a brief moment the silence persisted, then it was shattered by a gunshot. The 'log' jerked spasmodically, lashing the water to creamy foam before it disappeared. At the sound of the shot a flock of green parrots rose screaming from the nearby forest. Ginger drew himself up level with the hull, regarding intently the spot where the alligator had disappeared.

'Did you get him?' called Biggles from inside the machine.

'I don't think so, but I tickled him up a bit,' returned Ginger. 'It was the same big brute that was nosing round in the night.'

Silence returned as Ginger settled himself down on the hull and regarded the forest with keen, interested eyes. They travelled slowly up the mighty trunks of the trees that disappeared out of sight into a canopy of foliage high above; lianas wound round every bole and hung from every bough, passing from tree to tree like a fantastic network of cables. Below, in many places, the ground was strewn with the petals of flowers that bloomed far overhead. Climbing ferns and orchids, too, clung to the trees, sending down aerial roots that added to the tangle. Near the water magnificent tree-ferns flung out feathery fans twenty feet or more in width. Through the maze thus formed swept butterflies, the huge, metallic-blue *Morphos*, and yellow, swallow-tailed *Papilios*. A toucan, with a monstrous red-and-black beak nearly half as big as its body, sat on a branch, but flapped away heavily at the approach of a troop of spider-monkeys.

On the morning following the conversation with Carruthers the *Wanderer* had proceeded up the Unknown River, sometimes flying and sometimes taxiing. Three nights had been spent on the river itself before the lake on which the *Wanderer* now rested had been discovered – a smooth sheet of water that nestled in the jungle a hundred miles from the coast, and the same distance, therefore, from anything in the nature of civilization. It had been decided that the lake would make a good base from which to explore the surrounding country. So far nothing had occurred to interrupt the tranquillity of the cruise, for the *Wanderer* was well equipped with stores and such accessories as were likely to be required.

Ginger called down the hatchway, 'Are you fellows getting up?'

'Coming now,' answered Biggles.

Ginger grunted, for he was anxious to be off; he could not go ashore because the aircraft was moored some distance from the bank in order to avoid the mosquitoes and other insect pests which were all too plentiful. However, in a few minutes Biggles appeared, and the *Wanderer* was soon surging across the surface of the lake to take off on another survey flight. So far they had not seen any of the pyramids of which Carruthers had spoken, although according to Biggles's reckoning they were in the region of the two ancient cities, Tikal and Uaxactun, where the American Archaeological Society had carried out its excavations.

From the air, the scene presented was one of strange monotony. On all sides, as far as the eye could see, stretched the primeval forest, an undulating expanse of greens in various hues reaching to the horizon. In one direction only was it broken. Far away to the west the sun glinted on another lake, which Biggles supposed to be in Guatemala. Not that there was anything to mark the boundary. As in the case of most countries in tropical America, the frontier was assumed to be somewhere in the forest, but it was not possible to say precisely where. The *Wanderer* roared on, climbing steadily.

Presently there was a slight change in the scene, and it became possible to make out areas of open savannah, or rolling meadowland, although these were often broken by groups of trees and outcrops of rock. Biggles explained to the others that it was generally thought that these areas had originally been cleared by nations that had dwelt there in the past; the jungle, however, was steadily advancing over them again, so that they were fast being swallowed up by the forest.

It was Ginger who first spotted the apex of a pyramid. He caught Biggles by the arm and pointed. 'Take a look at that!' he cried.

Biggles cut the throttle and flew lower, so that there was no longer any doubt as to what it was. Near it, two other pyramids, not so high, could just be made out, peeping over the top of the green ocean.

'I should say that's Tikal,' observed Biggles.

'I vote we have a look at it from the ground,' suggested Ginger.

Biggles, surveying the panorama, noticed a lake nearer to the pyramids than the one they had left, but even so it was some distance away, and he shook his head doubtfully. Flying towards it, however, he came upon another and hitherto unsuspected sheet of water. It was much smaller, and not exactly a lake in the true sense of the word. It appeared rather to be a fairly extensive depression in the ground that had been flooded by a river – probably a tributary of the Unknown River. A stream flowed into it at one end, and out at the other.

'What about that stretch of water?' suggested Ginger. 'We ought to be able to get down on it.'

Biggles looked dubious. 'It's large enough,' he admitted. 'What I'm afraid of is obstructions. Trees are always falling into these rivers, particularly during the rainy season. If there happens to be any floating about in the middle of the lake, and we hit one of them, we shall be in a mess. We don't know how deep the water is, either. Not that all these hardwood trees float; if the water is shallow, and there are any lying on the bottom, we shall tear the keel off the boat.'

'It looks deep to me,' remarked Ginger encouragingly. 'Try that patch where there are no water-lilies.'

By this time Biggles was within a few feet of the water, leaning over the side eyeing it critically. 'All right,' he agreed, as he zoomed up to avoid the trees at the far end of the lake. 'We'll try it.'

Banking steeply, he turned and came back at landing speed. Very slowly, the aircraft sank towards the stretch to which Ginger had referred. There were no visible obstructions. The *Wanderer's* keel slashed the surface of the water, and then sank down with a surging rush that sent ripples racing towards the shore. The machine ran quickly to a standstill.

'Fine!' cried Ginger. 'Let's get nearer to the beach – at least, there seems to be a bit of sand over there.' He pointed.

Biggles taxied towards it, and brought the *Wanderer* to a standstill with her keel scraping gently on a shelving strip of sandy gravel. 'Well, here we are,' he announced.

Ginger was about to wade ashore when Biggles caught him by the arm. 'Just a minute,' he said tersely, staring fixedly at a certain spot.

'What is it?' asked Algy quickly, sensing danger from Biggles's tone of voice.

'Can you see what I see – or am I mistaken?' said Biggles quietly. 'Just on the edge of the timber, under that spray of crimson orchids.'

The others stared.

'Great heavens, it's a man!' breathed Algy.

'Get your guns,' ordered Biggles curtly, and, revolver in hand, he stepped down into the shallow water.

The man was lying half in and half out of the forest, his head towards the lake, with one arm outflung as though he had fallen while making a desperate effort to get to the water. That he was a native, or a coloured man, was by this time apparent. He wore only a ragged remnant of shirt and a pair of blue dungaree trousers, also in rags.

'He must be dead,' muttered Ginger as they approached.

'I don't think so,' returned Biggles quickly. 'If he was dead – or if he'd been dead more than an hour or two – he'd be half eaten by this time. There's a hungry army always on the prowl in the forest, looking for meat – and in the water, too, if it comes to that.'

Biggles dropped on his knees beside the man and turned him on to his back. He was unconscious. 'He's lost a lot of blood,' he continued, pointing to an ugly stain on the man's trousers. 'Let's see what caused the damage.' Taking his knife he cut a slit in the garment so that the wound was exposed. 'That's a gunshot wound,' he said crisply. 'How the dickens did it happen, I wonder? It looks as if there are other people in the forest besides us.'

'What on earth would the fellow be doing in a place like this, anyway?' put in Algy.

'I should say he's a chicle-collector – or else a rubber-tapper,' answered Biggles. 'As I told you, chicle is still collected wild in the forest.' He glanced up at Algy. 'Get the brandy flask and the medicine chest; we shall have to do what we can for the poor wretch.'

He cleaned the wound – a flesh wound in the thigh – and dressed it, while the others, with brandy and water, did what they could to restore consciousness. It did not take them long. The man opened his eyes. Instantly, with a gasp of terror, he tried to get to his feet, but they held him down.

'I wonder what language he speaks,' said Ginger.

'If he comes from Belize he'll probably speak English,' replied Biggles. 'If that fails I'll try Spanish.' He said a few words, and as soon as he saw that the man understood he told him that he had nothing to fear.

'He must be dead,' muttered George as they approached'

Together, they got him into a more comfortable position. Ginger, watching closely, noted that the man was older than he had at first supposed; he judged him to be not less than fifty years of age. He had a pleasant if rather wild countenance, and his skin was so dark that he appeared to have both Indian and negro in his ancestry.

Presently the man sat up and regarded his benefactors with incredulous eyes.

'What's your name?' asked Biggles.

The man uttered an unpronounceable word.

Biggles smiled. 'That's all right,' he told the others. 'We'll call him Dusky for short. What are you doing here, and who shot you?' he continued, again addressing the wounded man.

Before Dusky could answer there was a swift footfall near at hand. It brought the comrades round swiftly to face an enormous man who had just emerged from the forest. No one, perhaps not even he himself, could have guessed his nationality; his skin was more white than brown, but it was apparent that he was a half-caste of some sort. Well over six feet in height, and broad in proportion, with a gun over his arm he looked an ugly customer. The only garments he wore were a dirty shirt, open at the throat, and a ragged cotton suit. Nothing more. The lower part of his face was concealed in a tangle of black beard. His eyes were bloodshot and had an unpleasant glint in them. So much the comrades saw in their first appraising glance.

Biggles faced him squarely. Pointing at the wounded man, he said, 'Do you know anything about this?'

The stranger took a pace forward, his eyes, heavy with suspicion, darting from one to the other. 'What you doing here?' he demanded harshly.

'We might ask you the same question,' returned Biggles coolly. 'Did you shoot this chap?'

For a moment the man did not answer. He glanced at Dusky, scowling, and then looked up again at those who confronted him. For a moment he regarded them reflectively, malevolently.

'What do you here?' he questioned harshly, addressing Biggles.

'Why – have you bought the place or something?'

The scowl grew deeper. 'You git out – *pronto*.'

Biggles looked surprised. 'Are you presuming to tell us where we can go?'

'You git out, or mebbe you don't git out no more,' snarled the man.

Biggles appeared to consider the order. Actually, he was wondering if there was any point in staying. It was not as though they had any reason for remaining there.

'What you come here for, huh?' went on the man suspiciously.

'Believe it or not, we're just a picnic party.'

The sarcastic leer with which this remark was received made it clear that it was not believed.

'One lake is as good as another to us,' continued Biggles. 'If you feel that this one is your particular property, we'll pull out. In any case we should have done so, because we shall have to take this man' – Biggles indicated Dusky – 'to Belize. His wound needs treatment.'

The other started. 'No, you don't,' he grated.

'But I said we do,' returned Biggles calmly.

The man made a significant movement with his gun.

'I shouldn't try that if I were you,' Biggles told him evenly. Then, turning to the others, he said, 'Get aboard. You know what to do.'

Algy nodded, and touched Ginger on the arm. They returned to the aircraft.

Ignoring the stranger, Biggles turned to Dusky. 'Do you feel able to walk, or shall I carry you?'

'I can walk, boss.' Dusky got stiffly to his feet, standing on one leg.

The man took a quick pace forward as if he would prevent his departure, but stopped when Biggles turned on him with a crisp, 'Stand back! Take a look at the boat.'

The man glanced swiftly at the aircraft, over the side of which now projected a light machine-gun of the type known as the 'Tommy' gun. For a moment he hesitated, his lips drawn back, showing discoloured teeth; then, turning on his heel, he strode into the forest. An instant later the shrill blast of a whistle rent the air.

'He fetch de others,' said Dusky in a panic.

'Get into the boat,' snapped Biggles, and taking cover behind a tree, he watched the forest, whence now came answering cries. Not until Dusky had been hauled into the *Wanderer* did he abandon his position and follow him. He was only just in time, for barely had he joined the others when a gang of men, as unsavoury a crowd as could have been imagined, appeared in the gloomy recesses of the forest, running towards the spot. A shot rang out, and a bullet struck the machine somewhere near the tail.

'Get her off,' he told Algy, who was already in the pilot's seat. 'If we get mixed up in a brawl somebody's liable to be hurt, and then we may find ourselves in the wrong with the authorities.'

'Shall I give 'em a burst just to let 'em know that the gun isn't a dummy?' suggested Ginger tentatively.

'No – we may need our ammunition,' answered Biggles.

The last word was drowned in the roar of the engines as Algy started them. The *Wanderer* surged across the water and rose gracefully into the air.

The last they saw of the lake was a crowd of men on the beach they had just left. One, standing in front of the others, was shaking his fist.

'I should be sorry to run into that gang after this,' declared Ginger.

'I should have been sorry to run into them at any time,' returned Biggles curtly.

'Where shall I make for?' called Algy.

'Go back to the lake – the one we started from this morning,' ordered Biggles. 'I want to have a word or two with Dusky before we decide what we're going to do.'

CHAPTER III

Dusky Tells His Story and Ginger Learns a Lesson

It did not take them long to get back to the lake, for on a straight course it was not more than forty miles from the scene of their encounter. As soon as the *Wanderer* was safely down preparations were made for a meal, for it was lunchtime, and in any case it was obvious that Dusky was in a famished condition. Little was said until everyone was satisfied, although it was some time before Dusky stated that he had had enough. Ginger made coffee over the spirit lamp while Biggles examined Dusky's wound and dressed it again more carefully.

'It's nothing serious,' he announced. 'The bullet went right through, so we haven't got to extract it. Luckily it missed the bone. The flesh looks clean enough, so it should heal in a few days.'

In making this statement Biggles did not allow for the astonishing recuperative ability of a healthy native, and the wound actually healed at a speed that amazed him. Dusky, possibly because he was accustomed to pain and discomfort, treated it as a mere scratch.

616

As soon as they were settled Biggles asked Dusky to tell them just how he had come by his wound. Scenting a mystery, he wanted to know about the whole affair.

'Yes, massa, I tell you plenty,' answered Dusky eagerly.

'All right; make a start by telling us what you were doing in the forest and how that big stiff got hold of you.'

'You mean Bogat.'

'Is that his name?'

'*Si señor* – Cristoval Bogat.' Dusky spoke English with a soft negro accent, curiously broken by odd words of Spanish, a method of speech common enough in Central America.

'I'se chicle-collector, massa,' he went on. 'Me and my brudders we buy canoe and work for ourselves; take de chicle down de ribber to Belize. One time we do well, den we git scared because chicle-collectors who go up ribber don't come back no more. Den, we ain't got no more money, we make one more trip. We run into dees Bogat men. Dey shoot at us. Dey kill my brudders and capture me, and say me work for dem. Dey make me slabe.'

Biggles frowned. 'Slave? Do you mean that seriously?'

'Sure I do, massa.'

'But slavery was done away with long ago.'

Dusky shook his head sadly. 'Not up *dis* ribber, massa.'

'Which river are you talking about?'

'De Unknown Ribber.'

'But we're on a lake.'

'Dat so, but de ribber run fro de forest not far away.'

Biggles nodded. 'I see. Do the authorities know about this slave racket?'

Dusky shrugged his shoulders. 'Mebbe. De black trash along Belize talk plenty about it. Mebbe Gov'ment can't do nuthin'.'

'Who is this fellow Bogat?'

'He sorta right-hand man for de King of de Forest.'

Biggles wrinkled his forehead. 'King of the Forest? Great Scott! That's an ambitious title. Who is this precious monarch?'

'Ah dunno, boss. Nobody knows for sure. Some say he black man who kill Gov'ment man in Belize and run away; udders say he white man. Dey call him de Tiger. He mighty big boss, and eberyone mighty afraid of him. He boss tousands of Indians and all sorts of men. Dey say he got town up de ribber.' Dusky paused.

'Go ahead,' invited Biggles; 'this is getting interesting. Tell us all you know.'

Dusky scratched his short, curly hair. 'Der ain't much ter tell, massa.'

'Tell us what happened to you.'

'Dey capture me and set me to work wid gang ob chicle-collectors. Some gangs dey tap de rubber.'

'I get it. And the Tiger gets it all, eh?'

'Sure he does, massa.'

'What does he do with it?'

'Ah dunno fo' sure, but dey say it goes out ob de country de udder way, up de ribber and across de mountains.'

'That's a pretty state of affairs. The stuff is collected in British territory and then smuggled out of the country, presumably so that the Tiger doesn't have to pay duty on it. Go on, Dusky.'

'I work fer a year, mebbe more; I dunno. We slaves all sick wid bad food, and when we can't work dey beat us wid whips. Bogat, he's worse dan de debbil himself. Den one day two white men come. Dey ask ter go see de Tiger. Bogat take dem. Presently dey all together drinking like brudders. After dat we don't collect chicle no longer. We made ter go fro de forest to big old spooky city, and dere we dig.'

'What for?'

Dusky shook his head. 'Nobody knows – nobody 'cept de Tiger and de white men. But we reckon dey dig fer gold. Fust we dig under de old temple—'

'Did you find anything?' put in Ginger quickly.

'Not much. Some silber mugs. Den we go on digging udder places.'

'Why did they shoot you?' asked Biggles.

'Becos I run away. I can't stand dem whips no longer, so one night me and some frens, we run, think mebbe we get back ter Belize. Bogat and his gang shot at us – mebbe dey t'ink if we get back to Belize we say what's going on. De udders all get killed or else caught. I get shot too, but I run till I can't run no longer.'

'And these friends of yours who were shot – were they all chicle-hunters from Belize?'

'Sure dey were.'

Biggles looked at the others. 'This is a nice thing,' he muttered savagely. 'These fellows were British subjects – or at least under British protection. It seems to me that it's high time this self-appointed King of the Forest was shot out of his throne. It must be the fellow Carruthers told us about. I think the thing now is to go down the river and let Carruthers know about this. He may prefer to decide what we ought to do. There is this about it: we now have a useful ally in Dusky, who probably knows his way about this particular stretch of forest.'

'The only thing against us going back to the coast is that, as there has been trouble, Carruthers may not want us to come back. He seems to regard all travellers in his province as his responsibility,' observed Algy cautiously.

'I'll tell you how we could get over that,' declared Ginger. 'We needn't all go down the river. If two of us stay here the machine would have to come back to pick us up.'

'That's an idea,' agreed Biggles. 'Algy, suppose you run down to Belize and have a word with Carruthers? The rest of us will stay here. Tell him what we have learned and ask his advice. You could slip down today and come back tomorrow. There's no desperate hurry.'

'Okay, if you think that's a wise plan.'

'I can't think of anything better. Come on, let's get some stores ashore and make camp. Ginger will have a chance to collect more butterflies while we're waiting.'

Thus it was agreed, and shortly afterwards Biggles and Ginger, standing in front of a green canvas tent which they had erected, watched Algy in the *Wanderer* take off and head towards the coast. After it was out of sight they spent some time making the camp shipshape, stacking the stores and fixing up their hammocks and mosquito nets. Dusky rested quietly in the shade on a waterproof sheet, on a small area of ground which he had burnt to drive away insect pests.

When this task was completed, and there was nothing more they could do, Ginger took his butterfly-net and announced his intention of collecting some specimens. To his surprise, and somewhat to his indignation, Dusky protested, stating with sincere earnestness that this was a most dangerous thing to do. In response to Ginger's demand to be informed in what way it was dangerous, he declared that not only were there many pests, chiefly insect and reptile, in the forest, but there was also great danger of becoming lost. This Ginger found difficult to believe. As far as the pests were concerned, although he did not say so, he held the opinion that these were exaggerated. So far he had seen none except a few mosquitoes. He knew, of course, that such creatures as ticks and leeches abounded, but he felt that these were more likely to prove a source of annoyance than constitute any real danger to a well-dressed traveller.

Biggles did not forbid him to go, but he warned him to be careful. Ginger readily gave his promise to take no risks, and said that in any event he would not go far from camp. He carried a revolver in his hip pocket, and this, he asserted, would enable him to take care of himself. With his butterfly-net under his arm and a killing jar in his haversack, he set off into the forest.

At first he did not attempt to capture any butterflies, although he saw several, for he was too fascinated by his surroundings. In particular, the humming-birds of many species, all of brilliant colour, occupied his attention. Other birds were less common, although screaming macaws, in gorgeous liveries of yellow, blue and scarlet, occasionally flew overhead. There were also a number of toucans and tanagers, conspicuous in their black plumage with a fiery red blotch above the tail. Occasionally, too, he saw monkeys, but more often was only aware of their presence by the howling they set up as he approached.

At one place, near a pool, he saw numerous butterflies, large blue *Morphos*, and others. Some were drinking; others circled above the pool like a fountain of flowers. He also noted a great variety of wasps, beetles, bees and bugs such as he had never seen before.

He decided that he would endeavour to take some of the butter-flies that were hovering over the pool, but he found it difficult to approach from the side on which he stood. Generally speaking, the forest was fairly open, except of course for the festoons of lianas, but between him and the pool there was a screen composed of a lovely creeping plant, with pink and rose coloured blossoms. It grew so thickly as to be impassable.

When just before he had given his word that he would be careful not to lose his way, he had had every intention of observing it to the letter. Not even when he tried to reach the pool did he relax his vigilance, for he turned often to study the trees behind him so that he would recognize them again on his way back. Still taking note of his path, he started to make a detour in order to reach the pool from the far side. In doing this he came to a smaller pool, set in a sylvan glen of breathtaking beauty, and as there were as many butterflies here as round the larger pool, he decided that it would serve his purpose just as well. Forthwith he got busy, and had no difficulty in capturing as many butterflies as he could accommodate. He often took several with one sweep of his net, and afterwards spent some time sorting them out and admiring them. At length, having decided that he had enough, he set about the return journey, observing that he had been rather longer than he intended, for it was beginning to get dark.

It was now – as he afterwards realized – that he made his initial mistake. Some little distance away he saw the curtain of pink creepers that had prevented him from going straight to the larger pool, and thinking to cut off a corner, he went straight towards it. It was not until he reached the flowers, and saw no pool, that he realized that he had been mistaken in assuming that the flowers were those which he had originally seen. However, he was not in the least dismayed, for he could see the curtain of creepers a short distance ahead. Or he thought he could. It was not until he had reached them, and failed to find the pool, that he realized that these groups of creepers were common in the forest.

It now began to rain, and the big drops added to his discomfiture. Giving way to a sense of annoyance, he struck off in the direction in which he felt certain his outward trail lay; and indeed he may have been right; but if so, then he crossed the trail without seeing it. In another five minutes he knew that he was lost. To make matters worse, the foliage overhead was so thick that little light penetrated through it at the best of times; now, already, it was nearly dark. However, he did not lose his head. He did what in the circumstances was the wisest thing he could do. He stood still, and drawing his revolver, fired three shots in quick succession into the air. These were answered almost at once, and he drew a quick breath of relief to know that he was still within earshot of the camp. He started walking in the direction from which the answering shots had come, and this was, of course, his second mistake, although it was a natural one to make. When some minutes had passed, and he still did not meet Biggles, a doubt came into his mind, and he fired again – a single shot. It was answered by the report of a rifle, but it sounded a great distance away. In fact, it sounded farther off than it really was, for he had not yet learned that noises, and even shots, do not carry far in the density of the forest.

After another interval he fired again, but this time there was no reply. It was now quite dark. Angry with himself for behaving, as he thought, like a greenhorn, he decided to make a fire, and with this object in view he incautiously broke off a piece of dead wood from a branch near at hand. A cry of pain broke from his lips, and he dropped the branch as if it had been red hot, for a numbing sensation in the palm of his hand told him that he had been stung. In the darkness he could feel something crawling up his arm. With a shudder of horror he dashed it off. At the same moment another burning pain stung his neck, and he realized that he must have shaken one of the creatures – wasp, ant, he knew not what – off one of the upper branches.

For a minute or two he stood still, getting himself in hand, well aware that at all costs he must not give way to panic. With a soft swish something brushed his face as it flew past, and he broke into a perspiration of fear. The rain stopped, and strange rustlings could be heard in the undergrowth. Once there was a coughing grunt not far away, a sinister sound which could only have been made by a large animal or reptile. Perhaps his greatest horror was that he would accidentally step on one of the snakes with which the jungle abounded.

For how long he groped about in the darkness he did not know, but what with the pain from the many stings he received from insects and pricks from thorns, he became convinced that he would lose his reason long before dawn. Already he was on the border of delirium, and it was in sheer desperation that he fired his last shot.

To his amazement and joy, it was answered by a shout no great distance away, and presently he saw the glow of a torch coming towards him. It was held by Biggles. Dusky, hobbling on two sticks, accompanied him. He stood still until they joined him, after which Dusky led the way back to camp.

Ginger thought little about his butterflies when he got back, for although he had been in the jungle only a few hours he had been stung all over, and had been pricked by countless thorns. Leeches were clinging to his legs, although these were easily removed.

Weak and haggard from strain, he allowed Biggles to put some liniment on his wounds, and then retired to his hammock.

Biggles did not reproach him. 'I think you'd be wise to follow Dusky's advice in future,' was all he said.

'Don't worry, that was as much of the forest as I want – at any rate for the time being,' declared Ginger bitterly.

'Twenty-four hours of that is about as much as any man can stand,' Biggles told him seriously. 'And now I think we'd better turn in.'

CHAPTER IV

A Visitor, and a Mystery

It was shortly before noon the following day that the drone of the *Wanderer*'s engines announced the return of Algy. He landed, and taxiing up to the camp, shouted, 'I've brought a visitor!'

Biggles stared, and saw a man in white ducks sitting next to him. 'Great Scott!' he ejaculated for Ginger's benefit, 'it's Carruthers.'

The acting-Governor came ashore with Algy, bringing with him a tall, emaciated-looking man whose skin, yellow from recurrent bouts of fever, seemed to be drawn tightly over the bones. He carried a portfolio.

Carruthers greeted the others warmly, and introduced the tall man as Marcel Chorro, his head clerk.

'So you've run into trouble?' he queried.

'It doesn't seem to surprise you,' returned Biggles.

Carruthers shrugged his shoulders. 'Why should it? I've already told you that most people do, sooner or later, in this part of the world. If it isn't one thing it's another. But I must admit that you weren't long bumping into it.'

'I assume that Lacey has told you what has happened?' asked Biggles.

'Yes.'

'Good. Then let's sit down and discuss the matter. I'm anxious to hear your views. Ginger, you might bring something to drink.'

'Okay, chief.'

The party was soon arranged, and Carruthers opened the conversation.

'I think the first point to settle,' he began, 'is how you fellows feel about this affair. I mean, do you want to stay here or do you want to continue your pleasure cruise?'

'I've got an open mind about it,' confessed Biggles. 'Frankly, what we do depends largely on your advice. What do you want us to do? You know the country; moreover, you're in a position of authority, so we certainly shouldn't run counter to your orders. How do you feel about things?'

Carruthers sipped his drink and lit a cigarette before he replied. 'It's a bit difficult,' he admitted. 'As I told you, we had heard rumours of the existence of this man who calls himself King of the Forest. There has also been talk of his assistant Bogat; but as for who they are, you know as much as I do. I knew nothing about this slave traffic, or about these excavations that are being carried on. Nor did I know of the coming of the other two white men. I can't imagine who they are.'

'They aren't by any chance the survivors of the American party?' suggested Biggles.

'I should hardly think so. Why should they join up with brigands?'

'I take it you'd put a stop to this king business if you could?' questioned Biggles.

'Of course. Really, we ought to stop it.'

'Then why don't you?'

Carruthers raised his hands, palms upwards, indicating the forest on either side. 'My dear fellow, do you realize how far the jungle extends? You could drop an army in it, and then spend the rest of your life looking for it without finding it. You'd certainly need an army to do any good, and that's something we haven't got here. Think what it would cost to send even a small body of men, with the necessary stores and equipment, on such a job.'

'I'm afraid I can't agree with you,' returned Biggles imperturbably. 'If I had the handling of this situation I shouldn't think in terms of armies. Half of the men would be in hospital most of the time, anyway. This is a job for a small, mobile unit.'

Carruthers looked up sharply. 'You mean – like your party?'

'Put it that way if you like.'

Carruthers rubbed his chin. 'Perhaps you're right,' he admitted. 'All the same, it's quite obvious that you don't know what you're up against. What would you do? How would you start?'

'Clearly, the first thing would be to locate the headquarters of this gang, and then ascertain just what they're doing. If they're breaking the law – and there doesn't seem to be much doubt about that – then the next step would be either to take them into custody or drive them out of their retreat.'

'How?'

'You're going rather too fast. It would necessarily depend upon circumstances. There must be a way of doing it, though. I say that because I have yet to be faced by a problem for which there is no solution.'

Carruthers grimaced. 'It would be a dangerous business.'

'What's that got to do with it?'

The acting-Governor stared hard at Biggles. 'By Jingo! I like you,' he declared. 'I'm afraid we poor blighters who get stuck in the tropics get a bit slack. Seriously, would you, if I gave you the necessary authority, have a look round for me, and make some suggestions as to how we can put an end to this racket?'

'I should think so,' returned Biggles slowly. 'What do you mean by authority?'

'I could swear you in as special constables, but' – Carruthers laughed awkwardly – 'you realize that I've no funds to meet this sort of thing? You would only get constable's pay – three bob a day. All the same, if the affair was brought to a successful conclusion no doubt the finance people at home would refund your out-of-pocket expenses.'

'From a financial point of view I shouldn't call that an opportunity to be jumped at,' said Biggles, smiling. 'The Tiger must be robbing the State of thousands of pounds a year. If I apprehended him and secured a conviction I should expect a bonus.'

Carruthers laughed. 'Of course, if you did secure a conviction these fellows would get a pretty heavy sentence; they would have their money taken off them, in which case there might be funds to meet your case. Suppose you leave that to me?'

'Certainly. That's good enough,' agreed Biggles readily. 'I had to raise the point because we're not exactly millionaires. We should have to have a free hand, of course, so that we could go about the thing in our own way.'

'Naturally.'

'All right.' Biggles looked at the others. 'That's seems to be all there is to say. We'll see what we can do.'

'Splendid,' declared Carruthers. 'I'll leave the affair in your hands. And now, if that's all, I'd better be getting back to my office. I've plenty to do with the Governor away.'

'In that case we'll have a bite, and then I'll fly you back,' answered Biggles. 'It was good of you to come up here.'

'Not at all. On the contrary, I'm obliged to you for your help. Is there anything I can do for you?'

'Yes, there is,' returned Biggles promptly. 'One of my difficulties is going to be petrol. You see, we reckoned to cruise about always keeping within easy reach of Belize, where we could refuel. My machine has got a pretty useful range, but I've always got to keep enough petrol in the tanks to get back to Belize. That is to say, if I find myself far from Belize I shan't have much margin for cruising, and running up and down to the coast would be an expensive business. Could you send some petrol up to us? If you could send it up the river the boatmen could make a dump somewhere handy.'

'I see your point,' answered Carruthers. 'That can be arranged. In fact, I can send you some right away. There's a small supply at one of our posts not far down the river, for the use of the government launch. I'll send it up by express paddlers. The main supply can follow. Meanwhile, I'll get a message through to our nearest river post for the emergency petrol to be brought up to you. Keep an eye on the river. If you see the canoe coming it might be a good idea to land near it and tell the men where you want the stuff put.'

'That's a sound scheme,' agreed Biggles. 'It will save us a lot of trouble. I take it we can rely on this emergency supply coming? We should be in a mess if our tanks ran low and the stuff didn't arrive.'

'Don't worry. I'll see to it,' promised Carruthers.

'That's good enough for me,' declared Biggles.

And that was the end of the interview. After lunch Biggles flew the acting-Governor back to Belize, where he spent the night, leaving the others in charge of the camp.

He was in the cockpit early the following morning, anxious to get back to discuss ways and means of starting on their new project. Both for safety and simplicity he followed the river – for safety because it offered the only possible means of getting down should engine trouble develop, and for simplicity in that it marked an unmistakable course, and so enabled him to fly yet give his mind to other matters. Fortunately – as it transpired – he cruised along quietly, and there was never an occasion when he found it necessary to turn sharply, or otherwise put a strain on the aircraft. Not that there was anything unusual about this, for Biggles, like the majority of experienced pilots, never, in any circumstances, performed useless stunts.

He was about fifty miles short of his destination, and was on the point of leaving the river for the lake, when he noticed the loose turnbuckle. Just why he noticed it would be hard to say, except that it becomes an instinctive habit for a pilot to keep an eye on everything around him, even though there may not appear to be any immediate necessity for it. His roving eyes, passing over the turnbuckle which braced the flying wires between the starboard wings, stopped suddenly and remained fixed. A second later his left hand slid to the throttle and eased it back; at the same time he moved the joystick forward slightly so that the *Wanderer* began a slow glide towards the river, at this point about a hundred yards wide.

Although to anyone but a pilot it might have appeared a small thing, what he had noticed was this. The turnbuckle should have been screwed up so that none – or not more than one or two – of the threads on the cross-bracing wire were visible. At least six threads could now be seen, and as there were only eight or nine in all, it meant that the entire strain was being carried by two or three threads; even an ordinary strain on the wings might therefore be sufficient to pull the wire clean out of the buckle – which takes the form of a longish, rather fat piece of metal; and since the wings are held in place by these particular wires, should the wires break, or pull out of the turnbuckle, there would be nothing to prevent the wings from tearing off – that is, if one excludes the small fishplates which fasten the roots of the wings to the fuselage.[1]

Now, the turnbuckle concerned was on the starboard side. What made Biggles look at the turnbuckle on the port side he did not know; but he did, and to his alarm, and unspeakable amazement, he saw that the same thing had happened there. His face was pale as he brought the machine down as gently as he could, and a breath of relief broke from his lips as it settled safely on the water. It made him feel slightly weak to realize that the whole time he had been in the air a 'bump' might have been sufficient to take his wings off. Once on the water the strain was taken off the wires, and he sat still for a little while regarding the turnbuckles with brooding eyes. When he had first noticed the starboard one he had assumed, not unnaturally, that it had worked loose of its own accord; that it was one of those accidents which can occur to

[1] The cross bracing wires between the wings of a biplane are called respectively 'flying-wires' and 'landing-wires'. Flying-wires keep the wings of a plane *down* while the machine is in flight; landing-wires hold them *up* when the machine is at rest. Naturally, when a machine is in flight, the strain on the wings is upward, and the flying-wires hold them down. When the machine is at rest, the strain, imposed simply by gravity, is downward, and it is the landing-wires that hold them up.

any mechanical device. It should not, of course, be allowed to happen, and since the *Wanderer* was examined every day, it was not easy to see how it could happen. It would have been remarkable enough if only one turnbuckle had worked loose, but that two should become unscrewed at the same time by accident was incredible. In short, such a coincidence was enough to tax the imagination to breaking point.

Biggles's face was grim as he climbed out on the starboard wing and made the necessary adjustment. The turnbuckle was quite loose, and held the wire by only two threads. It was the same on the other side. Vibration alone might have been sufficient to give the turnbuckles the final twist that must have caused him to crash. Satisfied that they were now in order, he took off and flew over to the lake, where he found everything as he had left it. Algy and Ginger were there, waiting for him.

He taxied to the bank, switched off, and tossing the mooring rope ashore joined the others.

'Ginger, it was your turn yesterday to look over the machine,' he said quietly. 'You didn't forget by any chance, did you?'

Ginger looked hurt. 'Of course I didn't,' he retorted hotly. 'What made you ask?'

'Only that coming along this morning I happened to notice that the turnbuckles on both flying wires were loose – nearly off, in fact. I had to land on the river and fix them.'

There was dead silence for a moment.

'Did you say on *both* wires?' Algy burst out.

'I did.'

'Then somebody must have unscrewed them,' declared Algy, with such emphasis that he made it clear at once that he was not prepared to accept coincidence as an explanation.

'Yes, I think that's the only answer,' agreed Biggles.

'It couldn't have been done here, that's certain,' put in Ginger.

'I agree. That means it could only have been done in Belize.'

'You didn't put a guard over your machine last night?' queried Algy.

'No. Why should I? What possible reason had I for thinking that it might be interfered with? I shall take jolly good care it doesn't happen again, though.'

'Somebody must have deliberately tried to crash the machine.'

'He tried to do more than that. He tried to kill me at the same time.'

'But who on earth in Belize could have done such a thing?'

Biggles smiled faintly. 'That's something we may find out presently,' he said. 'The only possible enemies we can have in this part of the world are those connected with the Tiger, or his pal Bogat; it would seem therefore that the Tiger has friends in Belize.'

'That's the only solution,' murmured Ginger. 'The Tiger's ramifications evidently extend to the coast. Well, forewarned is forearmed, they say; we shall have to keep our eyes open.'

'We certainly shall,' agreed Biggles warmly. 'But come on, we may as well have a bite of lunch; it's too late to start anything today, so we'll get all set for an early move tomorrow. How's Dusky getting along?'

'Fine, he's hopping about already,' Ginger answered.

'Did you tell him that we're going to try to put a spoke in the wheel of the Tiger?'

'Yes.'

'What did he say?'

'He's flat out to help us,' declared Ginger. 'He hasn't forgotten that Bogat murdered his brothers.'

'Good. I think he's going to be useful,' returned Biggles. 'Now let's have a bite then talk things over.'

CHAPTER V

The Enemy Strikes

The upshot of the debate, in which Dusky took part, was this. They would turn in early, and, leaving the lake at dawn, proceed under Dusky's directions to that area in which the headquarters of the Tiger was assumed to be. Whether Dusky would recognize landmarks from the air remained to be seen; on the ground, at any rate, he appeared to have no doubt as to the general direction. Pending this survey, nothing could, of course, be done. As far as they themselves were concerned, the present camp would serve for the time being; if, later, a suitable base could be found nearer to the enemy, then they would move to it. Nothing further could be arranged immediately. This decided, they spent a little while preparing the camp for a more extended stay, clearing the bushes and piling them on the forest side of the tent. At nightfall, with the *Wanderer* moored close in, they got into their hammocks, closed the very necessary mosquito curtains, and went to sleep. There was a short discussion as to whether or not they should take turns to keep guard, but in the end they voted against it, a matter in which they were guided by Dusky, who said that as they were not in the region of savages there was no need for this precaution.

It was therefore with surprise that Ginger awoke some time later – what hour it was he did not know – to find Dusky in quiet conversation with Biggles. He realized that it was the sound of their voices that had awakened him.

Seeing that he was awake, Biggles said, 'Dusky swears that there is somebody moving about in the forest.'

'Does he mean that he's actually heard somebody?'

'Not exactly. I gather that there have been sounds made by night creatures that indicate that human beings are on the move. He believes that they are coming in this direction.'

'But nobody could possibly know that we are here.'

'That's what I've told him. All the same, he insists that he's right. You'd better wake Algy.'

'Perhaps it's a party of chicle-hunters – nothing to do with us?'

Dusky shook his head. 'Not *chicleros*,' he announced definitely. 'Dey not march at night – too mighty scared.'

'We should be foolish not to heed what Dusky says,' declared Biggles, starting to put on his clothes. 'Wake Algy, and both of you get dressed. We'll go outside the tent and listen. Bring your guns.' He himself picked up a rifle and slipped a cartridge into the breech.

Gathered outside the tent, they stood near the edge of the forest, listening intently. A crescent moon hung low in the sky, throwing a broad band of silver across the placid surface of the lake, but within the jungle profound darkness reigned. The air was heavy with heat and the tang of rotting vegetation; vague rustlings betrayed the presence of the invisible army of insects that dwelt in it.

For some minutes the silence continued; then a curious sound came from the forest; it was as though a branch was being violently shaken.

'What on earth was that?' muttered Biggles.

'De monkeys. Dey shake de branches when mens go underneath,' breathed Dusky, slightly hoarse with nervousness.

Biggles looked at the others. 'This is a funny business,' he said quietly. 'It's hard to know what to do for the best. Dusky is convinced that somebody is about, but that doesn't necessarily mean that we're being stalked. On the other hand, it may be Bogat's men – whether they're looking for us or not.'

'They couldn't possibly know we're here,' put in Algy.

'No, but they might guess it. They probably know of the existence of this lake, in which case they might have decided to investigate on the off-chance of finding us here. We're in no case to withstand a serious attack.'

'What's the time?' asked Algy suddenly.

Biggles glanced at his watch. 'Nearly five.'

'It will start to get light in an hour.'

Again, out of the forest, came the sinister rustling of branches. A monkey barked, and then broke off abruptly.

Biggles shook his head. 'I don't like this. I think we'd better start getting ready for a quick move. You two put the stores back in the machine. Don't make a noise about it. I'll walk a few yards into the forest with Dusky. If I shout an alarm, start the engine.'

Twenty minutes passed without further development, except that by the end of that time everything portable had been put on board. Algy and Ginger returned to the edge of the forest, where presently Biggles joined them.

'Dusky was right,' he said softly; 'I can hear them now, distinctly.'

'We've got everything on board except the tent,' announced Algy.

'Good – stand fast.'

'Where's Dusky?'

'In the forest, scouting.'

Hardly had the words left Biggles's lips when Dusky returned; he was shaking with excitement. 'Dey come, massa,' he panted.

'We'd better play safe until we see how many of them there are,' decided Biggles promptly. 'Into the machine everybody. Algy, get ready for a snappy take-off; Ginger, you man the gun, but don't use it until I give the word. Get going.'

Not until the others were aboard and the machine cast off did Biggles leave the bank. As he climbed into the aircraft he pushed it a few yards from the shore, leaving it in such a way that the nose faced open water.

'Absolute quiet now,' he ordered.

Silence settled again over the scene. The *Wanderer*, plainly visible from the bank, floated motionless, like a great bird asleep. Algy was in the pilot's seat with his hand on the starter, but Biggles and Ginger crouched by the gun, only their eyes showing above the top of the fuselage. The silence was uncanny, and Ginger found it hard to believe that human beings were abroad in the forest, creeping towards the site of the camp. Then he saw an indistinct shadow flit along the fringe of the forest a little way higher up, and he knew that Dusky's woodcraft had not been at fault.

'Here they come,' he breathed.

Another figure appeared, another, and another, until at last there were at least a dozen shadowy forms creeping towards the tent. Ginger made out the massive form of Bogat, and nudged Biggles; an answering nudge told him that his signal was understood.

With infinite stealth and patience the outlaws closed in on the tent. Then Bogat, gun at the ready, took the lead and advanced to the flap. He threw it open, and at the same time leapt back. 'Come out!' he shouted. The rest raised their guns, covering the entrance.

There was a brief; palpitating interval, then Bogat barked again. 'Come out! You can't get away.' He naturally assumed the airmen to be in the tent, for after a first penetrating stare at it, he ignored the aircraft.

'Don't move, Bogat; I've got you covered,' snapped Biggles. 'Do you want something?'

There was a unanimous gasp from the assembled men. Bogat swung round. He half raised his gun, and then, evidently thinking better of it, lowered it.

'I said, do you want something?' repeated Biggles. 'If you do it's waiting – a hundred rounds of nickel-coated lead. If you don't want anything, clear out of my camp.'

Bogat ducked like lightning, and at the same time fired his gun from the hip.

Ginger's gun spat. He swore afterwards that he didn't consciously pull the trigger; he declared that the shock of Bogat's shot caused his finger automatically to jerk the trigger. Above the uproar that instantly broke out Biggles's voice could be heard yelling to Algy to start up. The engines came to life, and the blast of air flung back by the propellers sent a cloud of fallen leaves whirling into the faces of the outlaws; it also struck the tent and laid it flat. The *Wanderer* surged forward across the water, with Ginger firing spasmodic bursts at the flashes that stabbed the darkness along the edge of the forest. Two or three bullets struck the machine, but as far as could be judged they did no damage. It was impossible to see if any casualties had been inflicted on the enemy. The *Wanderer*, gathering speed, rose into the air.

'Where to?' shouted Algy.

'Make for the river,' Biggles told him.

The stars were paling in the sky, but it was still dark. However, this did not worry Biggles, who knew that dawn would have broken by the time they reached the river, so that there would be no difficulty in choosing a landing place.

'We've lost the tent,' remarked Ginger angrily.

'But for Dusky we might have lost our lives, and that would have been a far more serious matter,' declared Biggles. 'We can always get another tent. I must say that I don't like being hounded about by these dagos, but it was a case of discretion being the better part of valour. Our turn will come. From now on it's open war.'

Nothing more was said. The *Wanderer* cruised on over the treetops. The rim of the sun crept up over the horizon and bathed them in a pink glow. The river appeared, winding like a gigantic snake through the jungle. Biggles took the joystick, and in a little while the aircraft was once more at rest, moored near the bank. The bullet-holes were quickly examined, and it was confirmed that nothing vital had been touched.

'Well, let's have some breakfast,' suggested Biggles. 'Then we'll move off.'

'Move off – where to?' asked Algy.

'To have a look round. What has happened need make no

difference to our programme. Bogat has declared war on us, so we know just how we stand.'

An hour later the machine was in the air again, heading northwest, following from a considerable height the course of the Unknown River. For the purpose of exploration Biggles would rather have flown lower, but this he dare not risk, for the nearer they flew to the source of the river the narrower it became, and places suitable for landing were fewer and farther between.

For a long time they saw only the same monotonous ocean of jungle, with the jagged peaks of a mountain group cutting into the blue sky far to the north. Dusky stated that the base of these mountains was generally regarded as the boundary between Honduras and Guatemala.

'We may as well have a look at them for all there is to see here,' announced Biggles. 'I'm beginning to wonder even if there is a city in the forest, whether we should notice it. These confounded trees hide everything. If we can't see anything from the air we might as well pack up. I'm not tackling the job on foot, not for Carruthers or anyone else. When I look at the forest from up here I begin to realize what we're up against. The mountains, at any rate, will be a change of scenery.'

Cruising at three miles a minute, instead of – as Dusky assured them – three miles a day, which could be reckoned as normal progress on foot, they reached the mountains in about a quarter of an hour, and from the altimeter it was possible to form a rough estimate of the height. It was necessary to fly at nearly six thousand feet to clear the highest peaks. The jungle persisted for some distance up the slopes, but for the most part the tops were clear of timber, and alternated between stark rock and, in the valleys, grassy savannah. Biggles remarked two or three places where it ought to be possible to land, although without having first examined the ground there would be a certain amount of risk involved.

It was Ginger who spotted the ruined city, although at first he did not recognize it as such. Gazing down on an unexpected plateau, he saw, on the very lip of the steep descent on the southern side, a jumble of rocks of such curious formation that he commented on it.

'That's a queer-looking collection of rocks,' he observed casually. 'Look how square they are. They might almost be houses.'

Biggles stared down at the spot indicated, and as he did so a strange expression came over his face. He pushed open the side window and looked again. 'You're dead right,' he said slowly. 'I'm by no means sure that they're *not* houses.'

'What!' cried Ginger incredulously. 'Let's go down and have a look.'

Biggles cut the throttle, and pushing the joystick forward, began to circle lower. Presently the *Wanderer* was flying at not more than a hundred feet above the plateau, and the matter was no longer in doubt. Apart from the shape of what Ginger had taken to be rocks, the regular manner in which they were laid out convinced them all that the work could have been done only by the hand of man.

'By gosh! Let's land somewhere. We must have a look at this,' declared Ginger excitedly.

Biggles's eyes were still on the city, around which it was now possible to make out the remains of a wall. 'It's deserted,' he said. 'If anyone was there, he would certainly come out to have a look at us.'

As he spoke Biggles studied the savannah beyond the town where it formed the plateau. It was too narrow to be an ideal landing-place, but there was plenty of length, and he decided that with care a landing might be made. He lowered the wheels, made a cautious approach, and settled down to a safe if somewhat bumpy landing.

Ginger was first out. 'Come on!' he shouted, starting off towards the ruins. 'I shouldn't wonder if the place is littered with gold.'

'I should,' returned Biggles dryly.

Leaving the machine where it had finished its run, they walked briskly to the ruins, for the buildings were no more than that, although it was obvious that at one time the place had been a town of importance. Certain buildings larger than the rest marked the sites of what had once been temples or palaces. The whole place, situated as it was on the edge of a chasm overlooking the southern forest, was in the nature of an eagle's eyrie.

Ginger's dream of gold was soon dispelled. With the exception of numerous broken potsherds, and a bronze hammer which Algy found, the houses – or as many as they visited – were empty.

'I'm afraid we're a few hundred years too late,' smiled Biggles. 'This place was either abandoned, or sacked, centuries ago. Still, it's an interesting discovery, and archaeologists concerned with ancient American civilizations will be tickled to death when they hear about it.' He pointed to an obelisk that stood in an open square, carved on its four sides. 'That's called a stele,' he remarked. 'There are any number of them in the forest. That weird-looking carving you can see is writing, but no one has yet learned how to read it. Mind you, I'm only speaking from what I've learned in books.'

'You don't think this is one of those old cities where excavations have been going on?' inquired Algy.

'Definitely not, otherwise there would be trenches and other signs,' answered Biggles. 'This is a new discovery.'

'What I should like to know,' put in Ginger, 'is how on earth the people who lived here got up and down from the forest – or did they spend their lives here?'

'Even if they spent their lives up here, as they may have done after they were driven out of the forest by the people who conquered them, there must have been some way of getting up,' replied Biggles. 'If we look around we may find it.'

It did not take them long to. Walking round the ruined wall, they came to an opening with the remains of an old gate, from which descended a staircase so fantastic that for a little while they could only stare at it with eyes round with wonder. It was partly natural and partly artificial. That is to say, a remarkable feat of Nature had been helped by the hand of man. It was fairly clear what had happened. At some period in the remote past, when the cliff – indeed, the whole mountain – was being formed, the rock, then in a plastic state, had settled down, leaving a narrow projecting cornice running transversely right across the face of the cliff, from top to bottom. The face of the cliff was not smooth, but in the form of gigantic folds, yet the cornice followed each fold faithfully. There were places where it disappeared from sight behind mighty shoulders of rock.

In its original form the cornice had no doubt been extremely rough, and of a width varying from two to six feet, and in that state a mountain goat might well have hesitated to descend by it. Then had come man, presumably one of the extinct nations of America. At any rate, men had worked at the cornice, cutting steps where they were required, so rendering the descent possible; but even so, the path was not one to be taken by a traveller subject to dizziness.

'Jacob's Ladder,' murmured Ginger.

Biggles nodded. 'It certainly is a remarkable piece of work. I should say that it can't be less than five or six miles from the top to the bottom, following the path, and therefore taking into account the irregular face of the cliff. I remember reading in a book about Bolivia about just such a path on the eastern slope of the Andes. An amusing tale was told of an engineer being paid an enormous salary to superintend a gold mine at the bottom of the staircase; but when he got to it, and saw where he had to go, he not only chucked up the job but declared that he wouldn't go down the path for all the gold in South America.'

'I don't blame him,' remarked Algy feelingly. 'I'd hate to go down this one.'

'Oh, I don't know; it isn't as bad as all that,' returned Biggles. 'After all, some of the cornice roads in the Alps are pretty grim, and people who live in the mountain villages have to go up and down them constantly.'

'It must have been a colossal task, cutting those steps,' put in Ginger.

'The ancients apparently liked colossal tasks,' replied Biggles. 'What about the pyramids of Egypt, and the Great Wall of China? This is nothing compared with them.'

At this juncture, Dusky, who had so far remained silent, interrupted with the surprising statement that he had seen the bottom of the stairway. Interrogation elicited the information that while he had been working for Bogat, clearing undergrowth from the ruins in the jungle near the foot of a cliff, he had come upon just such a flight of steps leading upwards. Asked by Biggles if he had revealed this discovery to Bogat, he said no, the reason being that, although he did not know where the steps led, he thought they might one day provide a means of escape. He had made the discovery about six months ago, as near as he could judge.

'Well, I must say it seems highly improbable that there can be two such stairways,' remarked Biggles. 'In that case, if we followed these steps we should come out either in, or very near, the excavations where the Tiger and the two white men are working. When you think about it, that is not altogether surprising; in fact, it seems quite a natural thing that there should be a town at the foot of these steps as well as at the top.'

'The question that seems to arise in that case is, has the Tiger discovered the staircase since the time Dusky was working at the bottom?' put in Algy.

'I should say not,' answered Biggles without hesitation. 'If the Tiger had discovered the steps he would most certainly have come up here, and even if he didn't start excavating – as seems probable – he would surely have left some traces of his visit: – old tins, or ashes of the fires where he did his cooking.'

'Yes, that's reasonable,' agreed Algy. 'What it comes to, then, is this. If Dusky's supposition is correct, we have discovered a way down into the Tiger's camp.'

'That's it,' nodded Biggles.

'What are we going to do?' queried Ginger eagerly. 'I'm all in favour of doing a bit of exploring up here on our own account.'

'We might have time to do that later on, but at the moment,

since our stores are not unlimited, I think we owe it to Carruthers to stick to our job.'

'You mean – go down the steps and try to get hold of the Tiger?'

'What else?'

Ginger looked at the stairway and drew back, shuddering. 'Strewth! I'm not so keen on that. I don't mind looking down from a plane, but to crawl down that dizzy path, with all that way to fall if we miss a step, doesn't strike me as a jaunt to be undertaken lightly.'

'Oh, that's all right,' replied Biggles calmly. 'All the same, I'm not entirely happy at the idea of all of us going. Somebody ought to stay to look after the machine. Apart from that, if we got in a jam going down we should all be in the same boat, whereas if somebody stayed behind he might be able to help the others.'

'That's sound reasoning,' murmured Algy.

'I'll tell you what: let's compromise,' decided Biggles. 'Algy, you and Dusky stay up here to keep an eye on things. Ginger and I will do a bit of exploring. If we find it's easy going all the way down we'll come back and let you know; on the other hand, if we find we can't get down, we shall have to come back anyway.'

'Good enough,' agreed Algy. 'When are you going?'

'Right away. There's no need to wait until tomorrow.'

'What about kit?'

'We'll take a tin of bully and some biscuits, a water-bottle and our rifles. That ought to be enough – for the first trip at any rate.'

This being agreed, the party returned to the machine, where

the necessary kit was obtained and a meal taken. They then returned to Jacob's Ladder. Biggles, with his rifle slung on his left shoulder, started down. Ginger, after a deep breath, followed.

CHAPTER VI

Down the Unknown Trail

For the first hundred steps Ginger's head swam to such an extent that he felt sick and dizzy; more than once he had to halt and lean weakly against the sheer wall of cliff that rose up on the right-hand side of the path, hardly daring to look at the frightful void that fell away on his left. In places the cliff was more than sheer; owing to faults in the rock, the path had been dug so far into it that the wall overhung the steps. There were places, too, where the path projected over the abyss in the manner of a cornice, so that one false step would mean a drop of four thousand feet or more to the forest. A slight heat haze hung over the treetops, making them look farther away than they really were; it also gave the forest an atmosphere of mystery, and created an impression of looking down upon another world. Thus, thought Ginger, might a man feel descending to Earth from another planet.

Biggles appeared to be little troubled by the terrifying drop. He strode on, rifle on his shoulder, whistling softly, and stopping only to warn Ginger of bad places, places where the wind and rain had worn the steps away so that no more than a smooth, narrow projection remained.

However, one becomes accustomed to anything, and after the first hundred yards Ginger began to breathe more freely. Once, while Biggles was waiting for him, he remarked, 'What would happen if we met somebody coming the other way? I should hate to try to pass anybody.'

Biggles laughed softly. 'I don't think we shall meet anyone on this path,' he observed lightly. 'Save your breath; we shall need it coming back.'

They went on. Condors appeared, stiff-winged, looking as big as gliders; they circled slowly, their heads turned always to face the invaders of their domain. Ginger eyed them nervously.

'We should be in a mess if they decided to attack us,' he said anxiously.

'So would they,' answered Biggles briefly, tapping his rifle.

Rounding the shoulder of rock that up to now concealed what lay beyond, they stopped for a moment to admire the stupendous view that unfolded before them; it seemed that the very world was at their feet. The path, after cutting into a colossal gorge, reappeared again on the far side, five hundred feet below; a mere thread it looked, winding down and down interminably. For the first time Ginger appreciated the full length of it.

'I shouldn't think the people who lived up top were ever invaded,' he opined. 'Why, a couple of men could hold this path against an army.'

'Easily,' agreed Biggles. 'I'd rather be the man at the top than one of the fellows coming up.'

After that, for an hour they walked on with hardly a word. The heat flung down by the sun, and radiated by the rock, always intense, became worse as they descended. As Ginger remarked, it was like going down into a furnace.

They were nearing the bottom – at least, they were more than three-quarters of the way down – when the steps ended abruptly in a veritable chaos of rock. At first Ginger thought they had reached the foot of the stairway, but Biggles pointed out that this was not so, and investigation soon proved his theory, which was that in the remote past a landslide had fallen across the path, carrying a section of it away.

'If we can find a way across this mass of detritus we ought to strike the steps again on the other side,' he declared. 'We know that the steps go right down to the forest, because Dusky saw them there.'

'Yes, of course,' answered Ginger.

'All the same, anyone coming up the steps, encountering this pile of debris, might well think that they had come to the end of the stairway,' resumed Biggles. 'Unless they persevered, and forced a way across the landslide, they would not know that the steps continued and went right on up to the top. Let's push on. Be careful where you're putting your feet, because some of this stuff doesn't look any too safe. If we started a movement the whole lot might slide again. Come on – this seems to be the easiest way.'

Biggles proceeded, choosing his path carefully, with Ginger following close behind. From his point of view there was now at least one advantage: there was no longer the precipice to fear, for the route Biggles had chosen traversed the landslide.

And so they came upon the village. It was entirely unexpected, for there had been absolutely nothing to indicate its presence. Reaching the bottom of a steep incline, across a confused jumble of mighty boulders, they found themselves confronted by a drop of some thirty or forty feet into a pleasant valley which the giant forest trees had failed to cross. That is to say, the valley marked the top limit of the big timber. Trees could be seen on the far side, and these, presumably, went right on down to the forest proper. There were no trees on the side where they stood regarding the scene. Nor were there any big trees in the valley, which was carpeted with verdant grasses and flowering shrubs. Up the centre of it ran a wide track, ending at a modern village. Actually, it appeared to be something more than a village, although they used the term for want of a better one. In the centre of a fairly extensive group of ramshackle buildings stood a fine bungalow, well built of heavy timber. At the back of it, and evidently a part of the premises, was a range of outbuildings roofed with corrugated iron. Radiating from this centre were rows of small houses. From a courtyard between the bungalow and the outbuildings smoke was rising lazily into the air from an outside cooking stove. A woman, conspicuous with a scarlet handkerchief tied round her head, did something at the fire and then disappeared into the house. Apart from some mules grazing higher up the valley, which appeared to end abruptly, there was no other sign of life.

As soon as Biggles and Ginger came in sight of this utterly unexpected feature they stopped, and after a few seconds' incredulous contemplation of it, sat down abruptly.

'Great Scott!' Biggles muttered. 'What the deuce is all this?'

Ginger, squatting beside him, answered, 'Don't ask me.'

Biggles regarded the village thoughtfully. 'There's only one answer,' he said slowly. 'The Tiger would never tolerate a second gang in the same area, so this must be part of his organisation. If that is so – and I'm convinced I'm right – then this might even be his secret retreat: the place Dusky spoke about. The fact that there are women – or at least one woman – here, proves fairly conclusively that this is a permanent settlement. The big house proves it, too, if it comes to that.'

'So what?' inquired Ginger. 'We should be taking a chance if we tried to cross that valley. There must be others here besides that woman we saw. We should be spotted for a certainty.'

'We may not have to cross the valley,' answered Biggles. 'I have a feeling that this is our objective.'

Ginger started. 'What do you mean – our objective?'

'Well, we were only going to the bottom of the stairway in order to locate the Tiger's headquarters. There was no other purpose in our going down. That bungalow, unless I am mistaken, is the palace of the King of the Forest, so there is no need for us to go any farther.'

'What are you going to do – go back and let Algy know what we've found?'

'I don't think so – not for the moment, anyway. We should only have to come down again.'

"If Carruthers and his police were here we could raid the place,' murmured Ginger.

'Quite, but they don't happen to be here. In any case, there wouldn't be much purpose in raiding the place if the Tiger wasn't here. He's the man we want – he and Bogat. Unless they were captured the racket would still go on.'

Ginger shrugged his shoulders. 'Well, you're the boss. What's the plan – or haven't you got one?'

'There's only one thing we can do, as far as I can see,' replied Biggles, 'and that's have a look round the village while we're here, while the place is comparatively deserted. We may not get another such chance. Don't forget that so far we have no actual proof of what the Tiger is doing – that is, proof that would carry weight in a court of law. It wouldn't be any use just talking vaguely about the Tiger being a crook, a slave-driver, a chicle thief, without evidence to prove it. This may be our chance to get such evidence. I'm going down into the village.'

Ginger stared aghast. 'Going down! You must be crazy.'

'We shan't collect any evidence sitting here.'

'We could watch them, though, and spot what was going on.'

'Even so, I can't see that we should learn more than we already know. We must get some concrete proof to secure a conviction. All the same, if we could capture the Tiger, or Bogat, and get back to the coast, we might hold him until we'd obtained the proof we need. Perhaps some of the slaves would give evidence. But we shan't get any of these things sitting here. I'm going down.'

'What do you want me to do? Shall I come with you, or stay here?'

Biggles thought for a moment. 'I think you'd better come with me,' he decided. 'I may need a witness if I find anything – otherwise I should only have my unsubstantiated word.'

'Suppose things go wrong? Algy won't know what's happened to us.'

'We can easily get over that.'

Taking his notebook from his pocket, Biggles tore out a page and scribbled a brief message to the effect that a village was in the valley just ahead, and they were going down into it. Returning to the stairway, he put the message under a stone in a conspicuous place, and built a little cairn beside it so that it could not be missed by anyone coming down. This done, they returned to the valley, and after hunting about for a little while found a way down into it.

'Keep this place in your mind's eye,' said Biggles quietly,

surveying the spot where they had descended. 'We may have to come back this way – in a hurry. Try to get a mental photograph of the silhouette of the rocks, in case we have to find it in the dark.'

This did not take long, after which Biggles turned towards the village.

'I think our best policy is to go straight up to the house,' he surprised Ginger by saying. 'In fact, I don't see that we can do anything else. There's no real cover, so even if we tried stalking tactics it is almost certain that we should be seen; and if we were spotted skulking like a couple of thieves, there would probably be an outcry. I think this is a case for bluff. All the same, we needn't expose ourselves unnecessarily; we'll just stroll along, and if nobody sees our faces we may get away with it.'

'You know best,' agreed Ginger, 'but it seems a risky business to me. I never was one for jumping into a lion's den without first making sure that the lion wasn't at home.'

Biggles smiled, and walked on towards the village, the nearest buildings of which were not more than a hundred yards away.

They had covered about half the distance when Biggles touched Ginger on the arm, and with an inclination of his head indicated something that he had seen. The boundaries of the valley were now apparent. Hemmed in by cliffs, sometimes high, and, in a few places, fairly low, such as at the spot where they had entered it, there was only one proper entrance. This was a narrow pass at the southern end of the track, a mere defile through the rock wall, presumably where those who lived in the village descended to the forest some four hundred feet below. At this natural gateway two men were on guard; at least, they were armed with rifles. Smoking, they lounged against the wall of the pass.

'If that is the only entrance to the valley, those fellows will wonder how the deuce we got in,' said Biggles softly. 'There is this about it, though; the people in the village – if there are any – knowing that men are on guard at the entrance, might suppose that we are here on business. My word,' he went on, glancing round, 'what a spot for a hideout. Carruthers was right. An army might have wandered about in the forest for years without even suspecting that this place was here. It would need an army to capture it, too, against a score of determined men.'

'There's one thing that puzzles me,' remarked Ginger. 'Dusky said he found the foot of the stairway. Anyway, he saw a stairway, so we must assume that it was the terminus of the path we came down. Yet, judging by the way he mentioned it – he was actually clearing the jungle, you remember? – it seems that those steps weren't used, which means there must be another way up. In fact, the Tiger may still not know that Dusky's stairway exists.'

'By jove! I didn't think of that,' returned Biggles quickly. 'You're dead right. Whether they have known about the stairway all along, or discovered it since Dusky was there, it seems unlikely that it is used. There is probably an easier way down. It doesn't matter at the moment, but we'll bear it in mind.'

By this time they had reached the village, still without seeing anyone apart from the two men on duty. A drowsy silence broken only by the hum of insects hung on the air. Biggles avoided the main street, a dusty track often interrupted by outcrops of rock, which wound a crooked course between the houses – most of them little better than hovels – and kept to the rear of the buildings, moving steadily towards the big bungalow. As they neared it they came suddenly upon a woman; she was on her knees, grinding maize; she looked surprised when she saw the strangers, but said nothing, and after they had passed they could hear her going on with her monotonous task.

'It would be a joke, wouldn't it, if this isn't the place we're looking for, after all?' murmured Ginger. 'It might turn out to be a perfectly legitimate village.'

'People don't post guards at the entrance to a perfectly legitimate village,' Biggles reminded him. 'Moreover, if this place was above-board, there would surely be some attempt at cultivation; and there would be no need for *chicleros* to sweat up and down four hundred feet of rock every time they went to work. All right – here we are; keep quiet now.'

They had reached the entrance to the yard that gave access to the outbuildings of the big house, the back door of which also opened into it. The fire which they had seen from the rocks was still burning; above it was suspended an iron cauldron from which arose an appetizing aroma.

'We'll try the outbuildings first,' said Biggles quietly, and walked over to them; but if he hoped to see what they contained he was disappointed, for they were locked, every one of them, and there were six in all, large and small. But from the far one they were granted a view of something which hitherto had been hidden by a corner of the house. It was a garden, a walled-in area, an unsuspected Eden. Grapes hung in purple clusters from an overhead trellis; scarlet tomatoes gleamed among the golden stalks of Indian corn; huge yellow gourds lay about among vines that wandered through flowers of brilliant colours. A bush loaded with great blue plums made Ginger's mouth water. This pleasant scene was enhanced by a pigeon-cote, where several birds were preening themselves. Into this unsuspected paradise Biggles led the way. Ginger made for the plums, but Biggles dragged him back into a shady arbour where a tiny fountain bubbled.

'Don't be an ass,' he muttered; 'we're on thin ice here. Don't you realize that we're in the king's garden? Stand fast.'

Peering through the creepers that covered the arbour, Ginger saw that they were now at the side of the house. A long, low window overlooked the garden. Near it was a door. It was open.

'We're doing well. Let's have a look inside,' murmured Biggles, and went on to the door, which gave access to the garden, but obviously was not the main entrance to the house. After a cautious peep inside Biggles took a pace over the threshold, Ginger at his elbow. He whistled softly as he looked around.

'And I should say this is the king's parlour,' he whispered.

The room was magnificently, if ostentatiously, furnished as something between a lounge and an office. An old, beautifully carved Spanish sideboard was disfigured by a lot of cheap, modern bric-a-brac. Bottles and glasses stood on a brass-topped table. A modern roll-top desk, littered with account-books and papers, stood near the far wall; but the piece that fascinated Ginger most was a fine, leather-covered chest. In strange contrast, near it stood an American steel safe. A second door led into the interior of the house. A strange foreign odour hung in the sultry air.

So much the visitors saw at a glance. After listening intently for a moment, Biggles walked over to the desk, where he began to scan the papers, but without disturbing them. He opened a ledger, and whistled softly as his eyes ran down the items.

'This is all we wanted to know,' he breathed. 'This is the Tiger's sanctum all right, and these are his accounts. There's enough documentary evidence here to hang him twice over. He's evidently a gentleman of some taste, too. Hullo, what's this?'

As he spoke Biggles picked up a tiny slip of flimsy paper that was lying on the desk, held in place by a cartridge used as a paper-weight. As he picked up the paper and read what was written on it his brow creased with anger and astonishment; he stared at it for so long that Ginger's curiosity could not be restrained.

'What is it?' he demanded.

'You might well ask,' replied Biggles through his teeth. 'It explains a lot of things. Take a look at that.' He passed the paper.

Ginger read the message, his lips forming the words:

'Keep watch for three Britishers in airplane. They are govern-ment spies sent to get you, acting for Carruthers. Names are Bigglesworth, Lacey and Hebblethwaite. They have been sworn in as police, and have got one of your peons, the man Bogat shot. They will use him as evidence.'
M. C.

'Did you note the initials?' inquired Biggles.

'Yes. Who on earth—'

'M. C. stands for Marcel Chorro – who else? He's the only man besides Carruthers who knows what we're doing. Evidently he is one of the Tiger's spies. My goodness! No wonder Carruthers found it hard to get evidence. Chorro must have been the swine who loosened my turnbuckles – yes, by gosh! Now we know how Bogat knew we were camping at the lake. He marched straight through the forest to attack us.'

'But how the dickens could Chorro have got a message through in the time?' gasped Ginger. 'The fastest canoe on the river couldn't get here much inside a week.'

'You saw the pigeon-cote outside, didn't you? Notice the thin paper used for the message.'

Ginger caught his breath. 'So *that's* it. Chorro and the Tiger run a pigeon post.'

'Undoubtedly. Come on, we've seen enough. It's no use tempting providence – we'll get back to Algy right away.'

Biggles started towards the door, but recoiled in horror. With staring eyes he clutched Ginger by the arm and held him back.

Ginger, following the direction of Biggles's eyes, felt his blood turn to ice. For some minutes he had been aware that the strange aroma had been getting more noticeable, now he saw the reason.

Emerging slowly from the chest that he had so much admired was a snake, but such a snake as not even a nightmare could have produced. As thick as a man's thigh, coil after coil was gliding sinuously out of the chest as though it would never end. Already fifteen feet of rippling horror lay stretched across the room, cutting them off from the door and the window.

CHAPTER VII

In the Claws of the Tiger

How long Ginger stood staring at the snake he did not know. He seemed to lose all count of time; he forgot where he was, and what he was doing. He was conscious of one thing only – the snake. Its little black eyes, glinting like crystals when the light caught them, fascinated him. After the first gasp of horror not a sound left his lips.

Pulling himself together with a mighty effort, he looked at Biggles, and saw that he, too, was at a loss to know what to do. He stared at the snake, then at the door, then back at the reptile. Once he braced himself as if he contemplated taking a flying leap; then he cocked his rifle and tried in vain to draw a bead on the swaying head.

'Go on – shoot,' urged Ginger, in something very near a panic.

'I daren't risk it,' muttered Biggles. 'That head is a small mark for a rifle, and if I miss, the shot will raise the place. If I only wounded the beast goodness knows what would happen.'

Curiously enough, the snake – which Biggles thought was a python – made no attempt to attack them; it lay across the floor, watching them in an almost human manner; it was as if it knew they were intruders, and had determined to prevent them from escaping. Every time they moved, it raised its head, hissing venomously, causing them to retire.

Torn by doubts and indecision, Biggles was still trying to think of a way out of their quandary when from outside came the sound of voices, followed a moment later by the trampling of footsteps; and almost before he was fully alive to their danger the inner door was thrown open and a man came into the room. He took one pace only and then stopped dead, staring at the spectacle that confronted him. Then his hand flashed to a holster that was strapped to his hip, and came up holding a revolver.

At first Ginger thought he was going to shoot the snake, but it was soon clear that this was not his intention, for he took not the slightest notice of the creature, although it had turned towards him and was now rubbing its sinuous body against his leg. Not until then did Ginger realize that the reptile was a pet, and not a wild creature that had invaded the house from the forest.

The newcomer, who was clearly the owner of the house, even if he were not the reputed King of the Forest, was a striking figure, but certainly not a pleasing one. He was a half-caste, the black predominating, of about fifty years of age; he was of medium height, but of massive, though corpulent, proportions. His arms and shoulders might have been those of a gorilla, but as an example of physique he was spoilt by a paunch of a stomach which, like his face, was flabby from overeating or self-indulgence, or both. His cheeks were puffy, but his chin was pugnacious. His eyes were small and dark; they were never still, but flashed suspiciously this way and that. His hair was long and luxuriant. An enormous black moustache drooped from his upper lip. He was dressed – or rather, overdressed – in a uniform so elaborate,

'His hand flashed to a holster, and came up
holding a revolver'

so heavy with gold braid, and of colours so brilliant that not even a cinema commissionaire would have dared to wear it. The general effect was that of a comic-opera brigand; but, looking at the coarse face, Biggles judged him to be a man of considerable mental and physical strength, vain, crafty, and unscrupulous; a man who would be brutal for the sheer pleasure of it, but who, at a pinch, might turn out to be a coward.

The newcomer broke the silence by calling out in a loud voice, 'Marita! Who are these men?' He spoke in Spanish.

A woman, evidently Marita, she who had tended the fire, appeared in the background. In the same language she answered, nervously, that she did not know the men. She had never seen them before – which was true enough.

The man came farther into the room. He spoke in a soft, sibilant voice to the snake, which writhed out of sight under the desk. Then he eyed Biggles suspiciously.

'What language you speak, eh?' he asked, talking now in English with an American accent, from which it may be concluded that he assumed the airmen to be either British or American.

'We speak English,' answered Biggles.

'What you come here for, huh?' rasped the half-caste. Then, before Biggles could answer, understanding flashed into his eyes. They switched to the desk, and Biggles knew that he had remembered the note from Chorro.

'Am I right in supposing that I'm speaking to the King of the Forest?' inquired Biggles calmly.

The half-caste's eyes narrowed. 'I am the king,' he said harshly. 'Where is the other man?'

'What other man?'

'There are three of you. Where is he?'

'What are you talking about?' demanded Biggles, although he knew well enough what was meant.

'Which of you is Bigglesworth?'

Biggles realized that it was useless to pretend. The Tiger knew they were in the district; he was also aware that the chances of any other white men being there were so remote as to be ignored.

'I'm Bigglesworth,' answered Biggles quietly.

An ugly smile spread slowly over the Tiger's face. He put a small silver whistle to his lips and blew a shrill signal. Instantly men came running. With them were two white men whom Biggles guessed were those to whom Dusky had referred. The first was tall and cadaverous; jaundice had set its mark on his face, leaving it an unhealthy yellow. The same unpleasant tint was discernible in the whites of his eyes, which were pale grey and set under shaggy brows. His mouth was large, with thin lips; nor was his appearance improved by ears that stuck out nearly at right angles from his head. His companion was a weedy-looking individual of nondescript type. Lank, hay-coloured hair covered his head; a moustache of the same tint straggled across his upper lip, stained in the middle with nicotine. An untidy, handmade cigarette was even then in his mouth.

The Tiger called them in and indicated the prisoners with a theatrical wave of his arm. 'The cops got here before us – that saves us the trouble of going to fetch them.' Then a look of doubt returned to his eyes. 'Where's the other one?' he purred.

'Oh, he's about,' returned Biggles evenly.

'Where is he?'

'Look around, maybe you'll find him ... maybe not.'

The Tiger changed the subject. 'How did you get here? Who brought you?'

Biggles smiled faintly. 'We brought ourselves.'

'That's a lie,' snarled the Tiger, crouching as though to spring, and Biggles began to understand how he had got his doubtful nickname. 'Somebody showed you the way in – who was it? I'll tear the hide off him.'

'Sorry,' said Biggles, 'but that's a pleasure you will be denied, for the simple reason that no such person exists.'

'How did you get past the guards?' The Tiger seemed to be genuinely worried by the fact that strangers had penetrated into his retreat.

'Oh, they were looking the other way,' returned Biggles truthfully.

The expression on the Tiger's face boded no good for the sentries, but Biggles was not concerned about their fate.

'Take them away,' snapped the Tiger.

Several men, a rag-tag but nevertheless picturesque set of ruffians, stepped forward and disarmed the prisoners. They offered no resistance, knowing it to be useless.

'What shall we do with them, your Majesty?' fawned the man who appeared to be in charge.

Biggles smiled at the words 'your Majesty'. It seemed that the title of King was actually enjoyed by the Tiger among his subjects.

The Tiger considered the prisoners reflectively; then a smile crept over his face. 'Put them next to Juanita; she must be getting hungry,' he ordered. 'When we get the other we will lift the bar and leave them together. All right; take them away.'

Rough hands were laid on the prisoners. Biggles did not

protest, perceiving that with the man with whom they had to deal it would be a waste of time. No doubt he had already been responsible for the deaths of scores of wretched slaves, so another murder, more or less, would not affect his conscience. In any case it was obvious that he thought himself safe in his secret retreat.

As they were marched towards the outbuildings, Ginger wondered who Juanita was, although that she was something unpleasant he had no doubt whatever. He was soon to learn. A door was opened, and they were pushed inside a shed. The door slammed, and a heavy bar crashed in place.

After the dazzling sunshine outside it seemed to be pitch black within, but as his eyes grew accustomed to the darkness Ginger began to make out some of the features of their prison. The first thing he saw was Biggles standing beside him, also peering about; next, a row of stout vertical bamboo bars that separated them from another compartment. This second stall had another barred wall, or part of a wall, beyond which was the open air. It needed no second glance to see that it was, in fact, a cage. Perhaps a better description would be to call the whole place a cage, divided by bars into two compartments. They were in one part. But what was in the other? Ginger looked for the occupant – for he knew that there must be one – but in vain. If proof that they were not alone were needed, a menagerie-like stench of wild beast provided it. Then he saw a small hole at the back of the next compartment, and he looked no farther; he knew that the beast, whatever it was, was inside, in its lair.

Biggles put a hand on the partition, and shook it. 'This is the bar the Tiger meant when he spoke about lifting it,' he remarked. 'Juanita is on the other side. Apparently, when feeding time comes, the partition is raised from the outside, leaving us all together.'

CHAPTER VIII

Algy Explores

Algy spent some time loafing about the ruined village, but as the day wore on, and Biggles and Ginger did not return, he became conscious of an uneasiness which presently turned to anxiety, and he took up a position at the top of the steps from which he could keep a lookout. Dusky said nothing, but knew well enough what was in his mind.

The day faded under a canopy of crimson glory; night fell, and still there was no sign of the explorers. Their failure to return put Algy in a quandary. He had been asked to remain on the plateau to look after the machine, and he was aware of the danger of leaving his post without letting the others know; all the same, he could not dispel the feeling that something had gone wrong. Ought he to go down Jacob's Ladder and investigate? There seemed to be little point in remaining where he was, for it was hard to see what could happen to the machine, which was still standing, an incongruous object, near the ruins. Again, he reasoned, if he met Biggles and Ginger coming up the path he could always come back with them. In the end he decided that if they had not returned by the time the moon rose he would go in search of them.

He was in some doubt what to do about Dusky, but thought it would be better if he remained behind; the old man, however, when the project was broached, had his own opinion on this, and declared that nothing would induce him to remain in a place which, without any doubt, was haunted by the ghosts of the past.

To this Algy had to submit, and as the silver moon crept up over the distant horizon he set off down the staircase, carrying his rifle, with Dusky following close behind.

By daylight the others had found it a difficult and dangerous journey, but in the uncertain moonlight Algy found the descent an unnerving ordeal. However, he did not hurry, but adopting the principle of slow but sure, moved cautiously down the cornice, hardly looking at the terrible void that fell away on his left. He still hoped to meet the others coming up, but there was no sign of life; no sound broke the heavy silence. He and Dusky might have been the only people on earth.

It was Dusky who, in the first light of the false dawn, spotted the cairn that marked the message which Biggles had left against just such an emergency. Algy picked up the paper, read it, and made Dusky acquainted with its contents.

'They may be all right, but it's strange they should stay away so long,' he said. 'The only thing we can do is go on to the valley and try to locate them.'

They had no difficulty in finding it, and making their way down the rocks, paused to consider the situation, for there was no indication as to which direction they should take; to march straight into the village struck Algy as being a dangerous undertaking, one that might do more harm than good.

Then, as they stood there, in the pitch blackness that precedes the true dawn, they became aware of a curious, not to say alarming, sound. It was a low snarling, punctuated from time to time by a crash, as if a heavy body was being flung against an obstruction. Having listened for a while, Algy asked Dusky what he thought it could be.

The old man answered at once that the snarling could only be caused by a wild beast. He thought it was in a cage, trying to free itself, and he offered to confirm this. Algy assenting to the proposal, he crept away into the darkness.

Not for a moment did it occur to Algy that the sound had any direct connection with Biggles and Ginger. There was no reason why it should. He had no objection to Dusky going off scouting, although for his part he preferred to remain where he was until it became light enough for him to get a better idea of his surroundings.

Pink dawn was beginning to flush the eastern sky when Dusky returned. He said no word, but beckoned urgently. Algy knew that the old man had discovered something, and without a question followed him. Descending to the foot of the rocks, they went on for some distance, keeping clear of the village, and after a while it became obvious that Dusky was making his way towards some outbuildings. As they drew nearer the snarling became louder, and it was clear that the beast, whatever it was, was in one of them. Then, in an interval of silence, came a low mutter of voices, and Algy thought he recognized Ginger's. He now took the lead, and went forward quickly.

Ten yards from the nearest building he stopped, listened for a moment, and then called sharply, 'Biggles – is that you?'

The answer came instantly. 'Yes, we're in here.'

Algy went forward again, and after a minute or two grasped the situation. He found that the building was, in fact, a cage divided into two compartments. In one of them was a black panther. As he came up it was tearing with its claws at the far side of its cage, but as soon as it saw him it turned its attention to him with a rush that made him take a quick pace backwards. However, when he saw that the bars held firmly he moved nearer, and, dimly, for it was not yet properly light, made out Biggles and Ginger in the background. Without waiting for explanations he cocked the rifle and took aim at the beast.

Biggles uttered a sharp cry. 'Don't shoot!'

'Why not?' demanded Algy, lowering the weapon. 'The shot will bring a crowd here,' Biggles told him tersely. 'Try to find a way of getting us out. It doesn't matter about the animal.'

Algy soon saw the wisdom of this, but a quick reconnaissance revealed that escape was not going to be easy. There was a door to the compartment in which the others were confined, but it was heavily built, and locked, and without the key he was helpless. He passed this information on to Biggles, and then explored farther. The door of the animal's cage was, he discovered, operated from above, as was also the partition, the raising of which would throw the two compartments into one.

'I'd better shoot the brute,' he told Biggles desperately. 'I could then lift the dividing bars, and by opening the door of the cage, let you out.'

'All right – go ahead,' agreed Biggles. 'As soon as we're out we'll make a dash for the stairway.'

Algy raised his rifle, but before he could fire a cry of alarm from Dusky brought him round facing the village. There was no need to look farther. A dozen men, mostly natives, but with some white men among them, were racing towards the spot. One fired a revolver as he ran.

673

Seeing that it was now too late to put his plan into operation, Algy's first thought was to take cover and try to hold the crowd at bay. Dusky was already on his way to the rear of the buildings, and he followed him, but even as he ran he got an idea that speeded him on.

'Help me up!' he shouted to Dusky, and using the old man's back as a vaulting horse, he scrambled on the roof of the building. Shouts from the oncoming crowd told him that he had been seen, but he gave no heed. Dropping the rifle, he seized the lever which operated the door of the animal's cage, and dragged it back. The door swung open. The panther was not slow to take advantage of the opportunity to escape, and shot out into the open, a streak of black, snarling fury. For a moment it crouched, as if uncertain which way to go; then it saw the crowd, which had stopped at its appearance, and the matter was no longer in doubt. It hated the men on sight, and went towards them like an arrow. The crowd fled, scattering.

Algy would dearly have loved to watch the rest, but there was no time. He raised the partition, and a moment later had the satisfaction of seeing Biggles and Ginger bolt out through the door by which the panther had vacated its prison.

'The stairway!' shouted Biggles. 'Make for the stairway.'

Algy snatched up his rifle, dropped to the ground, and in another second all four were in flight towards the rocks. A volley of shots made them look round, and they were just in time to see the panther fall. It had overtaken one of the white men and pulled him down, but the King of the Forest, with a courage worthy of a better cause, emptied his revolver into the animal's sleek flank.

'Keep going!' shouted Biggles. 'If we can reach the stairway we can hold them.'

Shouts told them that the Tiger was rallying his men to resume the pursuit, and they waited for no more. A few shots were fired as they scrambled up the rocks, but the shooting was wild and the bullets did no harm.

'Good,' panted Biggles as they reached the top. 'Take cover, everybody. Algy, lend me that rifle.'

Crouching behind a rock, he took quick aim and fired at the Tiger. But the run had unsteadied him, and the shot missed. However, it made their pursuers dive for cover. Not that they remained still. They spread out fanwise, and Biggles knew that no good purpose could be served by remaining where they were.

'We'll go on up and get back to the machine,' he decided.

In single file they began the long ascent, Biggles, still carrying the rifle, bringing up the rear. He knew, of course, that they would be followed, and was sorry in a way that it had been necessary to reveal the continuation of the staircase, of which, he felt sure, the Tiger was in ignorance.

For half an hour nothing happened, and they toiled on, naturally finding the ascent more arduous than the descent. Then, round a shoulder of rock far below them, appeared the Tiger and his men, also in single file, for the steps were not wide enough to permit the passage of two people abreast. Biggles knew that they, too, must have been seen. He did not shoot, for the range was considerable, and the mounting sun was already causing the air to quiver, making accurate shooting impossible. However, he kept an eye on their pursuers, and presently saw five men, natives, forge rapidly ahead.

'The Tiger has sent some Indians forward,' he told the others. 'They may be used to this sort of thing, and no doubt the Tiger hopes they'll overtake us. There's nothing to worry about at the moment; if they get too close we'll give them something that should discourage them. Keep going; we're still some way from the top.'

For an hour they stuck doggedly to their task, which, as time went on, strained their resources to the utmost. The heat became intense, and they were all breathing heavily, although they were still far from the top.

'I think it will pay us to take a breather,' announced Biggles presently. 'We shall never stand this pace right to the top.' He halted at a bend. 'This will suit us,' he continued, looking back.

Three hundred yards beyond them was another bend, beyond which it was not possible to see.

'The first man who pokes his nose round that corner is going to meet a piece of lead coming the other way,' announced Biggles, adjusting his sights, and holding the rifle at the ready.

Squatting on the steps, they recovered their breath. All were thirsty, but there was no water to be had, so no one commented on it. Ten minutes passed, and Biggles was just standing up preparatory to giving the order to march, when, at the lower bend, an Indian appeared. From the abrupt manner in which he stopped it was apparent that he was aware of his danger; but he did not withdraw; he said something to those behind him, the sound being clearly audible in the still air.

Biggles's rifle cracked, and the Indian vacated his position with alacrity, although whether he had been hit or not the comrades could not tell.

'That'll give them something to think about, anyway,' observed Biggles, giving the order to march.

Twice during the next hour he halted and surveyed the winding track behind them. There were places where it was possible to see for a considerable distance, but there was no sign of the Indians.

'I don't understand it,' he muttered, frowning. 'I can hardly think that they've gone back. However, as long as they don't interfere with us I don't care what they do.'

They went on and shortly before midday reached the top of the steps.

'The machine is still all right, anyway,' remarked Ginger, noting that it was standing as they had left it.

'We'll go across and have something to eat,' declared Biggles.

Hardly had the words left his lips when a rifle cracked, surprisingly close, and a bullet whistled over his shoulder to smack against the rock behind him. So astonished was he that he looked around in amazement, trying to make out the direction from which the shot had come, but there was nothing to indicate it. As, realising his danger, he dashed for cover, there came another shot.

'Where are they coming from?' exclaimed Algy, in tones of surprise and alarm.

'I don't know, but I suspect those Indians know more about this place than we do,' answered Biggles, peering cautiously at the surrounding rocks. 'Somehow they must have got level with us by another route. If we aren't careful they may outflank us. I think we'd better make a dash for the machine and find a healthier parking place.'

'You mean – take off?' queried Ginger.

'Yes.'

'Where are you going to make for?'

'The river – there's nowhere else we can go. Besides, we don't want to get too far away. We'll find a quiet anchorage and think things over. When I give the word, run flat out for the machine. We'll open out a bit, so as not to offer a compact target. Ready? Go!'

Jumping up, they all ran towards the machine, but the moment they left cover several shots were fired, which revealed that more than one rifle was being used. However, none of the shots came very close, which struck Biggles as odd until he saw a piece of fabric ripped off the hull of the aircraft.

'They're shooting at the machine!' he shouted. 'The rest of you get in and start up, while I hold them off.'

They were now within a score of paces of the *Wanderer*. Choosing a shallow depression, Biggles threw himself into it and opened a brisk fire on the spot from where the shots were coming. Puffs of smoke gave the enemies' position away, and he saw that in some way the Indians had reached the high rocks beyond the village, where they had taken cover. He emptied the magazine of his rifle and then dashed to the machine, the engines of which had now been started. As he jumped into the cabin there was a cry of dismay from Ginger.

'They've got the tank!' he shouted. 'The petrol is pouring out.'

Glancing at the main tank, Biggles saw that this was indeed the case. A lucky shot had struck the tank a glancing blow low down, making a jagged hole, through which petrol was pouring at a rate that must empty the tank in a few minutes. The danger was instantly apparent, for without petrol they would be stranded; the aircraft would be useless, and their only means of getting away would be on foot, down the stairway.

For a moment Biggles tried to plug the hole with his handkerchief; but the spirit still trickled through, and he knew that it could only delay the inevitable end. To make matters worse, shots were still striking the machine, and it could only be a matter of seconds before one of them was hit. He dashed to the cockpit. They had, he saw, just a chance of getting away. If he could only get the machine off the ground, and over the rim of the plateau before the tank emptied itself, they might be able to glide to the river even though the engines were dead.

Algy saw Biggles coming, and guessing what he had in mind, vacated the seat. Biggles flung himself into it, and with a sweep of his hand knocked the throttle wide open. The engines roared. The machine began to move forward. He held the joystick and waited, knowing that it was going to be a matter of seconds. If the engines would continue running for another half minute all might yet be well. If they failed – well, it was better not to think of that.

The machine, now with its tail up, raced on towards the rim of the plateau. Biggles eased the stick back gently, and it lifted. One engine missed fire, roared again, and then, just as the aircraft soared out over the blue forest far below, both died away altogether. The propellers stopped. An uncanny silence fell. But the machine was in the air, gliding towards the nearest loop of the distant river.

CHAPTER IX

New Perils

Had Biggles been asked if he thought the machine, now without motive power, would reach the river, and had he answered truthfully, he would have said 'no'; but he knew that it would be a near thing. He had about five thousand feet of height, and some five miles to go, which would normally be within the gliding range of a modern aeroplane. But the *Wanderer* was heavily loaded, and that made a lot of difference. Again, it was not gliding towards an aerodrome where he could be sure of a landing-ground free from obstructions. That part of the river towards which he was gliding – and this, of course, was the nearest part – was new to him, and even if he reached it, there was always a possibility of it turning out to be a death-trap, by reason of dead trees floating on the surface, or sand-banks, or even the giant water-lilies that flourished in many places. However, he had no alternative but to go on, hoping for the best.

The others were well aware of the gravity of the situation, but since they could do nothing about it either, they sat still, watching the grey ribbon of water grow ever more distinct.

Some minutes passed, the aircraft gliding sluggishly at little more than stalling speed. The altimeter now registered two thousand feet, and the river was still a good two miles away.

'You ought to just about do it,' Algy told Biggles calmly.

'Just about,' answered Biggles, smiling faintly.

The machine glided on, the air moaning softly over its wings. Nobody moved. Nobody spoke.

Ginger watched the river with a sort of helpless fascination. It seemed to float towards them, a narrow lane bordered by a spreading ocean of treetops. It was clear that the final issue would be a matter of inches.

Algy afterwards swore that he heard the topmost branches of the trees scrape against the keel as the aircraft just crept over them, to glide down on the water; but that was probably an exaggeration. Ginger sagged a little lower in his seat with relief as the immediate danger passed; provided that there were no obstacles floating on the river all would now be well. Actually there were obstructions, as Biggles afterwards found out, but partly by luck, and partly by skilful flying, he avoided them, and the *Wanderer* sent swarms of crocodiles scurrying as it surged to a standstill on a long, open reach.

Biggles sat back. 'Well, so far so good,' he announced. 'It's time we had a bite to eat. Ginger, get some grub out of the box.'

'Wouldn't it be better to make her fast to the bank first?' suggested Algy.

'It probably would – but how are we going to get to the bank?' returned Biggles.

Algy frowned as he realized the significance of Biggles's question. With the engine out of action they were as helpless as if they had been afloat on a raft without a paddle.

'I don't think we need worry about that,' resumed Biggles. 'We shall drift ashore presently, probably at a bend. As a matter of fact, it suits us to drift downstream, because sooner or later we ought to meet the petrol canoes coming up, and until we repair the tank, and get some juice into it, we're helpless.'

'And then what are you going to do?' inquired Ginger.

Biggles shrugged his shoulders. 'I don't know,' he confessed. 'It's a grim business, but we have at least discovered the Tiger's headquarters, and that's something. I feel inclined to go down to the coast and tell Carruthers about it, and leave it to him to decide on our next move. However, we'll go into that when we've had something to eat.'

Squatting on boxes in the little cabin, they made a substantial meal, leaving the *Wanderer* to choose its own course, and in this way perhaps half an hour passed.

It was Dusky who, not without alarm, suddenly called attention to the increased speed of the machine, which could be judged by the rate at which the forest trees on either side were gliding past. At Dusky's shout, the comrades broke off their conversation and climbed out on the hull.

One glance at the river ahead was enough to warn them of their peril, and Biggles could have kicked himself for not taking the possibility into account. Perhaps a quarter of a mile downstream the river plunged between two rocky hills; they were not very high, but they were quite sufficient to force the water into a torrent that boiled and foamed as it flung itself against boulders that had fallen from either side. Already the *Wanderer* was prancing like a nervous horse as it felt the surge of the current, turning slowly, sometimes floating broadside on in the middle of the river. Biggles looked swiftly at either bank in turn, but the nearest was a good fifty yards away, and this might as well have been a mile for all the hope there was of reaching it.

'If she hits one of those rocks she'll crumple like an eggshell!' shouted Algy, steadying himself as the machine gathered speed.

'I suppose it's no use trying to hook the bottom with an anchor?' suggested Ginger.

'No use at all,' answered Biggles promptly. 'Nothing will hold her now. Grab a spare spar, both of you, and try to fend her off when we come to the rocks. It's our only chance – but for heaven's sake don't fall overboard.'

So saying, he snatched up a spare strut and crawled forward until he was lying spread-eagled across the bows. His expression was hard as he looked at the rapids ahead, for there did not appear to be the slightest chance of the *Wanderer* surviving the ordeal that was now inevitable – at any rate, not unless the nose of the machine could be kept straight.

None of them could really say exactly what happened during the next ten minutes. The period was just a confused memory of foaming water and blinding spray. The *Wanderer* bucked and jumped like a live creature, yet somehow, between them, they managed to keep her fairly straight. The greatest mystery was that none of them fell overboard as they thrust with desperate energy at the rocks which seemed to leap up in their path. Then, suddenly, it was all over, and the machine floated smoothly on another stretch of tranquil water.

Biggles crawled back from his hazardous position on the bows, wringing the water from his hair and inspecting the palms of his hands, which had been blistered by the strut. The others were in much the same state, and they sank wearily down to recover their breath and their composure.

'In future we'd better keep an eye on where we're going,' muttered Ginger bitterly, gazing ahead as they rounded a bend.

His expression became fixed as he stared. Then, with a hoarse cry, he struggled to his feet. 'Look out, there's another lot ahead!' he yelled.

Biggles took one look in the direction in which Ginger was staring. Then he snatched up the end of the mooring-rope and dived overboard. Holding the line in his teeth, he struck out for the bank.

Had he not struck shallow water so that he could get his feet on the bottom sooner than he expected, it is unlikely that he would have reached it, for the *Wanderer* was already gathering speed as the river swept on towards the next lot of rapids. But having got his feet planted firmly on a shelving sandbank, he flung his full weight on the rope, and so caused the lightly floating aircraft to swing round near the bank lower down, close enough for Algy and Ginger to seize branches of overhanging trees, and hang on until the machine could be brought to a safe mooring.

'Who suggested this crazy picnic?' muttered Biggles sarcastically, as, dripping, he climbed aboard. 'I did,' grinned Ginger.

'Then perhaps you'll think of a way out of the mess we're in,' returned Biggles. 'There are rapids below us and rapids above us and our tank is dry. We look like staying here for some time. You might get the tank mended for a start – in case we need it again.'

'Okay,' agreed Ginger, and went to work. 'What are you going to do?' he inquired.

'Walk down the bank to the next lot of rapids, to see how bad they are,' answered Biggles. 'We've got to make contact with the petrol which Carruthers promised to send before we can do anything. Come on, Algy. You'd better come too, Dusky, in case we need your advice.'

Leaving Ginger alone, the others made their way, not without difficulty, down the riverbank, disturbing more than one alligator that lay basking in the stagnant heat. Presently it was possible to ascertain that the rapids stretched for nearly half a mile; they were worse than the first, and Biggles at once dismissed all idea of attempting to shoot them in the aircraft. Beyond the rapids the river resumed its even course, winding placidly through the tropical vegetation. They followed it for some time, but as there appeared to be no change, they were about to start on the return journey when Dusky halted, sniffing like a dog.

'What is it?' asked Biggles quickly.

Dusky's eyes opened wide as he whispered nervously that he could smell fire.

Biggles could not understand how this could be, for it seemed impossible that the green jungle, damp in the steaming heat, could take fire; but he followed Dusky, who was now creeping forward silently, every muscle tense, peering into the verdure ahead. After a little while he stopped, and, beckoning to the others, pointed.

Biggles, following the outstretched finger, saw that a little way in front, near the riverbank, the undergrowth had been cut and trampled down, obviously by human agency. In the centre of this area a fire still smouldered. Near it was a brown object, which presently he perceived was a human foot protruding from the debris. Flies swarmed in the still air.

'I'm afraid that fellow's dead, whoever he is,' murmured Algy in a low voice.

'Sure massa, he dead,' agreed Dusky.

Biggles went forward, and a moment later stood looking down at the dead body of a native; he wore blue dungaree trousers, and was clearly one of the more or less civilized natives of the coast. Biggles was still staring at the ugly scene, wondering what it portended, when a groan made him start, and a brief search revealed another native near the edge of the water. This one was not dead, but was obviously dying. Biggles knelt beside him and discovered a gunshot wound in his chest.

'Ask him who he is,' he told Dusky.

Dusky knelt beside the wounded man and spoke quickly in a language the others did not understand. The stranger answered weakly, and thereafter followed a disjointed conversation which went on for some minutes – in fact, until the wounded man expired.

Dusky stood up and turned a startled face to his companions. 'Dese men bring de petrol in one big canoe,' he announced. 'Dey get as far as dis and make camp; den Bogat's men come and dey all killed.'

'But where is the canoe, and the petrol?' asked Biggles in a tense voice.

Dusky pointed to the river, not far from the bank. 'De canoe sink dere,' he said. 'When Bogat's men rush de camp de paddlers try to get away, but bullets hit canoe and it sink.'

'When did this happen?'

'Last night, massa.'

Biggles turned to Algy and shrugged his shoulders helplessly. 'This is bad,' he said quietly. 'The petrol was our only chance of getting away.'

'But how on earth did the Tiger know that petrol was coming up the river?' demanded Algy.

Biggles laughed bitterly. 'Have you forgotten Chorro, Carruthers' assistant? He'd know all about it. As soon as Carruthers got back game as himself. He knew that it was not at all unlikely that his enemy was even then endeavouring to creep unseen to the cabin; but what the Indian would not expect, he told himself, was that he had left it. In fact, if that were so, then of the two positions he preferred his own, for it seemed to hold a certain advantage.

He had made his way for what he judged to be about two hundred yards when a gust of wind brought a flurry of snow-flakes with it. He stopped at once, almost overcome with dismay. It was no use going on. Not that there was much point in going back, he reflected bitterly. If there was going to be a heavy fall it would mean the end of everything. 'Still, I suppose I shall be better off inside than out here,' he thought morosely, as he stood up in the whirling flakes, knowing that there was no longer any need for him to remain prone. The snow effectually blotted out everything outside a radius of a few yards. Turning up his collar, he walked swiftly towards the cabin – or, since he could not see, where he imagined it to be.

It surprised him to find how far he had gone. Surely he should have reached the cabin by now? He began counting his paces. When he reached fifty he stopped, knowing that he must have passed his objective. Irritated, but without any alarm, he began to retrace his steps. Presently he broke into a run, only to pull up abruptly as he realized that he was lost. Even then he was not unduly perturbed, for he knew that the cabin could not be more than a hundred yards from where he stood. There was no need for him to lose his head, he told himself. Obviously, the thing to do was to retrace his steps in the thin mantle of snow which now covered the ground. But he soon discovered that this plan, while satisfactory in theory, was, in fact, impracticable, for his trail was obliterated almost as fast as he made it.

'Suppose Bogat's crowd is still hanging about?'

'I hadn't overlooked that possibility,' replied Biggles. 'We shall have to risk it. Come on, let's get back to the machine.'

They went back up the stream, and were relieved to find everything as they had left it. Ginger had just finished repairing the tank with a piece of sheet-metal. They told him of their discovery and what they proposed to do, and in a few minutes the necessary equipment for making a raft had been brought ashore – as well as weapons.

'I don't like the idea of leaving the machine,' muttered Algy.

'Nor do I, but we can't help it,' returned Biggles. 'If we work fast we ought to get the raft finished by nightfall, ready to start diving operations tomorrow as soon as it gets light. Let's go.'

They marched back to the site of the burnt-out camp, and after burying the unfortunate natives, set about collecting timber suitable for their purpose, in which respect they were guided by Dusky, who knew which wood was light and easy to handle. Some, although Ginger could hardly believe this until he had proved it, was so hard that it turned the edge of an axe.

The sun was sinking in the west by the time the task was finished, and a rough but serviceable raft, moored to a tree, floated against the bank, ready for the morning. Biggles decided that it was too late to start diving operations that day, so, picking up the tools, they made their way back towards the *Wanderer*.

They had not gone very far when, with squeals and grunts, a party of small, hairy pigs came tearing madly down the riverbank. Ginger's first impression was that the animals intended to attack them, but the peccaries – for as such Dusky identified them – rushed past with scarcely a glance. Nevertheless, Dusky eyed them apprehensively, and as they disappeared down the river he held up his hand for silence, at the same time adopting a listening attitude.

In the sultry silence Ginger was aware of vague rustlings in the undergrowth around them, and, exploring with his eyes, soon located the cause. Small creatures, the presence of which had been unsuspected, were leaving their nests in the rotting vegetation and climbing rapidly up the trunks of the trees. He saw a white bloated centipede, a foot long, its numerous ribs rippling horribly under its loathsome skin; a tarantula, a hairy spider as big as his hand, went up a nearby tree in a series of rushes, seeming to watch the men suspiciously every time it halted. This sinister activity gave Ginger an unpleasant feeling of alarm, but he said nothing. He was looking at Dusky askance when, from a distance, came a curious sound, a murmur, like the movement of windblown leaves in autumn.

Dusky muttered something and hurried forward, and there was a nervousness in his manner that confirmed Ginger's sensation of impending danger.

'What is it?' he asked anxiously.

'De ants are coming,' answered Dusky.

At the same time he broke into a run, and it was with relief that Ginger saw the *Wanderer* just ahead of them, for by this time the clamour around them had increased alarmingly. Insects and reptiles of many sorts were climbing trees or plunging through the undergrowth; monkeys howled as they swung themselves from branch to branch; birds screeched as they flew overhead. It was an unnecessary commotion about a few ants – or so it seemed to Ginger; but then he had not seen the ants.

It was not until they were within fifty yards of the machine that he saw them, and even then it was a little while before he realized that the wide black column which rolled like molten tar towards them just above the place where the machine was moored was, in fact, a mass of ants. Some, in the manner of an advance guard, were well out in front, and he saw that they were fully an inch and a half long. Nothing stopped the advance of the insects as they ran forward, surmounting with frantic speed every obstacle that lay across their path. The noise made by the main body, the movement of countless millions of tiny legs over the vegetation, was a harsh, terrifying hiss, that induced in Ginger a feeling of utter helplessness. This, he thought, was an enemy against which nothing could avail.

There was a wild rush for the *Wanderer*, and they reached it perhaps ten yards ahead of the insect army. Ginger gave an involuntary cry as a stinging pain, like a red-hot needle, shot into his leg; but he did not stop – he was much too frightened. He literally fell into the machine.

Biggles was the last to come aboard. The mooring-rope was already black with ants, so he cut it, allowing it to fall into the water. The machine at once began to drift with the current, so he ran forward, and dropping the anchor, managed to get it fast in weeds, or mud. At any rate, further progress was checked, for the current near the shore was not strong.

Ginger pulled up the leg of his trousers and saw a scarlet patch of inflammation where the ant had bitten him.

'Get some iodine on that,' Biggles told him crisply, and he lost no time in complying, for the pain was acute.

Having done so he joined the others on the deck, from where, in silence and in safety, they watched the incredible procession on the bank. Ginger could not have imagined such a spectacle. The ground was black. Every leaf, every twig, was in motion, as if a sticky fluid was flowing over it. It was little wonder that he stared aghast, not knowing what to say.

'I've seen armies of foraging ants before, but never anything like this,' remarked Biggles. 'They clean up everything as they go. Heaven help the creature, man, beast or insect, that falls in their path.'

'How far do they stretch?' asked Ginger, for as yet he could not see the end of the procession.

Biggles asked Dusky, who announced that the column might extend for a mile, perhaps farther. He had seen the same thing many times, and assured them that if the ants were unmolested they would soon pass on.

The comrades sat on the deck and watched until it was dark, but it was some time later before the volume of sound began to diminish. They then retired to the cabin, where Biggles switched on a light and produced some tins of food.

'We may as well eat, and then get some sleep,' he suggested. 'We've got to make an early start tomorrow.'

Ginger went to sleep, to dream of ants. The forest had taken on a new horror.

CHAPTER X

Swift Developments

Ginger was awakened in the morning by a wild shout from Biggles, a shout that brought him, still half dazed with sleep, to the deck. It was just beginning to get light, and it did not take him long to see what was amiss. The water, which normally was black, was now streaked with yellow, and was swirling past at a speed sufficient to cause the *Wanderer* to drag her anchor. There was, as far as he could see, no reason for this, and he said so.

'It must be raining higher up the river,' declared Biggles. 'The water is rising fast. We shall have to tie up to the bank – the anchor won't hold.'

By this time they were all on deck, and between them the machine was soon made fast to a tree-stump. Biggles stared for a minute at the sky, and then at the river.

'We've no time to lose if we're going to get that petrol,' he said urgently. 'Apart from the current, with all this mud coming down we soon shan't be able to see a thing under the water. Algy, you stay here and look after things. Ginger, Dusky come with me.' So saying, Biggles picked up a length of line, jumped ashore, and set off down the riverbank at a run, Ginger and Dusky following close behind. Ginger noted that there was little, if anything, to mark the passage of the ants.

It did not take them long to reach the raft, where the water was only just becoming discoloured. Biggles carried a large piece of loose rock on board, and pushed off; then, using the rock as an anchor, he brought the raft to a stop over the spot where the canoe had sunk – or as near to it as he could judge. Throwing off his jacket, and holding a spare piece of line, he prepared to dive.

'Here! What about the alligators?' cried Ginger in alarm.

'I shall have to risk it,' answered Biggles curtly. 'We've got to get some petrol, or we're sunk. Dusky, you keep your eyes open for danger.' With this Biggles disappeared under the water.

He had to make three dives before he located the sunken canoe. After this there was a short delay while the raft was moored directly over it. Then the work was fairly straightforward, and had it not been for the rising water, and the discoloration, it would probably have been possible to salve every petrol-can, for Biggles had only to tie the line to a handle while the others hauled it up. As it was, by the time seven cans had been recovered the river was in full spate, and the raft straining at its moorings in a manner which told them that their position was already perilous. With some difficulty they got the raft, with its precious load, to the bank, after which began the work of transporting the cans to the aircraft. By the time this was done the river was a swirling flood, bringing down with it debris of all sorts.

'It's getting worse,' announced Algy, with a worried frown, as they poured the petrol into the tank. 'We shall never hold the machine here in this, and if she gets into the rapids she's a gonner.'

'We'll go down the river to the coast and report to Carruthers,' declared Biggles. 'It's no use going on with our job while that rat Chorro is at large, advising the Tiger of all our movements. We've got just about enough petrol to do it. Get those empty cans ashore, and stand by to cast off.' So saying, Biggles went through to the cockpit.

Algy went forward to cast off the mooring-rope, but seeing that he was having difficulty with it, for the *Wanderer* was pulling hard, Ginger went to his help. At the same time Dusky started throwing the empty cans on the bank. In view of what happened, these details are important. Actually, just what did happen, or how it happened, none of them knew – beyond the fact that the line suddenly snapped. Ginger made a despairing grab at it, slipped, clutched at Algy, and dragged him overboard with him. The *Wanderer*, breaking free, bucked, and Dusky, caught in the act of throwing, also went overboard. All three managed to reach the bank, while the *Wanderer* went careering downstream. From the bank, Algy, Ginger and Dusky stared at it with horror-stricken eyes, too stunned to speak, helpless to do anything.

Ginger felt certain that the machine would be wrecked in the rapids. Not for a moment did he doubt it. And it was not until he heard the *Wanderer*'s engines come to life that he realized that Biggles still had a chance. He could no longer see the machine, for overhanging trees, and a bend in the river, hid it from view. But when, presently, the aircraft appeared in the air above them, and he knew that Biggles had succeeded in getting off, he sat down limply, weak from shock.

Algy looked at the machine, and then at the river.

'He'll never dare to land again,' he announced.

'He'd be a fool to try,' declared Ginger. 'At least, not until the flood has subsided,' he added.

They watched the *Wanderer* circle twice; then, as it passed low over them, something white fluttered down, and they made haste to collect it. It was an empty tin; in it was a slip of paper on which Biggles had written, 'Wait. Going to coast.'

'That's the wisest thing he could do – go down and fill the tank, and let Carruthers know about Chorro,' remarked Ginger. 'We shan't take any harm here for a few hours.'

'I hope you realize that we've no food, and that we haven't a weapon between us except Dusky's knife,' muttered Algy.

'In that case we shall have to manage without,' returned Ginger.

'Food – me find,' put in Dusky confidently, indicating the forest with a sweep of his arm.

'You mean you can find food in the forest?' asked Algy hopefully.

'Sure, boss, I find.'

'What sort of food?'

'Honey – roots – fruit, maybe.'

'Good. In that case we might as well start looking for lunch.'

'You stay – I find,' answered Dusky. 'Plenty fever in forest. I go now.'

'All right, if that's how you want it,' agreed Algy. Dusky disappeared into the gloomy aisles of the jungle.

For some time Algy and Ginger sat on a log gazing moodily at the broad surface of the river. There was little else they could do, for they dare not risk leaving the spot, in case Dusky should return and wonder what had become of them. It did not occur to either of them that they were in any danger. Perhaps they felt that in such a case Dusky would have warned them, although later they agreed that they were both to blame for what happened – but then it was too late.

They did not even see where the natives came from. There was a sudden rush, and before they realized what was happening they were both on their backs, held down by a score or more of savage-looking Indians armed with spears and clubs, bows and arrows. It all happened in a moment of time. Still dazed by the suddenness of the attack they were dragged to their feet and marched away into the forest, menaced fiercely by the spears of their captors. They could do nothing but submit.

In this manner they covered some five miles, as near as they could judge, straight into the heart of the forest before the party halted in an open space on the bank of a narrow stream on which several canoes floated. A few primitive huts comprised the native village. Into one of these they were thrown, and a sentry was placed on guard at the entrance.

Inside, the light was so dim that they could see nothing distinctly, and Ginger was about to throw himself down to rest, for the long march through the oven-like atmosphere had reduced him to a state of exhaustion, when, to his utter amazement, a voice addressed him in English.

'Say, who are you?' inquired the voice, with a strong American drawl.

'Who on earth are *you*?' gasped Ginger when he had recovered sufficiently from his surprise to speak.

'Eddie Rockwell's the name,' came the reply.

'What the dickens are you doing here?' demanded Algy.

'Guess that's what I should ask you.'

Algy thought for a moment or two. 'We're explorers,' he announced, somewhat vaguely. 'We've got a plane, but our chief has gone to the coast for petrol. While he was away this mob set on us and brought us here. That's all. What about you?'

'My tale is as near yours as makes no difference,' answered Eddie quietly.

As their eyes became accustomed to the gloom the comrades saw that he was a young man in the early twenties, but in a sad state of emaciation. His clothes were filthy, and hung on him in rags.

'Having more money than sense, I was fool enough to allow myself to be persuaded to start on a treasure-hunt,' continued Eddie. 'My father told me that the whole thing was a racket, and I reckon he was about right – but of course I wouldn't believe it.'

'A treasure-hunt?' queried Ginger.

'I saw an advertisement in a paper that a couple of guys knew where a treasure was waiting to be picked up. The map they had looked genuine enough, and I fell for it. I financed the expedition, and everything was swell until we got here. Then my two crooked partners just beat it with the stores and left me stranded. If you've tried getting about in this cursed jungle, you'll know what I was up against. However, I did what I could. I blundered about till I struck a stream, and then started down it, figuring that sooner or later, if I could hold out, I'd come to the sea. Instead, I bumped into a bunch of Indians and they brought me here. I didn't care much, because I was pretty well all in. I'd been staggering about without grub for a fortnight, and the Indians did at least give me something to eat. They brought me here, and here I've been ever since. That's all there is to it.'

An idea struck Ginger. He realized that these must be the three Americans about whom Carruthers was so concerned. 'You've been here for some time, haven't you?' he asked.

'Sure.'

'How long?'

'Say, ask me something easier. Weeks, mebbe months.'

'These partners of yours,' resumed Ginger. 'Was one of them a tall, thin, jaundiced-looking bloke, with pale grey eyes and a big mouth, and the other a weedy-looking rat with hay-coloured hair and a wisp of moustache, stained with nicotine?'

Eddie uttered an exclamation of surprise. 'Say, that's them,' he answered quickly. 'I reckon you must have seen them?'

'You bet we have,' said Ginger bitterly, and then told their own story with more detail, including the events which had brought them into contact with the two white men in the Tiger's secret village. He also mentioned that the disappearance of the party had caused the authorities some trouble.

'Say, now, what d'you know about that!' exclaimed Eddie when he had finished. 'Joe Warner and Silas Schmitt – they were my two precious partners – told me that there was a guy hereabouts who was boss of the whole works, but I didn't realize that he was such a big noise as you make out.'

'Your partners did, evidently,' put in Algy. 'They must have known that it was impossible for you to operate here without barging into him or his crowd, so it looks to me as if, having got you to finance them to the spot, they changed sides and left you in the lurch, knowing that you would never be able to get to the coast.'

'That's how it looks to me,' agreed Eddie. 'Can you talk the lingo these natives use?'

'Not a word.'

'What do you reckon they'll do with us?'

Algy shook his head. 'I've no idea, but judging from their behaviour so far it won't be anything pleasant.'

'Then you reckon we haven't a chance of getting away?'

'I wouldn't say that. Our chief is down the river, but he'll come back. Moreover, we've got a native servant about somewhere. It just happened that he was out of camp when the attack occurred, but when he gets back he'll guess what has happened, and he ought to be able to trail us. So, on the whole, things may not be as bad as they look.'

Eddie seemed to take encouragement from Algy's optimism. The conversation lapsed, Algy peering through one of the many flaws in the side of the hut in an endeavour to see what was going on outside. It seemed that the natives who had captured them were celebrating the event, with considerable noise.

He was still watching when, without warning, a volley of shots rang out from the edge of the jungle. Several Indians fell. More shots followed. There were wild shouts, and the assembled Indians broke up in disorder, scattering and flying for their lives, some into the forest, others flinging themselves into their canoes and paddling away in a panic. Among these was the native who had been on duty at the door of the hut, so there was nothing to prevent those inside from leaving.

For a few seconds Algy hoped that the attack might have been launched by Biggles, who in some miraculous way had returned with assistance; but when Bogat appeared, a rifle under his arm, followed by his gang, his heart, and his hopes, sank.

Bogat saw the three white men at once, and his lips parted in a villainous leer. He covered them with his rifle, and in another moment they were surrounded.

'It looks as if we've fallen out of the frying-pan into the fire,' murmured Ginger despondently.

'Who is this guy?' asked Eddie.

Briefly, Ginger told him. There was no time to go into details, for a rope was produced; the prisoners' hands were tied behind them, and a rope was passed from one to the other. Their captors, after setting fire to the huts, formed up in a rough column. Bogat took his place at the head of it, and the party moved off into the forest.

'Where do you suppose they're taking us?' asked Eddie.

'I should say we're on our way to see the King of the Forest,' returned Ginger.

A burly half-caste flourished a whip, and put an end to further conversation.

The prisoners trudged on in silence through the green jungle.

CHAPTER XI

The Snake

As it transpired, Biggles had just enough petrol to reach the coast. He at once sought Carruthers, who was not a little surprised to see him, and made him acquainted with all that had happened. Carruthers was furious when he heard of the fate of the emergency petrol canoe; but when the real character of Chorro was revealed he was aghast, for he had always regarded him as a trustworthy servant. Unfortunately, nothing could be done about him at the moment, for by a coincidence Chorro had just applied for, and had been granted, three weeks' leave of absence.

'Where's he gone?' inquired Biggles.

'Up the river,' answered Carruthers frankly. 'He is supposed to have a bungalow somewhere, a matter of two or three days' journey. He's been up the river before.'

Biggles smiled grimly. 'It's more likely that he's making a visit to the Tiger, to report on the situation.'

Carruthers nodded. 'I'm afraid you're right,' he replied slowly. 'Never mind; I'll deal with the scoundrel when he comes back.'

'If he does come back,' put in Biggles smoothly.

Carruthers gave him an odd look, but made no further comment on the subject. Instead, he asked Biggles what he intended doing.

'Have a bath, a square meal, fill up with petrol and take off again,' Biggles told him. 'I'm anxious to get back to the others.'

'I still don't see how we're going to get hold of the Tiger and his crew,' remarked Carruthers, with a worried frown. 'I'd come back with you, but at the moment, with the Governor away, I can't leave – at least, not for any length of time.'

'I must admit it isn't an easy proposition,' acknowledged Biggles. 'However, we're getting the hang of things, and sooner or later our chance will come.'

Further details were discussed, but nothing definite was arranged, and about two hours later, with full tanks, Biggles set off back up the river, relieved to see that the flood, which apparently had been caused by a local storm, had subsided.

He experienced a pang of uneasiness as he circled low over the camp and saw no sign of the others; but when he landed, taxied up to the bank and jumped ashore, still without them putting in an appearance, his uneasiness turned to alarm. For a few minutes he stood still, occasionally calling, but when this produced no result he began to examine the ground more closely.

Actually there was nothing to show what had happened – not until, in the long grass, he found a broken arrow. Even then he hoped that the arrow might be an old one that had lain there for a long time; but when he looked at the fracture, and saw that it was recent, he knew it was no use deceiving himself. Indians had been to the camp; this was so obvious that he no longer marvelled at the absence of Algy and Ginger. He spent some time hunting about in the bushes, dreading what he might find, and breathed a sigh of relief when his fears proved groundless. 'They're prisoners,' he told himself, and that was bad enough.

For once he was at a loss to know what to do for the best. He dismissed all thought of the Tiger. He was concerned only with Algy and Ginger, and, to a less extent, Dusky, whom he had left with them. Naturally, they would have to be rescued, but how he was to set about this in the jungle he could not imagine. No project that he could remember had seemed so hopeless.

Not for a moment did he relax his vigilance, for he realized that what had happened to the others might also happen to him. He lit a cigarette and tried to reconstruct the scene, and in so doing came upon the trail leading into the forest. This was a clue which he had not expected, for knowing that the Indians did most of their travelling by canoe, he had assumed that the attack had come from the river.

Now that he had something tangible to go on, he returned to the *Wanderer*, moored the aircraft securely to the bank and made it less conspicuous by throwing reeds and palm fronds over the wings. This done, he went to the cabin, selected a heavy Express rifle from the armoury, filled a cartridge-belt with ammunition and the pockets of his jacket with biscuits. Then, after a final glance round, he set off along the trail, which could be followed without difficulty.

He had not gone far when he was brought to an abrupt halt by a hoarsely whispered 'Massa.' He recognized the voice at once, but even so, his nerves tingled with shock.

'Dusky!' he called tersely. 'Where are you?' Dusky dropped out of a tree and hurried to him.

'What happened?' asked Biggles shortly, wondering how the old man had escaped.

This Dusky soon explained. In mournful tones he related how he had gone into the forest to find food, a quest which – fortunately for him, as it happened – had taken him into a tree. The tree was at no great distance from the camp, and the sound of the assault had reached his ears. From his hiding-place he had watched Algy and Ginger being led away into the jungle. He apologized for not going to their rescue, but pointed out that, as the only weapon he had was a knife, he was in no position to take on a crowd of Indians. This Biggles did not dispute. Indeed, when Dusky explained that he had remained in hiding, waiting for him to come back so that he could tell him what had happened, he congratulated him on his common sense.

'I suppose you've no idea where the Indians have gone?' asked Biggles.

Dusky shook his head, saying that he did not know the district, but gave it as a matter of opinion that the Indian village would not be far away.

'In that case we shall have to try to find it,' Biggles told him.

Dusky agreed, but without enthusiasm.

They continued on down the trail, Dusky now leading the way and stopping from time to time to listen. This went on for an hour, by which time, although they did not know it, they were getting near the village.

The first intimation of this came when shouts and yells reached their ears, sounds which Dusky interpreted correctly, as the Indian way of making jubilation over the capture of the white men.

They now proceeded with more caution, and were peering forward through the undergrowth hoping to catch sight of the village when a volley of shots sent them diving for cover. The shots, however, did not come their way, which puzzled Biggles more than a little. Dusky went up a tree like a squirrel, to return in a few moments with the unwelcome news that Bogat and his gang had attacked the Indians, scattered them, and taken over their prisoners. He also announced that there was another white man with Algy and Ginger.

Biggles wasted no time in futile guessing as to who this could be. He was too concerned about Algy and Ginger. He thought swiftly, undecided how to act.

'How many men has Bogat got with him?' he asked Dusky.

Dusky opened and closed his hands, twice.

'Twenty, eh?' muttered Biggles.

To attack twenty men single-handed – for Dusky could hardly be counted on – would be, he saw, a rash undertaking. With the advantage of surprise in his favour he might shoot two or three of them, but in the ensuing battle, even if he escaped, Algy and Ginger would be certain to get hurt. He perceived, too, that if he failed in an attempt at rescue now, the odds against him in future would be worse, for once his presence was revealed strict guard would be kept. Taking all the factors into consideration, he decided that it would be better to wait for a more favourable opportunity. Perhaps a chance would come after dark.

At this point Dusky, who had again ascended a tree, returned to say that Bogat and his men, with their prisoners, were moving off through the forest. This at once upset Biggles's plans, for he had assumed that Bogat would remain in the village for a while. To attack him while he was on the march was obviously out of the question, so he took the only course that remained open, which was to allow Bogat's party to go on and follow as close behind as was reasonably safe.

He told Dusky his plan, and the old man agreed, so after waiting for a little while to give Bogat a start, they once more took up the trail.

Biggles of course had not the remotest idea of where they were going, nor even if they were travelling north or south, for the green jungle hemmed them in on both sides, and overhead. Nor, for a long time, did Dusky know; but eventually the trail crossed another which he recognized as one he had used when collecting chicle for the Tiger.

'I reckon Bogat go to de Tiger's village,' he announced.

'But that's up in the mountains,' Biggles pointed out.

Dusky nodded. 'Sure. By-um-by we come to old ruins at bottom of steps. Maybe Bogat stop dere; maybe he go up steps to de king.'

'You're sure you know where we are?'

'Yes, I'se sure, massa.'

'How far is it from here to the foot of the steps?'

'Half an hour's march – maybe a little more, or less.' .

'If we're as close as that, then there must be a risk of our running into some of Bogat's Indians, chicle-collectors, or labourers.'

'Tha's right, massa.'

'In that case we'd better stay here and do a bit of thinking. Let's find a place where we can hide until it gets dark.'

Dusky turned aside from the trail and soon found a sheltered retreat.

Here they remained until the light, always dim beneath the towering treetops, turned to the gloom of evening. They saw no one, and heard nothing except the natural sounds of the forest. Once, a panther, as black as midnight, slunk past with twitching tail; it saw them, and its baleful yellow eyes glowed, but it made no attempt to attack them, and Biggles was relieved to see it pass on.

Dusky shivered. 'Dat's de debbil,' he muttered nervously.

'Forget it, Dusky. Devil or no devil, I warrant that he'd find an expanding bullet from this rifle a nasty pill to take.'

'He put a spell on you, den you can't shoot.'

'He won't put any spell on me, I'll promise you,' returned Biggles lightly.

'I reckon you don't believe in spells, massa?'

'No, I don't,' answered Biggles shortly.

'Den you watch out dem big snakes dey call anaconda don't get you. Why, everyone knows dey bewitch folks.' Dusky shivered again.

'I've heard that tale before, but I should have to see it before I believed it,' murmured Biggles cynically.

'Maybe if you stay in de forest long enough, you see,' whispered Dusky knowingly.

Biggles did not pursue the subject, and nothing more was said for some time.

'You know, massa,' said Dusky after a long silence, 'I reckon de gang don't work down here no longer. You remember I said about de gang working at de bottom of de steps?'

'What makes you think they've gone?'

'Cos I don't hear nothing. Dem boys would sure be hollerin'.'

'Hollering? Why?'

'When Bogat's men crack dere whips on dere backs.'

'I see. How can we make sure? Shall I go and have a scout round?'

'Not you, massa,' said Dusky quickly. 'I go. I don't make no noise. You stay right here. I find out what's going on.'

'You're sure you'll be able to find me again?'

'Sure, massa. Dere's a wide stretch of savannah just ahead – I go dat way.'

'All right,' Biggles agreed, somewhat reluctantly, and Dusky glided away, to be quickly lost in the shadows of the primeval forest.

An hour passed, so Biggles judged, and he began to get worried, for it was now quite dark, and he was by no means certain – in spite of Dusky's assurance – that the old man would be able to find him again.

As time went on and there was still no sign of him, Biggles became definitely concerned. He stood up and whistled softly, but there was no reply. Something – he could not see what – slithered away in the undergrowth.

Staring in the direction which Dusky had taken Biggles became aware of an eerie blue glow, but taking a few paces forward, he soon solved the mystery. It was moonlight shimmering on a thin mist that had formed in an open glade, evidently the savannah to which Dusky had referred. He was about to turn back to the rendezvous, for he had no intention of leaving it, when a movement on the edge of the blue light caught his eye. It was, he saw from the shape of the object, a human being. Moving quickly but quietly to the edge of the clearing, he saw, as he hoped, that it was Dusky; but what the old man was doing he could not imagine. His movements were peculiar. With his arms held out in front of him, and his head thrown back, he was walking slowly across the savannah, step by step, towards the middle of it, in the uncertain manner of a person walking in his sleep.

As Biggles watched this strange scene he became aware of a queer musty smell that reminded him vaguely of something, but he could not remember what it was. At the same time he was assailed by a sensation of impending danger far stronger than anything he had ever before experienced. It was so acute that he could feel his nerves tingle, and presently beads of perspiration began to form on his forehead. This was something new to him, but his response was irritation rather than fear – perhaps because he could not see anything to cause alarm. Alert for the first sign of danger, walking softly, he moved forward on a line that would intercept Dusky somewhere about the middle of the savannah.

He could still see nothing to account for it, but as he advanced his sensations approached more nearly to real fear than he could ever recall. The only object that he could see, apart from the surrounding vegetation, was what appeared to be a black mound rising above the rough grass, and it was towards this that Dusky was stepping with slow, mechanical strides. A sudden suspicion darted into Biggles's brain, and he increased his pace; and even as he did so the mound moved. Something in the centre of it rose up sinuously, and remained poised. It was the head of a snake, but of such a size that Biggles's jaw dropped in sheer amazement.

For a moment he could only stare, thunderstruck, while the great flat head began to sway, slowly, with hideous grace. Then Biggles understood, and, with knowledge, power returned to his limbs.

'Dusky!' he shouted hoarsely.

But he might have remained silent for all the notice the old man took.

'Dusky!' he shouted again. 'Stop!'

The old man continued to walk forward, arms outstretched, as though to embrace a friend.

A cry of horror broke from Biggles's lips, and he dashed forward. At a distance of ten paces from the mound, which he now saw was coil after coil of snake, he halted, and raising his rifle, tried to take aim. Perspiration was pouring down his face. The stench was now overpowering. The mist caused the target to dance before his eyes, yet he knew that it would be worse than useless

'Dusky!' he shouted. 'Stop!'

to fire blindly into the body of the creature. It must be the head or nothing.

To make sure, there was only one thing to do, and he did it. He ran in close, took deliberate aim at the squat head now turning towards him, and fired.

In the silent forest the crash of the explosion sounded like the crack of doom. It was followed, first, by a wild scream from Dusky, who fell flat on his face, and, secondly, by a series of furious smashing thuds, as if a tornado was flinging down the mighty trees. The mound was no longer there; instead, the centre of the clearing was occupied by seemingly endless coils which, with insensate fury, threshed and looped over and among the rank grass. The end of one such loop caught Biggles in the back and sent him spinning, but he was up again in an instant; waiting only to recover the rifle, which had been knocked out of his hands, he caught Dusky by the scruff of the neck and dragged him like an empty sack towards the edge of the jungle. Behind him, the crashing and thumping continued with unabated fury, and he recalled vaguely having read somewhere that even if it is decapitated, the anaconda, the great snake of the Central American forests, may take twenty-four hours to die.

Dusky began to howl, so Biggles stopped and dragged him to his feet. 'Shut up,' he snapped. 'You're not hurt.'

'Oh, massa, oh, massa, I thought dat ole snake had got me,' moaned Dusky.

'Come on, let's get out of this,' growled Biggles, who, to his disgust, was more unnerved than he would have cared to admit.

Dusky, with many a nervous backward glance, followed him obediently back to the rendezvous.

'What made you go blundering towards the snake as if you were crazy?' inquired Biggles, half angrily, half curiously.

'I didn't see no snake, massa,' answered Dusky weakly.

'Then how did you know it was there?'

'I dunno, massa. I just knew, that's all.'

'So you went up to it? What were you going to do – play with it?' sneered Biggles.

'I just couldn't help going,' protested Dusky. 'De snake called me, and I went. I told you dem ole snakes bewitch folks.'

'Well, that one won't do any more bewitching,' replied Biggles crisply. He knew it was useless to argue with the old man, for nothing would shake his inherent conviction that he had been bewitched. Indeed, Biggles, to his annoyance, had an uneasy feeling that there might be something in the superstition after all, for he himself had been conscious of a sensation for which he could not account.

He could still hear the dying monster flinging itself about in the savannah, but he knew there was nothing more to be feared from it.

'Come on, Dusky, pull yourself together,' he exclaimed. 'I've blown the snake's head off, so it can't hurt you now. I only hope that my shot was not heard by Bogat or the Tiger. Are you feeling better?'

Dusky drew a deep breath. 'Yes, massa,' he said shakily, 'I'se better now. But dat ole snake—'

'Forget about it,' snapped Biggles.

'Yes, massa.'

'Were you on your way back?'

'Yes, massa.'

'Then you've been to the bottom of the steps? What did you discover?'

'Just like I said, massa – dey's gone.'

'Gone? What do you mean?'

Dusky explained that he had been right up to the foot of the stairway, to the spot where, at the time of his escape, he had been forced to dig with the gang working among the ruins. These diggings were now abandoned except for one old man who had been left in charge of a store-shed. This old fellow was well known to Dusky; he was one of the forced labourers, and consequently had no love for his taskmasters. For this reason Dusky had not hesitated to reveal himself; but except for the fact that everyone, including the newly captured white men, had gone to some distant place far up the stairway to dig in some fresh ruins, he knew nothing.

'If he said distant place, it rather looks as if they've gone right up to the top – to the plateau where we landed the machine,' said Biggles thoughtfully. 'There are some ruins up there, as we know. Had they only gone to the valley where the king's house is situated, he would have said so.'

Dusky agreed.

'Then we shall have to go up there, too,' announced Biggles.

'We get captured fo' sure,' muttered Dusky dubiously.

'I can't see any alternative,' continued Biggles. 'We can't just sit here and do nothing – they might be up there for months.'

'How about de airplane?' suggested Dusky.

'That's no use. We couldn't land on the plateau without being seen or heard. No, Dusky I'm afraid it means going up on foot, but you needn't come if you don't want to.'

'I don't want to, but I'll come,' offered the old man courageously.

Biggles thought for a moment. 'I'll tell you what, though. I shall be pretty conspicuous in these clothes. If I could make myself look a bit more like one of the workmen I might be taken for a slave if we are seen. Is there any chance of getting an old pair of blue pantaloons, like those you wear?'

Dusky thought he could get a pair at the store-shed.

'That old man won't betray us, I hope?'

'No, sah,' declared Dusky emphatically. 'He like the rest, be glad if you killed de Tiger so dey can all go back to de coast. He'll help us. I make your face brown with berries, den you look like a no-good Indian.'

Biggles smiled in the darkness. 'That's a good idea. Let's start. There will be less chance of our being seen if we travel by night. Can you find your way to the store-shed? I can't see a blessed thing.'

'You foller me, massa; I show you,' said Dusky simply.

They set off. Dusky was never at fault, but the darkness was such that progress was necessarily slow, and it was some time before they reached the foot of the steps, where, in the store-shed, the old watchman crouched over a smouldering fire. He made no difficulty about finding a pair of ragged pantaloons, and this was the only garment Biggles put on. Really, in the steamy heat of the jungle, he was glad of an excuse to discard his own clothes, which the watchman hid under a pile of stones. Without guessing how much was to depend on them, Biggles transferred his cigarettes and matches to the pocket of his new trousers.

He was in some doubt about the rifle, for it was obvious that he could not carry it without it being seen. In the end he decided to take it, even if it became necessary to hide it somewhere later on. His automatic he strapped to his thigh, under his trousers. Meanwhile, Dusky and the old watchman, taking a torch, had gone into the forest, and presently returned with a load of red berries. These were boiled in an iron pot, and after the liquid had cooled Biggles more or less gave himself a bath in it. Fortunately, he could not see himself, or he might have been alarmed at the change, for instead of being white he was now the colour of coffee.

Thanking the watchman, and promising him deliverance from servitude in the near future, Biggles and Dusky set off on their long climb up Jacob's Ladder.

They came first to the valley in which the village was situated; but all was silent, so they wasted no time there. Continuing on up the steps, they found themselves just below the summit about two hours before dawn – as near as Biggles could judge.

Here he turned off into a narrow ravine, for he was tired to the point of exhaustion. Dusky appeared to suffer no such inconvenience, and offered to keep watch while he, Biggles, had a short sleep, an offer that Biggles accepted, and ordered Dusky to wake him at the first streak of dawn.

He appeared to have done no more than close his eyes when Dusky was shaking him by the shoulder. Before dropping off to sleep he had made his plan, and this he now put into execution.

'You're going to stay here,' he told Dusky. 'You can take charge of the biscuits and the rifle and wait until I come back. If I'm not back within forty-eight hours you can reckon that I've been caught, in which case try to make your way to the coast and let Mr. Carruthers know what's happened. All being well, I shall be back here, with the others, before very long. Keep under cover.'

With this parting injunction, Biggles went back to the steps, and after a cautious reconnaissance moved on towards the top. He now proceeded with the greatest care; and it was as well that he did, for while he was still a hundred feet from the top he was mortified to see a man sitting on a rock, a rifle on his arm, obviously doing duty as sentry. To pass him without being seen was clearly impossible, so Biggles, after exploring the cliff on his left for the best place, scaled it, and went on through a chaos of rocks towards the plateau. Guided now by distant shouts, and the occasional crack of a whip, he worked his way forward, and presently as he hoped, found himself in a position overlooking the plateau.

To his right, perhaps a hundred yards away, sat the sentry at the head of the stairway. With this man he was not particularly concerned – at any rate, for the time being. Immediately in front, and slightly below, lay the ruined village. Here a gang of men was working with picks and shovels, or carrying away baskets of earth. Altogether, there were about forty workmen, and Biggles had no difficulty in picking out Algy, Ginger, and the stranger. They were working close together. Watching the gang were six guards, standing in pairs. They carried rifles. Another man, an enormous Indian, walked amongst the labourers swishing a vicious-looking whip. Not far away, in the shade of a ruined house, squatted the Tiger and his two white companions. Close behind them stood two natives in tawdry uniforms; they also carried rifles, and were evidently a sort of bodyguard. Beyond, shimmering in the heat of the morning sun, the plateau lay deserted.

For some time Biggles lay still, surveying the scene thoughtfully. A big patch of grotesque prickly pear attracted his attention, and he saw that if he moved along a little to the left he could use this as a screen to cover an advance into the village. Once among the houses, it should, he thought, be possible to get right up to the gang of workmen, and so make contact with Algy and Ginger – which was his main object. Beyond that he had no definite plan.

Like a scouting Indian he backed down from his elevated position and began working his way towards the prickly pear.

CHAPTER XII

Ginger Gets Some Shocks

When Algy, Ginger and Eddie had been marched off through the forest by Bogat they did not know where they were being taken, but, naturally, they could make a good guess. Unless Bogat had some scheme of his own, it seemed probable that they would be taken to the Tiger. This suspicion was practically confirmed when they reached the foot of the stairway. Two hours later, utterly worn out, and in considerable discomfort from insect bites and scratches, they were standing before the King of the Forest, who eyed them with undisguised satisfaction.

In his heart, Ginger expected nothing less than a death sentence, but that was because he did not realize the value of labour in the tropics. It was, therefore, with relief that he received the news that they were to be put in the slave-gang. Algy, being older, perceived that this was, in fact, little better than a death sentence; that without proper food, clothes, and medical treatment, they were unlikely to survive long in a climate which sapped the vitality even of the natives. However, he agreed with Ginger's optimistic observation that while they were alive there was hope; for, after all, Biggles was still at large. Whether or not he would ever learn what had happened to them was another matter. They were not to know that Dusky had been a witness of the attack.

They were in evil case by the time they reached the plateau, for they had been given only a little maize bread and water, barely enough to support life. The stench of the stone building, little better than a cattle-pen, into which on arrival they were herded with the other slaves, all Indians or half-castes, nearly made Ginger sick. Life under such conditions would, he thought, soon become intolerable.

Tired as they were, sleep was out of the question, and they squatted miserably in a corner, waiting for daylight. At dawn the door was opened by a man who carried a heavy whip; behind him were six other men carrying rifles. A quantity of food, in the nature of swill, was poured into a trough; upon this the slaves threw themselves like animals, eating ravenously with their hands, scooping up the foul mixture in cupped palms. The three white men took no part in this performance.

A few minutes only were allowed for this meal, after which the gang was formed into line and made to march past a shed from which picks and shovels were issued. Thus equipped, they went to what had once been the main street of the village, where a shallow trench had been opened. The gang-boss cracked his whip and the slaves started work, deepening and extending the trench.

'What do you suppose we're doing?' asked Ginger, getting into the trench behind Algy.

'Probably laying the telephone,' returned Algy sarcastically.

'Ha, ha,' sneered Ginger. 'Very funny.'

The gang-boss advanced, brandishing his whip. 'No talking,' he snarled.

Ginger drove his pick viciously into the sun-baked earth, and thereafter for a while work proceeded in silence.

'Here comes the Tiger,' murmured Algy presently.

'I'll tear the stripes off his hide one day,' grated Eddie. 'They can't do this to me.'

'It seems as though they're doing it,' grunted Algy.

Ginger went on working. There was no alternative, for he had no wish to feel the whip across his shoulders.

A few minutes later, standing up to wipe the perspiration out of his eyes, he noticed something. It was nothing spectacular. He had already realized, from the nature of the ground, which consisted largely of broken paving-stones, that the trench was crossing the foundations of what must have been a large building. One or two of the supporting columns, although they had been broken off short, were still standing; one such column was only a few paces away on his right, and without any particular interest his eyes came to rest on it. They were at once attracted to a mark – or rather, two marks. At first he gazed at them without conscious thought; then, suddenly, his eyes cleared as he made out that the marks were initials.

There were two sets, one above the other. The lower ones had almost been obliterated by the hand of time, after the manner of an old tombstone, but it was still possible to read the incised scratches. They were the letters E.C., and were followed by the date, 1860. There was no need for him to look closely at the date of the initials above to see that they were comparatively recent. The letters were L.R., and the date 1937. A suspicion, dim as yet, darted into Ginger's mind. He threw a quick glance at the gang-boss to make sure that he was not being watched, and then leaned forward to confirm that his reading of the lower initials had been correct. In doing this he put his hands on the end of a stone slab in such a way that his weight fell on it. Instantly it began to turn as though on a pivot, and he flung himself back with a gasp of fear, for he had a nasty sensation that he had nearly fallen into an old well. Another quick glance revealed the gang-boss walking towards him, so he went to work with a will, aware that he was slightly breathless.

The lash swished through the air, but without actually touching him. It was a warning, and he took it – at least, while the boss was within hearing. Then he spoke to Algy, who was working just in front of him.

'Algy,' he whispered, 'you remember Biggles talking about a treasure supposed to have been discovered in these parts by a fellow named Carmichael?'

'Yes.'

'What was his Christian name, do you remember?'

'No – why?'

'Do you remember the date?'

'Yes – 1860.'

'Then this is where Carmichael came. I've just seen his mark. Go on working – don't look round.'

Ginger now spoke under his arm to Eddie, who was behind him.

'Eddie, you said you came here on a treasure-hunt?'

'Sure I did.'

'There was a map, I believe?'

'That's right.'

'Who drew it?'

'A guy named Roberts – Len Roberts.'

'And was there a date?'

'Sure. It was 1937. What's the idea? Do you reckon we're on a treasure-hunt now?'

'I'm certain of it,' replied Ginger. 'You see that paper the Tiger is looking at? Does that look like your map?'

'It sure does.'

'Then it's the treasure we're after. We're driving a trench right across the area where it is supposed to be.'

At this point, much to Ginger's disgust, further conversation was interrupted by an Indian, who dropped into the trench between him and Eddie.

'Here, you, get out of the way,' grunted Ginger, hoping that the man would understand what he meant.

'Go on digging,' answered a voice quietly.

Ginger started violently, and nearly dropped his pick. His nerves seemed to twitch, for there was no mistaking the voice. It was Biggles.

'Go on digging,' said Biggles again. 'Don't look round. Tell Algy I'm here.'

Ginger, who seemed slightly dazed, passed the incredible information on to Algy, first warning him to be ready for a shock. He then worked in silence for a little while, watching the guards.

Choosing a favourable moment, he snatched a glance behind him under his arm. 'How did you get here?' he whispered.

'Never mind that – I'm here,' breathed Biggles. 'Did I hear you say something about a treasure?'

'Yes, I reckon we're digging for it.'

'What makes you think so?'

'Take a look at that column on your right. Carmichael's initials are on it, and the date, 1860. Those above are those of the chap who made the map that brought Eddie here. He's the fellow behind you. Incidentally, he is one of the party of missing Americans Carruthers told us about. His partners abandoned him in the forest – they're the two fellows over there with the Tiger. He was caught by the Indians, and Bogat captured us together. Can you get us out of this jam?'

'That's what I'm here for.'

'Then for the love of Mike do something.'

'Don't be in a hurry,' said Biggles softly, pretending to work. 'I'm thinking. You go on as if nothing unusual had happened.'

'How did you know we were here?'

'I found Dusky, and he trailed you. He's back in a ravine waiting for us. Don't talk any more now, or that big stiff with the whip may get suspicious.'

Nothing more was said. The only sounds were the thud of picks, the scrape of shovels, the grunts of the slaves and the cracking of the whip.

Biggles considered the question of escape from every angle before making up his mind, but in the end he determined to act forthwith. There was no point in delaying the action, for the position was not likely to alter before sunset, and he had no intention, if it could be avoided, of passing the night under lock and key. In any case, he thought there might be an evening roll call, in which case the discovery of an extra man would be inevitable.

He told Algy, Ginger and Eddie to draw closer together so that they could hear what he had to say without making it necessary for him to raise his voice. He still knew practically nothing about Eddie apart from what Ginger had said, but it was obvious that he was a prisoner like the rest, in which case he would be anxious to escape. Apart from that, he would be an extra man on his side.

'Listen,' he said. 'We shall have to make a dash for it. There's no other way that I can see. We've got two useful factors on our side. The first is surprise – you can see from the way the guards are standing that the last thing they imagine is that they will be attacked. The second factor is my automatic. I'm afraid I shall have to use it. This is no time for niceties. This is what I'm going to do, and what I want you to do.'

Here Biggles had to pause and make a pretence of scraping earth from the bottom of the trench while the gang-boss went past. As soon as the man was out of earshot he continued:

'The next time those two nearest guards come this way I shall jump out of the trench and cover them with my gun to make them drop their rifles. If they refuse, I shall shoot. Either way, you'll grab the rifles and open fire on the other guards along the line. Don't get flustered. Be sure of hitting your man. In this way we ought to put four of them out of action before the others guess what's happening. If I know anything about it, when we start shooting they'll run.'

'What about the Tiger?' asked Ginger.

'Never mind about him for the moment. Having got the weapons, we'll fight a rearguard action to the top of Jacob's Ladder. If we can reach it, the rest should be easy. Is that all clear?'

The others, including Eddie, announced that it was.

'Then stand by,' whispered Biggles tersely. 'The guards are coming this way. Remember, speed is the thing.'

The two guards to whom Biggles had referred, both half-castes, were walking slowly along the line of workmen. Strolling would perhaps be a better word. Handmade cigarettes hung from their lips. One carried his rifle carelessly in the crook of his arm; the other held his weapon at the trail; and it was clear from their careless manner that they did not expect trouble. Thus does familiarity breed contempt, and Biggles judged correctly when he guessed that the men had performed their task every day for so long that they no longer apprehended danger. They sauntered along, smoking and chatting, throwing an occasional glance at the labourers. Biggles stooped a little lower in the trench, gripped his automatic firmly, finger on trigger, and waited.

He waited until they drew level. Then with a quick movement he stepped out in front of them, the pistol held low down on his hip.

'Drop those guns,' he rasped.

Never was surprise more utter and complete. The behaviour of the guards was almost comical. First they looked at Biggles's face, then at the pistol, then back at his face, while their expressions changed from incredulity to fear. Neither spoke. One of them dropped his rifle; or rather, it seemed to fall from his nerveless hands. The other made a quick movement as though he intended shooting. Biggles did not wait to confirm this. His pistol cracked, and the shot shattered the man's arm. The rifle fell, and he fled, screaming. This, the opening operation, occupied perhaps three seconds, and as it concluded Algy and Ginger played their parts. In a moment they had snatched up the fallen rifles and opened fire on the two guards next along the line. One spun round and fell flat. The other made a leap for the trench, but stumbled and fell before he reached it, the rifle flying from his hand.

'Come on,' snapped Biggles, and sprinted towards the spot.

The four white men had almost reached the second pair of rifles before the full realization of what was happening penetrated into the minds of the other people on the plateau – the Tiger, his two white conspirators, his bodyguard, the two remaining guards, and the slaves. An indescribable babble, like the murmur of a wave breaking on shingle, rose into the still air. Then, abruptly, it was punctuated by shots from several directions. Some of them came near the fugitives, but none of them was hit. Biggles saw a workman drop.

While Eddie picked up the two rifles he looked round and saw that the situation had changed but little. The two remaining guards had run for some distance; then, taking cover, they had started firing. The Tiger was shooting with a revolver and shouting orders at the same time, and the uproar he created was hardly calculated to encourage his bodyguard to take careful aim. They were shooting, but with more speed than accuracy. The two renegade white men were firing their revolvers, but the range was too long for accurate shooting.

'All right,' said Biggles crisply. 'Let 'em have it.'

Four rifles spat in the direction of the Tiger's party. One of the bodyguards fell; all the rest dived for cover, and disappeared behind the house.

'Start moving towards the stairway,' ordered Biggles. 'I'll cover you.'

He knelt down and opened a steady fire on the building behind which the Tiger and his party had taken refuge, while under his protective fire the others hurried towards Jacob's Ladder.

So far Biggles's plan had worked without a hitch, and it seemed as if the stairway would be reached without difficulty, and without serious danger. But, unfortunately, the man who had been on guard at the head of the steps, and who had disappeared at the first shots, now came back, and kneeling behind a boulder, opened a dangerous fire.

Biggles had assumed, naturally, that the man had bolted, but hearing the shots he looked round quickly and realized what had happened. He did not waste time wondering why the man had returned; he was concerned only with the danger he represented.

Biggles dashed on after the others. 'We shall have to work round that chap,' he said curtly. 'Algy, come with me. We'll go to the left. The others go to the right. We'll get him from the flank.'

But before this manoeuvre could be made, a new factor arose, one that instantly made Biggles's scheme impracticable. He realized why the guard, who had bolted down the steps, had returned. He had not come back alone. At the top of Jacob's Ladder now appeared Bogat, and behind him nearly a score of armed men. They took in the situation at a glance, and spreading out, taking cover behind rocks, effectually blocked the steps.

Biggles perceived that Bogat and his gang must have been actually coming up the steps all the time. It was unfortunate, but it couldn't be prevented. In any case, he was not to know it. It was one of those unexpected mischances that can upset the best-laid plan. To advance in the face of a score of rifles was obviously a hopeless proposition; nor could they remain where they were. In the circumstances he gave the only reasonable order, which was to retire.

'Get back to the village!' he shouted. 'We'll find cover in one of the buildings while we think things over. Keep together. Don't waste ammunition. Run for it.'

Dodging among the boulders, for shots were now whistling, they made a quick but orderly retirement to the buildings. It was fortunate that they had not far to go. Biggles selected a group of stone houses near the spot where, a few minutes before, they had been working.

'This will do,' he decided, and dived through the doorway to temporary safety. The others followed him.

'Anyone hurt?' he inquired.

Eddie had been slightly wounded in the forearm, that was all; he made light of it, and tore a strip off his shirt for a bandage.

'Sorry, chaps,' said Biggles apologetically. 'The show came unstuck. Bad luck we chose the moment that Bogat and his toughs were coming up the steps. Not being able to see through solid rock, I wasn't to know that. Still, I think we ought to be able to hold them off this place for some time – at any rate, long enough to enable us to work out a new plan. Keep watch through the windows, but don't show yourselves. Phew! Isn't it hot.'

Eddie drew his sleeve across his forehead. 'You're telling me.'

CHAPTER XIII

Strange Events

For some time they kept careful watch, but saw nothing of the Tiger or his associates. Sounds told them that the labourers had been herded back into their pen.

'What's going on, I wonder?' muttered Ginger at last.

Biggles answered. 'I should say that the Tiger, knowing we are on the plateau, has posted a strong guard at the head of the stairway. We are, he supposes, in a trap, and he has only to close the mouth of it to keep us in. Why should he hurry? He knows that we can't stay here indefinitely without food and water. No doubt he's watching the place from a distance. Then again, he may not be sure which house we are actually in, and doesn't feel like taking the risk of being shot in order to find out.'

'Did you come up the stairway?' asked Ginger.

'Not exactly,' returned Biggles. 'I came nearly to the top, but seeing a fellow on guard, made a detour and came in over the escarpment behind the village – at the back of those prickly pears.'

'Couldn't we get out that way?'

Biggles thought for a moment. 'Possibly. We could, of course, if no guards were posted, but I can't think that the Tiger would be such a fool as to shut the front door and forget to lock the back door – so to speak. The way I came must have been the way the Indians came when they chased us up the steps after we had escaped from the black panther. One thing is certain: it would be silly to try to get out of here in broad daylight. We'll wait for dark.'

It seemed a long wait – as indeed it was. Silence settled over the plateau. The sun struck down with bars of white heat. The only sound was the languid buzz of insects.

The shadows were lengthening when Ginger suddenly recalled the pivoting flagstone; he could see it from where he stood on guard at a window, not a score of paces away. In the rush of events following Biggles's arrival he had forgotten all about it.

'Here, Biggles,' he said, 'I've just remembered something.' In a few words he told the others of his curious discovery.

'Sounds interesting,' was Biggles's comment.

'You mean, the treasure might be in there?' put in Eddie. Biggles had by this time learned who Eddie was, and how he came to be with the party.

'It might be, but, to tell the truth, I wasn't thinking about that,' answered Biggles. 'It would be useful, of course, to locate the treasure, although I don't think we're in a position to clutter ourselves up with it at the moment. Our job is to get out. What I was thinking was that under Ginger's slab there might be a tunnel leading to another part of the plateau. At any rate, if there is a cave or something there it ought to be worth exploring.'

'Now?' queried Ginger.

'No. We'll wait till it gets properly dark.'

'There's no need for us all to go,' remarked Ginger. 'I know just where the thing is. I could explore, and then come back and let you know what's inside – if there is an inside.'

'That's a good idea,' agreed Biggles. And so it was decided.

Night came. The moon had not yet risen, but the sky was clear, and the stars gave as much light as was necessary for the reconnaissance.

'I'm afraid it's going to be a bit difficult, if there is a cave, or something, to get an idea of it without a light,' Ginger pointed out. 'I've no matches. All our things were taken away from us.'

'I've got some,' Biggles told him, remembering those which, with his cigarettes, he had put in his pocket. 'Take them, but go easy with them, and don't strike any in the open.'

Ginger took the box, and slipping through an opening that had once been a window, crept stealthily along a wall towards his objective, while the others covered his advance with their rifles. Hearing nothing, seeing no sign of life, pausing sometimes to listen, Ginger kept close against the wall until he reached the trench, which gave him all the cover he needed for the rest of his journey to the stone. Actually, there were several paving-stones, and in spite of his confidence, in the deceptive half-light he was some minutes finding the right one. It was an exciting moment when he felt it give under his weight, for, of course, he had not the remotest idea of what was underneath.

The stone moved slowly but easily; when the pressure was removed it swung back into place, and for this reason he was in some doubt as to how to proceed. He didn't like the idea of descending into the unknown without being quite certain that he would be able to get back. A closer examination revealed that the stone turned on a central pivot; for a primitive contrivance it was a beautiful piece of precision work, but before entering the void Ginger made sure of his exit by the simple expedient of fixing a loose piece of stone so that the slab could not entirely close. Then, rather breathless, he groped inside with his hands. He was not surprised when they encountered a step, also of stone.

If there was one, he reasoned, there should be more. And in this he was correct; but it was not until he was well inside that he risked lighting a match. He held his breath while it flared up, for he had no idea of what lay before him. He was prepared for anything.

Actually, the result of his first survey, while the match lasted, was rather disappointing. As far as he could see, a flight of well-cut steps led down, perfectly straight, to a room, a chamber so large that he could not see the extremities of it. There was no furniture. The walls appeared to be bare. He went on to the bottom of the steps and lit another match.

In its light everything was exposed to view, and it merely confirmed his first impression. He was in a large oblong room, the walls, floor and ceiling of which were of grey stone. At one end, the end farthest from the entrance, three broad, shallow steps led up to a dais, in the manner of an altar, on which squatted a hideous idol. It appeared to have been carved out of the living rock. Ginger went over to it, and by the light of the third match looked at it again. The image leered down at him, and he felt suddenly cold. For how many hundreds of years, perhaps thousands, it had been there, leering in the darkness, he did not know, but the effect of extreme antiquity affected him strangely. He struck yet another match, but there was nothing more to be seen. There was no door or passage leading to another room. If the treasure was in here, he thought, then they had been forestalled. It was certainly not there now, although it seemed likely that it had been there as late as 1937, or the explorer Roberts would not have carved his initials on the column.

It was a disappointing anti-climax, and feeling rather gloomy about the whole business, Ginger groped his way back up to the exit, from where, with due precautions, he returned to the house and told the others the result of his investigation.

'There's something funny about this,' declared Biggles quietly. 'Unless he was a first-class liar, Carmichael saw the treasure. So apparently did Roberts. Where has it gone? It seems very unlikely that anyone could have been on the plateau recently without the Tiger knowing about it, unless the explorers came as we did, by air, for they would have to come up Jacob's Ladder. Obviously, the Tiger didn't find the treasure, or he wouldn't be looking for it now – at least, I assume he's looking for it. I can't think what else he'd be looking for.'

'Just a minute,' put in Eddie. 'There was some writing in the corner of the map. I imagine Roberts wrote it.'

'What happened to this man Roberts?' asked Biggles curiously. 'Why did he dispose of the map? Why didn't he take the treasure?'

'His Indian porters deserted him. In fact, they tried to poison him.'

'So he couldn't carry the stuff?'

'That's right. It took him all his time to get back.'

'But why didn't he return afterwards?'

'He died.'

'How did these crooked partners of yours get hold of the map?'

'They bought it off Roberts's widow – so they said.'

'And this writing you just mentioned?'

'It was a list of instructions. I can't remember the words exactly, but there was something about a hinged stone – presumably the one Ginger discovered.'

'Roberts definitely saw the treasure – with his own eyes?'

'Oh yes. He brought a gold cup home with him.'

'Did you see it?'

'No. His widow sold it after he died.'

'Hm.' Biggles was silent for a moment. 'I should like to have a look at this place,' he announced.

'So should I,' said Eddie.

'Then let's all go,' suggested Biggles. 'We shall be no worse off there than we are here – in fact, it might turn out to be a better hiding-place. If we could get hold of some food and water we could lie low there for a week if necessary, in which case the Tiger might think we had in some way got off the plateau. Let's go. We can always come back if we don't like it. No noise. We'll go across one at a time. If we bump into trouble, rally here. Ginger, you know the way, so you'd better go first.'

Ginger, employing the same tactics as before, returned to the underground chamber. The others followed in turn, Biggles bringing up the rear. Everything remained quiet – from Biggles's point of view, suspiciously quiet. In spite of what he had said about the Tiger holding them in a trap by simply putting a guard on the stairway, he thought it was odd that no attempt had been made to dislodge them from the block of buildings in which they had sought refuge. Still, he did not overlook the fact that four desperate men, armed with rifles, made a formidable force to capture or shoot down by sheer frontal attack.

Before going down through the trap-door Biggles made a short excursion to collect some tufts of dried grass; then, after a final survey of the scene, he followed the others into the chamber and allowed the slab to sink slowly into place. As soon as he was inside he twisted the dried grass into a wisp – it could hardly be called a torch – and taking the matches from Ginger, set light to it. The grass blazed up brightly so that everything could be seen. Not that there was much to see.

Nobody spoke while the fire was alight. Biggles still had a little more grass, but as there seemed to be no point in burning it, he held it in reserve.

'Well, that's that,' he murmured, sitting on the bottom step. 'Did anyone notice anything interesting, or worth exploring?'

The others admitted that they had seen nothing worth mentioning.

'This is a funny business,' resumed Biggles. 'I still don't understand what became of the treasure.'

'I wish I had the map,' remarked Eddie. 'There may have been something on it that I have forgotten. If there was, and the Tiger ever finds this place, he'll know just what to do.'

'Well, there doesn't seem to be much *we* can do,' returned Biggles.

Ginger started groping his way round the walls, knocking on the stones with his knuckles. 'They sound solid enough,' he observed.

'Lumps of stone, weighing half a ton apiece, would sound solid, even if there was a cavity behind,' Biggles pointed out.

'What are we going to do?' asked Algy. 'I can't see any point in staying here.'

'There's not much point in going back to the house, if it comes to that,' answered Biggles. 'I don't want to be depressing, but I don't think we're in any shape to stay either here or in the house for more than another day. We might manage without food for a bit, but we can't do without water. I'm afraid that sooner or later we've got to risk breaking through the cordon, either by rushing the steps, or trying to get out over the rocks, the way I came in. I'll tell you what. I'll go and have a scout round.'

'That sounds pretty dangerous to me,' muttered Eddie dubiously.

Biggles laughed mirthlessly. 'Whatever we do is likely to be dangerous. I'll go and make sure that the escarpment is guarded. Either way, I'll come back. If it isn't guarded we'll try to slip out.'

'Why not all go?' suggested Ginger.

'Because four people are more likely to be seen than one, and the chances of making a noise become multiplied by four. No, this is a one-man job. I don't suppose I shall be very long. Here, Algy, you take the matches; you may need them.'

Biggles groped his way up the steps. There was a faint gleam of star-spangled sky as he went through the exit; then it was blotted out as the stone sank into place. Silence fell.

For a long time nobody spoke in the chamber. There seemed to be nothing to say – or it may have been that they were all listening intently for the first sign of Biggles's return. In such conditions it is practically impossible to judge time correctly, but when Biggles had been gone for what Ginger thought must be nearly an hour, he commented on it.

'He's a long time,' he said anxiously, almost irritably.

'I was thinking the same thing,' admitted Algy. 'If —'

Whatever he was going to say remained unsaid, for at that moment the silence was shattered by a deafening explosion. The chamber shuddered to the force of it. A moment later came the crash and spatter of debris raining down on the roof. It sounded like a roll of distant thunder.

Ginger flung himself flat, feeling sure that the whole place was about to collapse. This was purely instinctive, for he was beyond lucid thought. So were the others. The explosion would have been bad enough had it been expected, but coming as it did without warning, it was shattering. It took Ginger several seconds to convince himself that he had not been hurt. He was the first to speak.

'Are you fellows all right?' he asked in a strained voice.

The others answered that they were.

'What on earth was that?' continued Ginger.

'I don't know, but I'm going to find out,' replied Algy, groping his way up the steps.

Some time passed, but he did not speak again, although the others could hear him making strange noises. He seemed to be grunting with exertion.

'What's wrong?' asked Eddie.

'Plenty,' came Algy's voice in the darkness. 'Either some rocks have fallen on the slab or else the explosion has jammed it. It won't move.'

'You mean – we're shut in?' demanded Ginger.

'That's just what I do mean,' answered Algy, rather unsteadily.

Ginger squatted down on the stone floor. 'Not so good,' he remarked.

'What are you grumbling about? You wanted adventure,' Algy pointed out coldly. 'Now you're getting it. I hope you're enjoying it – but I'm dashed if I am.'

CHAPTER XIV

Biggles Makes A Capture

The first thing Biggles noticed when he left the underground chamber was that the moon was rising over the edge of the plateau. He had no time to weigh up the advantages and disadvantages of this, for as, lying flat, he began to worm his way towards the trench, he distinctly saw a dark shadow flit silently away from the side of the house which they had recently evacuated. An instant later a low mutter of voices reached his ears, but precisely where the sound came from he could not determine. The conversation was soon followed by the sound of retreating footsteps. That something was going on seemed certain, but there was no indication of what it was. Fearing that he may have been seen, he lay still for a little while, trusting to his ears to advise him of danger; but when nothing happened he felt that it was time he continued his reconnaissance.

With eyes and ears alert for danger, he reached the nearest house, and taking advantage of the deepest shadows, went on towards the ridge of rock which he could see silhouetted against the sky beyond the village. He reached the outlying boulders without incident, and there paused to survey the skyline for any movement that would reveal the position of sentries. His vigilance was rewarded when he saw the glow of a lighted cigarette. It was stationary. This at once fixed the position of at least one sentry, and Biggles was about to move forward on a course that would avoid him when a faint smell, borne on a slant of air, reached his nostrils and brought him to an abrupt halt. It was vaguely familiar, but it took him a second or two to identify it as the reek of smouldering saltpetre. Instantly realising the significance of it, he half rose up and looked behind him, hoping to discover the source of it. The next moment a column of flame shot into the air; simultaneously came the roar of an explosion, the blast of which flung him headlong. Knowing what to expect, he lay still with his hands over his head while clods of earth and pieces of rock rattled down around him and the acrid tang of dynamite filled the air.

As soon as the noise had subsided he looked back at the spot where the explosion had occurred, and saw, as he already suspected, that it was the block of houses in one of which they had first taken cover. The buildings were now a heap of ruins. It was easy enough to see what had happened. The enemy, fearing to make a frontal attack, had entered one of the rear houses and destroyed the whole block with a charge of dynamite.

Naturally, Biggles's first reaction to this unexpected event was one of thankfulness that they had left the house, otherwise they must have all been killed. That the enemy assumed this to be the case was made apparent by the way they now advanced, with much laughing and talking, from several directions. The sentries on the escarpment left their posts and joined their companions at the scene of the supposed triumph. In a few minutes the shattered houses were surrounded by groups of figures, some of which, Biggles saw with misgiving, were very near the underground chamber.

He waited to see what they would do, for upon this now depended his own actions. He was not particularly concerned about the others, although he guessed that the explosion must have given them a nasty shock. Being underground, they would be safe. He was not to know that falling masonry had piled itself on the entrance slab, making the opening of it from the inside impossible. His one fear was that Algy and Ginger would emerge in order to see what had happened, and so betray the secret hiding-place – as, indeed, might easily have happened had it been possible for them to get out. Biggles was relieved when nothing of the sort happened.

The question now arose in his mind, would a search be made at once for the bodies which were supposed to be under the ruins, or would the Tiger wait for daylight? The answer was provided when the Tiger began shouting orders, and the crowd started to disperse. As far as Biggles could gather, the Tiger had merely dismissed his men without giving any hint of his future plans. A number of figures, presumably the Tiger's personal party, remained near the ruins, and had it not been for this Biggles would probably have returned to the chamber forthwith. He did, in fact, wait for some time with this object in view, but when the Tiger showed no signs of leaving, he decided that it would be a good moment, an opportunity that might not occur again, to make contact with Dusky, who, if he did not soon show up, would presently be leaving the ravine. So Biggles decided that he would go down to him, tell him what had happened, recover his Express rifle and some biscuits, and then, if the Tiger had gone, return to the chamber. He thought it ought to be possible to do this before daylight.

His mind made up, he struck off towards the clump of prickly pear in order to leave the plateau as near as possible to the spot

by which he had entered it. He was not so optimistic as to hope
that he would be able to find his track through the chaos of rock,
but he had a pretty good idea of the general direction of the
ravine, and once he reached it there should be no great difficulty
in finding Dusky.

Actually, he was some time finding the ravine, for it was not
an easy matter to keep a straight course through the bewildering jumble of boulders; and when he did strike it he saw that
he was above the point where he had left it. This did not worry
him, however, and he started making his way towards the place
where he imagined Dusky would be. When he reached it the old
man was not there. He whistled softly, but there was no reply.
Rather worried, he continued on towards the stairway, no great
distance.

Had not he seen the moonlight glint on the barrel of the rifle
there might have been an accident, for he realized suddenly that
the rifle was covering him.

He dropped behind a rock. 'Is that you, Dusky?' he asked
sharply.

'Sure, massa, dat's me,' answered Dusky with a gasp of relief.
'I sure nearly shot you,' announced the old man with engaging
frankness.

'What are you doing here?' asked Biggles.

'When I hear all dat shootin' and bangin' I reckon you ain't
comin' back no more, so I was jest going off to fetch massa
Carruthers. I'd have gone down the steps by now if dat trashy
king hadn't come along.'

'King?'

Dusky explained that a few minutes earlier he was about
to descend the stairway when he heard someone approaching,

coming down the steps. Withdrawing into the ravine, he saw, or thought he saw, the Tiger, with only two men, go past.

Biggles perceived that if the king had left the scene of the explosion shortly after he himself had left, he would have had ample time to reach the spot. He thought swiftly, wondering how this new aspect could be turned to his advantage. If Dusky was right, then the Tiger had probably gone down to his palace – with only two men. If he could be captured, he would be a valuable hostage. With the king in his hands, he could dictate to Bogat and his crew. He remembered also that the Tiger had the treasure map, which was a valuable document for more reasons than one. If he captured the king he would also gain possession of the map. It was a tempting proposition, and the only doubt in Biggles's mind was what the others would think when he did not return. Still, he thought they ought to be able to take care of themselves. Making up his mind quickly he moved towards the steps.

'Where you go now, massa?' asked Dusky.

'I'm going down to the valley to capture the king,' answered Biggles shortly.

'You – what?' Dusky faltered. He shook his head sorrowfully, but followed as obediently as a dog.

The stairway was, as far as could be ascertained, deserted, and Biggles hurried down, for time was an important factor. Reaching the valley, he surveyed the scene. Everything was, as he hoped, quiet. The only sign of activity was a light that came from the palace. With his rifle over his arm, Biggles strode towards it, trusting that if he were seen his disguise would see him through.

As he drew nearer he observed that the light came from the French window which gave access to the room in which he and

Ginger had been trapped by the Tiger's pet snake. Suddenly a shadow moved across it, and he realized that a sentry was on duty. However, he went on into the garden and took cover behind a bush. It was now possible to see the sentry clearly. He carried a rifle at the slope.

Biggles leaned his Express against a bush and spoke quietly to Dusky. 'We've got to get that fellow out of the way,' he whispered. 'Can you think of any way of bringing him here?'

Dusky scratched his head. 'I dunno massa, but I'll try.' He whistled softly.

The sentry, who was pacing up and down, stopped abruptly.

'Who's there?' he called.

Biggles nudged Dusky, who whistled again.

The sentry, his curiosity aroused, began to walk slowly towards the spot. Dusky moved into the open where he could be seen. The sentry paused, then continued to move forward, his rifle at the ready.

'Who's that? What you doing here?' he asked sharply.

'I got a message,' answered Dusky.

'Who for?'

'For you.'

Upon this the sentry, seeing – as he thought – that he had only one man, a native, to deal with, proceeded with more confidence. He passed Biggles, and peered forward to see the face of the man in front of him. This was the moment for which Biggles had waited. The butt of his pistol came down on the sentry's head, and with a grunt the man collapsed at Dusky's feet. Biggles picked up the fallen rifle and thrust it into Dusky's hands.

'Stay here and watch him,' he ordered, and moving cautiously towards the building, saw what he had not previously noticed. The French window was open, probably on account of the heat.

Quietly, but without loss of time, taking his rifle with him, Biggles moved forward until he could see into the room. Two men were there, seated at a table with a bottle between them. One was Bogat and the other Chorro.

Biggles's first feeling was one of surprise; the second, disappointment; the third, mystification. Where was the Tiger? Bogat was still wearing his hat, as if he had only just arrived. Could Dusky have made a mistake?

While Biggles was still pondering the question Bogat spoke, and his first words explained the situation.

'No, the king is busy up top,' he said. 'When he heard that you'd arrived he sent me down instead to hear what you have to say. If you'd rather see him, or if it's something important, I'll take you up top.'

Biggles understood. In the darkness Dusky had been mistaken. The man he had seen come down the steps was not the Tiger, but Bogat. Chorro had arrived from the coast, and the Tiger had sent Bogat down to get in touch with him.

Biggles was annoyed, for had he known the truth he would not have come down; but now that he was here, with the two men practically at his mercy, he felt that it would be a pity not to take advantage of the situation. He could not very well blame Dusky for the mistake; the old man had acted for the best. Still, the new state of affairs called for an adjustment of plan.

Biggles withdrew a little into the darkness to think the matter over. It would, he thought, be an easy matter to capture the Tiger's two right-hand men, but what was he to do with them? It did not take him long to see that there was only one thing he could do with them, and that was take them to the coast. This would mean leaving the others for longer than he originally intended. Still, if he went back up the steps and rejoined them now it was not easy to see what he could do single-handed. On the other hand, if he went to the coast and explained matters to Carruthers, the acting-Governor might lend him some extra men. He should be able to get back some time the next day. If Algy and the others remained where they were they should be safe.

So Biggles reasoned as he stood in the shadow of the palace, confronted, for the third time within a few hours, with a decision not easy to make. Successive unexpected events had made his original plan a thing of the past. However, he felt that by securing Bogat and Chorro and taking them to the coast he would have achieved the first step forward in his declared intention of breaking up the Tiger's gang.

With the rifle in the crook of his arm ready for instant use, Biggles strolled into the room.

'Good evening, gentlemen,' he said evenly. 'Keep quite still. It should hardly be necessary for me to warn you that if either of you make a sound I shall have to employ your own methods to discourage you. Keep your hands on the table.'

The two men stared. Neither moved. Neither spoke. In the first place, at least, their obedience was probably due to shock. While they were still staring Biggles walked behind each in turn and removed his weapons.

'Now,' he continued, 'we're going for a walk. On your feet. Keep going. I shall be close behind you.'

When they reached the spot where Dusky was waiting, Biggles gave him Bogat's rifle and ordered him to lead the way down to the forest, the first part of the journey to the *Wanderer*.

It was now bright moonlight, but so much had happened that Biggles had only a hazy idea of the time. He was anxious to reach the foot of the steps before dawn, because there was less chance of meeting anybody on the way.

As a matter of fact it was earlier than he thought, and he found it necessary to wait for some time at the bottom of the steps, for he dare not risk losing his two dangerous prisoners in the darkness of the forest, where, of course, the moonlight did not penetrate. As soon as there was sufficient light to see he gave the order to continue the march, Dusky still leading the way and he himself bringing up the rear. So far the two prisoners had been passive, but Biggles felt certain that Bogat, at least, would make an attempt to escape. Once he got off the trail into the forest he would be safe from pursuit, and Biggles repeated his warning as to what would happen if either prisoner attempted it. They trudged on in silence. It was broad daylight by the time they reached the river.

Now all this time Biggles had the advantage of knowing where they were going, whereas the prisoners did not. They hoped, no doubt, that camp would presently be made, in which case an opportunity for making a dash into the jungle might present itself. But as soon as the aircraft came into view – for in spite of Biggles's rough camouflage, it could be seen from a little distance – the manner of both prisoners changed. They must have realized that unless they did something quickly their minutes of opportunity were numbered. Once in the machine, and in the air, there could be no escape.

Not for an instant did Biggles relax his vigilance, for he knew that this was the crucial moment. He was in fact ready for almost anything; yet in spite of that he was not ready for what did happen.

When they were only a score of paces from the machine Dusky suddenly pulled up dead. For a moment or two he stood rigid, leaning slightly forward, his big nostrils twitching, like a dog that catches the scent of its quarry. Then he turned his head slowly and looked at Biggles. His eyes were round with fear.

Even when he moved his lips, and opened them to speak, Biggles still had no idea of what the old man was going to say; but he sensed danger, and his muscles tightened as instinctively he braced himself. And as they all stood there, motionless, like a screen picture suddenly arrested in motion, the silence was broken by a curious sound, a sort of sharp *phut*.

Bogat started convulsively. Very slowly, as if it dreaded what it might find, his hand crept up to a face that had turned ashen, to where a tiny dart, not much larger than a darning needle, protruded. As his fingers touched it a wild scream burst from his lips, and he staggered back against a tree.

Chorro took one terrified look at him, and with the whimpering cry of a wounded dog, regardless of Biggles's order to stop, rushed into the forest.

Biggles raised his rifle, but he did not shoot. There was no need. For hardly had Chorro left the trail when there was a fierce crashing in the undergrowth, a crashing above which rose shrieks of terror. They ended abruptly.

Now all this had happened in less time than it takes to tell. Biggles knew, without Dusky's hoarse advice, that they had been ambushed by Indians, probably the same tribe that Bogat had so mercilessly attacked. He could do nothing for his prisoners. Chorro had disappeared, and it was not hard to guess his fate. Bogat was now on the ground, writhing and twisting in convulsions as the venom on the dart took effect.

Dusky panicked – which was hardly surprising. He fled back along the trail. Biggles followed, now concerned only with escape. He wondered vaguely whether it would be better to go back to the steps, or to try to reach the aircraft, although how this was to be done was not apparent. As he ran, wild shouts behind sent the parrots squawking into the air.

Dusky turned away from the trail like a hunted rabbit. Biggles followed blindly, not so much because he had any faith in his leadership – at least, in the present circumstances – as because he did not want to lose him. Presently he found himself splashing through mud, and saw the tall reeds that fringed the river just ahead. Dusky made for a tree on which the limbs grew low. Flinging aside his rifle, he went up it like a monkey. Biggles went after him, but kept his rifle, looping it over his shoulder by the sling to leave his hands free for climbing.

He thought Dusky would never stop going up, and for some absurd reason the memory of Jack and the Beanstalk flashed into his mind. The ground was about a hundred feet below when Dusky suddenly disappeared and Biggles, still following, found himself in a strange new world. They had arrived, so to speak, in a new jungle, a jungle with a fairly level floor from which sprang orchids and ferns, with great growths of moss and lichen.

Now, Biggles had heard of these different 'layers' of forest, raised one above the other, but this was the first time he had ever seen one, and he looked about with interest. It was easy to see how they were formed. Branches fell, but instead of falling to the ground, they were caught by the branches below them. Across these in turn fell other branches, twigs and leaves, to form eventually a substantial carpet. On this carpet seeds fell from the flowering treetops. Others were dropped by birds. These took root and flourished for a time; then, dying, the seedlings collapsed, to give extra thickness to the mat of rotting debris. Over a period of centuries this mat became as firm as the solid earth far beneath, and supported a flora and fauna of its own. Here among the green treetops dwelt birds, and rats, and other small creatures.

Biggles was recalled from his contemplation of this pleasant scene by Dusky, who whispered, 'We hide here.'

Biggles nodded. He was in no mood to argue. All the same, he began to regret that he had left the others. He wondered what they were doing. Could he have seen them he would have been a good deal more disturbed in his mind than he was.

CHAPTER XV

Desperate Diversions

If Biggles supposed that Algy, Ginger and Eddie were sitting quietly in the underground chamber waiting for him to come back – and there was no reason why he should think otherwise – he would have been wrong. Very wrong. Things had happened. Several things.

They began soon after Algy's discovery that, as a result of the explosion, the stone over the exit had jammed. At least, that is what they thought. As a matter of fact, a block of masonry had fallen on it. Masonry had fallen all over the place. Comparatively speaking, this particular piece was not heavy, but it was of sufficient weight to upset the finely adjusted mechanism of the pivot and so prevent the slab from being tilted open from the inside. Those below it did not know this. As Algy remarked, 'The thing has stuck.' They were not at first unduly perturbed, for they assumed that Biggles would return and do something about it. But when presently the sound of many footsteps could be heard overhead, Algy began to get worried. This was, of course, when the Tiger and his men gathered round the scene of the explosion.

Conversing in low tones, the comrades tried to visualize the scene outside, and as a result of their combined imaginations they arrived fairly near to the truth.

'They've either brought up a cannon and shelled the place, or else blown it up with a stick of dynamite,' declared Algy.

'I only hope they didn't get Biggles at the same time,' muttered Ginger.

'He'd been gone a fair while,' Algy pointed out. 'He should have got clear.'

'We shall have to wait until he comes back.'

'We should have done that in any case,' reminded Algy.

Time passed, a long time, and still Biggles did not return. There were no longer any sounds outside.

'Surely it's time he was back?' murmured Ginger. 'This is awful, sitting here doing nothing.'

'I'm afraid you're right,' agreed Algy. 'If everything had gone according to plan he should have been back by now. It begins to look as if something went wrong.'

'What can we do about it?'

'Nothing. At least, I can't think of anything. Have you any ideas, Eddie?'

Eddie answered that he had not. 'I must have been nuts to set out on this jaunt with a pair of cheap crooks,' he added disgustedly – which made it clear how he felt about the whole business.

'How about striking a match and having a look at the slab?' he suggested presently. 'Perhaps we shall be able to see what's happened.' They had of course been sitting in the dark.

'Yes, we might do that,' agreed Algy. 'But we shall have to go steady with the matches – there aren't many left.'

'Why is it nobody seems to have any matches when they are really needed?' remarked Eddie bitterly.

'I'll see it never happens to me again,' declared Ginger. 'Before I set out on another trip I'm going to have a special belt made,

751

one to go under my shirt. It will have little pockets all round it. In them I shall carry everything I've always wanted when I haven't had them – a box of matches, and an electric torch, a penknife with all sorts of gadgets in it, chocolates, string—'

'A few bombs and a Tommy gun,' sneered Algy. 'Pity you didn't think of it earlier. Stop romancing. Let's get down to brass tacks. I'm going to strike a match, so get ready to have a look round.'

As he spoke he struck the match. It flared up, dazzling them. As their eyes grew accustomed to the light they examined the slab eagerly, but there was nothing to indicate the cause of the trouble. Just as the flame was expiring a wild yell from Eddie nearly made Ginger fall off the step. The match went out.

'What's wrong? What are you yelling about?' snapped Algy.

'It's gone?'

'Gone? Who's gone? I mean, what's gone?'

'The idol.'

'You're crazy! Where could it go?'

'I tell you it's gone,' insisted Eddie. 'I happened to glance that way. It's no longer there.'

'Strike another match, Algy,' put in Ginger nervously. 'I don't like the idea of an image prowling about.'

In his haste Algy dropped all the matches, and several seconds passed – much to Ginger's irritation – before they could be collected.

'For the love of Mike get a move on,' he growled.

Another match flared, and they all stared in the direction of the image. One glance was enough. Eddie was right. It was no longer there.

With one accord, prompted by mutual curiosity, they started walking towards the place where it had been, but before they were halfway the match went out. Still, they had seen enough to give them an idea of what had happened.

'Strike another match,' urged Ginger.

'We can't go on striking matches at this rate,' protested Algy.

'Wait a minute. I'll tear a strip off my shirt,' offered Ginger. There came a noise of tearing material. 'All right, go ahead,' he resumed. 'I hope the stuff will burn.'

Another match blazed, and Ginger lighted the piece of material that he now held in his hands. 'That's better,' he said, as it flared up.

It was now possible to see precisely what had happened. The explosion had evidently been more severe than they had supposed, for there were several cracks in the walls and ceiling. With these they were not concerned. Their attention was riveted on a more interesting development. At first they could not understand what had become of the idol, but as they drew near they saw that the shock of concussion had caused it to tilt forward, revealing a square aperture behind it, a hole into which the base of the idol had previously fitted.

In order to reach this opening Algy had to climb on the back of the idol, but as soon as he touched it it swung still lower in a manner that explained how it operated. The idol was, in fact, a door, hinged at the bottom by a balancing device similar to the one that worked the slab above. So perfectly poised was the idol that the slightest pressure was sufficient to move it, but what hidden spring actuated it could not be discovered. With such precision did the ponderous stone with the carved face fit into the recess behind it, that, had not the explosion exposed the secret, it would not have been suspected.

'This is getting interesting,' murmured Algy.

'You bet it is,' declared Ginger enthusiastically. 'Go ahead. Let's see what's inside.'

'You've got the light, go ahead yourself,' invited Algy.

'Say, why argue? Let's all go,' put in Eddie. And in a moment they were all standing in the dark doorway, Ginger holding up the piece of burning stuff in order to throw the light as far as possible.

As a means of illumination the strip of shirt left much to be desired, but in its smoky yellow glow they saw three broad steps that led down into another chamber, a long, low room with what appeared to be heaps of debris piled at intervals on the floor. There was only one piece of furniture – a curiously carved chair.

'There doesn't seem to be anything to get worked up about,' observed Ginger in a disappointed voice, as they advanced slowly down the steps.

As Ginger trod on the bottom step it seemed to give under his weight, and he fell back with a cry of alarm. The light went out. Simultaneously, the chamber echoed to a dull, hollow boom.

Algy needed no invitation to relight the piece of rag. At first glance there appeared to be no change in the scene, and it was Eddie, who happened to glance behind him, who called attention to what had occurred. The entrance had disappeared. The idol had swung back into place.

'When I was a kid,' announced Eddie sadly, 'my Ma always swore that my inquisitiveness would be the death of me. I guess she was right. Unless we can find the gadget that tips old frosty-face, I reckon we're here for keeps.'

'Let's have a look round before we try to find it,' suggested Algy. 'You may not have noticed it, but that idol fits into its socket like a piston into a cylinder. So does the outside slab. In that case, how does it happen that the air in here is fresh? Look at the light. You don't suppose it would burn like that if the chamber wasn't ventilated somehow?'

'You're right,' agreed Ginger, sinking into the chair.

In an instant he was on his back, for the chair had collapsed in a cloud of dust. It did not break; it just crumbled, like tinder.

'That chair must have been standing there an awful long time,' said Eddie slowly.

Ginger, sneezing, sat on a pile of debris. It sank a little under his weight, and gave a soft metallic clink. A curious expression came over his face as he picked up a handful of the stuff. He said no word, but turning an amazed face to the others, allowed the pieces to drop one by one from his hand. They fell with a dull clink.

'For the love of Mike,' breathed Eddie. 'It's metal.'

Ginger laughed hysterically. 'Feel the weight of it,' he cried. 'It's gold!'

In a moment they were all on their knees examining their find, and soon established that the objects were not coins, but an extraordinary collection of small carved objects, trinkets, flowers, ears of corn, and the like. Digging into the pile, Algy pulled out a drinking-mug made in the form of a potato.

'It's the treasure all right,' he said in a strained voice, just as the light burnt out. 'Unfortunately, its no earthly use to us at the moment, but it's nice to know it's here. Rip another strip off your shirt,' he ordered. 'Let's see about getting out of this trap.'

Ginger obliged, and by mutual consent they returned to the steps, from where they made a close examination of the back of the idol. They tried coaxing it open, and failing in this, they tried force. But it was no use. They could see the cracks that marked the dimensions of the opening clearly enough, but nothing they could do would widen them.

'We're wasting our time,' said Eddie in a melancholy voice.

'Don't you believe it,' returned Ginger. 'The old priests, or whoever made this dugout, wouldn't fix the thing without making some way of opening it from the inside. There's a trick in it. All we've got to do is to discover it.'

'If they were cute enough to make a trap like this you can bet your sweet life the trick won't be easy to solve,' said Eddie. 'Only those in the secret could get in and out.'

'What I should like to know,' remarked Algy, 'is where the fresh air is coming from. It can't percolate through solid stone.'

'You're dead right,' affirmed Eddie. 'There must be a hole, or a feed-pipe somewhere. And I'll tell you something else. Even if there is a hole the air couldn't get in if we were below the level of the ground.'

'What are you talking about?' demanded Ginger. 'Of course we're below the level of the ground. We came downstairs.'

'Unless the guys who built this hideout installed a mechanical air-conditioning plant, which I'm not prepared to believe, then I say the air is coming in from some point below us,' declared Eddie.

'I think you're right,' agreed Algy thoughtfully. 'If we can find the hole we shall know more about it.'

Abandoning the sealed doorway, they set about exploring the chamber, starting with the walls; but everywhere the massive stones of which the chamber was composed fitted so perfectly that the task seemed hopeless. Eddie turned his attention to the floor, dropping on his knees to examine it more closely.

'You've got to remember that the ancients were clever engineers, but even so, their work was limited to simple mechanics,' he remarked. 'They had a primitive idea of hydraulics and levers, so—' The voice broke off abruptly. It was followed by a soft thud.

Algy looked round. So did Ginger. Then they stared at each other.

'Hi! Eddie!' shouted Ginger.

There was no answer.

Ginger turned wondering eyes to Algy. 'He's – he's gone!' he gasped.

'D'you think I'm blind?' sneered Algy with bitter sarcasm, which revealed the state of his nerves. 'Where was he when he disappeared?'

Ginger shook his head. 'I don't know. I was looking at the wall.'

'All right. Let's not get excited. There's dust on the floor. When we find the place where it has been disturbed we shall know where he was when he did the disappearing act.'

'I hope he isn't hurt,' muttered Ginger.

'He's probably groping about on the wrong side of one of these slabs, trying to get back,' asserted Algy, taking the light from Ginger's hand and starting to explore the flagstones which formed the floor.

'This is the place,' he announced presently. 'Apart from the dust, the cracks round this slab are wider than the others.'

'Perhaps it tilts, like the one up top,' suggested Ginger.

'That must be the answer, otherwise Eddie couldn't very well have fallen through,' replied Algy. 'Yes, that's it,' he went on quickly. 'The dust on this slab has disappeared. It probably fell into the hole, or whatever there is underneath, when Eddie went through. We're getting warm. I expect it's a case of applying weight to one particular spot. The most likely place would be near the edge, just here – Hi!'

Ginger grabbed Algy by the legs as the stone tilted suddenly and he started to slide. He nearly went in head first, and probably would have done had not Ginger dragged him back. As they struggled clear the stone swung back into place.

'Why did you let the hole close up again?' asked Ginger in a disappointed voice.

'Don't worry about that. We know the trick now,' answered Algy breathlessly. 'I don't want to land on my skull. We'll take this slowly: and as the trap closes automatically we'd better jam it open with something, otherwise it may close behind us and prevent us from getting back.'

Ginger went to one of the heaps of treasure and returned with what looked like a wand, or sceptre. 'This ought to do,' he said.

'Fine,' agreed Algy. 'Slip it in the crack when the stone moves. As soon as the crack is wide enough we'll drop a match in to see how deep the hole is underneath – if there is a hole.'

By the light of a match they ascertained that there was a drop, but only of about six feet; and the first thing they saw was Eddie lying crumpled up at the bottom, evidently unconscious.

Algy dropped down to him. There was no other way. Originally there had been a wooden ladder, but it now lay mouldering in a heap of dust. While Algy was examining Eddie, Ginger observed that the newly discovered cavity bore no likeness to the room they were in. It was more like an artificial cave, with the sides left rough. He also remarked a definite draught of air, refreshingly cool.

'How is he?' he called from above.

'He's got a nasty bruise on the forehead. He must have landed on his head; the blow knocked him out, but I don't think it's serious.'

'Is that a room or a tunnel you're in?'

Algy held up the match and looked round. 'It's a tunnel,' he said. 'You'd better come down. Jam the flags open so that we can get back if necessary.'

Ginger dropped into the cave. 'I say! A disturbing thought has just occurred to me,' he remarked.

'What is it?'

'If Biggles comes back and finds no one in the chamber he'll wonder what on earth has become of us.'

Algy clicked his tongue. 'I'm afraid he'll have to wonder,' he muttered wearily.

CHAPTER XVI

Carruthers Takes a Hand

Their fears in this respect, however, had they but known it,
were groundless. Biggles was miles away, sitting in a sylvan
paradise between earth and heaven, wondering what to do next.
Dusky, being a man of the country, was concerned only with the
immediate danger – the Indians, who could be heard laughing
and shouting some distance away.

'I'm glad they chose Bogat for a target, and not me,' remarked
Biggles.

'Dey know Bogat. Dey want him for a long time. Dey take you
for an Indian.'

Biggles thought that this was probably the correct explanation.
Not being a hypocrite, he made no pretence of being sorry for the
brutal Bogat, or the treacherous Chorro, who had got no more
than their deserts. An idea struck him.

'Is this carpet firm enough to walk on?' he inquired.

'Sure, massa.'

'There's no risk of falling through?'

'No risk,' declared Dusky confidently. 'This stuff thirty or forty
feet thick, maybe more.'

'In that case we ought to be able to work our way along so as to
get above the aeroplane. The river will serve as a guide.'

Dusky shook his head. 'If we walk, dem old parrots will set up a squawking and tell the Indians where we are. Better if we wait. Presently de Indians go.'

'Won't they smash the machine?'

'Dey too afraid to go near it,' said Dusky definitely. 'Dey tink, maybe, it's a new god.'

Biggles was not so sure of this, but he was content to rely on Dusky's judgement. After all, he reflected, the old man had spent most of his life among the Indians, and should know their habits.

'Did you know the Indians were there?' asked Biggles, while they were waiting. He remembered that Dusky had stopped before the Indians had revealed their presence.

'Sure, massa.'

'How did you know?'

'I smelled dem,' explained Dusky simply.

Biggles nodded. He was prepared to believe anything.

That Dusky had judged the situation correctly was presently proved when the Indians passed along the trail, in single file and in silence. As soon as they had disappeared into the dim corridors of the forest Dusky announced that it was safe to move. He did not descend straight to the ground, but kept to the treetops, picking his way carefully, with Biggles following. They were soon escorted by parrots and monkeys, which, coming close, but taking care to keep out of reach, set up a hideous clamour. Evidently they resented the intrusion into their domain, and left the invaders in no doubt as to their disapproval.

In several places there were holes in the floor, usually near the trunks of trees, such as the one through which they had made an entrance, and Dusky took care to keep well away from them.

Eventually, however, he selected one, and stamping with his feet to make sure that he was on a branch, worked his way towards the hole. He pointed, and Biggles, to his infinite relief, saw the *Wanderer* almost immediately below. There was no sign of any damage.

Getting down to the ground was tricky and hot work, and Biggles was not a little relieved to stand once more on terra firma. Watching the undergrowth closely, and with his rifle at the ready, he hurried to the machine, which, to his great satisfaction, appeared to be precisely as he had left it. Leaving Dusky on guard, he tore off the flimsy camouflage and prepared to cast off.

'Okay, Dusky, come aboard,' he said in a tired voice, for strain, exertion, lack of sleep, and the humid atmosphere were beginning to tell. He was weary, hungry and thirsty, not to say dirty.

'Which way we go, massa?' asked Dusky anxiously.

'I'm just wondering,' returned Biggles frankly, for now that the moment for departure had come he found himself in doubt. Two courses were open. The others, he knew, would be anxious about him, and he had an uncomfortable feeling that he had left them in the lurch. He had not stuck to his plan – not that this was entirely his fault. Algy and Ginger would no doubt agree that he had done the right thing when they knew what had happened, but in the meantime they would be worried. Nevertheless, it was not easy to see how he could rejoin them – anyway, until night fell. But apart from this he felt that the wisest course would be to go down the river and tell Carruthers what had happened. He might be able to make a suggestion. If not, Biggles reasoned, he would have to come back and carry on the war single-handed.

'We're going down the river,' he told Dusky abruptly, as he made up his mind.

He started the engines and took off with a vague feeling of surprise that at last something was going according to order. He half expected the engines to break down. Indeed, on the journey to the coast he listened to their note with as much anxiety as he could ever remember, for if they let him down now he hardly dared think what the fate of the others would be.

The engines did not let him down, and he offered up a silent prayer of thankfulness when the sea came into view. In twenty minutes, leaving Dusky in charge of the aircraft, he was in the presence of the acting-Governor.

Carruthers looked him up and down with real concern.

'I say, old man, you are in a mess,' he said sympathetically. 'You need a bath, a—'

Biggles broke in. 'I know. There are a lot of things I need, but I haven't time to attend to them now. Things have been happening – they're still happening, and I've got to get a move on. My friends don't know I'm here – but I'd better give you a rough idea of what has happened. While I'm doing that you might get me a spot of something to eat.'

Carruthers sent his servant for a drink and some sandwiches, and these Biggles consumed as he told his story as concisely as possible.

'By Jingo! You have been having a time,' exclaimed the acting-Governor when Biggles had finished. 'What do you want me to do?'

'To tell the truth, I don't know,' confessed Biggles. 'I thought you might be able to make a suggestion. After all, we're working under you, and apart from personal considerations, I don't want to do the wrong thing.'

'We've got to rescue your friends and this American, and, if possible, arrest the Tiger.'

'That's it,' agreed Biggles. 'We'll grab these two crooks Warren and Schmitt at the same time. They deserve hanging for abandoning young Rockwell in the jungle. The trouble is, I can't be in two places at once. I rarely ask for assistance, but this seems to be a case where a little help would be worth a deal of sympathy.'

'That's what I was thinking,' murmured Carruthers, his lips parting in a faint smile.

'Do you really mean that?' asked Biggles sharply.

'I might snatch a couple of days off to help you to clean up. If I could, what would you suggest?'

'Now you're talking,' said Biggles eagerly. 'You see, I can't be at both ends of that infernal stairway at the same time. The Tiger has got a guard posted at the top, to keep us trapped up there – at least, that's what he thinks. If we had some men at the bottom of the steps we could keep *him* trapped. Otherwise even if we landed an army on the plateau, he'd simply bolt down the steps and disappear into the forest. How many men can you spare?'

'Ten or a dozen – native police, of course. They're good fellows.'

'Got a machine-gun?'

'I could get one.'

Biggles thought quickly. 'Two good men under a reliable N.C.O., with a machine-gun, could hold the bottom of the stairway against an army. Three or four others arriving suddenly on the plateau, with another machine-gun, should be enough to stampede the Tiger's half-baked gang. Remember, I've already got three men up there. Let me see, by unloading most of my stores, at a pinch I could transport ten people up the river, including myself. Ten should be enough. We could land at the place where I just took off and unload Dusky, an N.C.O. and two men, with a machine-gun. Dusky would act as guide. He could show them where to place the gun so that it would cover the steps. Are you seriously thinking of coming?'

'Certainly.'

'Good. Very well. You and I, and four others, would take off again and land on the plateau, and make a rush for this underground chamber I told you about. The idea of that would be to let my friends out. We should then have a force of nine men, which should be plenty. When the Tiger sees you he'll guess the game's up and bolt for the steps. His gang will follow him. We shall then have the whole bunch between two fires, and unless he's a lunatic he'll surrender. Believe me, that stairway is no place to fight a defensive action.'

Carruthers nodded. 'That sounds a good plan. When shall we start?'

'The sooner the better. How soon could you be ready?'

'In an hour.'

'Fine. I'll refuel, have a bath, and meet you at the river in an hour from now. That will be one o'clock. If all goes well we ought to be back up the river by five – just nice time. There will be an hour or two of daylight left.'

'That suits me,' agreed Carruthers.

An hour later the heavily loaded aircraft, after a long run, took off and headed back up the river. Carruthers, with a service rifle across his knees, occupied the spare seat next to Biggles. Behind, packed in the cabin, was the little force of fighting men, all of whom were making their first trip in the air.

Biggles did not trouble about height – not that he could have gone very high with such a full load even if he had wanted to.

Generally speaking, he followed the river, so that he would be able to land his human freight safely should the emergency arise.

After some time the first landing-place, the bend where Bogat and Chorro had met their deaths, came into view, and Biggles set the *Wanderer* down gently on the water. Here four men were disembarked – Dusky, a sergeant, and two policemen. In addition to their small arms, they carried a Vickers machine-gun. They knew just what to do, for their part in the operation had been explained to them before the start. Under Dusky's guidance they were to proceed to the foot of the stairway and take up a position covering it. Anyone attempting to come down was to be arrested.

Biggles watched them file up the forest trail, and then, with an easier load, took off and headed for the plateau.

He tried to visualize what would happen when he landed. As he worked it out, the Tiger and his white associates would suppose that he was alone, in which case their mistake might cost them dear. Actually, he was not particularly concerned whether the Tiger fought or fled. His immediate concern was to get to the underground chamber and relieve Algy, Ginger and Eddie from their tiresome ordeal.

By air it was only a short distance to the plateau. Biggles did not waste time circling, for he knew there were no obstructions to be cleared. Lowering his wheels, he made for the spot he had chosen on the previous occasion.

'Tell your fellows to be ready to bundle out smartly as soon as the machine stops,' he told Carruthers. 'We're likely to come under fire right away, so get the machine-gun in action as quickly as possible. I don't think the Tiger will face it.'

'Leave it to me,' rejoined Carruthers quietly.

As he glided down to land Biggles could see men running from the village and many faces staring upward. It appeared as if the arrival of the machine had caused something like consternation. At the distance, however, he could not distinguish the Tiger.

The wheels touched; the machine rocked a little, and then ran on to a safe if bumpy landing. Kicking on hard rudder, and at the same time giving the engines a burst of throttle, Biggles guided the machine towards an outcrop of rock which he thought would make good cover. As soon as the *Wanderer* stopped he switched off, and grabbing his rifle jumped down. The others poured out behind him. Shots were already flicking up the dust, so the men, under Carruthers' leadership, made a dive for the rocks and there assembled the machine-gun.

About a dozen of the Tiger's men, led by the Tiger himself, were by this time sprinting towards the aircraft; but as the machine-gun started its devastating chatter they acted as Biggles expected they would. They turned and fled, leaving two of their number on the ground. Biggles picked off another man and then jumped to his feet.

'Come on! Let's get after them,' he said crisply.

But now things took a surprising turn, a turn for which Biggles thought he should have been prepared, but as a matter of fact the possibility had not occurred to him. The labourers, who were really nothing less than slaves, were working in the trench. Biggles had noticed them before he landed, but they did not come into his calculations. It seemed, now, as if they suddenly realized that deliverance was at hand. They were nearly all natives from the coast, and perhaps they recognized Carruthers' spotless white uniform. Be that as it may, with one accord, and with a wild yell, they leapt out of the trench and attacked their masters, using as weapons the tools they held in their hands. Biggles saw the gang-boss go down under a rain of blows from picks and shovels. The survivors of this onset, the Tiger among them, bolted for the steps, pursued by a yelling crowd. Some, in their desperate haste to escape, threw away their rifles.

'What on earth is happening?' cried Carruthers. 'It looks as if the Tiger's slaves have decided to take a hand,' answered Biggles grimly.

They could do nothing to prevent the massacre that followed, for they were still a good two hundred yards away, and the slaves were between them and the fugitives. Biggles ran on, followed by the others, hoping to save life if it were possible, and anxious to get to the chamber.

Just before he reached it he saw a fearful sight. Five or six brawny natives, fleeter of foot than the rest, overtook the two white men, Warren and Schmitt, at the head of the stairway. The hunted men screamed as hands fell on them and pulled them down. Carruthers, seeing what was likely to happen, shouted, but he might as well have saved his breath. For a moment there was a knot of struggling figures. Then they separated, and the two white men, clutching at the air, swung out over the awful void. Then they disappeared from sight, their screams growing fainter as they plunged to destruction.

Biggles left the rest to Carruthers. Feeling a trifle sick, he dashed to the chamber, and saw, for the first time, the effect of the explosion. He realized at once that the others must have been trapped.

He beckoned to some of the ex-labourers who were standing about talking in excited groups and made them clear the masonry. As soon as the slab was exposed he opened it.

'Hullo there!' he called cheerfully.

There was no answer.

Biggles felt his heart miss a beat. He went down the first few steps and struck a match, holding the light above his head. His fears were at once confirmed. The chamber was empty. And there he stood, flabbergasted, until the match burnt his fingers.

'Hullo!' he shouted again, in a voice that had suddenly become hoarse.

But there was no reply.

Slowly, hardly able to believe his eyes, he made his way back up the steps to the fresh air.

Carruthers appeared. 'What's the matter?' he asked quickly, noting the expression on Biggles's face.

'They're gone,' said Biggles in a dazed voice.

'Gone?' echoed Carruthers incredulously. 'Where could they have gone?'

Biggles shrugged his shoulders helplessly. 'Don't ask me,' he said bitterly. 'I'm no magician.'

CHAPTER XVII

Unexpected Meetings

Biggles might well have wondered what had become of Algy, Ginger and Eddie; and, as the idol had swung back into place, he might have searched for a long time without finding them. The earth had – as near as may be – opened and swallowed them up.

Eddie was a long time recovering from his fall, for only on the screen do people who have been stunned by a blow on the head recover in a few seconds. Algy and Ginger could do little to help him. They had not even any water. All they could do was squat beside him, rubbing his hands and fanning his face, at the same time debating whether they should try to carry him down the cave which they could see stretched for some distance – how far they did not know. It appeared to plunge down towards the centre of the earth.

They lost all count of time; indeed, they did not even know whether it was day or night when Eddie, after a few weak groans, eventually opened his eyes. Once consciousness returned he made fairly good progress, and presently was well enough to ask what had happened. He himself had no recollection beyond groping about on the floor looking for a trap-door.

'You found it,' Algy told him with humorous sarcasm. 'Having found it, you dived through and landed on your head.'

Eddie struggled into a sitting position. 'Where are we?'

'Ask me something easier,' returned Algy wearily. 'Still, if you;re well enough to get on your feet we'll try to find out. It's no use going back, so we may as well go forward.'

Now, all this time Ginger had kept a small fire going by tearing pieces off his shirt, with the result that there was very little of the garment left.

Eddie got up, rather unsteadily, while Ginger recklessly tore the remaining piece of shirt into strips to provide illumination. With this improvised torch he led the way, the others following, Eddie leaning on Algy's arm.

For some time nothing happened. The cave, a rough, narrow tunnel just high enough to enable them to stand upright, took a winding course downward at a steep angle. It seemed to go on interminably, but then suddenly opened out into a tremendous cavity in the earth, not unlike a cathedral. Enormous stalactites, like rows of organ-pipes, dropped from the roof to meet spiky stalagmites that sprang upwards from the floor. From all around came the faint drip, drip, drip, of water, an eerie sound in such a place.

'Now what have we struck?' asked Ginger in an awed voice, looking round. He took a pace forward, but backed hastily.

'What's wrong?' asked Algy.

'The floor's soft.'

'What do you mean – soft?'

'What I say. It feels like mud. It won't bear my weight.'

Algy stepped forward and tested it. 'You're right,' he said slowly. 'We seem to have struck a confounded bog.'

'It looks as if we shan't be able to get any farther.'

'Just a minute,' put in Eddie. 'Of course, there's always a chance that the bog has only been formed in recent years, but if it was always here, then surely there must be a way across, otherwise there would be no point in making the cave.'

'That's a reasonable argument,' agreed Algy. 'All the same, I can't see any bridge.' He began exploring the mud with his feet. 'Just a minute, what have we here?' he cried. 'It feels like a lump of rock just under the surface.'

Ginger tried it. 'That's what it is,' he said, standing on it. Groping with his foot, he found another. 'That's it,' he went on. 'There are stepping-stones, but either they've sunk or the mud has risen and covered them. Let's see if we can get across.'

'Gosh! I don't think much of this,' muttered Algy as he followed. 'What about you, Eddie? Can you manage?'

'Yes, I reckon so,' answered Eddie, holding on to the wall for support. He drew his hand away sharply. 'It's all right,' he went on quickly. 'It's only water. It's collected in a sort of basin in the rock. There must be a flaw, a fissure, in the rock, that lets the rain water in from above.'

'Water!' gasped Ginger. 'Let's have a drink. My throat's like dust.'

In a moment they were all drinking greedily out of their cupped hands.

'That's better,' exclaimed Ginger, rinsing his grimy face.

'You're sure right,' agreed Eddie. 'I feel a heap better for that.'

They now proceeded again, Ginger, carrying the flame, leading the way. Several times a false step got him into difficulties. Once he stepped off the path and sank up to the waist in slime. Algy had hard work to pull him out, while all around the disturbed area the mud quaked and threw up huge noisome bubbles.

'Phew! What a stink,' muttered Ginger disgustedly. 'We ought to have brought gas masks,' he added, trying to make light of the incident.

A moment later Eddie exclaimed, 'You're right at that.'

'About what?'

'Gas masks. My head's beginning to swim. There's sulphur in this gas. Push on, but don't fall in again, or you'll send up more gas.'

Ginger needed no second invitation, and it was with a shout of relief that he saw the stepping-stones ahead protruding above the mud. Once they could see them, progress became faster, and it was not long before they arrived at what appeared to be a continuation of the cave, although it was now much larger.

Ginger turned, and holding up the flame in such a way that it burned more brightly, took a last look at the subterranean mere.

'I say, you fellows, what's that?' he asked in a startled voice. 'I mean – that shadow – over there. It seems to be coming towards us.'

The others turned and looked, and saw, as Ginger had remarked, that a broad dark shadow was moving across the morass towards them. The strange thing about it was that it did not maintain an even rate of progress. It seemed to dart forward a little way, then pause, then come on again.

'Say! I don't like the look of that,' said Eddie. 'What could cause a shadow in here?'

'That isn't a shadow,' answered Algy in a hushed whisper. 'It's something – alive. I believe it's thousands of insects of some sort. Yes, by gosh, that's it. Just look at 'em. They look like whacking great water-spiders. What do they call those big spiders? Tarantulas. Their bite is poisonous.' He ended on a shrill note.

The others did not wait to confirm this. With one accord they turned about and fled up the cave.

After going a little way Ginger looked over his shoulder. 'Look out!' he yelled. 'They're coming!'

They blundered on. There was no longer any question of going back.

'The next time you want to go adventuring, my lad, you'll go alone,' panted Algy once, viciously.

It was more by luck than judgement that Ginger spotted the opening – or at least one opening, for there may have been others. They were not even thinking of one, for the cave still went downwards. Ginger happened to look up a side turning, and noticed a ghostly grey glow. He pulled up short.

'What's that?' he shouted.

The others stopped and looked. For a moment silence reigned.

'It's daylight!' yelled Algy.

There was a rush for the spot. Algy reached it first, and gave a cry of disappointment when he saw that the light came through a narrow crack only a few inches wide, although it was a yard or more long. A mouse might have got through it, but nothing larger. Beyond, showing as a strip of blue silk, was the sky. It was obvious that the crack was merely a flaw in the rock, due, no doubt, to the effect of wind and rain on the outside.

Ginger, holding up the light, looked behind, and a gasp of horror broke from his lips when he saw the vanguard of the tarantulas only a few yards away.

Algy saw them too, and it was in sheer desperation that he flung himself against the rock, near the crack. He had no genuine hope that it would widen sufficiently to allow him to go through, consequently he was utterly unprepared for what happened. The

'A gasp of horror broke from his lips when
he saw the tarantulas'

whole rock gave way under his weight, and after a vain attempt to save himself, he fell through behind it. The next moment he was clutching wildly at anything as he slid down a short but steep slope to what seemed certain destruction, for all he could see below him was a fearful void. A little avalanche of rocks preceded him to the brink. Loose boulders followed him down. He gave himself up for lost.

When his heels struck solid ground he could hardly believe his good fortune. Then, not before, did he see where he was. He was on the stairway. On either hand ran the narrow cornice. Even then he nearly went over the edge, for a piece of rock, catching him in the small of the back, sent him sprawling. He fell across the path with his legs in space. With frantic haste he drew them in, caring little that his rifle went spinning into the void.

Now Ginger's startled face had appeared at the aperture behind Algy, so he had seen everything that had happened. He also saw something which Algy did not see. Happening to glance up the steps, he saw to his amazement and alarm that somebody was coming down – running down. There was no need to look twice to ascertain who it was. It was the Tiger. Ginger let out a yell of warning.

'Here! Grab this!' he shouted, and allowed his rifle to slide down the slope.

At this moment he in turn was warned by Eddie that the tarantulas were on their heels, so half slipping and half sliding, he followed the rifle to the steps. Eddie came down behind him, and nearly knocked him over the edge. By the time they got down to him, Algy was covering the Tiger, who appeared to be unarmed, and shouting to him to go back.

Now, it must be remembered that none of them knew what had

happened on the plateau, so not for an instant did it occur to them that the Tiger was a fugitive. On the contrary, they supposed that either by luck, or by judgement beyond their understanding, he had deliberately aimed to intercept them. And when a yelling horde of Indians and half-breeds appeared round the bend higher up the steps, it only tended to confirm this. That the Indians were, in fact, pursuing the Tiger, did not occur to them. There was no reason why it should.

The Tiger pulled up when he saw the three white men in front of him. He threw a nervous glance over his shoulder, although this gave the impression that he was waiting for his men to come to his assistance. The situation appeared critical.

Algy addressed the Tiger. 'Get back,' he ordered. 'Get back and tell those men of yours to stop, or I'll shoot you.'

The Tiger appeared not to understand. He shouted something, either in Spanish or in a local dialect. Anyway, none of those below him knew what he said. Then he did a surprising thing. He looked up, then down the steps. Then he surveyed the face of the cliff. Before any of the watchers suspected his intention, with a cat-like leap he reached a narrow ledge above the path, a ledge that was not visible to those below. Along this ledge he made his way towards the hole from which the comrades had just emerged.

At first Algy thought he simply intended getting above them, but as soon as he realized what he was going to do, he shouted a warning. Again, either the Tiger did not understand or he took no notice. He disappeared into the hole.

He was out of sight only a moment or two. Then he reappeared, screaming, snatching and striking at a number of black hairy objects that were running over his body. He appeared to forget where he was, so it came as no surprise to the horrified watchers when he lost his balance and fell. He landed head first on the stairway amid a shower of rocks, and there he lay, limp in unconsciousness.

For a second or two Ginger stared blankly at the wretched man, his brain trying to keep pace with events. As in a dream he saw Algy bring his heel down viciously on a loathsome great spider, and shuddered. Then, remembering the Tiger's men, he looked up the steps and saw with fresh astonishment that they had stopped. One man now stood a little way in front of the others. It was a white man, in spotless ducks. He blinked and looked again. 'I'm going crazy,' he muttered.

Algy, looking rather pale, swung round. 'What are you talking about?' he snapped.

Ginger pointed. 'Is that Carruthers, or am I beginning to imagine things?'

Algy stared. He passed his hand wearily over his forehead. 'It's Carruthers, all right,' he said. 'If he's here, then Biggles shouldn't be far away.'

'I don't get it,' muttered Eddie in a dazed voice.

'Something seems to have happened while we were away,' murmured Algy.

Then Carruthers raised his hand in greeting, and shouted: 'What are you fellows standing there for? Come on up. We were wondering where you were. It's all over.'

Algy turned a stupefied face to Ginger. 'Did you hear that?' he said incredulously. 'It's all over.'

'What's all over?' demanded Ginger, whose nerves were beginning to crack.

'Let's go up and find out,' suggested Algy.

They went slowly up the steps. Carruthers went on ahead of

them. They could hear him shouting. By the time they reached the top Biggles was standing there.

'What do you fellows think you're playing at?' he inquired curtly.

'Playing!' snorted Algy. 'Playing! That's pretty good.' He laughed bitterly.

'I told you to wait until I came back.'

'So we should have done if somebody hadn't blown the place up.'

'What happened to the Tiger?' asked Biggles.

Algy told him. 'Some of the slaves are carrying him back up here,' he concluded.

Biggles nodded. 'That saves us a lot of trouble,' he observed. 'Let's go and meet him. I want to get that map. It should be in his pocket.'

'If you're thinking about the treasure you won't need it,' said Ginger with relish.

'Why not?'

It was Ginger's turn to smile. 'Because we've found it.'

Biggles started. 'So that's what you've been up to, is it? I might have guessed it. Well, let's go and have a look at it.'

'You can have a look at it – provided I can get to it again – when I've had a look at a square meal and a cake of soap,' promised Algy.

Biggles smiled. 'That's a fair proposition,' he agreed. 'Come on, I think we can fix you up.'

He led the way back to the machine, leaving Carruthers to attend to the business of sorting out the people on the plateau.

The rest of the story is soon told.

After a meal and a general clean-up, during which time Biggles ran over his adventures and the others gave him an account of what had happened during his absence, they all returned to the underground chamber. They wasted no time searching for the secret spring that actuated the idol, but with crowbars brought from the tool-store forced the panel open. The treasure was then carried into the open, where it could more easily be examined, and where Carruthers officially took possession of it in the name of the Crown.

It proved to be of even greater value than they had supposed, for there were some wonderful jewels, mostly rubies and emeralds, mixed up with the gold. It was a wonderful find, for many of the objects were unique examples of the craftsmanship of the early inhabitants of tropical America, and as such were likely to bring high prices from collectors of such things. As a matter of detail, most of the pieces later found their way into museums, the comrades, including Eddie, receiving a fair percentage in cash of the total sum they produced.

After the treasure had been examined it was taken to the *Wanderer* for transportation to the coast; and as their task was finished, the comrades flew straight back, taking Carruthers and the still unconscious King of the Forest with them. They stayed at the acting-Governor's bungalow while the official inquiry into the whole affair was held. The court, having heard the evidence, exonerated them from all blame in connection with the deaths of the leading conspirators, and unofficially congratulated them on their work in putting an end to a menace that had long been a scandal in the colony. This was very gratifying, and gave them all that satisfactory feeling of a job well done. The Tiger was still in prison, awaiting trial on several charges of murder – evidence of which had been furnished by the released slaves – when they left the colony, but they had little doubt as to what his fate would be.

The formalities over, Eddie, after trying in vain to persuade the others to go with him, returned to the United States. Dusky was given a responsible position in the native police. Then, as there was no reason for them to stay, they climbed once more into the *Wanderer* and continued their interrupted pleasure cruise, well satisfied with the result of their call at the little outpost of the Empire.